O F

LOVE

AND

LIFE

OF LOVE AND LIFE

Three novels selected and condensed
by Reader's Digest

The Reader's Digest Association Limited, London

The Reader's Digest Association Limited
11 Westferry Circus, Canary Wharf, London E14 4HE

www.readersdigest.co.uk

ISBN 0-276-42873-0

For information as to ownership of copyright in the material of
this book, and acknowledgments, see last page.

CONTENTS

PS, I love you

Cecelia Ahern

Holly, Sharon and Denise have been
friends since school. And of the three,
Holly has always been the one to do
things first: the first to fall in love, the
first to get married.
But into every life a little rain must
fall and Holly is discovering what it
is like to be the first to learn life's
hardest lesson.

One

HOLLY HELD the blue cotton sweater to her face and the familiar smell struck her immediately, an overwhelming grief knotting her stomach and pulling at her heart. Pins and needles ran up the back of her neck and a lump in her throat threatened to choke her. Panic took over. Apart from the low hum of the fridge and the occasional moaning of the pipes, the house was quiet. She was alone. Bile rose to her throat and she ran to the bathroom, where she collapsed to her knees before the toilet.

Gerry was gone and he would never be back. That was the reality. She would never again run her fingers through his soft hair, never share a secret joke across the table at a dinner party, never cry to him when she got home from a hard day at work and just needed a hug; she would never share a bed with him again, never be woken up by his fits of sneezes each morning, never laugh with him so much her stomach would ache, never fight with him about whose turn it was to get up and turn the bedroom light off. All that was left was a bundle of memories and an image of his face that became more and more vague each day.

Their plan had been very simple. To stay together for the rest of their lives. A plan that anyone within their circle would agree was accomplishable. They were best friends, lovers and soul mates, destined to be together, everyone thought. But, as it happened, one day destiny changed its mind.

The end had come all too soon. After complaining of a migraine for a few days, Gerry had agreed to Holly's suggestion that he see his doctor. This was done one Wednesday on a lunch break from work. The doctor

9

thought it was caused by stress and agreed that at the very worst he might need glasses. Gerry had been upset about the idea he might need glasses. He needn't have worried, since as it turned out it wasn't his eyes that were the problem. It was the tumour growing inside his brain.

Holly flushed the toilet and shakily steadied herself to her feet. Gerry had been thirty years old. By no means had he been the healthiest man on the earth, but he'd been healthy enough. When he was very sick he would joke bravely about how he shouldn't have lived life so safely. Should have taken drugs, should have drunk more, should have travelled more, should have jumped out of aeroplanes while waxing his legs . . . Even as he laughed about it, Holly could see the regret in his eyes. Regret for the things he'd never made time to do, the places he'd never seen. Did he regret the life he'd had with her? Holly never doubted that he loved her, but feared he felt he had wasted precious time.

Growing older became something he wanted desperately to accomplish, rather than merely a dreaded inevitability. How presumptuous they had been never to consider growing old as an achievement.

Holly drifted from room to room while she sobbed her fat, salty tears. Her eyes were red and sore. None of the rooms provided her with any solace. Gerry would not be happy with this, she thought. She dried her eyes and tried to shake some sense into herself.

Just as she had done every night for the past two months, Holly fell into a fitful sleep in the early hours of the morning. Each day she woke to find herself sprawled uncomfortably across some piece of furniture; today it was the couch. Once again it was the phone call from a concerned friend or family member that roused her. They probably thought that all she did was sleep.

'Hello,' she answered. Her voice was hoarse from all the tears, but she had long since stopped caring about maintaining a brave face.

'Oh, sorry, love, did I wake you?' Every morning Holly's mother called to see if she had survived the night alone.

'No, I was just dozing, it's OK.'

'Your dad and Declan have gone out and I was thinking of you, pet.' Why did that sympathetic voice always send tears to Holly's eyes? Her mother shouldn't have to be worried. Everything should be normal. Gerry should be here, rolling his eyes up to heaven and trying to make Holly laugh while her mother yapped on. So many times she would have to hand the phone to Gerry as her fit of giggles took over. Then he would chat away, ignoring Holly as she jumped round the bed pulling her silliest faces just to get back at him. It seldom worked.

'It's a lovely day, Holly. It would do you the world of good to go out for a walk. Get some fresh air.'

'Um, I suppose.'

'Maybe I'll call round later and we can have a chat.'

'No, thanks, Mum. I'm OK.'

Silence. Then, 'Well, all right, then. Give me a ring if you change your mind. I'm free all day.'

'OK. Thanks, though.'

'Right then . . . take care, love. Oh, I almost forgot. That envelope is still here on the kitchen table. It's been here for weeks.'

'It's probably just another card.'

'No, I don't think it is, love. Above your name it says . . . oh, hold on while I get it . . .' The phone was put down, then picked up again. 'OK, it says at the top "The List". I'm not sure what that means, love. It's worth just taking a . . .'

Holly dropped the phone.

'Gerry, turn off the light!' Holly giggled as she watched her husband undress before her. He danced round the room performing a striptease, slowly unbuttoning his white shirt with his long slender fingers. He raised his left eyebrow towards Holly and allowed the shirt to slide from his shoulders, caught it in his right hand and swung it over his head.

Holly giggled again.

'Turn off the light? What, and miss all this?' he grinned cheekily while flexing his muscles. He wasn't a vain man but had much to be vain about, thought Holly. His body was strong and perfectly toned. He wasn't a very tall man, but he was tall enough to make Holly feel safe when he stood protectively beside her five-foot-five body. When she hugged him her head would rest neatly just below his chin.

He lowered his boxers, caught them on the tips of his toes and flung them at Holly, where they landed on her head.

'Well, at least it's darker under here anyway,' she laughed.

Gerry dived into bed, snuggled up beside her and tucked his freezing-cold feet underneath her legs.

'Aaaagh! Gerry, your feet are like ice cubes.' Holly knew he had no intention of budging an inch. 'Gerry!'

'Holly,' he mimicked.

'Didn't you forget something?'

'No, not that I know of.'

'The light?'

'Ah yes, the light,' he said sleepily and pretended to snore loudly.

'Gerry!'

'I had to get out and do it last night, as I remember.'

'Yeah, but you were right beside the switch a second ago!'

'Yes . . . just a second ago,' he repeated sleepily.

Holly sighed. She hated having to get out of bed when she was nice and snug, step onto the cold wooden floor, then fumble around in the darkness on the way back. She tutted.

'I can't do it all the time you know, Hol. Someday I might not be here and then what will you do?'

'Get my new husband to do it,' Holly huffed, trying her best to kick his cold feet away from hers.

'Ha!'

'Or just remember to do it myself before I get into bed.'

'Fat chance, my dear. I'll have to leave a message on the light switch before I go just so you'll remember.'

'How thoughtful of you, but I would rather you just leave me your money.'

'And a note on the immersion. And on the milk carton.'

'Gerry. You're a very funny man. Hey, why don't you just leave me a list in your will of things to do if you think I'll be so incompetent?'

'Not a bad idea,' he laughed.

'Fine, then, I'll turn off the bloody light.' Holly grudgingly got out of bed, and switched the light off. She held out her arms in the darkness and slowly began to find her way back.

'Hello?!!! Holly, did you get lost? Is there anybody out there, there, there, there?' Gerry shouted out to the black room.

'Yes, I'm hhhhowwwwwwcch!' she yelped as she stubbed her toe against the bedpost.

Gerry snorted and sniggered underneath the duvet. 'Number two on my list: Watch out for bedpost—'

'Oh, shut up, Gerry, and stop being so morbid,' Holly snapped back, cradling her poor foot in her hand.

'Want me to kiss it better?' he asked.

'No, it's OK,' Holly replied sadly. 'If I could just put them here so I can warm . . .'

'Aaaaah! Bloody hell, they're freezing!!'

Which made her laugh again.

So that was how the joke about the list had come about. It was soon shared with their closest friends, Sharon and John McCarthy. It was John who had approached Holly in the school corridor when they were just fourteen and muttered the famous words, 'Me mate wants to know if you'll go out with him.' After days of emergency meetings with her friends, Holly eventually agreed.

'Aah, go on, Holly,' Sharon had urged, 'he's such a ride.'

How Holly envied Sharon right now. Sharon and John had married the same year as Holly and Gerry. Holly was the baby of the bunch at twenty-three, others were twenty-four. Some said she was too young and lectured her about how she should be travelling the world and enjoying herself. Instead, Gerry and Holly travelled the world together. It made far more sense that way because when they weren't together . . . well, Holly just felt like she was missing a vital organ from her body.

Tears once again rolled down Holly's face and she realised she had been daydreaming again. She sat frozen on the couch with the phone still off the hook beside her. The hours just seemed to pass her by these days without her knowing what time or even what day it was. She seemed to be numb to everything but the pain in her heart, in her bones, in her head. She was just so tired . . . Her stomach grumbled and she realised she couldn't remember the last time she had eaten.

She shuffled into the kitchen wearing Gerry's dressing gown and her favourite pink 'disco diva' slippers, which he had bought her. She was his disco diva, he used to say. Always the first on the dance floor, always the last out of the club. Huh, where was that girl now?

She opened the fridge and stared in at the empty shelves. Just vegetables and yoghurt long past its sell-by date. She smiled weakly as she shook the milk carton. Empty. Third on his list . . .

Christmas two years ago, Holly had gone shopping with Sharon for a dress for the annual ball they attended at the Burlington Hotel. Shopping with Sharon was always a dangerous outing, and Holly spent a disgraceful amount of money in Brown Thomas on the most beautiful white dress she had ever seen.

'Sharon, this will burn a huge hole in my pocket,' Holly said guiltily, running her fingers over the soft material.

'Aah, don't worry, Gerry can stitch it up for you,' Sharon replied, followed by her infamous cackle. 'Buy the damn thing, Holly. It's Christmas, after all, the season of giving and all that.'

'God, you are so evil, Sharon. I'm never shopping with you again. This is like, half my month's wages.'

'Would you rather eat, or look fab?' Was it even worth thinking about?

The dress was cut low, which showed off Holly's chest perfectly, and it was split to the thigh, displaying her slim legs. Gerry hadn't been able to take his eyes off her. It wasn't because she looked so beautiful, however.

He just couldn't understand how on earth that little slip of material had cost so much. Once at the ball, Ms Disco Diva overindulged in alcoholic beverages and succeeded in destroying her dress by spilling red wine down her front. While the men at the table drunkenly informed their partners that number fifty-four on the list prevented you from drinking red wine while wearing an expensive white dress, Gerry knocked his pint over, causing it to dribble off the table onto Holly's lap, and she tearfully announced, 'Rule fitty-fife: *neffer, effer* buy a 'spensive white dress.'

Was it possible that Gerry had kept his word and written a list for her before he died? She had spent every minute of every day with him up until his death, and he had never mentioned it. No, Holly, pull yourself together. She so desperately wanted him back that she was imagining all kinds of crazy things. He wouldn't have. Would he?

Holly was walking through an entire field of pretty tiger lilies; the wind was blowing gently, causing the silky petals to tickle the tips of her fingers as she pushed through long strands of bright green grass. All around her, birds whistled as they went about their business. The sun was so bright she had to shield her eyes, and with each brush of wind that passed her face, the sweet scent of the lilies filled her nostrils. She felt so . . . happy, so free.

Suddenly the Caribbean sun disappeared behind a looming grey cloud. The wind picked up and the air chilled. The petals of her tiger lilies were racing through the air wildly, blurring her vision. With every step, sharp stones scraped her feet. Something was wrong, and she felt afraid. In the distance a grey stone was visible. She wanted to run back, but she needed to find out what was ahead.

Bang! Bang! Bang! She raced over the sharp stones, collapsed to her knees in front of the grey slab and let out a scream of pain as she realised it was Gerry's grave. *Bang! Bang! Bang!* He was trying to get out! She could hear him!

Holly jumped from her sleep to a loud banging on the front door. 'Holly! Please let me in!' *Bang! Bang! Bang!* Confused and half asleep, she made her way to the door to find a frantic-looking Sharon.

'Holly, I've been banging on the door for ages!'

Holly looked around outside, still not fully alert. It was bright and slightly chilly—must be morning.

'Well, aren't you going to let me in?'

'Yeah, Sharon, sorry. I was just dozing on the couch.'

'God, you look terrible, Hol.' Sharon studied her face before giving her a big hug.

'Wow, thanks.' Holly rolled her eyes and turned to shut the door. Sharon was never one to beat about the bush, but that was why she loved her so much, for her honesty. That was also why Holly hadn't been round to see Sharon for the past month.

'It's so stuffy in here, when's the last time you opened a window?' Sharon marched round the house opening windows and picking up empty cups and plates. She brought them into the kitchen, where she then proceeded to tidy up.

'Oh, you don't have to do it, Sharon,' Holly protested. 'I'll do it.'

'When? Next year? I don't want you slumming it while the rest of us pretend not to notice. Why don't you go upstairs and shower, and we'll have a cup of tea when you come down.'

A shower. When was the last time she had even washed? Sharon was right, she must look disgusting with her greasy hair and dirty dressing gown. Gerry's dressing gown. But that was something she never intended to wash. She wanted it exactly as Gerry had left it.

'OK, but there's no milk. I haven't got round to . . .' There was no way she was letting Sharon look inside that fridge.

'Ta-da!' Sharon sang, holding up a bag Holly hadn't noticed her carrying in. 'Don't worry, I took care of that.'

'Thanks, Sharon.' Tears welled in Holly's eyes.

'Hold it! There will be no tears today! Just fun and laughter and general happiness, my dear friend. Now shower, quick!'

Holly felt almost human when she came back downstairs. She was dressed in a blue track suit and had allowed her long blonde hair to fall down on her shoulders. She gasped as she looked round the house. She couldn't have been half an hour, but Sharon had tidied and polished, vacuumed and plumped. She followed the noise she could hear to the kitchen, where Sharon was scrubbing the hobs.

'Sharon, you absolute angel! I can't believe you did all this! And in such a short space of time!'

'Ha! I was beginning to think you'd fallen down the plughole. You would and all, the size of you.' She looked Holly up and down. 'OK, so there's cheese and yoghurts, pasta and tinned foods. And microwave dinners in the freezer. How much weight have you lost?' Holly looked down at her track suit, sagging at the hips. 'There's biscuits to go with your tea. Jammy Dodgers, your favourite.'

That did it. The Jammy Dodgers were the icing on the cake. Holly felt the tears start to run down her face. 'Oh, Sharon,' she wailed, 'thank you so much. You've been so good to me and I've been such a horrible bitch of a friend.' She sat at the table and grabbed Sharon's hand. 'I don't know what I'd do without you.' This is what Holly had been dreading, breaking down in front of people, but she didn't feel embarrassed. Sharon sat opposite her patiently holding her hand as if it were normal.

'I'm your best friend, Hol. If I don't help you, then who will?' Sharon gave her an encouraging smile.

'Suppose I should be helping myself.'

'Pah!' Sharon waved her hand dismissively. 'Whenever you're ready. Grieving is all part of helping yourself anyway.'

'Thanks for coming round, Sharon, I really enjoyed the chat.' Holly gratefully hugged her friend, who had taken the day off work to be with her. 'I feel better already.'

'It's good to be around people, Hol. Friends and family can help.'

'Oh, I realise that now. I just thought I could handle it on my own.'

'Promise me you'll call round. Or at least get out of the house once in a while?'

'Promise.' Holly sighed. 'You're beginning to sound like my mum.'

'We're all just looking out for you. OK, see you soon, and *eat!*' Sharon added, poking her in the ribs.

Holly waved as Sharon pulled away in her car. It was nearly dark. They had spent the day laughing and joking about old times, then crying, followed by some more laughing, then more crying again. It had been good being with the living again instead of moping around with the ghosts of her past. Tomorrow was a new day and she intended to begin it by collecting that envelope.

Two

HOLLY STARTED her Friday morning well by getting up early. However, although she had gone to bed full of optimism, she was struck afresh by the harsh reality of how difficult every moment would be. Once again she woke to a silent house, but there was one small breakthrough. For the first time, she had woken up without the aid of a telephone call. She adjusted her mind, as she did every morning, to the fact that the dreams

16

of Gerry and her being together that had lived in her mind for the past ten hours were just that—dreams.

She showered and dressed comfortably in blue jeans, trainers and a T-shirt. She made a face at her reflection in the mirror. She had black circles under her eyes, her lips were chapped and chewed on and her hair was a disaster. First thing to do was to go down to her local hairdressers' and pray that Leo could fit her in.

Holly bounced out of the salon with delight. Without Gerry beside her, a few men looked her way, something that was alien to her and made her feel uncomfortable, so she ran to the safety of her car and prepared herself for her parents' house. So far, today was going well. It had been a good move to visit Leo.

She pulled up to the kerb outside her parents' house in Portmarnock and took a deep breath. To her mother's surprise Holly had called first thing to arrange a time to meet up. It was three thirty now, and Holly sat outside in the car with butterflies in her tummy. Apart from visits her parents had paid her over the past two months, Holly had barely spent any time with her family. She didn't want all the attention; she didn't want the intrusive questions about how she was feeling and what she was going to do next. However, it was time to put that fear aside.

Her parents' house was situated directly across the road from Portmarnock beach, the blue flag bearing testament to its cleanliness. She parked the car and stared across the road to the sea. She had lived here from the day she was born till the day she moved out to live with Gerry. She had loved waking up to the sound of the sea lapping against the rocks and the excited call of the seagulls. Sharon had lived round the corner, and on the hottest days of the year, the girls would venture across the road in their summer's best and keep an eye out for the best-looking boys. Sharon with her brown hair, fair skin and huge chest, Holly with her blonde hair, sallow skin and small chest. Sharon would shout to the boys and call them over. Holly would just fix her eyes on her favourite and not move them till he noticed.

Holly didn't intend to stay long, just long enough to have a little chat and collect the envelope. She rang the doorbell.

'Hi, love! Come in, come in!' said her mother with the welcoming, loving face that Holly just wanted to kiss every time she saw her.

'Hi, Mum.' Holly stepped into the house. 'You on your own?'

'Yes, your father's out with Declan, buying paint for his room.'

'Don't tell me you're still paying for everything for him?'

'Well, your father might be, but I'm not. He's working nights now so he has a bit of pocket money. Although we don't see a penny of it,' she chuckled and brought Holly to the kitchen, where she put the kettle on.

Declan was Holly's youngest brother and the baby of the family, a twenty-two-year-old studying film production at college. He constantly had a video camera in his hand.

'What job has he got now?'

Her mother rolled her eyes to heaven. 'He's joined some band. The Orgasmic Fish, I think they call themselves. Holly, if he goes on one more time about how famous they're going to be, I'll go mad.'

'Ah, poor Deco, don't worry, he'll find something eventually.'

'I know, and it's funny, because of all you darling children, he's the last one I worry about. He'll find his way.'

They brought their mugs into the living room and settled down in front of the television. 'You look good, love. Any luck with a job yet?'

'No, not yet, Mum. I haven't even started looking.'

Her mother nodded. 'Take your time and think about what you like, or else you'll end up rushing into a job you hate, like the last time.'

The last job Holly had had was working as a secretary for an unforgiving slimeball in a solicitor's office. She'd been forced to leave when the little creep failed to understand she needed time off to be with her dying husband. Now she had to look for a new job.

Holly and her mother relaxed, falling in and out of conversation until Holly finally built up the courage to ask for the envelope.

'Oh, of course, love. I hope it's nothing important, it's been there for a long time.'

'I'll find out soon enough.'

They said their goodbyes and Holly couldn't get out of the house quickly enough. Perching herself on the grass overlooking the sand and sea, Holly ran her hands over the thick brown envelope. Above the address label were two handwritten words, thick and bold:

THE LIST.

Her stomach did a little dance. Her trembling fingers gently tore at the package. She turned it upside-down and shook the contents out. Out fell ten tiny little envelopes, the kind you would expect to find on a bouquet of flowers, each with a different month written on it. Her heart missed a few beats as she saw a loose page underneath the pile.

With tears in her eyes, she read the familiar handwriting, knowing that the person who had sat down to write to her would never be able to do so again. She ran her fingers over his words, knowing that the last person to have touched the page was him.

PS, I LOVE YOU

My darling Holly,

I don't know where you are or when exactly you are reading this. I just hope it finds you safe and healthy. You whispered not long ago that you couldn't go on alone. You can, Holly.

You are strong and brave and you can get through this. We shared some beautiful times together and . . . you made my life. I have no regrets. But I am just a chapter in your life, there will be many more. Remember our wonderful memories, but please don't be afraid to make some more.

Thank you for doing me the honour of being my wife. For everything, I am eternally grateful.

Whenever you need me, know that I am with you.

Love for ever,

Your husband and best friend, Gerry

PS, I promised a list, so here it is. The envelopes must be opened when labelled and must be obeyed. I'm looking out for you, so I will know . . .

Holly broke down, sadness sweeping over her. Yet she felt relief that Gerry would somehow be with her for another little while. She leafed through the small white envelopes. It was April now. She had missed March, and so she delicately opened it. Inside was a small card with Gerry's handwriting on it:

Save yourself the bruises and buy yourself a bedside lamp!

PS, I love you . . .

Her tears turned to laughter. Gerry was back!

Holly read his letter over and over in an attempt to summon him to life again. Eventually, when she could no longer see the words through her tears, she closed her eyes and breathed in and out along with the gentle sighing of the waves. It was as though the sea were taking big deep breaths, pulling the water in while it inhaled and pushing it all back up onto the sand as it exhaled. She thought about how she used to lie by Gerry's side during his final days and listen to the sound of his breathing. She had been terrified to leave him just in case that was the time he chose to leave her. When she returned to his bedside she would sit frozen in a terrified silence and watch his chest for any movement.

But he always managed to hang on, baffling the doctors with his determination to live. Gerry kept his good humour right up until the end. He was so weak and his voice so quiet, but Holly had learned to understand his babbling new language. They would giggle together late into the night, and other nights they would hold each other and cry. Holly remained strong for him. Looking back on it, she knew that she needed him more than he needed her, needed to feel she wasn't just standing by helpless.

On the second of February at four in the morning, Holly held Gerry's hand tightly as he took his last breath. She didn't want him to be afraid, and she didn't want him to feel that she was afraid, because at that moment she wasn't. She had felt relief that his pain was gone, and that she had been there with him. She felt relieved to have known him, to have loved him and to be loved by him, and relief that the last thing he saw was her smiling face assuring him it was OK to let go.

The days after that were a blur. She occupied herself making funeral arrangements and greeting his relatives and old schoolfriends. She was thankful that after months his suffering was over. It didn't occur to her to feel the anger or bitterness she felt now. That feeling didn't arrive until she went to collect her husband's death certificate.

As she sat in the crowded health clinic waiting for her number to be called, she wondered why on earth Gerry's number had been called so early in his life. She sat sandwiched between a young couple and an elderly couple, and it all just seemed unfair. Squashed between the shoulders of her past and her lost future, she felt suffocated. She shouldn't have had to be there.

None of her friends had to be there.

None of her family had to be there.

It didn't seem fair. Because it just wasn't fair.

After presenting the official proof of death to bank managers and insurance companies, Holly returned home to her nest and locked herself away from the world. That was two months ago and she hadn't left the house until today. And what a welcome she had been given, she thought, smiling down at the envelopes. Gerry was back.

'Wow,' was all Sharon and John could say as the three of them sat round Holly's kitchen table in silence, staring at the contents of the package. Conversation between them had been minimal for the last few minutes as they all tried to decide how they felt.

'But how did he manage to . . .?'

'But why didn't we notice him . . . well . . .?'

'When do you think . . .? He was on his own sometimes . . .'

Holly and Sharon just sat looking at each other while John tried to figure out how his terminally ill friend had managed to carry out this idea all alone.

'Wow,' he eventually repeated after coming to the conclusion that Gerry had done just that.

'Are you OK, Holly?' Sharon asked. 'I mean, how do you feel about all this? It must be . . . weird.'

'I feel fine. Actually, I think it's the best thing that could have happened right now! It's funny, though, how amazed we are, considering how much we all went on about this list.'

'I think Gerry was the only one who took it really seriously,' Sharon said.

There was a silence. 'Well, let's study this more closely,' John said. 'There's how many envelopes?'

Holly sorted through the pile. 'There's March, which is the lamp one, April, May, June, July, August, September, October, November and December. A message for every month left in the year.'

'Hold on!' John's blue eyes twinkled. 'It's April now.'

'Oh, I forgot about that! Oh, no, should I open it now?'

'Go on,' encouraged Sharon.

Holly picked up the envelope and slowly began to open it. She wanted to treasure every second before it became another memory. She pulled out the little card.

A disco diva must always look her best. Go shopping for an outfit, as you'll need it for next month!
PS, I love you . . .

'Ooooh,' John sang with excitement. 'He's getting cryptic!'

Holly lay on her bed like a demented woman, switching the lamp on and off with a smile on her face. She and Sharon had gone shopping in Bed Knobs and Broomsticks in Malahide, and had eventually agreed on a beautifully carved wooden stand and cream shade, which matched the cream and wooden furnishings of the master bedroom. And although Gerry hadn't physically been there with her as she bought it, she felt as though they had made the purchase together.

She had drawn the curtains of her bedroom in order to test her new merchandise. How easily this could have ended their nightly arguments, but perhaps neither of them had wanted to end them. It had become a routine, something familiar that made them feel closer. How she would gladly get out of her cosy bed for him now, gladly walk on the cold floor, gladly bruise herself on the bedpost while fumbling in the dark. But that time was gone.

The sound of Gloria Gaynor's 'I Will Survive' snapped her back to the present. Her mobile phone was ringing.

'Hello?'

'G'day, mate, I'm hooooome!' shrieked a familiar voice.

'Oh my God, Ciara! I didn't know you were coming home!'

'Neither did I, actually,' said Holly's younger sister. 'But I ran out of money and decided to surprise you all!'

'Wow, I bet Mum and Dad were surprised all right.'

'Well, Mum's organising dinner tonight to celebrate. The whole family.'

'Did I mention that I'm going to the dentist to have all my teeth pulled out? Sorry, I can't make it.'

'I know, I know, I said the same thing to Mum, but we haven't all been together for ages. Sure, when's the last time you've even seen Richard and Meredith?'

'Oh, Richard was in flying form at the funeral. Had lots of comforting things to say like, "Did you not consider donating his brain to medical science?" Yes, he's a fantastic brother all right.'

'Oh, gosh, the funeral. I'm sorry I couldn't make it.'

'Ciara, don't be silly, it was far too expensive, flying from Australia. So when you say the whole family you mean . . .?'

'Yes, Richard and Meredith are bringing our little niece and nephew. And Jack and Abbey are coming. Declan will be there in body, and Mum, Dad and me, of course, and you *will* be there.'

Holly groaned. As much as she moaned about her family she had a great relationship with her brother Jack. He was only two years older than her so they had always been close growing up, always getting up to mischief (usually aimed at their eldest brother, Richard). Jack was similar to Holly in personality, and she considered him to be the most normal of her siblings. It also helped that she got along with Abbey, and when Gerry was alive the four of them often met up for dinner and drinks. When Gerry was alive . . . God, that didn't sound right.

Ciara was a whole different kettle of fish. Jack and Holly were convinced she was from the planet Ciara, population: one. Ciara had the look of her father: long legs and dark hair. She also had various tattoos and piercings as a result of her travels. A tattoo for every country, her dad joked. A tattoo for every man, Holly and Jack were convinced.

Of course this carry-on was all frowned upon by the eldest of the family, Richard, who had been born with the serious illness of being an eternal old man. His life revolved around regulations and obedience. When he was younger he had one friend and they had a fight when they were ten. After that Holly could never remember him bringing anyone home or going out to socialise. She and Jack thought it was a wonder he had even met his equally joyless wife, Meredith. Probably at an anti-happiness convention.

It wasn't as though Holly had the *worst* family in the world, it was just that they were such a strange mix. These huge clashes of personalities usually led to arguments at the most inappropriate times. They *could* get along, but that was with everyone really being on their best behaviour.

So was Holly looking forward to tonight? Absolutely not.

Holly reluctantly knocked on the door to her family home and immediately heard the pounding of tiny feet followed by a voice that should not belong to a child.

'Mummy! Daddy! It's Auntie Holly, it's Auntie Holly!'

It was Nephew Timothy, Nephew Timothy.

His happiness was suddenly crushed by a stern voice. 'Timothy! What did I tell you about running in the house! Go and stand in the corner and think about what I said. Do I make myself clear?'

'Yes, Mummy.'

'Ah, come on, Meredith, will he hurt himself on the carpet?'

Holly laughed to herself; Ciara was definitely home.

The door swung open and there stood Meredith, looking even more sour-faced than usual. 'Holly.' She nodded.

'Meredith,' Holly imitated.

Once in the living room, Holly looked round for Jack, but to her disappointment he was nowhere to be seen. Richard stood in front of the fireplace with his hands in his pockets, rocking back and forth from his heels to the balls of his feet like a man in mid-lecture. His lecture was aimed at their father, Frank, who sat in his favourite armchair, looking like a chastised schoolboy. Richard was so lost in his story he didn't see Holly enter the room. She blew her poor father a kiss, not wanting to be brought into their conversation. He smiled and pretended to catch it.

Declan was slumped on the couch wearing his ripped jeans and *South Park* T-shirt, puffing furiously on a cigarette, while Meredith invaded his space and warned him of the dangers of smoking. Ciara was hiding behind the couch throwing pieces of popcorn at Timothy who stood facing the wall in the corner, too afraid to turn round. Abbey was pinned to the floor by five-year-old Emily and an evil-looking doll.

'Hi, Ciara.' Holly approached her sister, who jumped up and gave her a big hug. 'Nice hair.'

'You like it?'

'Yeah, pink is really your colour.'

Ciara looked satisfied. 'That's what I tried to tell them,' she said, squinting her eyes at Richard and Meredith. 'So how's my big sis?'

'Oh, you know.' Holly smiled weakly. 'I'm hanging in there.'

23

'Jack's in the kitchen helping your mum if you're looking for him, Holly,' Abbey announced.

Holly raised her eyebrows. 'Really? Well, isn't he great?'

Holly's dad shifted in his seat. 'And all this happens in just one tiny test tube?'

Richard let out a disapproving sigh. 'Yes, but you have to understand these are so minuscule, Father, it's rather fascinating. The organisms combine with the . . .' And away he went.

Holly tiptoed into the kitchen, where she found her brother munching on some food. 'Ah, here he is, the Naked Chef himself.'

Jack smiled. 'There's my favourite sister.' He held out his arms to offer her one of his big bear hugs. 'How are you?' he said quietly into her ear.

'I'm OK, thanks.' Holly smiled sadly and kissed him on the cheek. 'Darling Mother, I am here to offer my services.' She planted a kiss on her mother's flushed cheek.

'Oh, aren't I just the luckiest woman in the world having such caring children,' Elizabeth said sarcastically. 'I hope you two won't be getting up to any mischief tonight. I would like this to be an argument-free zone for a change.'

'Mother, I am shocked the thought even crossed your mind.' Jack winked across to Holly.

'All right,' Elizabeth said, not believing a word of it. 'Well, sorry, there's nothing to be done here. Dinner will be ready in a few minutes.'

The three of them stared at the kitchen door, all thinking the same thing.

'No, Abbey,' squealed Emily, 'you're not doing what I tell you.' This was followed by a loud guffaw; Richard must have cracked a joke because he was the only one laughing.

'But I suppose it's important that we all stay here and keep an eye on the dinner,' Elizabeth added.

Everyone oohed and aahed as Elizabeth brought out the food. Holly had always loved her mother's cooking. 'Hey, poor little Timmy must be starving out there,' Ciara exclaimed to Richard. 'He must have done his time by now.'

She knew she was skating on thin ice but she loved the danger of it, and more important, she loved to wind Richard up. After all, she had to make up for lost time, she had been away for a year.

'Ciara, it's important that Timothy should know when he has done something wrong,' explained Richard.

'Yeah, but couldn't you just tell him?'

The rest of the family tried hard not to laugh.

'He needs to know that his actions will lead to serious consequences.'

'Ah well.' Ciara raised her voice a few octaves. 'He's missing all this yummy food. Mmm-mmm-mmm.'

'Stop it, Ciara,' Elizabeth snapped.

'Or you'll have to stand in the corner,' Jack added sternly.

The table erupted with laughter, bar Meredith and Richard, of course.

'So, Ciara, tell us about your adventures,' Frank moved swiftly on.

Ciara's eyes lit up. 'Oh, I had the most amazing time, Dad. I'd definitely recommend Australia to anyone.'

'Awful long flight, though,' Richard said.

'Did you get any more tattoos?' Holly asked.

'Yeah, look.' With that, Ciara stood up and pulled down her trousers, revealing a butterfly on her behind.

Mum, Dad, Richard and Meredith protested in outrage, while the others sat in convulsions of laughter. This carried on for a long time. Finally, when Ciara had apologised and Meredith had removed her hands from Emily's eyes, the table settled down.

'They are revolting things,' Richard said in disgust.

'I think butterflies are pretty, Daddy,' said Emily.

'Emily, I'm talking about tattoos. They can give you all sorts of diseases.' Emily's smile faded.

'Hey, I didn't get this done in a dodgy place sharing needles with drug dealers. The place was perfectly clean.'

'Well, that's an oxymoron,' Meredith said with disgust.

'Been in one recently, Meredith?' Ciara asked forcefully.

'I have never been in one, thank you.' Then she turned to Emily. 'They are dirty, horrible places, Emily, where only dangerous people go.'

'Is Aunt Ciara dangerous, Mummy?'

'Only to five-year-old girls,' Ciara said, and Emily froze.

'Richard, dear, do you think that Timmy might want to come in now for some food?' Elizabeth asked politely.

'It's Timothy,' Meredith interrupted.

'Yes, Mother, I think that would be OK.'

A very sorry little Timothy walked into the room with his head down and took his place silently. Holly's heart leapt out to him. How cruel to treat a child like that . . . Her sympathetic thoughts diminished immediately as she felt his little foot kick her shin underneath the table.

'So, Ciara, come on, did you do anything wild and wonderful out there?' Holly pushed for more information.

'Oh, yeah, I did a bungee jump actually, well, I did a few. I have a photo here.' She took out her wallet and passed the photo round the table. 'The first one I did was off a bridge and my head hit the water . . .'

'Oh, Ciara, that sounds dangerous,' her mother said.

'Oh, no, it wasn't dangerous at all,' she reassured her.

'Holly, what are you doing for your birthday?' Abbey asked.

'Oh, that's right!' shouted Ciara. 'You're gonna be thirty!'

'I'm not doing anything big,' Holly warned everyone. 'I don't want any party or anything, *please*.'

'Oh, you have to—' said Ciara.

'She doesn't have to if she doesn't want to,' Frank said.

'Thank you, Dad. I'm just going to have a girlie night out clubbing or something. Nothing mad, nothing wild.'

'Yes, I agree with you, Holly,' said Richard. 'Those birthday celebrations are always a bit embarrassing. Grown adults acting like children, drinking too much. You're quite right.'

'Well, I actually quite enjoy those parties, Richard,' Holly shot back. 'I just don't feel in the mood, that's all.'

There was silence for a moment before Ciara piped up: 'A girlie night it is then.'

'Can I tag along with the camera?' asked Declan.

'For what?'

'Just for some footage of clubs and stuff for college.'

'As long as you know I won't be going to trendy places.'

'No, I don't mind where you g—OW!' he shouted and stared menacingly at Timothy.

Timmy stuck out his tongue and the conversation continued on.

Three

HOLLY STOOD IN FRONT of the full-length mirror and inspected herself. She had carried out Gerry's orders and had purchased a new outfit. What for, she didn't know, but several times every day she had to drag herself away from opening the envelope for May. There were only two days left until she could, and the anticipation left her no room to think of anything else.

She had settled on wearing an all-black outfit to suit her current mood. Black fitted trousers tailored perfectly to sit over her black boots. A black corset that made her look like she had a bigger chest. Her hair, tied up, strands falling in loose waves round her shoulders.

She didn't feel thirty. But then again, what was being thirty supposed to feel like? When she was younger, she'd thought that a woman of that age would be so wise and knowledgeable, so settled in her life with a husband and children and a career. She had none of those things. There was nothing about being thirty worth celebrating.

The doorbell rang and Holly could hear excited chatter outside. She took a deep breath and plastered a smile on her face.

'Happy birthday!' Sharon, Abbey, Ciara and Denise—who she hadn't seen in ages—all yelled in unison.

She stared back at their happy faces and was immediately cheered up by their enthusiasm. She ushered them into the living room and waved hello to the camera being brandished by Declan.

'No, Holly, you're supposed to ignore him!' Denise dragged Holly by the arm onto the couch, where they all surrounded her and immediately started thrusting presents in her face.

'Open mine first!' squealed Ciara.

'I think we should pop open the bubbly first and *then* open the pressies,' said Abbey.

'Ciara, I promise to open yours first,' Holly said.

Abbey raced into the kitchen and returned with a tray full of champagne flutes. 'Anyone for champers, sweetie darlings?'

'Holly, you can do the honours.' Abbey handed her the bottle and everyone ran for cover.

'Hey, I'm not that bad!' Holly said, as she began to remove the cork.

The girls all cheered as they heard the pop, and crawled out of their hiding places.

'OK,' said Sharon. 'Here's to my bestest friend in the whole world who has had such a difficult year, but throughout everything has been the bravest and the strongest person I've ever met. She's an inspiration to us all. Here's to her finding happiness for the next thirty years! To Holly!'

'To Holly,' they all chorused, holding up their glasses. Everyone's eyes were sparkling with tears as they all took sips of their drinks, except for Ciara, who had knocked back her glass of champagne and was scrambling to give her present to Holly.

'OK, first you have to wear this tiara because you are our princess for the night, and second here's my present!'

The girls helped Holly put on the sparkling tiara that luckily went perfectly with her black, glittery corset. She carefully removed the tape from the parcel and looked inside the box. 'What is it?'

'Read it!' Ciara said excitedly.

Holly began to read aloud from the box, 'It's a battery-operated . . . Ciara! You naughty girl!' Holly and the girls laughed hysterically. 'Well, I'll definitely need this.'

Declan looked like he was about to throw up.

Holly gave her sister a hug.

'OK, me next,' Abbey said, putting her parcel on Holly's lap.

Holly opened Abbey's present. 'Oh, Abbey, it's beautiful!' She held up the sterling silver-covered photo album.

'For your new memories,' Abbey said softly.

'It's perfect,' Holly said, wrapping her arms round Abbey and squeezing her. 'Thank you.'

'Mine is less sentimental.' Denise handed her an envelope.

'Oh, brilliant!' Holly exclaimed as she opened it. 'A weekend of pampering in Haven's Health and Beauty Clinic! Oh, Denise, thank you!' Holly winked at Sharon. 'OK, last but not least!'

It was a large silver frame with a photograph of Sharon, Denise and Holly at the Christmas Ball two years ago.

'Oh, I'm wearing my 'spensive white dress!' Holly walked over to the fireplace. That had been the last ball that she and Gerry had been to. 'Well, this will take pride of place,' she announced, placing it beside her wedding photo on the mantelpiece.

'OK, girls,' screamed Ciara, 'let's get some serious drinking done!'

Two bottles of champagne and several bottles of wine later, the girls stumbled out of the house and piled into a taxi. Holly insisted on sitting in the passenger seat and having a heart-to-heart with Nick the driver.

'Bye, Nick!' they all shouted before falling out onto the kerb. They had decided to chance their luck at Dublin's most stylish club, Boudoir. It was reserved for the rich and famous only, and it was a well-known fact that if you weren't rich and famous, you had to have a member's card. Denise walked up to the door coolly waving her video store card in the bouncers' faces. Amazingly, they stopped her.

The only famous faces they saw as they fought to get in were a few newsreaders from the national TV station, to whom Denise kept repeating, 'Good evening,' very seriously. Unfortunately, after that Holly remembered no more.

Holly woke with her head pounding. Her mouth was dry. She leaned up on one elbow and tried to open her eyes, which were somehow glued together. She squinted round the room. It was bright, very bright, and it seemed to be spinning. Something very odd was going on. Holly caught sight of herself in the mirror and startled herself. Had she been in an accident last night? She collapsed flat on her back again. Suddenly the house alarm began wailing. Oh, take whatever you want, she thought, just bring me a glass of water before you go. After a while she realised it wasn't the alarm but the phone ringing beside her bed.

'Hello?' she croaked.

'Good, I'm not the only one,' said a desperately ill-sounding voice.

'Who are you?' croaked Holly again.

'Sharon, I think. The man beside me in bed seems to think I know him.' Holly heard John laughing loudly.

'Sharon, what happened last night? Please enlighten me.'

'Alcohol happened last night. Lots and lots of alcohol.'

'Any other information?'

'Nope,' Sharon said drowsily.

'Know what time is it?'

'Two o'clock. It's afternoon, Holly.'

'Oh. How did that happen?'

'Gravity or something. I was out that day from school.'

'Oh God, I think I'm dying. I think I'll go back to sleep. Maybe when I wake up, the ground will have stopped moving.'

'Good idea. Oh, and, Holly, welcome to the thirties club.'

Holly groaned. ''Night.' Seconds later she was asleep.

Eventually, at nine o'clock that night, she decided to treat herself to a Chinese takeaway. She sat snuggled up on the couch in her pyjamas watching Saturday night TV. Holly was surprised. It was the first time since Gerry had died that she was at ease with her own company.

Later that night Jack called. 'Hey, sis, what are you doing?'

'Watching TV, having a Chinese,' she said.

'Well, you sound in good form. Unlike my poor girlfriend.'

'I'm never going out with you again, Holly,' she heard Abbey scream weakly in the background.

'She says she can't remember anything.'

'Neither can I. Maybe it happens as soon as you hit thirty.'

'Or maybe it's just an evil plan you all hatched so you wouldn't have to tell us what you got up to.' He laughed. 'Anyway, I was ringing to ask if you're going to Declan's gig tomorrow night.'

'Where is it?'

'Hogan's pub.'

'No way. There is no way I'm ever setting foot in a pub again, especially to listen to some loud rock band.'

'Don't drink then. Please come, Holly, we hardly got a chance to talk at dinner.'

'Well, we're hardly going to have a heart-to-heart with The Orgasmic Fish banging out their tunes,' she said sarcastically.

'They're actually called Black Strawberries now, which has a nice sweet ring to it I think,' he laughed.

Holly groaned, 'Oh, please don't make me go, Jack.'

'You're going. Declan will be chuffed when I tell him, the family never usually goes to these things.'

Holly arrived at Hogan's and even on a Sunday the place was packed. Hogan's was a popular three-storey club situated in the centre of town. The first floor was a trendy nightclub that played all the latest music from the charts, where the young, beautiful people went. The ground floor was a traditional Irish pub for the older crowd. The basement was dark and dingy and it was where bands usually played. The tiny bar in the corner was surrounded by a huge crowd of young students in scruffy jeans and ripped T-shirts, pushing one another to be served. The bar staff also looked like they should be at college, and were rushing around with sweat dripping from their faces.

The basement was stuffy and Holly was finding it difficult to breathe in the smoky air. She waved at Declan to let him know she was there, but decided not to make her way over as he was surrounded by a crowd of girls. She wouldn't want to cramp his style. Holly had missed out on the whole student scene, having decided not to go to college and instead working as a secretary. Gerry had studied marketing at Dublin City University but he never socialised much with his college friends.

Finally, Declan made his way over.

'Well, hello, Mr Popular, I feel privileged you chose to speak to me.'

Declan rubbed his hands together cheekily. 'I know! This band business is great.' He scoured the crowds. 'And we were told there might be a record company guy coming to see us tonight.'

'Oh, cool!' Holly's eyes widened with excitement for her brother. She glanced around and tried to spot someone who might be a record company person. What would they look like? Finally, her eyes fell upon a man who seemed older than the rest of the crowd, more her own age. He was dressed in a black leather jacket, black slacks and a black T-shirt and stood staring at the stage.

'Over there, Deco!' Holly pointed at the man, who had stubble round his jaw. Declan looked excited and his eyes followed to where her finger pointed. Then his smile faded as he obviously recognised the man. 'No, that's just *Danny!*' he yelled, and he wolf-whistled to grab his attention.

Danny twirled round and nodded his head in recognition before making his way over. 'Hi, Declan, how are you set?'

'Yeah, OK,' Declan nodded unenthusiastically. Somebody must have told him acting like you didn't care was cool.

'Sound check go OK?'

'There were a few problems but we sorted them out.'

'Good.' He turned to Holly. 'Sorry for ignoring you. I'm Daniel.'

'Nice to meet you. I'm Holly.'

'Oh, sorry,' Declan interrupted. 'Holly, this is the owner; Daniel, this is my sister.'

'Hey, Deco, we're on!' yelled a blue-haired boy.

'See you two later,' and Declan ran off.

'Good luck!' yelled Holly. 'So you're a Hogan,' she said.

'Well, no, actually, I'm a Connelly,' Daniel smiled. 'I just took over the place a few weeks ago.'

'Oh.' Holly was surprised. 'So are you going to change it to Connelly's?'

'Can't afford all the lettering on the front, it's a bit long.'

Holly laughed. 'Well, everyone knows the name Hogan's; it would probably be stupid to change it.'

Daniel nodded. 'That was the main reason actually.'

Suddenly Jack appeared at the entrance and Holly waved him over. 'I'm so sorry I'm late,' he said, giving her a hug. 'Did I miss anything?'

'Nope. He's about to go on. Jack, this is Daniel, the new owner.'

'Nice to meet you,' Daniel said, shaking his hand.

'Are they any good?' Jack asked him, nodding at the stage.

'To tell you the truth, I've never heard them play.'

'That was brave of you!' laughed Jack.

'I hope not too brave,' Daniel said as the boys took to the stage.

The crowd cheered and Declan took on his moody persona as he lifted his guitar strap over his shoulder. The music started and after that there was no chance of carrying on any kind of conversation. The crowd began to jump up and down, and once too often Holly's foot was stomped on. *'Can I get you two a drink?'* Daniel yelled. Jack asked for a pint of Budweiser and Holly settled for a 7UP. Daniel returned minutes later with their drinks and a stool for Holly. The music wasn't Holly's type of thing, and it was so loud it was difficult for her to tell if the Black Strawberries were actually any good.

After four songs Holly had had enough, and she gave Jack a kiss goodbye. *'Nice meeting you, Daniel! Thanks for the drink!'* she screamed and made her way back to civilisation and cool, fresh air. Her ears continued to ring all the way home in the car. It was ten o'clock by the time she got there. Only two more hours till May. And that meant she could open another envelope.

Holly sat at her kitchen table nervously drumming her fingers. She gulped back her third cup of coffee and uncrossed her legs. It was 11.30 p.m. and she had the envelope on the table in front of her.

She picked it up and ran her hands over it. Who would know if she opened it early? No one would care.

But that wasn't true. Gerry would know. Each time Holly held the envelopes in her hand she felt a connection with him. She felt like they were playing a game together, even though they were in two different worlds. He'd know if she cheated.

The small hand of the clock eventually struck midnight. Once again she treasured every moment of the process. She carefully tore open the seal, slid the card out and opened it.

Go on, Disco Diva! Face your fear of karaoke at Club Diva this month and you never know, you might be rewarded . . .
PS, I love you . . .

The corners of her lips lifted into a smile and she began to laugh. Holly kept repeating *'no way!'* whenever she caught her breath. Finally she calmed down. 'Gerry! You bastard! There is absolutely no way I am going through with this!'

She felt Gerry watching her. He laughed.

'You know how I feel about this, and I refuse to do it.'

'You have to do it, you know,' laughed Gerry.

'I do not have to do this!'

'Do it for me.'

'I am not doing it for world peace. I hate karaoke!'

'Do it for me,' he repeated.

The sound of the phone caused Holly to jump in her seat. It was Sharon. 'OK, it's five past twelve, what did it say?'

'What makes you think I opened it?'

'Ha!' Sharon snorted. 'Twenty years of friendship qualifies me as being an expert on you; now come on, tell me.'

'I'm not doing what he wants me to do,' Holly stated bluntly.

'Why, what is it?'

'Oh, just Gerry's *pathetic* attempt at being *humorous*,' she snapped.

'Holly, spill the beans.' John was on the downstairs phone.

'OK . . . Gerry wants me to . . . sing at a karaoke.'

The other two burst out laughing so loud, Holly had to remove the phone from her ear. 'Phone me back when the two of you shut up,' she said angrily, hanging up.

A few minutes later they called back.

'OK.' Sharon had an overly serious 'let's get down to business' tone in her voice. 'I'm fine now. Don't look at me, John,' she said away from the phone. 'Holly, I'm sorry, but I kept thinking about the last time you—'

'Yeah, yeah, yeah,' Holly interrupted. 'It was *the most embarrassing day of my life.*'

'Oh, Holly, you can't let a stupid thing like that put you off! It was only a little fall—'

'Yes, thank you! Anyway I can't even sing, Sharon; I think I established that fact the last time!'

Sharon was very quiet.

'Sharon? Sharon, are you still there?'

There was no answer.

'Sharon, are you laughing?' Holly gave out.

She heard a little squeak and the line went dead.

'**H**appy birthday, Holly! Or should I say happy belated birthday?' Richard laughed nervously. Holly's mouth dropped open in shock at the sight of her older brother standing on her doorstep. This was a rare occurrence; in fact, it may have been a first. 'I brought you a mini Phalaenopsis orchid,' he said, handing her a potted plant. 'Shipped fresh, budding and ready to bloom.'

Holly fingered the tiny pink buds. 'Gosh, Richard, orchids are my favourite!'

'Well, you have a nice big garden here anyway, nice and'—he cleared his throat—'green. Bit overgrown, though . . .' He began that annoying rocking thing he did with his feet.

'Would you like to come in or are you just passing through?' Please say no, please say no. Despite the thoughtful gift, Holly was in no mood for Richard's company.

'Well, yes, I'll come in for a little while so.' He wiped his feet for a good two minutes at the door. He reminded Holly of her old maths teacher at school, dressed in a brown cardigan with brown trousers that stopped just at the top of his neat brown shoes.

Richard never seemed comfortable in his own skin. He looked like he was being choked to death by his tie, and his smile never managed to reach his eyes. Holly led him into the living room and placed the ceramic pot on the television.

'No, no, Holly,' he said, wagging a finger. 'It needs a cool, draught-free location away from sunlight and heat vents.'

'Oh, of course.' Holly picked the pot back up and searched the room for a suitable place.

'That little table in the centre, it should be safe there.'

Holly placed the pot on the table. 'Can I get you a tea or coffee?' she asked, expecting him to say no.

'Yes, great,' he said, clapping his hands together, 'tea would be splendid. Just milk, no sugar.'

Holly returned with two mugs of tea and placed them down on the coffee table. She hoped the steam rising from the mugs wouldn't murder the poor plant.

'You just need to water it regularly and feed it during the months of spring.' He was still talking about the plant. Holly nodded, knowing full well she would not do either of those things.

'I didn't know you had green fingers, Richard.'

'Only when I'm painting with the children. At least that's what Meredith says,' he laughed, cracking a rare joke.

'Do you do much work in your garden?'

'Oh, yes, I love to work in the garden.' His eyes lit up. 'Saturdays are my garden days,' he said, smiling into his mug of tea.

Holly felt as if a complete stranger were sitting beside her. She realised she knew very little about Richard and equally he knew very little about her. But that was the way Richard had always liked to keep things. He never shared news with the family. The first time the family had even heard of Meredith was the day they both came over for dinner to announce their engagement. Unfortunately, at that stage it was too late to convince him not to marry the flame-haired, green-eyed dragon. Not that he would have listened.

'So,' she announced, far too loudly, 'anything strange or startling?' Like why are you here?

'No, no, nothing strange.' He took a sip of tea. 'I just thought I would pop in and say hello while I was in the area.'

'Ah, right. What brings you to the dark and dangerous world of the north side?'

'Oh, you know, just a little business.'

'How are Emily and Timmy, sorry, I mean Timothy?'

His eyes lit up. 'Oh, they're good, Holly. Worrying, though.'

'What do you mean?' Holly asked.

'Oh, there isn't one thing in particular, Holly. Children are a worry in general.' He looked her in the eye. 'But I suppose you're glad you'll never have to worry about this children nonsense.'

Holly felt like she had been kicked in the stomach.

'So have you found a job yet?' he continued on.

Holly sat frozen with shock. She was insulted and hurt and she wanted him out of her house. 'No,' she spat out.

'So what are you doing for money? Have you signed on the dole?'

'No, Richard,' she said. 'I get *widow's* allowance.'

'Ah, that's a great, handy thing, isn't it?'

'Devastatingly depressing is more like it.'

The atmosphere was tense. Suddenly he slapped his leg. 'I better motor on so and get back to work,' he announced, standing up. 'Anyway, nice to see you and thank you for the tea.'

'You're welcome, and thank you for the orchid,' Holly said through gritted teeth. He marched down the path to his brown family car.

Holly fumed as she watched him drive off and then banged the door shut. That man made her blood boil so much she felt like knocking him out. He hadn't a clue about anything.

'**O**h, Sharon, I just *hate* him,' Holly moaned to her friend on the phone later that night.

'Just ignore him, Holly, he's an idiot.'

'But that's what annoys me. He's thirty-six. He should bloody well know when to keep his mouth shut. He says things deliberately.'

'I don't think he does it deliberately, Holly. I genuinely think he called round to wish you a happy—'

'Yeah! And what's that about?' Holly ranted. 'Since *when* has he ever called round to give me a birthday present? *Never!*'

'Well, thirty is more of a big deal than any other . . .'

'Not in his eyes it's not! He even said so at dinner the other day.' She mimicked his voice. '*I don't agree with silly celebrations blah-blah-blah, I'm a sap blah-blah-blah.*'

Sharon laughed. 'OK, so he's an evil monster!'

Holly paused. 'Well, I wouldn't go that far, Sharon.'

Sharon laughed. 'Oh, I just can't please you at all, can I?'

Holly smiled weakly. Gerry would know exactly how she was feeling, he would know exactly what to say and he would know exactly what to do. He would give her one of his hugs and all her problems would melt away. She grabbed a pillow from her bed and hugged it tight.

'Helloooo? Earth to Holly? Am I talking to myself again?'

'Oh, sorry, Sharon, what did you say?'

'Have you given any more thought to this karaoke business?'

'Sharon!' Holly yelped. 'No more thought is required!'

'OK, calm down, woman! I was just thinking that we could hire out a karaoke machine. What do you think?'

'No, Sharon, he wants me to do it in Club Diva.'

'Ah! So sweet! Because you're his disco diva?'

'I think that was the general idea,' Holly said miserably.

'Ah! That's lovely, although Club Diva? Never heard of it.'

'Well, if no one knows where it is, then I just can't do it, can I?' Holly said, satisfied she had found a way out.

They both said their goodbyes and Holly hung up. It was back to her empty, silent house.

Holly woke up the next morning still fully dressed and lying on her bed. She could feel herself slipping into her old habits again. All her positive thoughts were melting away. It was so bloody tiring trying to be happy all the time. Who cared if the house was a mess? Nobody but she was going to see it. Who cared if she didn't wear make-up or wash for a week? *Who bloody cared?* Her mobile phone vibrated beside her, signalling a message. It was from Sharon.

> club diva no 36700700
> think bout it. wud b fun.
> do it 4 gerry?

Gerry's bloody dead, she felt like texting back. But ever since she had begun opening the envelopes he didn't feel dead to her. It was as if he were just away on holiday and writing her letters, so he wasn't really gone. Well, the least she could do was ring the club and suss out the situation. It didn't mean she had to go through with it.

She dialled the number and a man answered. She couldn't think of anything to say so she quickly hung up again. Oh, come on, Holly, she told herself, it's really not that difficult.

Holly pressed redial. The same voice answered, 'Club Diva.'

'Hi, I was wondering if you do karaoke nights there?'

'Yes, we do, they are on a . . .' she heard him leafing through some pages, 'yeah, sorry, they're on a Tuesday night.'

'OK, em, well, I was wondering if, em . . .' Holly took a deep breath. 'My friend might be interested in singing and she was wondering what she would have to do?'

There was a long pause on the other end.

'Hello?' Was this person stupid?

'Yeah, sorry, I don't organise the karaoke nights, so . . .'

'OK.' Holly was losing her temper. It had taken courage to make the call and some underqualified little twit wasn't going to ruin it. 'Is there anyone who might have a clue?'

'Eh, no, there isn't, the club isn't actually open yet, it's very early in the morning still,' came the sarcastic response.

'Well, thank you very much, you've been a terrific help,' she said, matching his sarcasm.

'Excuse me, if you can just bear with me for a moment, I'll try to find out for you.' Holly was put on hold and forced to listen to 'Greensleeves' for five minutes. 'Hello? Are you still there?'

'Barely,' she said angrily.

'OK, I just made a phone call. What's your friend's name?'

Holly froze. 'Em, her name is Holly Kennedy.'

'OK, well, it's actually a karaoke competition on Tuesday nights. It goes on for a month and every week two people out of ten are chosen till the last week of the month, when six people sing in the final.'

Holly gulped. She didn't want to do this.

'But unfortunately, the names have all been entered in advance. Your friend could try again at Christmas. That's when the next competition is on.'

'Oh, OK.'

'By the way, the name Holly Kennedy rings a bell. Would that be Declan Kennedy's sister?'

'Eh, yeah, do you know her?' said a shocked Holly.

'I met her here the other night with her brother.'

Was Declan going round introducing girls as his sister? The sick and twisted little . . . No, that couldn't be right.

'Declan played a gig in Club Diva?'

'No, no. He played with his band downstairs in the basement.'

'Is Club Diva in Hogan's?'

'Yeah, it's on the top floor. Maybe I should advertise a bit more!'

'Is that Daniel?' Holly blurted out, and then kicked herself.

'Eh, yeah, do I know you?'

'Em, no! Holly just mentioned you in conversation, that's all.' Then she realised how that sounded. 'Very briefly.' Holly began hitting her head softly on the wall.

Daniel chuckled. 'Oh, OK, well, tell her if she wants to sing at Christmas I can put her name down now. You wouldn't believe the amount of people that want to sign up.'

'Really,' Holly said weakly. She felt like a fool.

'Oh, by the way, who am I speaking to?'

Holly paced her bedroom floor. 'Em . . . you're speaking to Sharon.'

'OK, Sharon, well, I have your number on caller ID so I'll call you if anyone backs out.' He hung up.

Holly leapt into bed, throwing the duvet over her head as she felt her face burn with embarrassment. Ignoring the ringing phone, she hid under the covers, cursing herself for being such a bimbo. Eventually she crawled out and hit the button on her answering machine.

'Hi, Sharon, I must have just missed you. It's Daniel here from Club Diva.' He paused. 'Em, I was just looking through the list and it seems somebody entered Holly's name a few months back, unless it's another Holly Kennedy . . . Anyway, call me back so we can sort it out. Thanks.'

Holly sat shocked on the edge of her bed, unable to move.

Four

HOLLY AND SHARON went to Bewley's Café overlooking Grafton Street, where they met up with Denise on her lunch break. Sharon said it was the best window-shopping she could ever do, as she had a bird's-eye view of all her favourite shops.

After lunch, the three girls linked arms and walked down the street, headed towards the clothes shop where Denise was manager. 'Right, you ladies of leisure, I'd better head back to work,' Denise said, pushing the door to her shop open. As soon as her staff saw her they stopped gossiping and began to tidy the clothes rails. Holly and Sharon tried not to laugh. They said their goodbyes and both headed up to Stephen's Green to collect their cars.

It was four o'clock by the time Holly started heading home to Swords. Sharon had convinced her to go shopping, which had resulted in her splashing out on a ridiculous top she was far too old to wear. She really needed to watch her spending from now on; her funds were running low, and without regular income she could sense tense times ahead. She had to start thinking about getting a job, but she was finding it hard enough to get out of bed in the morning as it was. Another boring nine-to-five job wasn't going to help matters. But it would pay the bills. Holly sighed loudly. The thought of it was just depressing her.

She phoned her mum and checked if it was all right for her to call round.

'Of course you can, love.' Then Elizabeth lowered her voice. 'Just as long as you know that Richard is here.' What was with all the little visits all of a sudden?

Holly contemplated heading straight home, but he was her brother. As annoying as he was, she couldn't avoid him for ever.

She arrived to an extremely loud and crowded house, and it felt like old times again. Her mum was setting an extra place at the table just as she walked in. 'Oh, Mum, you should have told me you were having supper,' Holly said, giving her a hug and a kiss.

'Why, have you eaten already?'

'No, but I hope you didn't go to too much trouble.'

'No trouble at all, dear, it just means that poor Declan will have to go without food for the day, that's all,' she said, teasing her son who was taking his seat. He made a face at her.

'So, Mr Hard Worker, why aren't you in college?' Holly said.

'I've been in college all morning,' Declan replied. 'And I'm going back in at eight o'clock, actually.'

'That's very late,' said her father, pouring gravy all over his plate. He always ended up with more gravy than food on his plate.

'Yeah, but it was the only time I could get the editing suite.'

'Is there only one editing suite, Declan?' piped up Richard.

'Yeah.' Ever the conversationalist.

'And how many students are there?'

'It's only a small class, there are just twelve of us.'

'Don't they have the funds for any more?'

'For what, students?' Declan teased.

'No, for another editing suite.'

'No, it's only a small college, Richard.'

'I suppose the bigger universities would be better equipped.'

And there was the dig they were all waiting for.

'No, the facilities are top of the range. And the lecturers are a bonus because they work in the industry. It's not just textbook stuff.'

Good for you, Declan, Holly thought.

'I wouldn't imagine they get paid well doing that.'

'Richard, working in film is a very good job; people have spent years studying for master's—'

'Oh, you get a degree for that, do you?' Richard was amazed. 'I thought it was just a little course you were doing.'

Declan stopped eating and looked at Holly in shock.

'What's your project on, Declan?' Frank asked.

'Oh, basically it's on club life in Dublin.'

'Oooh, will we be in it?' Ciara asked excitedly.

'I might show the back of your head or something,' he joked.

'Well, I can't wait to see it,' Holly said encouragingly.

'Thanks.' Declan started laughing. 'Hey, what's this I hear about you singing in a karaoke competition next week?'

'What?' Ciara's eyes nearly popped out of her head.

Holly pretended not to know what he was talking about.

'Ah, come on, Danny told me!' Declan turned to the rest of the table and explained, 'Danny owns the place I did the gig the other night and he told me Holly entered a karaoke competition in the club upstairs.'

Everyone oohed and aahed about how great it was. Holly refused to give in. 'Declan, Daniel's just playing games with you. Sure, if I was in a karaoke competition I *think* I would tell you all.'

Declan laughed. 'I saw your name on the list! Don't lie!'

'Holly, why didn't you tell us?' her mother asked.

Holly put her knife and fork down. 'Because I can't sing!'

'Then why are you doing it?' Ciara burst out laughing.

She might as well tell them, she figured; otherwise Declan would beat it out of her and she didn't like lying to her parents.

'OK, basically Gerry entered my name in the competition months ago because he really wanted me to do it, and as much as I *don't* want to do it, I feel I have to go through with it. It's stupid, I know.'

Her family stared at her.

'Well, I think that's a wonderful idea,' her dad announced.

'Yes,' added her mum, 'and we'll all be there to support you.'

'No, Mum, you really don't have to be. It's no big deal.'

'There's no way my sister is singing in a competition without me being there,' declared Ciara.

'Here, here,' said Richard. 'We'll all go so. I've never been to a karaoke before. When is it on?' He took out his diary.

'Eh . . . Saturday,' Holly lied, and Richard began writing it down.

'It is not!' Declan burst out. 'It's next Tuesday, you liar!'

Holly could not stop going to the toilet. She had got practically no sleep and she looked just the way she felt. There were huge bags under her eyes and her lips were bitten. The big day had arrived—her worst nightmare, singing in public. There was no better laxative than fear.

Her friends and family had been as supportive as ever, sending her Good Luck cards. Sharon and John had even sent her a bouquet of flowers, which she placed on the draught-free, heat-vent-free coffee table beside her half-dead orchid.

Holly dressed in the outfit Gerry had told her to buy in April and cursed him throughout. She piled on waterproof mascara because she could foresee the night ending in tears. She tended to have psychic powers when it came to facing the crappiest days of her life.

John and Sharon collected her in a taxi and she refused to talk to them, cursing everyone for forcing her to do this.

'Relax, Holly,' Sharon said, 'everything will be fine.'

'Bug off,' she snapped.

They finally reached Hogan's and, much to her horror, the club was packed. Her family had saved a table beside the Ladies, as requested.

Richard was sitting awkwardly on a stool, looking out of place in a suit. 'Tell me about these rules, Father. What will Holly have to do?'

Frank explained the 'rules' to Richard and Holly's nerves began to build even more.

'Gosh, that's terrific,' Richard said, staring round the club in awe. Holly didn't think he'd ever been in a nightclub before.

Jack was sitting with his arm draped round Abbey's shoulders; they both gave her a supportive smile.

'Hi, Holly,' Daniel said, approaching with a clipboard. 'OK, the order of the night is: first up is Margaret, then Keith and then you. OK?'

'That's all I need,' Holly snapped rudely. She just wished that everyone would leave her alone to wish evil thoughts on them all, but Daniel was still talking.

'Look, Holly, I'm really sorry to disturb you again, but could you tell me which of your friends is Sharon?'

'Over there.' Holly pointed to Sharon. 'Hold on, why?'

'Oh, I just wanted to apologise for the last time we spoke.'

'Why?' Holly said with panic in her voice.

'Oh, we just had a minor disagreement on the phone.' He headed over to Sharon. Holly leapt from her stool.

'Sharon, hi, I'm Daniel. I just wanted to apologise about the confusion on the phone last week.'

Sharon looked at him as though he had ten heads. 'Confusion? On the phone? What's your name again?'

'Em, it's Daniel.'

'And we spoke on the phone?' Sharon said politely.

Holly gestured wildly to her behind Daniel's back. He cleared his throat nervously. 'Yes, you called the club?'

'No, sweetie, you've got the wrong girl,' Sharon said.

Daniel appeared confused. Holly nodded her head frantically.

'Oh . . .' Sharon said, looking like she finally remembered. 'Oh, Daniel! God, I am so sorry, my brain cells seem to be going a bit dead. Must be too much of this,' she laughed, picking up her drink.

Relief washed over Daniel's face. 'Good, so you remember us having that conversation?'

'Oh, *that* conversation. Listen, don't worry about it.' She waved her hand dismissively.

'It's just that I only took over the place recently and I wasn't too sure of the arrangements for tonight.'

'Oh, don't worry, we all need time to adjust . . . you know?' Sharon looked at Holly to see if she had said the right thing.

'OK, then, well, it's nice to finally meet you in person,' Daniel said.

John and Sharon stared at him as he walked away.

'What was that all about?' Sharon asked Holly as soon as he was out of earshot.

'Oh, I'll explain it to you later,' said Holly as their karaoke host for the evening was just stepping up onstage.

'Good evening, ladies and gentlemen!' he announced.

'Good evening!' shouted Richard, looking excited.

'We have an exciting night ahead of us . . .' He went on and on in his DJ voice. 'First up we have Margaret from Tallaght, to sing the theme to *Titanic*, "My Heart Will Go On" by Celine Dion. Please put your hands together for Margaret!' The crowd went wild. Holly's heart raced.

When Margaret began to sing, the room became so quiet you could almost hear a pin drop. Her eyes were closed and she sang with such passion it seemed she had lived every line of the song.

'Wasn't that incredible?' the DJ announced as Margaret tripped back to her seat. The crowd cheered again. 'Next up we have Keith, you may remember him as last year's winner, and he's singing "America" by Neil Diamond. Give it up for Keith!'

Holly didn't need to hear any more and rushed into the toilet. She paced up and down trying to calm herself. Her knees were knocking, her stomach was twisted in knots. She looked at herself in the mirror and tried to take big deep breaths. The crowd applauded outside and Holly froze. She was next.

'Wasn't Keith terrific, ladies and gentlemen?' Lots of cheers again. 'Well, it doesn't get any better than that! Next we have a newcomer to the competition. Ladies and gentlemen, please put your hands together for Holly!'

Holly ran to the cubicle and locked herself in.

It was three years ago that Holly had taken to the stage for her debut karaoke performance. A huge crowd of her friends had gone to their local pub in Swords to celebrate the thirtieth birthday of one of the lads. Holly had been working overtime for two weeks. She really wasn't in the mood to go out partying. All she wanted was to have a nice long bath, put on the most unsexy pair of pyjamas she owned, eat lots of chocolate and snuggle up in front of the television with Gerry.

After standing on an overcrowded train all the way from Blackrock, Holly arrived at Sutton Station to see her local bus drive off and was forced to stand waiting for the next one in the freezing cold for half an hour. She arrived home to thumping music and crowds of people with cans of beer, some slumped on the couch she had intended to lie on. Gerry stood at the CD player acting DJ and trying to look cool. At that moment she had never seen him look so uncool.

'What is wrong with you?' he asked her after seeing her storming upstairs to the bedroom.

'Gerry, I am tired, I am pissed off, and you didn't even ask me if it was all right to invite all these people over. And, by the way, *who are they?*' she yelled.

'They're friends of Conor's and, by the way, *this is my house too!*' he yelled back.

Holly began to gently massage her temples. 'Gerry,' she said, trying to stay calm, 'it would be fine if you had planned it in advance, *then* I wouldn't care, but today of all days, when I am so so tired,' her voice became weaker and weaker, 'I just wanted to relax in my own house.'

'Oh, every day's the same with you,' he snapped. 'You never want to do anything any more. You come home in your cranky moods and bitch about everything!'

Holly's jaw dropped. 'Excuse me! I have been working hard!'

'*It's Friday,*' he yelled. '*It's the weekend!* Let your hair down for a change and stop acting like a *granny!*' And he stormed out of the bedroom and slammed the door.

After spending a long time in the bedroom hating Gerry and dreaming of a divorce, she managed to think about what he had said. And he was right. OK, he wasn't right in the way he had phrased it, but she *had* been cranky and she knew it.

Holly was the type of person who finished work at 5 p.m. and was running for her train by 5.01. She never took work home and she phoned in sick as many Monday mornings as possible. But owing to a momentary lapse of concentration when looking for new employment, she had found herself accepting an office job that forced her to work late. She hadn't gone out for weeks and she fell asleep the minute her head hit the pillow every night. Come to think of it, that was probably Gerry's main problem.

But tonight would be different. She intended to show her neglected friends and husband that she was still the fun and frivolous Holly who could drink them all under the table. This show of antics began by preparing homemade cocktails. These worked their magic and at eleven o'clock they all danced down the road to the pub where a karaoke was taking place. Holly demanded to be first up and heckled the host until she got her way. The pub was packed that night and there was a rowdy crowd who were out on a stag night.

The DJ gave Holly a huge build-up after believing her lies of being a professional singer. Gerry lost all power of speech and sight from laughing so hard, but Holly was determined to show him that she could still let her hair down. She decided to sing 'Like a Virgin' and dedicated it to the man who was getting married the next day. As soon as she started singing, Holly had never heard so many boos in her whole life, but she was so drunk she didn't care. Eventually, when people began to throw things at the stage, she handed back the microphone, tripped down the steps in her stilettos and fell flat on her face.

Gerry lost his voice from laughing so loudly and Denise and Sharon took photographs of the scene of the crime.

Holly vowed *never* to do karaoke again.

'**H**olly Kennedy? Are you here?' the karaoke host's voice boomed. The applause died down as everyone looked round in search of Holly. Well, they would be a long time looking, she thought as she lowered the toilet seat and sat down to wait for the excitement to settle so they could move on to their next victim. She closed her eyes and prayed for this moment to pass.

Outside the cubicle the toilet door open and slammed.

'Holly?' It was Sharon. 'Holly, I know you're in there, so listen, OK?'

Holly sniffed back the tears that were beginning to well.

'I know that this is an absolute nightmare for you but you need to relax, OK?' Sharon paused.

The DJ's voice said into the microphone, 'Ladies and gentlemen, it appears that our singer is currently in the toilets.' The entire room erupted in laughter.

'Oh, Sharon!' Holly's voice trembled in fear.

'Holly, you don't have to do this. Nobody is forcing you . . .'

'Ladies and gentlemen, let's let Holly know that she's up next!'

yelled the DJ. 'Come on!' Everybody began to chant her name.

'OK, well, at least nobody who cares about you is forcing you to do this. But if you don't do this, I know you'll never forgive yourself. Gerry wanted you to do this for a reason.'

'*Holly! Holly! Holly!*'

'Oh, Sharon!' Holly repeated again, panicking. Suddenly the walls of the cubicle felt like they were closing in on her; beads of sweat formed on her forehead. She burst through the door, her eyes red and puffy.

'Don't mind them, Holly,' Sharon said coolly, 'they can't make you do anything you don't want to do.'

Holly's lower lip began to tremble.

'Don't!' Sharon said. 'Don't even think about it!'

'I can't sing, Sharon,' Holly whispered.

'I know that! Screw them! You're never gonna see their ugly mugs *ever again!* Who cares what they think? I don't, do you?'

Holly thought about it for a minute. 'No,' she whispered.

'What? I didn't hear you. Do you care what they think?'

'No,' she said, a little stronger.

'Louder!' Sharon shook her by the shoulders.

'No!' she yelled.

'Louder!'

'NOOOOOOOOO! I DON'T CARE WHAT THEY THINK!' Holly screamed. The two of them began to giggle.

'Just let this be another silly Holly day so we can laugh about it a few months from now,' Sharon pleaded.

Holly took a deep breath and charged towards the door like a woman on a mission. She came face to face with her adoring fans, who were all chanting her name. She took an extremely theatrical bow and, to the sounds of claps and laughter, headed towards the stage.

Holly had everybody's attention now, whether she liked it or not. She stood with her arms folded and stared at the audience. The music started and her whole table held their thumbs up. It was corny but strangely comforting. Holding the microphone tightly, with an extremely shaky and timid voice she sang: '"What would you do if I sang out of tune? Would you stand up and walk out on me?"'

Denise and Sharon howled with laughter at the choice of song and gave a big cheer. Holly struggled on, singing dreadfully. Just when she felt she was about to hear boos her family and friends joined in. '"Ooh, I'll get by with a little help from my friends; yes, I'll get by with a little help from my friends."'

The crowd laughed and the atmosphere warmed a little more. Holly yelled at the top of her lungs, '"Do you *neeeed* anybody?"' A few people helped her out to sing, '"I need somebody to love."'

'"Do you *neeeed* anybody?"' she repeated and held the microphone out to the crowd and they all sang. Holly felt less nervous now and battled her way through the rest of the song. The people down the back resumed chatting, the bar staff carried on serving drinks. When she had finally finished singing, a few polite tables up the front and her own table were the only people to acknowledge her. The DJ took the microphone and managed to say between laughs, 'Please give it up for the incredibly brave Holly Kennedy!'

Her family and friends cheered. Denise and Sharon approached her with cheeks wet from tears of laughter.

'I'm so proud of you!' Sharon said, throwing her arms round Holly's neck. 'It was awful!'

'Thanks for helping me, Sharon,' she said as she hugged her friend.

Abbey cheered and Jack shouted, 'Terrible! Absolutely terrible!' Holly's mother smiled and Holly's father could barely look her in the eye he was laughing so much.

All Ciara could manage was to repeat over and over again, 'I never knew anyone could be so bad.'

Declan waved at her with a camera in his hand and gave her the thumbs-down. Holly hid in the corner at the table. She couldn't remember the last time she had felt so proud.

John shuffled over and leaned against the wall beside her. He said, 'Gerry's probably here, you know,' and looked at her with watery eyes.

Poor John, he missed his best friend too. She gave him an encouraging smile. He was right. Holly *could* feel Gerry's presence. She could feel him wrapping his arms round her and giving her one of the hugs she missed so much.

After an hour the singers had finally finished, and Daniel and the DJ headed off to tot up the voting slips. It was obvious Holly wasn't going to win, but on the off chance that she did, she shuddered at the thought of having to return to repeat the experience in two weeks' time. The DJ played a CD of a drumroll as Daniel took to the stage in his black leather jacket and slacks and was greeted by wolf whistles and screams from the girls. Richard looked excited and crossed his fingers at Holly.

'OK, so the two people that will be going through to the final are'— Daniel paused for dramatic effect—'Keith and Samantha!'

Holly jumped up and danced around in a huddle with Denise and Sharon. Richard looked on confused, and the rest of Holly's family congratulated her on her victorious loss.

Holly sat back down and sipped her drink thoughtfully. Sharon and John seemed engrossed in a heated discussion, Abbey and Jack were like love-struck teenagers as usual, Ciara was intent on getting to know Daniel better, and Denise was . . . Where was Denise?

Holly looked around the club and spotted her sitting on the stage striking a very provocative pose for the karaoke host. Holly's parents had gone, which left . . . Richard. Richard sat looking like a lost puppy taking a sip from his drink every few seconds.

Holly moved over and sat opposite him. 'You enjoying yourself?'

He looked up. 'Yes, thank you, I'm having fun, Holly.'

'I'm surprised you came, actually, I didn't think this would be your scene.'

'Oh, you know . . . you have to support the family.'

'So where's Meredith tonight?'

'Emily and Timothy,' he said, as if that explained it all.

'You working tomorrow?'

'Yes,' he said suddenly, knocking back his drink, 'so I best be off. You were a great sport tonight, Holly.' He looked round awkwardly at his family, debating whether to interrupt them and say goodbye, but eventually deciding against it. He nodded to Holly and off he went, manoeuvring his way through the crowd.

Holly was once again alone. As much as she wanted to grab her bag and run home, she knew she should sit this one out. There would be plenty of times when she would be the only singleton in the company of couples, and she needed to adapt. Holly wondered whether this had been Gerry's intention. She had stood on a stage and sung to hundreds of people, and now she was stuck in a situation where she was surrounded by couples. Whatever his plan was, she was being forced to become braver without him.

Holly smiled as she watched her sister nattering away to Daniel. Ciara was so carefree and confident. For as long as Holly could remember, Ciara had never managed to hold down a job or a boyfriend, she was always lost in a dream of visiting another far-off country. She turned her attention to Jack, still lost in a world with Abbey. She wished she could be more like him, the cool English teacher all the teenagers respected. Holly sighed loudly and drained her drink.

Daniel looked over. 'Holly, can I get you another drink?'

'Ah, no, thanks, Daniel, I'm heading home soon anyway.'

'Oh, Hol!' protested Ciara. 'It's so early! No, you're staying. Get her a vodka and Coke,' she ordered Daniel, 'and I'll have the same again.'

'Ciara!' Holly exclaimed.

'No, it's OK! I asked.' Daniel headed off to the bar.

'Ciara, that was so rude,' Holly gave out to her sister.

'What? It's not like he has to pay for it, he owns the bloody place,' she said defensively. 'Where's Richard?'

'Gone home.'

'No! How long ago?' She jumped down from her seat.

'I dunno, about five or ten minutes. Why?'

'He's supposed to be driving me home!' She threw everyone's coats into a pile while she rooted around for her bag.

'Ciara, you'll never catch him, he's been gone far too long.'

'No, I will. He's parked ages away and he'll have to drive back down this road to get home. I'll get him while he's passing.' She found her bag and legged it out of the door yelling, 'Bye, Holly!'

Daniel placed the drinks on the table and sat down again. 'Where's Ciara gone?'

'Oh, she's really sorry but she had to chase my brother for a lift.' Holly bit her lip. 'Sorry for being so rude to you earlier.' She started laughing. 'You must think we're the rudest family in the world. Ciara doesn't mean what she says half the time.'

'And you did?' he smiled.

'At the time, yes.' She laughed again.

'Hey, it's fine, just means there's more drink for you.' He slid the glass across the table towards her, then stared past her shoulder with amusement. 'Well, it looks like your friend is having a good night.'

Holly turned and saw Denise and the DJ wrapped round each other. Her provocative poses had obviously worked.

'Oh, no, not the horrible DJ who forced me to come out of the toilet,' Holly groaned.

'That's my friend Tom O'Connor from Dublin FM. He's working here tonight because the karaoke went out live on the radio,' Daniel said.

'What?'

His face broke into a smile. 'Only joking; just wanted to see the look on your face.'

'Don't do that to me,' Holly put her hand on her heart. 'Having the people in here hear me was bad enough, never mind the entire city.'

'If you hate it so much, why did you enter?' Daniel asked.

'Oh, my hilarious husband thought it would be funny to enter his tone-deaf wife into a singing competition.'

Daniel laughed. 'You weren't *that* bad! Is your husband here?' he asked, looking round.

Holly smiled. 'Yeah, he's definitely here . . . somewhere.'

Five

HOLLY SECURED her bedsheet onto the washing line with a peg and thought about how she had bumbled around for the remainder of May trying to get her life into some sort of order. Days went by when she felt so confident that her life would be OK, and then just as quickly the feeling would disappear and she would feel her sadness setting in once more. She had tried to find a routine she could happily fall into so that she felt like she belonged in this life, instead of wandering around like a zombie watching everybody else live theirs. Unfortunately, the routine hadn't turned out exactly as she had hoped. She found herself immobile for hours in the living room, reliving every argument they had had, wishing she could take back every horrible word she had ever said to him. She chastised herself for walking away from him when she should have hugged him; when she held grudges for days instead of forgiving him; when she went straight to sleep some nights instead of making love to him. The bad times had all been such a waste of time.

Then there were her happy days, when she would walk around in a daydream with nothing but a smile on her face, catching herself giggling when a joke of theirs would suddenly pop into her head. That was her routine. She would fall into days of deep, dark depression, then finally build up the strength to snap out of it for another few days. But the tiniest thing would trigger off her tears again. It was a tiring process, and most of the time she couldn't be bothered battling with her mind.

She reread Gerry's original letter over and over, analysing each word and each sentence, and each day she came up with a new meaning. But the fact was that she would never *really* know *exactly* what he meant because she would never speak to him *ever again*. It was this thought that she had the most difficulty trying to come to terms with.

June brought another envelope from Gerry.

Holly sat out in the sun, revelling in the new brightness of life, and read the fourth message. She loved the bumps of Gerry's handwriting under her finger as it ran over the dried ink. Inside, he had listed the items in the house that belonged to him and explained what he wanted Holly to do with them. At the bottom it read:

PS, I love you, Holly, and I know you love me. You don't need my belongings to remember me by, you don't need to keep them as proof that I existed or still exist in your mind. You don't need to wear my sweater to feel me around you; I'm always wrapping my arms round you.

Holly almost wished he would ask her to do karaoke again. She would have jumped from an aeroplane for him; run a thousand miles; *anything* except empty out his wardrobes and rid herself of his presence. But he was right and she knew it. The physical Gerry was gone.

It was an emotionally draining experience. It took her days to complete. She relived a million memories with every garment and piece of paper she bagged. Every time an item left her fingers it was like saying goodbye to a part of Gerry all over again. It was difficult; so difficult and at times too difficult.

Despite her wishes to do this alone, Jack had called round to offer some brotherly support, and she had appreciated it. Every item had a history and they would talk and laugh about the memories. He was there for her when she cried and he was there when she finally clapped her hands together, ridding her skin of the dust that remained.

She laughed as she bagged the dusty cassettes of his favourite rock band from his schooldays. He would blast the heavy-metal music from every speaker in the house to torment Holly with its screeching guitars and badly produced sound quality. She always told him she couldn't wait to see the end of those tapes. The relief didn't wash over her as once she hoped it would.

Her eyes rested upon a crumpled ball lying in the back corner of the wardrobe—Gerry's lucky football jersey. It was still covered in grass and mud stains from its last victorious day on the pitch. She held it close to her and inhaled deeply; the smell of beer and sweat was faint, but still there. She put it aside to be washed and passed on to John.

So many objects, so many memories. Objects that were once so full of life and importance but that now lay limp on the floor. Without him they were just *things*. Gerry's wedding tuxedo, his suits, shirts and ties that he would moan about having to wear every morning before going to work. The fashions of the years gone by, shiny suits and shell track suits bundled away. A snorkel from their first time scuba diving, a shell that he had picked up off the ocean floor ten years ago, his collection of beer mats. Letters and birthday cards from friends and family sent to him over the years. Valentine's Day cards from Holly. Childhood teddies put aside to be sent back to his parents. Records of bills, his golf clubs for John, books for Sharon, memories, tears and laughter for Holly.

His entire life bundled into twenty refuse sacks.

His and her memories bundled away into Holly's mind.

Each item unearthed dust, tears, laughter and memories. She bagged the items, cleared the dust, wiped her eyes and filed away the memories.

Holly's mobile began to ring, and she dropped the laundry basket onto the grass and ran to the kitchen to answer it. 'Hello?'

'I'm gonna make you a star!' Declan's voice screeched hysterically and he broke into uncontrollable laughter.

Holly searched her brain to figure out what he could be talking about. 'Declan, are you drunk?'

'Maybe jus a li'l bit, but that's completely irrelevant.'

'Declan, it's ten o'clock in the morning!' Holly laughed. 'Have you been to bed yet?'

'Nope. I'm on the train home now. I'm in Galway. The 'wards were on last night.'

'Oh, sorry for my ignorance, but what awards were you at?'

'The student media 'wards and I won!' he yelled, and Holly heard what sounded like the entire carriage celebrating with him. 'And the prize is that my film is gonna be aired on Channel 4 next week! Can you believe it?' There were more cheers this time and Holly could barely make out what he was saying. 'You're gonna be famous, sis!' was the last thing she heard before the line went dead.

Holly was delighted for Declan and rang round her family to share the good news, but they had all received similar phone calls. Ciara chattered on like an excited schoolgirl about how Daniel had offered Club Diva so they could watch the documentary next Wednesday on the big wall screen at Hogan's.

Holly sat at the kitchen table wondering what she should wear next week; she wanted to look sexy and gorgeous for a change. Maybe Denise had something in her shop. She picked up the phone and called her at work.

'Hello, Casuals,' answered a very polite Denise.

'Hello, Casuals, Holly here. I know I'm not supposed to call you at work but Declan's documentary won some student award thingy and it's gonna be aired on Wednesday night.'

'Oh, that's so cool, Holly! Are we gonna be in it?'

'Yeah, I think so. We're all meeting up at Hogan's to watch it. You up for that?'

'Oooh, of course! I can bring my new boyfriend,' she giggled.

'What new boyfriend?'

'Tom!'

'The karaoke guy?' Holly asked in shock.

'Yeah, of course! Oh, Holly, I'm so in love!' she giggled again.

'In love? But you only met him a few weeks ago!'

'I don't care; it only takes a minute . . . as the saying goes.'

'Wow, Denise . . . I don't know what to say! I mean . . . it's great news.'

'Oh, try not to sound too enthusiastic, Holly,' Denise said sarcastically. 'Anyway, I can't wait for you to meet him, you'll really *really* like him.' She rambled on about how great he was.

'Denise, aren't you forgetting that I've met him?' Holly interrupted in the middle of a story about how Tom had saved a child from drowning.

'Yeah, I know, but I'd rather you meet him when you're not acting like a demented woman hiding in toilets.'

Holly rolled her eyes. 'Look forward to it then . . .'

Holly arrived at Hogan's and pushed through the pub crowd to make her way upstairs to Club Diva. The traditional band was in full swing and the crowd was joining in on all their favourite Irish songs. It was only seven thirty, so Club Diva wasn't officially open yet. She was the first to arrive and settled herself at a table right in front of the big screen.

A smashing glass made her jump and she looked up to see Daniel behind the bar, a dustpan and brush in his hand. 'Oh, hiya, Holly.' He looked at her in surprise. 'I didn't realise anyone had come in.'

'It's just me, I came early.' She walked over to greet him.

'You're really early,' he said, looking at his watch. 'The others probably won't be here for another hour or so.'

Holly looked confused. 'But doesn't the show start at eight?'

'I was told nine, but I could be wrong . . .' Daniel reached for that day's paper. 'Yep, nine o'clock, Channel 4.'

'Oh, no, I'm sorry. I'll wander round town for a bit.'

'Don't be silly, the shops are all closed by now. You can keep me company—that's if you don't mind . . .'

'Well, I don't mind if you don't mind.'

'I don't mind,' he said, smiling. He leaned his hands against the taps in a typical barman's pose. 'So, now, what can I get you?'

'Well, this is great. I'll have a sparkling water, please.'

'Nothing stronger?' He raised his eyebrows.

'Better not or I'll be drunk by the time everyone gets here.'

'Good thinking.' He reached behind him to the fridge. He was wearing faded blue jeans and a light blue shirt that made his blue eyes twinkle. He slid the glass towards her.

'Can I get you anything?' she asked him.

'No, thanks, I'll take care of this one.'

'Please. You've bought me plenty of drinks. It's my turn.'

'OK, I'll have a Budweiser then, thanks.' He leaned against the bar.

'What? Do you want me to get it?' Holly laughed, jumping off her stool. 'I always wanted to work behind a bar when I was a kid,' she said, grabbing a pint glass and pulling down on the tap. She was enjoying herself.

'Well, there's a spare job if you're looking for one,' Daniel said, watching her work closely.

'No, thanks. I think I do a better job on the other side.' She took out her purse and handed him money. 'Keep the change,' she laughed.

'Thanks.' He turned to the cash register, then walked round the bar to join her. 'Has your husband deserted you again tonight?' he teased.

Holly bit her lip. She didn't want the poor man to ask her every time he saw her. 'Daniel, I don't mean to make you uncomfortable, but my husband passed away.'

Daniel blushed slightly. 'Oh, Holly, I'm sorry, I didn't know.'

'I know you didn't.' She smiled to show him it was all right.

'Well, I didn't meet him the other night, but if someone had told me, I would have gone to the funeral to pay my respects.' He sat beside her at the bar.

'Oh, no, Gerry died in February. He wasn't here the other night.'

'But I thought you told me he was here . . .' He trailed off, thinking he had misheard her.

'Oh, yeah.' Holly looked down at her feet with embarrassment. 'Well, he wasn't here,' she said, looking around the club, 'but he was here,' she put her hand on her heart.

'Ah, I see,' he said, finally understanding. 'Well, then, you were even braver the other night than I thought,' he said gently. Holly was surprised by how at ease he seemed. Usually people either wandered off or changed the subject. She felt she could talk openly without fear of crying. She briefly explained the story of The List.

'So that's why I ran off during Declan's gig that time.'

'It wasn't because they were so terrible by any chance?' Daniel joked, then he looked lost in thought. 'Ah, yes, that was the 30th of April.'

'Now you're getting the gist,' she laughed. 'I couldn't wait any longer to open it.'

'I have arrived!' announced Denise to the empty room as she

swanned in, dolled up to the nines. Tom strolled in behind her, unable to take his eyes off her.

'God, *you're* dressed up,' Holly remarked. In the end she had decided to wear just a pair of jeans, black boots and a very simple black top.

'Well, it's not every day I get to go to my own premiere, is it?'

Tom and Daniel greeted each other with hugs. 'Baby, this is my friend Daniel,' Tom said, introducing Denise to Daniel.

Holly shook Tom's hand after Denise had introduced her. 'Hi, Tom. I'm sorry about the last time I met you, I wasn't feeling very sane that night.'

'Oh, that's no problem,' Tom smiled. 'If you hadn't entered then I wouldn't have met Denise, so I'm glad you did.'

Holly settled down on a stool, feeling comfortable with these two new men, and after a while she discovered that she was enjoying herself. Later the rest of the Kennedy family arrived, along with Sharon and John. Holly ran down to greet them.

'Meredith not with you tonight?' she asked Richard boldly.

'No, she's not,' he snapped back, and headed over to the bar.

'Why does he bother coming at all?' she moaned to Jack while he held her head to his chest and consoled her.

'OK, everyone!' Declan stood on a stool. 'Because Ciara couldn't decide what to wear tonight, we're all late and *my* documentary is about to start any minute. So if you can just all shut up and sit down.'

'Oh, Declan.' Holly's mother admonished him for his rudeness.

Holly spotted Ciara glued to Daniel's side at the bar. She laughed to herself and settled down to watch the documentary. As soon as the announcer introduced it, everybody cheered.

The title *Girls and the City* appeared over a beautiful night-time shot of Dublin, followed by footage of Sharon, Denise, Abbey and Ciara all squashed in the back of a taxi.

Sharon was speaking. 'Hello! I'm Sharon and this is Abbey, Denise and Ciara.' Each of the girls posed for her close-up as she was introduced. 'And we're heading to our best friend Holly's house because it's her birthday today . . .'

The scene changed to the girls surprising Holly with shouts of 'Happy birthday' at her door. It returned to Sharon in the taxi.

'Tonight it's gonna be just us girls and *no men* . . .'

The scene switched to Holly holding the presents up to the camera. Then it returned to Sharon in the taxi. 'We are gonna do lots and *lots* of drinking . . .'

Now Holly was popping open the champagne, then the girls were knocking back shots in Boudoir, and eventually it showed Holly with the crooked tiara drinking out of a champagne bottle with a straw.

'We are gonna go clubbing . . .'

There was then a shot of the girls in Boudoir doing some embarrassing moves on the dance floor. Sharon was shown next, speaking sincerely. 'But nothing too mad! We're gonna be good girls tonight!'

The next scene showed the girls protesting wildly as they were escorted out of the club by three bouncers.

Holly stared in shock over at Sharon, who was equally surprised. The men laughed their hearts out and slapped Declan on the back. Holly, Sharon, Denise, Abbey and even Ciara slithered down in their seats with humiliation. What on earth had Declan done?

Holly held her breath. How drunk must they all have been to completely forget the events of that night? The truth terrified her.

Once again a new title took over the screen: 'Journey to the City'. It showed the girls scrambling over one another to get into the seven-seater taxi. Holly had actually thought she was quite sober at that stage. 'Oh, Nick,' she moaned drunkenly to the taxi driver from the passenger seat, 'I'm thirty today, can you believe it?'

Nick—who couldn't give a flying flute what age she was—glanced over at her and laughed, 'Sure you're only a young one still, Holly.' The camera zoomed in on Holly's face and she cringed at the sight of herself. She looked so drunk, so *sad.*

'But what am I gonna do, Jim?' she whinged. 'I have no job, no husband, no children and I'm thirty! Did I tell you that?'

'Ah, Holly, worry about all that shite tomorrow, love.'

The camera stayed with Holly as she leaned her head against the window, lost in thought for the rest of the journey. Holly couldn't get over how lonely she looked. She didn't like it. She looked round the room in embarrassment and turned back in time to see herself screaming to the girls on O'Connell Street.

'OK, girls. We are going to Boudoir and *no one* is going to stop us, *especially* any *silly bouncers* who *think* they own the place,' and she marched off in what she thought at the time was a straight line. All the girls cheered and followed after her.

The scene immediately jumped to the two bouncers outside Boudoir shaking their heads. 'Not tonight, girls, sorry.'

'But,' Denise said calmly, 'do you not know who we are?'

'No.' They both stared over their heads, ignoring them.

'Huh!' Denise put her hands on her hips. 'But this is the very, very famous . . . em . . . Princess Holly from the royal family of . . . Finland.'

On camera Holly frowned at Denise.

Her family howled with laughter. 'You couldn't write a script better than this,' Declan laughed.

'Oh, she's royalty, is she?' the bouncer with a moustache smirked. 'Finland got a royal family, Paul?'

'Don't think so, boss.'

Holly gave them both a royal wave. 'You see?' Denise said. 'You'll be very embarrassed if you don't let her in.'

'Supposing we let her in, then you'll have to stay outside.' Moustache Man motioned for the people behind them to pass.

'Oh, no, no,' Denise laughed. 'I'm her lady in waiting.'

'One *must* have a drink,' Holly said. 'One is *dreadfully* thirsty.'

Paul and Moustache Man snorted and tried to keep a straight face. 'No, honestly, girls, you need to be a member.'

'But I am a member, of the royal family!' Holly said.

Denise pleaded. 'The princess and I will be no trouble at all.'

Moustache Man raised his eyes to the sky. 'All right then, go on in,' he said, stepping aside.

'God bless you,' Holly said as she passed.

'She's out of her mind,' laughed Moustache Man, regaining his composure as Ciara's entourage approached.

'Is it OK if my film crew follow me in?' Ciara said confidently in a brilliant Australian accent.

'Hold on while I check.' Paul turned his back and spoke into the walkie-talkie. 'Yeah, that's no problem, go ahead.'

'That's that Australian singer, isn't it?' Moustache Man said.

'Yeah, good song that.'

'Tell the boys inside to keep an eye on the princess and her lady. We don't want them bothering that singer with the pink hair.'

As Holly watched the inside of Boudoir on the screen she remembered being disappointed by the club. There had always been a mystery as to what Boudoir looked like. The girls had read in a magazine that there was a water feature Madonna had apparently jumped into one night. Holly had imagined a huge champagne waterfall cascading down the wall of the club that continued to flow in little bubbling streams while the glamorous people sat round it and occasionally dipped their glasses into it. But instead of her waterfall, what Holly got was an oversized fish bowl in the centre of the circular bar. The room wasn't as big as she thought it would be, and it was decorated in rich reds and gold. On the far side was a huge gold curtain acting as a partition, which was blocked by another menacing-looking bouncer.

At the top of the room was the main attraction, a massive king-size bed, which was tilted on a platform towards the rest of the club. On top of the gold silk sheets were two skinny models dressed in gold body paint and gold thongs. It was all a bit too tacky.

'Look at the size of those thongs!' gasped Denise. 'I have a plaster on my baby finger bigger than those.'

Beside her in Club Diva, Tom began to nibble on Denise's baby finger. Holly returned her gaze to the screen.

'Good evening and welcome to the twelve o'clock news, I'm Sharon McCarthy.' Sharon stood with a bottle in her hand serving as a microphone. Declan had angled the camera so that he could get Ireland's famous newsreaders in the shot.

'Today, on the thirtieth birthday of Princess Holly of Finland, her royal self and her lady in waiting succeeded in being granted access to the famous celebrity hangout Boudoir. Also present is Australian rock chick Ciara . . . and it appears that Ireland's favourite newsreader Tony Walsh was seen smiling just moments ago. Here I have a witness to the fact. Welcome, Denise.'

'Well, I was just over there beside his table when I saw it happening.' Denise sucked in her cheekbones.

'Can you explain to us what happened?'

'Well, I was just standing there minding my own business when Mr Walsh took a sip of his drink and smiled.'

'Gosh, Denise, and are you sure it was a smile?'

'Well, it could have been trapped wind causing him to make a face, but others around me thought it was a smile.'

'So there were others who witnessed this?'

'Yes, Princess Holly here saw the whole thing.'

The camera panned across to Holly where she stood drinking from a champagne bottle with a straw. 'So, Holly, can you tell us, was it wind or a smile?'

Holly looked confused, then rolled her eyes. 'Oh, wind. Sorry, I think it's this champagne that's doing it to me.'

Club Diva erupted in laughter and Holly hid her face in shame.

'OK, then,' Sharon said, 'so you heard it here first. The night when Ireland's grimmest presenter was seen smiling. Back to you at the studio.' As she looked up and saw Tony Walsh standing beside her, Sharon gulped and said, 'Good evening,' and the camera was switched off. Everyone in the club was laughing at this stage, including the girls. The whole thing was just so ridiculous.

The camera was switched back on and focused on the mirror in the

Ladies. Declan was filming through a slit in the doorway and Denise and Sharon's reflections were visible.

'Where's Holly?' Sharon asked.

'Last time I saw her she was doing a few funky moves on the dance floor,' said Denise. The two of them laughed.

'Ah . . . our poor little disco diva. I hope she finds someone gorgeous out there and snogs the face off him.'

'Yeah,' agreed Denise. 'Come on, let's find her a man.'

Just after the girls left, a cubicle door opened and out stepped Holly. Through the crack in the door you could see her eyes were red from crying. She blew her nose and stared miserably at herself in the mirror.

The scene changed and the words 'Operation Gold Curtain' came up. Denise screamed, 'Declan, you bastard!' and rushed off to the toilet. Declan lit himself a cigarette.

'Time for Operation Gold Curtain,' Denise was announcing.

'Huh?' Sharon and Holly had collapsed in a drunken stupor.

'Operation Gold Curtain. Time to infiltrate the VIP bar!'

'You mean this isn't it?' Sharon said sarcastically.

'No! That's where the real celebs go!' Denise said excitedly, pointing at the gold curtain.

'I don't really care where the celebs are,' piped up Holly.

Denise groaned and rolled her eyes. 'Girls! Abbey and Ciara are in there, why aren't we?'

Jack looked curiously at Abbey, who shrugged her shoulders weakly. None of this was jogging anybody's memory except of course Denise's, and she had fled the room.

Once Sharon and Holly had heard that Abbey and Ciara were in the VIP bar, they sat up attentively and listened to Denise. 'OK, girlies, here's what we're gonna do!'

The camera followed the three girls as they very suspiciously approached the gold curtain and loitered around. Sharon finally built up the courage to tap the bouncer on the shoulder, causing him to turn round and provide Denise with enough time to escape under the curtain. She got down on her hands and knees and stuck her head through to the VIP bar. Holly kicked her in the bum to hurry her along.

'I can see them!' Denise hissed loudly. 'Oh my God! They're speaking to that Hollywood actor guy!' She took her head back out and looked at Holly, just as the giant bouncer turned his head towards them.

'No, no, no!' Denise said. 'This is Princess Holly of Finland. I am bowing to her. Join me!'

Sharon quickly got on her knees and the two of them began to worship Holly's feet. Holly looked around awkwardly as everyone in the club began to stare, and she once again gave the royal wave.

'Oh, Holly!' her mother said, trying to catch her breath after laughing so hard.

The big burly bouncer spoke into his walkie-talkie. 'Boys, got a situation with the princess and the lady.'

Denise looked at both girls in panic and mouthed, 'Hide!' The girls jumped to their feet and fled. The camera searched through the crowds but couldn't find them.

From her seat in Club Diva, Holly groaned loudly as it finally clicked with her what was about to happen.

Paul and Moustache Man rushed upstairs to the club and met a very big man at the gold curtain. 'What's going on?' Moustache Man asked.

'Those girls you told us to keep an eye on tried to crawl through to the other side,' the big man said. You could tell his previous job involved killing people.

'Where are they?' Moustache Man asked.

The big man looked away. 'They're hiding, boss.'

Moustache Man rolled his eyes. 'Well, start looking then.'

The camera secretly followed the three bouncers as they patrolled the club looking under tables and behind curtains. There was a bit of commotion at the top of the club and they headed towards the noise to sort it out. The two skinny dancers in gold body paint had stopped dancing and were staring with horrified expressions at the bed. The camera panned across. Underneath the gold silk sheets Sharon, Denise and Holly were rolling around, trying to make themselves as flat as possible so they wouldn't be noticed. A crowd gathered and soon the music was shut down. The three big lumps froze.

The bouncers counted to three and pulled the covers off the bed. Three startled-looking girls appearing like deer caught in headlights.

'*One* just had to get forty winks before *one* left,' Holly said.

Everyone watching the screen howled with laughter.

The scene changed to 'The Long Journey Home'. The girls were in the taxi. Abbey sat with her head hanging out of the window by order of the taxi driver: 'You're not throwing up in my cab.' Sharon and Denise had fallen asleep, with their heads resting on each other.

The camera turned to focus on Holly, who was sitting in the passenger seat once again. This time she wasn't talking the ear off the driver; she rested her head on the seat back and stared straight into the night. Holly knew what she was thinking as she watched herself.

Time to go home to that empty house alone again.

'Happy birthday, Holly,' Abbey's voice trembled.

Holly turned to smile at her and came face to face with the camera. 'Are you *still* filming with that thing? Turn it off!' and she knocked the camera out of Declan's hand. The end.

As Daniel went to turn the lights up in the club, Holly slipped quickly away through the nearest door. She needed to collect her thoughts before everyone started talking. She found herself in a tiny storeroom surrounded by empty crates. She sat down on one and thought about what she had just seen. She was in shock. She felt confused and angry with Declan; he had told her that he was making a documentary about club life. And he had literally made a show of her and her friends.

But the last thing she wanted to do right now was to scream at Declan in front of everyone. If it had been anyone else but her on the TV, Holly would have thought it very deserving of the award. But it *was* her . . . She didn't mind so much the bits of her and her friends being so silly, it was more the sneaky shots of her unhappiness that bothered her.

Thick salty tears trickled down her face. She had seen on television how she truly felt, lost and alone. She cried for Gerry, she cried for her-self with big, heaving sobs that hurt her ribs whenever she tried to catch her breath. She didn't want to be alone any more, and she didn't want her family seeing the loneliness she tried so hard to hide. She just wanted Gerry back and didn't care about anything else. She just wanted him. She heard the door open behind her and felt big strong arms wrap-ping themselves round her frail body. She cried as if months of built-up anguish were all tumbling out at once.

'What's wrong? Didn't she like it?' Declan ask worriedly.

'Just leave her be,' her mum said softly, and the door closed. Daniel stroked her hair and rocked her softly.

After crying what felt like all the tears in the world, she let go of Daniel. 'Sorry,' she sniffed, drying her face with her sleeves.

'There's no need to be sorry,' he said gently.

She sat in silence while trying to compose herself.

'If you're upset about the documentary, there's no need,' he said, sit-ting down on a crate opposite her.

'Yeah, right,' she said sarcastically, wiping her tears again.

'No, really.' He smiled. 'I thought it was very funny. You all looked like you were having a great time. Nobody but you noticed whatever it is that's upsetting you.'

Holly felt mildly better. 'Are you sure?'

'I'm sure I'm sure,' he said, smiling. 'Now, you really have to stop hiding in all the rooms in my club, or I might take it personally.'

'Are the girls OK?' There was loud laughter from outside.

'They're fine, as you can hear,' he said. 'Ciara's delighted everyone will think she's a star, Denise has finally come out of the toilet and Sharon just can't stop laughing. Although Jack's giving Abbey a hard time about throwing up on the way home.'

Holly giggled. 'Thanks, Daniel.' She smiled at him.

'You ready to go and face your public?'

'Think so.' Holly stepped outside to find everyone sitting round the table happily sharing jokes and stories. Holly sat beside her mum. Elizabeth gave her daughter a kiss on the cheek.

'So is it OK?' Declan asked Holly, afraid he had upset his sister.

Holly threw him a look.

'I thought you would like it, Hol,' he said worriedly.

'I hate surprises,' she said, rubbing her stinging eyes.

'Let that be a lesson,' Frank warned his son. 'You shouldn't film people without them knowing. It's illegal.'

'I bet they didn't know that when they chose him for the award,' Elizabeth agreed.

'You're not gonna tell them, Holly?' Declan asked worriedly.

'Not if you're nice to me for the next few months.'

Declan made a face; he was stuck and he knew it. 'Whatever,' he said.

Holly was standing over the sink with her sleeves rolled up, when she heard the familiar voice.

'Hi, honey.'

He stood at the open patio doors. 'Hello, you,' she smiled.

'Miss me?'

'Of course.'

'Have you found that new husband yet?'

'Of course I have, he's upstairs asleep,' she laughed.

Gerry tutted. 'Shall I go up and suffocate him for sleeping in our bed?'

'Ah, give him another hour or so. He needs his rest.'

He looked happy, she thought, fresh-faced and still as beautiful as she remembered. He was wearing her favourite blue top, which she had bought him one Christmas. He stared at her from under his long eyelashes with his big brown puppy eyes.

'Are you coming in?' she asked, smiling.

'No, I just popped by to see how you are. Everything OK?' He leaned against the doorjamb, hands in his pockets.

'So-so,' she said. 'Could be better.'

'I hear you're a TV star now,' he grinned.

'A very reluctant one,' she laughed. 'I miss you, Gerry.'

'I haven't gone far,' he said softly.

'You leaving me again?'

'For the time being.'

She smiled. 'See you soon.'

Holly woke up with a smile on her face and felt like she'd slept for days. 'Good morning, Gerry,' she said, happily staring up at the ceiling.

The phone rang beside her. 'Hello?'

'Oh my God, Holly, just take a look at the weekend papers,' Sharon said in a panic.

Six

HOLLY LEAPT OUT OF BED, threw on a track suit and drove to her nearest newsagent. She parked the car, walked into the shop and found the newsstand, where she began to leaf through the pages of a newspaper. The man behind the counter coughed loudly and Holly looked up at him. 'This is not a library, young lady, you'll have to buy that,' he said.

'I know that,' she said, irritated. Honestly, how on earth was anyone supposed to know which paper to buy if they didn't even know which paper contained what they were looking for? She ended up picking up every single newspaper and slammed them down on the counter, smiling sweetly at him.

The man started to scan them into the register one by one.

She stared longingly at the chocolate display in front of her and then grabbed two king-size bars from the bottom of the pile. One by one the rest of the chocolate bars began to slide onto the floor. Holly bent down with a red face to pick them up. So many had fallen she had to make several trips up and down. The shop was silent, apart from a few coughs from the queue forming behind her. Then she remembered she needed milk, so she rushed to retrieve a pint from the fridge.

She made her way back to the top of the queue and added the milk to her pile. The newsagent stopped scanning. 'Mark,' he yelled.

A spotty young teenager appeared from the aisles, a pricing gun in his hand. 'Yeah?' he said grumpily.

'Open the other till, will ya, son.' He glared at her.

Holly made a face at him.

Mark dragged his body over to the second till, and the queue rushed across to it. Holly grabbed a few packets of crisps from below the counter and added them to her purchases.

'Anything else?' the newsagent asked sarcastically.

'No, thank you, that will be all.' She paid her money and fumbled with her purse, trying to put the change back in.

'Next,' the newsagent nodded to the customer behind her.

'Excuse me,' Holly said. 'May I have a bag, please.'

'That'll be twenty cents.'

Holly found her money again, slammed the coin on the counter and began to fill the bag with her items.

'Next,' he said. Holly began stuffing the bag full in panic.

'I'll wait till the lady is ready,' the customer said politely.

Holly smiled at him appreciatively. As she turned to leave the shop, Mark, the boy behind the counter, startled her by yelling, 'Hey, I know you! You're the girl from the telly!'

Holly swirled round in surprise and the plastic handle of the carrier bag broke from the weight of all the newspapers. Her shopping went rolling in all directions.

The friendly customer got down on his knees to help her while the rest of the shop watched in amusement.

'It is you, isn't it?' the boy laughed.

Holly smiled up weakly at him from the floor.

'I knew it!' He clapped his hands together. 'You're cool!'

Holly's face went red. 'Em . . . could I have another bag, please?'

'Yeah, that'll be—'

'There you go,' the friendly customer placed a twenty-cent coin on the counter. 'I'm Rob,' he said, and held out his hand.

'I'm Holly.' She took his hand, a little embarrassed by his overfriendliness. 'Thanks for the help,' she said gratefully, getting to her feet.

'No problem.' He held the door open for her. He was good-looking, she thought, a few years older than her, and had the oddest coloured eyes, a kind of a grey-green colour.

He cleared his throat.

She blushed, suddenly realising she had been staring at him like a fool. She walked out to her car and placed the bulging bag on the back seat. Rob followed her over. Her heart did a little flip.

'Hi, again,' he said. 'Em . . . I was wondering if you would like to go for a drink?' Then he laughed, glancing at his watch. 'Actually, it's a bit too early for that. How about a coffee?'

He rested himself coolly against the car, his hands in the pockets of his jeans, acting as if asking a stranger out for coffee was the most natural thing in the world. Was this what people did these days?

'Em . . .' Holly thought about it. What harm could it do to go for a coffee with a man who had been so polite to her? The fact that he was absolutely gorgeous also helped. But, regardless of his beauty, Holly really craved company and he seemed like a nice, decent man to talk to.

She was just about to say yes when he glanced down at her hand and his smile faded. 'Oh, sorry, I didn't realise . . .' He backed away from her awkwardly. 'I have to rush off anyway.' He smiled quickly at her and took off down the road.

Holly stared after him, confused. Had she said something wrong? She looked down at her hand and saw her wedding ring sparkle back at her. She sighed loudly and rubbed her face tiredly. She wasn't in the mood to go home, she was sick of staring at the walls all day and talking to herself. It was only ten o'clock and it was beautifully sunny and warm. Across the road her local café, the Greasy Spoon, was setting up tables and chairs outside. Her stomach grumbled. She took her newspapers from the car with both hands, slammed the door and wandered across to the café.

A plump lady was cleaning the tables. 'Want to sit here, love?'

'Yes. I'll have the Irish breakfast.'

'No problem, love.' She waddled into the café.

Holly flicked through the pages of one of the tabloids and came to a small article in the review section that caught her eye.

GIRLS AND THE CITY A HIT IN THE RATINGS
by Tricia Coleman

For any of you unfortunate people who missed out on the outrageously funny *Girls and the City* last Wednesday night, do not despair. It will be back soon.

The hilarious fly-on-the-wall TV documentary, directed by Irishman Declan Kennedy, follows five Dublin girls out for a night on the town. They lift the lid on the mysterious world of celebrity life in trendy club Boudoir and provide us with thirty minutes of stomach-aching laughter.

Last Wednesday, the latest ratings reveal, four million people tuned in. The show is to be repeated on Sunday at 11 p.m. on Channel 4. This is must-see TV, so don't miss it!

Holly tried to keep her cool. This was obviously great news for Declan but disastrous for her. Having that documentary aired once was bad enough. She had let him off lightly the other night because he had been so excited, but she really needed to have a serious talk with him.

She flicked through the rest of the papers and saw what it was Sharon was ranting about. Every single tabloid had an article about the documentary and one had even printed a photograph of Denise, Sharon and Holly from a few years ago. How they had got their hands on it she did not know. And she wasn't too happy with the use of the words 'mad girls', 'drunken girls', and how they were 'well up for it'. What did that even mean?

Holly's food finally arrived and she stared at it in shock. The plate was piled high with sausages, bacon, eggs, hash browns, black and white pudding, baked beans, fried potatoes, mushrooms, tomatoes and five slices of toast. Holly looked around her with embarrassment, hoping no one would think she was a complete pig. She hadn't had much of an appetite lately, but she finally felt ready to eat.

When she reached her parents' house it was almost two o'clock. Holly rang the doorbell for the fourth time and still no one answered. She crossed the grass and pressed her face against the living-room window to see if there was any sign of life, and heard the screaming match.

'Ciara, get the damn door!'

'No, I said! I . . . am . . . busy.'

'Well, so am I!'

Holly rang the doorbell again just to add fuel to the fire.

'*Declan!*' Ouch, that was a bloodcurdling scream.

'Get it yourself, you lazy cow!'

Holly took out her mobile phone and rang the house.

'*Ciara, answer the phone!*'

'*No!*'

'Oh, for God's sake,' Holly snapped loudly and hung up. She dialled Declan's mobile number.

'Yeah?'

'Declan, open the door now or I'll kick it in,' Holly growled.

'Oh, sorry, I thought Ciara had answered it,' he lied.

He opened the door in his boxer shorts and Holly stormed in.

'Mum and Dad are out,' he said lazily and headed upstairs.

'Hey, where are you going?'

'Back to bed.'

'No you are not,' Holly said calmly. 'You are going to sit here with me. We're gonna have a long chat about *Girls and the City*.'

'No,' Declan moaned. 'Do we have to do this now? I'm really, really tired.' He rubbed his eyes with his fists.

'Declan, it's two o'clock in the afternoon. Sit!' she said.

He dragged his weary body over to the couch, where he stretched out along the entire thing, leaving no room for Holly. She rolled her eyes and dragged her dad's armchair close.

'I feel like I'm with a shrink,' he laughed, crossing his arms behind his head and staring up at her from the couch.

'Good, because I'm really going to pick your brains.'

'Oh, Holly, we talked about this the other night,' Declan whinged.

'Did you honestly think that was all I was going to say? "Oh, I'm sorry, Declan, but I didn't like the way you publicly humiliated me and my friends. See you next week"?'

'Obviously not.'

'Come on, Declan,' she said, softening her tone. 'I just want to understand why you thought it would be such a great idea not to tell me you were filming us.'

'You *knew* I was filming,' he said defensively.

'For a documentary about *club life*!'

'And it *was* about club life,' Declan laughed.

'Oh, you think you're so bloody clever.' She counted to ten to prevent herself from attacking him. 'Come on,' she said. 'Don't you think I'm going through enough right now?'

Declan sat up. 'I know you've been through hell, Holly, but I thought this would cheer you up. I wasn't lying when I said I was going to film the club, but when I brought it back to college to begin the edit, everyone thought it was so funny that I couldn't *not* show it to people.'

'Yeah, but you put it on TV, Declan.'

'I didn't know that was the prize, honestly,' he said, wide-eyed. 'Nobody knew, not even my lecturers. How could I say no to it when I won?'

Holly gave up and ran her fingers through her hair.

'I honestly thought you would like it,' he smiled. 'I checked with Ciara and *even she* said you'd like it. I'm sorry if I upset you.'

Holly froze. What had he just said? 'Ciara knew about the tape?'

Declan tried to think of a way to back out of it. Coming up with nothing, he threw himself back and covered his head with a cushion, knowing he had just started World War III.

'Oh, Holly, don't say anything, she'll kill me!' came his muffled reply.

Holly bounded out of her seat and stormed upstairs, thumping her feet and yelling threats. She pounded on Ciara's door.

'Don't come in!' yelled Ciara from inside.

'You are in so much trouble, Ciara!' Holly screamed. She opened the door and burst her way in, putting on her most terrifying face.

'I told you not to come in!' wailed Ciara, sitting on the floor with a photo album on her lap and tears streaming down her face.

'Oh, Ciara, what's wrong?' Holly said soothingly to her younger sister. She couldn't remember the last time she'd seen her cry, in fact, she didn't know Ciara even knew *how* to cry.

'Nothing's wrong,' Ciara said, snapping the album shut and sliding it under her bed. She wiped her face roughly.

'Something *is* wrong,' Holly said, crossing the room to join her sister on the floor. She wasn't sure how to deal with Ciara like this.

'I'm fine,' Ciara snapped.

'OK,' Holly said. 'But if there's something upsetting you, you know you can talk to me about it, don't you?'

Ciara refused to look at her and just nodded her head. Holly began to stand up to leave her in peace when all of a sudden Ciara burst into tears. Holly sat back down and wrapped her arms protectively round her, stroking her silky pink hair.

'Do you want to tell me what's wrong?' she asked softly.

Ciara gurgled some sort of reply and slid the photo album back out. She opened it with trembling hands and flicked a few pages.

'Him,' she said sadly, pointing to a photograph of her and some guy Holly didn't recognise. Holly barely recognised her sister. The photograph was taken on a boat in Sydney Harbour. Ciara was sitting happily on the man's knee with her arms round his neck. She had blonde hair and her features looked much softer.

'Is that your boyfriend?' Holly asked carefully.

'Was,' Ciara sniffed, and a tear landed on the page.

'Is that why you came home?'

Ciara gasped for breath. 'We had a fight.'

'Did he . . . He didn't hurt you or anything, did he?'

'No,' Ciara spluttered, 'it was just over something really stupid and I said I was leaving and he said he was glad . . .' She started sobbing again. Holly held her in her arms and waited. 'He didn't even come to the airport to say goodbye to me.'

Holly rubbed Ciara's back. 'Has he called you since?'

'No, and I've been home for two months, Holly,' she wailed, looking up with such sad eyes that Holly felt like crying too.

'Then maybe he's not the right kind of person for you.'

'But I love Mathew, Holly. I only booked the flight because I was angry, I didn't think he would let me go . . .' She stared for a long time at the photograph.

Ciara's bedroom windows were wide open and Holly listened to the familiar sound of the waves on the beach. She had shared this room with Ciara while they were growing up, and a strange sense of comfort embraced her.

Ciara began to calm down beside her. 'Sorry, Hol.'

'Hey, you don't need to be sorry at all. You should have told me all this instead of keeping it inside.'

'This is minor compared to what happened to you. I feel stupid crying about it.' She wiped her tears, angry with herself.

'Ciara, losing someone you love is always hard, no matter if they're alive or . . .' She couldn't finish the sentence.

'It's just that you've been so brave, Holly, I don't know how you do it. And here I am crying over a stupid boyfriend I only went out with for a few months.'

'Me? Brave?' Holly laughed. 'I wish.'

'Yes, you are,' Ciara insisted. 'Everyone says so. If I were you, I'd be lying in a ditch somewhere.'

'Don't go giving me ideas, Ciara.' Holly smiled at her.

'You're OK, though, aren't you?' Ciara said worriedly.

Holly slid her wedding ring up and down her finger. She thought about that question for a while.

'I'm lots of things, Ciara. I'm lonely, I'm tired, I'm sad, I'm happy, I'm lucky, I'm unlucky; I'm a million things every day, but I suppose OK is one of them.'

'And you're brave,' Ciara assured her. 'And in control.'

'No, you were always the brave one. As for being in control, I don't know what I'm doing from one day to the next.'

Ciara's forehead creased. 'I am far from being brave, Holly.'

'Yes, you are. All those things that you do, like jumping out of aeroplanes and snowboarding off cliffs . . .'

'Oh, no, that's not brave, that's foolish. Anybody can bungee jump off a bridge. You could do it *if you had to*.'

'Yes, and if your husband died you would cope *if you had to*. There's nothing brave about it. There's no choice involved.'

Ciara and Holly stared at each other, aware of the other's battle.

Ciara was the first to speak. 'Well, I guess you and I are more alike than we thought.' She smiled at her big sister and Holly hugged her tightly. 'So, was there something you were going to scream at me about earlier on?'

'No, forget about it, it was nothing,' Holly replied.

It was eight o'clock when Holly finally drove up her driveway, and it was still bright. The world never felt quite so depressing when it was bright. She had spent hours chatting with Ciara, who had changed her mind at least twenty times about whether or not she should call Mathew in Australia. By the time Holly left, Ciara was adamant she would never speak to him again, which probably meant she had called him by now.

She walked up the path to the front door and stared at the garden curiously. Was it her imagination or did it look a little tidier? Something about it looked different.

The sound of a lawnmower started and Holly spun round to see her neighbour, who was out working in his garden. She waved over to thank him, presuming it was he who had helped her, and he held his hand up in response.

It had always been Gerry's job to do the garden. He wasn't necessarily a keen gardener, it was just that Holly was an incredibly unkeen gardener, so somebody had to do the dirty work. Their patch of grass surrounded by a few shrubs and flowers now looked little more than an overgrown field. When Gerry died, the garden had died with him.

This thought now reminded Holly of the orchid. She rushed inside the house and poured water over the extremely thirsty-looking plant. She threw a chicken curry into the microwave and thought back over her day. She looked down at her wedding ring. When that man had walked away, Holly had felt so awful. He had given her that look as if she were about to initiate an affair. She felt guilty for even *considering* his invitation for coffee. She still *felt* married, and going for a coffee would have seemed like she was betraying her husband. Gerry had been gone almost five months now, but her heart and soul still belonged to him.

Holly twisted her ring round her finger. At what point should she take it off? Where was the rule book for widows that explained when exactly the ring should be taken off? And when it finally did come off, where would she put it, where *should* she put it? In the bin? Beside her bed so she could be reminded of him every single day? She wasn't ready to give up her Gerry yet; as far as she was concerned, he was still living.

The microwave beeped as her dinner was ready. She took the dish out and threw it straight in the bin. She had lost her appetite.

Later that night Denise rang her in a tizzy. 'Switch Dublin FM on quick!' Holly raced to the radio and flicked the switch. 'I'm Tom O'Connor and you're listening to Dublin FM. If you've just joined us, we are talking about bouncers. In light of the amount of persuasion it took the *Girls and the City* girls to blag their way into the club Boudoir, we wanna know what your thoughts on bouncers are. Do you like them? Do you understand why they are the way they are? Or are they too strict? The number to call is . . .'

Holly picked the phone back up. 'Well?' Denise said.

'What the hell have we started, Denise?'

'Oh, I know,' she giggled. 'Did you see the papers today?'

'Yeah, it's all a bit silly, really.'

They listened to the radio. Some guy was giving out about bouncers and Tom was trying to calm him down.

'Oh, listen to my baby,' Denise said. 'Doesn't he sound sexy?'

'Em . . . yeah. I take it you two are still together?'

'Of course.' Denise sounded insulted. 'Why wouldn't we be?'

'Well, it's been a while now, Denise, that's all.' Holly quickly tried to explain so she wouldn't hurt her friend's feelings. 'And you always said you couldn't be with a man for over a week!'

'Yes, well, I said I *couldn't* but I never said I *wouldn't*. Tom is different, Holly,' Denise said breathily.

Holly was surprised. 'Oh, so what's so different with Tom then?' She rested the phone between her ear and shoulder and settled down in a chair to examine her nails.

'Oh, there's just this *connection*. It's like he's my soul mate. He's so thoughtful, always surprising me with little gifts. He makes me laugh *all the time*, and I haven't got sick of him like all the other guys. *Plus* he's good-looking.'

Holly stifled a yawn. Denise tended to say this after the first week of going out with all her new boyfriends and then quickly change her mind. But then again, she and Tom had been together for several weeks.

'I'm very happy for you,' she said.

The next day Holly dragged herself out of bed to go for a stroll in the park. She needed to start doing some exercise and she also needed to start thinking about job-hunting. Everywhere she went she tried to picture herself working in that environment. She had definitely ruled out clothes stores (the possibility of having a boss like Denise had dissuaded her from that one), restaurants, hotels and pubs, and she certainly didn't want another office job, which left . . . nothing.

She sat down on a park bench opposite the playground and listened to the children's screams of delight. Why did people have to grow up? She wanted to be irresponsible, she wanted to be looked after. And then she could grow up all over again and meet Gerry all over again and force him to go to the doctor months earlier and then she would be sitting beside Gerry here on the bench watching their children playing. What if, what if, what if . . .

She thought about the stinging remark Richard had made about never having to bother with that children nonsense. She wished so much she could have a little Gerry running around the playground while she shouted at him to be careful and did other mummy things like spit on a tissue and wipe his podgy little dirty face. She and Gerry had just started talking about having children a few months before he was diagnosed. They had been so excited about it, and used to lie in bed for hours trying to decide names and create scenarios in their heads of what it would be like to be parents.

Well, think of the devil, Holly thought to herself, seeing Richard leaving the playground with Emily and Timmy. He looked so relaxed, and she watched in surprise as he chased the children round the park. They looked like they were having fun, not a very familiar sight. She zipped up her extra layer of thick skin in preparation for their conversation.

'Hello, Holly!' Richard, spotting her, walked across the grass.

'Hello!' Holly said, greeting the kids as they ran over to her and gave her a big hug. It made a nice change. 'You're far from home,' she said to Richard. 'What brings you all the way here?'

'I brought the children to see Grandma and Granddad, didn't I?' he said, ruffling Timmy's head.

'*And* we had McDonald's,' Timmy said excitedly, and Emily cheered.

'Oh, yummy!' Holly said. 'You lucky things. Isn't your daddy the best?' Richard looked pleased.

'Junk food?' Holly questioned her brother.

'Ah.' He waved his hand dismissively and sat down beside her. 'Everything in moderation, isn't that right, Emily?'

Five-year-old Emily nodded her head.

'One McDonald's meal isn't going to kill them,' Holly agreed.

Timmy grabbed at his throat and pretended to choke. His face went red as he made gagging noises and he collapsed on the grass and lay still. Richard and Holly laughed. Emily looked like she was going to cry.

'Oh dear,' Richard joked. 'Looks like we were wrong, Holly, the McDonald's did kill Timmy.'

Holly looked at her brother in shock for calling his son Timmy.

Richard got up and threw him over his shoulder. 'Well, we better go and bury him now.' Timmy giggled as he dangled upside-down.

'Oh, he's alive!' Richard laughed.

'No, I'm not,' giggled Timmy.

'OK, we best be off,' grinned Richard. 'Bye, Holly.'

'Bye, Holly,' the children cheered, and Richard walked off with Timmy slung over his shoulder as little Emily skipped and danced beside her father, gripping his hand.

Seven

BARBARA FINISHED SERVING her customers, and as soon as they left the building she ran into the staff room and lit up a cigarette. Melissa, her colleague, had called in sick that morning, so she was stuck all by herself today. And of course it was the busiest day they'd had in ages. As soon as November came, with those horrible depressing dark nights and sheets of rain, everyone came running in the door booking holidays to hot sunny countries.

With her boss out to run errands, Barbara was really looking forward to her cigarette break. Of course, just her luck, the bell over the door sounded just then and Barbara cursed, puffing on the cigarette furiously and spraying perfume all around so her boss wouldn't notice the smoke. She left the staff room expecting to see the customer sitting behind the counter, but instead he was still slowly making his way to the counter.

'Excuse me?' the weak voice called.

'Hello, sir, how can I help you?' she said, surprised at how young the man actually was. His body was hunched and the walking stick in his hand seemed to be the only thing preventing him from collapsing. His skin was very white and pasty, but he had big brown puppy eyes that seemed to smile at her. She couldn't help but smile back.

'I was hoping to book a holiday,' he said, 'but I was wondering if you could help me choose a place.'

Usually Barbara would have silently screamed at the customer for making her do this unbelievably impossible task. Most of her customers were so fussy that she could be sitting there for hours. But she surprised herself. 'No problem, sir. My name is Barbara. Why don't you take a seat and we'll search through the brochures.' She pointed to a chair and looked away so she didn't have to watch him struggle. 'Now,' she said, full of smiles, 'is there any country in particular you would like to go to?'

'Em . . . the Canary Islands. Lanzarote, I think. A summer holiday.'

They worked their way through the brochures and finally the man found a place he liked. Barbara was happy he took her advice into account, unlike other customers who just ignored her knowledge.

'OK, any month in particular?' she said.

'August?' he asked, and those big brown eyes looked so deep into Barbara's soul she just wanted to give him a big hug.

'August is a good month. Would you like a sea view or a pool view? The sea view is an extra thirty euros.'

He stared into space with a smile on his face. 'A sea view, please.'

'Good choice. Can I take your name and address, please?'

'Oh . . . this isn't actually for me.' Those brown eyes looked sad. 'It's a surprise for my wife and her friends.'

'Well, that's very thoughtful of you, sir.' She finished taking his details and he settled the bill. She began to print the arrangements from the computer to give to him.

'Oh, do you mind if I leave the arrangements with you? I'd be afraid of leaving papers around. I won't be telling her till July, so could it be kept quiet till then?'

'That's no problem at all, sir. Usually the flight times aren't confirmed till a few weeks before anyway.'

'Thank you for your help, Barbara,' he said, smiling.

'It's been a pleasure, Mr—?'

'It's Gerry.'

'It's been a pleasure, Gerry. Your wife will have a wonderful time. My friend went there and she loved it.' Barbara felt the need to reassure him his wife would be fine.

'Well, I'd better head back home. I'm not even supposed to be out of bed, you know.' He shrugged sheepishly.

Barbara jumped to her feet and ran round the other side of the counter to hold the door open for him. He smiled appreciatively as he walked past her and she watched as he slowly climbed into the taxi that had been waiting outside for him.

It was the first of July and Barbara sat grumpily behind the counter of Swords Travel Agents. It was the hottest day of the year, all her customers kept on bragging as they strolled in in their shorts and skimpy tops, filling the room with the smell of suncream. Barbara squirmed in her uncomfortable uniform and banged on the fan as it stalled.

'Leave it,' Melissa moaned. 'That'll only make it worse.'

'As if that could be possible,' Barbara grumbled.

'What is it with you today?' Melissa laughed.

'Oh, nothing much. It's just the hottest day of the year and we're stuck in this *crappy* job in this *stuffy* room.'

'Look, why don't you go outside to get some air and I'll deal with this customer.' Melissa nodded to the woman making her way in.

'Thanks, Mel,' said Barbara, grabbing her cigarettes.

'Hello, can I help you?' Melissa smiled at the woman.

'Yes, I was wondering if Barbara still works here?'

Barbara froze just as she was reaching the door. She groaned and headed back to her seat. She looked at the woman behind the counter. 'I'm Barbara.'

'Oh, good!' The lady dived onto the stool in front of her. 'I was afraid you might not work here any more.'

'She wishes,' Melissa muttered under her breath.

'Can I help you?'

'Oh God, I really hope you can,' the lady said a bit hysterically, and rooted through her bag. 'I received this today from my husband and I was wondering if you could explain it to me.'

Barbara frowned at the crumpled piece of paper on the counter. A page had been torn out of a holiday brochure and written on it were the words: *Swords Travel Agents. Attn: Barbara.* 'My friend went there on holiday, but other than that it means nothing to me. Can't you ask your husband for more information?'

'No, he's not here any more,' the lady said sadly.

'OK, maybe your name will come up on the computer.'

'It's Holly Kennedy.' Her voice shook.

'Holly Kennedy, Holly Kennedy,' Melissa repeated after listening in on their conversation. 'Oh, hold on, I was about to call you this week! I was under strict instructions not to ring you until July for some reason—'

'Oh!' Barbara interrupted. 'You're Gerry's wife?'

'Yes!' Holly threw her hands to her face. 'He was in here?'

'Yes, he was.' Barbara smiled. 'He was a lovely man.' She reached out to Holly's hand on the counter. Her heart went out to the lady. She was so young and it must be so hard for her right now. 'Melissa, can you get some tissues, please, while I explain to the lady exactly why her husband was here?'

She let go of Holly's hand to tap away at the computer and Melissa returned with a box of tissues. 'OK, Holly,' she said softly. 'Gerry has arranged a holiday for you and a Sharon McCarthy and a Denise Hennessey to go to Lanzarote for one week, arriving on the 28th of July to return home on the 3rd of August. He was adamant that he find the perfect place for you.' She tapped the crumpled page. 'You'll have a fab time, believe me. There are loads of restaurants and bars and . . .' She trailed off, realising Holly probably didn't give a damn whether she had a good time or not.

'When did he come in?' Tears poured from Holly's eyes.

Barbara tapped away. 'The 28th of November.'

'November?' Holly gasped. 'What time of day was this?'

'I really can't remember. It was a long time ago—'

'Yes, of course, I'm sorry,' Holly interrupted.

Barbara told her as much as she could remember until Holly could think of no more questions to ask.

'Oh, thank you, Barbara, thank you so much.' Holly reached over the counter and gave her a big hug.

'No problem at all.' Barbara hugged her back. 'Let us know how you get on,' she smiled. 'Here's your details.' She handed her a thick envelope and watched her walk out.

Holly eventually arrived at her house and waved to Sharon and Denise, who were sitting on her garden wall sunbathing. They jumped up and rushed over to greet her.

'Well, you both got here quickly,' she said, trying to inject energy into her voice. She felt utterly drained.

'Sharon left work as soon as you called and she collected me from town,' Denise explained, studying Holly's face.

'Oh, you didn't have to do that,' Holly said lifelessly as she put the key in the door.

'Hey, have you been working in your garden?' Sharon asked.

'No, my neighbour's been doing it, I think.' Holly pulled the key from the door and searched through the bunch for the correct one.

'You think?' Denise tried to keep the conversation going while Holly battled with yet another key in the lock.

'Well, it's either my neighbour or a little leprechaun lives down the end of my garden,' Holly snapped, getting frustrated with the keys. Denise and Sharon motioned to each other to stay quiet, as Holly was obviously stressed.

'Oh, sod it!' Holly yelled and threw her keys on the ground.

Sharon picked them up. 'Hey, hon, don't worry about it. I swear the bloody things jump around on the keyring just to piss us off.' She worked her way through the keys, the door opened and Holly rushed in to turn the alarm off.

'OK, why don't you two make yourselves comfortable in the living room and I'll join you in a minute.' Holly headed into the bathroom to splash cold water on her face. She needed to be as excited about this holiday as Gerry had intended. When she felt a little more alive she joined the girls in the living room and sat opposite them.

'OK. I opened the envelope for July today and this is what it said.' She handed them the small card:

Have a good Holly day!
PS, I love you . . .

'Is that it?' Denise wrinkled up her nose, unimpressed.

'Well, Holly, I think it's a lovely note,' Sharon lied. 'It's so thoughtful and it's . . . a lovely play on words.'

Holly had to giggle. 'No, you fool!' she said, hitting her over the head with a cushion. 'Sharon, you are so supportive you make me sick! This was inside.' Holly handed them the crumpled page.

She watched with amusement as the girls tried to figure out Gerry's writing. 'Oh my God!' Denise gasped.

'What what what?' Sharon demanded. 'Did Gerry buy you a holiday?'

'Girls,' Holly said, 'he bought *us* a holiday!'

The girls opened a bottle of wine.

'Oh, this is incredible,' Denise said after the news had sunk in. 'Gerry's such a sweetie.'

Holly nodded, feeling proud of her husband, who had once again managed to surprise them all.

'So you went down to see this Barbara person?' Sharon asked.

'Yes, and she was the sweetest girl.' Holly smiled. 'She sat with me for ages, telling me about their conversation.'

'That was nice.' Denise sipped her wine. 'When was it, by the way?'

'He went in at the end of November.'

'November?' Sharon looked thoughtful. 'That was after the second operation.'

They all nodded silently.

'Well, it looks like we're all off to Lanzarote!' Denise cheered and she held her glass up. 'To Gerry!'

'To Gerry!' Holly and Sharon joined in.

'Are you sure Tom and John won't mind?' Holly asked.

'Of course John won't mind!' Sharon laughed.

'And me and Tom can go away for a week another time. That way we're not stuck together for two weeks on our first holiday!'

'You practically live together anyway!' Sharon said.

Denise gave a quick smile but didn't answer and the two of them dropped the subject. That annoyed Holly, because her friends were always doing that. She wanted to hear how they were getting on in their relationships, but nobody seemed to tell her any of the juicy gossip. They seemed to be afraid to tell her about how happy they were or about the good news in their lives. Then again they also refused to moan about the bad things. So instead of being informed of what was really going on, she was stuck with this mediocre chitchat about . . . nothing.

'I have to say that leprechaun is doing a great job, Holly.' Denise cut into her thoughts as she looked out of the window.

'Oh, I know. I suppose I should go next door and thank him properly.'

After Denise and Sharon had headed off home, Holly grabbed a bottle of wine from the stash under the stairs and carried it next door to her neighbour. She rang the bell and waited.

'Hi, Holly,' he said, opening the door. 'Come in.'

Holly looked past him and saw the family sitting round the kitchen table eating supper. 'No, I won't disturb you, I just came to give you this'—she handed him the wine—'as a token of my thanks.'

'Well, Holly, this is really thoughtful of you, but thanks for what, if you don't mind me asking?'

'Oh, for tidying up my garden,' she said, blushing.

'But I haven't been tidying it, I'm sorry to say.'

'Oh. I thought you had been.' She laughed. 'You can keep that anyway.' She ran off down the driveway with her face burning with embarrassment. What kind of fool wouldn't know who was tidying her own garden?

She knocked on a few more doors and nobody seemed to know what she was talking about. Everyone seemed to have jobs and lives, and remarkably enough they didn't spend their days monitoring her garden. As she walked in through her door the phone was ringing.

She ran to answer it. 'Hello?' she panted.

'What were you doing, running a marathon?'

'No, I was chasing leprechauns.'

'Oh, cool.' Ciara didn't even question her. 'It's my birthday in two weeks.'

Holly had completely forgotten. 'Yeah, I know, Ciara.'

'Well, Mum and Dad want us all to invite friends to a barbecue. So will you tell Sharon and John, Denise and her DJ bloke, and that

Daniel guy too?' She laughed hysterically. 'He's yummy!'

'Ciara, I hardly know the man. Ask Declan to ask him.'

'No, because I want you to subtly tell him that I love him and want to have his babies.'

Holly groaned.

'Stop it!' Ciara gave out. 'He's *my* birthday treat!'

'OK, I'll call the others and . . .'

Ciara had already hung up.

Holly decided to get the most awkward phone call out of the way first and she dialled the number for Hogan's.

'Hi, can I speak to Daniel Connelly, please?'

'Yeah, hold on.' 'Greensleeves' belted out into her ear.

'Hello?'

'Hi, Daniel? It's Holly Kennedy.'

'Who?' he yelled.

Holly dived onto her bed in embarrassment. 'It's Holly Kennedy? Declan's sister?'

'Oh, Holly, hiya. Hold on a second while I go somewhere quieter.'

Holly was stuck listening to 'Greensleeves' again, and she danced round her bedroom and started singing along.

'Sorry, Holly.' Daniel laughed. 'You like "Greensleeves"?'

'Em, no, not really.' Her face went scarlet. 'I was just ringing to invite you to a barbecue.'

'Oh, great, yeah, I would love to come.'

'It's Ciara's birthday on Friday week—you know my sister, Ciara?'

'Er, yes, the one with the pink hair.'

Holly laughed. 'Yeah, well, she wanted me to invite you and to subtly tell you that she wants to marry you and have your babies.'

Daniel started laughing. 'Yes . . . that was very subtle all right.'

'Em, well, Denise and your friend Tom are coming, and Declan will be there, of course, so you'll know a few people.'

'Are you going?'

'Of course!'

'Good. I'll know even more people then, won't I?' He chuckled.

'Oh . . . great. Ciara'll be delighted you're coming.' She was just about to hang up when a thought popped into her head. 'Oh, one more thing. Is that position behind the bar still available?'

Thank God it was a beautiful day, Holly thought, as she walked round to the back of her parents' house. It had rained and rained this week. Ciara was in hysterics about what would become of her barbecue and she'd been hell to be with all week. Luckily for everyone's sake the weather had returned to its former splendour.

Holly followed the sounds of laughter and was glad to see that the garden was full with family and friends. Denise had already arrived with Tom and Daniel, and they had all flaked out on the grass. Sharon had arrived without John and she was sitting chatting to Holly's mum, no doubt discussing Holly's progress in life.

Holly frowned as she noted that Jack was once again not present. Ever since he had helped her to carry out the task of clearing out Gerry's things, he had been unusually distant. Even when they were children Jack had always been great at understanding Holly's needs and feelings without her having to point them out to him, but when she had told him that she needed space after Gerry's death, she didn't mean she wanted to be *completely* ignored and isolated. It was so out of character for him not to be in contact for so long. Nerves fluttered through Holly's stomach and she prayed that he was all right.

Ciara was in the middle of the garden, loving being the centre of attention. She was dressed in a pink bikini top and blue denim cut-offs.

Holly approached with her present, which was immediately grabbed and ripped open. 'Oh, Holly, I love it!'

'I thought you would,' Holly said, glad she had chosen the right thing. It was a butterfly bellybutton ring, which had a little pink crystal in each wing. She had chosen it so it would coordinate with Ciara's new butterfly tattoo and her pink hair, of course.

'I'm gonna wear it now, actually,' Ciara said, ripping out her current bellybutton ring and piercing the butterfly through her skin.

'Ugh,' Holly shuddered. 'I could have gone without seeing that, thank you very much.'

There was a beautiful smell of barbecued food in the air and Holly's mouth began to water. She wasn't surprised to see all the men huddled round the barbecue. Spotting Richard, she marched over and charged right in. 'Richard, did you tidy my garden?'

Richard looked confused. 'Excuse me, did I what?'

'Did you tidy my garden?' she repeated. She didn't know why she was acting angry, just a force of habit probably, because if he had tidied it he had done her a huge favour.

'When?' Richard looked around frantically, as though he had been accused of murder.

'I don't know when,' she snapped. 'During the past few weeks.'

'No, Holly, some of us have to work,' he snapped back.

Holly glared at him and went to join Denise, Tom and Daniel.

'Hi, Daniel.' She greeted him with a kiss on the cheek.

'Hi, Holly. Long time no see.' He handed her a beer.

'You still haven't found that leprechaun?' Denise laughed.

'No,' Holly said. She explained the story to Tom and Daniel.

'Do you think your husband organised it?' Tom blurted out.

'No.' Holly scowled at Denise for telling Tom.

Denise just held her hands up helplessly and shrugged.

'Thanks for coming, Daniel.' Holly turned to him.

'No problem at all. I was glad to come.'

He was dressed in a navy vest and combat shorts.

'You're very brown,' she commented.

'I was in Miami for a while last month.'

'Ooh, lucky you. Did you enjoy it?'

'Had a great time.' He nodded. 'Have you ever been?'

She shook her head. 'But at least us girls are heading off to Lanzarote next week. Can't wait.'

'Yes, I heard that. I'd say that was a nice surprise for you.' He gave her a smile, his eyes crinkling at the corners.

They chatted for a while about his holiday. 'I hope you didn't go with another woman or poor Ciara will be devastated,' she joked, and then kicked herself for being so nosy.

'No, I didn't,' he said. 'Laura and I broke up a few months ago.'

'Oh, I'm sorry to hear that. Were you together long?'

'Seven years.' He looked away and she changed the subject.

'By the way, Daniel, I just wanted to thank you for looking out for me after the documentary. Most men run away when they see a girl cry.'

'No problem at all, Holly. I don't like to see you upset.'

'You're a good friend,' Holly said, thinking aloud. 'Maybe I can get to know as much about you as you know about me.' She laughed.

'Yeah, I'd like that,' Daniel agreed.

'Oh, did you give Ciara that birthday present?'

'No,' he laughed. 'She's been kind of . . . busy.'

Holly turned and spotted her sister flirting with one of Declan's friends. So much for wanting Daniel's babies. 'I'll call her over, will I?'

'Go on,' Daniel said.

'Ciara!' Holly called. 'Got another pressie for you!'

'Ooh! What is it?' Ciara collapsed on the grass beside them.

Holly nodded over at Daniel. 'It's from him.'

Ciara turned excitedly to face him.

'I was wondering if you would like a job working behind the bar at Club Diva?'

Ciara's hands flew to her mouth. 'Oh, Daniel, that would be brill!' she squealed and threw her arms round him.

Any excuse, Holly thought. 'OK, OK, that's enough, Ciara. You don't want to kill your new boss.'

Suddenly the garden became very quiet and Holly's parents appeared with a large birthday cake singing 'Happy Birthday'. Someone followed behind them with a huge bouquet of flowers. Her parents placed the cake on the table in front of Ciara and the stranger behind them slowly removed the bouquet from his face.

'Mathew!' Ciara gasped. Her face went white.

'I'm sorry for being such a fool, Ciara.' Mathew's Australian accent echoed round the garden. He actually looked like he was acting out a scene from an Australian soap, but then drama always seemed to work for Ciara. 'I love you! Please take me back!' he announced. Everyone turned to stare at Ciara to see what she would say.

Her lower lip started to tremble. She ran over to Mathew and jumped on him, wrapping her legs round his waist and her arms round his neck.

Holly was overcome with emotion and tears welled in her eyes at the sight of her sister being reunited with the man she loved. Declan grabbed his camera and began filming.

Daniel put his arm round Holly's shoulders. 'I'm sorry, Daniel,' Holly said, wiping her eyes. 'I think you've just been dumped.'

'Not to worry,' he laughed. 'I shouldn't mix business with pleasure, anyway.' He seemed relieved.

Holly smiled at the jazz band as she passed and looked around for Denise. They had arranged to meet up in the girls' favourite bar, Juicy, known for its extensive cocktail menu and relaxing music. Holly had no intentions of getting drunk tonight, as she wanted to be able to enjoy her holiday as much as she could, starting the next day. She spotted Denise snuggling up to Tom on a large black leather couch in the conservatory area overlooking the River Liffey. Dublin was lit up for the night and all its colours were reflected in the water. Daniel sat opposite Denise and Tom sipping a strawberry daiquiri.

'Sorry I'm late,' Holly apologised, approaching her friends. 'I just wanted to finish packing before I came out.'

'You're not forgiven,' Daniel said quietly into her ear as he gave her a welcoming hug and kiss.

Denise looked up at Holly and smiled, Tom waved slightly and they returned their attention to each other.

'I don't know why they even bother inviting other people out. They just sit there staring into each other's eyes, ignoring everyone else,' Daniel said, sitting down again and taking another sip from his glass. He made a face at the sweet taste. 'And I really need a beer.'

Holly laughed. 'It sounds like you've been having a fantastic night.'

'Sorry,' Daniel apologised. 'It's just been so long since I've spoken to another human being, I've forgotten my manners.'

'Well, I've come to rescue you.' Holly picked up the menu and surveyed the choice of drinks before her. She ordered a drink with the lowest alcohol content and snuggled down in the cosy chair. 'I could fall asleep here,' she remarked.

Daniel raised his eyebrows. 'Then I would *really* take it personally.'

'Don't worry, I won't,' she assured him. 'So, Mr Connelly, since you know absolutely *everything* about me, tonight I am on a mission to find out all about you. So be prepared for my interrogation!'

Daniel smiled. 'OK, I'm ready.'

Holly thought about her first question. 'Where are you from?'

'Born and reared in Dublin.' He took a sip of the red cocktail and winced again. 'And if any of the people I grew up with saw me drinking this stuff and listening to jazz, I'd be in trouble.'

Holly giggled.

'After I finished school I joined the army,' he continued.

Holly raised her eyes, impressed. 'Why did you decide to do that?'

He didn't even think about it. 'Because I hadn't a clue what I wanted to do with my life, and the money was good. Anyway, I only stayed with the army for a few years.'

'Why did you leave?' Holly sipped on her lime-flavoured drink.

'Because I realised I had urges to drink cocktails and listen to jazz music and they wouldn't permit it in the army barracks,' he explained.

Holly giggled again. 'Really, Daniel.'

He smiled. 'Sorry, it just wasn't for me. My parents had moved down to Galway to run a pub and the idea of that appealed to me. So I moved down to Galway to work there. Eventually my parents retired and I took over the pub, but I decided a few years ago that I wanted to own one of my own. I worked really hard, saved my money, took out the biggest mortgage ever and moved back to Dublin and bought Hogan's. And here I am, talking to you.'

Holly smiled. 'Well, that's a wonderful life story, Daniel.'

'Nothing special, but a life all the same.' He returned her smile.

'So where does the ex come into all this?' Holly asked.

'She's right in between running the pub in Galway and leaving to come to Dublin.'

'Ah . . . I see,' Holly nodded, understanding. She drained her glass and picked up the menu again. 'I think I'll have Sex on the Beach.'

'When? On your holidays?' Daniel teased.

Holly thumped him playfully on the arm. Not in a million years.

Eight

'WE'RE ALL GOING on our summer Holly days!' the girls sang in the car all the way to the airport. John had offered to drive them but he was fast regretting it. Holly felt like she was back at school and off on an excursion. Her bag was packed with sweets and magazines, and they couldn't stop singing cheesy songs. Their flight wasn't until 9 p.m., so they wouldn't arrive until the early hours of the morning.

They reached the airport and piled out of the car. John lifted their suitcases from the boot, they gave him a hug and then dragged their luggage across the departure lounge to the long check-in queue.

'I told you we should have come earlier,' Sharon moaned.

'We'd just wait at the boarding gate,' reasoned Holly.

'Yeah, but at least there's a bar there,' Denise pointed out.

After thirty minutes of queuing they finally checked in.

'Why is that girl staring at me?' Denise said through gritted teeth, eyeing up the girl at the end of the bar.

'Probably because you're staring at her.' Sharon checked her watch. 'Only fifteen more minutes.'

'No, honestly, girls. I'm not being paranoid here.'

'Well, why don't you ask her, then,' Sharon sniggered.

'Oh, here she comes,' Denise sang and turned her back.

Holly looked up and saw a skinny, blonde-haired girl heading towards them. 'Hi, there!' the girl squeaked. 'I didn't mean to be rude by staring, but I just had to see if it was really you!'

'It's us all right,' Sharon said sarcastically, 'in the flesh.'

'Oh, I just *knew* it!' the girl squealed. 'My friends kept telling me I was wrong but I *knew* it was you! That's them over there.' She pointed to the end of the bar and the other four girls twinkled their fingers back. 'My name's Cindy and I just love that show you're all in. And you play

Princess Holly, don't you?' She pointed a manicured nail in Holly's face.

Holly opened her mouth to speak but Cindy kept on talking. 'When are you making the next one?'

'Oh, we're in discussions right now,' Denise lied.

'Fantastic!' Cindy clapped her hands. 'What's it about?'

'Well, we can't really say, but we have to go to Hollywood.'

Cindy looked like she was going to have a heart attack. 'Oh my God! Wow!' She looked down at Denise's boarding pass on the table. 'Wow, you girls are going to Lanzarote?!'

Denise grabbed her pass and shoved it in her bag.

'I'm going there too. We're staying in a place called Costa Palma Palace. Where are you guys staying?'

Holly's heart sank. 'Oh, I can't remember, girls, can you?'

Sharon and Denise shook their heads vigorously.

'Oh, well, not to worry. I'll see you when we land anyway!' Cindy gave them each a big hug and tottered back to her friends.

Four hours later the plane glided over the sea and landed at Lanzarote Airport. The girls made their way to the luggage reclaim and stood for almost an hour waiting for their bags while the crowd headed out to their coaches. Finally they headed off to meet their holiday rep.

'Kennedy, McCarthy and Hennessey?' the young woman dressed in a red uniform said in a thick London accent.

The girls nodded.

'Hi, I'm Victoria and I'll show you to the coach.' She led them outside.

It was two o'clock in the morning, and yet a warm breeze greeted them. Holly smiled to the girls, who felt it too; now they were really on holiday. They stepped onto the coach.

'Woo-hoo,' Cindy waved at them. 'I kept you all a seat back here!'

The girls trudged down to the back seat of the bus.

Forty-five minutes later they reached Costa Palma Palace and the excitement once again returned to Holly's stomach. Tall palm trees lined the centre of the drive and a large fountain was lit up with blue lights outside the main entrance. The girls were booked into a studio apartment with twin beds and a sofa bed. Holly stepped onto the balcony and looked out to sea. Although it was too dark to see anything, she could hear the water gently lapping up against the sand. She closed her eyes and listened.

At nine o'clock that morning Sharon woke Holly up. 'The Germans have nicked all the sunbeds at the pool,' she said grumpily. 'I'll be down on the beach if you want me.' Holly sleepily mumbled some response.

At ten o'clock Denise jumped on her in bed and they decided to get up and join Sharon.

The sand was hot and they had to keep moving so as not to burn the soles of their feet. They spotted Sharon sitting under the shade of an umbrella.

'Oh, this is so beautiful, isn't it?' Denise looked around.

Sharon looked up from her book and smiled. 'Heaven.'

Holly looked around to see if Gerry had come to the same heaven. Nope, no sign of him. All around her there were couples: couples massaging suncream onto each other's bodies, couples walking hand in hand along the beach. Holly didn't have any time to be depressed, as Denise had stepped out of her sundress and was hopping around on the hot sand in nothing but a skimpy leopardskin thong.

'Will one of you put suncream on me?'

Sharon put her book down. 'I'll do it.'

Denise sat at the end of Sharon's sunbed. 'You know what, Sharon? You'll get an awful tan line if you keep that sarong on.'

Sharon looked down at herself. 'What tan? I never get a tan. I've nice Irish skin, Denise. Besides, I look like such a blob these days I wouldn't want to scare everyone off.'

Holly looked at Sharon, annoyed at her for calling herself a blob. She'd put a little weight on but was by no means fat.

'Why don't you go up to the swimming pool then and scare all those Germans away?' Denise joked.

'Yeah, girls, we really need to get up earlier tomorrow,' Holly suggested. 'The beach gets boring after a while.'

The girls relaxed by the beach for the rest of the day, occasionally dipping themselves into the sea to cool down. They ate lunch at the beach bar. Holly gradually felt all the tension working its way out of her muscles, and for a few hours she felt free.

That night they enjoyed dinner in one of the many restaurants not far from the complex.

'I can't believe it's ten o'clock and we're heading back to the apartment already,' said Denise.

People overflowed from the bars onto the streets, music vibrating from every building. Holly could almost feel the ground pulsing beneath her. There was loud laughter, clinking glasses and singing. Neon lights flashed and tanned young bodies hung out in big groups around outdoor tables.

Looking at the average age of the clientele, Holly felt old. 'Well, we can go to a bar if you want,' she said uncertainly.

Denise scanned the bars in order to choose one.

'All right, beautiful.' A very attractive man flashed his pearly whites at Denise. 'Are you coming with me?'

Denise stared at the young man for a while, lost in thought. Sharon and Holly smirked at each other, knowing that Denise wouldn't be going to bed early after all.

Finally Denise snapped out of her trance. 'No, thank you, I have a boyfriend and I love him!' she announced. 'Come on, girls!' she said to Holly and Sharon, and walked off in the direction of the apartment.

The two girls remained on the street, mouths open in shock. They had to run to catch up with her. 'Who are you?' Sharon said. 'And what have you done with my man-eating friend?'

'OK.' Denise held her hands up in the air and grinned. 'Maybe being single isn't all it's cracked up to be.'

Holly lowered her eyes and kicked a stone along the path as they made their way back to their resort. It sure wasn't.

A silence fell between them as the music faded away slowly, leaving only a beat of the bass in the distance.

'That street made me feel so old,' Sharon said suddenly.

'Me too!' Denise's eyes widened. 'Since when did people start going out so young?'

Sharon began to laugh. 'Denise, *we* are getting older.'

'Well, it's not like we're *old* old. I mean, we could stay out all night if we wanted to, we just . . . are tired. We've had a long day . . . oh God, I do sound old.' Denise rambled on.

Sharon watched Holly. 'Holly, you haven't said a word.'

'Yeah, I was just thinking about Gerry.'

'Let's go down to the beach,' Denise suggested, and they slipped out of their shoes and allowed their feet to sink into the cool sand.

The sky was clear black and a million little stars twinkled; it was as if someone had thrown glitter up into a massive black net. The full moon rested low over the horizon where the sea met the sky. The girls sat in its path, the water gently lapping before them. The air was warm but a slight breeze brushed past Holly. She closed her eyes and filled her lungs with fresh air.

'That's why he brought you here, you know,' Sharon said, watching her friend relaxing.

Holly's eyes remained closed and she smiled.

'You don't talk about him much, Holly,' Denise said.

Holly's eyes opened. 'I know.'

Denise drew circles in the sand. 'Why not?'

Holly thought for a while. 'I don't know whether to be sad or happy when I talk about him. It's like, if I'm happy, certain people judge and expect me to be crying my eyes out. When I'm upset it makes people feel uncomfortable.' She stared out to the sparkling sea. 'I can't tease about him in conversation like I used to because it feels *wrong*. I can't talk about things he told me in confidence because they're *his* secrets.'

The three girls sat crosslegged on the soft sand.

'John and I talk about Gerry all the time.' Sharon looked at Holly with glittering eyes. 'We talk about the times he made us laugh, which was *a lot*. We even talk about the things he did that *really* annoyed us.'

Holly raised her eyebrows.

Sharon continued, 'Because to us, that's just how Gerry was. He wasn't all nice. We remember *all* of him.'

There was a long silence.

Denise was first to speak. 'I wish my Tom had known Gerry.'

Holly looked at her in surprise. A tear ran down her cheek.

'Gerry was my friend too,' Denise said, tears pricking in her eyes. 'So I try to tell Tom things about him just so he knows that one of the nicest men on this earth was *my* friend. But I can't believe that someone I now love so much doesn't know a friend I loved for ten years.'

Holly reached out to hug her friend. 'Well, then, we'll just have to keep telling Tom about him, won't we, Denise?'

They didn't bother meeting up with their holiday rep the next morning, as they had no intention of going on any tours or taking part in any silly sports tournaments. Instead, they headed over to the beach.

'Do you ever hear from Gerry's parents, Holly?' Sharon asked as she and Holly lounged on their Lilos in the sea.

'Yeah, they send me postcards every few weeks.'

'So they're still on that cruise? Do you miss them?'

'To be honest, I don't think they feel we have any connection any more. Their son's gone and they have no grandchildren.'

'That's bull, Holly. You're their daughter-in-law.'

'Oh, I don't know,' Holly sighed.

'They're a bit backward, aren't they?'

'Yeah, *very*. They hated me and Gerry "living in sin", as they said. Couldn't wait for us to get married. And *then* they couldn't understand why I wouldn't change my name.'

'Yeah, I remember that,' Sharon said.

'Hello, girls.' Denise floated out to meet them.

'Hey, where have you been?' Holly asked.

'Oh, chatting to some bloke from Miami. Nice guy.'

'Miami? That's where Daniel went on holiday,' Holly said.

'Hmm,' Sharon mused, 'nice guy, Daniel, isn't he?'

'Really nice,' Holly agreed. 'Very easy to talk to.'

'Tom was telling me he's been through the wars recently,' Denise said, turning to lie on her back.

Sharon's ears pricked up at the sound of gossip, 'Why's that?'

'Oh, he was engaged to some chick called Laura, and it turned out she was sleeping with someone else. That's why he moved to Dublin and bought the pub, to get away from her.'

'Where did he live before?' Sharon asked.

'Galway. He used to run a pub there,' Holly explained.

'Oh,' Sharon said. 'He doesn't have a Galway accent.'

'Well, he grew up in Dublin and joined the army, then he left and moved to Galway to work in his parents' pub. When his father retired, he took over the pub. He met Laura and they were together for seven years. When they broke up he moved back to Dublin and bought Hogan's.' Holly caught her breath.

'Don't know much about him, do you?' Denise teased.

'Well, if you and Tom had paid the slightest bit more attention to us the other night in Juicy's, maybe I wouldn't know so much about him,' Holly replied playfully.

Denise sighed loudly. 'God, I really miss Tom,' she said sadly.

'Did you tell the guy from Miami that?' Sharon laughed.

'No, I was just chatting to him,' Denise said defensively. 'To be honest, nobody else interests me. It's really weird.'

Sharon smiled at her. 'I think they call it love, Denise.'

They lay in silence for a while, all lost in their own thoughts, allowing the gentle motion of the waves to soothe them.

'Bloody hell!' Denise yelled. 'Look how far out we are!'

Holly sat up immediately. They were out so far from shore everybody on the beach looked like ants.

'Oh God!' panicked Sharon, and as soon as Sharon panicked Holly knew they were in trouble.

'Start swimming, quick!' Denise yelled, and they all lay on their stomachs and started splashing. After just a few minutes they gave up, out of breath. It was no use, the tide was moving out too quickly, and the waves were just too strong.

'Help!' Denise screamed at the top of her lungs and waved her arms around wildly.

'I don't think they can hear us,' Holly said.

'Oh, could we be any more stupid?' Sharon gave out and ranted on about the dangers of rafts in the sea.

'Oh, forget about that, Sharon,' Denise snapped. 'We're here now so let's all scream together.'

They all sat up on their rafts. 'OK, one, two, three . . . HELP!' They all waved their arms frantically.

Eventually they stopped screaming and stared at the dots on the beach.

'Tell me there aren't sharks out here,' Denise whimpered.

'Oh, please, Denise,' Sharon snapped viciously, 'that is the last thing we need to be reminded of right now.'

Holly gulped and stared down into the sea. The once-clear blue water had darkened. Denise continued her bloodcurdling screams.

'Jesus, Denise,' Sharon snapped, 'the only thing that's gonna respond to that is a dolphin.'

Holly wasn't sure whether to laugh or cry. 'At least one good thing came out of this,' she said.

'There's a good thing?' Sharon said.

'Well, the three of us always talked about going to Africa,' she giggled. 'And by the looks of things, we're halfway there.'

The girls looked out to sea, to their future destination.

'It's a cheaper mode of transport too,' Sharon joined in.

Denise stared at them as if they were mad, and just one look at her, lying in the middle of the ocean naked but for a leopardskin thong, was enough to set the girls off laughing.

'What?' Denise looked at them wide-eyed.

'I'd say we're in deep, deep trouble here,' Sharon giggled.

'Yeah,' Holly agreed, 'we're in way over our heads.'

They lay there laughing and crying for a few minutes more till the sound of a speedboat caused Denise to start waving frantically again.

'It's just like a regular night out with the girls,' Sharon giggled, watching Denise being dragged to the boat by a muscular lifeguard.

'I think they're in shock,' one lifeguard said to the other as they pulled the remaining hysterical girls onto the boat.

'Quick, save the rafts!' Holly managed to blurt out.

'Raft overboard!' Sharon screamed.

The lifeguards looked at each other worriedly, as they wrapped warm blankets round the girls and sped back to shore.

As they approached the beach, a large crowd was gathering. The girls looked at one another and laughed even harder. When they were lifted off the boat there was huge applause. 'They clap now, but where were they when we needed them?' Sharon grumbled.

'There they are!' Cindy and the Barbie Brigade pushed their way through the crowd. 'Oh my God!' she squeaked. 'I saw the whole thing through my binoculars and called the lifeguards. Are you OK?' She looked to each of them frantically.

'Oh, we're fine,' Sharon said. 'We were the lucky ones. The poor rafts never even had a chance.' They all cracked up laughing and were ushered away to be examined by a doctor.

That night the girls realised the seriousness of what had happened and their mood drastically changed. They sat in silence throughout dinner, all thinking about how lucky they were to have been rescued and kicking themselves for being so careless. Holly had reacted unusually out there on the water, and it bothered her to think about why she had. After the initial panic of thinking she was going to die, she had become feverishly giddy as she realised that if she did die she knew she would be with Gerry. It bothered her to think that she didn't care whether she lived or died. She needed to change her perspective on life.

The next morning Holly woke to the sound of Sharon throwing up in the toilet. She followed her in and gently rubbed her back and held her hair back.

'You OK?' she asked worriedly after Sharon had stopped.

'Yeah, it's just those bloody dreams I had all night. I dreamt I was on a boat and on a raft. I think it was just seasickness.'

'I had those dreams too. It was scary yesterday, wasn't it?'

Sharon smiled weakly. 'I'm never going on a raft again.'

When the three of them arrived down at the swimming pool, Denise and Sharon joined the Barbie Brigade. Well, it was the least they could do, seeing as they were the ones who had called for help. But before Holly was dragged into any conversation she signalled to Sharon that she was leaving, and Sharon gave her an encouraging wink, knowing why she was disappearing.

Holly wrapped her sarong round her hips and carried her small beach bag down to the shore. She couldn't believe that she'd fallen asleep before midnight the previous night. She had planned to get up quietly, without waking the others, sneak out onto the balcony and open Gerry's sixth message. Now she found a quiet corner, away from all the excited shouts of children playing and stereos blaring out the latest chart songs, and made herself comfortable on her beach towel. It was still early and already the sun was hot.

Holly carefully pulled Gerry's envelope out of her bag as if it were the most delicate thing in the world, and she ran her fingers along the neatly written word, 'August', and gently tore open the seal.

Hi, Holly,

I hope you're having a wonderful holiday. You're looking beautiful in that bikini! I hope I picked the right place. It's the place you and I almost went for our honeymoon, remember? I'm glad you finally got to see it.

Apparently, if you stand at the very end of the beach near the rocks and look round to the left, you'll see a lighthouse. I'm told that's where the dolphins gather. I know you love dolphins . . . tell them I said hi.

PS, I love you, Holly . . .

With shaking hands, Holly put the card back into the envelope and secured it safely in a pocket of her bag. She felt Gerry's eyes on her as she stood up and rolled up the beach towel. She ran to the end of the beach, which suddenly stopped because of a cliff. She put her trainers on and began to climb the rocks.

And there it was.

Exactly where Gerry had described it, the lighthouse sat high on the cliff, bright white as though it were some sort of torch to heaven. Holly carefully climbed over the rocks and made her way round the little cove. She was on her own now. It was completely private. And then she heard the noises. The squeaks of dolphins playing near the shore away from all the tourists on the beaches. Holly collapsed on the sand to listen to them talk.

Gerry sat beside her.

He may even have held her hand.

Holly felt happy enough to head back to Dublin, relaxed, destressed and brown. Just what the doctor ordered. That didn't stop her from groaning when the plane landed in Dublin Airport to heavy rain.

'Well, it looks like the leprechaun didn't do any work while you were away,' Denise said, looking at the garden as John reached Holly's home.

Holly gave her friends a hug and a kiss. There was a horrible musty smell inside her quiet, empty house and she went to open the patio doors to let the fresh air circulate.

She froze just as she was turning the key in the door.

Her entire back garden had been transformed.

The grass was cut. The weeds were gone. The garden furniture had been polished and varnished. A fresh coat of paint gleamed from her garden walls. Flowers had been planted and underneath the great oak sat a wooden bench. Holly looked round in shock; who was doing all this?

Nine

IN THE DAYS FOLLOWING her return from Lanzarote, Holly kept a low profile. It wasn't something she, Denise and Sharon talked about, but after living in each other's ears for a week, Holly was sure they all agreed it was healthy to spend some time apart. Ciara was impossible to get hold of, as she was either working at Daniel's club or spending time with Mathew. Jack was down in Cork and Declan was . . . well, who knew where Declan was.

Now she was back, she wasn't exactly bored with her life, but it just seemed so . . . nothing and so pointless. She'd had the holiday to look forward to, but now again she felt she had no real reason to get out of bed in the morning. And compared to last week in Lanzarote, Dublin was wet and ugly.

Some days she never even got out of bed, she just watched television and waited . . . waited for next month's message from Gerry, wondering what journey he would take her on next. When he was alive she'd lived for him, and now that he was gone she lived for his messages. Everything was about him.

Something that she did feel she should do was to catch the leprechaun. After further interrogation of her neighbours she still knew nothing more of her mystery gardener, and she was beginning to think the whole thing had just been an awful mistake. Eventually she had herself convinced that a gardener was working on the wrong garden, so she checked the post every day for a bill that she was going to refuse to pay. But no bill arrived, of that variety anyway. Plenty of others arrived, electricity bills, phone bills, insurance bills. Everything that came through her door was a bloody bill, and she hadn't a clue how she was going to continue paying them all. But she had become numb to all those irrelevant problems in life. She just dreamed the impossible dreams.

One day Denise called. 'Hiya, how are you?' she asked.

'Oh, full of the joys of life,' Holly said.

'Oh, me too!' she giggled in response.

'So what's happening?'

'I'm calling to invite you out for dinner tomorrow night. It's short notice, so if you're busy . . . cancel whatever you've planned!'

'Hold on and let me check my diary,' Holly said sarcastically.

'No problem,' Denise said seriously, and was silent while she waited. Holly rolled her eyes. 'Oh, whaddaya know? I appear to be free tomorrow night.'

'Oh, goody!' Denise said happily. 'We're meeting at Chang's at eight.'

'Who's we?'

'Sharon and John and some of Tom's friends. We haven't been out together for ages, so it'll be fun!'

'OK then, see you tomorrow.' Holly hung up feeling angry. Had it completely slipped Denise's mind that Holly was still a grieving widow and that life just wasn't fun any more? She stormed upstairs and opened her wardrobe. Now what piece of old and disgusting clothing would she wear tomorrow night, and how on earth was she going to afford an expensive meal? She could barely afford to keep her car on the road. She grabbed all her clothes from her wardrobe and flung them across the room, screaming her head off until she finally felt sane again.

Holly arrived at the restaurant at eight twenty, as she had spent hours trying on different outfits. Eventually she settled with the one she had been instructed to wear by Gerry for the karaoke, just so she could feel closer to him.

As she was walking towards the table her heart sank.

Couples R Us.

She paused halfway there and quickly sidestepped behind a wall. She wasn't sure she could go through with this. She hadn't the strength to keep battling with her emotions. She looked around to find the easiest escape route; the fire escape beside the kitchen door. The moment she stepped out into the cool fresh air she felt free again. She walked across the car park, trying to formulate an excuse to tell Denise.

'Hi, Holly.'

She froze and slowly turned round. She spotted Daniel leaning against his car, smoking a cigarette.

'Hiya, Daniel. I didn't know you smoked.'

'Only when I'm stressed.'

'You're stressed?' They greeted each other with a hug.

'I was figuring out whether to join the Happy Couples.' He nodded towards the restaurant.

Holly smiled. 'You too?'

He laughed. 'Well, I won't tell them I saw you if that's what you want.'

'So you're going in?'

'Have to face the music some time,' he said, grimly stubbing out his cigarette with his foot.

Holly thought about what he'd said. 'I suppose you're right.'

'You don't have to go in if you don't want to. I don't want to be the cause of you having a miserable night.'

'On the contrary, it would be nice to have another loner in my company. There are so very few in existence.'

Daniel laughed and held out his arm. 'Shall we?'

Holly linked her arm in his and they made their way towards the restaurant. It was comforting to know she wasn't alone in feeling alone.

'By the way, I'm getting out of here as soon as we finish the main course,' he laughed.

'Traitor,' she answered, thumping him on the arm. 'Well, I have to leave early anyway, to catch the last bus home.' She hadn't had the money to fill the tank in the car for the past few days.

'Well, then, we have the perfect excuse. I'll say I'm driving you home and you have to be home by . . .?'

'Half eleven?' At midnight she was planning to open the September envelope.

'Perfect time.' He smiled, and they made their way into the restaurant, feeling slightly reinforced by each other's company.

'Here they are!' Denise announced as they reached the table.

Holly sat beside Daniel. 'Sorry we're late.'

'Holly, this is Catherine and Mick, Peter and Sue, Joanne and Conal, Tina and Bryan, John and Sharon you know, Geoffrey and Samantha, and last but not least, this is Des and Simon.'

Holly smiled and nodded at all of them.

'Hi, we're Daniel and Holly,' Daniel said smartly.

'We had to order already,' Denise explained. 'But we ordered loads of dishes so we can all share them.'

Holly and Daniel nodded.

Everyone fell into conversation and Daniel turned to Holly. 'Did you enjoy your holiday?'

'Oh, I had a fabulous time,' she answered. 'We took it easy and relaxed, didn't do anything wild and weird.'

'Just what you needed,' he smiled. 'I heard about your near-death experience, though.'

Holly rolled her eyes. 'I bet Denise gave you the exaggerated version.'

'Well, she just told me about how you were surrounded by sharks and had to be airlifted by a helicopter.'

'She didn't!'

'No, not really,' he laughed.

'OK, everyone,' Denise called. 'You're probably wondering why Tom and I invited you all here tonight. Well, we have an announcement to make.' She smiled.

Holly's eyes widened.

'Myself and Tom are getting married!'

Holly's hands flew up to her mouth in shock. 'Oh, Denise!' she gasped, and walked round the table to hug them. 'That's wonderful news! Congratulations!'

She looked at Daniel's face; it had gone white.

They popped open a bottle of champagne and everyone raised their glasses for a toast. 'Hold on! Hold on!' Denise stopped them. 'Sharon, did you get a glass?'

Everyone looked at Sharon. Tom poured her a glass.

'No, no, no! Not for me, thanks,' she said.

'Why not?' Denise huffed.

Sharon looked at John. 'Well, I didn't want to say anything . . .'

Everyone urged her to speak.

'Well . . . John and I are going to have a baby!'

Holly just froze in shock. Tears filled her eyes as she went over to congratulate Sharon and John. Then she sat down and took deep breaths. This was all too much.

'So let's make a toast to Tom and Denise's engagement and Sharon and John's baby!'

Everyone clinked glasses and Holly ate dinner in silence, not really tasting anything.

'You want to make that time eleven o'clock?' Daniel asked quietly, and she nodded in agreement.

After dinner they made their excuses to leave and nobody really tried to persuade them to stay. Holly left her last thirty euros towards the bill.

For a while, they sat in the car in silence. Holly wanted to feel happy for her friends, but she couldn't shake off the feeling of being left behind. Everyone else's lives were moving on except hers.

'That was some night, wasn't it?' Daniel said at last.

Holly shook her head with disbelief. 'Daniel, I have known those girls all of my life, and I did *not* see any of that coming. Although Sharon wasn't drinking when we were away, and she did throw up a few mornings, but she said it was seasickness . . .' Her brain went into overdrive as things started to add up.

'Seasickness?' Daniel asked, confused.

'After our near-death experience,' she explained.

95

'Oh, right.' This time neither of them laughed.

'It's funny,' he said, 'the lads always said that myself and Laura would be the first to get married. I didn't think Laura would marry before me.'

'She's getting married?' Holly asked.

'He used to be a friend of mine, too.' He laughed bitterly.

'Obviously he's not any more.'

'Nope.' He pulled up outside her house. 'Ah, well, we all get our fair share of bad luck. You know that better than anyone.'

'Huh, fair share,' she repeated.

'I know, there's nothing fair about it, but don't worry, we'll have our good luck, too.'

They sat in silence for another while, then Holly glanced at her watch.

Daniel read her mind. 'So how're the messages from above going?'

Holly sat forwards. 'Well, I've another one to open tonight, actually. So . . .' She turned to look at him.

'Oh, right,' he said. 'I'd better let you go, then.'

Holly bit her lip. 'Thanks a million for the lift, Daniel.'

'No problem at all.' They gave each other a quick hug.

'See you soon,' she said. She waved him off, then headed for the house and let herself in. 'Right, Gerry,' she said, walking into the kitchen. 'What have you got in store for me this month?'

Holly held the tiny envelope tightly and glanced up at the kitchen clock. It was five past twelve. Usually Sharon and Denise would have called her by now, but so far neither of them had phoned. It seemed news of an engagement and a pregnancy beat the news of a message from Gerry these days. Holly scorned herself for being so bitter. She wanted to be back in the restaurant right now celebrating with her friends like the old Holly would have done. But she couldn't bring herself even to smile for them.

She was jealous of them and their good fortune. She was angry with them for moving on. Even in the company of friends she felt alone; in a room of a thousand people she would feel alone. But it was when she roamed the rooms of her quiet house that she felt most alone.

She couldn't remember the last time she'd felt truly happy. She missed going to bed at night with absolutely nothing on her mind. She hated the butterflies in her tummy every time she remembered Gerry. She missed the feeling of being loved, of knowing Gerry was watching her as she watched television or ate her dinner. She missed sensing his eyes on her as she entered a room; she missed his touches, his hugs, his words of advice, his words of love.

She hated counting down the days till she could read another one of his messages because they were all she had left of him, and after this one there would be only three more. And she hated to think of what her life might be like when there would be no more Gerry.

She slowly opened her seventh envelope.

Shoot for the moon, and if you miss you'll still be among the stars.
Promise me you will find a job you love this time!
PS, I love you . . .

Holly read and reread the message, trying to discover how it made her feel. She had been dreading going back to work for such a long time, had believed that she wasn't ready. But now she knew she had no choice. If Gerry said it was to be, it would be. Holly's face broke into a smile. 'I promise, Gerry,' she said happily. She studied his writing for a long time as she always did, and when she was satisfied she had analysed every word, she rushed over to the kitchen drawer, took out a notepad and pen and began to write her own list of possible jobs.

1. FBI agent?—Am not American. Do not want to live in America. Have no police experience.
2. Lawyer—Hated school. Hated studying.
3. Doctor—Ugghh.
4. Nurse—Unflattering uniforms.
5. Waitress—Would eat all the food.
6. Beautician—Bite my nails and wax as rarely as possible. Do not want to see areas of other people's bodies.
7. Secretary—NEVER AGAIN.
8. Actress—Could not possibly outdo my wonderful performance in the critically acclaimed *Girls and the City*.
9. Hotshot businesswoman in control of life—Hmm . . . Must do research tomorrow . . .

Holly finally collapsed onto her bed and dreamed of being a big hotshot advertising woman making a huge presentation on the top floor of a skyscraper overlooking Grafton Street. Well, he did say aim for the moon . . . She woke up early and walked to her local library to look up jobs on the Internet.

The librarian directed her to the row of computers on the far side of the room. 'It's five euros for every twenty minutes online.'

Holly handed over ten euros. It was all she had managed to take out of her bank account that morning. She couldn't believe that was all she had left.

'No, no,' the librarian said, handing back her money, 'you can pay when you finish.'

Holly reached the computers and realised that there were none free. She stood drumming her fingers on her handbag and looking around. Her eyes nearly popped out of her head as she spotted Richard tapping away. She tiptoed over and touched him on the shoulder. He jumped with fright and swirled round in his chair.

'Hiya,' she whispered.

'Oh, hello, Holly. What are you doing here?' he said uneasily, as if she had caught him doing something naughty.

'I'm just waiting for a computer,' she explained. 'I'm finally looking for a job,' she said proudly.

'Oh, right.' He shut down his screen. 'You can use this one.'

'Oh, no, you don't have to rush for me!' she said quickly.

'Not at all. I was just doing some research for work.'

'All the way over here?' she said, surprised. 'Don't they have computers in Blackrock?' She wasn't quite sure what it was that Richard did for a living, and it would seem rude to ask him after he'd worked there more than ten years. She knew it involved wearing a white coat, wandering round a lab and dropping colourful substances into test tubes.

'My work brings me everywhere,' Richard joked awkwardly. He said a quick goodbye and made his way over to pay at the desk.

Holly sat down at the computer and quickly became engrossed in her job-hunting.

Forty minutes later she made her way to the desk. The librarian tapped away on the computer. 'That's fifteen euros, please.'

Holly gulped. 'I thought you said five for twenty minutes.'

'Yes, that's right.' She smiled at her.

'But I was only online for forty minutes.'

'Actually, you were on for forty-four minutes, which cuts into the extra twenty minutes.'

Holly lowered her voice. 'Look, this is really embarrassing, but I actually only have the ten on me now. Is there any way I can come back with the rest later on today?'

The librarian shook her head. 'I'm sorry, but we can't allow that. You need to pay the entire amount.'

'But *I don't have* the entire amount,' Holly protested.

The lady stared back blankly.

'Fine,' Holly huffed, taking out her mobile.

'Sorry, but you can't use that in here.' She pointed to the NO MOBILE PHONES sign on the counter.

Holly looked up slowly at her and counted to five in her head. 'So we have a little problem here, don't we? May I go outside to use the phone?'

'As long as you stand in front of the entrance.' The lady shuffled papers and pretended to go back to work.

Holly stood outside the door and thought about who to call. She didn't want Denise and Sharon to know about her failures in life now that they were both so blissfully happy. She couldn't call Ciara because she was on a day shift at Hogan's pub. Jack was back teaching at the school, Declan was at college and Richard wasn't even an option.

Tears rolled down her face as she scrolled down the list of names in her phone book. The majority hadn't even called her since Gerry had died. She turned her back on the librarian so she wouldn't see that she was upset, and dialled the first number that came into her head.

'Hi, this is Gerry, please leave a message after the beep and I'll get back to you as soon as I can.'

'Gerry,' Holly said crying, 'I need you . . .'

Watching her mother's happy face as she drove in and parked in the car park brought back memories. Her mum used to collect her from school every day when she was little, and she was always so relieved to see that familiar car come to rescue her after her hellish day at school. Holly had always hated school—well, she had until she met Gerry. Then she would look forward to going to school each day so they could sit together.

Holly's eyes filled with tears again as Elizabeth rushed over to her and wrapped her arms round her.

'OK, love, why don't you wait in the car and I'll go in and deal with the librarian?' Holly did as she was told and sat in the car, flicking through radio stations.

Minutes later, her mother climbed back in and glanced over at her daughter, who looked so lost. She started the car. 'Why don't we go home and we can relax?'

Holly smiled gratefully and a tear trickled down her face. Home. She liked the sound of that.

In the living room at Portmarnock, Holly snuggled up on the couch with her mother.

'I rang you last night at home, were you out?' her mum said. She took a sip of her tea.

Oh, the wonders of the magical tea. The answer to all of life's little problems. You have a gossip and you make a cup of tea, you get fired from your job and you have a cup of tea, your husband tells you he has a brain tumour and you have a cup of tea . . .

'Yeah, I went out to dinner with the girls and about a hundred other people.' Holly rubbed her eyes tiredly.

'How are the girls?' Elizabeth said fondly. She had always got on well with Holly's friends.

'Sharon's pregnant and Denise got engaged,' Holly said.

'Oh,' Elizabeth squeaked, not sure how to react. 'How do you feel about that?'

Holly stared down at her hands and tried to compose herself. She wasn't successful and her shoulders began to tremble and she tried to hide her face behind her hair.

'Oh, Holly,' Elizabeth said sadly, putting her cup down and moving closer to her daughter. 'It's perfectly normal to feel like this.'

Holly couldn't manage to get any words out of her mouth.

The front door banged. 'We're hoooome!' Ciara announced.

'Great,' Holly sniffed, resting her head on her mum's chest.

'*Where is everyone?*' Ciara shouted.

'Just a minute, love,' Elizabeth called out.

'*I have news!*' Ciara's voice got louder. Mathew burst open the door carrying her in his arms. 'Me and Mathew are moving back to Australia!' she yelled happily into the room. She froze as she saw her sister in her mum's arms, quickly jumped down and led Mathew out.

'Now Ciara's going too, Mum.' Holly cried even harder, and Elizabeth cried softly for her daughter.

Holly stayed in the guest bedroom that night and woke up to a madhouse the following morning. She smiled at the familiar sound of her brother and sister running around the house screaming about how they were late for college and late for work. The world went on, simple as that, and there was no bubble big enough to protect her.

At lunchtime Holly's dad dropped her home and squeezed a cheque for five thousand euros into her hand.

'Dad, I can't accept this,' Holly said, overcome with emotion.

'Take it,' he said, gently. 'Let us help you, love.'

'I'll pay back every cent,' she said, hugging him tightly.

Holly stood at the door and waved her father off down the road. She looked at the cheque in her hand and immediately a weight was lifted from her shoulders. She could think of twenty things she could do with this cheque, and for once buying clothes wasn't one of them.

On the table in the hall she noticed the red light flashing on the answering machine. She sat on the stairs and hit the button.

She had five new messages.

One was from Sharon ringing to see if she was OK because she hadn't heard from her all day. The second was from Denise ringing to see if she was OK because she hadn't heard from her all day. The two girls had obviously been talking to each other. The third was from Sharon, the fourth was from Denise and the fifth was just someone hanging up. Holly pressed delete and ran upstairs to change. She wasn't ready to talk to Sharon and Denise yet.

She sat in the spare room in front of her computer and began to type up a CV. It took her two hours to finally print out something half decent, but reading back over it she decided that she had somehow managed to make herself look intelligent and even she would hire herself. She dressed smartly and drove down to the recruitment office in the car, which she had finally managed to fill with petrol. There was to be no more time-wasting. If Gerry said to find a job, she was going to find a job.

A couple of days later Holly sat out on her newly renovated garden furniture in her back garden, sipping on a glass of red wine. She looked around at the neat, landscaped lines and decided that whoever was working on her garden had to be a professional. She breathed in and allowed the sweet scent of the flowers to fill her nostrils. It was eight o'clock and already it was beginning to get dark. The bright evenings were gone, and everybody was once again preparing for hibernation for the winter months.

She thought about the message she had received on her answering machine that day. It had been from the recruitment agency and she had been shocked to receive a reply from them so quickly. The woman on the phone said that there had been a great response to her CV, and already Holly had a job interview lined up. Butterflies fluttered around her stomach at the thought of it. It was for a job selling advertising space for a magazine that circulated throughout Dublin. It was something she had no experience in, but Gerry had told her to shoot for the moon . . .

Holly also thought about the phone call she had just received from Denise. Denise had been so excited on the phone she didn't seem to be at all bothered by the fact that Holly hadn't talked to her since they'd all met up for dinner. She had been all talk about her wedding on New Year's Eve, and all Holly had to do was make a few noises to let her know she was still listening . . . although she wasn't.

Sharon hadn't called since the day after she had announced her pregnancy, and Holly knew she would have to call her soon, but she just couldn't bring herself to do it. She was still trying to get her head round the fact that Sharon and John were managing to achieve everything that everyone had always assumed Holly and Gerry would do first. Sharon had always said she hated kids, Holly thought angrily. Holly would call Sharon when she was good and ready.

It began to get chilly and Holly took her glass of wine inside. All she could do was wait for her job interview and pray for success. She went into the living room, turned on her and Gerry's favourite album of love songs on the CD player and snuggled up on the couch with her glass of wine, where she closed her eyes and pictured them dancing round the room together.

The following day she was woken by the sound of a car in her driveway. She got out of bed and threw on Gerry's dressing gown. She peeped out of the curtains and jumped back as she saw Richard step out of his car. She really wasn't in the mood for one of his visits. She paced her bedroom floor, feeling guilty as she ignored the doorbell ringing. She knew she was being horrible, but she just couldn't bear sitting down with him for another awkward conversation.

She breathed a sigh of relief as she heard his car door bang shut. She stepped into the shower and allowed the warm water to run over her face and she was once again lost in a world of her own. Twenty minutes later she padded downstairs in her disco diva slippers. A scraping noise from outside made her prick her ears up and listen closely. There it was again. A scraping noise and a rustling . . . Holly's eyes widened as she realised that her leprechaun was outside.

She crept into the living room and got down on her knees. Peering above the windowsill she gasped as she saw Richard's car still sitting in the driveway. What was even more surprising was the sight of Richard on his hands and knees with a small gardening implement, planting new flowers. She crawled away from the window and sat on the carpet in shock.

A few minutes later she stood up and brushed the dust off her clothes. She peeked out from behind the curtain again and saw Richard packing up his gardening equipment. Holly kicked off her slippers and shoved her feet into her trainers. As soon as Richard drove down the road she ran outside and hopped into her car. She was going to chase her leprechaun.

She managed to stay three cars behind him just like they did in the movies, and she slowed down as she saw him pulling over. He parked his car and went into the newsagent, returned with a newspaper and crossed the road to the Greasy Spoon.

She backed into a free space, crossed the road and looked inside the café. Richard was sitting with his back to her, hunched over his paper and drinking a cup of tea. She marched over happily with a smile on her face. 'God, Richard, do you ever go to work?' she joked loudly, causing him to jump. She was about to say more but stopped herself as he looked up with tears in his eyes and his shoulders began to shake.

Ten

HOLLY PULLED OUT A CHAIR and sat down beside Richard. She looked at him in shock, not knowing what to do or what to say. Tears rolled down his face and he tried with all his might to stop them.

'Richard, what's wrong?' She awkwardly patted his arm.

The plump lady made her way round the counter and placed a box of tissues on the table beside Holly.

'Here you go,' Holly said, handing Richard a tissue. He wiped his eyes and blew his nose loudly.

'I'm sorry for crying,' he said, embarrassed.

'Hey, it's my new hobby these days, so don't knock it.'

He smiled sadly. 'Everything just seems to be falling apart.'

'Like what?' she asked, concerned at her brother's transformation into somebody she didn't know at all. Come to think of it, she had seen so many sides to him over the past few months he had her slightly baffled.

Richard took a deep breath and gulped back his tea.

'Richard, I've recently learned that talking about things helps,' Holly said gently. 'And coming from me that's a huge tip, because I used to think I was superwoman, able to keep all my feelings inside. Why don't you tell me about it?'

He looked doubtful.

'I won't laugh, I won't say anything if you don't want me to. I won't tell a soul what you tell me,' she assured him.

He focused on the salt and pepper shakers at the centre of the table and spoke quietly. 'I lost my job.'

Holly remained silent and waited for him to say more. After a while, Richard looked up to face her.

'Richard, I know you loved your job, but you can find another one.'

'I lost my job in April, Holly.' He spoke angrily. 'It is now September. There's nothing for me, not in my line of work.'

'Oh.' Holly didn't know quite what to say. 'But Meredith is working, so you still have a regular income. Just take the time you need to find the right job—'

'Meredith left last month.' This time his voice was weaker.

Holly's hands flew to her mouth. 'The kids?'

'They're living with her,' he said, and his voice cracked.

'Oh, Richard, I'm so sorry,' she said, fidgeting with her hands. Should she hug him or leave him alone?

'I'm sorry too,' he said miserably.

'It wasn't your fault, so don't tell yourself it was.'

'Wasn't it?' he said, his voice beginning to shake. 'She told me I was a pathetic man who couldn't even look after his own family.' He broke down again.

'Oh, never mind that silly bitch. You are an excellent father and a loyal husband,' she said, and realised she meant every word of it. 'Timmy and Emily love you because you're fantastic with them, so don't mind what that demented woman says.' She wrapped her arms round him and hugged him while he cried.

Richard's tears finally subsided and he pulled away from her and grabbed another tissue. Holly's heart went out to him; he had always tried so hard to do the right thing and to create a perfect life and family.

'Where are you staying?' she asked.

'In a b. and b. down the road,' he said, pouring another cup of tea.

'You can't stay there. Why didn't you tell any of us?'

'Because I thought we could work it out, but we can't . . . She's made up her mind.'

'What about Mum and Dad?' she asked.

Richard shook his head. 'No, I wouldn't want to dump myself on them. I'm a grown man now.'

'Oh, Richard, don't be silly.' She made a face. 'There is absolutely nothing wrong with returning to the house you grew up in now and again. It's good for the soul.'

He looked uncertain. 'I don't think that's such a good idea.'

'Ciara's heading back to Australia in a few weeks.'

His face relaxed a little.

Holly smiled. 'So, what do you think?'

Richard smiled too, but it quickly faded. 'I couldn't ask Mother and Father, Holly, I wouldn't know what to say.'

'I'll go with you, and I'll talk to them for you. Honestly, Richard, they'll be delighted. You're their son and they love you. We all do,' she added, placing her hand over his.

'OK,' he finally agreed, and she linked her arm in his as they headed out to their cars.

'Oh, by the way, Richard, thank you for my garden.'

'You know?' he asked, surprised.

She nodded. 'You have a huge talent.'

Her brother's face relaxed into a shy smile.

Two days later Holly looked at herself in the toilet mirror of the office building where her interview was taking place. She had lost so much weight since she had last worn her old suits that she had had to go out and purchase a new one. It was just the right fit, black with light blue lines going through, and she matched it with a light blue top underneath. She felt like a hotshot advertising businesswoman in control of her life, and all she needed to do now was to sound like one.

She took her seat again and looked around the office while she waited. The colours were warm and light poured in from the large Georgian windows. The ceilings were high and there was a lovely feeling of space. Holly could sit there all day thinking. Her heart didn't even jump as her name was called.

Shoot for the moon, she whispered to herself, shoot for the moon.

Holly knocked lightly on the door and a deep gruff voice told her to enter. 'Hello,' she said more confidently than she felt. She walked across the room and held out her hand to the man who had stood up from his chair. He greeted her with a big smile and a warm handshake. He looked to be in his late fifties, with a big physique and silver hair.

'Holly Kennedy, isn't it?' he said, taking his seat and glancing down at her CV. She sat opposite him.

'That's right,' she said, placing her handbag on the floor and resting her sweaty hands on her lap.

He put his glasses on the end of his nose and flicked through her CV in silence. Holly glanced round his desk and her eyes fell upon a silver photo frame with three pretty girls close to her age, all smiling happily at the camera. When she looked up she realised he had put the CV down and was watching her.

'Before we start talking about you, I'll explain who I am and what the job entails. I'm Chris Feeney, founder and editor of the magazine. As you know, the running of any media organisation is hugely reliant on the advertising we receive. Unfortunately, our last man had to leave in a hurry, so I'm looking for somebody who could begin work almost immediately.'

Holly nodded. 'That would be no problem at all. In fact I'm eager to begin work as soon as possible.'

'I see you've been out of the work force for over a year now, am I correct in saying that?' He stared at her over the rim of his glasses.

'Yes, that's right. Unfortunately my husband was ill, and I had to take time off work to be with him.'

'I see. Well, I hope he's fully recovered now.'

Holly wasn't sure, did he want to hear about her personal life? He continued to look at her and she realised he was waiting for an answer.

'Well, no, actually, Mr Feeney. Unfortunately he passed away in February. He had a brain tumour.'

'I'm very sorry,' Chris said. 'It must be hard for you being so young and all.' He looked down at his desk. 'My wife lost her life to breast cancer just last year, so I understand how you may be feeling.'

'I'm sorry to hear that,' Holly said sadly, looking at the kind man across the desk.

'They say it gets easier.' He smiled.

'So they say,' Holly said grimly. 'Apparently gallons of tea does the trick.'

He started to laugh, a big guffaw of a laugh. 'Yes! I've been told that one too, and my daughters inform me that fresh air is also a healer.'

Holly smiled. 'Are they your daughters?' She looked at the photograph on the desk.

'Indeed they are,' he said, smiling also. 'My three little doctors who try to keep me alive,' he laughed. 'Unfortunately the garden no longer looks like that, though,' he said, referring to the background in the photograph.

'Wow, is that your garden?' Holly said, wide-eyed. 'It's beautiful. I presumed it was the Botanic Gardens, or somewhere like that.'

'It was Maureen's speciality. You can't get me out of the office long enough to sort through that mess.'

'Oh, don't talk to me about gardens,' Holly said, rolling her eyes. 'I'm not exactly Ms Greenfingers myself. My place looks like a jungle.' Well, it did look like a jungle, she thought to herself.

They looked at each other and smiled.

'Anyway, getting back to the interview,' Mr Feeney said. 'Have you experience working with the media at all?'

'Yes, I have, actually.' She returned to business mode. 'I worked in an estate agent's advertising new properties, so I was on the other end of what this job requires.'

'But you have never actually worked on a magazine?'

Holly racked her brains. 'I was responsible for printing up a weekly newsletter for a company I worked for . . .' She rambled on and on, grasping at every little straw she could as she went through every job she'd ever worked at. Eventually she grew bored with the sound of her own voice. She was underqualified for this job and she knew it, but she also knew that she could do it if he would just give her the chance.

Mr Feeney took off his glasses. 'I see. Well, Holly, you have a great deal of experience in the workplace, but I notice you haven't stayed in any job for longer than nine months.'

'I was searching for the right job for me,' Holly said.

'So how do I know you won't desert me?'

'Because this is the right job,' Holly said seriously. She took a deep breath as she felt her chances slipping away from her. 'Mr Feeney, I'm a very hard worker. When I love something I give it one hundred per cent. What I don't know I am more than willing to learn so that I can do my best for myself and for the company. If you put your trust in me, I won't let you down.' She stopped herself just short of getting down on her knees and begging for the damn job. Her face blushed as she realised what she had just done.

'Well, then, I think that's a good note to finish on,' Mr Feeney said, smiling at her. He stood up and held his hand out. 'Thank you for taking the time to come down here. We'll be in touch.'

Holly decided to drop in on Ciara at work, where she could have a bite to eat. She rounded the corner and entered Hogan's pub. It was packed with smartly dressed people on their lunch breaks, some even having a few sneaky pints before heading back to the office. Holly found a small table in the corner.

'Excuse me,' she called out loudly, and clicked her fingers in the air, 'can I get some service here, please?'

The people around her threw her looks for being so rude to the staff. Ciara swirled round with a scowl, but it broke into a smile when she spotted her sister grinning at her. 'I was about to smack the head off you,' she laughed, approaching the table.

'I hope you don't speak to all your customers like that,' Holly teased.

'Not *all* of them. You having lunch here today?'

Holly nodded. 'Mum told me you were working lunches, but I thought you were working in the club upstairs?'

'That man has got me working all the hours under the sun. He's treating me like a slave,' Ciara moaned.

Daniel walked up. 'Did I hear someone mention me?'

Ciara's face froze. 'No, no, I was just talking about Mathew. He has me up all hours of the night, I'm like his sex slave . . .' She wandered over to the bar to get a notepad and pen.

'Sorry I asked,' Daniel said, staring at Ciara. 'Mind if I join you?' he asked Holly.

Holly pulled out a stool for him. 'OK, what's good to eat here?' she asked, looking through the menu.

Ciara mouthed, 'Nothing' behind Daniel's back.

'The toasted special is my favourite,' Daniel suggested, and Ciara shook her head wildly at Holly.

'What are you shaking your head at?' Daniel said, catching Ciara in the act again.

'Oh, it's just that . . . Holly is allergic to onions.'

Holly nodded her head. 'Yes . . . they, eh, make my head bloat.' She blew her cheeks out. 'Terrible things, onions. Fatal in fact.' Ciara rolled her eyes at her sister.

'OK, leave the onions out,' Daniel suggested, and Holly agreed. Ciara stuck her fingers in her mouth and pretended to gag as she walked away.

Daniel studied Holly's outfit. 'You're looking very smart today.'

'Yes, well, I was just at a job interview.' Holly winced at the thought of it. 'Let's just say I won't expect a call anytime soon.'

'Oh, well, not to worry,' Daniel said, smiling. 'Still have that job upstairs if you're interested.'

'I thought you gave that job to Ciara.'

'Holly, you know your sister; we had a bit of a *situation*.'

Holly laughed. 'What did she do this time?'

'Some guy at the bar said something she didn't quite like so she served him his pint over his head.'

'Oh, no!' Holly gasped. 'I'm surprised you didn't fire her!'

'Couldn't do that to a Kennedy family member, could I?'

Ciara arrived with Holly's food, slammed the plate down on the table and turned on her heel.

'Hey!' Daniel frowned, taking Holly's plate away. 'There are onions in it. Ciara must have given the wrong order again.'

'No, no, she didn't.' Holly grabbed the plate back. 'I'm only allergic to red onions,' she blurted out.

'How odd. I didn't think there was a huge difference.'

'Oh, there is. They may be part of the same family but the red onion contains deadly toxins . . .'

'Toxins?' Daniel said disbelievingly.

'Well, they're toxic to me, aren't they?' she mumbled, and bit into the sandwich to shut herself up.

'Have you spoken to Denise or Sharon lately?'

'Just Denise,' she said, looking away. 'You?'

'Tom has my head done in with all this talk of weddings. Wants me to be his best man.'

'How do you feel about it?'

'Ah,' Daniel sighed. 'Happy for him, in a selfish and bitter kind of way.' He laughed.

'Know how you feel,' Holly nodded. 'You haven't spoken to your ex lately or anything?'

'Who, Laura?' he said, surprised. 'Never want to see the woman again.'

'Is she a friend of Tom's?'

'Not as friendly as they used to be, thank God.'

'So she won't be invited to the wedding then?'

Daniel's eyes widened. 'You know, I never even considered that.' There was a silence as Daniel contemplated the thought. 'I think I'm meeting up with Tom and Denise tomorrow night to discuss the wedding plans, if you feel like coming out.'

Holly rolled her eyes. 'Gee, thanks, well, that just sounds like the best fun ever, Daniel.'

Daniel started laughing. 'I know, that's why I don't want to go on my own. Call me later, if you decide to come.'

Holly nodded.

'Right, here's the bill,' Ciara said, dropping a piece of paper on the table and sauntering off. Daniel watched after her and shook his head.

Holly's heart began to pound as she spotted Sharon's car outside her house. It had been a long time since Holly had spoken to her. She should have been to visit Sharon first and she knew it. She pulled up and got out, walked towards Sharon's car and was surprised to see John stepping out. There was no Sharon to be seen. Her heart began to pound; she hoped Sharon was OK.

'Hi, Holly,' John said grimly, banging the car door behind him.

'John! Where's Sharon?' she asked.

'I just came from the hospital.'

Holly's hands flew to her face. 'Oh my God! Is she OK?'

John looked confused. 'Yeah, she's just having a checkup. I'm going back to collect her after I leave here.'

Holly's hands dropped down by her sides. 'Oh,' she said, feeling stupid.

'You know, if you're that concerned about her then you should call her.' John's icy blue eyes stared straight into hers.

Holly bit her lip, feeling guilty. 'Yeah, I know. Why don't you come inside and I'll make us a cup of tea.'

She flicked the switch on the kettle and busied herself while John made himself comfortable at the table.

'Sharon misses you, you know.'

Holly carried the mugs over to the table. 'I miss her too.'

'It's been a while now, Holly, and you know the two of you used to speak to each other every day.' John took the mug from her hand and placed it in front of him.

'Things used to be very different, John,' Holly said angrily.

'Look, we all know what you've been through—'

'I know you all *know* what I've been through, John, but you don't seem to understand I'm *still* going through it!'

There was a silence.

'I can't just move on with my life like you're all doing and pretend nothing's happened.'

'Do you think that that's what we're doing?'

'Well, let's look at the evidence, shall we?' she said sarcastically. 'Sharon's having a baby. Denise is getting married—'

'Holly, that's called living. You seem to have forgotten how to do that. I miss Gerry too. He was my best mate. We went to school together, we played on the same football team. I was his best man at his wedding and he was at mine! Whenever I had a problem I went to Gerry, whenever I wanted to have a bit of fun I went to Gerry. I told him some things that I would never have told Sharon and he told me things he wouldn't have told you. Just because I wasn't married to him doesn't mean that I don't feel like you do.'

Holly sat stunned. John took a deep breath.

'Yes, it's difficult. Yes, it's horrible. Yes, it's the worst thing that has ever happened to me in my whole life. But I can't just stop going to the pub because there's two blokes laughing and joking on the stools Gerry and I used to sit on. I can't stop going to football matches just because it's somewhere we used to go together all the time.'

Tears welled in Holly's eyes and John continued talking.

'Sharon knows you're hurting but you have to understand that this is a hugely important time in her life, too, and she needs her best friend to help her through it. She needs your help just like you need hers.'

Holly sobbed hot tears. 'I'm trying, John.'

'I know you are.' He grabbed her hands. 'But Sharon needs you. Avoiding the situation isn't going to help anyone.'

'But I went for a job interview today,' she sobbed childishly.

John tried to hide his smile. 'That's great news, Holly. And how did it go?'

'Shite,' she sniffed, and John started laughing. He allowed a silence to fall between them before he spoke again.

'She's almost five months pregnant, you know.'

'What?' Holly looked up in surprise. 'She didn't tell me she was pregnant when we were in Lanzarote.'

'She was afraid to,' he said gently. 'She thought you might get mad at her and never want to speak to her again.'

Holly wiped her eyes aggressively. She looked away. 'I meant to call her, I really did. I picked up the phone every day but I just couldn't do it. Then I'd say that I'd call the next day, and the next day I would be busy . . . Oh, I'm sorry, John. I'm truly happy for the both of you.'

'Thank you, but it's not me that needs to hear this.'

'But I've been so awful! She'll never forgive me now!'

'Oh, don't be stupid, Holly. It's Sharon we're talking about here. It will all be forgotten about by tomorrow.'

Holly raised her eyebrows at him hopefully.

'Well, maybe not *tomorrow*. Next year perhaps . . . and you'll owe her big-time.' His icy eyes warmed and twinkled at her.

'Stop it!' Holly giggled. 'Can I come with you to see her?'

Butterflies fluttered around in Holly's stomach as they pulled up outside the hospital. Sharon stood alone outside, waiting to be collected. She looked so cute Holly had to smile at the sight of her friend. As Holly looked at Sharon dressed in a polo neck and jeans, she could see the swelling of a bump. Holly stepped out of the car and Sharon's face froze.

Oh, no, Sharon was going to scream at her. She was going to tell her she hated her and that she was a crappy friend and that . . .

Sharon's face broke into a smile and she held her arms out. 'Come here to me, you fool,' she said softly.

Holly ran into her arms. There, with her best friend hugging her tight, she felt the tears begin again. 'Oh, Sharon, I'm so sorry, I'm a horrible person. I'm so so so so so so sorry, to—'

'Oh, shut up, you whiner, and hug me.' Sharon cried too, and they squeezed each other for a long time as John looked on.

'Ahem.' John cleared his throat loudly.

'Oh, come here, you.' Holly smiled and dragged him into their huddle.

'I presume this was your idea.' Sharon looked at her husband.

'No, not at all,' John said, winking at Holly. 'I just passed Holly in the street and told her I'd give her a lift . . .'

'Yeah, right,' Sharon said sarcastically, as the three of them walked towards the car and got inside.

'So what did they say?' Holly asked Sharon from the back. 'Is it a boy or a girl?'

'It's an "it" for now,' Sharon said. 'They're not too sure yet.'

'Would you want to know if they could tell you?'

Sharon scrunched her nose up. 'I don't know, I haven't figured that out yet.' She looked across at John again, and the two of them shared a secret smile.

A familiar pang of jealousy hit Holly and she sat quietly while the three of them headed back to Holly's house in John's car. Later, sitting round her kitchen table, they made up for lost time.

'Sharon, Holly went for a job interview today,' John said when he managed to get a word in edgeways.

'Oooh, really? I didn't know you were job-hunting already!'

'Gerry's new mission for me,' Holly smiled.

'Oh, was that what it was this month? I was just dying to know! So how did it go?'

Holly grimaced and held her head in her hands. 'Oh, it was awful, Sharon. I made a total fool of myself.'

'Really?' Sharon giggled. 'What was the job?'

'Selling advertising space for that magazine, X.'

'Ooh, that's cool, I read that at work all the time.'

'What kind of magazine is it?' asked John.

'Oh, it has fashion, sports, culture, food, reviews . . .'

'And adverts,' Holly joked.

'What was so wrong with the interview? You can't have been that bad.' Sharon looked intrigued.

'Oh, I think it's bad when the interviewer asks if you have any experience and you tell him you once printed up a newsletter.' Holly banged her head playfully off the kitchen table.

Sharon burst out laughing. 'I hope you weren't referring to that crappy little leaflet you printed up on the computer.'

John and Sharon howled with laughter.

'Ah well, it was *advertising* the company . . .' Holly giggled.

'Remember, you made us all go out and post them round people's houses? It took us days to do!'

'Hey, I remember that,' John laughed. 'Remember, you sent me and Gerry out to post hundreds of them one night?'

'Yeah?' Holly was afraid to hear what came next.

'Well, we shoved them in the skip at the back of Bob's pub and went in for a few pints.'

Holly's mouth dropped open. 'You sly little bastards! Because of you two the company went bust and I lost my job!'

'Oh, I'd say it went bust the minute people took a look at those leaflets, Holly,' John teased.

'Shut up, you,' Holly laughed. 'Hey, what else did you and Gerry get up to that I don't know about?'

John's eyes danced. 'Ah, a true friend never reveals secrets.'

But something had been unlocked. And for the first time since Gerry had died, the three of them laughed and laughed, and Holly learned how to talk about her husband again. It used to be that the four of them gathered together: Holly, Gerry, Sharon and John. This time three gathered to remember the one they had lost. Soon they would be four again, with the arrival of Sharon and John's baby.

Life went on.

That Sunday, Richard called by to visit Holly with the kids. She had told him he was welcome to bring them whenever it was his day with them. They played outside in the garden while Richard and Holly finished off their lunch and watched them through the patio doors.

'They seem really happy, Richard,' Holly said.

'Yes, they do, don't they?' He smiled as he watched them chasing each other around. 'I want things to be as normal for them as possible. They don't quite understand what's going on.'

'What have you told them?'

'Oh, that Mummy and Daddy don't love each other any more and that I moved away so that we can be happier.'

'And they're OK with that?'

'Timothy is OK but Emily is worried that we might stop loving her and that she will have to move away.' His eyes were sad.

Poor Emily, Holly thought, watching her dancing around with her scary-looking doll. She couldn't believe that she was having this conversation with Richard. He seemed like a different person these days. But then again, they now had something in common. They both understood what it was like to feel lonely and unsure of themselves.

'How's everything going at Mum and Dad's house?'

Richard swallowed a forkful of potato and nodded. 'Good. They're being extremely generous.'

'Ciara bothering you at all?'

'Ciara is . . . Ciara,' he smiled. 'We don't see eye to eye on a lot of things.'

'Well, I wouldn't worry about that,' Holly said. 'The majority of the world wouldn't see eye to eye with her.' She sat back in her seat, trying to decide how to phrase what she was going to say. 'We're all different, Richard. Ciara is eccentric, Declan is a dreamer, Jack is a joker, I'm . . . well, I don't know what I am. But you were always very controlled. It's not necessarily a bad thing.'

'I've always thought you were very thoughtful,' Richard said, after a long silence.

'When?' Holly asked incredulously.

'Well, I wouldn't be sitting here eating lunch with the kids running around having fun outside if you weren't thoughtful now, but I was referring to when we were children.'

'Jack and I were always so awful to you,' she said softly.

'You weren't *always* awful, Holly.' He gave her an amused smile. 'Besides, that's what brothers and sisters are for, to make each other's lives as difficult as possible. It forms a great basis for life, toughens you up. Anyway, I was the bossy older brother.'

'So how does that make me thoughtful?' Holly asked.

'You idolised Jack. You used to follow him around and you would do exactly what he told you to do.' He started laughing. 'I used to hear him telling you to say things to me and you would run into my room terrified and blurt them out and run away again.'

Holly looked at her plate, feeling embarrassed.

'But you always came back,' Richard continued. 'You would always creep back into my room silently and watch me working at my desk, and I knew that was your way of saying sorry.' He smiled. 'None of our siblings had a conscience in that house. Not even me. You were the only one, always the sensitive one.'

He continued eating and Holly sat in silence. She didn't remember idolising Jack, but she supposed Richard was right. Jack had always been her favourite brother; Gerry had always got along with Jack the best. However, she realised she had been making excuses for him every time he didn't call round or phone her when he said he would. In fact, she had been making excuses for him ever since Gerry died.

The next day, Holly jumped around the house ecstatically as she replayed the message on the answering machine for the third time.

'Hi, Holly,' came the gruff voice. 'This is Chris Feeney here from magazine X. I'm just calling to say that I was very impressed with your interview. Em . . .' He stalled a bit. 'Well, no doubt you'll be delighted to know that I've decided to welcome you as a new member of the team. I would love you to start as soon as possible, so call and we'll discuss it.'

Holly rolled around her bed in terrified delight and pressed the PLAY button again. She had aimed for the moon, and she'd landed!

Eleven

HOLLY STARED UP at the tall Georgian building and her body tingled with excitement. It was her first day of work and she felt that good times were ahead of her in this building. It was situated in the centre of town, and the busy offices of magazine *X* were on the first floor above a small café. Holly had got very little sleep the night before due to nerves and excitement; however, she didn't feel the same dread that she usually felt before starting a new job. Her family and friends had been ecstatic when they heard the news, and just before she left the house that morning she had received a beautiful bouquet of flowers from her parents, wishing her luck on her first day.

But although she had felt excited when she sat down to eat her breakfast, she had also felt sad. Sad that Gerry wasn't there to share her new start. They had performed a little ritual every time Holly started a new job. Gerry would wake Holly up with breakfast in bed and then he would pack her bag with ham and cheese sandwiches, an apple, a packet of crisps and a bar of chocolate. Mind you, they only ever did that on her first day, every other day they would tumble out of bed late as usual, race each other to the shower and then wander around the kitchen half asleep, grumbling at each other while they grabbed a quick cup of coffee. They would give each other a kiss goodbye and go their separate ways, then start all over again the next day. If Holly had known that their time was so precious . . .

This morning, she had woken to an empty house in an empty bed to no breakfast. She had allowed herself to imagine that when she woke up Gerry would miraculously be there to greet her, but with death there were no exceptions. Gone meant gone.

Now, poised at the entrance, Holly checked herself to see that she looked presentable and made her way up the wooden staircase. She entered the waiting-room area and the secretary she recognised from the interview came from behind the desk to greet her.

'Hi, Holly,' she said happily, shaking her hand. 'Welcome to our humble abode.' She looked about the same age as Holly and had long blonde hair.

'I'm Alice, by the way, and I work out here in Reception, as you know. Well, the boss man's waiting for you.'

'I'm not late, am I?' Holly asked, worriedly glancing at her watch.

'No, not at all,' Alice said, leading her down to Mr Feeney's office. 'Don't mind Chris and all the other lot, they're all workaholics. I think Chris actually lives in his office. The man isn't normal,' she said, tapping on his door lightly and leading her in.

'Who's not normal?' Mr Feeney asked, standing up from his chair.

'You.' Alice smiled and closed the door behind her.

'See how my staff treat me?' Mr Feeney's handshake was once again warm and welcoming, and Holly felt immediately at ease.

'Thank you for hiring me, Mr Feeney,' she said genuinely.

'You can call me Chris, and there's no need to thank me. Follow me and I'll show you round the place.' He started leading her down the hall. The walls were hung with framed covers of every X magazine published for the last twenty years.

'In here is our office of little ants.' He pushed open the door and Holly looked into the huge office. There were about ten desks in all, with people all sitting in front of their computers and talking on the phone. They looked up and waved politely. Holly smiled at them. 'These are the wonderful journalists who help pay my bills,' Chris explained. 'That's John-Paul, the fashion editor; Mary, our food woman; and Brian, Sean, Gordon, Aishling and Tracey. Everyone, this is Holly!' They smiled and waved again and continued talking on the phone.

Chris led her to the room next door. 'This is where all our computer nerds hide. That's Dermot and Wayne, and they're in charge of layout and design, so you'll be keeping them informed about what advertisements are going where. Lads, this is Holly.'

'Hi, Holly.' They both stood up and shook her hand and then continued working on their computers.

'I have them well trained,' Chris chuckled, and headed back down the way they had come and Holly glanced at the walls feeling excited. This was like nothing she had ever experienced before.

'In here is your office,' he said.

Holly couldn't stop herself from smiling as she looked around at the small room. She had never had her own office before. It was just big enough to fit a desk and filing cabinet. There was a computer sitting on the desk with piles and piles of folders. Opposite the desk was a book-case crammed with stacks of old magazines. A huge Georgian window practically covered the entire wall behind her desk, and the room had a bright and airy feel to it.

She placed her new briefcase on the desk. 'It's perfect,' she said.

'**R**ight, Ciara, are you sure you've got your passport?' Holly's mum asked for the third time since leaving the house.

'Yes, Mum,' Ciara groaned. 'I told you a billion times, it's right here.'

'Show me.' Elizabeth twisted round in the passenger seat.

'No! I'm not showing it to you. You should just take my word for it. I'm not a baby any more, you know.'

Declan snorted and Ciara elbowed him. 'Shut up, you.'

'Ciara, just show Mum the passport so you can put her mind at rest,' Holly said tiredly.

'Fine,' she huffed, lifting her bag onto her lap. 'It's in here, look . . . no, hold on, it's in here . . . no, actually maybe I put it in . . . Oh, crap!'

'Bloody hell, Ciara,' Holly's dad growled, slamming on the brakes and turning the car round.

'What?' she said defensively. 'I put it in here, Dad. Someone must have taken it out,' she grumbled, emptying the contents of her bag in the car.

'Ciara,' Holly moaned as a pair of knickers went flying over her face.

Holly sat squashed in the back seat with Declan and Ciara. Richard was driving Mathew and Jack, and they were probably at the airport already. This was the second time they had returned to the house, as Ciara had forgotten her lucky nose ring and demanded that her dad turn the car round earlier. An hour after setting off, they reached the air-port in what should have been only a twenty-minute drive.

'Pet, keep in touch with us a lot more this time, won't you?' Elizabeth cried as she hugged her daughter.

'Of course I will. Oh, please, don't cry, Mum, or you'll get me started.'

A lump formed in Holly's throat as she stood on the tips of her toes to hug the enormous Mathew. 'Take care of my sister.'

'Don't worry, she's in good hands,' he smiled.

'Look after her now, won't you?' Frank smacked him on the back. Mathew was intelligent enough to know it was more of a warning than a question and gave a very persuasive answer.

'Bye, Richard,' Ciara said. 'Stay away from that Meredith bitch now. You're far too good for her.' She gave him a big hug and Declan too. 'You can come over any time you like, Dec, maybe make a movie or something about me. And, Jack, look after my big sis,' she said, squeezing Holly tightly. 'Ooh, I'm gonna miss you,' she said sadly.

'Me too,' Holly's voice shook.

'OK, I'm going now before all you depressing people make me cry,' she said, trying to sound happy.

Holly stood in silence with her family and they all watched as Ciara and Mathew walked away, hand in hand. Even Declan had a tear in his eye, but pretended he was about to sneeze.

'Just look at the lights, Declan.' Jack threw his arm round his baby brother. 'They say that helps you sneeze.'

Declan stared up at the lights and avoided watching his favourite sister walking away. Frank held his wife close as she waved at her daughter, while tears rolled down her cheeks.

Holly drummed her fingers on her desk and stared out of the window. She was absolutely flying through her work this week. She didn't know it was possible to actually *enjoy work* so much. She had stayed in happily through lunch breaks and had even worked late. But it was only her third week, after all; give her time. The office had developed a light-hearted banter and she loved feeling that she was a part of the team, as if she were actually doing something that made a real impact on the finished product. Every time she made a deal she thanked Gerry for pushing her all the way to the top.

She heard the radio go on in Chris's office next door. On the hour without fail, he turned on the news, and all the news seeped into Holly's brain. She had never felt so intelligent.

She glanced back down at her work again; a freelancer had written an article on how he travelled around Ireland trying to find the cheapest pint. It was very amusing, but there was a huge gap at the bottom of the page and it was up to Holly to fill it. She flicked through her book of contacts and an idea came to her immediately. She picked up the phone and dialled.

'Hogan's.'

'Hi, Daniel Connelly, please.'

'One moment.'

Bloody 'Greensleeves' again. She danced around the room to the music while she waited.

'Hello?'

'Daniel? Hiya, it's Holly.'

'How are you doin', Holly?'

'I'm grand, thanks, you?'

'Couldn't be better. How's that snazzy job of yours?'

'Well, actually, that's why I'm calling.' Holly sounded guilty.

He laughed. 'So what's up?'

'Do I remember you saying you needed to advertise Club Diva more?' Well, he had actually thought he was saying it to Sharon, but she knew he wouldn't remember that minor detail.

'I do recall saying that, yes.'

'How would you like to advertise it in *X*?'

'Is that the name of the magazine you work on?'

'No, I just thought it would be an interesting question, that's all,' she joked. 'Of course it's where I work!'

'Oh, *of course*, I'd forgotten. That's the magazine that has offices just round the corner from me!' he said sarcastically. 'The one that causes you to walk by my front door every day, and yet you still don't call in. Why don't I see you at lunchtime?' he teased. 'Isn't my pub good enough for you?'

'Oh, everyone here eats their lunch at their desks,' she explained. 'So what do you think?'

'I think that's very boring of you all.'

'No, I mean what do you think about the ad?'

'Yeah, sure, that's a good idea.'

'OK, well, I'll put it in the November issue. Would you like it placed monthly?'

'Would you like to tell me how much that would set me back?'

Holly totted up the figures and told him.

'Hmm,' he said. 'I'll have to think about that, but I'll definitely go for the November edition.'

'OK, that's great. You'll be a millionaire after this goes to print.'

'I'd better be,' he laughed. 'By the way, there's a launch party for some new drink coming up next week. Can I put your name down?'

'Yeah, that would be great. What new drink is it?'

'Blue Rock, a new alco-pop drink that's apparently going to be huge. Tastes like shite but it's free all night.'

'Wow, you're such a good advertisement for it,' she laughed. 'When is it on?' She took out her diary and made a note of it. 'That's perfect, I can come straight after work.'

'Well, make sure you bring your bikini to work in that case. The party has a beach theme.'

'But it's almost winter, you nutter.'

'Hey, it wasn't my idea. The slogan is "Blue Rock, the hot new drink for winter".'

'Ugghh, how tacky,' she groaned. 'OK, thanks, Daniel. Have a think about what you want your ad to say and get back to me.'

'Will do. What time do you finish work?'

'Six.'

'OK, why don't you come round here at six, and I'll take you somewhere to have a bite?'

'Great.' She hung up the phone and then froze. Had she just agreed to go on a date with Daniel? She sat quietly as she went over the conversation in her head. Finally she stood up and went next door to Chris's office, a new thought occurring to her.

'You finished dancing in there?' he chuckled.

'Yeah, I just made up a routine. Came in to show you,' she joked. 'No, actually, it's just an idea.'

'Take a seat.' He nodded to the chair in front of him. 'What's the idea?'

'Well, you know Hogan's round the corner?'

Chris nodded.

'I was just on to the owner to place an ad and he was telling me that they're having a launch party for a new alco-pop drink. It has a beach theme, all the staff will be in bikinis and that kind of thing.'

'In the middle of autumn?' He raised his eyebrows.

'It's apparently the hot new drink for winter.'

He rolled his eyes. 'Tacky.'

Holly smiled. 'That's what I said. Anyway, I just thought it might be worth covering.'

'That's great, Holly. I'll get one of the lads onto it.'

Holly smiled happily. 'By the way, did you get your garden sorted yet?'

Chris frowned. 'I've had about ten people come down to look at it. They tell me it'll cost six grand.'

'Wow, six grand! That's a lot of money.'

'Well, it's a big garden, so they have a point.'

'What was the cheapest quote?'

'Five and a half grand, why?'

'Because my brother will do it for five,' she blurted out.

'Five?' His eyes nearly popped out of his head. 'Is he good?'

'Remember I told you my garden was a jungle?'

He nodded.

'Well, it's a jungle no longer. He did a great job on it, but he works alone, so it takes him longer.'

'For that price I don't care. Have you his business card?'

'Eh . . . yeah, hold on and I'll get it.' She stole some impressive-looking card stock from Alice's desk, typed up Richard's name and mobile number in fancy writing, and printed it out. She cut it into a small rectangular shape, making it look like a business card.

'That's great,' Chris said, reading it. 'I think I'll give him a call now.'

'No, no,' Holly said quickly. 'He's up to his eyeballs today. You'll get him easier tomorrow.'

Holly couldn't concentrate during the last hour of work; she kept on watching the clock, willing the time to go more slowly. Why didn't it go this fast when she was waiting to open her messages from Gerry? She opened her bag for the millionth time that day to double-check that Gerry's eighth message was still tucked safely in the inside pocket. As it was the last day of the month she had decided to bring the October envelope with her to work. She wasn't sure why, but she couldn't face leaving it sitting on the kitchen table. She was only hours away from being that much closer to Gerry again, but she was also dreading her dinner with Daniel.

At six o'clock on the dot she heard Alice switch off her computer and clatter down the wooden stairs. She prayed that Chris would dump another load on her desk just so she would have to stay late and cancel dinner. She and Daniel had been out together before, so why was she worrying now? Something was niggling at the back of her mind. There was something in his voice that worried her, and something happened to her stomach when his voice came on the phone that made her feel uneasy about meeting up with him.

She slowly shut down her computer and packed her briefcase with meticulous care, then finally headed outside. Her heart beat wildly as she spotted Daniel walking down the road to meet her. The cool autumn months had arrived, so he was back to wearing his black leather jacket with blue jeans. His black hair was messy and stubble lined his chin. He had that just-out-of-bed look. Holly's stomach lurched again and she looked away.

'I'm so sorry, Daniel,' she apologised. 'I should have come to Hogan's, but I got tied up and I couldn't call,' she lied.

'Don't worry about it, I'm sure it was important.' He smiled at her and she felt instantly guilty. This was Daniel, her friend. What on earth was wrong with her?

'So where would you like to go?' he asked.

'How about in there?' Holly said, looking at the small café on the ground floor of her office building. She wanted to go to the least intimate and most casual place possible.

Daniel scrunched up his nose. 'I'm a bit hungrier than that, if you don't mind. I haven't eaten all day.'

They walked along together and eventually he settled on an Italian restaurant. Inside it was quiet, with just a few candlelit tables occupied by couples.

'They make you sick, don't they?' Daniel laughed, following Holly's gaze to a couple on the far side of the room who were kissing across the table.

'Actually no,' Holly said quietly. 'They make me sad.'

Daniel hadn't heard her, as he was busy reading through the menu. 'What are you having?'

'A Caesar salad. I just don't have a very big appetite.'

Holly tried to control the conversation, steering it into safe territory, and they spent the evening talking about the ad, what angle to take and what information to give. She left the restaurant feeling a little panicked about why she had been so uncomfortable with a man that she was certain only wanted to be her friend.

She stepped outside for a breath of fresh air while Daniel kindly paid the bill. He was extremely generous, there was no denying that, and she was glad of his friendship. It just didn't feel quite right to be eating in a small intimate restaurant with anyone other than Gerry. She should be back at home sitting at her kitchen table waiting until midnight.

She froze as she spotted a couple walking towards her. 'Holly, is that you?' she heard the familiar voice.

'Hello, there!' She tried to sound surprised.

'How are you?' the woman asked, giving her a feeble hug. 'What are you doing standing out here in the cold?'

'Oh, you know . . . I was just having a bite to eat,' Holly smiled pointing at the restaurant.

'Well, good for you.' The man patted her on the back. 'It's good to get out and do things on your own.'

She glanced at the door. 'Yes, it's nice to do that . . .'

'There you are!' Daniel laughed, stepping outside. 'I thought you had run off on me.' He wrapped his arm loosely round her shoulders.

Holly smiled at him weakly and turned to face the couple.

'Oh, sorry, I didn't see you there.' Daniel smiled.

The couple stared back at him stonily.

'Daniel, this is Judith and Charles. They're Gerry's parents.'

Holly cursed at the driver in front of her. She was fuming. She was mad at herself for feeling that she had been caught in a bad situation last night, when really there was nothing to it. She had a headache and the traffic was driving her insane. Poor Daniel, she thought. Gerry's parents had been so rude to him. Oh, why did they have to see her the one time she was happy? They could have come round to the house any other day and found her living the life of the perfect grieving widow. Well, screw them, she thought angrily.

She decided Ciara would cheer her up, but just as she pulled up outside her parents' house, she remembered that Ciara wasn't there.

She rang the doorbell and Declan answered. 'What's wrong with you?'

'Nothing,' she said, feeling sorry for herself. 'Where's Mum?'

'In the kitchen with Dad and Richard. I'd leave them alone for a bit.'

'Oh, OK.' She felt lost. 'What are you up to?'

'I'm just watching what I filmed today. It's for a documentary on homelessness. Do you wanna watch it?'

'Yeah.' She smiled gratefully and settled herself down on the couch. A few minutes into the video and Holly was in tears, but for once they weren't for herself. Declan had done an incisive, heart-rending interview with a remarkable man who was living on the streets of Dublin. The fact that Gerry's parents had bumped into her and Daniel now seemed such a stupid thing to worry about.

'Oh, Declan, that was excellent,' she said, drying her eyes when it had finished. 'Are you happy with it?'

'It's hard to be happy about the fact that what he has to say is *so* bad that it's making a great documentary.' Declan shrugged. 'Anyway I'm off to bed, I'm knackered.' He kissed her on the top of the head as he passed, which really touched Holly. Her baby brother was growing up.

Holly glanced at the clock on the mantelpiece and noticed it was almost midnight. She reached for her bag and took out the October envelope from Gerry. She was even more intrigued by this one, as the envelope was larger than the others. She ran her fingers over the writing once again and tore the seal open. Holly slid the card out and a dried sunflower fell onto her lap, along with a small pouch of seeds. Her hands shook as she touched the delicate petals. His message read:

A sunflower for my sunflower. To brighten the dark October days you hate so much. Plant some more, and be safe in the knowledge a warm and bright summer awaits.
PS, I love you . . .
PPS, Could you please pass this card on to John?

Holly lifted the second card that had fallen onto her lap and read the words through her tears and laughter.

To John,
  Happy 32nd birthday. You're getting old, my friend, but I hope you have many, many more birthdays. Enjoy life and take care of my wife and Sharon. You're the man now!
  Lots of love, your friend Gerry

Holly read and reread every single word Gerry had written. She stood up from the couch. She felt a new bounce in her step and she couldn't wipe the grin off her face. She tapped lightly on the kitchen door.

'Come in,' Elizabeth called.

Holly stepped in and looked round at her parents and Richard sitting at the table with cups of tea in their hands.

'Oh, hello, love,' her mum said, happily getting up to give her a hug and a kiss. 'I didn't hear you come in.'

'I was just watching Declan's documentary.' Holly beamed at her family and felt like giving them all a hug.

'It's great, isn't it?' Frank stood up to hug her.

Holly joined them at the table. 'Have you found a job yet?' she asked Richard.

He shook his head sadly as if he were going to cry.

'Well, I did.'

He looked at her, disgusted that she could say such a thing. 'Well, I know *you* did.'

'No, Richard.' She grinned. 'I mean I got *you* a job.'

'You what?'

'You heard me. My boss will be calling you tomorrow.'

His face fell. 'Oh, Holly, that's very nice of you indeed, but I have no interest in advertising. My interest is in science.'

'And gardening.'

'Yes, I like gardening.' He looked confused.

'That's why my boss will be calling you. To ask you to work on his garden. I told him you'll do it for five thousand; I hope that's OK.' She smiled at him as his mouth dropped open.

He was completely speechless so Holly kept on talking. 'And here are your business cards.' She handed him a pile of cards.

Richard and her parents picked up the cards and read them in silence. Suddenly Richard started laughing, jumped out of his chair pulling Holly with him, and danced her around the kitchen while her parents looked on and cheered.

Twelve

'OK, THIS IS THE LAST ONE, I promise, girls!' Denise called as her bra was sent flying over the changing-room door.

Sharon and Holly groaned and collapsed onto their chairs again. 'You said that an hour ago,' Sharon complained, kicking off her shoes and massaging her swollen ankles.

'Yeah, but I mean it this time. I have a really good feeling about this dress,' Denise said, full of excitement.

'You said *that* an hour ago too,' Holly grumbled, resting her head back on the chair and closing her eyes.

They had been dragged to every single wedding-gown boutique in the city and Sharon and Holly were exhausted and extremely fed up. Whatever excitement they had felt for Denise and her wedding had been drained from their systems. And if Holly heard Denise's irritating squeals one more time . . .

'Oooh, I love it!' Denise shrieked.

'OK, here's the plan,' Sharon whispered to Holly. 'If she walks out of there looking like a meringue that has sat on a bicycle pump we are going to tell her she looks beautiful.'

Holly giggled. 'Oh, Sharon, we can't do that!'

'Oooh, wait till you see!' Denise shrieked again.

'On second thoughts . . .' Holly looked at Sharon miserably.

'Ta-da!' Denise stepped out of the dressing room and Holly's eyes widened. She looked at Sharon uncertainly and tried not to laugh at the look on her face.

'Do you like it?' Denise squealed, and Holly winced.

'Yes,' Sharon said unenthusiastically.

'Are you sure?'

'Yes.'

'Do you think Tom will be happy when he looks down the aisle and sees me walking towards him?'

'Yes,' Sharon repeated.

'Do you think it's worth the money?'

'Yes.'

'It'll be nicer with a tan, won't it?'

'Yes.'

'Oh, but does it make my bum look enormous?'

'Yes.'

Holly looked at Sharon, startled, and realised that she wasn't even listening to the questions any more.

Denise carried on, obviously not even listening to the answers. 'So will I get it?'

'No!' Holly interrupted before Sharon said yes again.

'No?' Denise asked.

'No,' Holly confirmed.

'Oh.' Denise turned to face Sharon. 'Do you agree with Holly?'

'Yes.'

'OK then, I trust you two,' Denise said, sadly. 'To be honest I wasn't really that keen on it myself.'

Sharon put her shoes back on. 'OK, Denise, let's go and get something to eat before I drop dead.'

The three of them trudged into Bewley's Café and managed to grab their usual spot overlooking Grafton Street.

'Oh, I hate shopping on Saturdays,' Holly moaned, watching people bump and crush one another on the busy street below.

'Gone are the days of shopping midweek, now you're no longer a lady of leisure,' Sharon teased, as she picked up her club sandwich.

'I know, and I'm *so* tired, but I feel like I've earned the tiredness this time,' Holly said happily.

'Tell us about the little episode with Gerry's parents,' Sharon said with a mouthful of food.

Holly rolled her eyes. 'They were just so rude to Daniel.'

'They can't tell you who to see and who not to see,' Sharon gave out.

'Sharon, I'm not seeing him.' Holly tried to set the record straight. 'I have no intentions of seeing anyone for at least twenty years. We were just having a business dinner.'

'Oooh, a *business* dinner!' Sharon and Denise giggled.

'Well, that's what it was, but it was also nice to have a bit of company,' Holly admitted. 'When everyone else is busy it's nice to have someone else to chat to. Especially male company.'

'Yeah, I understand,' Sharon nodded. 'It's good for you to get out and meet new people anyway.'

Denise giggled. 'Well, Holly, I'm glad you get along with him, because you're going to have to dance with him at the wedding.'

'Why?' Holly looked at Denise confused.

'Because it's tradition for the best man to dance with the maid of honour.' Her eyes sparkled.

Holly gasped. 'You want me to be your maid of honour?'

Denise nodded, full of excitement. 'Don't worry, I already asked Sharon and she doesn't mind.'

'Oh, I would love to!' Holly said. 'But, Sharon, are you sure?'

'I'm happy just being a blown-up bridesmaid. I'll need to borrow Denise's marquee to wear as a dress!'

'I hope you don't go into labour at the wedding.' Denise's eyes widened.

'Don't worry, Denise, I won't be due till the end of January. Oh, by the way, I forgot to show you the photograph of the baby!' Sharon pulled a small photograph from her bag.

'Where is it?' Denise moved the scan closer.

'There.' Sharon pointed out the area.

'Whoa! That's one big boy,' Denise exclaimed.

Sharon rolled her eyes. 'Denise, that's a leg, you fool, we still don't know the sex yet.'

'Oh,' Denise blushed. 'Well, congratulations, Sharon, it looks like you're having a little alien.'

'Oh, stop it, Denise,' Holly laughed. 'I think it's beautiful.'

'Good.' Sharon looked at Denise and Denise nodded. 'Because I wanted to ask you something. John and I would love it if you would be our baby's godmother.'

Holly gasped with shock for the second time that day, and tears filled her eyes.

'You didn't cry when I asked you to be maid of honour,' Denise huffed.

'Oh, Sharon, I would be honoured!' Holly gave her friend a big hug.

Holly pushed through the crowds in Hogan's pub and made her way upstairs to Club Diva. Her jaw dropped as she approached the door. A group of young muscular males dressed in swimwear were banging out Hawaiian drumbeats. Skinny female models in skimpy bikinis greeted all the guests by wrapping beautiful multicoloured garlands of flowers round their necks. Holly could barely recognise the club; it had been completely transformed. A water feature came into view as they entered. Aqua-blue water cascaded down from rocks.

Holly looked around for Denise and Tom and saw her friend being photographed as she held her hand up to the camera to show off her sparkly engagement ring. Holly laughed at the big celebrity couple.

The bar staff were also dressed in bikinis and swimwear and they lined the entrance with trays of blue drinks in their hands. Holly lifted a drink from a tray and took a sip, trying not to make a face from its overly sweet taste. The floors were scattered with sand; each table was sheltered by a huge bamboo umbrella; the bar stools were all big kettle drums; and there was a wonderful smell of barbecue in the air. Holly darted to the nearest table, helped herself to a kebab and found herself facing Daniel.

'Em, hello. The place looks great,' she said.

'Yeah, it worked well.' He looked pleased. Daniel wore faded blue jeans and a blue Hawaiian shirt with big pink and yellow flowers. He still hadn't shaved and Holly wondered how painful it would be to kiss him with that sharp stubble . . . Why was she even wondering about it?

'Daniel,' she said, 'once again I'm really sorry about the other night.'

'Oh, there's no need to apologise again, Holly. I just felt uncomfortable for you.' He smiled and placed his hands on her shoulders as though he were going to say something more, but someone called him over to the bar.

Holly hoped that Daniel didn't think there was more to the dinner than there really had been. He had called her almost every day since that episode, and she realised she looked forward to his calls. There was that niggling thing at the back of her mind again. She wandered over to Denise and joined her on the sunbed, where she was sipping on the blue concoction.

'So what do you think of the hot new drink for winter?' Holly indicated the bottle.

Denise rolled her eyes. 'Tacky. I've only had a few and my head is spinning already.'

Denise banged the till closed with her hip and handed over the receipt. 'Thanks.' Her smile faded as soon as the customer turned away from the counter. She sighed loudly, staring at the long queue in front of the cash register, grumpily grabbed the item of clothing from the next customer, de-tagged it, scanned it and wrapped it.

'Excuse me, are you Denise Hennessey?' she heard a deep voice ask, and she looked up to see where the sexy voice had come from. She frowned as she saw a police officer before her and tried to think if she had done anything illegal in the past few days. When she was satisfied she was crime-free she smiled. 'Yes, I am.'

'I'm Officer Ryan and I was wondering if you would accompany me to the station, please.'

It was more of a statement than a question, and Denise's mouth dropped open in shock. He was no longer the sexy officer. He was the lock-you-up-for-ever-in-a-cell-type officer. She gulped. 'What for?'

'Everything will be explained to you down at the station.' He walked round the counter and Denise looked at the long line of customers helplessly. Everybody just stared back at her.

'Check his ID, love,' one of the customers shouted.

Her voice shook as she demanded to see his ID, which was a completely useless operation, as she had never seen a police ID before nor did she know what a real one would look like. Her hand trembled as she studied it closely, but she didn't read a thing. She was too self-conscious of the customers and staff that had gathered, who must all be thinking the same thing: she was a criminal.

'I refuse to go until you tell me what this is about.'

'Ms Hennessey, if you just work with me here, then there will be no need to use these.' He took out a pair of handcuffs from his trouser pocket. 'There's no need to make a scene.'

'But I didn't do anything!' she protested, starting to panic.

'Well, we can discuss that down at the station, can't we?' He began to get irate.

Denise crossed her arms across her chest. 'I said I will *not* go with you until you tell me what this is about.'

'OK then,' he shrugged. 'If you insist.' He opened his mouth to speak and she yelled as she felt the cold silver handcuffs being slapped round her wrists. She was in so much shock she couldn't speak as he led her out of the shop.

'Good luck, love,' the customer shouted again.

Images of sharing a cell with a psycho murderer jumped into Denise's mind. Maybe she would find a little bird with a broken wing and nurse it and teach it to fly to pass the years inside . . .

Her face reddened as they stepped out into Grafton Street, and the crowds immediately scattered. Denise kept her eyes down to the ground, hoping nobody she knew would spot her. Her heart beat wildly and she briefly thought of escape, but she was already being led towards a blue minibus with blacked-out windows. Denise sat in the front row of seats behind the driver and, although she could sense people behind her, she sat rigidly in her seat, too terrified to turn round.

'Where are we going?' she asked as they drove past the police station. The female police officer driving the bus and Officer Ryan ignored her.

'Hey! I thought you were taking me to the station!'

No answer.

'*I haven't done anything wrong!*'

Still no answer.

'Dammit! I'm innocent, I tell you!'

Denise started kicking the seat to get their attention. Her blood started to boil when the female officer pushed a cassette in the player. Denise's eyes widened at the choice of song.

Officer Ryan stood up, a big grin on his face. 'Denise, you have been very naughty.' He stood up and made his way in front of her. She gulped as he started to gyrate his hips to the song 'Hot Stuff'.

She was about to give him a great big kick between his legs when she heard whooping and laughing. She twisted herself round and spotted her sisters, Holly, Sharon and about five other friends. She finally figured out what was really happening when her sisters placed a veil on her head screaming, 'Happy hen party!'

'Oh, you bitches!' Denise spat at them until she had used every curse word invented, and made up a few of her own.

The girls continued to hold their stomachs, doubled up with laughter.

'Oh, you are so lucky I didn't kick you in the balls!' Denise screamed at the gyrating policeman.

'Denise, this is Ken,' her sister Fiona giggled, 'and he's your stripper for the day.'

Denise narrowed her eyes. 'I almost had a heart attack, I hope you know! What will my customers think? And my staff! Oh my God, my staff think I'm a criminal.'

Sharon giggled. 'They were all just playing along.'

'When I go back to work I'm going to fire the lot of them.'

'Don't worry,' her sister said. 'We told your staff to inform the customers after you left the shop.'

Denise rolled her eyes. 'Well, knowing *them* they deliberately won't, and I will be *so* fired.'

'Denise! Stop *worrying*!' Fiona said. 'Your boss thought it was *funny*, now relax and enjoy the weekend.'

'Weekend? Where are we going for the weekend?' Denise looked round at her friends, startled.

'We're going to Galway, and that's all you need to know,' Sharon said.

The room was still spinning. Having closed her eyes, Holly was now unable to sleep. It was five o'clock in the morning, which meant that she had been drinking for almost twelve hours. Her stomach became queasy and she sat up on the bed and tried to keep her eyes open so she could avoid the feeling of seasickness.

She turned to face Denise on the bed so that they could talk, but the sound of her friend's snores ended all thought of communication between them. Holly sighed and felt her way across the bedcovers in the dark for the remote control. She watched as the television demonstrated a new knife to slice oranges without spraying yourself in the face with the juice. Eventually she rushed to the toilet and hung her head over the toilet seat, prepared for whatever might come. She wished she hadn't drunk so much, but with all the talk of husbands and happiness she had dreaded to think what the next two days would be like. Denise's friends were twice as bad as Denise. They were loud and hyper and acted exactly the way girls should on a hen weekend, but Holly just didn't have the energy to keep up with them.

It felt like only yesterday that Holly had had her own hen party, but in fact it was more than seven years ago. Back then she had been so excited and the future had looked so bright. She was to marry the man of her dreams and they would live the rest of their lives together. Now, life had become a nightmare for her.

Yes, she had finally managed to drag herself out of bed every morning. Yes, she had succeeded in finding a new job. But these were just formalities, something else to check off on the 'things that normal people do' list. It was as if her body had become one great jigsaw, just like the green fields with their pretty grey stone walls connecting the whole of Ireland. She had started working on the corners and the edges of her jigsaw because they were the easy bits, and now she needed to do all the bits in between, the hard parts. Nothing she had done so far had managed to fill that hole in her heart.

Holly pretended to have a coughing fit just so the girls would wake up. She needed to talk, she needed to cry, she needed to vent all her frustrations and disappointments. But what more advice could they give her? She repeated the same old worries over and over. Sometimes her friends would succeed in getting through to her and she would feel positive and confident, only to find herself thrown back into despair.

Tired of staring at the four walls, she threw on a track suit and made her way downstairs to the hotel bar.

Charlie groaned with frustration as the table down the back began to roar with laughter again. He wiped down the bar counter and glanced at his watch. Five thirty and he was still here working. He had thought he was so lucky when the girls from the hen party had gone to bed, earlier than expected, and he was about to go home when this overbearing crowd arrived from a nightclub in Galway city. And they were still here. They weren't even residents of the Galway Inn, but the group included the daughter of the owner, who had brought them.

Her and her arrogant boyfriend, and he couldn't stand them.

'Don't tell me you're back for more!' he laughed as one of the women from the hen party walked in. She bumped into the wall as she tried to make her way to the high stool.

'I just came down for a glass of water,' she hiccupped.

'There you go.' Charlie placed a glass of water on a beer mat.

She squinted at his name tag. 'Thanks. Charlie?'

'Did you girls have fun tonight?'

Holly sighed. 'I suppose.'

'Are you OK?' Charlie watched her. He had a horrible feeling she was going to cry, but he was used to it.

'I miss my husband,' she whispered. Her shoulders trembled.

'How long are you here for?' he asked.

'The weekend,' she told him.

'Have you never gone the weekend without him?'

'Only once. And that was at my own hen party seven years ago.' A tear spilled down the woman's face.

Charlie shook his head. 'Seven years lucky, isn't that what they say? Don't worry, your husband's probably miserable without you.'

'Oh God, I hope not.' Holly's eyes widened.

'That's the spirit.' Charlie smiled, then jumped as he saw his boss's daughter coming towards the bar with one of those looks on her face.

'Hey, Charlie,' she yelled. 'Maybe if you stopped chatting and did a bit of work, me and my friends wouldn't be so thirsty.'

Holly's mouth dropped open. That woman had a nerve. And her perfume was so strong it made Holly start to cough.

'I'm sorry, do you have a problem?' The woman looked her up and down.

'Yes, actually,' Holly slurred. 'Your perfume is disgusting and it's making me want to throw up.'

Charlie dropped to his knees behind the counter, pretending to look for a lemon to slice, and tried to block out the sounds of the two women snapping at each other.

'What's the delay here?' a deep voice enquired. Charlie shot to his feet at the sound of her boyfriend's voice. He was even worse. 'Sit down, honey, and I'll bring the drinks over,' he said.

'Fine, at least someone is polite around here.' She stormed back to her table. Holly watched her hips go boom-boom-boom as they went from side to side. She must be a model or something, she decided. That would explain the tantrums.

'So how are you?' the man beside Holly asked.

'I'm fine,' Holly replied, staring straight ahead.

'I'm Stevie,' he said, holding out his hand to her.

'I'm Holly,' she mumbled and took his hand lightly.

'Holly, that's a lovely name.' He held her hand for much too long and Holly was forced to look up into his eyes.

'Eh . . . thanks,' she said, and her face flushed.

'Can I buy you a drink, Holly?' Stevie asked smoothly.

'No, thanks, I have one here.' She sipped on her water again.

'OK, well, I'm just going to bring these drinks down and I'll be back to buy the lovely Holly a drink.' He walked away.

'Who the hell is that idiot?' Holly asked, looking bewildered, and Charlie laughed.

Charlie lowered his voice. 'That's Stevie, boyfriend of that blonde bitch who was here a minute ago.'

Holly stared at the beautiful woman thinking nasty thoughts. 'Good night, Charlie.'

'You off to bed?'

'It's about time. I hope you get home soon,' she smiled.

'I wouldn't bet on it,' he replied, and watched her leave the bar. Stevie followed after her and Charlie made his way closer to the door just to make sure she was OK. The blonde, noticing her boyfriend's sudden departure, left her table at the same time. They both stared down the corridor in the direction Holly and Stevie had headed.

The blonde gasped and her hand flew to her mouth.

'Hey!' Charlie called out angrily as he witnessed a distressed Holly pushing a drunken Stevie away from her.

Holly angrily wiped her mouth, disgusted with his attempts to kiss her. She backed away from him. 'I think you've got the wrong idea here, Stevie. Go back to the bar to your girlfriend.'

Stevie wobbled on his feet and slowly turned to face his girlfriend.

'Stevie!' she shrieked. 'How could you?' Tears streaming down her face, she ran from the hotel.

The next day Holly and Sharon went for a long walk on the beach just outside Galway city. Although it was October, the air had warmth in it and Holly didn't need her coat. She stood and listened to the water gently lapping.

'Are you OK?' Sharon wrapped her arm round Holly's shoulders.

Holly sighed. 'Every time someone asks me that question, Sharon, I say, "I'm fine, thank you," but to be honest, I'm not. Do people *really* want to know how you feel?' Holly smiled. 'The next time I'm going to say, "Well, actually, I'm not very well at all, thank you. I'm feeling a bit depressed and lonely." Then say how it pisses me off when everyone says time is a healer when at the same time they also say absence makes the heart grow fonder, which really confuses me, because that means that the longer he's gone the more I want him. Nothing is healing at all and every morning I wake up in my empty bed it feels like salt is being rubbed into those unhealing wounds. And then I'll say how much I miss my husband and how I feel like I'm just waiting for my world to end so that I can join him.' Holly took a deep breath. 'What do you think?'

'Oooh!' Sharon jumped and her arm flew away from Holly's shoulders.

'Oooh? I say all that and all you can say is "Oooh"?'

Sharon placed her hand over her bump and laughed. 'No, you silly, the baby kicked! Feel it!'

Holly placed her hand over Sharon's swollen belly and felt the tiny little kick. 'Oh, Sharon, if only every minute of my life were filled with perfect little moments like this I would never moan again.'

'I think this little boy is going to be a footballer like his daddy!' Sharon laughed.

'Boy?' Holly gasped. 'You're having a boy?'

Sharon nodded happily. 'Holly, meet baby Gerry. Gerry, meet your godmother Holly.'

Holly smiled as she flicked through the November magazine's pages. It would be out in the shops tomorrow, the first of November, and she felt so excited. Her first magazine would be on the shelves and she could also open Gerry's November letter. Tomorrow would be a good day.

Although she had only sold the ad space, she felt great pride in being a member of a team that managed to produce something so professional-looking. And she felt that she had really proved herself. She had taken her job by the reins and guided it through to success.

Time to get working on the December edition. But before she started work, first she had to call Denise.

'Hello? Ridiculously expensive clothes shop. Pissed-off manager speaking, how can I help you?'

'Denise! You can't answer the phone like that!'

Denise giggled. 'Oh, don't worry, I have caller ID so I knew it was you.'

'Hmm.' Holly was suspicious; she didn't think Denise had caller ID on her work phone. 'I got a message you called.'

'Oh, yeah, I was just ringing you to confirm that you are coming to the Christmas Ball. Tom is going to buy a table this year. It's on the 30th of November.'

'Oh, the 30th . . .' Holly paused and pretended to flick through some pages on her desk very loudly. 'No, Denise, I can't. Sorry. I have a deadline. I'll be far too busy . . .' Well, she did have a deadline, but the magazine would be out in the shops on the 1st of December. She didn't really need to be in work on the 30th at all.

'Well, that makes a change,' Denise muttered under her breath.

'What did you say?' Holly asked, getting slightly angry.

'Nothing,' Denise said shortly.

'I heard you. You said "that makes a change", didn't you? Well, it just so happens that I take my work seriously, Denise, and I have no plans to lose my job because of a stupid ball. And you might not understand this, Denise, but funnily enough I would find it *a bit difficult*, to say the least, to go to a place that Gerry and I had been going to together for the past ten years.' She slammed the phone down and burst into tears.

Her weeping eventually died down into little sobs as she realised that everyone must have heard everything she'd said. She felt so embarrassed she was afraid to go to the toilets for a tissue. She wiped her eyes on the end of her shirt, then sat up to attention as she heard a light rapping sound on her door.

'Come in.' Her voice shook.

Chris entered her office with two cups of tea in his hands.

'Tea?' he offered, raising his eyebrows at her. She smiled weakly, remembering the joke they had shared on the day of her interview. He placed the mug down in front of her and relaxed in the chair opposite.

'Having a bad day?' he asked as gently as his gruff voice allowed.

She nodded as tears rolled down her face. 'I'm sorry, Chris.' She swallowed hard as she tried to compose herself. 'This won't affect my work,' she said shakily.

He waved his hand dismissively. 'Holly, I'm not worried about that. You're a great worker.'

She smiled, grateful for the compliment. At least she was doing something right.

'Would you like to go home early?'

'No, thanks. Work will keep my mind off things.'

He shook his head sadly. 'That's not the way to go about it, Holly. I should know. I've buried myself inside these walls and it doesn't help things. Not in the long run, anyway.' He handed her a tissue. 'You need to love more than just your job. I know I'm not the greatest example, but I'm learning too.' He placed his hand on the desk and started to brush away imaginary crumbs while he thought about what to say next. 'I heard you don't want to go to this ball.'

Holly cringed at the fact he had heard her phone conversation.

Chris continued. 'There were a million places I refused to go to when Maureen died. We used to go for walks in the Botanic Gardens every Sunday, and I just couldn't go there any more after I lost her. There were a million little memories contained in every flower and tree that grew in there. The bench we used to sit on, her favourite rose garden, just everything about it reminded me of her.'

'Did you go back?' Holly asked, sipping the hot tea.

'A few months ago,' he said sadly. 'It was a difficult thing to do, but I did it and now I go every Sunday again. You have to confront things, Holly, and think of things positively.' He leaned forwards in his chair and stared directly into her eyes. 'Some people go through life searching and never find their soul mates. They *never* do. You and I did, we just happened to have them for a shorter period of time. It's sad, but it's life. So you go to this ball, Holly, and you embrace the fact that you had someone whom you loved and who loved you back.'

Tears trickled down Holly's face as she realised he was right. She needed to remember Gerry and be happy about the love they shared. She thought of the line he had written in his last letter: *Remember our wonderful memories, but please don't be afraid to make some more.*

She wanted to hang on to every single shred of memory of the two of them together. It was scaring her that she was forgetting his face. When she dreamed about him now he was always somebody she made up in her mind. She still rang his mobile phone, paying the mobile company every month just to hear his voice on his answering machine. His smell had faded from the house; his clothes were long gone. He was fading from her mind, but she couldn't let go because he was all she had.

'I'm so sorry, Denise,' Holly apologised to her friend. They were sitting in the staff room at Denise's workplace. 'I didn't mean to lose my temper on the phone. Just because I'm feeling extra-sensitive these days, it doesn't give me the right to take it out on you.'

'No, I've been so excited by this wedding that I didn't stop to think about how you might be feeling.' Her eyes rested on her friend, whose face looked so pale against her dark jacket.

'But you were right to be excited,' Holly insisted.

'And you're right to be upset,' Denise said firmly. 'I didn't think. I just didn't think.' She held her hands to her cheeks as she shook her head. 'Don't go to the ball if you don't feel comfortable, Holly. We'll all understand.' She reached out to hold her friend's hands.

Holly felt confused. Chris had succeeded in convincing her to go to the ball, but now one of her best friends was saying it was OK not to go. She got up and hugged Denise goodbye, promising to call her later to give her a decision.

Just before reaching the office, Holly poked her head into Hogan's. She was feeling much more at ease with Daniel. Since that evening in the restaurant, where she had felt so uncomfortable, she had realised that she was being ridiculous. She understood now why she had felt that way. Before, the only close friendship she'd had with a man was with Gerry, and that was a romantic relationship. The idea of becoming so close to Daniel seemed strange and unusual. Holly had since convinced herself that there didn't need to be a romantic link for her to share a friendship with an unattached man. Even if he was good-looking.

And the ease she now felt had become a feeling of companionship. They could talk for hours, discussing her feelings, her life, his feelings, his life, and she knew that they had a common enemy: loneliness. She knew that he was suffering from a different kind of grief but they were helping each other through the difficult days.

'Well?' he said, walking round from behind the bar. 'Will Cinderella go to the ball?'

Holly smiled and scrunched up her nose, about to tell him that she wouldn't be going, when she stopped herself. 'Are you going?'

He smiled and scrunched up his nose and she laughed. 'Well, it's going to be another case of Couples R Us,' he said. He pulled out a high stool for her at the bar and she sat down.

Holly giggled. 'We could just be terribly rude and ignore them.'

'Then what would be the point of going?' Daniel sat beside her and rested his leather boot on the footrest of her stool. 'You don't expect me to talk to you all night! We've talked the ears off each other!'

'Fine then!' Holly pretended to be insulted. 'I was planning on ignoring you anyway.'

'Phew!' Daniel wiped his brow. 'I'm definitely going then.'

Holly became serious. 'I think I really need to be there.'

Daniel stopped laughing. 'Well, then, we shall go.'

Holly smiled at him. 'I think it would be good for you too, Daniel.'

His foot dropped from the footrest and he turned his head away to survey the lounge. 'Holly, I'm fine,' he said unconvincingly.

Holly hopped off her stool and kissed him roughly on the forehead. 'Daniel Connelly, stop trying to be all macho and strong. It doesn't wash with me.'

They hugged each other goodbye and Holly marched back to her office, determined not to change her mind again.

Thirteen

'OH, HOLLY, you look fabulous!' Sharon said excitedly.

'I look like crap,' Holly grumbled.

'Oh, stop saying that,' Sharon said angrily. 'I look like a blimp and do you hear me complaining? Accept the fact that you're a babe!' She smiled at her in the mirror. 'You'll be fine.'

'I just want to stay home tonight, Sharon. I have to open Gerry's last message.' Holly couldn't believe the time had come to open the last one. She wanted to stay in and savour the last special moment.

'I know, but that can wait a few hours, can't it?'

Holly was just about to say no when John shouted up the stairs. 'Come on, girls! The taxi's waiting! We have to collect Tom and Denise!'

Before Holly followed Sharon downstairs she slid open the drawer of her dressing table and took out the November letter from Gerry that she had opened weeks ago. She needed his words of encouragement to help her out now. She slid the card from the envelope and read:

Cinderella must go to the ball this month. And she will look glamorous and beautiful and have the time of her life just like always . . . But no white dresses this year . . .

PS, I love you . . .

Holly took a deep breath and followed Sharon downstairs.

'Wow,' Daniel said, 'you look fabulous, Holly.'

'I look like crap,' Holly grumbled, and Sharon shot her a look. 'But thanks,' she quickly added. Denise had helped her choose a simple black halter-neck dress.

They all piled into the seven-seater taxi, and after picking up Tom and Denise, they made it to the hotel in record time.

They stepped up to the table just inside the function room. The woman sitting behind it smiled. 'Hello, Sharon; hello, John; hi, Denise . . . Oh, gosh! Hello, Holly. It's so good of you to come considering . . .' She flicked through the guest list to tick off their names.

'Let's go to the bar,' Denise said, linking Holly's arm.

As they walked across the room to the bar, a woman Holly hadn't spoken to for years approached her. 'Holly, I was sorry to hear about Gerry. He was a lovely man.'

'Thank you.' Holly smiled and was dragged away again by Denise. They finally reached the bar.

'Hi there, Holly,' a familiar voice behind her said.

'Oh, hello, Patrick,' she said, turning to face the man who sponsored the charity. He was large and overweight with a bright red face, probably due to the stress of running one of Ireland's most successful businesses.

'You're looking as lovely as always.' He gave her a kiss on the cheek. 'Can I get you a drink?'

'Oh, no, thanks,' she smiled.

'Ah, let me.' He held his hand up to attract the barman's attention. 'What'll you have?'

Holly gave in. 'A white wine then, please, if you insist.'

'I might as well get a drink for that miserable husband of yours,' he laughed, searching the room for Gerry. 'What's he having?'

'Oh, he's not here,' Holly said, feeling uncomfortable.

'Ah, why not? What's he up to?' Patrick asked loudly.

'Em, he passed away early in the year, Patrick,' Holly said gently, hoping not to embarrass him.

'Oh,' Patrick reddened even more and stared down at the bar. 'I'm very sorry to hear that.' He looked away.

'Thank you,' Holly said, counting the seconds in her head till he left the conversation. He left after three seconds, saying he had to take his wife her drink. Denise had made her way back to the group with their drinks, so Holly picked up her glass of wine and headed over.

'Hi, Holly.'

She turned to see who had called her name.

'Oh, hello, Jennifer.' She was faced with another woman she knew only from attending the ball. She was dressed in an over-the-top ball gown and dripping in expensive jewellery.

'How are you? You look fab.' She sipped her champagne and looked Holly up and down. 'Gerry not with you tonight?'

'No, he passed away in February,' she said.

'Oh, gosh, I'm so sorry to hear that. I had no idea. He was so *young*.' She placed a hand on Holly's arm. 'You must feel miserable. How on earth did you come here tonight? With all these couples around?'

'Yes, it is hard, but I'm dealing with it. Trying to be positive, you know? You just have to learn to move on.' Holly smiled. 'Anyway, speaking of moving on, I'd better go and join my friends,' she said, politely. She made her way over to the table and took her seat.

'Are you OK?' Daniel asked quietly from beside her.

'Yes, I'm fine, thank you,' she replied, taking a sip of wine. She glanced over at Jennifer, who was in a huddle with her female friends talking and staring over at Holly and Daniel.

'You don't have to give me that answer, Holly. It's me,' he laughed.

Holly groaned. 'I feel like I'm back at Gerry's funeral again. Having to pretend to be all strong and superwoman-like even though all some of them want is for me to be devastated because it's so *awful*.' She mimicked Jennifer and rolled her eyes.

He nodded. 'When Laura and I broke up, for months everywhere I went I was telling people.'

'Any word on Laura?' Holly asked.

Daniel's eyes lit up. 'Yes, actually. A friend who works as a barman in Laura's dad's hotel told me her boyfriend tried to come on to some other woman and Laura caught him, so they split up.' He laughed evilly.

Holly froze. 'Daniel, what hotel does her father own?'

'Oh, the Galway Inn. It's brilliant, isn't it? I can tell you, if I ever met the woman who split them up I would buy her the most expensive bottle of champagne I could find.'

Holly smiled weakly. 'Would you now . . .?' He'd better start saving his money then. Holly stared at his face curiously. She would have bet all her money against those two ever being together; Laura didn't seem his type, whatever his 'type' was. 'Em, Daniel, I was just wondering . . . Laura seems to sound like a bit of a bitch, to be honest.' She bit her lip and studied his face to see if she had insulted him. 'Well, my question is really, whatever did you see in her? You're so different, well, at least you *sound* like you're so different.'

His lips broke into a sad smile. 'Laura isn't really a bitch, Holly. Well, for leaving me for my best friend she is . . . but when we were together, never. Dramatic, yes.' He smiled. 'You see, I loved the drama of our relationship. I found it exciting; she *enthralled* me.' His face became animated. 'I loved waking up in the morning and wondering what kind of mood she would be in that day, I loved the passion of our fights and I loved how we would make love after them. She would make a song and dance about most things, but I suppose that's what I found attractive about her. Our temperaments contrasted, but we made a good team . . .' He looked into the face of his new friend and saw her concern. 'She didn't treat me badly, Holly, she was just . . .'

'Dramatic,' Holly finished for him. He nodded.

Holly watched his face as he got lost in another memory.

'You miss her,' she said gently, putting her hand on his arm.

Daniel snapped out of his daydream and stared deeply into Holly's eyes. A shiver went down her spine. 'Wrong again, Holly Kennedy.' He nodded his head and frowned, as though she had said the most bizarre thing ever. 'Completely and *utterly* wrong.'

After dinner and a few bottles of wine, Daniel took Holly by the hand and led her to the dance floor. As soon as they reached it the song ended and Eric Clapton's 'Wonderful Tonight' began. The floor began to empty out and Holly was left facing Daniel. She gulped. She hadn't planned on this. She had only ever danced with Gerry to this song.

Daniel placed one hand lightly on her waist and gently took her hand and they began to circle round. Holly was stiff. Dancing with another man felt wrong. She shuddered. Daniel must have thought she was cold because he pulled her closer as if to keep her warm. She was led round the floor in a trance until the song ended and she made the excuse of having to go to the toilet. She locked herself in a cubicle and leaned against the door, taking deep breaths. She had been doing so well. Even with everyone asking her about Gerry she had remained calm. But the dance had shaken her. Perhaps it was time to go home, while the going was good.

Holly made her way back to the table and started to say goodbye to everyone. Daniel stood up to go with her. 'You're not leaving me here on my own,' he laughed. 'We can share a cab.'

Holly was slightly irritated when Daniel hopped out of the taxi and followed her to her house, as she was looking forward to opening the envelope from Gerry. It was a quarter to twelve, which gave her fifteen minutes. She called another taxi to arrive at her house in half an hour, just to let him know he couldn't stay too long.

'Ah, so this is the famous envelope,' Daniel said, picking it up from the kitchen table.

Holly's eyes widened; she felt protective of that envelope, and she wasn't happy with him touching it, removing Gerry's trace from it.

'December,' he said, reading the outside and running his fingers along the lettering. Eventually he placed it back on the table and Holly breathed a sigh of relief and continued to fill the kettle.

'How many more envelopes are left?' Daniel asked, taking his overcoat off and walking over to join her at the counter.

'That's the last one.' Holly's voice was husky.

'So what are you going to do after that?'

'What do you mean?' she asked, feeling confused.

'Well, as far as I can see, that list is like the Ten Commandments. What the list says goes, as far as your life is concerned. So what will you do when there aren't any more?' His blue eyes twinkled.

'I'll just live my life,' she replied, turning her back and flicking the switch on the kettle.

'Will you be able to do that?' He walked closer to her. 'You'll have to make your own decisions then,' he said softly.

Holly rubbed her face tiredly. 'Daniel, what's this about?'

'I'm asking you this because I'm going to say something to you now, and you are going to have to make your own decision.' He looked her straight in the eye and her heart beat wildly. 'There will be no list, you'll have to follow your own heart.'

Holly backed away a little. A feeling of dread pulled at her heart. 'Daniel, I don't think that this is the right time to talk about—'

'This is a perfect time,' he said. 'You already know what I'm going to say to you, Holly, and I *know* you already know how I feel about you.'

Holly's mouth dropped open and she glanced at the clock.

It was midnight.

Gerry touched Holly's nose and smiled to himself as she wrinkled up her nose in her sleep. He loved watching her sleep; she looked like a princess, so beautiful and peaceful.

He tickled her nose again and smiled as her eyes slowly opened. 'Good morning, sleepyhead.'

'Good morning, beautiful.' She cuddled closer to him and rested her head on his chest. 'How are you feeling today?'

'Like I could run the London marathon,' he joked.

'Now that's what I call a quick recovery.' She lifted her head and kissed him on the lips. 'What do you want for breakfast?'

'You,' he said, biting her nose.

'Not on the menu today unfortunately. How about a fry?'

'No,' he frowned. 'That's too heavy for me,' and his heart melted as he saw Holly's face fall. He tried to perk himself up. 'But I would love a big, huge bowl of vanilla ice cream!'

'Ice cream!' she laughed. 'For breakfast?'

'Yes,' he grinned, 'I always wanted that for breakfast when I was a kid but my darling mother wouldn't allow me to have it. Now I don't care any more.' He smiled bravely.

'Then ice cream you shall have,' Holly said happily, hopping out of bed. 'OK, I'll be back in a minute.' He heard her racing downstairs and clattering around in the kitchen.

Lately he had noticed her racing around every time she left his side. It was as if she were afraid to leave him for too long on his own, and he knew what that meant. Bad news for him. He had finished his radiation therapy, which they had prayed would target the residual tumour. It had failed, and now all he could do was lie around all day, as he felt too weak to get up most of the time. It just seemed so pointless to him because it wasn't even as if he were waiting to recover. His heart beat wildly at the thought. He was afraid; afraid of where he was going, afraid of what was happening to him and afraid for Holly. She was so strong; she was his rock and he couldn't imagine his life without her, but he needn't worry about that scenario, because it was she who would be without him. He felt angry, sad, jealous and scared for her. He wanted to stay with her and carry out every wish and promise they had ever made to each other, but he knew he was fighting a losing battle. After two operations the tumour had returned, and it was growing rapidly inside him.

He and Holly had become even closer over the past few months, which was something he knew was a bad idea, for Holly's sake, but he couldn't bear to distance himself from her. He was enjoying the chats till the early hours of the morning, and giggling just like when they were teenagers. But that was on their good days.

They had their bad days, too.

He wouldn't think about that now. And his new little project was keeping him busy. As he mapped out his plan to remain with Holly even when he was gone, he was also fulfilling a promise.

He heard Holly thudding up the stairs; his plan was working.

'Babe, there's no more ice cream left,' she said sadly. 'Is there anything else you would enjoy?'

'Nope,' he shook his head. 'Just the ice cream, please.'

'Oh, but I have to go to the shop to get it,' she complained.

'Don't worry, hon, I'll be fine for a few minutes.' He lifted his mobile off the bedside table and placed it on his chest.

'OK.' Holly bit her lip. 'I'll only be down the road.'

She threw on a track suit, gave him a long kiss and raced downstairs.

As soon as Gerry knew it was safe, he pulled back the covers. He sat on the edge of the mattress waiting for the dizziness to pass, then he made his way to the wardrobe. He took out an old shoe box from the top shelf that contained nine full envelopes. He took out the tenth, empty envelope and wrote 'December' on the front. Today was the 1st of December, and he moved forward one year, knowing he wouldn't be around. He imagined Holly to be a karaoke genius, relaxed from her holiday in Spain, and hopefully happy in a new job she loved.

He imagined her on this very day in one year's time and he thought hard about what to write. Tears filled his eyes as he placed the full stop beside the sentence; he kissed the page, sealed it in the envelope and hid it back in the shoe box.

He wiped the tears from his eyes and slowly made his way back to his bed, where the phone was ringing.

'Hello?' he said, trying to control his voice, and he smiled when he heard the sweetest voice on the other end. 'I love you too, Holly . . .'

'No, Daniel, this isn't right,' Holly said, upset, and pulled her hand away from his grip.

'But why isn't it right?' he pleaded.

'It's too soon,' she said, feeling so confused.

'Too soon because that's what people have been telling you, or because that's what your heart's telling you?'

'Oh, Daniel, I don't know!' she said, pacing the kitchen floor. '*Please* stop asking me so many questions!'

Her heart beat wildly and her head was spinning. It all felt so wrong. 'I can't, Daniel. I'm married! I love Gerry!'

'Gerry?' he asked, his eyes widening as he went over to the table and grabbed the envelope. 'This is Gerry! This is what I'm competing with! It's a *list*, Holly. A list you have allowed to run your life. Now you have to think for yourself. Gerry's gone,' he said gently, walking back over to her. 'Gerry's gone and I'm here. I'm not saying I could ever take his place, but at least give us a chance.'

She took the envelope from his hand and hugged it close. 'Gerry's not gone,' she sobbed. 'He's here, every time I open these.'

There was a silence as Daniel watched her crying. She looked so lost and helpless, he just wanted to hold her. 'It's a piece of paper,' he said softly, stepping closer to her again.

'Gerry is *not* a piece of paper,' she said angrily through her tears. 'He was a living, breathing human being I loved. Gerry is a million billion happy memories.'

'So what am I?' Daniel asked.

'You'—she took a deep breath—'are a kind, and incredibly thoughtful friend who I respect and appreciate—'

'How do you feel about me?' His voice shook slightly.

She stared at the ground. 'I feel strongly about you, Daniel, but I need time.' She paused. 'Lots of time.'

'Then I will wait.' He smiled sadly and wrapped his strong arms round her weak body.

The doorbell rang. 'That's your taxi.' Holly's voice shook.

'I'll call you tomorrow.' He kissed her on the top of the head and made his way to the front door. Holly stood in the middle of the kitchen, going over and over the scene that had just occurred.

Still in shock, she eventually made her way slowly upstairs. She slipped out of her dress and wrapped herself in Gerry's dressing gown. She climbed into bed like a child and flicked on the bedside lamp. She stared at the envelope, thinking about what Daniel had said.

She took the phone off the hook and switched the power off her mobile. She needed to savour this special and final moment, to say goodbye to Gerry's contact with her.

She slowly tore open the envelope, trying not to rip the paper.

Don't be afraid to fall in love again. Open your heart and follow where it leads you . . . and remember, shoot for the moon . . .
PS, I will always love you . . .

'Oh, Gerry,' she sobbed, and her shoulders shook as her body heaved from the pain of her tears.

She got very little sleep that night and the times she did nod off, her dreams were obscure images of Daniel's and Gerry's faces and bodies mingled together. She awoke in a sweat at 6 a.m. and decided to get up and go for a walk to clear her jumbled thoughts. Her heart felt heavy as she walked. She had bundled herself up well to protect herself from the stinging cold, yet her head felt hot. Hot from the tears, from her brain working overtime.

How on earth had she found herself in this situation? Just as soon as she was getting round to picking up the pieces of her shattered life, she dropped them all again. She wasn't looking to become entangled in some ridiculous love triangle. The third person wasn't even around. And, anyway, if she were in love with Daniel, wouldn't she be the first person to realise it? If she didn't love him, then she should come right out and say it . . . but she was thinking about it . . .

And why was Gerry urging her to find a new love? What had he been *thinking* when he wrote that message? Had he already let go of her before he died? Had it been *so* easy for him to resign himself to the fact that she would meet someone else?

After hours of tormenting herself, she headed back to her house. 'OK, Gerry,' she announced as she stepped inside. 'I've been for a walk and I've thought deeply about what you said. And I've come to the conclusion that you had lost your mind when you wrote that message.'

She had three weeks left at work until she could take her Christmas holidays, which meant she would have to avoid Daniel for fifteen working days. That seemed possible. She hoped that by the time of Denise's wedding she would have made a decision. But first she had to get through her first Christmas alone.

'OK, where do you want me to put it?' Richard panted, dragging the Christmas tree into her living room. A trail of pine needles led all the way out of the living-room door, down the hall and out to her car. Holly sighed, she would have to vacuum the house again. They smelt so fresh, but damn, were they messy.

'Holly!' Richard repeated, and she jumped from her thoughts to face him.

'You look like a talking tree, Richard.' She giggled. All she could see were his brown shoes sticking out.

'Holly,' he grunted, losing his balance slightly under the weight.

'Oh, sorry,' she said quickly. 'Just by the window.'

He made his way over. 'There now,' he said, wiping his hands and stepping back to look at his work.

Holly frowned. 'It looks a little bit bare, don't you think?'

'Well, you will have to decorate it, of course.'

'Richard, I was referring to the fact that it only has about five branches left. It's got bald patches,' she moaned.

'I told you to buy a tree earlier, Holly, not to leave it until Christmas Eve. I sold the best ones weeks ago.'

Holly frowned. She really didn't want a Christmas tree this year. Richard had insisted, though, and Holly felt that she had to help him out with his new Christmas tree-selling venture, in addition to his flourishing landscaping business. But the tree was awful and no amount of tinsel could hide that.

She couldn't believe it was Christmas Eve already. She'd worked overtime to get the January issue of the magazine ready. She had ignored all Daniel's calls and had ordered Alice to tell him she was in a meeting if he ever called the office. He called the office nearly every day. She didn't intend to be rude, but she needed time. Richard's stare snapped her back to reality. 'Sorry, what?'

'I said would you like me to help you decorate it?'

Holly's heart fell. That was her and Gerry's job, nobody else's. Every year without fail they would put the Christmas CD on, open a bottle of wine and decorate the tree . . .

'I'm sure you've better things to be doing.'

'Well, actually I would quite like to do it,' he said. 'Usually myself, Meredith and the children do it together . . .'

'Oh.' Holly hadn't even thought about Richard's Christmas as being difficult. 'OK, then, why not?' she smiled.

Richard beamed and he looked like such a child.

'Oh, but the only thing is I'm not too sure where the decorations are. Gerry stored them in the attic somewhere . . .'

'No problem,' he smiled encouragingly. 'That used to be my job too.' He bounded up the stairs to the attic.

Holly opened a bottle of red wine and pressed PLAY on the CD player; Bing Crosby's 'White Christmas' played softly in the background. Richard returned with a black sack slung over his shoulder and a dusty Santa hat on. 'Ho-ho-ho!'

Holly giggled and handed him his glass of wine.

'No, no,' he waved his hand, 'I'm driving.'

'You can have one glass at least, Richard,' she said, feeling disappointed.

'No, no,' he repeated, 'I don't drink and drive.'

Holly threw her eyes up to heaven and knocked back his glass of wine, before beginning on her own. By the time Richard left she had finished the bottle and was opening another. She noticed the red light flashing on the answering machine. Hoping it wasn't a message from who she thought it was from, she hit the PLAY button.

'Hi, Sharon, it's Daniel Connelly here. Sorry to bother you, but I had your phone number from when you called the club months ago . . . I was hoping you could pass on a message for me. Denise has been so busy I couldn't rely on her to remember.' He laughed. 'Anyway, I was wondering if you could just tell Holly that I'm going down to my family in Galway for Christmas. I haven't been able to get through to her on her mobile, and I don't have her home number . . . so if you could just tell her that I'll have my mobile with me if she wants to reach me.' He paused. 'Anyway, I'll see you all at the wedding next week. OK, thanks.'

The second message was from Denise telling her that Daniel was looking for her, the third message was from Declan also telling her that Daniel was looking for her and the fourth message was from Daniel again. 'Hi, Holly, it's Daniel here. Declan gave me your number. I can't believe you never gave me your home number, yet I've a sneaking suspicion I've had it all along without realising . . .' There was a silence as he exhaled. 'Anyway, I really need to talk to you, Holly. I think it should be before we see each other at the wedding. Please, please take my calls.' Another deep breath and exhalation. 'OK, well, that's all. Bye.'

Holly pressed PLAY again, lost in thought.

She sat in the living room, staring at the tree. She cried. Cried for her Gerry and for her balding Christmas tree.

Fourteen

'HAPPY CHRISTMAS, LOVE!' Frank opened the door to a shivering Holly standing on the doorstep.

'Happy Christmas, Dad.' She smiled, and gave him a big bear hug. The beautiful smell of pine mixed with wine and Christmas dinner cooking in the kitchen filled her nostrils, and she was hit with a pang of loneliness. Christmas was Gerry. It was their special time together when they would hide from the stresses of work and just relax and entertain their friends and family and enjoy their time alone. She missed him so much it gave her a sick feeling in the pit of her stomach.

She had visited the graveyard that morning to wish him a happy Christmas. It was the first time she had been there since the funeral. Gerry had wanted to be cremated, which meant that she had to stand in front of a wall that had his name engraved on it. She told him about her year and what her plans were for the day; she told him Sharon and John were expecting a baby boy and they were calling him Gerry; she told him that she was to be his godmother; that she was to be maid of honour at Denise's wedding. She explained what Tom was like, because Gerry had never met him, and she talked about her new job. She wanted to get some deep spiritual feeling that Gerry was there with her, but she really just felt like she was talking to a drab grey wall.

All in all, it hadn't been a good morning.

'Oh, happy Christmas, dear!' Elizabeth announced, walking out of the kitchen with open arms. Holly started to cry. Elizabeth's face was flushed from the heat of the kitchen and the warmth of her body warmed Holly's heart.

'I'm sorry.' She wiped her face. 'I didn't want to do that.'

'Hush,' Elizabeth said, hugging her even tighter.

Holly had called round to visit her mother the previous week in a panic about what to do about the Daniel situation.

'So how do you feel about him?' Elizabeth had asked.

'I like him, Mum, I really do, but I don't know if I'll *ever* feel ready for another relationship. He's not Gerry, but I'm not expecting him to be. What I feel now is a different kind of feeling; but a nice one, too.'

'It's important not to rush into things, Holly, but whether it's with Daniel, the man on the moon, or alone, I just want you happy.'

As comforting as her mother had been to her that day, Holly was no closer to making her decision. First, she had to get through Christmas without Gerry.

The rest of Holly's family joined them in the living room and greeted her with hugs. They gathered round the tree and exchanged gifts and Holly allowed the tears to flow throughout. She hadn't the energy to hide them; she hadn't the energy to care. But the tears were a strange mixture of happiness and sadness. A peculiar sensation of feeling alone yet loved.

She sneaked away from the family so she could have a moment to herself; her head was a jumble of thoughts that needed to be sorted and filed. She found herself in her old bedroom, staring out of the window into the dark, blustery day. The sea was fierce and threatening and Holly shuddered at its power.

'So this is where you're hiding.'

Holly turned to see Jack watching her from the bedroom door. She smiled weakly and turned round to face the sea again, uninterested in her brother and his recent lack of support. She listened to the waves and watched the black water swallow the sleet that had begun to fall. She heard Jack sigh loudly and felt his arm round her shoulder.

'Sorry,' he said softly.

Holly raised her eyebrows, unimpressed, and continued to stare ahead.

He nodded to himself slowly. 'You're right to treat me like this, Holly, I've been acting like a complete idiot lately. And I'm so sorry.'

Holly turned to face him and her eyes glistened. 'You let me down, Jack.'

He closed his eyes slowly as though the very thought of that pained him. 'I know. I just didn't handle the whole situation well, Holly. I found it so hard to deal with Gerry . . . you know . . .'

'Dying,' Holly finished for him.

'Yeah.' He clenched and unclenched his jaw and looked like he had finally accepted it.

'It wasn't exactly easy for me, you know, Jack.' A silence fell between them. 'But you helped me pack away all his things. You went through his belongings with me and made the whole thing so much easier,' Holly said, feeling confused. 'You were there with me for that, why did you just suddenly disappear?'

'God, that was so tough to do.' He shook his head sadly. 'You were so strong, Holly . . . you *are* strong,' he corrected himself. 'Getting rid of his things just tore me up, being in the house and him not being there just . . . *got* to me. And then I noticed you were getting closer to Richard, so I just figured it would be OK for me to take a step back because you had him . . .' He shrugged his shoulders and blushed at the ridiculousness of finally explaining his feelings.

'You fool, Jack,' Holly said, thumping him playfully in the stomach. 'As if Richard could ever take your place.'

He smiled. 'Oh, I don't know, you two seem very pally these days.'

Holly became serious again. 'Richard has been very supportive over the past year, and, believe me, people haven't failed to surprise me during this whole experience,' she added pointedly. 'Give him a chance, Jack.'

He stared out to the sea and nodded slowly, digesting this.

Holly wrapped her arms round him and felt the familiar comforting hug of her brother. Hugging her even tighter, Jack said, 'I'm here for you now. I'm going to stop being so selfish and take care of my little sister.'

'Hey, your little sister is doing just fine on her own, thank you very much,' she said sadly as she watched the sea crash violently against the rocks, its spray kissing the moon.

They sat down for their meal. Everyone oohed and aahed at the spread of food before them.

'I got an email from Ciara today,' Declan announced. 'She sent this picture.' He passed round the photograph he had printed off.

Holly smiled at the sight of her sister lying on the beach eating barbecued Christmas lunch with Mathew. Her hair was blonde and her skin was tanned, and they both looked so happy. After travelling round the world searching and searching, Ciara, she reckoned, had finally found contentment.

'They're saying it might snow today,' Holly announced.

'No, it won't snow,' Richard said. 'It's too cold for that.'

Holly frowned. 'Richard, how could it be too cold to snow?'

He wiped his fingers on the napkin that was tucked into his black woolly jumper with a Christmas tree emblazoned across the front. 'It needs to get milder before it can snow.'

Holly giggled. 'Richard, it's about minus a million in the Antarctic and it snows there. That's hardly mild.'

'That's the way it works,' he said matter-of-factly.

'Whatever you say.' Holly rolled her eyes.

'He's right, actually,' Jack added after a while, and everyone stopped chewing to stare at him. That was not a phrase they often heard. Jack went on to explain how snow worked and Richard helped him out on the scientific parts. Abbey raised her eyebrows at Holly and they shared a secret look of shock.

'You want some vegetables with your gravy, Dad?' Declan asked seriously, offering him a bowl of broccoli.

Everyone looked at Frank's plate and laughed.

'Ha-ha,' Frank said, taking the bowl from his son. 'Anyway, we live too close to the sea to get any.'

'To get what? Gravy?' Holly teased and they laughed again.

'Snow, silly,' he said, grabbing her nose like he used to when she was a child.

'Well, I bet you all a million quid that it snows today,' Declan said, eagerly glancing around.

'Then you'd better start saving, Declan, because if your brainiac brothers say it ain't so, it ain't so!' Holly joked.

'Better pay up then, boys.' Declan nodded towards the window.

'Oh my God!' Holly exclaimed. 'It's snowing!'

'So much for that theory, then,' Jack said to Richard, and they laughed.

Everyone deserted the dinner table and threw on their coats to run outside like excited children. Elizabeth wrapped her arms round her daughter's shoulders. 'Well, it looks like Denise will have a white Christmas for her white wedding,' she smiled.

Holly's heart beat wildly at the thought of Denise's wedding. In just a few days she would have to confront Daniel. As if her mother had been reading her mind she asked quietly, 'Have you thought about what to say to Daniel yet?'

Holly glanced up at the snowflakes glistening down from the black, star-filled sky in the moonlight. The moment felt so magical; right there and then she made her final decision.

'Yes, I have.' She smiled and took a deep breath.

'Good.' Elizabeth kissed her on the cheek. 'And remember, God leads you to it and takes you through it.'

'He'd better. I'm going to need Him a lot the next while.'

'Sharon, don't carry that case, it's too heavy!' John yelled at his wife, and Sharon dropped the bag angrily.

'John, I am not an invalid. I am *pregnant!*'

'I know that, but the doctor said not to lift heavy things!' He walked to her side of the car and grabbed the bag.

'Well, screw the doctor, he's never been bloody pregnant,' Sharon yelled, watching John storm off.

Holly banged down the boot of the car loudly. She had had enough of John and Sharon's tantrums; she had been stuck listening to them bicker all the way down to Wicklow in the car. Now all she wanted was to go and relax in the hotel.

She grabbed her bag and glanced up at the building. It was more like a castle. As the venue for their New Year's Eve wedding, Tom and Denise couldn't have picked a more beautiful place. The house was covered in dark green ivy climbing up its ageing walls and a huge fountain adorned the front courtyard. Acres and acres of beautifully kept lush green gardens surrounded the hotel. Denise didn't get her white Christmas wedding, after all; the snow had melted minutes after it had arrived.

Still, it had been a beautiful moment for Holly to share with her family on Christmas Day, and it had succeeded in lifting her spirits for a short time. Now all she wanted to do was find her room and pamper herself. She dragged her bag behind her over the cobblestones and was suddenly jerked forwards and sent flying as someone tripped over her luggage.

'Sorry,' she heard a singsong voice say and she watched the tall blonde's hips go boom-boom towards the hotel. Holly frowned. She knew that walk from somewhere, but . . .

Laura.

Oh, no! she thought, panicking. Tom and Denise had invited Laura after all! She had to find Daniel quickly so that she could warn him. And then if the moment was right she would finish off that chat with him. She rushed towards the reception area, which was crowded with angry people and luggage. Denise's voice was instantly recognisable above all the noise.

'Look, I don't *care* if you've made a mistake! *Fix it!*' Denise held her hand up in a very startled receptionist's face. 'I don't want to hear any more excuses! Just get ten more rooms for my guests!'

Holly spotted Tom and headed over to him, beating her way through the crowd.

'Hi, Holly,' he said, looking very distracted.

'What room is Daniel in?' she asked quickly.

'Daniel?' he asked, looking confused.

'Yes, Daniel! Your best man.'

'I really don't know; ask Denise.'

Holly gulped. Denise looked possessed, and she had no intention of asking her in that mood. She queued in line behind the other guests and twenty minutes later she reached the front.

'Could you tell me what room Daniel Connelly is in, please?'

The receptionist shook his head. 'I'm sorry, we can't give out guests' room numbers.'

'Look, I'm a friend of his,' Holly smiled sweetly.

The man smiled politely. 'I'm sorry, it's against policy—'

'Listen!' she yelled and even Denise shut up screaming beside her. 'It's very important you tell me!'

'Holly.' Denise placed her hand on her arm. 'What's wrong?'

'I need to know what room Daniel's in!' Holly yelled.

Denise looked startled. 'It's room three forty-two.'

Holly stormed off in the direction of the elevators. When she arrived at the right floor, she rushed down the corridor dragging her bag behind her and checking the door numbers. When she reached his room she knocked furiously on the door. As she heard footsteps approaching the door she realised she hadn't even thought about what she was going to say. She took a deep breath as the door was pulled open.

She stopped breathing.

It was Laura.

'Honey, who is it?' Daniel walked out of the bathroom, a towel wrapped round his body.

'You!' Laura screeched.

Holly glanced from Laura to Daniel and back to Laura again. She gathered from their seminakedness that Daniel had already known Laura was coming to the wedding. He hung on to his towel tightly, his face a picture of shock. Nobody spoke for a while. Then eventually someone spoke and Holly wished it hadn't been that particular person. 'What are *you* doing here?' Laura hissed.

Holly's mouth opened and closed like a goldfish's. Daniel's forehead wrinkled in confusion as he stared from one woman to the other. 'Do you two . . . do you two know each other?'

'Ha!' Laura's face twisted in contempt. 'I caught this little bitch kissing my boyfriend!'

'Your *boyfriend*?' Daniel yelled, crossing the room to join them at the door.

'Sorry . . . ex-boyfriend,' Laura mumbled, staring at the floor.

Holly crossed her arms over her chest. 'Yeah, Stevie, wasn't it? A good friend of Daniel's, if I remember correctly.'

Daniel's face reddened as he looked at them both. 'You kissed Stevie?' he said, slowly getting the gist of the story.

'No, I did *not* kiss Stevie.' Holly looked at Laura and laughed. 'I take it you're back with Daniel, so what does it matter anyway?' She then turned to Daniel. 'We were down in Galway for Denise's hen weekend and Stevie was drunk and tried to kiss me in the hotel.'

'Oh, you're such a liar,' Laura said. 'I saw what happened.'

'And so did Charlie, the barman,' Holly told Daniel. 'So you can go there and ask him, if you don't believe me. But I really don't care. I came to have that chat with you but you're obviously busy.' She marched off down the corridor to the elevator, dragging her suitcase behind her.

She pressed the button and breathed a sigh of relief. When the doors opened, she stepped in and closed her tired eyes. She didn't even feel angry with Daniel; in fact, in a really childish way, she was glad he had done something to stop them from having their little chat. So she had been dumped and not the other way round. But Daniel couldn't have been that much in love with her, she reasoned, if he was able to go back to Laura so quickly. Ah well, at least she didn't hurt his feelings . . . But she did think he was a complete fool for taking Laura back.

Denise looked at Holly excitedly as someone rapped a spoon against their glass and the speeches began. Holly fumbled nervously with her hands in her lap, going over and over her speech in her head. She should have written it down because now she couldn't remember the start of it.

Her heart beat wildly as Daniel sat down and everyone applauded. She was next. Sharon grabbed her hand and Holly smiled back at her shakily. Denise's father announced that Holly was going to speak and the room turned to face her. All she could see was a sea of faces. She stood up and glanced down the room and spotted John sitting at a table with his and Gerry's friends. John gave her the thumbs up and Holly's speech went out of the window as a new one formed in her head.

'Please forgive me if I get a little emotional while I speak, but I am just so happy for Denise today. She is my best friend . . .' she paused and glanced down at Sharon. 'Well, one of them.'

The room laughed.

'Finding someone you love is a wonderful feeling. But finding a true soul mate is an even *better* feeling. A soul mate understands you like no other, loves you like no other, will be there for you *for ever*, no matter what. I know a thing or two about that, and I know that Denise has found a soul mate in Tom.' A lump formed in Holly's throat and she took a moment to compose herself. 'I am honoured to have been asked to share this beautiful day with Denise and Tom, and here's to them having many more beautiful days like this together.'

Everyone cheered and reached for their glasses.

'However!' Holly held her hand up. The noise died down and once again all eyes were on her.

'However, some here today will be aware of the list a marvellous man thought up.' John's table cheered. 'And one of its rules was to *never, ever* wear a 'spensive white dress.'

John's table went wild and Denise broke down in hysterics.

'So, on behalf of Gerry,' Holly said, 'I will forgive Denise for breaking that rule only because she looks so amazing. And I will ask you all to join me in a toast to Tom and Denise and her very, very 'spensive white dress. I should know, because I was dragged round every bridal shop in Ireland!'

The guests all held up their glasses. 'To Tom and Denise and her very, very 'spensive white dress!'

Holly's face beamed as John's table held their glasses up to her and cheered. And then the party began.

Tears formed in Holly's eyes as she watched Tom and Denise dancing together for the first time as husband and wife, and she remembered that feeling. That feeling of excitement, of hope, of pure happiness and pride, a feeling of not knowing what the future held but being so ready to face it all. And that thought made her happy; she wouldn't cry about it, she would embrace it. She had enjoyed every second of her life with Gerry, but now it was time to move on. Sure it would be difficult, but it didn't feel as difficult as it had a few months ago.

She had been given a wonderful gift: life. Sometimes, cruelly, it was taken away too soon, but it was what you did with it that counted.

'May I have this dance?' She looked up to see Daniel smiling at her.

'Sure.' She smiled back and took his hand.

'May I say that you're looking very beautiful tonight?'

'You may,' Holly smiled again. She was happy with how she looked. Denise had chosen a beautiful lilac-coloured dress for her with a corset top, and there was a large slit up the side.

'That was a lovely speech,' he told her. 'I realise that what I said to you was selfish of me. You said you weren't ready and I didn't listen.'

'That's OK, Daniel; I don't think I'll be ready for a long, long time. But thank you for getting over me so fast.' She nodded over at Laura, sitting moodily on her own at the table.

Daniel bit his lip. 'I know it must seem crazy fast to you, but when you didn't return any of my calls, even I got the hint you weren't ready for a relationship. And when I went home for the holidays and met up with Laura, that old flame just sparked again. You were right, I never got over her. Believe me, if I hadn't known with all my heart that you weren't in love with me, I never would have brought her to the wedding.'

Holly smiled at Daniel. 'Sorry for avoiding you all month. I was having a bit of "me" time. But I still think you're a fool.' She shook her head as she watched Laura scowl back at her.

Daniel sighed. 'I know she and I have a lot to discuss over the next while and we're really going to take things slowly, but like you said, for some people love just lives on.'

Holly threw her eyes up to heaven. 'Oh, don't start quoting me on that one,' she said, laughing. 'Ah well, as long as you're happy, I suppose. Although I don't see how you ever will be.' She sighed dramatically and Daniel laughed too.

'I am happy, Holly. I guess I just can't live without the drama.' He glanced over at Laura, and his eyes softened. 'I need someone who is passionate about me, and for better or for worse, Laura is passionate. What about you? Are you happy?' He studied Holly's face.

Holly thought about it. 'Tonight I'm happy. I'll worry about tomorrow when tomorrow comes. But I'm getting there . . .'

Holly gathered in a huddle with Sharon, John, Denise and Tom and awaited the countdown.

'Five . . . four . . . three . . . two . . . one! HAPPY NEW YEAR!' Balloons of all colours of the rainbow fell from the ceiling.

Holly hugged her friends happily with tears in her eyes.

'Happy New Year.' Sharon kissed her on the cheek.

Holly placed her hand over Sharon's bump and held Denise's hand tightly. 'Happy *New* Year for all of us!'

Epilogue

HOLLY FLICKED through the newspapers to see which one contained a photo of Denise and Tom on their wedding day. It wasn't every day that Ireland's top radio DJ and a girl from *Girls and the City* got married. That's what Denise liked to think anyway.

'Hey!' the grumpy newsagent yelled at her. 'This is not a library. You either buy it or put it down.'

Holly sighed and began to gather every newspaper from the news-stand once again. She had to take two trips to the counter due to the weight of the papers. Once again a queue had formed behind the till. Holly smiled to herself and took her time. She made her way with the last of the papers and began to add chocolate and packets of sweets to the pile.

'Oh, and may I have a bag too, please.' She batted her eyelashes and smiled sweetly.

The old man stared at her as though she were a naughty schoolgirl. 'Mark!' he yelled angrily.

The spotty teenager appeared from the shopping aisles.

'Open the other till, son,' he was ordered. Half the queue behind Holly moved over to the other side.

'Thank you.' Holly smiled and made her way to the door. Just as she was about to pull it open it was pushed from the other side, causing her purchases to spill out all over the floor.

'I'm so sorry,' the man said, bending down to help her.

'Oh, it's OK,' Holly replied politely.

'Ah, it's you! The chocoholic!' Holly looked up startled.

It was the friendly customer with the grey-green eyes who had helped her before.

Holly giggled. 'We meet again,' she said.

'Holly, isn't it?' he asked, handing her the chocolate bars.

'That's right. Rob, isn't it?' she replied.

'You've a good memory,' he laughed.

'As do you,' she grinned. She piled everything back into her bag, and got back onto her feet.

'Well, I'm sure I'll bump into you again soon.' Rob smiled and made his way over to the queue.

Holly stared after him in a daze. Finally she walked over. 'Rob, is there any chance you'd like to go for that coffee today? If you can't, that's fine . . .' She bit her lip.

He smiled and glanced down nervously at the ring on her finger.

'Oh, don't worry about that,' she held her hand out. 'It only repre-sents a lifetime of happy memories these days.'

He nodded his head. 'Well, in that case I would love to.'

They crossed the road and headed to the Greasy Spoon.

Holly smiled to herself as she sat at the table waiting for him to bring back the drinks. He seemed nice. She relaxed back in her chair and gazed out of the window into the cold January day that caused the trees to dance wildly in the wind. She thought about what she had learned.

She was a woman who had taken advice from a man she loved and she had tried her hardest to help to heal herself. She now felt confidence within herself to reach for what she wanted.

She was a woman who made mistakes, who sometimes cried on a Monday morning or at night alone in bed. She was a woman who often became bored with her life and found it hard to get up in the morning. She was a woman who sometimes questioned what reason she had to live on this planet and who sometimes just got things wrong.

On the other hand, she was a woman with a million happy memories, who knew what it was like to experience true love and who was ready to experience more life, more love and make new memories. Whether it happened in ten months or ten years, Holly would obey Gerry's final message. Whatever lay ahead, she knew she would open her heart and follow where it led her.

In the meantime, she would just live.

CECELIA AHERN

When twenty-two-year-old Cecelia Ahern sold her first novel, *PS, I Love You*, for a seven-figure sum, no one was more surprised than the author herself. 'It was amazing. Even now I can hardly believe it's happened.'

Having completed a degree in journalism and media communications at Dublin's Griffith College, she was about to start a Masters in film production when the idea for the novel 'just popped into my head one day when I was daydreaming'. She decided that she had to stop everything and write it down. 'I just knew that I had something special, and as I wrote I passed on the pages to my mum. She read them, and laughed and cried in all the right places, and she was so encouraging that I continued. Then one day we were watching Irish author Cathy Kelly on the television and my mum said that she played golf with Cathy's publicist.' The publicist gave Cecelia the name of an agent in Ireland and she sent off four chapters of her novel. 'Then she asked for another chapter, then another,' Cecelia remembers. 'After ten chapters she said she would represent me—I was shocked because I was just looking for advice really. She is a wonderful agent and had worked passionately hard for months and months to get me the right publishing deal. I was in a shop changing-room when she called me to say she had been successful. I don't remember getting dressed afterwards. When I got home I had to check that I hadn't accidentally walked off in stolen gear!'

Cecelia wrote *PS, I Love You* mainly at night. 'I would start writing at around ten and write until six or seven in the morning. I'm a night-time

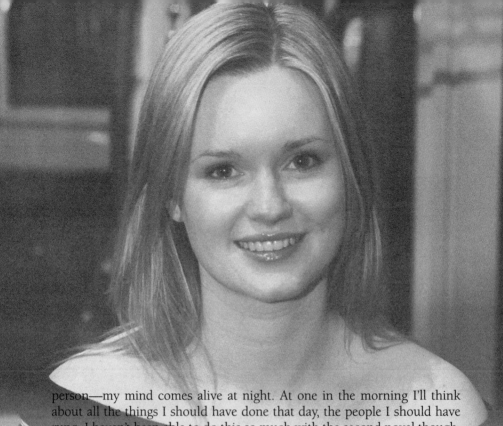

person—my mind comes alive at night. At one in the morning I'll think about all the things I should have done that day, the people I should have rung. I haven't been able to do this so much with the second novel though, because there are more demands on my time. I'm now living with my boyfriend in a flat we have bought recently and my mum's not there to answer the phone or do the chores!'

Holly Kennedy, the main character in *PS, I Love You*, is certainly not Cecelia Ahern in disguise—'in fact I went out of my way to make her very different from me'—but when she was writing about Holly, Cecelia says she took on many of her heroine's moods. 'If Holly was upset then I was upset, if she was drunk then I felt a little wobbly—and I don't even drink alcohol!'

Blonde and strikingly pretty, Cecelia Ahern is dressed in her favourite pink when I meet her and I'm struck by how young she is, but also, when discussing her writing, by her maturity and level-headedness. It's clear that the overnight success has not gone to her head, but then as daughter of Irish prime minister Bertie Ahern, and sister-in-law of Nicky Byrne of the Irish band Westlife, Cecelia is well used to the spotlight . . . plus her boyfriend is Irish hurdler, David Keoghan, who is hoping to qualify for the Olympics. 'This is a big year for both of us,' Cecelia says. 'We've got different jobs but both jobs are our passion. Hopefully, with my head full of ideas I can keep going for a long time. It's hard work but I'm going to give it my all.'

Jane Eastgate

MICHELLE PAVER

Fever Hill

*As the old steam train rattles through the hill
pastures on its journey to Montego Bay, Sophie
Monroe sighs and thinks: I'm home. For three long
years she has dreamed of coming back to Jamaica,
of seeing her sister Madeleine again and visiting
her inheritance, the old house at Fever Hill.
Now she is so close she can smell the sugar cane.
But her fear is that home will no longer be as
magical as her memories of it.*

PART ONE:
Jamaica 1903
CHAPTER ONE

THE DOCTORS SAID SHE HAD tuberculosis, and blamed it on invisible creatures called 'bacilli', but Sophie knew better.

She was ill because the duppy tree was trying to kill her. The washer-woman's little girl had told her so, and Evie knew all about things like that, for her mother was a witch.

The following year when Sophie was twelve, she recovered. But she still had bad dreams about duppy trees. So one night her brother-in-law took her up into the hills to meet one, and when they reached the great tree in the glade on Overlook Hill they sat on the folded roots, and ate the fried plantain and johnny cake that Madeleine had packed for them. Sophie felt scared, but safe, because Cameron was with her.

And as she sat beside him in the blue moonlight, watching the little lizards darting up and down the enormous trunk, she realised that she must have been mistaken about the tree wanting to kill her. And after that she wasn't scared of duppy trees any more. Instead, she became passionately interested in them, and tried to grow one in a pot.

'Sophie's making one of her about-turns,' said Cameron with a laugh. And Maddy smiled at him, and helped her little sister to find a place for the potted duppy tree on the verandah, where it gradually died.

Thinking of that now as the train rattled through the hill pastures on its way to Montego Bay, Sophie felt a sudden uprush of love for them both—and a tug of concern. She needed to see for herself that they were happy and well. She needed to dispel the vague impression she had gathered from Maddy's last letter that something wasn't quite right.

Pushing the thought aside, she turned her head and watched the pastures slipping past. Acid-green guinea grass rippled in the wind, dotted with ambling white Hindu cattle. On a dusty red track, a black woman carried a basket of yams on her head with easy grace.

I'm home, thought Sophie. She still couldn't believe it. For three years she had dreamed of coming back to Jamaica. Then it all seemed to happen in the blink of an eye. School was over, and she was on her way out from Southampton. Now here she was on the last leg of the journey.

On the opposite seat, Mr van Rieman cleared his throat. 'According to this,' he said, tapping the journal in his hand, 'the Jamaican sugar planter is becoming an endangered species. It says that since the slaves were freed, hundreds of plantations have been turned over to cattle, or simply abandoned.' He regarded Sophie over his wire-rimmed spectacles. 'I take it, Miss Monroe, that such will not be the fate of your brother-in-law's estate?'

She shook her head and smiled. 'Somehow Cameron always manages to keep Eden afloat.'

'Indeed,' said Mr van Rieman, looking slightly put out.

'Eden,' said Mrs van Rieman brightly. 'What a lovely name.'

Sophie threw her a grateful look, and almost forgave the fact that for most of the journey the Americans' small, baleful son Theo had been surreptitiously kicking her leg whenever his mamma wasn't looking.

The train pulled into Appleton for the lunchtime stop, and they stepped stiffly down into the blaze of the November sun. Jamaica broke over them like a wave. Pickneys raced about between people's legs. Higglers crowded the platform, plying their wares. *Butter-dough! Paradise plums! All sort a mango! Paperskin, Christmas, cherry-cheek!*

Luncheon at the Station Hotel was awkward, with the van Riemans questioning Sophie in ringing tones, while the rest of the dining room listened with open ears. Sophie swallowed her pride and answered as best she could, for the Americans had been kind to her when they'd met in the ticket office at Kingston—albeit politely appalled at the notion of a young lady of nineteen travelling alone.

'If I have this right, Miss Monroe,' said Mrs van Rieman, 'you're ten years younger than your sister, who has two darling little children?'

Sophie's mouth was full of pepperpot, so she could only nod.

'And what about you?' said Mrs van Rieman with an arch twinkle. 'Any sweethearts yet?'

Sophie gave her a fixed smile. 'No,' she replied.

'Miss Monroe is above such trivial concerns,' put in Mr van Rieman. 'Miss Monroe is a bluestocking! She intends to study medicine.'

'I'm only thinking about it,' said Sophie quickly. 'There's a clinic near my brother-in-law's estate, and I thought I'd try to get some experience there, and see if I like it.' She flushed. There was no need to tell them all that. But she always talked too much when she was embarrassed.

'I believe you spent your early childhood in London?' said Mrs van Rieman. 'Then you came out to Jamaica, as you had family here?'

Again Sophie nodded. Then, because she was nearly home and feeling a little reckless, she said, 'Also I was ill, and Maddy thought the tropics would do me good. I had TB.'

There was a small silence.

'Tuberculosis,' repeated Mr van Rieman. His wife put her hand to her throat. The other diners applied themselves to their food.

'Tuberculosis of the knee,' Sophie explained. 'But I've been free of it for the past seven years. There's no danger of infection.'

'Of course not,' said Mrs van Rieman faintly.

'Did you have a splint?' Theo said loudly.

'Yes,' said Sophie. 'A big clumpy iron one that I had to wear all the time for two years. I hated it.'

'Do you limp?' said Theo with a hint of contempt.

'*Theo!*' said Mrs van Rieman.

'No,' lied Sophie. In fact she did limp a little, when she was tired or self-conscious. But she wasn't going to tell that to the entire Station Hotel. They were already feeling sorry enough for her as it was: the sickly, bookish younger sister without a sweetheart.

'If you never took the splint off,' said Theo, 'how did you wash?'

'That's enough,' snapped Mrs van Rieman, and the subject was dropped.

As they rejoined the train, Sophie considered offering to move to another compartment. But she guessed that that would only embarrass the van Riemans. So instead they all settled back into their seats with self-conscious smiles, and Sophie gazed out of the window.

Gradually, the cattle pastures gave way to cane-pieces. They were in sugar country now, and the heavy scent of molasses drifted in through the window. The smell of home.

The familiar names flashed past. Ginger Hill, Seven Rivers, Catadupa. And far in the distance, she glimpsed the eerie blue-grey humps of the Cockpits: a harsh wilderness of treacherous sinkholes and oddly conical hills, which had fascinated her as a child. Her pulse quickened. On the other side of the Cockpits, with its face to the sea, lay Eden.

The train halted at Montpelier for the final rest-stop, scarcely ten miles from Montego Bay. Mr van Rieman hurried off to the third-class compartment to consult his courier, and Mrs van Rieman went inside the station building to use the facilities, leaving her son with Sophie.

They waited at the top of the station steps in the shade of a big silk-cotton tree, and watched the ox wagons trundling past, piled high with sugar cane. Then Theo resumed the attack.

'How *did* you wash?' he said with quiet insolence.

'I didn't,' said Sophie without turning her head.

Theo digested that. 'I bet that's an untruth,' he muttered.

Sophie did not reply.

'I don't *like* Jamaica,' said Theo.

'I'm not surprised,' Sophie replied. 'It's a very frightening place for a little boy.'

'I don't mean that I'm scared,' retorted Theo.

'Well, you should be. Jamaica's full of ghosts.'

Theo blinked.

'Some of them live in caves in the hills,' she said calmly, 'but mostly they live in trees like this one behind you.'

Theo jumped. 'You're making that up,' he said belligerently. 'It's just an old tree.'

'Actually it's not; it's a duppy tree. Ask anyone. Duppy is Jamaican for ghost. D'you see the folds in the trunk? That's where they live. They come out at night and make people ill.'

Theo swallowed.

'I used to believe that a duppy tree was making me ill,' she went on. 'But then a brave boy sorted things out for me, and after that I got better.'

Theo looked pale but defiant. '*How* brave?'

'Extremely. He was a street urchin from London.'

'What was he called?'

'Ben.'

'What happened to him?'

'Nobody knows. After he dealt with the duppy tree he was never seen again.'

Across the road, a young groom jumped down from his carriage to check the harness on his horses. Something about the way he moved reminded her of Ben.

Strange the way memory works. She hadn't thought about him in ages, and now suddenly she could almost see him. Thin as an alley cat, with filthy black hair and a grimy, sharp-featured face, and narrow green eyes. The ten-year-old Sophie had been captivated.

'You know an awful lot about Jamaica,' said Theo humbly.

She felt a twinge of remorse. 'Actually,' she said, 'there's one thing I forgot to tell you about duppy trees. They never attack Americans.'

Theo looked uncertain. 'But how will they know that I *am* American?'

'They can always tell.'

He nodded, and some of the colour returned to his lips.

'Come along,' said Sophie, 'let's find your mamma.' But as she took his hand and turned to go, she glanced back over her shoulder at the young groom. His master and mistress were approaching down the street, and he was waiting for them. Suddenly Sophie's heart lifted. The young groom's master and mistress were Madeleine and Cameron.

She forgot the proprieties and yelled her sister's name. 'Maddy! Cameron! Over here!'

They didn't hear her. And at that moment a wagon laden with sugar cane trundled down the street and hid them from view.

She let go of Theo and picked up her skirts and ran down the station steps to the edge of the street. Impatiently she waited while the oxen plodded past. And as the red dust slowly cleared, she saw them across the street: beautiful, unmistakable Maddy, with her luxuriant black hair piled beneath a wide straw hat, and her magnificent figure swathed in her favourite bronze silk dust coat. She was leaning on Cameron's arm, and he was bending over her, and she was wiping her eyes and nodding, and trying to smile.

At that moment Cameron turned to speak to the groom, and Sophie saw with a jolt that it wasn't Cameron at all. Cameron was tall and broad-shouldered and in his early forties, with unruly fair hair and features that possessed great strength and undeniable charm. The man to whom her sister was clinging—*clinging*—was also fair-haired, but much slighter and more delicate, and only in his late twenties, like Maddy herself. Sophie had never seen him before in her life.

'Miss Monroe?' said Mrs van Rieman, coming up behind her. 'The train is about to leave . . . Is something wrong?'

Sophie turned and tried to say something, but her words were drowned out by another ox wagon. And when she looked back, and the dust had settled again, the carriage and groom and the fair-haired young gentleman and her sister had gone.

Suddenly she was desperate to get to Montego Bay. But as Mr van Rieman informed her with grim pleasure, the train was delayed. A wagon had overturned just outside Montpelier, spilling its load of logwood across the tracks. It would take at least half an hour to clear.

As Sophie paced up and down outside the train, she talked herself out of panic. After all, there couldn't be anything seriously wrong, or Maddy would have sent her a wire. Wouldn't she?

At last, after nearly forty-five minutes, they got under way again, and the train began its lumbering descent towards the plains of the north coast. They trundled through acre on acre of green cane-fields. Then Mrs van Rieman exclaimed with pleasure at the view of Montego Bay spread out below them—at the tidy red-roofed houses and the royal palms, and the glittering turquoise sea. Sophie hardly saw it. Surely, surely Maddy and Cameron would be waiting at the station, just as they'd promised?

They drew into the station in a cloud of steam. The platform was thronged with higglers of every shade of black and brown, and Mrs van Rieman barely registered Sophie's muttered thanks and hasty leave-taking.

Then suddenly there they were—*both* of them. Her knees nearly buckled with relief. There was Maddy in her bronze silk dust coat, pushing her way up the platform steps with a brilliant smile on her lovely face—and here was Cameron coming forward and sweeping Sophie off the ground in a hug. The delicate-featured young gentleman was nowhere to be seen.

'What a relief!' cried Sophie, when Cameron had set her down and she could breathe again. She turned to Maddy. 'I saw you at Montpelier, I shouted, but you were gone before I could catch your eye.'

'Montpelier?' said Maddy, laughing as she stooped to free her dust coat from the wheels of a passing trolley. 'Sorry, but it wasn't me.'

'But Maddy,' said Sophie, astonished. 'I saw you.'

Madeleine straightened up and looked at her in amusement. 'So now I've got a double up at Montpelier, have I? How very exciting.'

'But—'

'Sophie, I've been shopping in Montego Bay all afternoon. Now come along. You must be exhausted. And there's so much to talk about. I can't believe it . . . *three years*! We've planned it all out. Cameron's riding behind, so we'll have the dog cart to ourselves. And Braverly's making a special dinner, and the children are staying up for a treat. They're absolutely wild with excitement. Come along!'

Sophie woke at daybreak with a dragging tiredness and a sense of unease that wouldn't be reasoned away. She drew back the mosquito curtain and lay watching the sunlight warming the terracotta floor tiles.

She remembered when she used to wake up in this same room at dawn, and slip down to the river to meet her best friend Evie, who had run up through the cane-pieces from Fever Hill. They would go off to one of their secret places in the woods, and ask the spirits to get rid of Evie's freckles, and keep the bacilli out of Sophie's knee, and watch over Ben Kelly, wherever he was.

She turned and pressed her face into the pillow. Why think of him now? It was as if her thoughts were determined to revert to the unresolved and the unexplained. The boy who'd briefly been her friend, and then left without saying goodbye. The sister who was behaving so inexplicably.

She got out of bed and went to the window, flexing the stiffness out of her knee. Her room looked east, over a jungle of huge-leaved philodendron and wild almond trees, towards the stables at the bottom of the slope. Through the green-gold fronds of a tree fern beneath the eaves, she saw Cameron mount his horse and give a last word to Moses the groom. He looked as he always did: hurried and untidy, but utterly capable. Surely, she thought, he'd show it if something were wrong?

Turning back to the room, she saw with what care her sister had prepared it for her return. There were new curtains of blue and white, and a desk amply stocked with paper and ink; a washstand with eau de cologne and rosewater, and, on a shelf, a substantial pile of books.

And touchingly, Madeleine had brought up the great map of the Northside from Jocelyn's study at Fever Hill, and hung it where it could be seen from the bed. As Sophie climbed back under the covers, she could almost hear her grandfather's sharp, no-nonsense voice telling her tales of the family history. How Benneit Monroe and his friend Nathaniel Lawe had come out to Jamaica to fight the Spanish in 1655, and then carved up the Northside between them. Benneit Monroe had taken the land to the west of Falmouth, and Nat Lawe—Cameron's ancestor—that to the east. And, as Jocelyn never tired of telling her, they had always retained their properties back 'home': the Lawes' estate in Dumfriesshire, and the Monroes' at Strathnaw.

'But there aren't any boy Monroes left, are there?' Sophie would say with a frown. 'Only Maddy and me, so—'

'So what?' snapped Jocelyn. 'When I'm gone, you shall have Fever Hill, and Madeleine shall have Strathnaw. As long as the land remains in the family, that's good enough for me.'

She thought about that now as she lay in bed, trying to summon up the sound of her grandfather's voice. It didn't seem possible that there was no Jocelyn Monroe waiting for her at Fever Hill. And it didn't seem possible that Madeleine was deceiving Cameron. She loved him, and he loved her. There must be some other, quite innocent explanation.

She turned on her side, and met the eyes of her mother, gazing at her from the faded daguerreotype in its leather travelling frame.

Rose Durrant had been darkly beautiful, like Maddy, and had died when Sophie was born. Sophie knew her only through family gossip. Rose Durrant had flouted convention and ruined lives—including her own—by running off to Scotland with Jocelyn's married son and heir.

Sophie gazed into her mother's wilful, long-dead eyes. *The trouble with the Durrants*, a family friend had once told her, *is that they always went too far*. Had Maddy inherited more from her mother than her striking good looks and her talent for photography? Had she also gone too far?

Turning that over in her mind, Sophie fell asleep.

When she woke again it was nearly noon, and the dawn freshness had given way to heat. She dressed and went out into the raftered hall that served as sitting room, dining room and general dumping-ground.

In the flurry of last night's arrival she had hardly noticed her surroundings, but now she saw with dismay how much shabbier everything had become. Clearly money at Eden remained as scarce as ever.

Compared with many a Jamaican great house, Eden was small, with only a single storey of living quarters over an undercroft of storerooms and Madeleine's darkroom. Bedrooms, the nursery, and Cameron's study were arranged around the central sitting room, while a loggia on the southeast side led out to the bathhouse and the cookhouse beyond.

Sophie went out onto the verandah, and found her sister sitting on one of the big cane sofas, mending a cushion cover.

Madeleine looked up at her and smiled. 'Braverly saved you some breakfast,' she said. 'But it'll be time for lunch soon, so I expect you'd rather wait?'

Sophie nodded and said that would be fine.

'And you're not going to like this,' said Madeleine, biting off a thread, 'but I've accepted an invitation to a tea party at the Trahernes'. I know it's a bore on your first day, but Sibella wanted to welcome you home. Well, that's what she said. Actually I think she wants to ask you to be her bridesmaid. I hope you don't mind?'

I hope you don't mind? Since when had Maddy been so polite with her? 'Not at all,' she said, hearing her own false politeness with disbelief. 'It'll be nice to see her again.'

She looked out over the garden. From where she stood, a graceful double curve of white marble steps swept down to the rough green lawn. In the borders, hummingbirds flashed and hovered in a jungle of tree ferns and hibiscus. She caught the brilliant orange and cobalt of strelitzia and the cloudy blue of plumbago. At the bottom of the lawn, the Martha Brae slid by between banks overhung with scarlet heliconia and giant bamboo.

She gripped the sun-hot balustrade. 'Cameron was out early,' she said.

Madeleine sighed. 'Actually, that was late for him. These days I hardly see him. I hate to think what it'll be like at crop time.'

'But I thought he'd got a manager for Fever Hill.'

'He has. But you know Cameron. He has to see things done for himself.'

Sophie nodded. Below her on a banana leaf, a small green lizard regarded her with a swivelled and ancient eye.

'Sophie,' Madeleine said quietly, 'you don't need to worry.'

Sophie turned and met her sister's eyes. 'Then why won't you tell me what you were doing in Montpelier?'

Madeleine sighed. 'Because I wasn't in Montpelier.'

'But—'

'Sophie. Enough. As I said, you don't need to worry.'

Angrily, Sophie turned back to the garden.

Down by the river she caught a flash of red. Belle—small, determined, and dark as her mother—emerged from the bamboo, wearing a pinafore dress of scarlet twill. A flash of blue sailor suit, and six-year-old Fraser, tall and fair like his father, exploded after his little sister, closely followed by a mastiff puppy with flapping caramel-coloured ears. They were happy children growing up in a happy, secure home. If Madeleine was doing anything to threaten that, Sophie would never forgive her.

The next instant she felt mean and disloyal for even thinking such a thing. 'You've got a new dog,' she remarked, to make amends.

'That's Scout,' said Madeleine, sounding relieved that they'd moved onto neutral ground. 'He's a pest, but the children adore him.'

Sophie drew a circle on the balustrade. 'Yesterday at Montpelier—'

'Oh, Sophie, do stop.'

'I saw someone who looked like Ben.'

Madeleine blinked. 'Which Ben?'

'Our Ben. Ben Kelly. From years ago.'

Madeleine looked down at her sewing. 'Good heavens. Well, don't mention that to Cameron, will you?'

'Why not?' said Sophie sharply.

'Surely you remember? He never did understand how we could have been friends with a boy of that . . . sort.'

'Is that the real reason you don't want me to mention it?'

'Of course,' snapped Madeleine. 'What's the *matter* with you?'

There was an edgy silence.

Sophie watched Madeleine's needle flashing in and out, and thought how strange it was that they never talked of Ben, or of the old days in London, or of Cousin Lettice, the grim little martinet who had brought them up. Nor did Madeleine speak of her childhood in Scotland, or their parents, or their early days at Fever Hill. She felt a pang of unease. Madeleine was so very like their mother. That glossy black hair, those beautiful dark eyes, the extravagantly curved red mouth. *A secretive lot, the Durrants. And they always went too far.*

'If I know Rebecca Traherne,' whispered Madeleine as they followed the butler across the echoing marble ballroom, 'this tea party will be irreproachably English. You'll see. We could be at a tea party in Kent.'

'Except for the servants,' murmured Sophie, as they passed a tall black footman in the house livery of azure and silver.

To her surprise, Sophie found herself battling nerves. She had forgotten how grand the great house at Parnassus actually was. An enormous three-storey pile of golden cut-stone, it dominated the Coast Road into Falmouth, staring down from acres of Italian gardens and French parterres. The contrast with Eden couldn't have been starker.

It was too hot for tea in the grounds, so the little gilt tables had been set out in the cool south gallery, which had been transformed into an artificial garden of potted orange trees and ferns. The china was Wedgwood and the tea had been shipped out from Fortnum's. Only the lobster salad carried a taint of Jamaica, but it was rendered respectable by being the tea-time favourite of His Majesty the King.

None of it, thought Sophie with a pang, would have fooled her grandfather for a second. Jocelyn Monroe had detested the Trahernes—whose ancestor Owen Traherne had been a blacksmith—and he had always regarded them, with the exception of his daughter-in-law Clemency, as insufferable *parvenus*. And so they were—at least, to a Monroe who could trace his ancestry back seven hundred years.

Everyone who was anyone was attending the tea party, and Sophie knew them all. And because she was a Monroe, albeit an illegitimate one, they accepted her with open arms. She talked to Rebecca Traherne's beautiful house guest, a Mrs Dampiere from Spanish Town, and sat with Olivia Herapath and fielded a flood of scurrilous gossip and a barrage of loud, well-meaning questions about 'that dratted knee'.

She took refuge with old Mrs Pitcaithley and plied her with scones, for the gentle old lady's income shrank yearly, and she had strict notions of *noblesse oblige*, choosing to go hungry herself rather than see her staff less than amply fed.

Finally, Madeleine introduced her to a succession of eligible young men. Sophie was relieved when they lost interest after she politely declined the pleasure of watching them play billiards.

'Don't be such a *blue*,' whispered Sibella as she descended on her in a flurry of primrose spotted muslin.

'I'm not,' protested Sophie. 'How was finishing school?'

'A bore,' said Sibella.

'You're looking awfully pretty. Being engaged agrees with you. Congratulations.'

Sibella rolled her eyes. 'If I'd known how much work it was going to be . . .' But she accepted the compliment as a matter of course.

And she did look enchanting. Plump and fair-haired, she had her father's slightly protuberant blue eyes, and a pert little nose.

She squeezed Sophie's hand. 'You will be my bridesmaid, won't you?'

'Of course, if you want—'

'But first I must ask. You didn't become a suffragist, did you?'

'What?' said Sophie, startled.

'A suffragist! You know, votes for women. You didn't join them, did you?'

'I didn't join anything,' said Sophie with perfect truth, although she had attended several suffragist meetings.

Sibella breathed a sigh of relief. 'Thank heavens! I hate them. Nasty, ugly women who can't get husbands. And Mrs Palairet would never have stood for it.' Mrs Palairet was her future mother-in-law, and the matriarch of one of the oldest families in Trelawny.

Sophie was nettled. 'Why should it matter to Mrs Palairet what I do?'

'Oh, Sophie, what a question! You're going to be my bridesmaid. Think how it would reflect upon me.'

Then Sophie knew that she had not been chosen as a bridesmaid out of friendship, but because she was a Monroe, and would add cachet to the wedding, while not being pretty enough to outshine the bride. Oddly, she didn't resent that. Sibella probably wasn't even aware of it herself. Now she pulled Sophie over to a side table on which lay two large gilt-edged volumes sumptuously bound in pale blue morocco.

'Look, this one's my Gift Book. Isn't it heavenly?'

'What's a Gift Book?' said Sophie.

'For the *wedding*! It has columns for Sender, Description and Category of Gift, and Date of Thank-you Note. And that'—she indicated the companion volume—'is the Trousseau Register.'

Idly, Sophie opened the Register and scanned the first page. She blinked. 'Good heavens, Sib, twelve dozen pocket handkerchiefs? What are you going to do with those?'

'Oh, Sophie, where have you been? Any fewer would be impossible! And Mrs Palairet quite approves. She—'

'Ah, then it must be correct.'

Two spots of colour appeared on Sibella's plump cheeks. 'Presumably laughing at one's friends is the newest style of London wit. But I confess I don't find it the least bit amusing.'

'I wasn't laughing at you,' Sophie said insincerely.

Sibella stroked the Register. 'It's just that I want things to be perfect,' she muttered. 'It's such a lot to live up to, marrying a Palairet.'

Sophie looked at her. 'But, Sib . . . you do love Eugene, don't you?'

'Of course I do,' she snapped. 'But this is real life, Sophie, not some novel. And it's jolly hard work.'

Can that be true? Sophie wondered. Does one really have to leave it all behind in novels? On the drive over she had asked Madeleine about Sibella's fiancé. 'Fat, self-satisfied, and a little too fond of the tote,' her sister had said. Sibella was the same age as herself, and an heiress at the top of the social tree. She had no need to marry anyone she didn't love. So why on earth was she doing it?

Thinking about that, Sophie went out into the gallery, and found a cup of tea. She turned to look for a seat, and came face to face with the delicate-featured young gentleman from Montpelier.

The sounds of the tea party fell away, and she nearly dropped her cup and saucer. He was startlingly good-looking, with pale blue eyes and chiselled features and fine, silky golden curls.

'I'm afraid you don't know who I am, do you?' he said gently.

She opened her mouth, but couldn't think of anything to say.

He held out his hand. 'Alexander Traherne.'

Awkwardly fielding cup and saucer, she took it. 'Sibella's brother?'

He bowed. 'Guilty as charged.'

She swallowed. 'You've been away, I suppose?'

'Eton. Oxford. The usual round. What about you?'

'Cheltenham Ladies' College.'

'Does that mean you're a frightful blue?'

'Frightful, I'm afraid.'

'Dear me, what a pity. But how odd that we've never met.'

'As it happens,' she said smoothly, 'I saw you yesterday in Montpelier.'

For a moment his smile faltered, but he recovered fast. 'But how fascinating,' he said, 'particularly since I spent the day at the races.'

'Are you sure?'

He laughed. 'Regrettably, yes. I dropped five hundred guineas in the Subscription Plate at Mandeville.'

'Then I wonder who it was that I saw at Montpelier.'

'So do I. Ordinarily I should be loath to suggest that a lady could ever be mistaken. But in this case, I rather fear that you are.' He met her gaze without blinking but she knew that he was lying, and he knew that she knew it, too. 'Oh, look,' he said, with a hint of relief, 'here's Davina, coming to bear you away. If you ever solve the mystery, do let me know.'

'I shall make a point of it,' she said.

She made her excuses to his sister, and passed swiftly through the gallery, and out into the grounds. There were people strolling beneath the pergola, so she walked quickly round to the front of the house, and down a flight of shallow stone steps into the great formal parterre. As she left the shade of the royal palms, the heat hit her like a wall. She didn't care. She needed to be alone. She was beginning to be genuinely angry with her sister. What on earth was she playing at? *Alexander Traherne? God, Maddy. Do you have any idea of the risks you're running?*

The sunlight was so stark that it hurt her eyes. The parterre lay stunned beneath the sun: a joyless formal arrangement of dry grey lavender and small clipped lime trees. To her right, beyond the low stone wall of the parterre, an avenue of copperwoods demarcated the formal gardens from the stables beyond. In front of the stables, on a broad expanse of hard brown grass, a groom was walking a pretty little bay mare back and forth, presumably to cool her down.

Sophie climbed the steps and leaned against the parterre wall to watch. Then she shaded her eyes with her hand and frowned. The groom walking the mare was the same one she'd seen in Montpelier. She recognised the way he moved: that graceful, straight-backed wariness that reminded her of Ben Kelly.

The groom took off his cap and wiped his forehead on his wrist, and she realised that he didn't just remind her of Ben Kelly. He was Ben Kelly. She wasn't even all that surprised. In some way, she had known it was him from that first moment in Montpelier.

It was Ben Kelly—and yet it wasn't. The Ben Kelly she remembered—the image she'd carried around with her—had been a whip-thin street urchin of fourteen or so. The young man she was looking at now must be—what, about twenty-two? Still thin, but clean-shaven, with straight black hair and a sharply handsome but resolutely unsmiling face.

She remembered what Madeleine had said on the verandah when she'd taxed her with seeing him in Montpelier. *Which Ben? Good Heavens. Don't mention that to Cameron, will you?* Madeleine had known it was him all along. And she'd never said a word.

Well, my God, thought Sophie angrily, you shan't wriggle out of it this time, Maddy. And neither shall that simpering Alexander Traherne.

She pushed herself off the wall and took a step forward. 'Hello, Ben,' she said. 'Remember me? Sophie Monroe.'

He did not reply. He just stood there in the blazing sunlight, staring at her. Beside him the little mare playfully nuzzled his shoulder.

'I saw you yesterday,' said Sophie, 'in Montpelier. But you'd gone before I could come across and say hello.'

Still he did not reply. Instead he gave her a slight bow—the perfect groom—and then, to her astonishment, put his cap back on and turned and started leading the mare towards the stables.

'Ben!' she called out sharply. 'Come back here. I need to talk to you.'

But he threw her a glance over his shoulder, and shook his head. Then he walked away. She moved to follow him, but her knee buckled and she had to steady herself on the parterre wall.

Somewhere behind her, a woman tittered. Sophie glanced round and saw Mrs Dampiere standing on the steps by the house, watching her.

And when she turned back to the stables, Ben Kelly had gone.

He thought he was doing all right until he saw Sophie. Second groom at Parnassus, and it's only a matter of time till they put old Danny out to pasture and make him head. Ben Kelly, head groom. That's not bad for starters. Then yesterday he was walking Trouble round to cool her off, and suddenly there she was: Sophie Monroe, but all grown up.

He hasn't thought of her in years. Not once. It's an easy trick to master when you get the hang of it. You just slam the lid down and put your thoughts to something else. Just slam the lid down hard.

At least, he thought that was how it worked. But then yesterday, just for a moment, everything blew wide open, and he was back where it started. Nine years ago, in that photo shop in the Portland Road, with this posh kid in the stripy red pinafore trying to give him a book.

'I thought you might care to have it,' she said, like it was the most natural thing in the world. 'And then you'll be able to read too.'

For the life of him he couldn't work out what she was after. Giving him things? What for? It made him go hot and prickly in his chest.

And yesterday, as she'd stood there in the glare, telling him to come back and talk to her, he'd got that hot prickly tightness again.

Ah, sod it. She'll get over it. What's she expect?

It's still dark, and in the bunkhouse everyone else is fast asleep. He can't stand it no more, so he pulls on his togs, and puts Sophie out of his mind, and goes out to see to his horses.

After he's done his horses, he fetches a bit of sweet hay for Trouble, his favourite, to get her appetite going. What a daft name, Trouble. Whoever called her that didn't know about horses, cos this one wouldn't hurt a fly. She's too busy puzzling out what people want of her, so she can obey them and not get thrashed.

So now she's happily snuffling up the hay, and he's scratching her ears, when all of a sudden she jerks up her head, all startled and worried. It's Master Alex, come for an early ride. Trouble's scared of him.

'Now then, my lad,' he goes, 'saddle her up, there's a good fellow.'

'What, sir?' goes Ben, playing for time.

Master Alex gives an irritated little laugh. 'The mare. Saddle her up. That is, if you have no objection.'

As it happens, Ben does. The thing about Trouble is that somewhere down the line, she had a bad time of it. She was in a right state when she come here: running with lice and scared of her own shadow. Ben worked on her for months. He talked to her all the time, so she'd know he wasn't going to hurt her. And now she has a nice glossy coat and the free step of a really good mover.

Not that Master Alex would know about that, as he hasn't been allowed to ride her yet. Ben's seen to that. The last thing she needs is a heavy-handed idiot like him yanking her about.

'When you're ready, my lad?' goes Master Alex, all sarky. Funny how Ben's always 'my lad', even though they're pretty much of an age.

'Yessir,' goes Ben, tipping his cap. 'It won't take a moment to give her the once-over with a bit of soft soap.'

Master Alex frowns. 'Whatever for?'

'On account of the lice, sir. She's nigh on free of them. But it's always them last little few that do like to hang on.'

Master Alex shoots him a look, like he *thinks* he's being played, but he's not quite sure. At least, not sure enough to risk the lice. So in the end he gets up on Eagle, a big flashy chestnut with no staying power. They're made for each other, them two. Ben bites back a grin as he watches them go.

'Watch youself, bwoy,' says Danny Tulloch on his way to the tack room. 'That likkle mare belong to Master Alex, not you. You run you mouth with him, he put you out the door quick-time.'

Ben shrugs. 'Well, then, I'll watch myself, won't I?'

Danny gives a sour grin and shakes his head.

By now Master Alex is well gone, so Ben slips a head collar on Trouble and gets up on her bareback, and takes her down the beach.

It's all right, the beach. Willow trees and white sand, and that clear water: as clear as gin. When he first come to Jamaica, he used to sleep out here. It was the only place where he could find a bit of peace. Everywhere else got him all twisted up inside.

The trouble was, there was too much of everything. Every kind of fruit you could think of, just growing wild by the side of the road. All the flowers and the coloured parrots, and the warm, clean, spicy-smelling air. It made him think about Kate and Robbie and the others back in London, rotting away in their freezing, muddy graves. It made him feel so bad. That's when he learned to slam the lid down hard.

But Trouble likes the beach. So they have a bit of a gallop. After a bit Ben slips off her back and they take a walk in the sea. He lets go of the reins and she follows him like a dog, giving little snorty blows to tell him she's enjoying herself. And when he jumps back on, she twists round and nibbles his knee. That's horse talk for 'We're mates, you and me', so he returns the favour by finger-nibbling her neck.

The last time he saw Sophie—before she went to England, that is— she was scratching her pony's neck, too. She was out riding with her grandpa, a little ways past Salt Wash. She must've been about fourteen. And she was chattering, of course, and scratching her pony's neck.

She didn't see Ben. He was in a weeding gang in the cane-piece, and she never noticed. Well, why should she? He could've called out to her, but he didn't. What's the point? She's quality and he's not. It's all very well when you're kids, but you don't want to go mixing things up later on.

Madeleine understands that. The other day at Montpelier, they'd glanced at each other, and she'd smiled and said, 'Hello, Ben, you're looking well,' but after that she'd hardly said a word. And she was right. They might've been mates in London, but you can't go mixing things up.

That's what Sophie needs to understand. The way she'd looked at him yesterday. Sort of puzzled, and maybe a bit hurt that he wouldn't stop for a word. But then—oh, how she'd glared at that Mrs Dampiere, when her knee went, and she laughed at her! So she's still got a temper on her, just like the old days.

One time back in London, they were in the kitchen of that Cousin Lettice's, and he was standing by the door, ready to cut the lucky at the first sign of trouble, while Madeleine and Sophie and Robbie were sitting at the table, eating soup. And all of a sudden Sophie twisted round in her chair and hiked up her pinafore dress a few inches, and peeled back her stocking. 'Look, Ben, I've got a bruise.' And she pointed to a tiny pink swelling on the cleanest knee he'd ever seen.

'That's no bruise,' he snarled.

'Yes it jolly well is,' she flashed back.

Oh, she had a temper all right. But the rum thing is, she was also easy to hurt. Like when she give him the picture book and he snapped at her, and for a moment her honey-coloured eyes filled with tears.

So did he hurt her yesterday, when he walked away? Ah, who cares?

He puts Trouble into a canter, and they cross the Coast Road and go up through the gates of Parnassus. The lodges are big stone affairs with blind windows and a Latin motto on the front. *Deus mihi providebit.* Danny's brother Reuben, who's a preacher at Coral Springs, says that means 'God will provide for me'.

Well, that might be true if you're Alexander Traherne or Madeleine Lawe or Sophie Monroe, but it don't mean a thing if you're Ben Kelly. God leaves the Kellys to shift for themselves. So what? It's the way of the world. But the point is, you don't want to go mixing things up.

It's midday when he gets back, and the stable yard's silent and still beneath a hammering sun. Nothing but the red dust shimmering, and the crickets loud in your ears. He gives Trouble a rubdown, and now it's the afternoon, and the ladies are going out calling. They always like Ben to drive, as it adds a bit of class to have a white groom instead of a darkie, so he's got to get all poshed up in his buckskin breeches and top boots, and the tight blue tunic with the high collar.

This afternoon it's just Madam doing the rounds, so he's back in time for tea. Only there's a riding party going out, and four horses wanting tacking up, so no tea. Master Alex and Master Cornelius are taking that Mrs Dampiere up to see Waytes Lake. They've both got the hots for her, and they're dragging Miss Sib along to keep it respectable. But an hour later Master Cornelius is back again, hot and cross. Miss Sib's mare's gone lame. Ben's to take her a fresh horse, and then walk the lame one back.

So off he goes on Samson, heading southwest through the cane-pieces of Waytes Valley, and finds them up at the southern end. He swaps round the saddles and helps Miss Sib up onto Samson. The mare's lame, all right. It'll be a long walk back.

But now the quality are having a squabble. Miss Sib's got a headache and wants to go home, but she don't want 'the groom' taking her, as that'd be too slow; she wants her brother and Mrs Dampiere. Master Alex isn't having any of that, he wants to take Mrs Dampiere to the lake by hisself. Well, he would, wouldn't he?

In the end, of course, Miss Sib wins, and Master Alex has to do the gentlemanly thing and take her back. That's when Mrs Dampiere puts in her oar. 'I'd so set my heart on seeing the lake,' she goes, all apologetic. 'I wonder, Alex dear, could the groom possibly show me the way?'

She's a pretty bit of muslin. Very young, with pale gold hair and grey eyes, and a little soft pink mouth. The sort that always gets their way.

And Master Alex grits his teeth and smiles at her, and says, 'Why, of course.' Then he tells Ben to walk the lame mare up to the house at Waytes Point, pick up a fresh horse, then take the lady on to the lake.

'Yessir,' goes Ben. Like he hasn't thought of that already.

So now they're off to Waytes Point, him and Mrs Dampiere. And pretty soon they've left the lame mare grazing in the paddock, and Ben's up on Gambler, who's only too glad of an outing. Mrs Dampiere rides behind and don't say a word, which is fine by Ben. He's not sure about her. Why did she have to laugh when Sophie nearly took a tumble?

He slams the lid on that, and in half an hour they get to the lake. It's not much of a lake. Just a cut-stone dam to catch the run-off from the hills, with a sheet of stinking green water behind. But Mrs Dampiere don't seem to notice. They stop beneath a clump of trees by the dam, and she tells him to help her down. It's the first thing she's said to him all afternoon.

While he's seeing to the horses, she walks out onto the dam wall. It's smooth underfoot and over a yard wide, but on one side there's a nasty drop into some thorn bushes, and on the other that slimy green water, so he goes after her, to see her all right. Master Cornelius would have his hide if she took a tumble. Halfway along she nearly does, and he offers her his arm, and she takes it without a word. She's wearing a dark blue riding habit and long black gloves with black pearl buttons, and a glossy top hat with a dark blue spotted veil. He can see a wisp of pale gold hair escaping at the nape.

For some reason, that puts him in mind of Sophie when she was a kid. Her hair wasn't fine like Mrs Dampiere's, but thick and coarse like a horse's mane, and strawberry blonde. Only now that she's grown up it's darker, sort of light brown. Apart from that, she hasn't changed much. She never was a beauty, not like Madeleine. She's too skinny, and she looks like trouble. Them straight dark eyebrows, and that mouth of hers. Little shadowy dents at the corners, that get deeper when she's in a sulk. No, she's not a beauty. But she's grown up into the kind of girl that you'd give a second look.

Shut it, he tells himself angrily. You just shut it about Sophie Monroe.

'So this is where you go swimming,' says Mrs Dampiere, cutting across his thoughts.

He shoots her a look. 'I spose some people do, ma'am.'

'But not you?'

'No, ma'am.'

She leans over the edge and studies the water lilies. 'What is your name?' she asks without looking round.

'Kelly, ma'am.'

'Kelly. So you're Irish?'

'My pa was Irish, ma'am.' And may the bastard burn in hell.

'Ah. Your colouring is Irish. So you take after your father?'

'No,' he goes quickly, before he can stop himself.

But she can see that she's got to him, and her mouth twists in a smile. That's when he understands what she's about. It's simple. She's a flirt.

Across the pond, a big blue heron hitches itself off a log and flies away. Mrs Dampiere watches till it's just a speck in the sky. 'They beat their women,' she says without turning round.

'Ma'am?' he goes. It give him a bit of a start.

'The Irish. They beat their women. Or so I understand.' She turns and looks up at him. 'I wonder, Kelly, do you beat yours?'

He stoops and flicks a grass seed off his boot. 'It's time we were starting back, ma'am,' he says. The perfect groom.

She gives him a wry smile. 'Just so, Kelly. Just so.'

So they start back towards the horses, and he's well relieved, because she's acting like nothing's happened. She's pointing out the trees with her riding crop and asking him the names. She says she's new to Jamaica, and it's all a bit unfamiliar.

So of course he goes along with it. 'That's a guango, ma'am.'

'And the one with the feathery leaves?'

'Poinciana. And the one beside it,' he adds on the spur, as he's still narked at her for taking advantage, 'that's a mimosa, ma'am. What the darkies call shame o' lady.'

That makes her laugh. She's got some brass, all right.

When she gets to the shade of the poinciana tree, she stops. He thinks she's waiting for him to fetch her horse, but then she unhooks the little pearl buttons on her glove, and starts drawing it off.

Oh, shit. *Shit.* Not now. Not with Sophie still in his head.

'You know, Kelly,' she says, as she gives each finger a sharp little tug, 'Master Cornelius tells me that you can ride anything. Is that true?'

He don't say nothing. But then, she's not expecting him to.

She drops the first glove in the grass, and then the second, then puts up her veil, unpins her hat and lays it on the ground. 'You don't like to show your feelings, do you, Kelly?'

'I don't have any, ma'am. I'm a groom.'

'Oh, indeed? No feelings? I don't believe you.'

He clears his throat. 'I'll fetch your horse, ma'am. We should—'

'If you don't do as I say,' she cuts in, 'I shall tell Master Cornelius that you were impertinent. I shall have you dismissed.'

For two pins he'd say to her, 'Well go on then.' But why should he let her get him sacked? Besides, if he left Parnassus, who'd look after Trouble? Anyway, why is he hesitating? It's not as if he don't know how.

She comes up close to him, smiling, then puts up her hand and unfastens the top button of his tunic. Her nails scratch his throat, and he flinches.

Her smile widens. 'Don't worry. I'm not going to hurt you. Although I'm very much hoping that you'll hurt me.'

The thing about Ben Kelly was that he had never lied to her. He had been scornful and harsh, and once he'd nearly made her cry. But he had never lied. 'What's the bloody point?' he would have said if she had asked. 'If you can't take the truth, that's your lookout.'

The first time they met was in London in 1894, at the photography studio in the Portland Road where Maddy did a little ladylike helping out. Early one foggy March morning she had taken Sophie along with her for a tenth-birthday treat, and they stumbled upon two unbelievably filthy urchins looking for something to steal.

Neither Sophie nor Madeleine had ever met an urchin before. So instead of summoning a policeman, Maddy grabbed a wooden rifle from the props shelf and cried, 'Stop, thief!', with what Sophie thought was incredible presence of mind. And as neither boy could tell a real gun from a fake, they froze like cornered animals.

'What have you got in your pockets?' snapped Maddy, looking fierce.

With grim obedience the urchins emptied their pockets, and several rotten apples and a pear thudded wetly onto the counter.

The girls were astonished. Every week Mr Rennard, the studio proprietor, bought a bowl of fruit in case any of his sitters needed livening up with what he called 'a bit of background'. But this week he hadn't got round to replacing it.

'What were you going to do with those?' said Maddy, voicing the question in Sophie's mind.

'Eat them,' snapped the older boy, as if she'd said something idiotic. 'Whatcha think?'

'But they're rotten,' said Maddy. 'We were going to throw them away.'

'Shows how much you know,' he muttered.

Sophie was captivated. She had never met anyone like him. In fact, she hadn't met too many people at all, because Cousin Lettice didn't allow them to mix with company. And of course the Poor were doubly out of bounds, since they lacked moral fibre and harboured disease.

He said his name was Ben Kelly, and his brother's name was Robbie, and he spat out his answers in a voice sharp with scorn, for he knew that he'd seen more of the world than they.

Sophie caught her breath and tried not to stare. He was grey with dirt and he smelt like a sewer rat, but for her that only heightened his glamour. Then she noticed his eyes. She had never seen anyone with green eyes. He was like some kind of exotic and perilous birthday present.

She could tell that he was older than her, but to her amazement he didn't know *how* old, and he didn't seem to care. 'I dunno,' he said with a shrug. 'Thirteen? What's it to you?'

But what does he do about birthdays? she wondered.

She felt sorry for Robbie, who was a hunchback, but she never felt sorry for Ben. Right from the start she just wanted to be his friend.

So to get his attention, she plucked up her courage and decided to show him her new book. 'It was my birthday last week,' she said, speaking quickly, as she always did when she was nervous. 'I didn't have a party, as we don't know anyone. That's why it's so nice to meet you—'

'Sophie—' muttered Maddy with an admonitory glance.

'But Maddy gave me *Black Beauty*,' she went on, throwing her sister a beseeching look, 'and it's absolutely wonderful, I've read it twice already.' She put it on the counter and pushed it over to where he could see it.

He glanced at the calfskin binding. Then his eyes returned for a closer look. She felt a thrill of triumph as she watched him put out one grimy forefinger and trace the gilded curve of the horse's neck. Then he caught her watching him, and his face closed. 'So you can read. So what?'

She blinked. 'But . . . everyone can read.'

She noticed that Maddy was shaking her head and giving her that lopsided grin which meant 'Oh, Sophie, really!' and she suddenly perceived her mistake. She was appalled. It had never occurred to her that there might be people who couldn't read.

'I'm most awfully sorry,' she said earnestly. 'I didn't mean . . . um . . . can't you read?'

'I know my letters,' he snapped. It was the closest that he ever got to telling her a lie. She found out later that he had gone to school only once, for a couple of weeks when they were giving out soup tickets. And because he was clever, he had picked up most of the letters, although he hadn't yet learned how to string them together into words.

At the time, though, she didn't know any of that. 'Maddy keeps a few books for the clients' children,' she said, running to the drawer behind the counter and giving her sister a questioning look.

Maddy nodded, hefting the gun on her hip.

'It's to keep them amused,' Sophie went on breathlessly. She glanced at him over her shoulder, met his narrow, unsmiling gaze and turned back to the drawer in confusion. 'I thought you might care to have one,' she went on. 'It's about a cavalry horse in the Crimean War. I thought you might enjoy it.'

She thought he would be pleased, or perhaps even a little grateful. Instead he glanced from her to the picture book with scowling incomprehension. His face worked as if she had flung him a deadly insult. 'Not going to read it, am I?' he snarled as he snatched it from her hand. 'Going to sell it, that's what.'

She thought she must have misunderstood. She tried to smile, and told him that when he had finished this book, he could come back and she would give him another. But to her horror, that only made things worse. 'You cracked or what? Why would I come back?'

By this time she was blinking back tears.

Luckily that was when Maddy stepped in and glared at Ben, and he backed down, and Sophie's self-respect was saved. A moment later he muttered, 'Come on, Robbie, time we was off,' and they left.

Sophie stood at the door swallowing tears as she watched them disappear into the fog. She didn't understand what she had done wrong.

It was only later that she realised that he simply hadn't known how else to react. He was like a dog who has experienced nothing but beatings, and can only snarl when someone offers it a bone.

She thought that she would never see him again, but a few months later he came back. It was just after Cousin Lettice's husband had died and left them bankrupt. Madeleine had explained that bankrupt meant extremely poor—at least, poor by Cousin Lettice's standards, for they had to dismiss Cook, and have their clothes dyed black instead of buying new ones. But it didn't mean poor like Ben and Robbie. Even Sophie understood that.

It was a hot, sticky day in August. Cousin Lettice had gone to lie down, and Sophie and Madeleine were in the kitchen making lunch. Suddenly the basement door opened, and there they were.

Sophie's heart swelled painfully. 'Maddy, look! It's Ben and Robbie!'

It turned out that he'd heard about Cousin Septimus 'popping his clogs and going all to smash', and found out where they lived by 'asking around', and just dropped by 'to see what was what'.

Maddy darted him a cool look and told him to shut the door, so it fell to Sophie to make them welcome. 'Can I show them into the morning room?' she begged her sister.

Maddy vetoed the idea of the morning room on the grounds that they would only steal things. Sophie thought that shockingly rude, but Ben didn't seem to mind at all. In fact, he shot Maddy a sharp, feral grin and said with approval, 'Now you're learning.'

Sophie was determined that this time she wouldn't offend him. So when Maddy asked her to lay the table, she didn't even look at him as she went to the dresser and fetched four of everything and set it on the table. Yes, he could have some soup if he wanted—but it was entirely up to him. Nobody would say a word about it either way.

Maddy poured out four bowls of soup and set them on the table, but when she, Robbie and Sophie sat down, Ben remained by the door. Ten minutes later he was still leaning there, so Sophie decided to take matters into her own hands. 'Look, Ben,' she said, 'I've got a bruise. I fell down the steps and banged my knee.'

'Sophie . . .' mumbled Madeleine through a mouthful of soup.

Sophie ignored her. Greatly daring, she twisted round in her chair and peeled back her stocking to show him.

He snorted. 'That's no bruise.'

'Yes it jolly well is,' she snapped, 'and it hurts, too.'

She was furious with herself for flaring up, but to her astonishment he merely gave a harsh bark of laughter. Then he sidled over and sat down, and worked his way with frowning concentration through three bowls of soup. She felt a glow of triumph. She had got him to the table.

They talked a little about their respective parents, and established that both sets of fathers and mothers were dead. Well, that's a point in common, thought Sophie happily.

Then Robbie lifted his head from his bowl long enough to recite one of his by-rote narratives. 'Ma had red hair like me, but Pa's was black like Ben's, and Pa knocked her about so she died. Then Ben took me away and Pa died too and Ben said good riddance. Ma used to send us hop-picking, that's why Ben's so strong, but I had to stop home on account of I was too little. And we had two whole rooms in East Street and a separate bed for the kids, and every Sunday Ben had to fetch the dinner from the bakehouse, brisket and batter pudding and spuds.'

Sophie was fascinated. Only two rooms? And from the sound of it, they hadn't had a kitchen of their own. She wanted to ask questions, but Ben cuffed Robbie around the head and told him to belt up, and Robbie grinned and did as he was told. That fascinated her, too. Ben was like a sheepdog with his brother: making him do what he wanted and snapping at him if he didn't, but also fiercely protective.

Maddy was a little like that with her, although without the cuffing. So when they finished the soup and Maddy told Sophie to take Robbie out and show him the garden, she didn't hesitate, although she desperately wanted to stay behind with Ben. How was she to know that Maddy was going to mess things up, and give him the book, *The Downfall of the Dervishes*, which Sophie herself had picked out weeks ago and bought with her own personal money, in case he ever came back?

She was outside with Robbie, showing him Cousin Lettice's potted ferns, when they heard Ben yelling angrily. 'Rob, look sharp! We're off!'

Robbie jammed on his cap and scuttled inside, and by the time Sophie reached the kitchen they were both on their way out—Ben with a face like thunder, *The Downfall of the Dervishes* tucked under his arm.

Sophie was incandescent. '*I* was going to give it to him!' she shouted at her sister when they'd gone. '*I* bought it, it was *my* present!'

'I'm sorry,' said Maddy. 'I forgot.'

'What did you say to him to make him go off like that?'

'Nothing,' said Maddy. 'We were just talking about how to make money. And . . . things like that.' Maddy could be infuriatingly secretive.

For weeks afterwards, Sophie loitered in the kitchen, on the offchance that Ben would come back. But he never returned. Then, suddenly, she fell ill. The small pink bump on her knee turned into a painful swelling. She became feverish at night, and floppy and tired in the mornings. Finally the doctor was called, and he prodded her knee, and pronounced the dreaded word.

'The condition first makes its appearance,' said the medical book which Maddy borrowed from Mudie's library, 'with a slight lesion such as a knock or contusion, into which the tuberculosis bacilli are thought to gain entry to the organism.' The organism. That meant her.

Her world shrank to her bedroom.

Cousin Lettice was outraged that any 'charge' of hers should have fallen so shamefully ill. Maddy became secretive and anxious. She saw Ben Kelly a couple of times more—without Sophie, of course—and, under questioning, she admitted that she'd told him about the TB.

Sophie was furious. Then, when he failed to come and see her, in despair. She knew it was because of the TB. He was never coming back.

But she never stopped hoping that he might.

She wrote about him in a secret code in her journal. She debated how she would behave if she saw him again: whether she would be angry and aloof, or just pretend not to have noticed that he'd ever been away.

Of course when it finally happened, she was neither.

It was July 1895, and they'd been living at Fever Hill for just over eight months, when one day Maddy suggested—in a voice that brooked no opposition—that Sophie should take a little drive with Jocelyn to Falmouth, 'for a change of air'.

The truth was that Maddy was worried about her. They all were. Although her health had improved when they had first arrived in Jamaica, over the past few weeks she had been getting steadily worse. And no one knew that better than herself. She had become horribly thin and yellow, and so weak that when she practised walking with the hated splint and the calliper on the other leg to even up the lengths, she hardly had the strength to manipulate her crutches.

It was market day in Falmouth, and the square was heaving with people as she sat on the bench on the courthouse verandah and waited for Jocelyn to come and collect her. It was a noisy, colourful sight: the cassia trees dripping with great festoons of yellow blossom, the Negro ladies raucous and brilliant in their green, mauve and orange print gowns. Sophie hardly saw any of it. She felt anxious and alone.

Things at Fever Hill were going from bad to worse. Maddy had become unhappy and withdrawn, and wouldn't tell her why. The house was full of whispers; they were surrounded by illness and death. A duppy tree had stolen her shadow and she was going to die.

There was no one she could talk to. She couldn't tell the old people like Jocelyn and Great-Aunt May, and Clemency. And worst of all, Maddy had become unapproachable; she seemed to have too many dark secrets of her own to be able to spare time for Sophie's.

There was absolutely nobody to help.

Then, suddenly, through a haze of red dust at the other end of the square, there was Ben. *Her* Ben, from London. It wasn't possible that he could be here in Jamaica . . . After the initial shock she struggled to her feet and yelled his name. 'Ben! Ben! Over here!' She waved her sunhat so wildly that she nearly overbalanced on her crutches.

After what seemed like an age, he finally heard her, and stopped dead. No smile. Just a sudden wary stillness as he spotted her.

She scarcely noticed. She was too busy laughing and crying and shouting his name. As she watched him shoulder his way through the crowd towards her, she saw how he had changed. He was taller and stronger— she later learned that he had worked his passage to Jamaica on a sugar boat—and most noticeable of all, he was clean. His black hair was glossy, his skin lightly tanned, and he wore blue dungarees and a calico shirt.

'What's up, Sophie?' he said as he jumped up onto the verandah. He took off his straw hat and sat down at the other end of the bench. Then he threw her a questioning look, as if he had seen her only the day before.

She sat down clumsily, scattering her crutches. 'You've grown so tall and brown,' she gabbled, 'and you've got new clothes, and . . . .'

'And I don't pong no more,' he said, flashing his feral grin and rescuing the crutches.

She gave a self-conscious laugh.

'And look at you,' he said. Then his grin faded. She could tell that he was trying to think up something else to say, but couldn't, because she looked so awful, and he wouldn't lie to her.

She smoothed her skirt over her knees. 'I thought I'd never see you again,' she said. 'You never came to say goodbye.'

'Couldn't,' he said. 'Bluebottles were after me.'

'Bluebott—? Oh, you mean policemen.' She decided not to ask what kind of trouble he'd been in. It was enough to know that he hadn't kept away because of her illness.

'Where's Robbie?' she asked.

He sucked in his breath like a wince. 'He's not here,' he muttered.

Then she knew. Dead, she thought. Poor Robbie. Poor Ben. She wondered how he had died, and if she would meet him when she went to heaven herself. These days, she thought about dying a lot.

'Oh, B-Ben,' she stammered, 'I'm so glad you're here.' Then she burst into tears.

She cried for what seemed like ages: great noisy hiccupy sobs. Through the sobs she felt him briefly touch her arm, then brush off her sleeve as if he had made her dusty. 'What's up, Sophie?' he said brusquely.

Then out it all came. The tension at Fever Hill. The terror of the duppy trees. Her dragging conviction that she was going to die.

To her relief he simply listened without interrupting. Then he sat for a moment in silence. 'Right,' he said flatly. 'You leave it to me. I'll sort it out. But you got to do your bit. All right?'

She nodded, and shakily blew her nose. 'What . . . what do I do?'

'You don't say nothing to nobody, you stop fretting, and you start getting better.'

And somehow, knowing that he was in Jamaica, she had. From that day her appetite came back, and she slept peacefully for the first time in weeks. But she never saw him again. Once more he had dropped out of sight.

At least, he had until now.

CHAPTER TWO

'SOPHIE, WHAT DO YOU think you're doing?' asked Madeleine as she watched her sister drawing on her gloves.

'I'd have thought that was obvious,' replied Sophie. 'I'm going out to make a call.' She put on her hat and jammed a hatpin into the crown.

'But you hate making calls. And yet suddenly you can't stay away from Parnassus.'

'I'm not going to Parnassus.'

'You know what I mean. The only reason you're going to Fever Hill is because it's Sibella's day to call on Clemency, and . . .'

'And I can see Sibella as well as Clemmy,' put in Sophie. 'Precisely. Two birds with one stone.'

'Don't you mean three?'

Sophie did not reply. Since the Trahernes' tea party she had veered between anger at the risks Madeleine was running, and frustration that she was being kept in the dark. But she hadn't confronted her sister over Alexander Traherne. What was the point? She'd only deny everything.

No, the only way to get at the truth was to corner Ben and make *him* tell. He had never lied to her in the past, and she was fairly sure that he wouldn't now.

'You don't need to go to Fever Hill to see Sibella,' said Madeleine. 'You'll be seeing her in a few days at the Historical Society picnic.'

'But Clemency won't be there, will she?' Sophie said sweetly. 'And I really ought to see her, oughtn't I?'

Madeleine sighed. 'Well, whatever you do,' she said quietly, 'don't make trouble for Ben. It wouldn't be fair.'

Sophie paused with another hatpin in her hand and looked at her in surprise. 'So you admit that he's at Parnassus?'

'Well, of course. He's been there for nearly two years.'

'But . . . Maddy. Why did you never tell me before?'

'Sophie—'

'He was my friend.'

'That's precisely why I didn't tell you.' Frowning, she picked at the lacquer on the looking-glass frame. 'Listen, Sophie. You had a schoolgirl crush when you were little—'

'I did not,' said Sophie indignantly.

'But things are different now. You're no longer a child. You can't go around making a spectacle of yourself like you did at Parnassus.'

'I didn't,' muttered Sophie without much conviction.

'Yes, you did. Sibella saw you, and so did that house guest of Rebecca's, and half the staff.'

'I wouldn't have needed to "make a spectacle of myself",' she replied, 'if you'd been more open with me.'

They met each other's eyes in the glass. 'Why can't you have a little faith in me?' said Madeleine. 'Why can't you just let things be?'

'How can I? If I see something going wrong, how can I just stand by and "let it be"?'

Madeleine opened her mouth to reply, then shook her head. 'You always do this. You get hold of something and you just will not let go.'

She's treating you like a child, Sophie told herself angrily as she crossed the bridge at Romilly and drove north along the Eden Road. Keeping you in the dark as if you're not ready to handle the truth. It was horrible to feel so angry with her own sister. But she couldn't help it.

In the dog cart beside her, Fraser whistled tunelessly through his teeth, happily unaware that he had been brought along as a pretext. Once they reached the house and found Sibella safely ensconced with Clemency, Sophie intended to take him down to the stables 'to see the horses'.

At the big guango tree she turned left onto Fever Hill land and headed west through the cane-pieces of Bellevue. Two miles in, the track veered north, and followed the trickle of the Green River, until presently the great house loomed up ahead: huge, shuttered and lonely on its bare brown hill.

She felt a twinge of guilt about Clemency. It was hardly fair to call on her simply as an excuse for questioning Ben. Clemency deserved better than that. And she needed help. 'She hasn't been off the estate in years,' Cameron had told her the night before. 'Scarcely eats a thing—except for laudanum, of course. She mixes it with pimento dram to hide the taste. Try to make her see sense and come and live with us.' As a sop to her conscience, Sophie had resolved to do just that.

But to her frustration there was no one about when they drew up at the steps. No sign of Sibella's pretty little buggy, or of Clemency and her niece taking tea in the gallery.

Fraser sucked in his lips importantly, and jumped down and ran to the horse's head. 'Shall I take the carriage down to the stables?'

'Just tie it up here,' murmured Sophie, gazing up at the blank, shuttered façade. Her anger had drained away, leaving only self-doubt. Perhaps Maddy was right. Perhaps she shouldn't interfere.

Dead leaves rattled sadly across the steps as they climbed to the gallery. It was empty and dim, and smelt of desolation and decay. The floor was soft with dust, the cane furniture mildewed and broken. On the side table, next to a battered paraffin lamp, stood a gleaming silver frame containing the familiar funeral photograph.

'Clemency?' called Sophie. Her voice echoed through the shadowy house. 'Clemmy?'

No answer. She felt a curious reluctance to go inside. It had always been a strange house: a place of shadows and whispers, turned in upon itself. In his last years Jocelyn had hardly moved from his library, while his ancient aunt, known to all the family as Great-Aunt May, had lived in implacable isolation in the upper gallery, and Clemency flitted between her rooms and the family burying-place.

But now Jocelyn was dead, and Great-Aunt May was living in a town house in Falmouth. Only Clemency remained, attended by Evie's mother, Grace McFarlane, who made the daily climb from her home in the old ruined slave village at the bottom of the hill.

Fraser kicked the dust with the toe of his boot. 'Aunt Clemmy will probably be at the burying-place. That's where she has her tea.'

'But I cannot possibly leave,' whispered Clemency, handing Sophie her cup and fluttering her hands at the dead. 'How could I leave all this?'

Once again Sophie bit back her frustration. They had found Clemency alone, sitting on the bench beneath the poinciana tree that shaded the graves. There was no sign of Sibella. When Sophie asked if she was expected, the older woman simply looked blank.

'Sometimes Miss Traherne comes later,' offered Fraser. Then he ran off to set out his toy soldiers on a tombstone.

Sophie hoped he was right. Stifling her impatience, she turned back to Clemency, and grimly resolved to do her duty. 'You'd love it at Eden,' she said, 'and the children would adore to have you with them.'

But to her astonishment, Clemency's china-blue eyes widened with alarm. 'Oh, hush! You'll make Elliot feel left out!'

Sophie hesitated. 'Clemmy, darling. Elliot has been dead for twenty-nine years.' Clemency's son had died in 1873, two days after he was born.

'*Hush!*' whispered Clemency again, as if the inhabitant of the little white marble tomb might hear and be offended. 'I am very well aware of that, Sophie. But I fail to see that it signifies.'

Sophie put her teacup back on the tray and tried again. 'You'd only be an hour's ride away. You could come here every day, if you wished.'

'It wouldn't be the same,' said Clemency. She took a little flask of pimento dram from her pocket, poured a measure into her cup and drank it down, giving Sophie her wincing, apologetic smile.

Sophie forced herself to smile back. As always with Clemency, she felt a twinge of vicarious guilt. This submissive yet stubborn woman had once been married to her father. Married, and then deserted for Rose Durrant.

Clemency had never uttered a word of reproach. Indeed it was doubtful she even remembered that she'd had a husband, for she had married only because her brother Cornelius had told her to. The defining event of her life had not been her husband's desertion but the death of her child. For nearly thirty years she had worn nothing but white mourning. And when her hair had failed to turn white from grief, she had simply dyed it grey.

Sophie stirred her tea and fought the downturn in her spirits that this place always brought about. Her grandfather Jocelyn lay close by, reunited after five lonely decades with his adored young wife Kitty. And her father Ainsley lay beneath the low slate slab on which Fraser now paraded his lead hussars. Her father, who had left a trail of ruined lives: an unwelcome reminder of the risks that Madeleine was running.

'Oh, look,' said Fraser, glancing up, 'here's Miss Traherne.'

Thank God, thought Sophie. She got to her feet and gave Clemency a brisk smile. 'I've just remembered, I promised Fraser I'd take him to see the horses. Do you mind? I'll be back very soon.'

Her heart was beating uncomfortably fast as they crossed the hard brown lawns and started down the croton walk towards the stables. Fraser raced ahead like a puppy, doubling back every so often to make sure that she was following.

'You'll never guess who's in the stable yard,' he told her breathlessly as he tugged at her hand to make her go faster. '*Evie!* She can make animals out of cane-trash. She made a giraffe for my birthday.'

Oh no, thought Sophie. She wanted to see Evie again, but not here. Not now, when she needed to talk to Ben.

Apprehensively, she emerged from the croton walk into the glare of the stable yard. At the far side she could see Sibella's little buggy. Beside it, Ben, hatless and in shirtsleeves, was setting down a pail of water for the horse. On the seat of the buggy sat a coloured girl in a pink print dress, chatting to him and swinging her legs.

Fraser raced across the yard, and Evie turned and smiled down at him. Then she saw Sophie, and said a word to Ben. He straightened up, wiped his hands on his breeches and threw Sophie a wary, unsmiling look.

She felt horribly self-conscious as she walked towards them across the yard. It was a struggle not to limp. 'Hello, Ben,' she said with as much ease as she could muster. 'Hello, Evie. It's good to see you again.'

Out of the corner of her eye, she saw Ben roll down his shirtsleeves and reach for his tunic and cap. He did not respond to her greeting.

'Hello, Sophie,' murmured the coloured girl with a shy smile. 'It's good to see you, too.'

As a child, Sophie had always been a little in awe of Evie, who, apart from being a year older, had been prettier and healthier, and had a mother who was a witch. Now Sophie saw that the child had grown into a breathtakingly beautiful young woman. She had dark, almond-shaped eyes with an almost oriental slant, chiselled features and flawless, coffee-coloured skin. Sophie felt overdressed in her fussy, unflattering gown.

She turned her head and nodded at Ben in what she hoped was a friendly manner. He nodded back, but didn't meet her eyes. In the old days, Ben would have flashed her his feral grin and said, 'What's up, Sophie?' But this wasn't the old days.

Hating herself for her cowardice, she turned back to Evie. 'I was wondering when we'd bump into each other,' she said brightly. 'I didn't know that you'd taken a position at Fever Hill.'

'I haven't,' replied Evie in her soft Creole accent. 'I teach school over at Coral Springs.'

She was too polite to show offence at being mistaken for a maid, but Sophie's cheeks burned. Evie had always been bright and ambitious. How could she have made such a blunder?

But Evie good-naturedly smoothed things over by telling her about the teacher's dissertation on local history that she was writing.

'My grandfather had lots of old estate papers,' Sophie said quickly, to make amends. 'You must make use of the library whenever you like.'

Evie thanked her, but they both knew that she never would.

How pompous I sound, thought Sophie. The white lady bountiful patronising the coloured girl. She summoned what remained of her courage and turned to Ben. 'Hello, Ben,' she said. Then she remembered that she'd already greeted him.

He tipped his cap to her with wary respect. 'Is it about the horse, miss?' he muttered, looking at the ground.

'The horse?'

'Your horse, miss. He's still out front. I took him a pail of water, but were you wanting me to bring him down here?' He still wasn't meeting her eyes, and his face wore a determined look, as if he'd worked out beforehand how he would behave.

'Um . . . no. No, thank you, that's quite all right.' She bit her lip. 'Ben . . . I'm sorry if I embarrassed you the other day. I mean, at Parnassus.'

'You didn't, miss,' he muttered. 'And . . . it's Kelly, miss. Not Ben. Better like that, if you understand.'

Again she felt herself colouring. So that's how it's to be, she thought. Madeleine was right after all. Things are different now.

'Just as you wish,' she said. 'Well, I won't take up too much of your time; I just needed to ask you something. I think I saw you in Montpelier. On Monday?'

He frowned at his boots. 'I don't remember, miss.'

Oh, no, she thought with a sinking heart. Not you too. 'Are you sure?' He nodded.

There was another awkward silence. Evie sat in the buggy, studying her shoes. Ben turned his cap in his hands and frowned.

Sophie wondered why she had come. What was she doing here?

What could she possibly achieve, except to make everyone, including herself, supremely uncomfortable?

It was Fraser who came to her rescue. Perhaps sensing that something was wrong, he moved across and took her hand and looked up at her and smiled: a small tow-headed ally in a sailor suit.

She felt a rush of gratitude. 'Well,' she said, looking down into his big grey eyes, 'Fraser and I must be getting back. Goodbye, Evie, And good luck with your dissertation. Goodbye . . . Kelly.'

'Goodbye, Sophie,' said Evie, with her shy smile.

'Miss,' said Ben with a nod.

The croton walk seemed endless, and she knew that she limped. She could feel their eyes on her all the way.

But when she glanced back, she saw with a pang that Ben was bending down under the horse's belly to adjust its harness. Only Evie was looking after them, with a curiously intent expression on her lovely face.

Night's coming down quick at the old slave village, and Evie's sitting out on the step, eating fufu with her mother, and trying to keep the black uneasiness from creeping into her heart. Mosquitoes are humming, the crickets and the whistling frogs are starting up their night song, and Patoo's going hoo-hoo up in the calabash tree. Evie shivers. Sophie's in trouble, or she will be soon. What that trouble is, or when it will come, Evie doesn't know. But she's seen the sign. It always starts the same way. A sudden rush of sweet-sweet smell, then the cold fear creeping down the back of her neck. A spirit looks just like a regular person but you always know that it's dead. It's got no sound to it, and the wind never lifts a hair of its head. It's in the wrong time and the wrong world. And for a while, when she sees it, Evie's in that world too.

Like the time when she was twelve, and saw blind old grandmother Semanthe, who'd died when she was little, sitting by the hearth, as sharp as sin. Two weeks after that, Evie's brother died. For years she blamed herself. Maybe if she'd told, he would have lived. But how was she to know that nana Semanthe had meant it for a warning?

And last month she'd seen a spirit-girl standing behind Ben. A thin, sad spirit-girl with red hair and blue shadows under her eyes, just standing there. Evie hasn't told Ben yet. What good would it do, since she doesn't know what it means? Thinking on that, she gets up quickly and starts off into the dark, moving noiselessly between the tumble-down slave houses mounded over with creepers. All the houses are ruined, except for theirs. They're the only ones who live here. Apart from the duppies. Halfway between the gates to the Fever Hill Road and the busha house up on the hill. That's my home, she thinks in disgust. A halfway place for a halfway girl who's neither black nor white.

She reaches the old aqueduct at the edge of the village, and curls up on the ancient cut-stone wall. When they were children, she and Sophie used to come down here looking for treasure: for one of the big jars of Spanish gold that the nanas say got lost from ages back. Of course they never found one. But once they found a little calabash baby rattle from slave time. They tossed for who should keep it, and Sophie won. She was always the lucky one. It's no different now.

Evie stretches out her legs and studies her brown canvas shoes with dislike. This afternoon at the stables, Sophie looked so pretty and fine in that beautiful flounced dress, with those lovely high-heeled shoes with the little pearl buttons on the straps.

Jealousy curdles within her. *How are you, Evie? I didn't know that you'd taken a position here.* As if Evie's some kind of maid!

The truth is, it wasn't Sophie's fault. She meant no harm, and she was mortified by her mistake. It's Evie McFarlane who's got this black, uneasy confusion in her heart. There's trouble coming for Ben because of that red-haired spirit-girl. And some kind of trouble for Sophie, too. But how bad? And when? And what should she do?

Maybe she should talk to Ben. She can tell him most things, for he's like a brother to her; sometimes she even calls him her 'buckra brother'.

Thinking of that, she brings out the little bag on the cord at her neck. Not the guard with the piece of her caul inside, but the other one: the silk bag that she calls her 'buckra charm', for it contains the gold chain that she can never openly wear. If she did, her mother would ask questions, and the man who gave it her would know that he can have her.

But she's no fool, is Evie McFarlane. He's had no kisses from her, and no hand's play, either. She's a decent girl and she knows her worth.

And yet . . . sometimes it feels good just to take out the fine gold chain and pour it from palm to palm, and remember that she only has to crook her finger at him, and everything will change. No more slave village. No more fufu out in the yard. And best of all, no more four-eyed nonsense. No more dead-bury spirits walking about under the sun.

Because all that four-eyed talk is just so much cane-trash, Evie, it's just so much trash. You're not four-eyed. You've got no spirit-sight. You never saw nana Semanthe sitting out on the step, or the red-haired spirit-girl standing behind Ben.

And you did *not*, this afternoon at the stables, see old Master Jocelyn following Sophie up the croton walk, stooping a little and leaning on his silver-topped cane, like he always did before he died.

Sophie always was pretty bad at hiding her feelings. So when she ran into a spot of bother it wasn't long before all Trelawny knew. Including Ben.

Moses Parker and his niece Poppy heard it first, up at Eden. They told their cousins the McFarlanes down at Fever Hill, and they told *their* cousins, Danny and Hannibal Tulloch, at Parnassus. And on to Ben.

It turns out that Miss Sibella saw Sophie chatting to Evie in the stable yard, and then 'had a quiet word' with her about getting too familiar with the coloureds. Sophie didn't take too kindly to that. In fact, the very same afternoon she rode over to see that Dr Mallory at his darkie clinic at Bethlehem, and started helping out.

That was a week ago, and since then things have been limping along quietly enough. But today it's the Historical Society picnic, and it looks like the ladies are ganging up on Sophie again.

The picnic's a big posh charity affair with a lunch and tea. This year, Master Cornelius is the host, so it's no expense spared. Huge stripy marquee and a band, and all sorts of fancy nosh. The only thing is, it's up at Waytes Lake. Not Ben's favourite place. The last time he was here was with Mrs Dampiere. He can see her now, talking to Master Cornelius. She catches his eye and tries not to smile. She thinks it's funny. Ben don't. He feels like everybody's watching him, like everybody knows. And it only makes it worse that Madeleine and Sophie are here too.

So now it's tea-time, and Madeleine's off by the lake talking to Master Alex, and Sophie's sitting in the marquee with Miss Sibella and old Mrs Pitcaithley and Mrs Herapath, and that's when they start in on her about the clinic. All very ladylike and polite and 'for her own good', but still having a go. Hannibal Tulloch's on serving duty, and hears it all. Though why he thinks Ben cares one way or the other is anybody's guess.

But still. He takes a little walk past the doorway, to see what's what. And when he does, he gets a surprise. He'd expected her just to be a bit narked. After all, she's not the sort to be fazed by a telling off. But when he sees her she's sitting by the tea urn, all alone, and with that look on her face that she gets when she's trying not to show she's upset. It puts him in mind of when she was a kid, and she give him the picture book and he went for her. It puts him in mind of the other day at Fever Hill.

A while later, he's standing by the carriage with Trouble when he sees her again. Master Alex and Madeleine are still by the lake, and she's making straight for them, very determined. Up she goes to Master Alex—not a glance at her sister—and draws him aside and starts talking to him, all sweetness, but very, very firm. To begin with, Master Alex is looking down at her and smiling, the perfect gentleman, then his smile fades, like he's just had a nasty surprise. Then he looks over at Ben.

Shit, thinks Ben as he watches them coming towards him. What's she gone and said to him?

'It seems that Miss Monroe has hurt her wrist,' goes Master Alex, looking a bit pink about the cheeks. 'You're to drive her home at once.'

Ben shoots Sophie a look, but she's turned away, very composed. What's her game? Her wrist was fine ten minutes ago when she was pouring the tea. He scratches round for an excuse. 'Trouble didn't ought to be pulling a carriage in the first place,' he tells Master Alex, 'let alone traipsing all the way up to Eden and back.'

Master Alex raises an eyebrow. 'I think, my lad, that you may safely leave me to make the decisions.'

For a moment, Ben meets the pale blue eyes. He can tell that Master Alex isn't best pleased about it neither, but for some reason he's going along with it. Maybe Sophie said a word to him about what she saw at Montpelier, to persuade him to toe the line. She's not stupid, is Sophie.

So Ben heaves a sigh and tips his cap at Master Alex, and jumps up into the driver's seat and stares stonily ahead.

So now it's been twenty minutes since they set off, and she still hasn't said a word, but he's buggered if he'll be the first to speak. He didn't ask to drive her home. They come out of Waytes Valley onto the Fever Hill Road, and that's when he realises that he'll *have* to speak first, to ask her which way she wants to go. Oh, bugger. *Bugger.*

He tips his cap and turns his head sideways. 'D'you want to go by town, miss, or cut through Fever Hill?'

'Fever Hill,' she replies. 'That is, if you think you can find your way.'

He sets his teeth. He can find his way blindfold, as she well knows. What's her game? Is she needling him because he give her a time of it at Fever Hill? Well, what's she expect? She's grown up now, and a lady. It's not her place to talk to grooms.

So after a quarter of a mile they turn into the Fever Hill carriageway. They go up through the cane-pieces of Alice Grove, and past the old ruined sugar works that got burnt in the Rebellion, past the slave village where Evie lives, and the tumbledown aqueduct. They skirt the bottom of the hill and the great house stables, then go across the trickle of the Green River and out into the cane-pieces of Bellevue. It's a hot afternoon for the beginning of December, and everything's breathless and still. Even the crickets are half asleep. All he can hear is the clip-clopping hoofs and the creak of the carriage, and the blood thumping in his ears.

They start down the slope towards the bridge over the Martha Brae, This time of year the river's a sluggish, muddy green and he catches the familiar smell of greenstuff and rottenness. The bridge is soft with moss, and over on the other side he can see the ruins at the edge of Eden. Only a couple more miles, he thinks with relief.

It's a rum old place, the ruins at Romilly. Tumbledown walls tangled over with strangler fig. And in among the creepers, these strange little twisted mauvy-white flowers. Evie says they're orchids. All Ben knows is that they've got a thick, sweet scent that makes him think of graves. The darkies say that years back Romilly was some kind of slave village like the one at Fever Hill. That's why they don't come here, on account of all the duppies. When Ben was a lad he used to sleep out here. Darkie ghosts? What are they to him? He's got a packload of ghosts of his own.

'When you get across the bridge,' says Sophie, making him jump, 'just pull up on the other side.'

What? Christ. What's she up to now?

He gives the reins a flick. 'Very good, miss,' he mutters.

'After that, you may help me down.'

'Yes, miss.'

'And stop calling me miss.'

'All right.'

When they're over the bridge he pulls up. Then he jumps down to help her out. As she puts her foot on the step she stumbles, and has to steady herself on his arm. She don't look at him, but he can tell that she's angry with herself. She always hated that knee of hers. She don't limp or nothing, but it looks like it buckles now and then.

He ties Trouble to a clump of giant bamboo, then stands by her head with his hand on her coarse black mane.

He watches Sophie walk to the riverbank and pace up and down, her arms crossed about her waist. She's in pale green. Floaty pale green frock, lace gloves, and a big straw hat with a pale green ribbon down her back. It's pretty, but it don't look right on her.

He tells hisself that she's just some posh bint like that slimy Mrs Dampiere. But it don't work. It never did with Sophie.

'I used to come here with Evie,' she says, looking down at the river. 'We used to give offerings of rum to the River Mistress, and make a wish. I always made the same wish. I asked the River Mistress to make sure that, wherever you were, you'd be all right.'

Christ, she can talk straight when she wants. He'd forgotten that. It gives him that hot, prickly tightness in his chest.

'It looks as if the River Mistress heard me,' she goes on, 'although it did take rather a long time to find out.' She turns and shoots him a look. Her face is stubborn and set: little shadowy dents at the corners of her mouth deeper than usual. 'I know you don't want me to talk to you,' she says, 'but I don't care. Just this once I shall do as I please and you can't stop me.'

She's right about that. He can hardly put her in the dog cart if she don't want to go, can he? And he can't just leave her here to walk home. Although that's what she deserves for putting him on the spot.

'Ever since I got back,' she says, 'everything's been different. Eden. Maddy. You. I've tried to pretend it isn't so, but what's the use?'

So what d'you want me to do about it? he tells her silently. If you're asking me to make you feel better, you've come to the wrong bloke.

She takes a couple of steps towards him, and lifts her chin. 'When I was little,' she says, 'you helped me get better.' She says it almost angrily, like an accusation. 'I don't know what you did. Perhaps it was just seeing you, and knowing I had a friend, or . . . or merely thinking that I did. You can pretend all you like that none of that happened, Ben Kelly, but I don't believe that you can have forgotten everything.'

'Well of course I haven't forgotten,' he snaps. 'Forgotten? How could I sodding well forget?' Suddenly he's so angry that he wants to shake her. He pulls off his cap and wipes his forehead on his wrist, and takes a few paces in a circle. Then he comes back to face her and stands with his hands on his hips, glaring down at her. 'Do you think that when I was a kid, people used to just give me things? Me? A sewer rat? Well, do you?'

She blinks as if he's hit her.

'*Blackie the Charger* and *The Downfall of the Dervishes*,' he goes, counting them off on his fingers. 'Plus a whole load of soup, and that fruit on the first day. Of course I haven't forgotten.'

She chews her lip and looks down at her feet, then back to him.

'Just because somebody don't talk about it, it don't mean they don't remember. But what's the good in raking it up? What's the point?'

She starts to say something, but he cuts the air with his palm. 'No. Don't start. I know what you're going to say.'

The dents at the corners of her mouth deepen, but this time it's a bit of a smile. 'No you don't.'

'Yes, I do. You're going to have another go at me about Montpelier. Well, I'll save you the trouble, shall I? You're right, I was there, just like you said. So was Master Alex, and so was your sister.'

Her mouth falls open. 'Why were you there? What were they—?'

'That's enough!' he shouts. 'I'm not telling you no more. I promised Madeleine I wouldn't, and I'm not going back on that now.'

There's a silence while she takes that in. Then she looks up into his face. She's very intent, but for once he hasn't a clue what she's feeling. He can see the little flakes of gold in her eyes, and the way her eyelashes are tipped with gold, so that you can't tell how long they really are till you're right close up. Again he gets that prickly tightness in his chest.

'Why can't you just trust Madeleine?' he says. 'She's your big sister, she's only looking out for you. You're bloody lucky to have her.'

That makes him think of his own big sister, Kate, and for a moment a horrible feeling wells up inside of him. It's frightening. Like everything's about to crack wide open. He has to slam the lid down hard.

He gives himself a shake, and turns on his heel and goes over to the giant bamboo and unties the reins with a snap. 'You said we was friends,' he tells her over his shoulder, 'but that's in the past. We're not kids no more, and we're not friends, neither. The only reason you can make me talk to you is because I'm a servant, and you can order me about. That's not being friends.'

She opens her mouth to reply but he talks her down.

'You didn't ought to've done this,' he says, yanking down the carriage step and jerking his head at her to climb up.

'Ben, I'm sorry.'

'I don't want sorry. I just want you to promise—*promise*—that you won't pull a trick like this again.'

She catches her lip between her teeth, and those eyebrows of hers draw together in a frown. Then she nods. 'Very well. I promise.'

They made the rest of the journey in awkward silence. Sophie watched Ben's rigid back, and wondered what he was thinking. But not once did he turn round or say a word to her.

They reached the house, and she was startled to see Moses waiting by the door, looking scared. '*Jesum Peace*, but I glad to see you, Missy Sophie!' he cried, wringing his hands and getting in the way as Ben was letting down the carriage steps. 'Master Camron into a *rage*, missy! Swearing like half past midnight, and blazing at Mistress—'

'At Mistress?' said Sophie as she stepped down. 'But Mistress isn't home yet, I left her at Waytes Lake.'

Moses tried to swallow and shake his head and talk, all at the same time. 'No, Missy. Master Camron sent for her to come straight home, and now they on the verandah, and he *blazing* into her, lip-lashing and throwing black words! Missy Sophie, I about ready to take foot and run!'

Sophie threw an anxious glance at Ben, but he ignored her. She watched in disbelief as he jumped back into the driver's seat, turned the phaeton round and headed off down the road without a backward look.

Pushing thoughts of Ben to the back of her mind, she glanced apprehensively at the house. Something must be very wrong. Cameron was the last man to lose his temper with his wife, let alone send her a peremptory summons and then swear at her when she arrived. Squaring her shoulders and dreading what she might find, Sophie went inside.

'How could you do it?' came Cameron's voice from the verandah. 'How could you bring yourself to do such a thing?'

Sophie's heart sank. It could mean only one thing. He'd found out about Montpelier. And God knew what else. She crept across the hall, but was only halfway to her room when Cameron spotted her.

'Sophie?' he called brusquely from the doorway. 'Could I trouble you to come out here for a moment?'

She floundered for an excuse, and came up with nothing. 'Er . . . of course. Just give me a minute to take off my hat.'

When she reached the verandah he was prowling up and down, his light grey eyes glassy with anger. Madeleine sat very straight on the sofa, her face rigid and defiant. Scout the puppy was pressed against her skirts. He was trembling, his ears flat against his skull. Sophie halted in the doorway and put on what she hoped was a noncommittal smile.

Cameron shot her a look and continued to pace. 'I dare say you know all about this,' he said between his teeth.

She glanced at her sister. But Madeleine's eyes were fixed on some point in the middle distance. 'Know about what?' said Sophie.

Cameron threw up his hands. 'Why, the simple matter of my wife selling her inheritance behind my back.'

Sophie's mouth fell open. 'What?'

'You mean to say you didn't know? It's true. Strathnaw. The Monroe family seat. Sold. Behind my back.' Again he began to pace. 'My God, how people will laugh when they find out—'

'Nonsense,' put in Madeleine robustly. 'No one can laugh if they don't know about it, and I went to enormous trouble to keep it secret.'

'Yes,' said Cameron, 'secret from your own husband.'

'If you'd known beforehand you would have stopped me.'

'Well, of course I'd have stopped you!' he roared.

This was too much for Scout. He gave a yelp and hurtled down the steps with his tail between his legs.

Quietly, Sophie made her way to the sofa and sat down beside her sister. Madeleine turned her head and made an attempt at a smile. Sophie couldn't smile back. She felt too ashamed. To have suspected her own sister of infidelity—infidelity with a thoughtless young cub like Alexander Traherne—while all the time she had only been trying to sell that grim old Scottish barrack to save the home she loved.

How could you have been so blind, Sophie berated herself, to have failed utterly to perceive that Eden was in danger of going under? All the signs had been there. The long hours Cameron worked. Madeleine turning her own gowns instead of ordering new ones, making the children's clothes herself. And what made Sophie go hot and cold with shame was that through it all they had financed her without complaint. The Ladies' College at Cheltenham, the first-class passage home, even the little pony trap for taking her to that wretched clinic.

She watched her sister put her hands to her temples and smooth back her hair. Ever since Sophie could remember, Madeleine had done that when she was under pressure.

'Surely you can understand why I did it?' said Madeleine to Cameron's back. 'Eden is our home. For sixteen years you've put your heart and soul into this place. I will not stand by and watch it taken away by the bank.'

'Strathnaw was your inheritance. There have been Monroes on that land for over four hundred years, Madeleine. How could you sell it? How would Jocelyn have felt if he'd lived to see this? Did you think of that?'

'Of course I thought of it! I thought of very little else!'

Sophie reached out and took her hand, and gave it a squeeze. 'I think you were immensely brave,' she said. 'Who did you find to buy it?'

Madeleine gave her a wan smile. 'I don't even know. I didn't want to. The Trahernes handled all that.'

'*The Trahernes?*' said Cameron in disbelief. 'Oh, God in heaven.'

Madeleine looked perplexed. 'But they were wonderful. Both Cornelius and Alexander.'

Cameron snorted. 'I'm sure they were. A young rake like Alexander and an old lecher like Cornelius? Superlative choice of conspirators, my darling. What were you thinking of?'

'I was thinking of saving Eden,' she retorted. 'Which clearly was horribly wrong of me. I do apologise.'

He gave her a narrow look.

'Cameron, do come and sit down,' said Madeleine. 'All this looming is giving me a headache.'

He glanced from Sophie to his wife, and back again. The he rubbed the back of his neck, and sighed, and went to a chair and threw himself down. He put his elbows on his knees and shook his head. 'We would have found a way,' he muttered. 'We would have found some way to dig ourselves out of this mess without selling an acre.'

Madeleine looked at him for a moment. Then she rose and went to sit on the arm of his chair, and put her hands on his shoulders. 'And what was I supposed to do? Watch you work yourself into an early grave?'

'Madeleine—'

'I did it for us,' she said firmly. 'And I would do it again. Tomorrow.' She smoothed a lock of his hair back from his temple. 'I know it's a blow to your pride. I know that. But you've suffered worse in the past, and lived.'

He gave a snort of laughter.

'And you'll live with this,' she went on. 'But I will not let us be forced out of Eden. And there's an end of it.'

'Maddy, why didn't you tell me?' said Sophie the following afternoon when she'd finally caught up with her sister alone. They were walking together in the garden, and watching the children chasing an exuberant Scout around the lawn.

'How could I tell you?' said Madeleine. 'That would have been asking you to lie for me. To lie to Cameron.' She turned away, and for the first time Sophie realised what the weeks of deception must have cost her.

'Oh God, Maddy. I'm so sorry.'

Madeleine wiped her eyes with her fingers. 'Whatever for?'

'For being such an idiot. For pestering you all the time.'

'Good heavens, in your place I'd have done far worse. No, I'm the one who's sorry. What a homecoming for you! I couldn't believe it when Alexander told me we had to go to Montpelier on the very day you were arriving. I didn't sleep all night.'

'But . . . why did you have to go on that particular day?'

'It was the only time the attorney could come. He was bringing the papers for me to sign from Spanish Town.' She shuddered. 'I was terrified that we wouldn't get back to Montego Bay in time to meet you. That was our one piece of luck, when the train got delayed.'

Sophie frowned. 'I still don't quite understand. When you met me at Montego Bay, you were with Cameron. How—?'

'I told him I was going in early, to do some shopping, and I'd meet him there. Another lie, I'm afraid.'

Sophie paused. 'All that was three weeks ago. Once it was done, why didn't you just tell us?'

'Because it wasn't done. The attorney had to perfect the title, or something. I don't understand the details, but I did know that I had to wait until it was irrevocable before I told Cameron, or he'd put a stop to it.'

'How did he find out?'

Madeleine gave a hollow laugh. 'Oh, that was the most wonderful mix-up! The letter from the attorney came through yesterday, confirming that it had all gone through. But the clerk addressed it to Cameron by mistake. He picked it up when he went to town to collect the post.'

'Oh, Lord,' said Sophie.

'Quite,' said Madeleine. 'Oh well. We'll get over it.'

Sophie was silent for a moment. 'You do know that you can have Fever Hill, don't you? Just say the word and I'll sell it tomorrow, and you can have the money.'

'My goodness, what an offer! Whatever would Clemency say?'

'It's not a joke, Maddy. I mean it.'

Madeleine put a hand on her arm and tried to smile. 'I know you do. And it's wonderful of you. But there's no need to sacrifice your inheritance just yet. Strathnaw will see us through for a good many years. And who knows, the price of sugar may soar, and we'll all become millionaires!'

Sophie saw that she was determined to make light of it. And perhaps that was the best way of dealing with it.

Madeleine put her arm through Sophie's. 'There's something else I need to talk to you about,' she said in a low voice.

Sophie made a face. 'My goodness, you mean there's more?'

She'd meant it as a joke, but Madeleine didn't smile. 'I'm afraid so,' she said. 'It's about Ben.'

Sophie braced herself. 'If it's about yesterday—'

'Not exactly. At least, I don't think it is.'

'What does that mean?'

Madeleine looked down at her feet and frowned. 'Susan told me just now. She heard it from Moses.'

'What did she hear? Is anything wrong?'

'I'm afraid they sacked him, Sophie.'

Sophie stopped and stared at her.

'Apparently, Cornelius gave him his notice last night.'

'But . . . why?'

'I don't know. Something about insolence. But I get the impression that that was just an excuse.'

Sophie cast about in dismay. 'Of course it's an excuse! It's because of us, isn't it? It's because I got him to tell me about Montpelier, and somehow Alexander found out, and—'

'No, that's just jumping to conclusions—'

'Well, then, maybe it's because I kept him talking at Romilly and he was late getting back. Either way, it's our fault.'

Madeleine did not reply. But Sophie could see from her face that she thought so too.

'It's so unfair,' said Sophie, nearly in tears. 'He was doing so well at Parnassus. And now we've spoilt it for him.'

'We don't know that for sure, Sophie.'

'Yes, we do. He's lost his job, and it's all our fault.'

It takes him a while to work out why he's got the sack, on account of it all came a bit out of the blue. One minute he was in the tack room cleaning stirrup irons, and the next thing there was Master Cornelius giving him two weeks' notice without a character. 'I'm disappointed in you, Kelly. Disappointed and severely displeased.'

Me too, thought Ben, putting down the stirrup iron on a bale of hay. Sacked? What for? Coming home late? What?

He watched Master Cornelius walking up and down the tack room. He's a short, meaty, good-looking man in his late fifties: the sort of man you take to at first, but never quite trust. There's too much of the lizard in him for that. Bulgy pale blue eyes, always swivelling about for the next bit of skirt. Red lips that never look dry. Scaly lizard hands.

'You know, Kelly,' he said, picking up a jar of paraffin wax and frowning at the label, 'you brought this on yourself. Perhaps in future you'll keep a civil tongue in your head. Especially when there's a lady present.'

A lady? What lady? What's this about?

Two years down the plughole. That's what it's about. And without a character there's precious little chance of another situation, at least not around here. Which means no more accidentally-on-purpose drives up to Eden, and no more bickering with Sophie.

And that's a *good* thing, he tells himself the next day. You were right when you said it had to stop. You were right to make her promise.

He's in the loose box with Trouble, showing Lucius the ropes. He's still got two weeks' notice to work, but he wants to make sure that Lucius gets the hang of it. 'She don't like being tied up when you're grooming her,' he tells him.

Lucius nods. He already knows but he also knows that Ben needs to say it. He's all right, is Lucius.

'And sometimes,' goes Ben, 'she gets a bit of a swelling in the off hind pastern. Bran poultice'll sort that out.'

'I hear you, Ben.'

Ben strokes her nose for a bit, then gets the hell out of the loose box.

Just then there's a clatter of hoofs, and in come Miss Sib, Mrs Dampiere and Master Alex back from their ride. Master Cornelius is out in the yard too, smoking a cigar and watching Mrs Dampiere. As she rides past Ben she glances down and throws him a cool look. Ben glances from her to Master Alex, then to Master Cornelius, and back to her. And suddenly he knows why he got the sack.

Two years down the plughole, he thinks. And all for a bit of snug that you never even wanted.

Just then, Master Alex jumps down from the saddle and chucks him the reins, and tells him to clean the tack *properly* for a change. And Ben looks down at the reins trailing on the ground, and something inside him just gives, like a worn-out stirrup leather. 'You know what?' he goes. 'Why don't you do it yourself?'

It's quite funny, really. Suddenly you can hear a pin drop in that yard.

Master Cornelius takes his cigar out of his mouth, and Master Alex gapes, like he can't credit what he's just heard. Miss Sibella's mouth is open too, but you can tell she's enjoying it. This'll give her something to tell the ladies over tea. Mrs Dampiere is still in the saddle, carefully rearranging her habit and not looking at nobody.

Ben stoops for a bit of straw to wipe off his hands. No time now to go back to the bunkhouse for his kit. He'll have to leave his spare shirt and breeches and that special curry comb he saved up for. Shame about that. And now he definitely won't be seeing Sophie no more, and it's a shame about that too. Oh well. Way of the world. 'So I reckon I'll be off,' he says.

'You still have two weeks to work,' says Master Cornelius.

Ben snorts. 'Two weeks? You can shove that.'

A horrified gasp from Miss Sibella. A choky splutter from Lucius.

'*What* did you say?' says Master Alex.

'You heard me,' snaps Ben. He sweeps off his cap and gives them all a mock bow. Then the devil in him remembers Mrs Dampiere. 'You know what?' he goes to Master Alex and Master Cornelius. 'The funny thing is, I never even wanted her.' He jerks his head to make sure they know who he means. 'She made all the running. You can have her and welcome. Besides, she isn't even that good.'

And that, he tells himself as he starts off down the carriageway, is what you might call burning your boats.

To Sophie's consternation, Madeleine had flatly refused to give Ben a job at Eden, and Clemency didn't need a groom at Fever Hill. That was why she went to Falmouth to see her Great-Aunt May.

As she followed the silent butler Kean to the upstairs drawing room, Sophie felt oddly apprehensive. She told herself that she had nothing to fear from an old lady of eighty-four, but it wasn't entirely true. Great-Aunt May possessed a grim talent for exposing weaknesses.

It took a moment for Sophie's eyes to adjust to the gloom. The louvres were shut, and the mahogany wall panelling swallowed most of the light that filtered through. No outside sounds penetrated. The drawing room was deathly still. Great-Aunt May sat very straight on a hard mahogany chair, with her gloved hands crossed atop her ivory-headed cane. She was just as narrow and rigidly upright as Sophie remembered, encased in a tight, high-collared gown of stiff grey moiré, which made no concession to the heat. Great-Aunt May despised concessions, just as she despised sickness, pleasure and enthusiasm.

Behind her hung the famous Winterhalter portrait of her in presentation dress. At the age of eighteen she had been imperiously lovely: golden-haired and statuesque, with ice-blue eyes and a porcelain complexion that had never seen the sun. Sophie felt the portrait's gaze on her as she made her way across the parquet and tried not to limp.

'Well, miss,' said Great-Aunt May in her hard, dry voice. 'I had not expected that you would be so prompt to call. It can scarcely be more than three weeks since your ship docked at Kingston.'

'You're very well informed, Great-Aunt May,' said Sophie, ignoring the jibe.

'Why have you come? You have never had the slightest regard for me, and you must be aware that I have never entertained any liking for you.'

'I know that. But—'

'I must have things about me that are beautiful. You are not beautiful. Moreover you are ill.'

'Actually, I've been better for years.'

The old lady rapped the floor with her cane. 'You are ill, I say! Why, you are practically a cripple. I saw you limp. Now answer my question. Why have you come?'

Sophie paused for a moment, to bring herself under control. 'I've heard that you're in need of a coachman,' she said evenly.

'Upon my word, miss, you surprise me! What conceivable interest can you have in my household arrangements?'

'Well, I know of someone who was recently dismissed from another establishment, and might suit.'

'Dismissed, you say. For what infraction?'

'For insolence. But that was—'

'Indeed. A pretty notion you have of the quality of manservant I might care to retain.'

'I think it may have been a misunderstanding. Mr Traherne'—she paused to give weight to the name—'has always had the highest regard for the servant in question.'

Something flickered in the inflamed blue gaze.

Sophie kept very still. If the old lady sensed that she was being manipulated, she would be intractable. And yet . . . if there was any possibility of vexing the Trahernes . . .

It was common knowledge on the Northside that Great-Aunt May hated the entire clan with a deep, corrosive hatred that had no end. Six decades before, she had suffered the ignominy of an offer of marriage from Cornelius's father, and had never got over the humiliation. The great-grandson of a blacksmith—and he had the effrontery to aspire to the hand of Miss May Monroe! Sixty-six years later, her rancour remained undimmed. It was probably the only thing keeping her alive.

Again she rapped her cane on the floor. 'I will not be influenced.'

'I know that, Great-Aunt May.'

'Should anyone apply for the post, I shall consider him, if I see fit. But I will not be influenced. Now tell me the truth. What possible interest can you have in a manservant of Mr Traherne?'

Sophie hesitated. 'None.'

The old lady pounced on the hesitation. 'Then why are you here?'

Sophie felt herself colouring.

'Shall I tell you, miss? Shall I tell you why you show such inappropriate interest in your inferiors?'

'I don't,' said Sophie between her teeth. 'It's just that in this case there are reasons—'

'Do not attempt to exonerate yourself! I have heard reports of your behaviour. Your involvement in that . . . clinic, do they call it?' She leaned forwards, and her hot blue eyes bored into Sophie's. 'You are drawn to your inferiors because you know that you are unfit for anyone else.'

Sophie got to her feet. She didn't have to take this. Not even for Ben.

But Great-Aunt May had her prey in her talons, and she wasn't about to let go. 'You have no breeding,' she continued. 'You are not a true Monroe.'

'I'm as much a Monroe as you.'

'You are a Durrant. Your mother had the instincts of a guttersnipe, and so have you.'

Sophie turned on her heel and ran. She slammed the drawing room doors behind her, pushed past a startled Kean, and ran down into the street. She stood there panting, blinded by the glare. *You are drawn to your inferiors because you know that you are unfit for anyone else. Your mother had the instincts of a guttersnipe, and so have you.*

It wasn't true. None of it was true. She felt angry with herself for allowing Great-Aunt May to upset her. And, which was worse, for showing it. Why should she be troubled by the rantings of an evil old witch?

She started slowly up the street, and as she walked, the sunny peace of the little town had its effect. She began to feel better. What did it matter what Great-Aunt May had said to her? She'd achieved what she'd set out to do. She'd shown the old witch a way to discountenance the Trahernes.

Now it was up to Ben to apply for the position. Although of course, she remembered, he doesn't know about it yet. So now you've got to find him.

CHAPTER THREE

EVIE SITS DREAMING on the aqueduct wall. A ground dove waddles along the track towards her, and she flaps her hand to shoo it away. 'Out! Outta here, you duppy bird!' She reaches inside her bodice and grasps the little green silk bag that contains the buckra gentleman's gold chain. She closes her eyes and holds it tight, like a talisman.

'Hello, Evie,' says Sophie at her shoulder.

Evie jumps, and nearly topples into the aqueduct.

'I'm sorry,' says Sophie, 'I startled you.' She's nervous, twisting her riding crop in her hands. Looking at her, Evie feels the familiar confusion of jealousy and liking and self-loathing. She hates that she's been found in her old print dress and her canvas shoes, in this rundown ruin of a place. She hates that she's pleased to see Sophie.

Sophie turns and gazes out over the scummy green water, then back to Evie. 'I need to see Ben,' she says. 'Can you tell me where he is?'

I should have guessed, thinks Evie. Sophie always did have a peculiar deep regard for Ben. 'Ben's gone,' she says. 'Don't know where.'

Sophie doesn't believe her. 'You see, I've found him a position, and I need to tell him, or it'll get filled. It's in Duke Street, at Great-Aunt May's.'

'Miss May?' Evie's surprised.

Sophie grins. 'I saw her yesterday, and she still frightens the life out of me. But you see, she really does need a coachman. It's ridiculous, she only ever drives eight hundred yards to church, but I thought that if Ben were to apply, she'd probably take him. It would appeal to her, to cock a snook at the Trahernes.'

Clever Miss Sophie. Clever, unwise Miss Sophie, walking into trouble with her eyes wide open and blind. 'Better stay away from him,' she says.

'Everyone keeps telling me that.' Sophie taps her riding crop against her boot. 'Will you at least see that he gets the message?'

Well, and why not? thinks Evie. After all, you're not really friends with Sophie any more, so why worry about keeping her out of trouble? And why worry about Ben? Ben can look after himself. He always has.

'Evie . . . please.'

She sighs. 'All right.'

'Thank you.'

After that Sophie doesn't stay long, and then Evie hears her mother, calling her to supper. She gets up and brushes off her skirts.

When she reaches the yard, her mother glances up from the hearth. 'What did Miss Sophie want?' she asks as she hands her daughter a bowl of steaming fufu.

Evie shrugs. 'Nothing. Just to visit.'

For a while they eat in silence. Then Grace says, 'You know, you're better not spending time with her, girl.'

Evie blows on her fufu and frowns. 'Why not?'

'You know why. She's from a different class of ideas and life.'

'Mother, I'm a teacheress. I can spend time with who I like.'

'But it does no good to go meddling with carriage folk. You know that.'

Evie sets her teeth. 'Meddling with carriage folk?' she says quietly. 'But Mother, you're the one who did that. Not so? You "meddled" with a buckra gentleman, and—'

'Evie—'

'And I'm the result. Not so, Mother? You went with a buckra gentleman, though you never would tell me his name.'

Grace gives her a black hard look, but Evie's blood is rising and she don't care. 'So please don't tell me who I can't spend time with, Mother. I'm half white. I can—'

'Half white is no white,' snaps Grace. 'Don't you know that yet?'

Evie can't take any more. She throws down her bowl, runs to her room and fetches her little wooden writing box from under the bed. Then she makes her way out to the end of the yard and seats herself on her grandmother's tomb under the garden cherry tree. She takes out her pen and ink and a sheet of her special notepaper, and quickly writes: *I shall be taking the air in Bamboo Walk tomorrow, at four o'clock. EM.* Then she seals it with a little stump of sealing wax.

This has nothing to do with her mother, she tells herself. In fact this only proves that these days a mulatto girl can receive admiration and respect from a buckra gentleman. From Cornelius Traherne.

A slumbrous afternoon at the clinic, and not a patient in sight. Dr Mallory had gone off in disgust, leaving Sophie on her own. She sat by the open door at the rickety little table, struggling to concentrate on *Diseases of the Lungs*. But the words conveyed nothing to her. It had been five days since her conversation with Evie by the aqueduct, and still there had been no word of Ben. Perhaps he'd left Trelawny, or taken ship back to England, or Barbados or Panama or America.

She put her chin on her elbows and heaved a sigh. What was she doing here? These days she felt constantly dissatisfied: edgy and tearful, and full of vague yet insistent longings. What was wrong with her? What did she *want*?

Bethlehem itself was a pleasant little place. The people were friendly but stubborn, and reluctant to betray their own bush doctors for a 'doctor-shop' where they couldn't buy Calvary powder or dead-man oil. Most days, Sophie had little to do except dole out cough linctus.

She wouldn't have minded if it hadn't been for Dr Mallory. A clever, bitter, distressingly fat widower, he detested the practice of medicine, and had only become a doctor because God had told him to. He made no secret of resenting Sophie's presence, even though it had been his own idea that she should help him.

This afternoon, the village was more than usually quiet, for it was market day, and most people were away. Through the open door Sophie could see an old man sitting under a pawpaw tree at the far side of the clearing, polishing his Sunday shoes. Chickens pecked the dust. Beneath the breadfruit tree, Belle squatted on her haunches and admonished her toy zebra, Spot. She had conceived a passionate devotion for Sophie, and had badgered her mother until she was allowed to accompany her aunt.

With a tact that Sophie appreciated, Madeleine rarely enquired about the clinic. Cameron, however, was more outspoken. 'Sophie, it's been what, two weeks?' he had said after dinner the night before. 'Isn't it time to call it a day? After all, old Mallory doesn't need you, and you don't need him, and heaven knows the blacks don't need either of you.'

He was right, of course. But how could she back down now? Was this to be yet another of her famous 'about-turns'?

Belle's voice outside the door cut across her thoughts. She was asking someone just beyond Sophie's line of vision to take a look at Spot's hoof. 'It's wobbly because Fraser pulled it,' she said. 'Aunt Sophie gave me some carbolised dressing.'

'Dressing's not much use for a broken cannon bone,' said Ben.

Sophie's heart jerked.

'What's a cannon bone?' said Belle.

'The bit above the fetlock,' said Ben. 'It's broken all right. Flopping about all over the place.'

Very quietly, Sophie got to her feet and backed away from the door. She moved to the high louvred window, and stood on tiptoe to peer out. Ben was squatting down to Belle's level in the shade of the breadfruit tree. He wore his usual breeches and top boots and a collarless blue shirt, but instead of his groom's cap, a battered straw hat lay beside him in the dust. He was frowning and turning the zebra in his hands.

'Will he get better?' asked Belle, standing before him with her hands clasped behind her back.

He shook his head. 'Best make an end of him.'

'Oh. What does that mean?'

'Put a bullet in him.'

Belle blinked. 'You mean I ought to shoot him?'

He handed the toy back to her. 'Best thing for him. He'll never walk on four legs again.'

'But if I carry him.'

He shrugged. 'Suit yourself. If you want to carry a stripy horse all day, that's your lookout.'

She nodded, and hugged Spot under her chin. 'Actually he's not a stripy horse. He's a zebra.'

'What's a zebra?'

'Um. A sort of stripy horse.'

Ben smiled.

It was the first time that Sophie had seen him smile—really smile—since he was a boy. It made her want to cry. Standing there with her hands on the windowsill, she felt a sudden shattering rush of feeling for him. It took her breath away. It made everything clear.

He *mattered* to her. He always had. Ever since that day in the photographer's studio, when he'd stood at bay before Madeleine's imitation gun: an alley cat of a boy, who had snapped and snarled, and then been reduced to captivated silence by a gilded horse on the binding of a book. He mattered to her because his mind worked the same way as hers, and because he could sense what she was feeling, and because . . . because he just did. And now at last she understood why she'd never been attracted to any of the young men she'd ever met. It was because they weren't Ben.

The windowsill was rough beneath her hands, and she clung to it. She felt dizzy and shaken. And hopelessly sad. She couldn't tell him what she felt. She couldn't tell anyone. No one must know, because it was impossible. Even she could see that. Holding her breath, she watched him reach for his hat and look about him, then make for the door. Quickly, before he spotted her, she drew back from the window and sat down, and bent over her book.

When his shadow cut across the doorway, she glanced up, and made what she thought was a creditable job of appearing surprised. She was on the verge of tears, and she was sure that it showed in her face, but if he noticed, he made no sign. He just stood in the doorway and gave her his unsmiling nod. 'Can I come in?'

She clasped her hands together on the book, and nodded.

He tossed his hat on the medicine trolley, and went to lean against the opposite wall, glancing about him at the bottles and jars on the shelves.

'So this is the clinic,' he said.

She cleared her throat. 'Yes. This is it.'

'I worked for a hospital once. Runner for St Thomas's. Learned all the names of the medicines.'

'Was that before you knew me and Madeleine?'

He nodded.

She wondered where he had been for the past five days. His clothes were dusty but clean, and he didn't look as if he'd been sleeping rough.

She looked down at her hands, and saw that they had tightened into fists. 'So what happened to that promise you made me give you,' she said, 'about not seeing you again?'

He crossed his arms on his chest. 'Yes, but *I* never promised nothing, did I? Anyway. I just come to say thanks. That's all.'

'For what?'

'For putting in a word for me at your great-aunt's.'

'I take it that this means you've got the position?'

He nodded. 'Scary old cat, isn't she? But I think we'll muddle along.'

She remembered Great-Aunt May's imperious declaration: *I must have things about me that are beautiful.* 'I imagine,' she said, 'you'll do very well.'

'So why d'you do it, then?'

'Why did I do what?'

'Put in a word for me with Miss Monroe?'

'It was the least I could do, since I got you dismissed.'

'You didn't.'

'Yes I did. That day when you drove me home, you had words with Alex—Master Alex—I mean, with Alexander Traherne.'

'That's not why I got the sack.'

'Then why did you?'

He did not reply. A faint redness stole across his cheekbones.

'Sibella mentioned some incident at the stables, but she didn't say what. Just that Cornelius and Alexander were both incandescent.'

'Does that mean angry?'

'You know it does. Sibella said you were insolent.'

'Well. They had it coming.'

'But why antagonise the most powerful family in Trelawny?'

He turned his head and studied the jars on the shelf. Then he shrugged. 'I don't know. I suppose because I knew it wouldn't last.'

'What wouldn't last?'

'The job. It was too good. So I made it end. That's what I do.' He turned back to her, and they regarded one another in silence.

She was still sitting behind the table, and he was standing by the shelves against the opposite wall. There was six feet between them.

Only six feet, she thought. All you've got to do is get up and cross that little distance. But you can't do it, can you? Because you're not brave enough. Because what if he doesn't feel as you do?

Belle appeared in the doorway. She was carrying the injured Spot— who now sported a handkerchief bandage—and she was scowling as she held it up for Ben's inspection. 'Will this help?'

Ben shook himself, and glanced down at her and blinked. 'Um . . . a bit. Just don't let him put any weight on that hoof.'

Belle nodded. 'Can I have some cyanide ointment?'

'No,' said Ben and Sophie together.

Belle thrust out her lower lip, and stalked out of the clinic.

When she'd gone, there was silence. Then Ben shook himself again, and reached for his hat. 'I'd better be off,' he muttered. 'I start work tomorrow, and I've still got to get down to town.'

'Will you come again?' she said quickly.

'No.'

'Why not?'

'Because it's not a good idea.'

'Why?' Now that they were talking again, she felt stronger. She might lack the courage to go to him, but she had the courage to argue. 'You're friends with Evie,' she pointed out. 'Why can't you be friends with me?'

'Because I can't, that's all.'

'Why not?'

She watched him walk the length of the room, then back again. 'You can't go saying things like that,' he told her angrily. 'Not to me.'

'Why not to you?'

'Because I'm common. Because I grew up in a slum.'

'I know that, but—'

'That's just it, you don't know.' He shook his head. 'You don't know.'

'Perhaps not. But that's all in the past. What does it matter?'

'Of course it sodding well matters.' He looked down at his hat, then tossed it back on the trolley. 'Look. When I was the same age as that little girl out there, we lived in two rooms on East Street, for the eight of us. We used to sleep six kids to a bed. D'you know what that's like?'

She shook her head.

'Bedbugs and lice, and all the girls and boys mixed up together. So not much sodding chastity, if you take my meaning.'

She felt her face growing hot.

'One night,' he went on, 'when my sister Lil's about twelve, our Jack—he was our big brother—he gets into her. You know what that means?'

She swallowed. 'Yes. I think so.'

'So the next day she finds herself a fancy man, and she's off on the streets, doing tricks for a tanner. And that's *good*. Because now it means she's earning her keep.'

She dug her fingernail into a crack in the binding of the book she was still holding. 'Why are you telling me this?'

'To make you see the difference between you and me. I'm just the same as Jack. Christ, I was getting into girls when I was eleven.'

She raised her head and looked at him steadily. 'You're right,' she said between her teeth, 'it does make a difference. It makes me feel horrified, and sorry for you. There. Are you satisfied?'

He met her eyes, then glanced away.

'What happened to Lil?' she asked suddenly.

'What d'you mean?'

'Well, something must have happened to her. Did she get some disease? Did she get pregnant? Did she have to go to a . . . an angel-maker? It's what they call them, isn't it? When they get rid of unwanted babies?'

He flinched as if she'd hit him.

'Why do you always do this?' she demanded, angrily blinking back tears. 'Always pushing me away when I get too close.'

'Well, I've got to, haven't I? Otherwise you'd just blunder in and get hurt. Anyone gets too close, and they get hurt. You take my word for it.'

'No. No, I don't believe that.'

'That's because you don't know nothing. And the worst of it is, you don't even know that you don't know.'

'Well, then, tell me!' Without thinking, she got up and went round to his side of the table. 'You say that I don't know anything, but whenever I ask, you won't answer my questions.'

He drew a deep breath. 'Look. I didn't tell you those things to make you feel sorry for me.'

'I know that.'

'I told you to show you what I am, so you'll stay away.'

She did not reply. She stood with her hands by her sides, looking up into his face. She was close enough to see that the green of his eyes was ringed with turquoise at the edges, and split by little spokes of russet.

Green eyes, she thought, aren't as noticeable as blue; you don't remark on them straight away, but when you do, it's like sharing a secret.

'Christ, Sophie,' he muttered. Then he closed the distance between them and laid his warm hand on her cheek, and bent and kissed her quickly on the mouth.

It only lasted a moment. She just had time to feel the warmth of his lips on hers, and to catch his dry spicy smell, and then he'd twisted away and was making for the door. In a daze she heard the jingle of a bridle and a horse trotting, and a man's voice, suddenly nearer. She turned, blinking in the glare, and saw Cameron standing in the doorway.

When he saw her, his face lit up with a smile. Then he recognised Ben, and froze.

Dawn. The glade of the great duppy tree on Overlook Hill. It was only an hour's ride from the house, and yet it seemed a world away, for this was the start of the Cockpits. Vapour rose from the great tattered leaves of philodendrons, and beaded the spokes of spiders' webs strung from tree to tree. Curtains of strangler fig and clots of Spanish moss hung down from the outstretched arms of the oldest silk-cotton in Trelawny.

Sophie sat on one of its folded roots, and watched her horse cropping the ferns. Her eyes felt scratchy with fatigue. She hadn't slept all night.

Cameron hadn't said a word at the clinic. He'd simply glanced at Sophie, and given Ben a long, unreadable look, and then gone back outside and scooped up Belle, and ridden out of Bethlehem. Ben had stood in the doorway watching him go, then he had shaken his head, and walked out of the village without a backwards glance.

Dinner that night had been a fraught affair, with Sophie braced for an attack that didn't come. Cameron was courteous as always, but silent and withdrawn. It was clear from Madeleine's constrained attempts at conversation that he had told her everything.

But after all, Sophie kept telling herself, what could Cameron have seen? By the time he had reached the doorway they had already drawn apart. He hadn't seen them kiss. All he had seen was their taut faces. But that would have been enough for a man as perceptive as Cameron.

Somehow Sophie had got through dinner, and then pleaded a headache and gone early to bed. She had half expected Madeleine to come to her room and have it out, but she hadn't. And that made it worse. All night she had lain awake, staring up at the mosquito net, her feelings in turmoil. Exasperation at Cameron for making her feel guilty; anger at herself for getting Ben into trouble again; a welter of emotion when she remembered that kiss. If she shut her eyes, she could summon up the exact feel of him against her mouth. His lips had been hot and dry and surprisingly gentle, his hand warm on her cheek. She could still smell his sharp, indefinable smell.

It had happened so quickly that she hadn't had time to respond. But how, she wondered, how *does* one respond? What does one actually do? She had never kissed a man before.

She put her hand on the tree's rough bark, and gazed up at the great spreading canopy, laden with tiny scarlet orchids and spiky wild pines. Years ago, Cameron had brought her up here to help overcome her terror of duppy trees. And under this same tree, nearly three decades before, her sister had been conceived. Rose Durrant had called it the Tree of Life. She had told Madeleine stories of how she and her lover Ainsley Monroe had met in secret in the forest at midnight. She had been almost as young as Sophie was now: blinded by love and utterly reckless. Like mother like daughter? wondered Sophie, looking up at the tree. It had not escaped her notice that a few weeks ago she'd been suspecting Madeleine of the Durrant taint of recklessness, when it turned out to be she herself who most resembled their improvident mother.

When she got back to Eden, there was a letter waiting for her from Sibella. Sensing trouble, she took it to her room to read.

Parnassus, 15th December 1903

Dear Sophie,

How could you disgrace me so? You positively engineer an assignation with one of my own father's servants at the Historical Society picnic, and then your brother-in-law is forced to drag you away from yet another assignation in some ghastly slum. Are you deaf to all sense of propriety? Most of all, are you deaf to your obligation to me?

It pains me to say this, but I feel it my duty to tell you that you have utterly degraded yourself by this unnatural partiality. Moreover you have, by association, degraded me. I had thought that I was bestowing a favour upon you by asking you to walk up the aisle behind me as my chief bridesmaid. And this is the thanks I get.

It grieves me unutterably to say this, but you have left me no choice. I must absolutely rescind my offer, and make Amelia Mordenner chief bridesmaid. Perhaps this will teach you the folly of . . .

There was more. Four close-written pages of it. Sophie read it to the end, then tore it up and burnt the pieces in the washbasin. She was surprised to find that Sibella's arguments left her unmoved.

She sat on her bed for several minutes, thinking. Then she went to her desk and dashed off two short notes. One was to Sibella, wishing her luck with Amelia Mordenner. The other was to Ben, asking him to meet her at Romilly Bridge on the day after tomorrow.

Quickly, before she could change her mind, she sealed the notes and took them to the stables, where she gave Quaco, the stable boy, a shilling to deliver them at once and in secret. Then she went back inside and sat down at the breakfast table.

To her relief, Cameron had already left for the works, and she only had to face Madeleine and the children. 'What did Sibella want?' asked Madeleine, pouring the tea.

'To excommunicate me,' she replied.

Fraser looked up from his milk. 'What does ex—?'

'I'll tell you later,' said his mother, putting a slice of toasted johnny cake on his plate and starting to butter it. She threw her sister an enquiring glance. 'Does that mean you won't be coming with us on Boxing Day?'

'What?' said Sophie.

'The Boxing Day Masquerade. At Parnassus?'

'Oh,' said Sophie, 'I'd forgotten all about that.' It was *the* Christmas event on the Northside, and everyone would be there. Even Great-Aunt May always sent her carriage as a mark of recognition, along with her butler Kean. And this year, of course, it would be driven by her new coachman. Sophie put her hands to her temples and stared down at her plate. Sibella would be watching her like a hawk. And by then, too, she would have met Ben at Romilly.

Madeleine got up and came and sat beside her, and put an arm round her shoulders. 'Personally, I've always detested masquerades. The drumming gives me a headache, and the masks give me nightmares. Don't go if you don't want to.'

Sophie kneaded her temples. 'But what about Sibella?'

'Bother Sibella,' said Madeleine robustly. 'Listen. Cameron and I will go because we must, but there's no reason why you should be martyred, too. Send a line on the day, to say you're unwell.'

Sophie looked at her in bemusement. So far, Madeleine hadn't said a word to her about Ben, and what Cameron had or hadn't witnessed at the clinic. And now she was being so understanding about Sibella. Why?

Madeleine took a deep breath. 'Sophie,' she began with a slight frown.

Sophie braced herself. Here it comes, she thought. A lecture about Ben.

'I know it sometimes seems as if I'm . . . rather too conventional,' Madeleine said quietly. 'I mean, too keen on making calls and leaving one's card, and that sort of thing.'

Sophie glanced at her in surprise. It was the last thing she'd expected.

'But you see,' Madeleine went on, 'I know what it's like to be on the outside.' She bit her lip. 'You were too young to remember, but for me it's as if it were yesterday. That dreadful sense of being inferior. Never being allowed to mention one's parents. Never being allowed to make friends.'

'I remember,' said Sophie.

Madeleine turned and looked into her eyes. 'But do you? I wonder.'

Sophie sighed. 'But Maddy, we're not in London now. This is Trelawny. Things are different out here.'

'No, they're not. That's just it. It may seem as if they are . . . as if they're more relaxed. Certainly, people will turn a blind eye to matters of birth if one's a Monroe of Fever Hill, or a Lawe of Eden. But that doesn't mean they'll overlook . . . well, indiscretion.' She softened that with an anxious smile. 'People can turn on you, Sophie. It can happen in a moment. And it's a cold place to be: on the outside, looking in. I don't want that for you.'

Sophie did not reply. She'd been expecting a row. But this was far more devastating. She thought of the note she had sent to Ben. What would Madeleine feel if she knew about it?

'Well,' said Madeleine, giving her hand a little pat. 'Just think about what I've said. That's all I ask.'

It's been five days since Evie met Master Cornelius in Bamboo Walk, but she can still feel the throb of the bite mark on her breast, and the scratches on her arms and thighs. He'd very nearly got what he wanted.

It's been five days since it happened, and she still can't get her balance. One moment she's close to tears, and the next she's into a rage. She wants to shout and scream and cry. She wants to holler like a pickney.

He'd been strong, but she'd fought like a cat. She dreams of it every night. She thinks of it all day. Even now, as she's coming out of Dr Mallory's clinic with a little bottle of iodine for the scratches, she can't get it out of her mind. His rough wet tongue. The yellow ridges on his fingernails. The oniony smell of his sweat. Thinking of him makes her feel dirty. It's like he's leaving slimy snail trails in her mind.

With a flush of shame she remembers her pitiful self-deception: that he respected her; that he wanted to further her career. How could she have been such a fool? How many times has her mother warned her that when a buckra gentleman starts sniffing around a coloured girl he's only after one thing? Well, Grace McFarlane was right.

Evie crosses the clearing and starts for home, heading north between the coffee walks and the little plots of cane.

She's approaching the edge of Greendale Wood when she bumps into Ben. He's leading a big chestnut gelding and wearing his new coachman's uniform, a dark green tunic and breeches which suit him wonderfully. He looks handsome-to-pieces, and unusually carefree and at ease.

'What you doing up here?' she says tartly. 'What about that new job of yours?'

He grins. 'This job! I got nothing to do all day except exercise the horse. So I thought I'd nip along and see Sophie.'

'She didn't come to the clinic today.'

He frowns. 'Why not? She in trouble?'

'How should I know? I'm not her sister.'

He gives her a considering look, then falls into step beside her, with his hands in his pockets. His horse ambles behind him like a dog, with the reins slung over the saddle.

'You won't keep your job long,' Evie tells him, 'if you go gadding about like this.'

Another grin. 'Ah, that's where you're wrong. This *is* the job. Turns out the old witch likes me to go out and pick up the odd bit of news. It's called "exercising the horse".'

'What kind of news?'

He shrugs. 'Gossip. And the grimmer the better. Who's just dropped dead. Who's just gone all to smash and blown out his brains and left his kids to take their chances on the parish.'

Who's just escaped being raped in a cane-piece, thinks Evie.

'The way it goes,' he explains, 'is that I mention it to Kean, sort of in passing, and it filters through to her.'

'And you think that's a good thing, do you?' she says between her teeth. 'Passing on bad news?'

'So she likes to find out the worst of people. So what? She's paying.' He gives her a narrow-eye look. 'What's up with you, then?'

'Nothing.'

'Oh, yeah? So how'd you get them bruises on your arms?'

'I fell off a verandah.'

'Since when did that get you a set of fingermarks on your neck?'

She turns away. Damn him for being so sharp.

'Tell me who he is,' he says calmly, 'and I'll give him a going over. Next time he claps eyes on you he'll run a mile.'

His tone is utterly without swagger, but she knows that he'll do it. And for a second she feels a flash of gratitude. But she shakes her head. 'You'd only get into trouble.'

He laughs. 'Me? Never.' Then his smile fades. 'So this bloke who give you the bruises. Did he get what he wanted?'

'No! Now leave me be!'

They walk on in silence. As they near the river, the trees become taller, the undergrowth thicker. They push through great waxy leaves, and Evie blunders into a spider's web. It's only after she's brushed it away and walked on fifty yards that she realises what she's done. Every pickney knows that you've got to be polite to Master Anancy spider-man, or he'll bring you bad luck. And if you tear up his place, you need to say sorry fast. But it's too late to say sorry now.

Automatically her hand goes to her neck to find her charm-bag, but of course it isn't there. It got torn off in the struggle in Bamboo Walk, along with the little green silk bag that contained his golden chain. Strange. Since she became a woman, she's looked down on ignorant superstitions like charm-bags. But without its weight against her heart, she feels vulnerable and afraid.

'So,' says Ben, startling her, 'have you seen Sophie, then?'

'No. I told you.'

He rubs the back of his neck. 'Oh, well. I'll see her soon enough.'

'What do you mean?'

'I'm sposed to be meeting her, day after tomorrow.'

'Where?'

But he just shakes his head. He's trying to keep from smiling, but he can't, and suddenly she knows what's different about him. He's happy. She didn't realise it before because it's so rare with him, but now she sees it in his eyes and his mouth, and the way he moves. It puts her into a rage. Why should he be in love when she's so wretched?

'Ben,' she says in a hard voice, 'You got to stay away from Sophie Monroe.'

He stoops for a stone and sends it whizzing low over the ferns. 'Now tell me something I don't know.'

'No, *listen*. Do you know what I see sometimes when I look at you?'

'What?'

'I see a red-haired girl standing at your shoulder.'

Oh, Jesum Peace, but he's not expecting that. He stops in his tracks and stares at her. His face has gone blank with shock.

She'd not thought it'd have this strong an effect on him, and it frightens her. But she can't stop now. 'Long red hair,' she says, 'and a white face. Like she's sickening for something.'

'No,' he whispers. 'No.'

'She died in pain, didn't she, Ben? Blue shadows under her eyes. Fever-sweat on her skin. And one side of her face turned all to pulp.'

The blood's gone from his cheeks. His lips are grey. 'How can you know?' he says in a cracked voice. 'I never told you about her.'

'She came for a reason, Ben. They always do. She's warning you.'

He's shaking his head. A fine sheen of sweat has broken out on his forehead. 'You can't've seen her,' he says dully. 'She's dead. Kate's dead.'

'Oh, I know it,' she says. 'I always know when I see a dead one.'

But he's not hearing her. He's staring past her into nothingness.

'It's a warning, Ben. You got to heed what she's telling you.'

'A warning?' His gaze swings round to her. 'Why would Kate want to warn me? I'm the one that got her killed.'

CHAPTER FOUR

IT'S TWENTY-FOUR HOURS since Evie told him, but it feels like a month. He can't sleep. Can't eat. He hasn't felt this bad since Robbie died. He didn't think he could, not with all of them gone. But now things long buried are pushing their way to the surface.

Kate's back. She's back.

Is she here now, as he's riding Viking down the Eden Road? Is she walking beside him? Gliding in and out of the shadows, and trailing her dead hand over the grass? Would he know it if she was? He keeps thinking of Kate as she was that last summer. He was only about ten, but the memory's so sharp he can almost see her. That coppery hair that used to crackle and spark when she brushed it. The warm, clever blue eyes.

He read once in a penny newspaper that each man kills the thing he loves. Well, it's true for him. When he was a kid he loved his big sister, though he didn't know it at the time. She was more of a mother than his ma. She walloped him when he nicked things, and she walloped the big boys when they beat him up. He loved her, and he killed her.

So maybe that's why sometimes, when he's thinking of her, he gets a picture of Sophie. Because it's a warning, only Evie got it the wrong way round. It's not Sophie who's going to hurt *him*. It's him who's going to hurt Sophie. So all in all, it's the right thing to do, not turning up at Romilly tomorrow. It's for the best.

But ah God, she'll be so hurt. She'll think it's because there's something wrong with her. That she's not pretty enough, or it's because of her knee. She won't understand. And he can't tell her. But it's the only thing to do. He just wishes he could get her out of his head. That moment before he kissed her. He's never felt so close to another person. And the strange thing was that he didn't mind. He didn't get that prickly tightness in his chest. He was just falling, falling into those honey-coloured eyes.

A distant pounding of hoofs jolts him back to the present. It's some horse in a flat-out gallop over to his left, only he can't see, on account of the trees. Viking skitters about a bit, and Ben tells him to pack it in. 'Listen,' he says, 'if some crazy planter wants to take a gallop in this heat, that's his lookout. You just thank your stars I got more sense.'

Viking snorts, and tosses his head in agreement.

They leave the trees behind and the cane-pieces open out around, and that's when he catches sight of the crazy planter. He's just come a cropper on a cane-track, and broken his horse's knees.

Ben turns Viking's head and puts him forward through the cane. 'You all right?' he shouts. Not that he cares much one way or the other.

The planter struggles to his feet and gives a rueful laugh. 'Does it look as if I am?'

Ben ignores him. He jumps down and tethers Viking to a stand of cane, and walks past him to check on the horse. She's got her head down, and she's shaking like a leaf: foam all over her, blood streaming from her shattered knees, and the left front cannon bone's snapped clean through. She smells him coming and manages a welcoming nicker, and . . . oh, no. No. It's Trouble.

'Christ Almighty,' he snarls over his shoulder. 'You bloody fool. Look what you done.'

Behind him the man gives an astonished laugh. 'Steady on, old fellow. It was an accident.'

That's when Ben turns and recognises Master Alexander Traherne.

Master Alex recognises him at the same moment, and goes still. The pale blue eyes flicker over him, sizing him up. Maybe he's thinking how Ben made a fool of him over Mrs Dampiere, and what about getting his own back? But then he takes in the empty cane-pieces, with nobody to lend a hand if things get rough. So instead he just gives himself a shake and straightens his necktie.

'Lend me your mount,' says Master Alex calmly, 'there's a good fellow.'

Ben snorts. 'As if I would.'

Master Alex studies him for a moment, then brushes off his hands. 'Watch yourself, my lad. No sense in talking back to your betters. Now lend me your mount and we'll call it quits.'

'I'm not your lad,' snarls Ben. 'I never was.'

Beside him, Trouble keeps looking from one to the other, twitching her ears and trying to follow, in case they're giving her an order. That makes Ben feel sick and ashamed. Because this is his fault. If he hadn't spent so much time schooling her, Master Alex would've never ridden her. He done this to her. Each man kills the thing he loves.

A movement at his shoulder, and he turns to see Master Alex walking off down the track. It seems he's given up on getting a ride home, and decided to hoof it. 'Oi!' shouts Ben. 'Where d'you think you're going?'

'Home,' calls Master Alex. 'Not that it's any business of yours.'

'What about Trouble?'

'What about her?'

'You can't just leave her. You got to finish her off.'

'I'll send a boy to do that.'

'But that'll take hours! Look at her. You can't leave her in this state.'

But Master Alex just waves a hand irritably and keeps going.

Ben thinks about fetching him back, then gives it up as a bad job. It's Trouble he's got to think of now.

She tries to move towards him, but she can't. She just stands there trembling. Watching him. Please don't leave me, she's asking him.

'Don't worry, sweetheart,' he tells her. 'I'm not going nowhere.'

He takes out his knife and keeps it behind his back as he walks over to her, talking all the time so as not to frighten her. When he gets up close, he puts his free hand on her wet, shivering withers, and moves it gently up her neck, under her mane. She's boiling hot and running sweat. That idiot must've ridden her like a madman. 'All right, sweetheart,' he murmurs. 'Soon be over now.' His eyes are stinging, and there's a lump in his throat, but somehow he manages to keep his voice steady. More or less.

He moves his free hand up to her forelock, then down to cover her eye. For a moment that he'll never forget he feels the long, bristly lashes trembling under his palm. Then he raises his other hand and brings the knife up under her ear, and with a single thrust he drives it deep into her brain.

For a moment, she stiffens, then a shudder goes through her. Then she's crashing down onto her side. He kneels beside her, stroking her cheek and watching the great velvet eye glazing over, and murmuring, 'All right now,' over and over again. The hot blood bubbles over his thighs. Black spots dart before his eyes. He feels dizzy and sick, and suddenly very, very tired.

'What the devil d'you think you're doing? Who gave you permission to kill my horse?' says Master Alex, behind him.

In a daze, Ben turns and squints up at him.

Master Alex has retraced his steps, and is standing about a yard away: hands on hips, sun at his back, face dark against the glare.

'I . . . I done you a favour,' mutters Ben. 'You left her—'

'That's my property. Who gave you permission?'

Wearily, Ben stands up. He glances down at the knife in his hand. How did that get there? He drops it in the dust. He's so tired. Why can't Master Alex stop yapping?

'I said, who gave you permission?'

'Shut up,' mutters Ben.

'You think you're special, don't you?' says Master Alex. 'You actually think you're entitled to speak to your betters as if . . .'

There's more, but Ben's not listening. He squints into the sun, and takes a swing, and lands Master Alex a short, hard punch on the jaw.

Master Alex grunts, and goes down hard in a cloud of dust.

Ben stands over him, blinking and shaking the feeling back into his hand. 'I told you to shut up,' he mutters. Then he walks over to Viking and unties him, and swings up into the saddle and rides away.

'Are you sickening for something, girl?' says Grace McFarlane with her hands on her hips.

Evie shakes her head.

'You working too hard. Always got your nose in some damn book.' Grace gives a small proud smile and squats down to poke the fire.

It's nearly supper-time, and dark in the yard. But it's not total dark, for beyond the village Master Cameron's burning off the cane. They always burn off the cane at night, so that they can spot the stray sparks and stamp them out. Then, early in the morning, they start taking off the crop. It's much easier with the trash all burnt off, but you got to work quickly, before it spoils.

Lying in bed listening to them burning off the cane is one of Evie's best memories of when she was a pickney. The sound of the men calling to each other, the crackle and roar of the flames. She used to lie in bed and picture the men bringing to life this great hungry fire-animal—but always hemming it in, never letting it escape. She used to find cane-fires oddly reassuring.

She doesn't tonight. Tonight everything's wrong-side and tangle-up. She's full of worry-head about Ben. Why did she tell him about the red-haired girl? And why did she tell him then, on that particular day, when she'd been keeping silent for months? Was it chance? Or was she being used by some spirit of darkness?

With Christmas only a week away, the dawn air was cool, and Sophie's breath steamed as she waited at Romilly Bridge. It would be hot by midday, but now everything was deliciously fresh, and the colours sharp and clean. Black swallows dipped to drink at the turquoise river. She caught the saffron flash of a wild canary, the iridescent green of a doctor-bird. Putting her hands on the sun-hot parapet, she took a deep breath of the fresh, green-smelling air, and watched her horse cropping the ferns, and nearly laughed aloud. She felt scared and exhilarated, and appalled at what she was doing.

She had hoped to find him waiting when she arrived. But of course, she reminded herself, it was a good six miles from Falmouth, and he wouldn't find it easy to get away.

She walked down to the riverbank and snapped off a stem of scarlet heliconia. She tossed one of the big gold-tipped claws into the sliding current. By the time you've thrown them all in, she told herself, he'll be here.

He wasn't.

Perhaps he hadn't received her note. Perhaps Great-Aunt May had taken it into her head to change the habit of a lifetime, and go for an early morning drive.

Or perhaps, she thought with a sudden sense of falling, perhaps you've made a mistake. Perhaps when he kissed you it was just the impulse of the moment. After all, why should he want to see you again? He's so good-looking, and you're not nearly pretty enough. And you limp.

'How do you know he isn't after your money?' Cameron had said with his customary bluntness the night before, when he had asked her to take a turn with him in the garden after dinner.

'You only say that,' she had retorted, 'because you don't know him.'

'And you do?'

'Yes.'

'Are you sure?'

She did not reply. Until he said it, the thought of money hadn't occurred to her. She knew that that was naive, but she also knew that it hadn't occurred to Ben, either.

At the edge of the clearing, someone was coming. Sophie froze.

It was a small boy pickney on his way to school. Barefoot, in patched but scrupulously clean calico shirt and shorts, he was kicking an unripe mango before him like a football, and whistling between his teeth.

He caught sight of Sophie and gave her a brilliant smile. 'Morning, Missy Sophie,' he called politely.

She forced an answering smile and returned the greeting.

When he'd gone, she watched the dust settling softly back to earth.

It was getting warmer. The rasp of the crickets was gathering strength. He isn't coming, she told herself, and the words thudded in her heart. He isn't coming.

One of the darkies stamps on Ben's knee, and pain unfolds like a black flower. Pain like that probably means it's broken, he tells himself. So if it's broken anyway, and if they just keep hitting you there, you'll be all right.

But of course they don't.

They came on him on the Arethusa Road as he was heading back from a ride: three big, silent darkies he's never seen before. Which stands to reason. Master Alex couldn't get the lads from Parnassus to beat up one of their own.

They came up behind him and yanked him off Viking and dragged him into a cane-piece. He managed to give one of them a good bash in the ribs and another a broken cheekbone before they brought him down. But they know what they're about. Measured. Precise. Nothing too visible.

Happy Christmas, he thinks. He starts to laugh. Once he's started he can't stop. He's heaving and gasping as they're hitting him.

Did one of them mutter 'enough', or did he only hope they did? It's hard to tell, as things are getting a bit floaty.

Sorry, Sophie, he tells her inside his head. Sorry, love.

That's his last thought before it goes black.

'Apparently he had some kind of accident,' said Madeleine as they were coming out of church on Christmas Day.

'What do you mean, an accident?' demanded Sophie. 'When?'

Madeleine paused in the aisle to make way for a trio of old ladies who, like the church decorations, were wilting in the heat. It had been a long service, and everyone was eager for luncheon.

'When?' Sophie said again as they moved out onto the porch.

Madeleine scanned the throng of carriages for Cameron. He never attended services, but sometimes for her sake he collected them from St Peter's and said a word to the rector, thereby quashing suspicions of out-right heathenism. 'Some time last week,' said Madeleine, spotting him waiting for them further up the street.

'Last week? Maddy, how could you not tell me?'

'Because it isn't serious. He's *fine*.'

'Then why isn't he here? Why did Great-Aunt May have to get some-one else to drive her to church?'

'Oh look,' said Madeleine, 'there's Rebecca Traherne. Now remember, you're going to be ill tomorrow, so don't appear too healthy.'

They dealt with Rebecca, then Sophie resumed the attack. 'How did you find out?' she asked.

'From the servants, of course,' said Madeleine.

Sophie chewed her lip. 'Just how bad is it?'

'I told you, he's fine. He was found by a weeding gang a couple of miles out of town. He must have fallen from his horse—'

'Ben? He's the best rider in Trelawny.'

'Anyway,' said Madeleine with a quelling glance, 'they took him to Prospect because it's nearest, and one of Grace's cousins patched him up. Cuts and bruises, a chipped knee bone, and some bruised ribs. So you see, I do care enough to have made enquiries. But that's all I know.'

Sophie took that in silence. Around them churchgoers chatted in little groups, and carriages departed in a haze of dust.

Madeleine fiddled with the clasp of her reticule. Plainly she was also worried about Ben, and Sophie guessed that she hadn't told everything.

'Is he still at Prospect?' Sophie asked.

Madeleine shook her head. 'They took him to Bethlehem.'

Sophie tossed her head in frustration. It would have to be Bethlehem, just when Dr Mallory had closed the clinic for what he grimly called 'the festivities'.

In silence they started making their way up the street to where Cameron was waiting with the carriage. Fraser sat beside his father, clutching his presents on his lap. When he caught sight of Sophie he leapt to his feet, waving so hard that he would have tumbled out of the carriage if Cameron hadn't transferred the reins to one hand and gripped a handful of sailor suit with the other.

Just before they got within earshot, Madeleine turned to Sophie and said quickly, 'Sophie, you can't go to see him. I need you to promise me that you won't.'

It was Sophie's turn to look stubborn.

'What possible good could it do?' said Madeleine. 'Grace and her people can look after him just as well as you could.'

'But—'

'Leave him alone, Sophie. Don't make things worse for him than they already are.'

Sophie stared at her. 'What do you mean by that?'

Madeleine looked unhappy.

'Maddy . . . it was an accident, wasn't it?'

But by then they were at the carriage, and Fraser was jumping down, brandishing his new red kite, and there was no more time to talk.

On the drive back to Eden, Sophie debated what to do. Ben was in some sort of trouble, and he was hurt. That much she knew. And she was pretty sure that Madeleine wouldn't tell her any more. In the end, she decided not to do anything—at least, not today. After all, she could hardly saddle her horse and ride off to Bethlehem in the middle of Christmas lunch.

Fortunately, Cameron was preoccupied with crop time, and Madeleine had her hands full with the children, so neither of them noticed that Sophie hardly said a word. After lunch, Sophie wrote to Rebecca Traherne, excusing herself from tomorrow's Masquerade, then she pleaded a sick headache and went early to bed.

Boxing Day was cloudy and cool—'bleaky', as the servants called it— and everyone was subdued and slightly cross. Madeleine took the dog cart to fetch Clemency from Fever Hill. Clemency had flatly refused to desert her dead child on Christmas Day, but after much persuasion had consented to come for Boxing Day and stay the night, to help Sophie look after the children while Madeleine and Cameron were at Parnassus.

They ate an elaborate lunch in Clemency's honour. Then Madeleine withdrew to bathe and dress for the Masquerade, and Clemency and Sophie kept the children amused. At five o'clock, Madeleine and Cameron were ready to leave.

'We'll be back at some unearthly hour around dawn,' said Madeleine, rolling her eyes. 'Rebecca always lays on an enormous breakfast, and by then everyone's so exhausted, they fall on it.'

Poppy, the nursemaid, was already getting the children ready for an early bed. Belle was still a little frail after shaking off a slight fever the week before, while Fraser had simply eaten too many sweets. 'I've hidden the rest,' said Madeleine, drawing Sophie aside, 'but he'll work on Clemency, he always does, so I'm counting on you to be strong.'

Did Sophie imagine it, or did her sister give special emphasis to that 'I'm counting on you?' *You can't go to see him. I need you to promise me that you won't.*

At last the carriage departed in a cloud of dust, and the house settled into peace. It was twenty past five. It would be light for about another two or three hours, and after that there would be a nearly full moon. Plenty of time to ride to Bethlehem and see Ben. She'd be home by eight. And Clemency and Poppy could look after the children.

Clemency came out onto the verandah and perched on the sofa, and gave Sophie one of her wincing smiles. 'They're fast asleep,' she whispered. 'Exhausted, poor little dears. I must say, I am too.'

Sophie forced a smile. 'D'you know, I think I need some air. Should you mind dreadfully if I take myself off for a ride?'

Clemency's pretty young-old face lit up with relief. 'Darling, not at all! In fact, I was just going to ask if you'd mind if I went to my room for a little lie-down, and perhaps a short prayer?'

Sophie felt a twinge of sadness. A *short prayer* probably meant hours on her knees, apologising to Elliot for having deserted him. 'Of course I don't mind,' she said. 'You do whatever you like, Clemmie. I shall be back in a couple of hours, but don't worry if I'm late.'

Enough agonising, she told herself briskly as she changed into her riding skirt and pulled on her boots. For once, simply *act*.

In old times, the slaves had three days' holiday a year: Christmas Day, Boxing Day and New Year's Day. They made good use of them. They shed their drab clothing and dressed up in the brightest prints they could find, with anklets of scarlet john-crow berries, necklaces of blue clay beads and fearsome horned masks. Then, for those three days, they yelled, danced and drummed their way through towns, villages and estates, in a make-believe return to the African homeland they had lost.

The Masquerade at Parnassus was a tidy anglicised version of the old parade. A sedate Britannia headed the procession, followed by the Montego Bay Coloured Troupe playing patriotic songs. Then came a carnival king and queen in flowing robes and gilt paper crowns, and an entourage of servants in fancy dress and papier-mâché masks: the Sailor, the Jockey, the Messenger Boy; and finally a civilised version (in nautical dress) of the traditional ringleader, 'Johnny Canoe'.

But at Bethlehem, on the edge of the Cockpits, the parade was the real thing: a throwback to a darker, wilder past. No one mentioned 'Johnny Canoe'. *Jonkunoo* was king. Jockeys and sailors were nowhere to be seen; in their place were half-naked men in grotesquely horned masks: Devil, Horsehead, Pitchy-Patchy, the Bull—leaping, dancing and yelling to the harsh rhythms of pipe and drum.

As Sophie tied her horse to a tree at the edge of the village, she was sharply aware that she was the only white person there. Pushing her way through the crowd, she caught sight of Evie, and relief washed over her.

The coloured girl was sitting with her mother and the village nanas beneath the breadfruit tree. When she saw Sophie, her lips parted in a little 'O' of surprise. She glanced about her, signalled to Sophie to stay where she was, and got up and ran over to her. 'What are you doing here?' she said in a hoarse whisper.

'Where's Ben?' asked Sophie.

Evie bit her lip. Then she drew Sophie aside into the comparative privacy of a coffee-tree walk behind the houses.

'Evie, you've *got* to tell me. He's not at Great-Aunt May's, I checked. She sacked him. So—'

'He's all right,' said Evie. 'Not to fret, Sophie. He's all right.'

Sophie was close to tears. She hadn't realised until now how worried she'd been. 'What happened? Maddy said it was an accident, but—'

'An accident?' Evie snorted. 'No, he had a fight with Master Alex.'

'Master Alex?' Sophie looked at her in bemusement. 'But . . . you can't mean that Alexander Traherne managed to beat him up?'

Evie burst out laughing. 'Course not!' She wiped her eyes, suddenly much more her usual self. 'No, they met on the road, and got to argifying—I mean, arguing. Why they were arguing, I don't know, but then Ben hit him. And the next day, he got set on by some men, and beaten up.'

'What men?'

Evie shook her head. 'Strangers from foreign.'

'Strangers,' Sophie repeated. Presumably hired thugs of 'Master Alex'. 'And where is he now?'

'I don't know, Sophie. He left yesterday. Got a lift partway with Uncle Eliphalet on his mule, but I don't know to where.'

'What direction? North? South?'

'Northwest.'

'Towards the river?'

'I think so. But truly, I don't know.'

I do, thought Sophie.

It was nearly eight o'clock by the time she reached Romilly, and the light was fading. She tethered her horse to an ironwood tree and made her way on foot along the river path, which led to the innermost ruins of the old slave compound. Giant bamboo turned the path into an airless, shadowy tunnel. A thick carpet of leaves muffled her footsteps.

Ben had set up camp in a roofless ruin a few yards from the river. He hadn't heard her approach. He was in shirtsleeves, sitting on a block of cut-stone beside a small fire, with one leg stuck out in front of him, and a pair of bamboo crutches laid on a blanket on the ground.

The side of his face that was turned towards her was unmarked, but she saw the patchwork of purplish-yellow bruises on both forearms, and the bandage round his knee. His shirt was open to the waist, revealing lower ribs strapped with tape. By the crutches lay a calabash, probably containing one of Grace's special salves, with a roll of tape beside it, a pair of rusty scissors, and a can of water that he'd been heating on the fire. It looked as if he'd started to change the dressings, and then lost interest.

As he turned to poke the fire, she saw the dark bruising down his right cheekbone and around the eye, the crusted blood on a deep vertical cut bisecting his eyebrow.

She stepped out from under the giant bamboo, and he saw her, and went still. 'I thought I'd find you here,' she said.

He did not reply. But plainly he was horrified to see her.

Suddenly she saw herself as she must appear to him: her hair coming loose, her jacket and riding skirt covered in dust. The bedraggled bluestocking, trailing after her unwilling prey.

But still she floundered on. 'Why didn't you stay at Bethlehem? I mean, they were looking after you there, so why—?'

'Because I wanted to come here,' he cut in. In the leaping firelight his cheeks were dark with stubble. It made him look older, rougher, and startlingly unfamiliar. 'I wanted to be on my own. All right?'

'Does that mean you want me to go?'

'Yes,' he said without looking at her. 'You shouldn't've come.'

'But I couldn't just—'

'I thought you'd be down at Parnassus. At that party.'

'I sent them a note to say I was ill.'

'Why'd you do that?'

'Why d'you think? I was worried about you.'

'That's daft,' he snapped. 'You shouldn't've come.' He reached for one of the crutches to poke the fire, but dropped it with a clatter, and swore under his breath. His movements were awkward, and without his usual grace. Somehow that gave her the courage to take a step forward, and remove her hat, and sit down on a corner of the blanket, a safe distance from him.

'What happened to your leg?' she asked.

'What's it to you?'

'Oh, absolutely nothing,' she retorted. 'That's why I'm here.'

He drew a breath. 'Grace says I've bruised the knee bone.'

She considered that. 'Your ribs—do they hurt?'

'No.' He shrugged. 'A bit.' He reached for the can of hot water and knocked it over. '*Bugger.*'

She leaned forward and righted the can, then took her handkerchief from her pocket and held it out. 'Here. Use this.'

He looked at it for a moment, then took it with a scowl. She remembered a thirteen-year-old boy being offered a book, and snarling like a fox cub because he didn't know how to accept a kindness.

She watched him dip the handkerchief in what remained of the water, and make a clumsy job of cleaning a long, bloody bruise on his side. Then she had to look away. He was finely muscled, and below the sunburn that ended at the base of the throat his skin was pale and smooth. He looked both familiar and unfamiliar: boy and man, known and unknown. It made her want to cry.

Around them, night settled on the river. Fireflies spangled the creepers that choked the low ruined walls. The crickets' rasp had given way to the clear pulse of the whistling frogs, and on the breeze Sophie caught a drifting sweetness. Glancing about her, she saw a cluster of cockleshell orchids clinging to a block of cut-stone to her left. The pale, twisted petals seemed to catch and hold the moonlight. Their scent was heavy and sweet.

Raising her head, she saw with a shock that Ben was watching her, his expression unreadable in the moonlight. She said quietly, 'Why didn't you meet me at the bridge?'

'I couldn't.'

'Why not?'

He turned back to the fire. 'Look. I know I hurt you. And I'm sorry. But I had to stay away. If I'd met you on the bridge, I'd've hurt you more.'

'I don't understand.'

'You don't have to.' He sighed. 'It's nothing to do with you. It's nothing to do with you, or your knee.'

Nothing to do with your knee. Was she so easy to read? So transparent and pitiful? She tugged at a snag in the blanket.

'Sophie,' he said quietly.

She raised her head and glowered at him.

'Christ, Sophie,' he said, 'when are you going to forget about that bloody knee?'

'That's easy for you to say. You don't limp.'

He nodded at his bandaged leg. 'I do now.'

'Not permanently.'

'What would you know? You don't either.'

'I do when I'm tired.'

'So what? Sophie . . . look at me.'

She met his eyes. He was close enough for her to see the black blood crusting his eyebrow, and the bruises down the side of his face, and the gleam of his teeth between his lips. And as she looked at him, she realised that he did want her to stay, after all.

'Let me see it,' he said, startling her.

'What?'

'Your knee. Let me see it.'

'No!' She drew in her riding skirt and tucked it under her.

He studied her face for a moment, then nodded. 'All right.'

She rubbed her palm up and down her thigh. 'It's just that I don't like anyone touching it.'

'Why, does it still hurt?'

'Of course not.'

'Then why?'

'I don't know, I just don't.'

Again there was silence between them. In the river a fish splashed. In the trees an owl hooted..

Without looking at Ben, Sophie pulled her riding skirt a fraction above her knee. 'Promise you won't touch.'

'All right. I promise.'

Catching her lower lip in her teeth, she reached under her skirt and unclipped the stocking from the suspenders, then started rolling the thin black silk down her thigh.

'Let me do that,' he said.

'No!'

'Yes.'

Suddenly she was breathless and shaking. She watched him take his crutch and lever himself painfully off the block of cut-stone and onto the blanket beside her. His face was tense and serious as he put out his hand and gently rolled the stocking down over her knee. His fingers were trembling. She hissed as they brushed her shin.

He stopped. 'You all right?'

She nodded. She wanted to tell him to stop, but she couldn't. She couldn't breathe.

He looked down, and his dark brows drew together in a frown. 'D'you remember when we was kids, in that kitchen of yours, and you showed me your knee?'

Again she nodded.

'You said, "Look, Ben, I got a bruise." Only I couldn't see nothing.' He paused. 'You were the cleanest person I'd ever seen.'

She wanted to touch his cheek, but she couldn't. She couldn't move.

He peeled back the stocking to just above her riding boot, and put his warm hand on her shin, lowered his head and softly blew on her knee. She felt his hair brushing her skin, then the gentle caress of his hand.

'You said you wouldn't touch,' she whispered.

He raised his head and met her eyes. Then his gaze dropped to her mouth. 'I lied.'

He moved closer to her, and she caught the aromatic tang of Grace's salve on his skin, and beneath it his own smell: the sharp clean scent of red dust and wind-blown grass. He kissed her lightly on the mouth.

Then he kissed her again, and this time he pressed harder, opening her mouth with his. For the first time she felt the heat and strength of his tongue. She was frightened and curious and excited. She didn't know how to respond. She tried to do what he was doing, and put her arm round his neck and kissed him back.

With that first real kiss she left everything behind; she struck out into unknown territory. And she knew that it was the same for him, because although he'd done this before, he'd never done it with her. With that first deep kiss they left their old selves behind and crossed over for ever from being friends to being lovers. And as she felt the roughness of his cheek against hers, and the softness of his hair beneath her wrist, she experienced not only the first deep stab of desire, but also a new tenderness for him, because he was in this with her, taking in the strangeness and the unbelievable closeness, and trembling against her. She buried her face in his throat and clutched his shoulder—and heard him wince. 'Sorry,' she mumbled, and against her neck he gave a crooked smile; then she felt him shake, and the warmth of his laughter on her skin. He raised his head to hers and looked at her for a moment, and his smile slowly faded, and he kissed her again, harder and deeper.

They moved closer against one another—carefully, because of his ribs—and he ran his hand down her thigh and under her hips, and she slid her hands beneath his shirt and grasped the hard muscles of his back.

Suddenly, he broke away with a cry.

'What's wrong?' she whispered. 'Oh God, did I hurt you?'

He shook his head. He was sitting hunched over, breathing painfully through his teeth. 'We can't do this,' he muttered, still shaking his head.

She put her hand on his shoulder but he shook it off. 'Yes, we can,' she said. 'I want to.'

'No. No.'

'Why?'

'I don't . . . I don't want to hurt you.'

'Ben—'

'The first time it hurts, Sophie. It hurts.'

'I know.' She tried to make light of it. 'I managed to pick up something in my medical studies. But I . . . don't expect it'll hurt too much. I've done lots of riding, and always astride, and that's supposed to—'

'Sophie, shut up,' he said softly.

She bit her lip. He was right, she was talking too much. But she was so nervous. She couldn't believe she was doing this. Sitting in a ruin, trying to seduce a man. She looked about her at the pale clustered orchids and the thick cords of the strangler fig, and finally at Ben, scowling down at his hands with a strange, angry expression which made him seem very young. 'Do you love me?' she said in a low voice.

He did not reply. She watched him run his hand through his hair, then grind the heel of his hand into his good eye.

'Do you love me?' she said again.

He drew a raw breath. Then he nodded.

'Then it'll be all right.'

'You don't know that. You don't know nothing about it.'

'Then tell me. Show me.' She lay back on the blanket, and drew him down towards her.

It was past midnight when she got back to Eden. Madeleine and Cameron weren't back from Parnassus and everyone else had gone to bed. Someone had left a lighted hurricane lamp on the sideboard.

She led her horse down to the stables, untacked her, gave her a drink and checked her manger for hay. Then she walked round the side of the house to the garden. Scout clattered down the steps to greet her, settled himself beside Sophie on the bottom step and shoved his nose under her hand. She stroked his silky ear and breathed in the scents of the moonlit garden: the smell of the tree ferns and the perfume of star jasmine.

She felt exhausted, but incredibly alive. She could still feel the faint throbbing ache inside her, and the tenderness on her inner thighs. She could still feel the weight of his body on hers; she could still smell him on her skin. And if she shut her eyes she could almost summon up the closeness, the unbelievable closeness.

'Meet me here tomorrow,' he'd whispered as they lay together, watching the fireflies and feeling the sweat cooling their skin.

'Aunt Sophie?' said a small voice at the top of the stairs.

She turned to see Fraser standing in his nightshirt, squinting down at her. She got to her feet. 'Darling, you should be in bed,' she said quietly.

'My tummy hurts.'

Sophie climbed the steps and took his hand. It was warm but not feverishly hot. She bent and planted a kiss on his sleep-creased cheek. 'You'll live,' she said.

'But it hurts,' he insisted crossly.

'Come along then, and I'll take a look at you.'

Together they went inside, and when they reached the pool of light from the hurricane lamp, Sophie knelt and put the back of her hand to his forehead. 'You haven't got a fever,' she told him, 'and no swollen glands. You've just had too many sweets, darling.'

'I didn't have a single one after Mamma left,' he grumbled, 'except what Clemency gave me.'

The qualification made her smile. 'Then I'm sure you'll feel better very soon. Come along. I'll make you some rhubarb powder in milk. Then it's back to bed.'

A quarter of an hour later she was curled up in her own bed, wide awake, watching the slatted moonlight on the tiles. Outside the window, a tree fern nodded against the louvres. In the distance an owl hooted. Drifting in on the night air came the cloying sweetness of stephanotis.

She buried her face in the pillow and slept.

At Bethlehem, the scent of stephanotis tells Evie that something is wrong. She asks if her mother can smell it too, but Grace only gives her a narrow-eye look and shakes her head.

It's about four in the morning, and the Jonkunoo parade has broken off for food. Grace has brought Evie a slice of her favourite dish, but she can't eat a bite. Something is bad wrong.

A couple of days ago, Ben told Evie that she made a mistake about that red-haired girl: that it wasn't meant as a warning for him, but for Sophie. If she was wrong about that, then was she wrong about old Master Jocelyn, too? She thinks back to that day at Fever Hill, when she watched old Master Jocelyn following Sophie up the croton walk. Sophie and little Master Fraser. And suddenly she knows what was wrong, and the knowledge is a cold certainty in her belly. Old Master Jocelyn wasn't following Sophie. Not Sophie.

She grabs her mother's arm. 'Something's wrong. We've got to get to Eden, quick-time.'

Sophie was shaken awake by a frightened Clemency. Fraser was ill. She didn't know what to do.

'How ill?' mumbled Sophie, still heavy with sleep.

'I'm afraid I don't know, dear.' She stood by the bed like an ineffectual ghost, twisting her waxy hands and shaking her head so violently that her dyed grey braids brushed against Sophie's face.

But she was right about Fraser. When they reached the nursery he was thrashing about in the bedclothes, and battling against a terrified Poppy, who was trying to hold him down. Belle was curled up on the other bed, sucking her toy zebra's ear and staring at them.

As Sophie leaned over Fraser, a cold kernel of fear settled inside her. His eyes were shut against the light, and his breathing was fast and shallow. 'It hurts!' he moaned, pummelling Poppy with his fists.

'Where, darling?' said Sophie. 'Tell me where.'

'All over! Aunt Sophie, make the hurts go away!'

Sophie took his small fist in hers. It felt cold. What did that mean? She glanced at the nursery clock. A quarter to two. Two hours before, he'd had nothing worse than a tummy-ache.

'It *hurts!*' screamed Fraser. He threw off the bedclothes and would have fallen out of bed if Sophie hadn't caught him. In the lamplight she saw a pink rash splashed across the smooth skin of his calves.

God, she thought. What's that? 'Clemency,' she said without turning round, 'take Belle and go and sleep in the servants' quarters. D'you understand? Tell Braverly to stay with you, and *not* to come inside. Whatever this is, it could be catching.'

Clemency's hands crept to her throat.

'Poppy,' said Sophie over her shoulder. 'You run and wake Moses and tell him to saddle Master Cameron's horse and ride as fast he can and fetch Dr Mallory. He's to tell Dr Mallory it's an emergency, and to come at once. And he's to send a man for Dr Pritchard, too, and another down to Parnassus to fetch Master and Mistress. Now go!'

Poppy fled.

Please God make it the measles, Sophie thought, when they'd left her alone with Fraser. Or something else that we know how to fight.

'When will the hurts go away?' Fraser mumbled.

'Soon. Soon. When the doctor comes.' She felt a pang of guilt at deceiving him. It would be at least two hours before Dr Mallory got there, and Dr Pritchard would arrive some time after that. All she could do was to try to reassure him, and get him to sip a little water.

And always at the back of her mind was the gnawing dread that this might in some way be her fault. What if she'd been here all the time, and could have spotted some subtle sign of impending illness, and sent for the doctor straight away?

The rash was worse. It had spread all over his legs and arms, and when she raised his nightshirt she saw with horror that it now covered his whole body. How could anything spread so quickly?

A terrible thought gripped her. She reached for her *Introductory Primer on Diagnostic Medicine*, and turned to the index. The words blurred and shifted, and she couldn't find what she was looking for. Then she had it. 'Brain fever: see Meningococcal Disease; also Meningitis.'

Dawn is commencing to light when Evie and her mother reach Eden. By the look of things, Master Cameron and Miss Madeleine have just gone inside, for the carriage is still at the door, and the horse has its head down, blowing hard.

In an instant, Evie takes in all the wrongness of the house. Miss Madeleine's bronze satin evening mantle dropped in the dust and trampled under the horse's hoofs. Miss Clemmie and little Missy Belle standing in the carriageway in their nightgowns, wide-eyed and frightened. Moses hanging on to the horse's bridle like he can't let go.

And there in the doormouth sits Sophie, rigid on the threshold in her dressing gown, her lips bluish-grey, her eyes staring into darkness.

'Sophie?' says Grace.

Sophie raises her head and tries to find the source of the sound, as if she's having trouble focusing.

'Sophie,' says Evie, going to sit beside her and putting her arm round her shoulders.

'It was brain fever,' says Sophie. Her voice sounds flat, as if she had nothing left inside. 'Dr Mallory came, and Dr Pritchard, and they said—'

At that moment from inside the darkened house comes a terrible, wrenching scream. Evie has never heard such a sound in her life.

Sophie's face crumples. 'I was holding him,' she says. 'I was holding him. And he died.'

CHAPTER FIVE

SOPHIE WAS BUSY in her room when there was a knock at the door, and Cameron asked if he might come in. His eyes went to the packing cases around her, but he made no comment. 'I wonder, do you have a moment?'

She glanced at the folded blouses in her arms, and put them on the bed. 'Of course. Shall we go out onto the verandah?'

He nodded, and stood aside to let her pass.

She wondered if he too was aware of the new formality between them. Her mourning gown of dull black parramatta seemed to impose on her a rigidity of which even Great-Aunt May would have approved.

Cameron took one end of the old cane sofa, and Sophie the armchair opposite. Scout heaved himself up and trotted over to his master, and then slumped down again at his feet.

Cameron looked exhausted. January was the busiest time of the year, when the works at Maputah and Fever Hill had to run twenty-four hours a day or the cane would spoil, and bankruptcy would follow hard on bereavement. Sophie wondered when he found time to grieve. She herself had done with crying. Now she was too hollowed out to feel anything but a desperate fatigue and a longing for peace.

'Is anything wrong?' she asked.

There was silence while they both considered that. *Is anything wrong?* Everything was wrong. Fraser Jocelyn Lawe had been lying out on the wooded slope behind the house for three weeks now: the first inhabitant of Eden's new burying-place. Clemency had said that his white marble tomb was almost as beautiful as Elliot's, but Sophie hadn't seen it for herself. She couldn't bear to. Nor had she attended the funeral. Instead she had stayed at the house, while Cameron had followed the hearse to Falmouth, and stood in the churchyard surrounded by his workers, and finally ridden back for the burying.

Clemency had been one of the few ladies to attend, and the sole female representative of the Monroes had been Great-Aunt May. Madeleine had not attended. She'd simply announced that she wouldn't be going to church any more, that she was finished with God.

Cameron studied Sophie for a moment before he spoke. 'Moses tells me that you've ordered the carriage for Monday. For Montego Bay.'

Sophie put her hands together in her lap. 'I hope that's all right,' she said carefully. 'I shall be catching the eight forty-five to Kingston. I'll be booking a passage on Tuesday's packet to Southampton.'

'Don't go,' he said.

'I think I must.'

But she sounded more certain than she felt. Half of her thought she was wrong—that she was running away when Madeleine needed her most. The other half told her that it was the only thing to do. Madeleine didn't want her here any more. They hadn't talked about it—they hadn't talked at all. But Sophie could feel it. Perhaps Madeleine blamed her for Fraser's death. Or perhaps she simply couldn't forgive the fact that Sophie had been with him in his final hours, while she, his mother, had not.

And always at the back of Sophie's mind was the thought of how much worse Madeleine would feel if she ever found out that on the night when her son was dying, her sister had been with Ben.

'Sophie,' said Cameron, dragging her back to the present. 'If you go back to England now, you'll be running away.'

'No. No, I'll be making it easier for everyone.'

'Not for me,' he said quietly. 'Not for Madeleine.'

'How is she?' Sophie asked. 'I mean, really?'

Cameron shook his head. 'I don't know. She won't talk to me. That is, she talks to me, but she isn't there.'

'Cameron,' said Sophie quietly. 'You do understand why I have to go?'

He hesitated. 'Sophie . . . it wasn't your fault.'

'How do you know that?'

'Because,' he said evenly, 'you sent for the doctor as soon as he became ill. And you did everything for him—everything that could be done.'

Sophie sat in silence, and her eyes grew hot. She wanted to believe him. If she could believe him, she could remain at Eden. Perhaps she could even see Ben again. But, she couldn't do it. She'd been with Ben, and then Fraser had died. She couldn't think of Ben without seeing Fraser's wide grey eyes.

'So that's where you were that night,' said Madeleine between her teeth, as she paced up and down the verandah the following afternoon. 'You were with Ben Kelly.'

Sophie sat on the sofa and watched her sister twisting her hands together, and held her breath. It had happened without warning, like a thunderclap. She'd come out to join Madeleine for tea, and found her alone and tautly waiting. Apparently, the previous evening, Ben had sent word by Moses, asking Sophie to meet him on Overlook Hill—and somehow Madeleine had intercepted the message.

'I *asked* you not to go to him,' Madeleine said accusingly. 'You promised that you wouldn't.'

Sophie opened her mouth to say that she'd never promised. Then she shut it again. What was the use?

'Did you sleep with him?' Madeleine asked suddenly.

Sophie looked down at her fists, clenched in her lap.

'My God,' said Madeleine, 'you did, didn't you? He summoned you, so you left Fraser to go to him. And then he—'

'It wasn't like that.'

'Did he hurt you?'

'No!'

'My God. My God.' She put both hands to her temples. Then she looked at Sophie. Her face had a rigidity that Sophie had never seen before. 'I'll never forgive him,' she said in a low voice.

Sophie stared at her. They both knew that she didn't just mean Ben. She meant her sister, too. Sophie spread her cold hands on her knees. 'Madeleine . . .' she began. 'It wasn't his fault. It wasn't—'

Madeleine turned on her. 'Don't you ever speak of this again. D'you understand? I'll never forgive him. I hope he rots in hell.'

Vapour misted the tree ferns as Sophie led her mare up the overgrown track on Overlook Hill and the woods echoed with early morning bird-calls. It had been shamefully easy to get away. Cameron had left for the works at daybreak, and Clemency was still asleep. Belle was in the nursery and Madeleine hadn't yet woken up. After the scene on the verandah the day before, she had gone to her room. She hadn't emerged for dinner, and Cameron had told Sophie that she'd taken a powder and gone to bed. He had given Sophie a thoughtful look, and she'd wondered how much he knew. She hadn't had the courage to ask.

She kept seeing that look in Madeleine's eyes. That hard, accusing stare that told her what her sister couldn't bring herself to say out loud. *I'll never forgive you.*

And who could blame her? She had begged Sophie not to go to Ben, but she had, and then Fraser had died. The two events were unrelated, but not in her heart. Sophie understood that, because she felt it herself. And now more than ever she knew that she had to get away. Away from Madeleine and Cameron, and Eden and Ben.

She reached the glade of the great duppy tree. Ben was waiting beneath it. His face lit up when he saw her. He came towards her and took the reins and tethered her horse, and helped her down. He had dispensed with the crutches, and his bruises had faded.

'I missed you so much,' he said, putting his hand against her cheek.

'I missed you too,' she muttered. But when he bent to kiss her she twisted her head away. She felt sick at the thought of what she was about to do. Sick and empty inside.

'You all right?' he said.

'No. I'm not.' She looked down and saw that she was gripping her riding-crop with both hands, her knuckles straining her gloves.

She heard him move closer, then felt his arms about her as he drew her against him. For a moment she shut her eyes and relaxed against him, and listened to his heart beat. Then she gently pushed him away. 'What about you?' she said without meeting his eyes. 'How's your leg? And . . . and your ribs? Are you all right?'

'Me?' His lip curled. 'I'm always all right.'

Oh God, I hope that's true, she thought.

'I'm sorry about the little lad,' he said, running his hands up and down her arms, as if to warm her. 'I was going to write Madeleine a note, only I didn't have no paper. Tell her I'm sorry.'

'That's not a good idea.'

There was a silence. Then his arms dropped. 'You told her about us.'

'She found out when you sent the message to Moses. I had to tell her the rest.'

'Oh, Sophie.' He stepped back a pace. 'What did she say?'

She hesitated.

'She blames me,' said Ben. 'That's it, isn't it?' He rubbed a hand over his face, then shook his head. 'Christ, Sophie. Christ.'

She felt a spark of anger at him. Why was he thinking only of them, when Fraser lay dead in the little marble tomb behind the house? Suddenly she wondered if she'd ever really known him. Looking at him standing there, he seemed rough and unfamiliar. How was it possible that three weeks ago they'd been lovers? Three weeks. She was a different person now. She forced herself to meet his eyes.

'I came to see you, because I need to tell you . . .' She moistened her lips. 'I'm leaving for England tomorrow. I won't be coming back.'

To her surprise, he only looked startled. 'That's a bit sudden.'

'I can't stay here any longer.'

He scratched his head, then nodded. 'Fair enough. But it'll take me a while to follow you. I got to get up the fare, and—'

'No, you can't follow me. It's over, Ben. That's what I came to tell you. We can't see each other any more.'

She watched the understanding dawn; the stillness come down over his features. 'No,' he said flatly. 'You can't . . . no.'

'I have to.'

'No, listen. Come with me. I got it all worked out. We can go to Panama. Or America. We'll do all right there. We can be together.'

'Ben. I can't be with you. Not anywhere. Not after this.'

He stood with his hands by his sides, watching her. 'Don't do this, Sophie,' he said at last.

She pushed past him and ran to her horse. 'I've got to go. I can't stay here any more.' She was amazed at how calm she sounded, when inside she was breaking. She was amazed at the steadiness of her hands as she threw the reins over the mare's head, put her foot in the stirrup and swung herself into the saddle.

'If you do this,' he said, 'it's for ever. Don't you know that?'

'Of course I do,' she flung back at him, 'but what choice do I have? How can I be with you after what happened?'

After what's happened, Evie just wants to get away. Away from Fever Hill and her mother, away from Sophie and Ben and that poor dead child. And most of all, away from her own self. Away from Evie Quashiba McFarlane, the four-eyed daughter of the local obeah-woman.

So here she is, sitting on the train in an empty third-class compartment, craning out of the window as the whistle goes, and Montego Bay drops away behind her. In her whole life she's never been further than Montpelier, ten miles down the line, but now she's clutching a ticket all the way to Kingston. Even as the john crow flies, that's more than a hundred miles. But she's glad. She's been so full of black feeling that it's a fat relief to be on her way. Home, family, friends. Leave it all behind.

At one point, a few hours before she caught the mail coach, she thought about going to see Miss Madeleine. Perhaps it might ease her heart to know that old Master Jocelyn had been waiting to take her little one's hand and help him over to the other side. But then she thought better of it. Just leave it. Leave it all behind.

It's early evening when Ben reaches the sea, and by then he's drunk. He stumbles onto the beach somewhere east of Salt Wash, peers at the bottle, and takes another long, blistering pull. He's been walking all day, stopping only to buy a bottle of proof rum at Pinchgut. First thing tomorrow, he'll be down at the quay and get the first job going.

A shiver runs through him. He's lost his hat, and the sun's sickeningly hot, but the odd thing is, he can't stop shivering. It's been hours since he watched Sophie ride away, but he still can't get warm. And he's got this pain in his chest. Worse than his cracked ribs. Deeper than any bruise.

He's had it before, years ago when Kate died, and then again when Robbie went. It feels like someone's taken a chopper to his breastbone and split him down the middle. But how can he be feeling that now, when he swore then that he'd never feel it again?

'Because, you idiot,' he mutters, 'you let it happen. Didn't you? You went and let her in.'

Forget about it, Ben Kelly. Slam down the lid on the whole rotten, stinking mess. Slam it down hard.

PART TWO:
London 1910
CHAPTER SIX

A COLD, WET AFTERNOON in early April. Rain rattled the windows of the dingy little office. In the street, a pair of sodden dray horses hauled a wagon piled with coal from Lambeth Pier. The rumble of Waterloo Station grew to a roar as a train thundered across the bridge at the end of Centaur Street.

Sophie put the box file on her desk in a puff of dust, and looked about her with satisfaction. This was the sort of work she liked: peaceful, predictable and solitary. The Reverend Agate was upstairs in his study working on his History, and the rain was keeping the applicants away, so she had the office of St Cuthbert's Charitable Society to herself. Nothing to do but sort through old records. And absolutely no need to deal with that other matter, the unposted letter in her bag.

Pushing the thought away, she opened the box file and gave the contents a cursory glance. Twenty-year-old receipts from the Poor Law Guardians; reports from the Charity Organisation Society. Oh, good: another volume of the daily Register of the Reverend Agate's predecessor, the Reverend Chamberlaine. She was developing a strange fascination for his granite cynicism.

January 3rd, 1888, he had written in his tiny backward-sloping hand. *Mrs Eliza Green, aged 27, 10 Old Paradise Street. She may be 'Green' by name, but looks anything but verdant, & her complexion is unappealingly yellow. Works as a scrubber at St Thomas's. Has borne 10 children, 4 living. Husband in the Madhouse—and yet she has the temerity to seek a Maternity Certificate to finance her next confinement! Told her that if she chooses to indulge in impropriety, she must face the consequences. Application refused.*

'Still on the same box?' said the Reverend Agate, making her jump.

He was standing in the doorway, forcing his lipless mouth into an uneasy smile. 'It's only the important items we wish to retain. No need to trouble yourself with old Chamberlaine's Registers.'

Serenely she returned the smile. 'Yes, of course.'

'Capital. Capital. Any applicants while I was upstairs?'

'Only two. I gave one a certificate for the infirmary, and the other some oil of turpentine.'

His mouth tightened. 'You must feel free to summon me if—'

'You're most kind. But I didn't think it necessary to trouble you. It was only an abscess and a case of croup.'

'Ah. To be sure.'

They both knew that if he'd been there there would have been no certificate and no free medicine. It was a little game they played. Sophie would let through as many applications as she could, while he did his best to prevent her. It wasn't that he was ill-natured, just ferociously mean. And he could conjure up almost as many reasons for refusing an applicant as the Reverend Chamberlaine.

'Capital!' he said again, rubbing his hands. 'Well, well. I shall be upstairs at my desk, should you need me.'

'Thank you,' she said, and turned back to the Register. But to her irritation, she could no longer concentrate. The Reverend Agate had broken the spell of peaceful tedium and let in the outside world.

The rain was showing no signs of easing off, and she had forgotten her

umbrella, so she was going to get soaked going home. And she remembered that she had to be back by four, as she had rashly promised Sibella
that they would go for a cup of chocolate at Charbonnel's. And of course
she must decide what to do about the letter.

For the past fortnight she had been carrying it around in her bag. It
had accompanied her on her daily Underground journey from Baker
Street to Lambeth North, on her lunchtime walks to the street market in
The Cut, and during her solitary evenings in Mrs Vaughan-Pargeter's
drawing room in New Cavendish Street. It was becoming ridiculous.
The following morning her attorney would receive her instructions, and
within a day she would be free. So why couldn't she post it?

The answer was simple. She had forgotten how to make decisions.
She had so constructed her life that she didn't need to. She had freed
herself from doubt, and—apart from Madeleine's stilted little bi-
monthly letters—from the past. But was she doing the right thing?
What would Madeleine think? And Cameron? And Clemency?

If only I could be sure, she thought. If only I could have some indica-
tion that I'm right.

Sibella's brougham was outside the house in New Cavendish Street, and
Sibella herself was waiting impatiently in the drawing room.

'Did you order tea?' Sophie asked as she drew off her gloves.

'I thought we were going out,' said Sibella with a frown. 'You don't
mean to say that you've forgotten?'

Sophie repressed a flicker of irritation. She was tired, and she needed
to be alone. But clearly, chocolate at Charbonnel's was immovable.
Thank heavens that Sibella was going home next week.

She tried a change of subject. 'What did you do today?'

'Mrs Vaughan-Pargeter took me about,' said Sibella in an accusatory
tone. 'We went to that new department store.'

'Selfridge's? Oh, isn't it grand?'

'Personally, I think it far too large and rather vulgar. And the clothes!
"Hobble skirts"? And something ghastly called a "tube frock". They're all
very well for you, but if one has any sort of figure, they're absolutely the
end.' It was her most frequent complaint. She had put on flesh since her
marriage, and even now, in widow's black, she looked very nearly fat.

Sophie sat on the sofa and kneaded her temples, and wondered how
she had got herself into this position.

She had been astonished when Sibella's letter had arrived the previous
month, for they hadn't corresponded since Sophie had left Jamaica. *As
no doubt you already know*, Sibella had written after a brisk introduction,

I recently lost my darling Eugene. Of course Sophie had heard. Madeleine's letters, while short, were informative.

I have been inconsolable, Sibella wrote crisply, *so Papa is sending me to London for a change of air. I would have come years ago if it hadn't been for the beastly price of sugar and the earthquake in '07. Such a trial. Dear Eugene's town house quite went up in smoke, and even Papa's interests were damaged.*

I shall be in London for a month, and I shall want you to show me about, as I'm sure that Alexander will be perfectly useless. But I'm afraid that I shall be staying at an hotel, as Papa had to sell our place in St James's Square. Isn't it frightful? So many changes. It's too unfair.

So many changes. For the past three weeks that had been Sibella's constant refrain. Now she fiddled idly with one of Mrs Vaughan-Pargeter's cushions, and studied Sophie's plain grey costume with disapproval. 'Everything is different from when I was here last,' she muttered.

'That's life,' said Sophie unsympathetically.

'And it's not just London. Trelawny is absolutely going to the dogs. You ought to come back and see for yourself.' Her tone implied that Sophie had been getting off scot-free for years, and should jolly well mend her ways. 'It's dreadful,' she went on. 'Estates going to smash every day. Why, old Mowat absolutely shot himself.'

'You already mentioned that.'

'And I was counting on London to cheer me up.' She sounded aggrieved, as if London were somehow in breach of contract. 'All these horrid motor-omnibuses. And "underground railways". What a ridiculous idea. Who wants to go on a beastly train under the ground?'

Sophie sighed. Sibella had, quite simply, lost her nerve. She hadn't been to London for a decade, and it frightened her. Watching her fiddling with the cushion, Sophie felt a flash of sympathy. After all, were they so very different? She too had lost her nerve.

It was a shaming thought, and it lent her the resolve she needed. She jumped to her feet and went to the bell pull and rang for the parlour maid. To Sibella she said, 'I just need to give something to Daphne, and then we can go.' Then she opened her bag and unearthed the letter.

'Daphne,' she said quickly, as soon as the maid appeared, 'would you take this and see that it's posted at once?'

'Yes 'm,' murmured the girl, looking less than delighted at the prospect of running to the postbox in the rain. But as she took the letter her hand touched Sophie's icy fingers and she glanced up in alarm. 'You all right, 'm?'

'I'm fine,' said Sophie with a brief smile.

Sibella had seen none of this. She was standing by the chimneypiece, inspecting her new mourning bonnet in the looking glass. 'I do think it's amazing,' she remarked, 'that they found anyone to buy the old place.'

'Which place?' murmured Sophie, going to the window. There now, she told herself. That wasn't so hard, was it?

'Old Mowat's place, of course. Arethusa.'

Sophie drew back the curtain and looked down into the street. The rain was coming down in sheets. She could see a tall, very thin gentleman paying off a hansom cab, and Daphne huddling beneath an umbrella as she ran to post the letter.

You did the right thing, she told herself. But she felt shaky and sick.

'I can't imagine who they found to buy it,' said Sibella again.

'Buy what?' said Sophie.

'*Arethusa*. Aren't you listening?'

'I expect someone took a fancy to it,' Sophie said with her eyes still on the street. 'A coffee planter or a rich American.'

Sibella snorted. 'Easier said than done in times like these.'

'Oh, I don't know,' said Sophie, turning back from the window. 'I've just sold Fever Hill.'

Sibella's expression would have made her laugh if she hadn't been on the verge of tears. Her friend's eyes opened theatrically wide and her jaw dropped, then shut with an audible click.

'Don't say a word,' said Sophie. 'I don't want to talk about it.'

'But—'

'Sib, *please*. Can we just go to Charbonnel's and have a quiet cup of chocolate, and pretend I didn't say it? I'll tell you all about it tomorrow.'

She turned back to the window. The hansom was moving away, and the tall, thin gentleman was unfurling his umbrella.

The Honourable Frederick Austen cast a wistful glance at the brougham waiting outside the elegant little town house, then shook himself and walked round the corner into Mansfield Street.

What a confounded idiot he was. To have paid off his cab in the pouring rain three streets from his employer's house, simply for the chance of catching a glimpse of the fascinating young widow who seemed to be a daily visitor to New Cavendish Street. He had only seen her face once, but it had been enough. She was enchanting. Wide blue eyes; a small, soft mouth; and a truly magnificent figure. Surely one so beautiful must also be sweet-tempered?

But of course he would never find out, for why should she speak to him? He was the last man on earth to find favour with a lady. He looked like an ostrich. All the Austens did. They had long thin necks and large beaky noses. So all things considered, it was better if they never met.

He headed for the tall stone house in Cavendish Square of which his employer was already tiring. A restless man, his employer. Moody. Discontented. Unpredictable. A rough diamond. Very rough indeed.

'We'll call you my secretary,' he'd said at that extraordinary interview in the Hyde Park Hotel. 'I'll pay you three times over the odds, but you'll be earning it. It'll be your job to teach me whatever I want to know.'

A singular requirement, particularly when it was made by an ex-street-Arab (and probably worse) to a member of the aristocracy. But as Austen had four unmarried sisters, and a ninety-room country seat in Tipperary, which was largely lacking a roof, he took the position. And so began the most exhausting, alarming and entertaining year of his life.

Whatever I want to know turned out to be everything. What to read and how to talk; how to dress and what to eat; where to live and where to ride one's horses. In short, how to be a gentleman.

To his surprise, Austen found himself enjoying the job. He enjoyed the discussions and arguments. He liked his employer's cleverness and his flat-on view of the world. He liked his cavalier attitude to his wealth—acquired, he vaguely explained, through a 'prospecting syndicate' with his business partner in Brazil. He liked the fact that although he worked to improve his accent, he didn't carry it to extremes. 'I can't be talking like I've just come out of Eton,' he said drily, 'because I haven't.' Most of all, Austen admired his employer's indifference to the opinion of others, for that was so utterly unlike himself. Austen could suffer paroxysms of self-consciousness quite literally at the drop of a hat.

But there was another side to his employer that he found unsettling and incomprehensible. Black, silent moods that could last for days. And a distance that must never be crossed. Two months before, as they were preparing to leave Dublin, Austen had been astonished when his employer gave orders to sell his prized thoroughbreds.

'But . . . I thought you were attached to them,' he had ventured.

His employer had looked at him with eyes grown suddenly cold. 'I'm not attached to anything,' he had said softly. 'Not to my horses. Not to you. Remember that, my friend.'

Always that distance.

And it hadn't taken long to learn that 'why' was not a question one ought to ask. Why do you never go out into Society? Why do you bother to improve your speech, when you don't care a pinch of snuff for what people think? Why have you hired a private detective? And why, since we've been in London, do you go out alone every afternoon?

True to form, his employer was out when Austen reached the house. Only Mr Walker was at home, as Austen discovered to his discomfort when he went upstairs and opened the drawing-room doors.

Mr Walker, in an easy chair, froze with a teacup in one hand and the *Daily Mail* in the other. Their unease was mutual. Mr Walker was far more conventional than his business partner, and far more cautious—which was probably why they had made such a good team in Brazil. But that also meant that he was uncomfortable with people like Austen, whom he knew to be his betters.

For his part, Austen simply didn't know how to behave. Until a year ago he had never spoken to a black man in his life—let alone lived with one under the same roof. He liked the man well enough, and in a way he even respected him. But he couldn't relax with him.

Downstairs the front door slammed, and moments later Austen saw his employer coming up the stairs. He breathed a sigh of relief.

His employer glanced from Austen to his business partner, and he grinned. 'What's up, Austen? You been squabbling with Isaac again?'

Austen's cheeks burned. 'Oh, I say, sir, I wouldn't dream—'

His employer touched his shoulder. 'I didn't mean it.' He went over and poured himself a cup of cold tea and drank it off in one go, then threw himself down into a chair. 'So what you been up to, mate?' he asked Mr Walker. Sometimes with his business partner he lapsed into his old mode of speech. Austen suspected that he did it to tease his secretary.

'Been down the docks,' said Mr Walker.

'God Almighty, Isaac, what for?'

Mr Walker shrugged. 'I dunno. Old times.'

Austen cleared his throat.

His employer turned his head. 'What is it, Austen?'

'Not "God Almighty",' said Austen gently. 'Might I suggest "Dear Lord"?'

His employer studied him for a moment, then burst out laughing. 'Why don't you come over here and have some tea? And if you ever catch me saying "Dear Lord", you can shoot me. All right?'

Austen permitted himself a shy smile, and edged towards the sofa. 'Very well, Mr Kelly,' he said.

Ben woke with a start as Norton drew back the curtains. For a moment he didn't know where he was. His heart was pounding. He lay still, fighting the pull of the dream. He couldn't shake it off. All the little details. Kate's blue frock. Her bright blue eyes and hair like copper wire. His terror that she might leave home to live with her sweetheart, Jeb Butcher. Twenty years on, and he hadn't forgotten a thing.

Outside it was still dark. The street light shone in his eyes. Seven o'clock, and a fire was already blazing in the grate. Some time around five a housemaid would have crept in and made it up. She hadn't woken him. Since coming to London he slept like the dead. And now he was dreaming of them, too.

Rubbing his face, he propped himself up on one elbow. The unflappable Norton set the coffee tray on the table, poked the fire, turned the gas on low, then went through into the dressing room to lay out his master's clothes.

Ben got out of bed, shrugged on his dressing gown and stood looking down at the fire. Even without it the room would have been warm, for he always took houses with hot-water pipes in every room.

He turned to survey the bedroom. In the golden glow of the gaslight, the furnishings were opulent but not ostentatious. The deep patina of well-polished mahogany. The dark blue sheen of silk damask hangings. What would Jack have made of it? Or Lil, or Kate?

Why dream of them now, suddenly, after all these years? That bloody dream! Until he'd got to London he'd never had a single one. Panama. Sierra Leone. Brazil. He'd slept like a baby. Maybe it was coming to London that had done it. After all, London held other memories apart from Kate and Jack and the others. Cavendish Square wasn't very far from the Portland Road. The other day he'd even thought of walking down it, just to see if the photographer's studio was still there. He'd stopped himself in the nick of time. So maybe it was thinking of that— or trying not to think about her—that had got him all churned up.

Involuntarily he glanced at the picture above the chimneypiece. It was an oil painting of Montego Bay that he'd seen in Paris and taken a fancy to. It wasn't very good, but at least the artist knew what royal palms look like, and poinciana trees and bougainvillaea.

Funny, but he still missed Jamaica. It was probably why he'd ended up in Brazil: because he'd felt at home there, with the parrots and the darkies. And now that he was in London, he sometimes went all the way down to the gardens at Kew, just to stand in the Palm House and breathe in that hot, wet, green smell, and see if the vanilla was in flower.

Norton appeared at the dressing-room door and discreetly cleared his throat. 'Shall you be going riding this morning, sir?'

'No,' snapped Ben. 'No riding. I'm going to Kew.'

'Very good, sir,' said Norton.

'But Kew,' said Sibella crossly, as the train rattled through the suburbs, 'is so frightfully middle-class. I fail to see why we can't go to Richmond.'

'Because,' answered her brother with an amused glance at Sophie, 'it's a cold, dank morning, and we wish to be pleasantly warm in the Palm

House, rather than shivering with a lot of undernourished deer.'

Sibella turned to the window and studied her reflection. When she was satisfied with her new pouched walking coat with the sable collar, she renewed the attack. 'All those ghastly terraced houses. And tramways, and . . . and day-trippers.'

Sophie wondered in amusement why Sibella believed that they themselves fell outside the term. 'I imagine,' she said, 'that we'll be safe from the crowds on a Wednesday morning in April.'

'Don't try to humour me,' said Sibella, turning back to the window.

Again Sophie and Alexander exchanged glances, and Alexander rolled his eyes. He had joined them at the last minute, much to Sophie's relief. Sibella had been impossible ever since she'd heard about Fever Hill.

'But it's your family *seat*,' she had said in a scandalised tone over her chocolate, having ignored Sophie's request that the subject be deferred.

'We don't have a family seat,' Sophie had replied, taking refuge in pedantry. 'We're not aristocracy. But even if we did, our "seat" would have been Strathnaw. And if you remember, Madeleine sold that years ago.'

She had thought that a powerful argument in her favour, but Sibella had brushed it aside. 'I dread to think what Aunt Clemency will say.'

That put Sophie on the defensive. 'Clemency could hardly go on living at Fever Hill by herself. Anyway, I hear that she already spends a good deal of her time at Eden.'

'But still—'

'Sibella, it's done. I've signed the papers. I've—'

'But why?'

Then Sophie had gone into her prepared speech: about feeling morally obliged to repay Cameron for her education, and wishing to recompense Mrs Vaughan-Pargeter more adequately for her keep.

Her real reason for selling Fever Hill was simple and stark. She needed to sever her ties with Jamaica. By getting rid of Fever Hill, she was cutting herself loose from all the pain and regret. She was finally setting herself free. So why wasn't she feeling any better?

You did the right thing, she told herself as she and Alexander wandered through the dripping green jungle of the Palm House. They were alone together, for Sibella had declined to 'play gooseberry', and had gone off to inspect an adjacent greenhouse. You needed to cut yourself off, and you did. And now you're free.

So what was she doing in the one place in London that reminded her of Jamaica? She raised her head and studied the intricate green-gold fronds of a tree fern that wouldn't have been out of place in the gardens at Eden.

Alexander reached up and held a frond out of the way of her hat. 'I'm told,' he said, 'that there's a rather fine display of orchids in Greenhouse Number Four. Shall you care to see it?'

'Not really,' she replied. 'I don't care for orchids.'

'To tell you the truth, neither do I. I dare say I'm the most dreadful philistine, but I've always thought that they look rather badly made.'

She smiled. Charming, handsome, undemanding Alexander. How he had changed from the old days. If someone had told her that they would become friends, she wouldn't have believed it. Alexander Traherne? That indolent, conceited young man?

But as Sibella never tired of pointing out, Alexander had reformed. He had given up gambling and had cleared all his debts. 'And as for that business of the groom,' Sibella had confided to Sophie, 'why, no one could have been more mortified than Alexander when he found out that Papa had had the fellow thrashed. He moved heaven and earth to make amends, but of course by then he'd fled the country.'

The fellow. With her talent for rearranging the truth, Sibella had pretended to have forgotten Ben's very name—not to mention the fact that her friend had once been in love with him. But her quick sideways glance to see how Sophie was taking it gave her away.

They turned into one of the quieter paths running along the side of the Palm House, and Alexander tapped his cane on the flags and frowned. 'Sophie,' he began, without looking at her.

'Yes?'

He hesitated. 'That work you do. That . . . volunteer affair?'

'You mean at St Cuthbert's?'

He nodded. 'I suppose you're frightfully attached to it, and all that?'

She was surprised. 'I suppose I am,' she said. 'It makes me feel useful.'

He nodded. 'You see, I was wondering. Why the slums? You could be useful, as you put it, just about anywhere. Couldn't you? You're not inextricably linked to Lambeth, or . . . or even London?'

He was right, of course. But 'Why the slums?' was a harder question than it appeared. She herself had never come up with a satisfactory answer, although sometimes in her darker moments she wondered if Lambeth wasn't some means of retaining a link with Ben.

But of course that was absurd. And the only reason she'd thought of it now was because she was still upset about Fever Hill. 'I could leave it tomorrow,' she said, with a sharpness that made Alexander blink.

'Ah,' he said. 'I was rather hoping you'd say that.'

They walked on in silence. Then Alexander came to a halt and took off his hat, and ran his hand through his golden curls. 'I dare say you've some idea of what's coming next.'

'Alexander—'

'Please. Hear me out, old girl. I promise I shan't take long.' He paused. 'I know that in the past I haven't always run quite the right side of the post. I mean, I've dabbled a bit with cards, and . . . well, that sort of thing.'

She bit back a smile. 'That sort of thing' probably encompassed champagne suppers in Spanish Town with ladies of doubtful reputation, and running up racing debts at the speed of a cane-fire.

'But I truly believe,' he went on earnestly, 'that at last I've got myself straight. I know you don't exactly love me.'

'I'm very fond of you,' she replied.

He gave her a slight smile. 'Well, you see, old girl, I'm rather more than fond of you. And I do believe, though it sounds frightfully arrogant to say so, that I could make you happy.'

She believed it too. He was considerate, gentlemanly and handsome. And everyone she knew would thoroughly approve of the match. Of course he would make her happy. At least, as happy as she deserved to be. 'I think you're probably right,' she said.

Again that slight smile. 'Does that mean you'll consider it?'

She stood looking up at him. In the greenish light his eyes were a clear, arresting turquoise, and his face had the smooth planes of a classical statue. 'I'll consider it,' she said.

They moved along the narrow path towards the end of the Palm House. Ahead of them, a tangle of peacock ferns dripped moisture. Beneath its fronds, Sophie saw, with a jolt, a small clump of orchids. They had tubular, leafless stems and insignificant pale green flowers. They were not, she told herself, cockleshell orchids. Certainly not.

Suddenly she wondered if people put orchids on graves. She wondered what sort of flowers Madeleine put on Fraser's grave: on the grave that she, Sophie, had never seen.

'You see,' she said without turning round, 'I'm happy as I am.'

'And yet you miss Jamaica.'

'No.'

'Sophie—yes. I've seen how you fall silent when we come here to look at the palms. You miss it, and you're afraid of it.'

She glanced at him, surprised that he could be so shrewd.

'You're afraid of Eden,' he went on, 'because of what happened to your nephew. And yet you miss it terribly. But don't you see? Here's your chance. You could go home, without going home. You could be happy at Parnassus, I'd make sure of it. And no one would put the least pressure on you to go to Eden, not if you didn't want to.'

She turned her head and looked out through the glass walls of the

Palm House. A pair of ladies in enormous hats and modish draped coats tottered across the lawns towards the Tea Rooms. A slender dark-haired man in an astrakhan coat emerged from the adjacent greenhouse and walked swiftly away. Something about the way he moved reminded her of Ben. He had the same grace. The same taut air of watchfulness.

What's wrong with you? she told herself angrily. Why should every good-looking dark-haired man suddenly remind you of Ben?

But of course she knew the answer. It was because of Fever Hill, and those wretched cockleshell orchids. Because of the hundred little daily coincidences that were always reminding her of Jamaica.

Alexander was wrong. She couldn't go home. Not ever.

She turned her head and looked up into his face. 'Dear Alexander,' she said softly. 'I'm so sorry. But I can't marry you.'

His features contracted slightly, but he managed a strained smile. 'It's because you don't care for me,' he said quietly. 'That's it, isn't it?'

'That isn't it at all,' she said with perfect truth. On the contrary, she didn't want love. She just wanted peace.

He squared his shoulders and gave her another slight smile. 'Well, I give you fair warning, old girl. I shall ask you again in a month or so. And who knows, if I'm very lucky, you might even say yes.'

She put all thoughts of Fever Hill and cockleshell orchids and Ben firmly from her mind, and returned his smile. 'Who knows?' she said.

Sibella took her brother's walking stick and hammered on the roof of the brougham, and told the driver to keep circling the park. Then she turned back to Alexander and pursed her lips. 'It's high time that you faced it,' she said importantly. 'You've simply got to marry money.'

'But that's what I'm trying to do,' he protested. 'It's scarcely my fault if she said no.'

'I don't believe,' she said severely, 'that you fully appreciate the gravity of your position. Sophie Monroe is positively your last chance.'

'My last chance?' he said indignantly. 'Hang it all, Sib. I'm fond of Sophie, but you've got to admit she has some pretty serious drawbacks.'

'Such as?'

'Well, for one thing, she was born on the wrong side of the blanket. And she's a frightful blue. And definitely damaged goods, what with that illness, and that appalling business about the groom.'

'It's because of those "drawbacks" that you even stand a chance,' she snapped. 'Any other girl with a fortune like hers wouldn't touch you with a polo stick.'

'Oh, I say—'

'Well, it's true! Tell me, Alexander. Give me a rough estimate. How much do you actually owe on the horses?'

Alexander ran his forefinger along his bottom lip, and wondered what to tell her. 'At a rough estimate, I should say . . . about five thousand?'

His sister's eyes became enormous. 'Alexander! I never dreamed it would be as much as that!'

Oh, yes, you did, he told her silently. And wouldn't you be delighted if you knew that he actually owed Guy Fazackerly four times as much. But the bill only fell due on New Year's Day, eight months away. Plenty of time for him to marry Sophie. And plenty of time for Sib to snag that rich financier their father had in his sights for her, which would be an additional comfort. So why was she trying to worry him like this?

He turned to her and gave her his most charming smile. 'Sib, darling, isn't this a tad academic? After all, the governor won't live for ever, and then I shall be a landowner, just as the Almighty intended.'

'Haven't you been listening? Papa is losing *patience* with you! He wants your proposal, in detail, as to how you plan to settle your debts.'

'But I can't,' cried Alexander. 'I haven't any money.'

It was all so confoundedly disagreeable. Why was everyone so hard on him? His needs were so few. An agreeable house, a few decent horses and a string of polo ponies. To be tolerably dressed, to give the odd dinner for one's friends, and to keep a dear girl in a pretty little apartment.

He allowed his mind to wander to the dear girl he had left behind in Jamaica. He ought to buy her something when he was next in the West End. Perhaps one of those Japanese paper sun-umbrellas? It wouldn't cost much, and she would be so grateful. Girls like that were easily pleased.

'What you have to appreciate,' said Sibella, 'is that Papa isn't going to stand much more of this. He is talking seriously of cutting you out of his will, and making Lyndon his heir.'

Alexander's mouth went dry.

'Of course we must put a stop to that,' said Sibella. 'And as a first step, you absolutely *must* clear your debts.'

Alexander thought for a moment. 'When you marry this financier fellow the governor's got in his sights, surely he—'

'Mr Parnell is quite horribly strait-laced,' said Sibella severely. 'The merest hint of gambling debts and he'll be off for good. And if that were to happen, which God forbid, then I'd be without a husband, and Papa would be without a business partner, and you, brother mine, would be out in the cold for good.'

'Which brings us neatly back to Sophie Monroe.'

'Precisely.'

'Sophie, do hurry up,' said Sibella, raising her voice above the determined grizzling of Mrs Carpenter's baby. 'I can't let the carriage wait for much longer in a place like this.'

'I'll be ready in a moment,' said Sophie, watching in relief as the Reverend Agate beat a retreat upstairs. She handed Mrs Shaughnessy her certificate, and took a bottle of quieting syrup from the shelf and gave it to Mrs Carpenter. 'A teaspoonful three times a day,' she said.

'There,' she breathed, when the door tinkled shut. She sat down at her desk and put her elbows on the pile of the Reverend Chamberlaine's Registers and her head in her hands. Her eyes felt scratchy with fatigue. She hadn't slept properly for days. She'd been worrying about Fever Hill, and whether Madeleine had got her letter yet.

Sibella stared in horrified fascination as Mrs Carpenter made off down the street, hoisting the wailing infant on her hip. 'Sophie, how can you bear this?'

Sophie did not reply. She was looking down at the topmost Register, lying open on the pile. *Jan. 22nd, 1889*, she read. *Mrs Bridget Kelly, 39 East Street.* Something about the address was vaguely familiar.

East Street. The Kellys of East Street.

'We lived in two rooms on East Street,' he'd told her that day at the clinic. She hadn't thought of it in years—hadn't wanted to think of it— but now the memory was so sharp that she could almost see him.

'If you've finished,' said Sibella impatiently, 'then we can go. Sophie? Are you listening?'

'What? In a moment.' She put out a tentative hand and touched the Register. Suddenly she was frightened. She didn't want to know what it said. Why should she? That was all over years ago.

Mrs Bridget Kelly, she read, *39 East Street. Immigrant Irish. Aged 32, but looks 50, she is so raddled & unkempt. Husband Padraig a coal-heaver & a low radical, currently 'indisposed' (i.e., he drinks), who got himself dismissed for attending a 'union' meeting, and is now learning that the world can do without him. The family owes 5 wks' rent at 10/- per week, landlady requires 15/- down, which Mrs Kelly says she has not got; she says they must remove to cheaper lodgings if it cannot be found. She makes 2/6d a week by piecework, & the children contribute. The eldest boy, Jack, 14, works as a ganger at 4/- per week. The girls, Katherine, 15, & Lilian, 13, are silk-winders at 2/- each, but widely reported to be engaged in immoral activities. Benedict, 8, is 'supposed at school'; Robert, 2, is a defective; and the babe in arms is yellow & ill-favoured.'*

Benedict, she thought numbly. I always thought it would have been Benjamin. Or simply Ben. She didn't attempt to convince herself that this was some other family. Of course it was his.

'Sophie,' said Sibella. 'I really am about to lose my patience.'

'Coming,' she murmured.

Manifestly, wrote the Reverend Chamberlaine, *the Kellys are far from respectable, and undeserving of any kind of aid. I told Mrs Kelly so in no uncertain terms, and suggested that, as they are Catholics, she might apply to the authorities at St George's. She said that St George's had turned her down, & that we were her last resort. Scarcely complimentary! Application refused.*

Sophie sat blinking at the crabbed, backward-slanting writing. Then she shut the Register, and grabbed hold of the whole pile of volumes, and crammed them into the waste-paper basket. Then she stuffed an old newspaper on top, to cover them up.

She got to her feet, and wiped her palms on her thighs, as if to rub away the last trace of them. 'There,' she said. 'There.' Then she turned to Sibella. 'I'll fetch my hat, and we can go.'

Everything's different since Pa got the sack. When they lived in East Street, Ben was always out on the click with Jack or Lil. But now they've moved north of the river, and Lil's down Holywell Street all the time, and Jack's got a job down the docks, and moved into a dosshouse on the West India Dock Road. Ben never thought he'd miss him but he does.

He never thought he'd miss Ma neither, nor the baby, but he does. They just hadn't woken up one day. No one questioned why. Pa's down the Lion all the time, and when he's back he's yelling at Kate or watching her like a cat. And Kate gets this wary look when Pa's around, and she don't laugh no more.

Soon as Ben gets home he knows there's trouble. All yelling and banging coming from upstairs—from their place. All of a sudden the door opens, and out comes Pa. He stumbles down the stairs, then sees Ben and lurches to a stop. He's well basted, but steady enough to grab Ben and shake him like a rat. Then he chucks Ben against the wall, and lumbers out. Rubbing his shoulder, Ben picks hisself up off the floor. Couple of minutes later, Kate comes out onto the landing. She's all poshed up in her blue frock. One eye is swelling shut, and she's lost the buttons down the front of her jacket. Then he sees the carpetbag in her hand, and his heart goes still.

She comes down the stairs and sits on the bottom step. 'Come here, Ben,' she goes. Her good eye is very blue, but red round the rim. 'Ben,' she says, rubbing his arm as if to make it better. 'I got to go, Ben. I can't stop here no more.'

He opens his mouth but nothing comes out.

'I'm going to Jeb,' she says. 'But you got to promise not to tell Pa.'

'Kate . . . no.' He grabs her hand. 'I'll come with you.'

Her face crumples. 'Jeb can't take you too, Ben. How can he? He can't afford to take me, let alone you and Robbie—'

'*I don't care about Robbie!*'

'*Well, you got to. You got to stop here and look after him. You're the big brother now.*'

'*No, Kate, no!* No!'

Someone knocked on the door of the study, and Ben raised his head from his hands and looked about him without recognition. He drew a deep breath and rubbed his face. 'What is it?' he said.

The butler opened the door. 'A Mr Warburton to see you, sir.'

Ben glanced at the clock on the desk. Ten o'clock in the morning. Warburton was on time, as usual. Private detectives seemed to make a point of that. He gazed at his hands on the green morocco desktop, and struggled to get back to reality. It was three hours since he'd woken from the dream, but he still couldn't shake it off. It had left him feeling drained, with a gnawing sense of loss.

Discreetly, the butler cleared his throat.

Ben squared his shoulders. 'Send him in,' he said.

Sophie heard the front door opening and closing with conspiratorial softness. She moved out onto the landing to listen.

Down in the entrance hall, Mrs Vaughan-Pargeter shooed away the housemaid and tiptoed forward to extend a tremulous greeting to Sibella Palairet. 'I'm *so* sorry, my dear,' she whispered, 'but I'm terribly afraid that she won't see anyone at all.'

'Not even me?' murmured Sibella, aghast.

Mrs Vaughan-Pargeter shook her head. 'The thing is, she's still so frightfully *down*. Won't eat a morsel. Can't seem to get up an interest in anything. It's all the fault of that dreadful, dreadful man.'

'But surely . . .'

Their voices faded as they moved into the drawing room.

Sophie went back into her room, shut the door and leant against it. She slid down onto the floor and clasped her arms about her knees.

That dreadful, dreadful man.

But the Reverend Agate wasn't dreadful. He was simply right. He had been right to be angry and horrified, and relieved. He had been right to lose his temper. 'You could have *killed* that child!' he'd bellowed, brandishing the offending bottle. An opiate strong enough to put a grown man deeply to sleep—and Sophie had given it to Mrs Carpenter for soothing her baby.

Of course the Reverend Agate had lost his temper. What did he care that Sophie had simply made a mistake? What did he care that the baby

259

had eventually awoken with no ill effects? The point was, he was responsible. There had been questions from the rector and the St Cuthbert's Guardians, and a stern note from the doctor at the infirmary.

You could have killed that child.

Every time she thought of it she broke out in a cold sweat. She had handed the wrong bottle to Mrs Carpenter and sent her away. If the child had been a little weaker, or Mrs Carpenter a little more generous with the 'quieting syrup', Sophie Monroe would have killed a child.

She could never go back to St Cuthbert's. She could never face anyone again. All thoughts of Ben, and the Reverend Chamberlaine's Register, had been pushed aside. Fever Hill no longer mattered. All it took was a single mistake, and a child was dead. The wrong bottle taken from a shelf in an unguarded moment. The slightest symptom missed or mistaken. The seemingly innocuous stomachache that turns out to be a deadly brain fever.

As if it were happening all over again, she remembered those first terrible days after Fraser's death. Everybody kept telling her that it wasn't her fault. But it was. She knew. *She knew.*

The private detective perched on the edge of his chair. 'To date,' he said, anxiously scrutinising his notebook, 'a degree of progress has been made on your . . . on . . . the mother, sir.' He paused. 'Unfortunately, the . . . er, remains, are proving somewhat inaccessible.'

Ben tapped the desktop with his fountain pen. 'Meaning?'

The detective ran a finger inside his celluloid collar. 'There has been a degree of, er . . . construction work over what was once the churchyard.'

'What kind of construction work?'

'A . . . a brewery.'

Ben thought for a moment. Then he burst out laughing. Poor old Ma. She'd never had much luck when she was alive, and now they'd gone and built a bloody brewery on top of her. He stopped laughing as abruptly as he'd started. 'What about . . . the older daughter?' It annoyed him that he couldn't bring himself say her name.

'Ah, yes,' said the detective, relieved to be back on track. 'Katherine.' His face fell. 'I regret, sir. Nothing as yet.'

Ben put down the pen and kneaded his temple.

'But the younger brother,' said the detective, brightening, 'now that is beginning to look reasonably promising.'

Ben shot him a look. 'Are you sure it's him?'

'Why . . . yes, I believe so.'

'I don't want belief. I want certainty.'

The detective swallowed. 'Of course, sir. I have noted down here all the . . . the means of identification.' He held up the notebook as evidence. 'Depend upon it, sir. There will be no mistake.'

'There'd better not be,' said Ben softly, still holding the detective's gaze. 'I shall know it if you play me false.' He leaned back in his chair and passed a hand across his eyes. All this effort, and he still couldn't find Kate. And she wanted him to. That was what this was all about. The dreams. And that time in Jamaica when she'd appeared to Evie.

Jamaica. He sat up. Was that what she was trying to tell him?

His heart raced. He forgot about being tired. *Jamaica.*

He'd been planning on going back for some time now; just to show them what he'd made of himself, and maybe teach one or two of them a lesson. So why not take his dead along too? Why had he never thought of it before? It was perfect. The clean, sweet air. The warmth. The colours. It was everything they'd never had when they were alive.

He glanced at the detective, who sat meekly with his head down. 'In a few days,' said Ben, 'I shall be leaving London for good.'

The detective raised his head and gave him a small, defeated smile. 'Very good, sir.'

'I shall be going to Jamaica. I shall want you to redouble your efforts. I'll pay you a monthly retainer. Say, ten pounds. Will that do?'

The detective's mouth fell open. Two spots of colour appeared on his sallow cheeks. 'Yes, sir. Of course, sir. More than generous—'

'I shall want a report every week, without fail. My secretary will sort out the details. But be sure and address the reports to him, rather than to me. The Honourable Frederick Austen, Fever Hill, Trelawny.'

The detective nodded, and wrote it all down in his notebook.

The curtain had gone down on the first act of *Il Trovatore*, and Sibella had hurried away to talk to an acquaintance in another box, having dispatched Alexander to order champagne.

Sophie didn't want any champagne, but Sibella insisted. 'You can't come to the opera and not have champagne.'

'Can't we have champagne without the opera?' suggested Alexander.

'Ridiculous boy,' said Sibella. 'Now go and fetch.'

Sophie sat and fiddled with the tassel on her evening bag, and hoped they would come back soon. It was her first time out of the house in a fortnight, and she couldn't shake off the sense that everyone was looking at her. *There's that woman who almost killed a baby. Deplorable.*

It was ridiculous, of course, for no one knew or cared about Mrs Carpenter's baby. But she couldn't help herself.

To her relief, Alexander swiftly returned with a waiter in his wake bearing an ice bucket, glasses and two bottles of champagne. She felt a surge of gratitude. Over the last weeks she had become dependent on him and Sibella. Once, she had believed she could be self-reliant, that she could achieve something by herself. Now she knew that to be a mistake. St Cuthbert's had taught her that.

'Sophie,' said Alexander, as he handed her a glass of champagne. 'Sophie . . . I wonder, could I talk to you?'

'That's what you're doing,' she said with a smile. She took a sip of champagne. It was just what she needed: icy and dry and delicious.

'Quite so,' he murmured. He paused, as if composing his words.

She knew what was coming next. She had thought about it a great deal. And she knew that what she was about to do was right.

'I don't know if you remember,' he began, 'but a few weeks ago, I said that I would wait a while, before I asked you whether you would—'

'Yes,' she said.

He gave her an enquiring glance.

'Yes,' she said again. 'The answer, Alexander, is yes.'

CHAPTER SEVEN

FEVER HILL TOOK BEN by surprise. He'd never expected to like it. He'd only bought it on a whim, but when he got there, he fell in love with it. He arrived in May, just after the rains, when the whole estate was bursting with life. The trees were in full flower: lemon-yellow cassias and dusty pink oleanders, vermilion poincianas and powder-blue jacaranda.

One morning he stood on the great marble steps and looked out over the shimmering cane-pieces and thought in astonishment, Yes. I'm home. For the first time in his life he was at peace. No more restlessness, no more black moods. No more dreams of the old days. He was finished with all that. He'd left it behind in London.

For two months he lived peacefully on the property. He left the running of the estate to the manager who'd handled it under Cameron Lawe, and bought half a dozen thoroughbreds, and set about schooling them. Isaac came to stay for weeks at a time, preferring to walk and survey the hills, rather than to run his own place at Arethusa, on the other side of Falmouth. Even Austen was enjoying himself, having confessed somewhat sheepishly to a passion for birdwatching.

Then, in the middle of July, the telegram arrived from the private detective. *Your brother Robbie, sisters Lilian and Katharine found. Report follows. Request instructions.*

Robbie and Lil and Kate. Found. After all this time.

Two days later, he and Austen caught the train to Kingston, and plunged headlong into arrangements for bringing out the bodies. They spent hours in shipping offices and the Telegraph Department, then, when Ben couldn't stand it any longer, he left the rest to Austen, and took Evie out to lunch at the Constant Spring Hotel.

She loved the great hotel with its magnificent dining-terraces, and the enormous French menu. She wore a gown of green silk and a wide-brimmed hat of fine pale straw, elegantly trimmed with cream silk flowers. Both hat and gown looked expensive, and Ben wondered how she could afford them on a teacher's salary. But he dismissed that as none of his business, and told her that she looked enchanting.

She acknowledged the compliment with a stately little nod, then leaned towards him and whispered, 'Our fellow diners probably think I'm your mistress.'

'I wondered about that,' he replied. 'Do you mind?'

She smiled and shook her head, then threw him a mischievous glance. 'So, Ben. What *about* that? Have you got yourself a mistress yet?'

'You know very well that I haven't,' he said mildly.

'Cho!' she said, lapsing into *patois* to tease him. 'You must be the despair of every Society matron on the Northside!'

'Very sad, I agree,' he said drily. 'Now what about you? When am I going to be introduced to your mysterious sweetheart?'

Evie snorted. 'Never! You'd grill him like a snapper and chase the poor man away. Sometimes you act as if you're my big brother.'

'Sometimes that's how I feel.'

The waiter came and refilled their glasses, and Evie applied herself to her pineapple ice, stabbing at it delicately with her spoon. 'So why'd you buy it, Ben?' she said suddenly. 'Why'd you go and buy Fever Hill?'

He took a cigar from his case and turned it in his fingers. 'I felt like it.'

She studied him for a moment, and her almond-shaped eyes were impossible to read. Then she put down her spoon and took a sip of champagne. 'You bought it because it belonged to Sophie,' she said calmly. 'Because you can't forget her. Because she broke your heart.'

'I bought it,' he said between his teeth, 'because it came on the market, and I liked the idea of annoying Cornelius Traherne. Now can we please talk of something else?'

She put down her glass and looked at him, and smiled. 'Annoying Cornelius Traherne. Now that's something with which I can sympathise.'

He pretended to be amused, but she wasn't fooled. She had spoilt the day, and she knew it. They finished their lunch with a strained attempt at good humour, then he drove her back to her pretty little house.

Back at the hotel, he found a note from Austen. *Complications re shipping have sent me back to Port Royal. Irritating, but capable of resolution. Should be back by six. A.* Ben cursed under his breath. He didn't want to be on his own. He didn't want a chance to brood on what Evie had said.

He went out onto the verandah and ordered tea and a newspaper, and stood with his hands in his pockets, gazing at the groups of tourists strolling beneath the royal palms.

The Myrtle Bank Hotel occupied a magnificent position on Harbour Street with views of the sea. Like much of Kingston, it had been destroyed by the earthquake three years before, but had since been rebuilt. Everything about it was rich and recently established. Rather like me, thought Ben. The idea amused him, and made him feel a little better.

The tea arrived, and with it the *Daily Gleaner*. He sat down and forced himself to read every page, determined to keep the black mood at bay. He ploughed through the foreign news and the local happenings. He learned whose horse had won at the Spanish Town meeting, and that the Governor's daughter was leaving for England on the *Atranta*.

Underneath that was a small paragraph that he nearly missed.

Arrived by the mail steamer yesterday morning, Mr Augustus Parnell the noted City financier, travelling with Mr Alexander Traherne of Parnassus Estate, Mrs Sibella Palairet, and Miss Sophie Monroe, latterly of Fever Hill Estate. The party will be staying at the Myrtle Bank Hotel before travelling on to Trelawny. It is with great pleasure that this correspondent has learned that Mr Traherne and Miss Monroe have recently become engaged to be married.

Sophie had been dreading her arrival in Jamaica. The *Atranta* had been due to dock on Friday at seven in the morning, and two hours before she was on deck with a scattering of sleepy American tourists awaiting their first glimpse of Kingston harbour. Alexander, Sibella and Gus Parnell were all still asleep, which was just as she had planned. When at last the sharp green mountains rose above the horizon, she felt a shock of painful longing, and a strange kind of dread.

An hour later she stood on the quay with the others, assailed by the din of the West India Regimental Band, which had come to greet the packet, and the thunder of street cars and trams and drays. She picked her way past iridescent piles of snapper and parrotfish, and higglers' handcarts laden with the last of the June plums and the first of the oranges. She was only too glad to let Alexander take the lead.

He had been taking the lead for the past two months, and after the initial strangeness she had discovered that it was a relief. He had seen to everything. He had placed the engagement notice in *The Times*, and made arrangements with Mrs Vaughan-Pargeter about packing up her things; he had even conspired with his sister over the trousseau. Finally, he had booked their passage to Jamaica, and gently told Sophie that of course she must stay at Parnassus; she needn't think of going anywhere else.

They both knew that 'anywhere else' meant Eden, but that she couldn't face it yet. In her brief letters to Madeleine she had avoided the question of a visit, and she noticed that her sister did the same, confining herself to expressions of slight surprise at the suddenness of the engagement, and cautious approval. Bizarrely, Madeleine said nothing about Fever Hill.

It was Monday afternoon, their fourth day in Kingston, and Sophie and Sibella had just returned to their hotel after a day's shopping. Sibella had declared herself absolutely *finished*, and gone upstairs to lie down. Disinclined to do the same, Sophie wandered out into the grounds, found a table in a shady corner and ordered tea. She sat back in her chair and gazed up at the wild almond tree overhead: a shifting pattern of enormous dark green leaves and small pale green blossoms, and little chinks of hot blue sky.

'I don't believe it,' said a man's courteous voice directly behind her. 'Can this really be Sophie Monroe, back in Jamaica after all this time?'

The voice was startlingly familiar . . . and yet unfamiliar. She twisted round, shading her eyes with her hand, but he was standing with his back to the glare, and at first she couldn't see his face. Then the sun went black. Dark spots darted before her eyes. *It couldn't be him.*

He was standing looking down at her with his head slightly to one side and an amused expression on his face. He wore a white linen suit and a Panama hat, and looked completely at his ease. 'It is you, isn't it?' he said again. 'May I sit down for a moment, or are you expecting someone?'

She swallowed hard. Then, still unable to speak, she clumsily indicated the cane chair on the other side of the little round tea table.

Nothing was real any more. She wasn't sitting under a wild almond tree in the gardens of the Myrtle Bank Hotel. Ben wasn't standing beside her . . . And it really was him. The same narrow green eyes, the same sharply handsome face, the same lean, graceful figure. He was the same . . . but he wasn't. He was utterly changed. The slender gentleman before her now was dressed with a casual, unstudied elegance, and spoke with distant courtesy, and not a trace of a Cockney accent.

'Ben?' she said stupidly. It came out as a croak.

He sat down and put his hat on the ground beside his chair. He crossed his legs, leaned back and smiled at her. It was a charming smile—a social smile. He told her that she was looking remarkably well, and asked what she'd been doing with herself since he'd last seen her.

She mumbled something about St Cuthbert's.

A charity volunteer, he said, how interesting. And have you been in Jamaica long?

Four days, she said.

Indeed, he said. I was in London a couple of months ago, we must have been there at about the same time. Isn't it extraordinary how one's always missing people one knows, just by a whisker?

Then he noticed the sapphire and diamond cluster on her finger, and asked whom he ought to be congratulating, and she steeled herself and told him that it was Alexander Traherne. He looked mildly surprised, then faintly amused. I hope you'll be very happy, he said.

The tea arrived, and she asked in a strangled voice if he'd care to join her. He reached for his hat and got to his feet and said, thank you, no, I ought to be going. But you go ahead, you must be parched.

She stared at the tea things. She couldn't touch them. If she did she would drop the teapot or break a cup. There was an awkward silence. At least, she felt it to be awkward, but Ben merely stood with one hand in his pocket, slowly fanning himself with his hat.

'I don't understand,' she said suddenly.

He smiled down at her. 'What don't you understand?'

'I don't . . . I mean, you're . . . you're—'

'Rich?' he put in gently.

'Well . . . yes.'

'And you really haven't heard a whisper about it?'

She shook her head.

He gave a slight laugh. 'Well, then, it seems we're both hopelessly ill-informed! Although I have to say, I think I've more of an excuse than you. You see, I never bother with newspapers at Fever Hill.'

The ground tilted. 'Fever Hill?' she said.

He was laughing and shaking his head. 'Really, Sophie, don't you know about that either? You're going to have to administer a sharp rebuke to that sister of yours for not keeping you better informed!'

'I thought it best to wait,' said Madeleine over tea at Parnassus, 'and tell you face to face.'

Sophie caught the glance that passed between her sister and Sibella, and realised with a jolt that Sibella had known about Ben all along.

'According to Olivia Herapath, he knocked around Panama for a while, then took up with some coloured engineer—the one who's bought Arethusa. They went to Sierra Leone to look for gold, but they didn't find any, so then went to Brazil, where they did. Cameron says they bought up the rights very cheaply and then sold them on to mining companies at enormous profit. Mr Walker provided the surveying expertise, while Mr Kelly was the brains behind it.'

Mr Kelly. How bizarre to hear Madeleine calling him that. The last time she'd spoken of him, she'd been cold-eyed and savage with grief. *I'll never forgive him*, she had cried. *I hope he rots in hell.*

'It was something of a nine days' wonder,' Madeleine went on, 'but it's all blown over now. And of course, Mr Kelly never goes out into Society.'

'I should think not,' said Sibella, pink with indignation.

Sophie pictured the consternation at Parnassus when they'd first got the news. An erstwhile groom—their groom—the new owner of Fever Hill! Cornelius would have been incandescent, poor Rebecca prostrated. 'But has it really blown over?' she asked.

'There's been a certain amount of gossip,' Madeleine said carefully.

There was an awkward silence. Then Sibella stepped into the breach by loudly admiring the presents that Sophie had brought from London. Sophie did her best to join in, but she knew that she failed. She was painfully aware of how different this homecoming was from her last. Seven years before, she hadn't needed presents to buy approval. Her welcome had been genuine, Jamaican, and at Eden. Now they sat on Italian wrought-iron chairs under Rebecca Traherne's rose pergola, and skated like mayflies over the surface. Even when Sibella tactfully left her alone with Madeleine, they didn't mention Fever Hill. Or Ben.

They strolled the length of the pergola, and watched Belle emerging from the croton bushes, scowling as she beamed the torch that Sophie had brought her from London directly into her eyes.

'She's going to be beautiful,' said Sophie for something to say.

Madeleine sighed. 'She's a dreadful tomboy. Rides all over the estate, always giving the grooms the slip. Cameron wants to send her away to school. But I don't think she's ready.'

Of course not, thought Sophie with a pang. Madeleine had already lost one child. How could she lose another, even if it was only to a girls' academy in Kingston? 'I'm sure you're right,' she agreed.

'Am I? I don't know. Cameron has a point. She rarely sees children her own age, and she's got a morbid streak, which worries me.'

Sophie glanced at her in surprise. Was this her way of bringing the conversation round to Fraser?

'She never seems to play with her dolls,' Madeleine went on with her eyes on her daughter. 'Just holds funerals for them.'

'But lots of children do that. Don't they?'

'Yes, but Belle's are so elaborate. Proper Jamaican nine-nights, with parched peas in the pockets and cut limes on the eyes.'

'That's to stop them becoming duppies,' said Belle, who'd heard her name mentioned, and sidled up.

'Oh, I can understand that,' Sophie told her. 'At your age I was fascinated by duppies. I was very ill, you see, and I—' She broke off in confusion. 'I was fascinated.' She'd been going to say that she'd been scared of dying and becoming a duppy herself, but stopped just in time.

Belle was looking up at her with new respect. 'How did you get better? Did you ask a duppy tree?'

'As a matter of fact, I did.'

Belle's mouth fell open. 'How? Did you give it an offering?'

'Belle,' said her mother, 'that's enough. Run along and ask Mrs Palairet if you can go to the stables and say hello to the horses.'

As Sophie watched Belle reluctantly trailing off, she felt a pang of recognition. She had been about Belle's age when she'd first come out to Jamaica. She had adored Fever Hill, and lived in terror of the duppy tree across the lawn; she had idolised her older sister, and—although she hadn't known it at the time—she'd had a hopeless crush on Ben.

He had been like some dark, bright-eyed spirit from another world: filthy, savage, but always vividly aware of whatever she felt. How could he have transformed into that polite man in the white linen suit?

At her side, Madeleine asked when it was to be.

'When is what to be?' said Sophie.

'The wedding. I was talking of the wedding.'

'Oh. I don't really know. We haven't fixed a date.'

'Ah.'

They walked on a few paces. Then Madeleine said, 'I was so looking forward to seeing Alexander, but I understand he's—'

'In Kingston, yes. You see, we'd been planning on staying there a fortnight, but then I changed my mind, and he still had business to complete, so he had to go back.' She knew she was talking too much, but this polite fencing was beginning to wear her down.

'Sophie,' said Madeleine, 'you do love him, don't you?'

Sophie was startled. She had forgotten how direct her sister could be. 'What are you talking about?'

'It's just that it seemed . . . well, rather sudden. So I wondered.'

'I'm extremely fond of Alexander,' said Sophie.

'Oh, Sophie.'

'Why "Oh, Sophie"? It's true. It really is.' Then an unwelcome thought occurred to her. 'I should perhaps mention . . . Alexander doesn't know anything about Ben. I mean, he knows that I was . . . attached to Ben. But he doesn't know anything about what happened . . . that night.'

Madeleine's face had gone still. 'I'm sure that's for the best,' she said, scarcely moving her lips.

'I thought so too,' said Sophie. *What happened that night.* What an anodyne way of putting it. Suddenly she was alarmingly close to tears. She snapped off a rose and started pulling it to pieces. 'How could you let me come back without warning me that he was here?' she said harshly.

Madeleine's face contracted. 'For heaven's sake, Sophie, we thought you *knew.* You'd just sold him Fever Hill!'

'But I didn't know it was him. I had no idea.'

'And we had no idea that you were selling it.' Madeleine's eyes glittered with angry tears. 'I cannot imagine why you took it into your head to sell it. And I cannot imagine why you didn't tell us first.'

'Because you'd have tried to stop me.'

'Well, of course we would!'

'Madeleine, I'm sorry. I'm sorry I didn't tell you. But you still should have warned me about Ben.'

'No,' said Madeleine, raising her hand as if to ward off an attack. 'No. We won't talk about him any more. It's different for you, Sophie, you've been away, you've been out of it. But for me nothing's changed. Can't you understand? Nothing's changed.'

Sophie looked at her sister's beautiful, agonised face, and wondered how she could ever have hoped that things might be different between them. 'Of course,' she said gently. 'I understand. Nothing's changed.'

The early-morning sun played prettily on Evie's chintz counterpane, and on the hat and gloves and parasol laid out in careful readiness. Even though it was a Saturday, she'd been up for hours, for she always gave herself plenty of time to get ready when her sweetheart took her out. Saturday was their day. Which was why she'd had to do some fancy rearranging when Ben had carried her off to Constant Spring last week.

She smiled at the recollection. Lord God, if those two ever met, how the fur would fly! That was the thing about Ben. He might look different from the way he had seven years before, he might dress and talk differently too, but underneath he was just the same. And you never knew what he might do. Her sweetheart, on the other hand, was a perfect gentleman. In fact, he was perfect in every way.

Downstairs, the key turned in the lock. Her heart leapt. She'd made him a present of a latchkey two days before, but this was the first time he was using it. A latchkey for a lover. What a shocking, unteacher-like thing to do. But she couldn't help herself. She was in love with him.

She heard his well-known step on the stairs, and stared at her reflection as she listened to him reach the landing and come to a halt outside the door. In the mirror her eyes were bright, her lips moist and full.

On the other side of the door, the familiar voice called softly, 'Evie?'

'I'm here,' she called. 'You may come in, if you wish.'

A muffled laugh. 'If I wish? Well, I rather think that I do!'

Then the door was flung open, and in a heartbeat she was in his arms, and he was pressing his mouth to hers. She sank her fingers into his golden curls and murmured, 'Alexander, Alexander. I've missed you so.'

'I fail to understand,' said Miss May Monroe coldly, 'why you have done me the honour of calling, Mr Kelly.' Her ice-blue gaze fixed on Ben, then slid sideways to Austen, who visibly shrank.

Ben repressed a smile. The old cat knew perfectly well why he'd come. She just liked her little game. And why not? At ninety-one she was remarkable. She still held court in her shadowy drawing room; still sat rigidly upright, scorning to touch the back of her chair; and still dressed impeccably, in a high-collared gown of pewter silk that made no concession to the stifling September heat.

'It's good of you to see me, Miss Monroe,' he said evenly.

'So it is. Now answer the question. Why have you called?'

He met the unblinking blue gaze. 'I've a mind to go into Society. So naturally my first thought was to call on its *de facto* head.'

A wintry compression of the lips, which may have been a smile. 'You have acquired Latin, Mr Kelly. How very droll.'

Ben did not reply.

'But I regret that I cannot assist you. It is impossible for you to go into Society. You are a coachman.'

Beside him, Austen gasped. 'I've been a lot worse things than a coachman,' Ben said with a slight smile. 'But you could have declined to see me, Miss Monroe. You didn't. So I think I can allow myself to hope.'

'That does not follow at all.'

'Then why did you let me come up?'

'Because it amuses me to see how you have turned out.'

There must be more to it than that. The old cat despised amusement.

'You are a very clever young man, Mr Kelly,' she said coldly, 'but I repeat, what is it that you want?'

Ben hesitated. 'No doubt you're aware,' he said, 'that this summer's ball at Parnassus was cancelled—out of respect for the death of the King.'

The old lady inclined her narrow grey head. 'So it was given out.'

He nodded. 'And it was the proper thing to do.' He paused. 'The fact that sugar prices are the lowest they've ever been is of course irrelevant to a man like Cornelius Traherne. Saving money had nothing to do with it.'

The gloved claws adjusted their grip on the ivory-headed cane. Now she was interested. Any chance to discountenance the Trahernes.

'So I was thinking,' continued Ben, 'that I might step into the breach, and give some kind of . . . entertainment. Perhaps at Christmas.'

The blue eyes glittered. 'But what is it that you want of me?'

Ben met her gaze. 'I was hoping you might agree to come. Then everyone else would too.'

'I never go out.'

'I thought you might make an exception. Or at least send your carriage and your man.'

'I repeat. I never go out.'

Austen shifted uneasily on his chair, but Ben let the silence grow. He'd expected this. No city falls at the first assault. And he was damned if he was going to beg.

When the silence had gone on long enough, he picked up his hat and rose to take his leave. But as he did so, the doors opened, and Kean announced Mrs Sibella Palairet.

Plump and pretty in modish black and white half-mourning, the young widow swept in, all smiles for Miss Monroe. She didn't notice Ben. Austen leapt to his feet and turned red as Miss Monroe introduced him. The young widow's smile became gracious when she learned that he was an Honourable. It congealed when she turned and recognised Ben.

'Mrs Palairet,' he said with a nod and a slight smile.

She drew herself up. 'I do not believe, sir, that we have been introduced.'

Ben laughed. 'One rarely is to one's groom.'

That earned him a wince from Austen and an unreadable look from Miss Monroe.

The old lady flexed her claws on the head of her cane, and turned to him. 'Concerning your plans, Mr Kelly. It may be that I shall see fit to send my carriage and my man.' The ice-blue eyes held his for a moment, then slid to Mrs Palairet, and back to him. 'It may be,' she said again.

What the hell is she after? Ben wondered. He glanced at the little widow, then back to the old witch. Could it be, he thought suddenly, that she planned all this? That it wasn't mere chance that his visit coincided with that of Sibella Palairet? Sibella Palairet—*née Traherne*.

Then understanding dawned. It was outrageous. The old witch was proposing some kind of bargain. The social countenance of her carriage and her man at his Christmas entertainment, in return for a fling with the plump little widow.

No, that can't be it, he told himself. Not even Miss Monroe would . . .

And yet, when one thought about it, she might. And it would be savagely effective. A scandal like that would topple the Trahernes from social pre-eminence and frighten off the wealthy Mr Parnell, thereby scuppering Cornelius's hopes for shoring up his flagging finances. And seventy-three years after being insulted by a parvenu's offer of marriage, Miss May Monroe would finally have her revenge.

Provided, of course, that Ben decided to play along with it. He felt angry and disappointed. What an idiot he'd been to have hoped that the old witch would admit him to her charmed circle on his own merits.

What naivety! He ought to have known that social acceptance was only ever going to be had at a price. And in his case, that price was a roll in the hay with Sibella Palairet. Once a groom, always a groom, it seemed.

Abruptly, he took his leave, giving no sign that he'd understood her little game.

September gave way to October, and the rains did not come. The heat increased. Tempers grew short. And Sophie began to realise that she'd made a huge mistake by agreeing to marry Alexander.

When they'd first arrived in Jamaica, she had simply been grateful for being cosseted and kept safe from the outside world. But as the months passed, she had become increasingly restless. At Parnassus, ladies were not encouraged to be active. Alexander gently let it be known that he disapproved of her riding out alone; nor did he wish her to see her old friend Grace McFarlane. 'It doesn't do to fraternise with these people,' he said with his most winning smile. 'Particularly not the McFarlanes.'

'But why not?' she asked in surprise. 'I've been friends with Evie since we were children.'

'Yes,' he said patiently, 'but you aren't a child now.'

He might be right about that, but it didn't alter her conviction that she was living a lie. She didn't belong at Parnassus. She didn't fit in.

But how could she jilt Alexander—Alexander who was always so kind and considerate, and who hadn't done anything wrong. Besides, even if she did get up the courage to break it off, where could she go? She still hadn't been back to Eden, not even for an afternoon, so seeking refuge there would be out of the question. The days merged into weeks and she did nothing. She had bitter arguments in her head. She called herself a hypocrite and a coward. She let things slide.

In the middle of October, the rains finally came, turning the roads to rivers and confining Sophie to the house. One afternoon during a particularly thunderous downpour, she couldn't take it any more, and determined to have it out with Alexander.

She found him in his study, reading a newspaper. 'Alexander,' she said as soon as she got through the door, 'we need to have a serious talk.'

'You're absolutely right,' he said, glancing up with a smile. 'I've been a brute. Going off to Kingston all the time, and leaving you on your own.'

'It's not about that—'

'But I promise it'll be different when we're married,' he cut in earnestly. 'For one thing we'll be living at Waytes Valley, so you'll have your own house. That'll give you something to do.'

She gritted her teeth and wondered how to begin.

Alexander must have seen something in her face, for he put down his newspaper and came over to her, and put his arms on her shoulders. 'You know, old girl, we really ought to fix a date. How about it, eh?'

As gently as she could, she twisted out of his hands. 'That's what I wanted to talk to you about.'

His face lit up. 'I can't tell you how delighted I am! So, when is it to be?'

She looked up into his face. He was so undemanding. So unfailingly good-natured. And so happy. 'Um . . . next spring?' she said. *Coward, coward, coward. Now you've just made it ten times worse.*

'Oh, I say,' he murmured with the slightest of frowns, 'isn't that an awfully long wait? I was thinking rather of November.'

Her stomach turned over. 'But . . . that's next month.'

'I know I'm a brute to press you, but it's just that I'm tired of waiting.'

'November's too soon,' she said. 'How about after Christmas?'

For a moment he hesitated. Then he smiled. 'So be it. January. I'll run and tell the governor. He'll be over the moon.'

She gave him a tight smile.

The weeks that followed were a whirlwind of activity. The invitations were sent out; the wedding breakfast was planned like a military operation; every day Sophie resolved to say something, and every day passed with nothing being said. Then, on the 25th of November, something happened that made matters a great deal worse.

MICHELLE PAVER

Scores of engraved, gilt-edged invitations of impeccable simplicity went out to everyone who was anyone in Trelawny.

Mr Benedict Kelly, At Home on Monday the 26th of December, at 8 o'clock. Masquerade. Dancing. RSVP.

Northside Society had a wonderful time being completely appalled.

'Outrageous,' declared Sibella, opening her eyes very wide.

'The man's a cad,' said Gus Parnell with satisfaction.

'Of course he is, my dear fellow,' chuckled Cornelius, slapping him on the back. 'Only a blackguard would flout the rules by not making a single call, then expecting everyone to kowtow, simply because of his money.'

'I've always rather liked him,' said Clemency, startling everyone. She had adapted surprisingly well to the move from Fever Hill, and now often made the trip from Eden to Parnassus in her little pony trap.

'Oh, Aunt *Clemmy*,' cried Sibella impatiently, 'you've never even met the man!'

'Yes, I have, dear,' replied Clemency mildly. 'Years ago, when he was a boy. I gave him ginger bonbons.'

'What on earth does that signify?' snapped Sibella. 'The point is, no one can possibly go. That's the point.'

'I agree,' said Alexander, glancing at Sophie. 'Don't you agree, my love?' She put on her blandest smile and said that of course she agreed.

They would have been astonished if they had known the savagery of her reaction. For a week she had been berating herself for her cowardice in not breaking it off with Alexander, but now all that was swept away in her fury at Ben. Boxing Day? The very night when she'd gone to him at Romilly . . . when Fraser had died. How could he do it?

A week later, the fashionable world was set agog for a second time, when word got round that no less a personage than Miss May Monroe herself had *accepted* her invitation: at least to the extent of letting it be known that she would send her carriage and her man Kean.

'I suppose that that makes it all right?' asked Rebecca Traherne with her hand to her cheek.

'I should rather say that it does,' said Cornelius. 'Everyone will go, simply because they can't bear to be left out. I hear that even old Ma Palairet hasn't the courage to stay away.'

Only Clemency declined, out of loyalty to Madeleine and Cameron, who had sent their regrets by return of post.

'We can't possibly go,' said Sophie later to Alexander, having sought him out in his study.

'Why not, my love?' he said, looking up with a smile from the letter he'd been writing. 'I rather think that we ought.'

She stared at him. 'But I couldn't. I couldn't possibly.'

He stood up and came round the side of the desk and took her hand. 'That,' he said gently, 'is precisely why we must. We must show everyone that the man means nothing to you now.'

She felt her blood rise. 'So I am to attend Mr Kelly's Masquerade simply because he means nothing to me, while I'm barred from seeing Evie McFarlane, precisely because she's my friend. I don't see the logic at all.'

'I hardly think that you need to,' he crisply replied. 'All you need to do is to be guided by me.'

After Sophie had gone, slamming the door behind her, Alexander sat for a moment in silence, kneading his temples. Everything was such a *muddle*. Sophie was dragging her feet, and the governor was looking thunderous. The debt was due on New Year's Day and now, to cap it all, there was this other unpleasantness.

On the blotter before him lay Evie's letter. He'd been rereading it when Sophie came in. Now he took it up again with weary distaste.

Dearest Alexander,

Why have you not come to see me or written? It has been weeks since I told you my news, and I have heard nothing from you. You promised to help me. I am so alone. I can't tell anyone, and I don't know what to do. My love, I need you now more than ever . . .

Confound it all. How could he possibly have known that she would be careless enough to get herself with foal?

With a sense of being greatly ill-used by the world at large and by women in particular, he took up his pen and began to write.

Dear Evie,

I particularly asked you never to write. By doing so, you have made things confoundedly difficult for me. You must understand that when you told me your news the other week, I was so taken aback that I scarcely knew what I was about. And forgive me, but I must ask you: are you absolutely sure that it is mine? If you tell me that it is, then of course I must take your word for it.

I might add that your timing in this matter could hardly be worse, given my impending marriage. However, no one can say that I have ever neglected my obligations. I therefore enclose a five-pound note, which I trust will enable you to take care of your little difficulty promptly, permanently, and to your satisfaction.

Yours, AT.

CHAPTER EIGHT

Where are the spirits when you need them? thought Evie as she sat hunched on her grandmother's tomb.

Every night since she'd got back to Fever Hill, she'd come out here to the bottom of her mother's yard, and asked the spirits for some sign as to whether she should have the child or get rid of it. But nothing came.

Lord God, what a fool she'd been! How could she ever have imagined that she was good enough for Alexander Traherne?

A hot wave of shame washed over her as she recalled her secret fantasy: that he would realise that he couldn't marry Sophie, and marry her instead . . . All the lies. The kisses, the caresses, the burning promises. Sophie didn't mean anything, he had said. It was just a marriage of convenience. It was Evie he loved. What did it come to in the end? A paper sun-umbrella and a five-pound note.

She had the money now, tucked into her bodice, just like the gold chain his father had once given her, which she'd lost in the struggle in Bamboo Walk. His father. Why hadn't she realised they were just the same?

A noise behind her, and she opened her eyes to see her mother standing by nana Semanthe's tomb, looking down at her with her hands on her hips. 'What's wrong with you, girl?' she said quietly. 'Sweetheart trouble? Sweetheart trouble out in foreign?'

Evie thought for a moment, then nodded.

'Some sugar-mouth buckra man.'

Evie's head jerked up. 'Why you say that, Mother?'

'Tcha! I not no fool. What the name he got, this man?'

But Evie shook her head. One thing was certain: her mother must never find out. Grace McFarlane had done some dark things in her time. If she ever learned who'd done this to her daughter, he wouldn't live long. And then Grace would be hanged for murder. And the Trahernes would have won.

'Mother,' she said, swinging her legs off the tomb, 'Don't worry about me. It's all over now. Now I'm tired, I'm going to bed.'

The next morning she awoke to a new clarity. It wasn't that she knew what to do, but she felt sure that today she would make her decision.

She put on her town clothes, and told her mother that she was going up to the busha house to see Mr Kelly.

'Is he the sweetheart?' said her mother narrowly.

'Oh, Mother! Of course not! He's like a brother to me. You know that.' And I hope, she added silently, that he'll be like a brother to me now.

But to her dismay, Ben wasn't at home. 'I'm afraid he's out riding,' said the ugly black man who came out onto the verandah. He was very dark, with a clever, bony face that reminded her of a younger version of her cousin, Danny Tulloch. She took an instant dislike to him.

'My name's Isaac Walker,' he said, smiling as he extended his hand.

She gave him the barest of nods and ignored the hand. 'Evie McFarlane,' she muttered.

His smile widened as he took in the name. 'Grace McFarlane's daughter? I've been looking forward to—'

'Please tell Mr Kelly that I called,' she said coldly, and turned to go.

'Are you sure you won't wait? Or . . . d'you want me to give him a message?'

She looked him up and down with the disdain that only a beautiful woman can fling at an ugly man. 'No message. Good day to you, sir.'

She walked down the carriageway in a towering rage. Don't you start your sugar talk with me, she told Isaac Walker silently. You with your trickified smiles and your lying, sweet-mouth ways. Her anger lasted about a mile and a half. By the time she'd come out into the Fever Hill Road, all that remained was a cold, heavy dread. She realised now that her plan to see Ben had been nothing more than a delaying tactic. Ben couldn't tell her what to do. She had to decide that for herself.

It was dark by the time she got back to her mother's place, and the fufu was bubbling on the hearth. 'You know is past eight o'clock?' Grace said sharply. 'Where you been all day?'

'Out,' muttered Evie. 'Cousin Moses gave me a lift to Montego Bay, and I did a little shopping.' Which, in a way, was true.

'Shopping? Cho! Don't seem to me that you bought anything.'

'I didn't.' That was a lie. The bush doctor's little brown bottle of physic in her pocket had eaten up over half of Alexander's five pounds.

Her mother gave the embers a prod, and came to sit beside her. 'Evie,' she began, 'that sweetheart you got.'

Evie tensed.

'Now don't give me no back-answer, girl. Just listen.' She paused. 'You know it does no good to tangle-up with that kind a man.'

Evie gave a weary smile. 'Yes, Mother, I know.'

Beside her, her mother took up a stick and drew a circle in the dust. 'You know, Evie, you father was a buckra gentleman.'

Evie bridled. 'I know that, Mother. But just because you took up with one doesn't mean that you can tell me what—'

'No, that's not what I intending.' She tapped the circle with the stick and frowned. 'I going to tell you a thing, Evie. I didn't take up with you father. He took up with me.'

Evie shot her a look. 'What do you mean?'

Grace shrugged. 'You know what I mean. Years back, I'm setting out for Salt Wash one afternoon. I'm cutting through Pimento Piece, heading over towards Bulletwood, and he's out riding and he sees me. And he's too strong for me.' She opened her hands to take in the rest.

Evie tried to speak but no sound came. She cleared her throat. 'You mean . . . he forced you?'

Her mother snorted. 'Well, I sure as hell didn't ask him,' she said drily.

Evie licked her lips. In all her musings about her father, it had never occurred to her that he might have forced himself on her mother. Grace McFarlane? The Mother of Darkness? It wasn't possible.

'Did you ever tell anyone? You could have gone to the magistrates—'

Her mother put back her head and hooted. 'Merciful peace, girl! What anybody coulda done if I did even tell? The man too *strong*! You hearing me? Too strong in every damn way.'

'But . . . what did you do?'

She shrugged. 'Thought about lot, lotta things. Thought about running away to foreign. Or letting the River Missis take care of it. Or going up into the far country and taking bush medicine to kill it dead inside a me.' She frowned. 'To kill you, I meaning to say.'

Evie flinched. Until now she'd only thought of the thing inside her as the most desperate of problems. For the first time she realised it was a child. Would she have the courage—or the wickedness—to do what her own mother could not?

Grace lifted the lid of the pot, and the familiar smell of thyme and fragrant hot peppers filled the air. 'But I'm glad at the way it turned out,' she said as she stirred the fufu. 'My own self daughter.'

Evie blinked. Her mother never said such things to her. Why was she saying them now? Was this the sign she'd been waiting for? Were the spirits telling her to throw away the physic and have the child?

'Mother,' she said slowly. 'Why did you never tell me before?'

'Because it all in the past.'

'Forgive and forget? That's not like you.'

'Vengeance will come to him in the end. But not from me.'

'Who was he?' Evie asked abruptly.

Grace sighed. 'Now, Evie. What good—?'

'Tell me. I ought to know the name of my own father.'

A long silence. Her mother raised the spoon to her lips and blew off the steam to taste the fufu. Then she tossed in a little more thyme, gave a satisfied nod, and replaced the lid. 'Well, maybe you right, maybe it time.' She got to her feet and took hold of Evie's wrist. 'Come.'

She led her to the tombs at the bottom of the yard. At great-grandmother Leah's she stopped, and put her daughter's hand flat on the cold stone. 'First you got to swear. Swear on great-grandmother Leah that you never will try for to confront him or face him down.'

Evie thought for a moment. Then she swore.

Her mother gave a satisfied nod. 'Well, all right. So now I tell. You father. He's that Cornelius Traherne.'

Evie swayed. Then she leaned over the side of the tomb and retched.

The crossroads at the foot of Overlook Hill marks the edge of Eden land. If you stop there with the estate behind you, you have a choice of three ways. To your right the track disappears into the deep woods on Overlook Hill, climbing all the way to the glade of the great duppy tree, then winding down the rocky western slope to the Martha Brae and the bridge at Stony Gap. To your left runs the familiar, unthreatening dirt road that heads east past the works at Maputah, and then on towards Bethlehem. But straight ahead—straight ahead and due south—that's the narrow, stony track that winds up towards the distant hamlet of Turnaround, and the start of the Cockpits.

The Cockpits belong to no one. They are the province of mountain people and duppies. The Cockpits are a vast, hostile wilderness of deep ravines and tall, green, weirdly conical hills. Sudden precipices await the unwary, and haunted caves and hidden sinkholes..

'Turnaround means exactly that,' Belle's mother always told her. 'So what do you do when you reach the crossroads?'

'Turn around,' Belle would reply.

That was why Muffin now stopped out of force of habit when they reached the crossroads after giving Quaco the slip.

It was half past ten in the morning, and Belle could feel the sun beating down on her hat and shoulders. The rasp of the crickets was deafening. So was the pounding of her heart. But, surely, she reasoned, her promise to her mother could be set aside in an emergency?

In the pocket of her riding skirt was the list of wishes she had drawn up two weeks before, after she'd seen her parents quarrelling on the verandah. *Mamma and Papa to be happier and never quarrel again. Sugar prices to go up or treasure to be found, so that Papa will not have to work so hard. Aunt Sophie to come for a visit and make up with Mamma.*

Her plan had seemed so easy in the safety of her own room. Of all the wishes on her list, 'treasure to be found' was the most straightforward. In *Tales of the Rebel Maroons* there was a story about the Spanish Jars that the buccaneers had filled with gold doubloons and hidden in caves in the Cockpits. And according to the map in her father's study, there were caves just off the track to Turnaround.

So why was she even hesitating? It was now the 19th of December—two whole weeks since the row on the verandah—and she was tired of calling herself a coward. Besides, she'd been enormously careful to protect herself and Muffin from the duppies: she'd pinned a sprig of rosemary and Madam Fate to her belt, and tied another big bunch to the pony's browband. They ought to be fine. Thus telling herself, she gathered the reins and put Muffin forward along the track to Turnaround.

It was noon when she found it. The path had forked often, but she'd made sure to mark each turn with a distinctive knot of grass, as her father had taught her. She was thinking of him as she rounded a corner and spotted it: a mouth of pure darkness about twenty yards up the slope. It was half hidden by a thorn tree, but unmistakably a cave.

She touched the rosemary at her waist. It felt woefully inadequate. What use were herbs against duppies? But she'd come too far to turn back now. She tied Muffin to a thorn bush, and started to climb.

As she got closer, she saw that the mouth of the cave was fringed with spiky wild pine, and a small creeping plant with grey-green stems and tiny nubbly green flowers. Orchids, she thought, her heart pounding. Ghost orchids. She wished she hadn't remembered the name.

Inside the cave, something moaned.

Belle froze.

Another moan. This time it sounded like a wounded animal. Clutching the herbs in her fist, she edged closer. At first she couldn't see anything, but as her eyes grew accustomed to the dimness she made out a dirt floor, and, in a corner, a crumpled blanket of homespun.

Her heart lurched. Beside the blanket lay a woman, motionless and as grey as a duppy. It was Evie McFarlane.

That girl sick bad, said the voices in the cave walls. *Baby dead. And sure as sin, that girl ready to dead too.*

Drip, drip, drip went the spring at the back of the cave. Pain burns her belly. She screams. But the only sound she makes is a nightmare wheeze.

A while back, a little girl came and gave her water. She felt the butterfly brush of soft hair on her neck, and the sweet child-breath on her cheek. But then the little girl pressed a sprig of rosemary into her palm and whispered that she was going for help.

Now all Evie can hear is the dripping of the spring and the murmur of the cave people. *What you doing in this old stone-hole, girl? This no place for you . . .*

'Christ, Evie, Christ . . .' mutters the man kneeling beside her.

Ben? What's Ben doing up here in the hills? Is he dead too? Is he stuck in this old stone-hole alongside all the whispering spirits?

She hears the skitter of pebbles as he scrambles down the drop at the back of the cave towards the spring. Then his returning footsteps, and the clink of the bucket as he sets it down. 'Christ, Evie, Christ . . .' His voice is shaking, and he's swearing continuously under his breath.

Coolness floods her mouth. She swallows, splutters, and tries to swallow again. Coolness curls down inside of her, down where the fire lives.

He starts washing her neck and arms. Where'd he get the bucket? Oh yes, she remembers now. She brought it with her, didn't she? She planned it all out. The bucket and the blanket and the little bottle of bitter brown physic. The thought of that makes her want to retch.

Ben raises her in the crook of his arm to help her drink. He takes off his jacket and rolls it up to make a pillow. It feels soft as he lays her down on it. It smells of horses and cigars, and it's warm from his body.

When she woke again, the cave people were gone. All she could hear was the murmur of the wind in the thorn tree at the mouth of the cave, and the high, lonely cry of a red-tailed hawk. The pain was still there, but it was duller now, no longer burning her up. *Baby dead, him dead.* Tears stung her eyes. She turned her head, and the glare at the mouth of the cave sent splinters of glass into her brain. She moaned.

A dark rock by the thorn tree moved and resolved into Ben. He came and knelt beside her and held his cupped hand to her lips for her to drink. The water tasted of earth and iron.

'How long have you been here?' she asked. She was astonished by the weakness of her voice.

'A few hours,' he replied.

She turned her head away. 'What did you do with the blanket?'

'I burnt it,' he said.

She tried to swallow, but her throat was too tight. She shut her eyes tight, but the tears squeezed out just the same.

When she'd stopped crying, Ben said, 'Evie. Who is the father?'

She did not reply.

'Evie?'

'Ben . . . no. I'm not telling.'

Another silence. Then he said softly, 'Evie, why didn't you come to me? I would have got you the best doctors.'

'The best doctors are white. They wouldn't treat a mulatto girl.'

'Then I'd have got you a black doctor.'

'There's only one black doctor on the Northside, and he's my cousin.'

'And you don't want anyone to know. That's it, isn't it? That's why you came up here?'

She nodded. 'And it's got to stay that way, Ben. Promise me that.'

He nodded. But something in his eyes made her uneasy.

'How did you find me?' she asked.

He told her how he'd been riding in the hills, and met a frightened little girl on a pony. 'She was babbling about something she'd found in a cave, so we came back here, and . . . there you were.' He cleared his throat. 'I did what I could for you, then I took Belle home. Well, at least I saw her safely to the crossroads.'

She frowned. 'Her name was Belle?'

'Yes, Isabelle Lawe.'

She shut her eyes in dismay. She pictured Belle excitedly telling her parents all about her adventure in the hills, which would mean that by now most of Trelawny knew, including her mother.

'Don't worry about Belle,' said Ben, guessing her thoughts. 'She won't breathe a word. Once we reached the crossroads, all she could think about was how she was going to catch it from her parents for venturing into the Cockpits. So I suggested a pact. I wouldn't rat on her, if she didn't rat on you.'

'And you're sure she'll stick to that?'

His lip curled. 'Oh, yes.'

She studied his face. 'There's something you're not telling.'

He turned his head to look at the cave mouth, then back to her. 'I sent for help.'

Her heart sank. 'What sort of help?'

He ran his thumb across his lower lip. 'I met young Neptune Parker, and sent him for supplies and horses. '

Oh, no! Neptune Parker was her second cousin!

Again Ben read her thoughts. 'He doesn't know you're up here. As far as he's concerned I've just found something interesting in a cave.'

But still she sensed that there was more to come. 'Was it only for supplies that you sent Neptune?'

Again he glanced away. 'No. I also sent him to deliver a note.'

'A note? Who'd you send for, Ben? Who?'

'She won't tell anyone, Evie. You know you can trust her.'

In a horrifying flash she realised who he meant. And she should have known. With Ben it always came back to the same woman. Always.

Sophie had no idea what Ben imagined she could do, but his request was so extraordinary that she obeyed it at once.

E.M. needs you. Bring medicine. Tell no one (including Neptune). B.K.

A pencilled scrawl on a scrap of notepaper. In seconds, she went from astonishment that he should seek her help, to indignation at his arrogance, to sharp anxiety for Evie. *Bring medicine.* Medicine for what?

By great good luck she was alone when the note arrived, and it had been surprisingly easy to get away without being seen—although that was probably due to the network of servants conspiring to help her. Neptune Parker was related to Danny Tulloch, the head groom, and also to Hannibal, the second footman.

But to her consternation, Neptune wouldn't tell her a thing about where they were going. He was polite and respectful, but immovable as they rode through the cane-pieces and into the Cockpits.

An hour later, Neptune reined in beside a stunted calabash tree and dismounted. He indicated the half-hidden mouth of a cave some twenty yards above the track. Ben was nowhere about.

His absence astonished her. She'd just ridden ten miles cross-country in the baking sun, and he didn't even have the decency to be here when she arrived. Setting her teeth, she dismounted, tethered her horse and unbuckled the saddlebag containing the hasty collection of medicines she'd cobbled together with the help of the Parnassus housekeeper. She glanced at the mouth of darkness gaping in the hill. It looked horribly quiet and still. What would she find inside? And what did Ben imagine she could do? She wasn't a doctor. She wasn't even a nurse.

She drew a deep breath and gave Neptune a reassuring smile. 'Well, then,' she said briskly. 'If Master Ben comes back from wherever on earth he's got to, perhaps you'd be kind enough to tell him where I've gone.' Then she shouldered the saddlebag and began to climb.

An hour later she emerged from the cave, drying her hands on her handkerchief. And there he was: sitting on the ground halfway down the track, with his back to her and his elbows on his knees.

'How is she?' he demanded, jumping to his feet.

No greeting. No 'Thank God you came'. What did he care that she had dropped everything for a one-line summons. What did he care that she felt shaky and sick from the stink of blood and hopelessness in that cave? Biting back on her anger, she put her finger to her lips and motioned to him to follow her down the slope.

Neptune must have gone off to water the horses, because all that remained beneath the calabash tree was a stack of supplies. Sophie found a wooden box in the shade, sat down and closed her eyes.

'How is she?' Ben said again.

'I gave her a febrifuge and a sleeping powder,' she muttered. She took off her hat and tossed it on the ground, and kneaded the back of her neck. She looked up. 'She's extremely weak and very low in spirits, which is hardly surprising. And furious with you for summoning me.'

She intended 'summon' as a reproach, but he ignored it. 'But she'll be all right?' he insisted.

'As far as I can tell, yes.'

She wondered if he was the father of Evie's child. But if he were, surely he would have looked after her better than this.

He turned back to her. 'Did she tell you who the father is?'

She shook her head. 'Who is he? D'you know?'

'Of course not. That's why I'm asking you.' He saw something in her face, and tossed his head. 'You thought it was me.'

'It crossed my mind.'

'Do you honestly think that if I were the father I would have let her come up here?'

'I only said that it crossed my mind. I didn't—'

'Sooner or later,' he cut in, 'she'll have to tell me his name. And when she does, I'll rip his spine out.'

She could see that he meant it. She almost envied Evie for inspiring such fierce concern.

He turned back to her and searched her face. 'Are you absolutely sure that she's going to be all right?'

'I told you, I'm as sure as I can be.'

He looked at her for a moment. Then put his head in his hands.

It was only then that Sophie realised just how worried he'd been. And as she watched him, something stirred at the back of her mind. That day at the clinic, when she'd asked him about his sister Lil. 'Did she get pregnant? Did she have to go to an . . . an angel-maker?' He had flinched as if she'd struck him. Perhaps what had happened to Evie had brought bad memories to the surface.

As he straightened up, she looked at his face. Wealth seemed to have given him authority, but it didn't seem to have brought him happiness or peace. He was hatless and dishevelled, in riding breeches, dusty top boots and shirtsleeves rolled to the elbow. He looked just the same as he had in the old days. It was almost as if the last seven years had never happened. As if she'd simply gone riding one afternoon, and come across him up in the hills.

There was an awkward silence. Then he said, 'I suppose I ought to thank you for coming.'

'Oh, please,' she said tartly, 'don't do anything just because you "ought".'

That seemed to surprise him. Then his lip curled. 'I take it that this won't cause problems for you?'

'What kind of problems?'

'I mean, with your . . . fiancé.'

She felt herself reddening. Until that moment she had forgotten all about Alexander. It simply hadn't crossed her mind that by coming here she had flouted his prohibitions: not to see Evie McFarlane, and not to have anything to do with Ben Kelly. 'There won't be any problem,' she said firmly. 'Neptune was very discreet.'

She watched him draw out his watch and frown at it, then snap it shut. 'It's getting late,' he said, standing up and brushing off his hands. 'Neptune will be back soon with the horses. He'll take you home.'

'Thank you,' she replied, 'but I'll wait and help you bring Evie back.'

'She wants to stay up here till she's better.'

'*What?* But she can't.'

'Try telling her that.'

'In a *cave*? But—'

'Look, she doesn't want anyone to know, especially not her own family. You don't need to worry. She'll be all right. I'll stay with her tonight. And tomorrow—'

'Tomorrow I'll come up and see how she is.'

'That won't be necessary.'

'Oh, I think that it will.'

He sighed. 'You couldn't manage it without your fiancé knowing.'

'You leave that to me,' she snapped. She wasn't sure exactly how she *would* manage it, but she was damned if she was going to be dismissed like some servant who had outlived her usefulness.

He put his hands on his hips and took a few paces up the track, then turned back to her. She thought he meant to remonstrate with her, but instead he said simply, 'I think I need to apologise to you.'

She was astonished. 'For what?'

'That day in Kingston. I gave you a bad time of it. I overdid things.'

She thought about that. Then she raised her chin. 'Do you know,' she said in a cut-glass accent, 'I rather fancy that you did.'

He laughed. 'All right, I deserved that. In my defence, I think I was still a bit angry with you. But that's all over now.'

She felt a gentle sinking in the pit of her stomach.

In the distance, Neptune appeared with the horses. Ben watched them for a moment, then turned back to her. 'Seven years ago,' he began, then cut himself off with a frown.

'Yes?' she said. 'Seven years ago, what?'

Again he glanced at Neptune, who was still out of earshot. 'Just this,' he said. 'I was a fool, and you were right. You were right to break it off. It would never have worked.'

Slowly she pushed herself to her feet. Then she picked up her hat and dusted it off. 'Probably not,' she said.

He nodded, his face grave. 'I just thought it needed saying, that's all.'

'I see.'

'Well. I'll tell Neptune to take you back.'

'Yes. Thank you.'

He thought for a moment, then held out his hand. 'Goodbye, Sophie.'

She looked at it without speaking. Then she shook hands with him, and looked up into his face and tried to smile. 'Goodbye, Ben,' she said.

CHAPTER NINE

SOPHIE SAT IN HER BALL GOWN beside Alexander—this man who overnight had become a stranger to her—as the phaeton made its way slowly up the carriageway towards the great house on Fever Hill.

It had been seven days since that strange meeting with Ben up in the Cockpits, and since then she had led a double life. Polite, sleepwalking days at Parnassus were punctuated by wild rides into the hills to see Evie. No one noticed her absence. Nothing seemed real any more.

She turned and regarded Alexander. He had chosen the Sailor for his costume, and the tight white uniform with its gold braiding suited him to perfection. No wonder, she thought, that Evie fell in love with him.

She still couldn't quite believe it. Two days before, she had taken Evie some books, and found her swiftly regaining her strength—and with it, her anger. An unguarded word about Parnassus had slipped out. Sophie had guessed the rest.

Evie and Alexander. All those visits to Kingston 'on business'.

Evie had lifted her chin and given her a look of cool defiance from which she couldn't banish the anxiety. 'If it's any comfort,' she had said, 'it started long before you met him in London.'

'I don't need comfort,' Sophie had replied. 'It's just . . . unexpected. That's all. I don't even mind. I really don't.'

But in the days that followed, she discovered that that wasn't entirely true. She *did* mind. She minded that he'd been after her money.

And what breathtaking hypocrisy! Calmly to caution her against the impropriety of befriending a mulatto girl, when he himself had impregnated that same girl, and then thrown her aside.

My God, she thought, as the phaeton trundled up the carriageway, how did everything get so twisted? Here you are with this weak, mendacious, unfaithful man, whom you intend to jilt as soon as decently possible after Christmas—here you are, making your way to Fever Hill, for a masked ball to be given by Ben. None of it makes sense. It isn't real.

She hadn't seen Ben since that day in the hills, for he'd contrived to be away whenever she visited Evie. But she was glad of that. She didn't want to see him again. And she didn't want to see him tonight. What was the point? It was all over now. That's what he said.

'Apparently,' said Alexander, cutting across her thoughts, 'our Mr Kelly has brought his family out for Christmas. Isn't that sweet? Although of course, the fact that they're dead does rather put a dampener on things.' He paused. 'I hear he's got the coffins up at the hothouse ruins. Just beyond your family burying-place.'

'I know,' she said with an edge to her voice. 'Sibella heard it in town three days ago.'

'Ah yes. Darling Sib. She seems to have developed quite a fascination for our handsome Mr Kelly.' He slapped his gloves lightly against his thigh. 'It must have been devilish tricky, getting the blacks to handle the coffins at all. Don't you think?'

She did not reply.

'And there's even talk of a mausoleum. I call that vulgar in the extreme.'

'Other people have mausoleums,' she said.

He smiled. 'I knew that in the end you'd leap to his defence.'

'Why do you say that?'

'My darling, I wonder you can even ask, when you've been meeting him in secret up in the hills.'

Ah. So that was it. She turned and met his eyes.

He was still softly slapping his gloves against his thigh, and looking very slightly pained. 'I'm sorry I had to bring it up,' he said.

'How did you know about it?' she asked. 'Did you have me followed?'

'Does it matter?'

She shook her head. After what he'd done to Evie, none of it mattered. And yet, ridiculously, she felt guilty. 'If it's any consolation,' she said, 'it wasn't an assignation. There's nothing between me and Mr Kelly.'

'I never for a moment imagined that there was. The problem is,' he added delicately, 'other people won't see it that way.'

She looked down at the mask in her lap. It was a deep midnight blue, like her gown, and edged in tiny brilliants. She couldn't wear it now. She was sick of masks.

She raised her head. 'I went into the hills to help Evie,' she said calmly. 'Do you remember Evie? Evie McFarlane?'

He took that without a flicker.

'She needed help,' she went on. 'You see, someone—some man—has let her down rather badly.'

'So she ran off into the hills?' He raised an eyebrow. 'Good Lord, the things these people do.'

'Alexander,' she said wearily, 'let's do away with the pretence. I can't marry you. I know about Evie.'

Another silence. He ran his thumb across his bottom lip, then gave her a small, rueful smile. 'Well? And what of that?'

She blinked.

'I'm most awfully sorry if I've hurt you, old girl,' he said gently, 'but what you must understand is that it didn't mean a thing.'

'It meant something to Evie.'

'Well it oughtn't to have done. I never made her any promises.'

'Does that make it all right?'

'It makes it . . . well, it makes it the sort of thing that happens.' He took her hand and squeezed it. 'You want to punish me. I understand that. And I admit, I've been most frightfully wicked. But I promise that I'll never do it again. No more wild oats. I shall be the most faithful spouse in Christendom. You have my word.'

She opened her mouth to reply, but he put his finger to her lips.

'Be reasonable, my darling. I think you ought to forgive me my little trespass, as I forgive you yours.'

'You . . . forgive me?' she said in disbelief.

He smiled. 'Well, of course.'

'For what? I told you, there's nothing between me and—'

'But there was, though, wasn't there?'

Again, she met his eyes.

'Seven years ago, you . . . how can I put this without descending to indelicacy . . . you knew the man, in the biblical sense.'

She swallowed. 'How long have you known?'

'Oh, for absolutely ever. Darling Sib put two and two together from something your sister let slip just after you'd left for England. And of course she simply had to tell me.' He paused. 'It's really quite astonishing, the double standards that the world applies to this sort of thing.'

'What do you mean?' she said uneasily. She was beginning to see where he was heading.

'If word got out, I shudder to think what the scandal would do to your sister, and that little girl of hers. People can be so horribly ill-natured.'

She opened her mouth to reply, but just then they swept up to the house, and liveried footmen ran forward to open the doors.

It looked to Ben as if everyone was having a bloody good time. Except, that is, for the host. To Northside Society's surprise, it had found that, thanks to Austen, everything was being 'done rather well'. So it had decided to enjoy itself.

Even Isaac and Austen were having a good time. Isaac—one of about a dozen fancy-dress Sailors—was chatting to a cluster of wealthy banana farmers from Tryall, and even Austen was circulating with that inborn sociability that the shyest of the gentry seems to know how to affect. He'd chosen the Doctor for his costume, and the dark frock coat and severe black mask suited him, and somewhat disguised his nose. And as he was a good dancer, he hadn't lacked for partners. He'd even stood up with Sibella Palairet, although he'd been too abashed to say a word.

Ben could see the little widow now, circling the ballroom with Augustus Parnell. She'd been one of the first to arrive, with her mother-in-law, with whom she was spending Christmas.

For the festivities she'd interpreted half-mourning liberally, and wore a heavily corseted creation of mauve satin, with a prettily ineffectual gold lace mask and a headdress of mauve silk lilacs.

She had spotted him watching her. Self-consciously she turned and spoke to Parnell, with a sidelong glance of studied insouciance that must have fooled no one.

Oh, God, thought Ben wearily. He'd been putting it off for weeks, but tonight he'd have to decide. Either he must seduce the little widow, or he must come clean and tell Miss May Monroe he did not intend to keep his side of their bargain.

It was a humiliating thought, and it made him feel more apart than ever. He looked about him at the enormous, glittering ballroom. What was he doing here? How had it come to this?

Fever Hill—his beloved old house of peace and silence and mellow sunlight—had been overrun. Everywhere he turned he saw a blaze of electric chandeliers, a brilliant blur of satin, an artificial forest of ferns and huge oriental bowls of orchids.

Those bloody orchids. He'd intended them as a little dig at Sophie. 'Just keep the tone Jamaican,' he'd told Austen when they were discussing the arrangements. 'The food, the decorations, all of it Jamaican. And plenty of orchids. Make sure of that.'

That had been before he'd met her up in the hills. But since then he'd forgotten to change his instructions, so orchids were everywhere. The heavy perfume reminded him painfully of Romilly. Yes, the whole thing had spectacularly backfired. A Boxing Day Masquerade! Why had it occurred to him to do it? Buying Fever Hill. Coming back to Jamaica. Throwing this bloody party. It was all because of Sophie. But what did she care? She was going to marry Alexander Traherne.

A footman glided past with a tray of champagne, and Ben exchanged his empty glass for a full one. Eleven o'clock. Another seven hours to go.

And there she was, coming up the main steps on the arm of her fiancé.

Ben saw her before she saw him, and he was grateful for that. She wore a narrow-skirted, high-waisted gown of midnight blue, shot through with changing sea-green. It was cut in a deep V at front and back—so deep that it left the pale shoulders bare, and was only held up by two slender blue straps. No jewels and no mask. The wavy light-brown hair was tied back at the temples and hung loose down her back, restrained only by a narrow bandeau of blue silk.

He knew at once what the costume was meant to be. She was the River Mistress—the shadowy siren who haunts Jamaican rivers and entices men to their doom. Years ago, she had told him that as a child she used to go down to the Martha Brae and ask the River Mistress to watch over him. Had she forgotten that? Or was this some kind of sly dig, just as the orchids were with him?

He moved forward to greet them. 'I thought the River Mistress only ever appeared at noon,' he said as he briefly took her hand.

She gave him a practised smile. 'Occasionally I make an exception.'

'I'm honoured that you made one for me.' He turned to Alexander Traherne and held out his hand.

'How do, Kelly?' said the fiancé, just touching the tips of his fingers.

'How do, Traherne?' Ben replied, mimicking his tone.

Traherne ignored that. 'I see you're exercising the host's prerogative, and eschewing both mask and fancy dress. I must say, I envy you the tailcoat. This sailor's uniform is confoundedly heating. And I never could abide a mask.'

'Then don't wear it,' said Ben with a smile. He turned back to Sophie. 'You know, I was surprised when I saw that you'd accepted. I never thought that you would.'

'Alexander said that we ought,' she replied sweetly.

'So you obeyed your fiancé,' he remarked. 'How very proper.'

She didn't like that. The little dents at the corners of her mouth deepened ominously. 'Was that Great-Aunt May's carriage we saw by the steps?' she asked. 'So she really has been as good as her word?'

God, she was quick. If you stung her, she stung right back.

'We're all agog,' she went on. 'What did you have to do to persuade her to send him?'

He flinched. She couldn't possibly know anything about that sordid little arrangement. 'I struck a bargain,' he said lightly.

'What kind of bargain?'

'I can't say.'

Alexander swallowed a yawn. 'How desperately intriguing,' he murmured. 'Come along, darling, we oughtn't to monopolise our host.'

But Sophie had seen Ben flinch, and she was onto it. 'And when shall you keep this mysterious bargain,' she asked, 'whatever it is?'

At that moment Sibella Palairet appeared in the gallery. She looked flushed and pretty, and slightly pitiable.

'I don't know,' murmured Ben. He glanced from Sophie Monroe to her fiancé, and back again. Ah, but what does it matter? he thought in disgust. She's getting married in a couple of weeks.

'I think,' he said slowly, 'I shall keep my side of the bargain tonight.'

Every time Sibella saw Ben Kelly, her stomach turned over.

She had never felt like this before, and she hated it. Ben Kelly terrified her. He made her feel breathless and confused: desperate to see him again, but speechless with fear when she did. And since that never-to-be-forgotten episode on the Fever Hill Road three weeks before, she had dreamed of him every night. It did no good telling herself that he was a gutter-born scoundrel with not a drop of decent blood in his body. She didn't care about that. She just wanted him to kiss her again.

That was why she was here now, in this great crowded ballroom, counting the minutes until she could go to him. *The burying-place, midnight,* his note had said. *If nothing else, to return that token you let fall the other day.* Every time she thought of it she felt faint.

He hadn't danced with her or said a word to her all evening, apart from the briefest of greetings when she'd arrived. If it hadn't been for that note slipped inside her invitation, she could have pretended that she had imagined the whole thing.

It had all begun so innocently, when she had been returning home from Yarmouth along the Fever Hill Road in the pony trap, and fancied that Princess, her little grey mare, had developed a limp. Sibella had judged it prudent to pull up in the shade of a giant bamboo and wait until someone should come by to assist her.

Fortunately, after a few minutes, Ben Kelly arrived. 'It's probably just a stone,' he said, dismounting and coming round to take a look at the mare.

He lifted Sibella down from the trap and she stood beside him in a whispering, shadowy tunnel beneath the giant bamboo. She watched him gently lifting the grey's foreleg and exploring the tender underside with his fingers, and her heart had begun to pound.

'Here we are,' he said. He had taken a small, pearl-handled knife from his pocket and deftly prised a pebble from the mare's hoof.

Sibella looked at the line of his jaw, and the way the dark hair fell into his eyes, and her stomach turned over.

'You'll be able to walk her home now,' he said, flicking back his hair as he looked up into her face. 'But go gently. She mustn't be rushed.'

She nodded. She was watching his mouth and didn't hear a word. As he straightened up, she couldn't trust herself to speak. He was still look-ing into her eyes and caressing the mare's neck with one hand. Then he took out his handkerchief and brushed off his hands. 'You know,' he said calmly, 'I've been thinking about you.' He put his hands lightly on her shoulders and bent and kissed her.

Never in her life had she experienced anything so wonderful as that kiss. The heat, the dizziness, the spiralling down into a pleasure she'd never known or imagined could exist. She clung to him until she could no longer breathe, then he broke from her and, without a word, led her back to the pony trap, took her by the waist and lifted her into the seat.

In a blur she watched him walk to his horse. But then he stopped and stooped for something in the dust. It was the pink foulard scarf and little diamond brooch that she had been wearing.

He walked back to her as if to return it, then seemed to think better of it. He folded the scarf and put it in his breast pocket. 'Perhaps some other time,' he said with a curl of his lip.

That had been three weeks ago. *The burying-place, midnight.* In half an hour they would be alone together. Absolutely alone. She pictured the long pale grass glowing in the moonlight. She saw herself laid out like a sacrifice on a marble tomb. Passive. Surrendering to him . . .

Suddenly she couldn't bear the ballroom a moment longer. She pushed through the crowds and ran out to the verandah, then down the steps onto the lawns. She took deep breaths of the warm night air.

'Are you unwell?' said a man's voice behind her.

She spun round. Her heart jerked with disappointment. Augustus Parnell stood on the bottom step, watching her. 'N-no,' she stammered. 'That is, I am quite well. Thank you.'

His costume was that of the Doctor: the same as poor ugly Freddie Austen. But unlike Austen, it didn't suit Parnell. It made him look like an undertaker. 'Forgive me,' he said, 'but you appear a trifle flushed.'

'It was the crush in the ballroom. Such an unseasonably hot night. Don't you agree?'

'I'm afraid I'm not in a position to say what is seasonable and what is not, since this is my first Christmas in the tropics.'

'Oh, of course. I was forgetting.'

'However, perhaps you would care for an ice.'

She forced a smile. 'How thoughtful. Would you be so kind as to fetch me one?'

'I should consider it a privilege.'

She watched him go. Then she picked up her skirts and ran round the corner of the house and onto the lawns on the west side, so that he wouldn't be able to find her when he returned.

Alexander watched his sister dispatching Gus Parnell on yet another pretext, and swore under his breath. What did she think she was playing at? Couldn't she see that Parnell wouldn't stand for much more of this? Did she imagine that rich, admiring bankers grew on trees?

He snatched another brandy from a passing tray and downed it in one. Then he descended the steps to the lawns, to smoke a cigar.

Everything was going to blazes, and he didn't know what to do. He needed Parnell, and he needed Sophie. But now Sophie was cutting up rough because of that wretched little mulatto. He could hardly force her to marry him. Despite his attempt in the phaeton, they both knew that.

So what was he to *do*? What if Sib made a fool of herself and Parnell slipped the hook? What if Sophie couldn't be brought round? What if New Year's Day came and went and the debt remained unpaid?

He would be finished. Word would spread like wildfire that Alexander Traherne had welshed on a debt. He would be blackballed at every club he'd ever put his name to. The governor would cut him off without a penny. He'd be a nobody. He might as well slit his throat.

And all for a paltry gambling debt. It was so horribly unfair.

He threw away his cigar and stood for a moment, irresolute. He must do something. But what? At his feet, the cigar flared briefly in the darkness. Frowning, he ground it out under his heel, and turned back to the house. It was all so outrageously unfair.

It was a quarter to midnight, and Sophie had had enough. She had danced a slow gavotte with Cornelius, and another with Alexander, who had scarcely spoken a word to her all evening. She hated being back at Fever Hill. For her it would always be a magical place of shadows and whispers, wearing its dilapidation with a faded elegance. She hated to see it brightly illuminated and swarming with brittle, inquisitive gossips. And what was worse, it reminded her of Maddy. Maddy, a thousand miles away at Eden. It was all wrong.

She caught sight of Alexander at the other end of the gallery, and moved behind one of those wretched bowls of orchids. Why, she wondered, had he thought it necessary to make that clumsy attempt at a threat? He must know that he couldn't force her to marry him.

But what about Eden? There was the rub. Alexander was vindictive enough to start some scandalous rumour about her and Ben. And when Cornelius, the most powerful financier on the Northside, learned that she wasn't going to marry his son, his goodwill towards the Lawes would evaporate like mist. Again she would have brought trouble to Eden.

And after Parnassus, where would she go? Back to England? Her heart sank. Something told her that if she left Jamaica again she would never return. It would be the ultimate defeat.

She could see Ben now, standing by the doors amid a throng of people, watching the waltz. He hadn't spoken to her since that edgy greeting out on the steps. But he hadn't avoided her, either. Several times in the course of the evening their paths had crossed, and he'd simply given her a polite nod, and moved away.

She watched him stoop to speak to the woman at his side. The woman turned to listen, and with a shock Sophie recognised Sibella Palairet. She was looking up at Ben with total concentration, her lips slightly parted, her eyes fixed on his mouth. Sophie glanced from Sibella to Ben, then back again. And she remembered the ancient brougham stationed at the edge of the carriageway, with Great-Aunt May's man inside. Suddenly, she had a sensation of falling. Could it be that this was the mysterious 'bargain'?

It wasn't possible. And yet . . . what a fine revenge for Great-Aunt May it would be: to put an end to the Parnell–Palairet match, and bring down scandal on the Trahernes at a single stroke. And all it would take was one vain, stupid, little widow, gift-wrapped in mauve satin and gold lace.

And Ben would do it, too. He couldn't have forgotten what the Trahernes had done to him . . . That, she thought, is what this whole wretched ball has been about: to show the Trahernes how far he's come, and to bring them down.

And the worst of it, she thought, plucking an orchid from a bowl and shredding it in her fingers, the very worst of it is that he must have known all about it that day in the hills. She felt shaky and sick. She could never have imagined that he would change so much, that he could be capable of an act so calculated, so sordid and so destructive.

This, she told herself, really is the end. The Ben you knew is gone for ever. She opened her hand and watched the shredded petals drifting down around her feet. Then she raised her head and searched for him through a blur of tears.

He was no longer there. Neither was Sibella.

'For the last time,' yells Pa, 'where's Kate?'

'I don't know,' mumbles Ben.

Pa grabs his arm and yanks him to his feet and wallops him. Bam, bam, bam. The rooms goes round. Lights burst in his eyes.

Robbie's hunched in the corner with his face to the wall, rocking from side to side. Good boy, Ben tells him silently. Stay there and let me take care of this.

'Where's she gone?' goes Pa, shaking him by the arm.

'I don't know,' mumbles Ben between his teeth.

Pa knocks him about some more, then slams him against the wall. More lights flare. Salty-sweet blood fills his mouth. He slides down in a heap.

Pa stands over him, swaying. The brewery stink is hot and strong, but he's miles from passing out, worse luck for Ben. 'So you're not going to tell me, eh?' he says, very low and quiet.

Shakily, Ben wipes his face on his sleeve. He tries to move but he can't.

Pa turns and stumbles over to the corner and grabs Robbie by the ankle, and hoists him upside-down. Robbie don't say nothing, not even a yelp. He just dangles there like a sewer rat.

'Leave him alone,' mutters Ben, wiping the blood from his eyes.

'So you're not going to tell me, eh?' goes Pa over his shoulder. He swings Robbie round by the legs, like he's going to take at bash at the door frame with Robbie's head. 'You sure about that?'

'Pack it in,' whispers Ben.

'Robbie or Kate? What's it to be?'

Ben struggles to his feet and props hisself against the wall. 'Pack it in!'

'Why should I? Robbie don't mind, do you, Rob?' And all the time he's swinging round and round, taking that little carroty head closer to the door; and Robbie's not making a sound, but his mouth's going big and square. 'Come on, Ben,' goes Pa. 'You got to choose.'

Ben twists round and grinds his forehead into the wall. His eyes are stinging and hot. How can he choose?

Kate's big and strong, he tells hisself. She can hold her own against Pa, and she's got Jeb to look after her, too. But Robbie can't hold his own against anyone. And he's only got Ben.

'Come on, Ben,' goes Pa. 'Which is it to be? Robbie or Kate?'

'Ben?' wails Robbie. 'Ben!'

'Slippers Place,' croaks Ben through big jerky sobs.

'What?' goes Pa. 'What's that you say?'

Ben grinds his head against the wall, mashing the plaster to a soggy pulp of blood and tears. 'She's at Slippers Place. Now let him go!'

Sunlight hit him in the eyes and he woke up. He was sweating. His heart was pounding. He didn't know where he was.

You shouldn't have told him, Ben. You made the wrong choice, didn't you? You shouldn't have told him about Kate.

He put his hand to his cheek and wiped away tears. You lost Kate, he told himself, and then you lost Sophie. That's why the dreams keep coming. One loss conjuring up another.

The silent maidservant moved from the window to the bed, and held out a salver on which lay a small cream-coloured envelope.

'What's that?' he muttered, propping himself up on his elbow. On the bedside table his watch told him that it was nine o'clock in the morning. Christ. He'd only been asleep for just over an hour. The last guest had left sometime after seven.

'Message, Master Ben,' murmured the maid, her eyes politely averted. 'Carriage waiting for reply. They says it's urgent.'

Cursing under his breath, he snatched the envelope and tore it open. He scanned the contents. It was from the little widow. He crumpled the note and threw it across the room.

Well, who did you think it was from? he told himself in disgust. Sophie Monroe, writing to thank you for the party?

He remembered how she had looked as she'd ascended the steps with her fiancé. The sardonic gleam in her honey-coloured eyes; the twist of mockery in her mouth. And when shall you keep this mysterious bargain?

He rubbed a hand over his face. He felt exhausted and still slightly drunk, heavy with fatigue and self-disgust.

Beside the bed, the maidservant cleared her throat. 'Carriage waiting, Master Ben, waiting for reply.'

He thought of the little widow in her over-upholstered dress and her artificial flowers. *You shouldn't have done it, Ben.*

There was a sour taste in his mouth. He reached for the carafe and poured himself a glass of water and drained it in one go. 'Tell the boy there's no reply,' he muttered.

Half an hour later, he was dressed and coming downstairs when he saw Isaac in the hall. His partner was in his town clothes, and there was a large portmanteau at his feet.

Ben stopped on the bottom stair, and gripped the banister with a sudden, surprising clutch of panic. Isaac had been threatening to leave for days—they hadn't been getting along too well since he'd got some ridiculous idea into his head about Ben and Evie—but he'd always allowed himself to be talked into staying. At least, until now.

Don't go, Ben told him silently. Not now. Not today. Please. Out loud he said, 'So you're going, then.'

Isaac turned his head and waited while a trio of manservants passed through with potted orange trees in their arms. When they'd gone he said, 'I'll be at Arethusa for another week or so. Then I'm off.'

'Where?'

'I don't know. That depends.'

'Isaac—'

'I'm thinking of selling up. If I do, I'll get the lawyer to give you first refusal on Arethusa.'

'For Christ's sake, Isaac! I don't care about that.'

Isaac looked up at him, and his face was taut. 'What do you care about, Ben?'

Ben ignored that. 'For the last time, there's nothing between me and Evie McFarlane. Nothing but friendship.'

'Then tell me where she is.'

Ben hesitated. 'No.'

'Why?'

'She doesn't want to be found.'

'I don't believe you. I will find her, Ben. With or without your help. That girl's in some sort of trouble. I could tell when she came up here that day. She needs a friend.'

'She's got a friend.'

Isaac shook his head sadly. 'You still don't trust me, do you?'

'Of course I trust you.'

'No, you don't. You don't trust anyone. You never have.' He put on his hat and picked up his portmanteau. 'Goodbye, Ben. And good luck. Something tells me you're going to need it.'

Ben stayed on the stairs, listening to the clatter of the carriage dying away. Wrongdoing and loss, he thought. He couldn't remember when he'd felt so bleak. He forced a shrug, and put his hands in his pockets, and wandered through the house and out onto the south lawns, where the clearing up was in full swing.

He walked round the side of the house, found a patch of shade on the bench beneath the breadfruit tree, and sent for champagne. He drank the first glass in one, and waited for the artificial lightening of the spirits.

A shadow cut across his sun, and he glanced up to see Austen standing before him. 'Hello, Austen,' he said. 'Sit down and have a drink.'

Uncertainly, Austen perched on the far end of the bench, but waved away the champagne. 'No, thank you, Mr Kelly.'

Ben shot him a look. These days, Austen only called him 'Mr Kelly' when he was on his dignity. 'So,' he said, pouring himself another drink. 'What's on your mind?'

Austen cleared his throat and frowned at his feet. 'I understand that there was a carriage here. And a note from . . . from a lady.'

'That's right.'

More throat-clearing. 'Mr Kelly. I need to talk to you. Not as employer and secretary. Man to man.'

Ben glanced at him in surprise. He hadn't given his secretary credit for such strength of purpose. 'Go on, then,' he said.

'Last night I saw something,' Austen said. 'I mean, I saw you and Mrs Palairet . . . talking, and then . . . then you both disappeared. So I thought'—his face was burning—'I had witnessed enough to give me cause for concern.'

Ben found such delicacy intensely irritating. 'Well, of course you did,' he snapped. 'You saw, but you didn't take part. That's the story of your life, isn't it?'

Austen pulled at his nose. 'Mr Kelly. I need to ask . . . Are you . . . that is, do you intend to marry her?'

Ben blinked. 'Who?'

'Mrs Palairet.'

Ben looked at him, then burst out laughing. 'Sibella? Of course not!'

Again Austen pulled at his nose. Then he put both hands on his knees, and stood up very quickly. 'Then I regret to inform you that I cannot remain in your employ for another day.'

Ben looked up at him for a moment. Then he waved his hand. 'Don't be ridiculous, Austen. You don't even know what—'

'With respect, Mr Kelly, it's not ridiculous at all. It's the only honourable thing for a fellow to do.'

Ben was astonished. He'd read about men who put women on pedestals—he'd often teased Austen for being one—but he hadn't really believed it until now. 'Austen,' he said wearily, 'don't be an ass. There really is no need for us to quarrel.'

'On the contrary, Mr Kelly,' Austen said quietly, 'I'm as certain as I could be that there is.'

He was in earnest. Ben's spirits plunged. First Isaac, now Austen.' He leaned forward with his elbows on his knees. 'I can explain about Mrs Palairet,' he said in a low voice. 'But, please. I'm asking you . . . I'm *asking* you . . . to stay.'

Austen's face worked. Then he shook his head, turned and walked away across the lawn.

Sophie was woken by a maidservant tapping her on the arm. Blearily she raised her head. The maid told her that Miss Sibella was downstairs in the drawing room, and that she needed to speak to her 'quick-time'.

Sophie was instantly awake.

'I had to see you,' cried Sibella as soon as Sophie reached the drawing room. Sophie glanced over her shoulder to check that the door was closed, then turned back to Sibella. She looked terrible, her gown haphazardly fastened, her face puffy and blotched from crying.

Sophie couldn't find it in herself to feel sorry for her. She could only remember how Sibella had gazed up at Ben as they'd stood together in the ballroom. 'What d'you want?' she said harshly.

Sibella twisted the rings on her plump fingers. Then she threw herself onto the sofa and burst into tears. 'I feel so ashamed,' sobbed Sibella. 'So dirty and . . . and humiliated. I . . . I wrote to him. I begged. I even waited at the house for a reply.' She made a sound in her throat. 'Do you know what he did?' She pushed back her hair and her eyes were red-rimmed and outraged. 'He sent word that there was no reply. Can you *imagine*?'

Sophie didn't want to imagine anything. She was trying hard not to picture Ben and Sibella together.

But Sibella clutched her hand and pulled her down beside her onto the sofa. 'You've got to go and talk to him.'

'*What?* But—'

'Sophie, you've got to! There's no one else who can help.'

Sophie tried to withdraw her hand from the feverish grasp, but Sibella clung to it. 'You're not making any sense,' Sophie told her as gently as she could. 'You're overwrought. You need to go to bed.'

Sibella stared at her with incomprehension, then broke down again.

Gradually, reluctantly, Sophie pieced together the story. There was something about a missing scarf and a diamond brooch, both gifts from Gus Parnell, and a promise by Ben to return them—a promise that hadn't been kept—and a midnight tryst at the burying-place. The idea of the tryst hurt more than anything. A lovers' tryst among the Monroe tombs. It felt like a calculated stab at herself.

And now, according to Sibella, Parnell was 'cutting up rough' and demanding that she produce the wretched things, and Papa was being horrible to her, and what was she to *do*?

'You've got to get them back,' she cried, clutching Sophie's hand so tightly that her rings bit into the flesh. 'He's a liar and a scoundrel, but he'll listen to you, I know he will.'

'Sibella,' she said wearily, 'he won't listen to anyone. Least of all me.'

Sibella took a shaky breath and wiped her eyes with her fingers. 'But there's no one else. You're my only, only friend. Say you'll go. Oh, Sophie, *do* say you'll go!'

What can you possibly say to him? she wondered as she rode between the great cut-stone gatehouses of Fever Hill. Twice she reined in and resolved to turn back. Let Sibella sort out her own sordid little affairs. Thoughtless, insensitive Sibella, who—if she remembered it at all—had doubtless assumed that Sophie had got over her feelings for Ben years ago.

The men taking down the coloured lanterns strung between the palms watched her pass with undisguised curiosity. She ignored them. For the hundredth time she cursed Sibella.

At last she reached the house, and there was no more time for second thoughts. A boy ran out to take her horse. A maid came down the steps to conduct her inside. She was shown straight into his study.

It had been her grandfather's study, and she was surprised to see how little it had changed. It still had books from floor to ceiling, and oil paintings of Jamaica on the walls, and at the far end, in front of the doors leading onto the south verandah, a great walnut desk.

Ben was sitting behind it with a sheaf of what looked like blueprints spread out before him. When she was shown in, he stood up, and his face briefly lightened. Then he caught her stony expression. He looked pale and tired, with dark shadows under his eyes.

As well he might, she thought grimly, remembering Sibella's blotchy, tear-stained face. *I feel so ashamed. So dirty and humiliated.*

Ben and Sibella at the burying-place. It didn't seem possible. She pushed away the images that kept floating before her eyes. 'I didn't think you'd see me,' she said as she walked the length of the study.

'I didn't think you'd come,' he replied. He motioned her to a chair on the other side of the desk, and resumed his own.

She sat down and clasped her hands in her lap. They felt shaky and cold. 'How could you do it?' she said quietly.

He raised his eyebrows. 'What have I done this time?'

'I've just come from Sibella. She's in a terrible state.'

'I take it that means she didn't enjoy the party.'

She looked down at her hands. It didn't seem possible that he could treat this as a joke. 'I know it's because she's a Traherne,' she said in a low voice. 'But I never thought . . . I never imagined you'd sink this low.'

'And you do now?' He gave her a slight smile. 'You're quick to believe the worst of me, aren't you?'

'You used her. You used her to curry favour with Great-Aunt May.'

A flush darkened his cheekbones. But he recovered swiftly. 'And of course, in polite society,' he said drily, 'nobody ever uses anyone. I'm always forgetting that.'

'The least you can do,' she said between her teeth, 'is give me back these trinkets of hers.'

'Ah, so that's why you've come.' He leaned back in his chair. 'She's in trouble with her sweetheart—her sweetheart whom, I might add, she cordially detests—and now she's sent you to do her dirty work.'

Sophie coloured.

'You see,' he went on, frowning, 'you indicated just now that I was a blackguard for using her. But to the uninitiated, it might appear that *she* was using *you*. Although that's impossible, isn't it, because in polite society nobody ever uses anyone. I mean, she isn't using Gus Parnell to buy herself a comfortable future. And her father isn't using her, or Parnell, to buy himself back to financial security. And her brother certainly isn't using you to get out of his own little spot of trouble.'

'Alexander isn't in any trouble,' she snapped. Then she felt annoyed with herself for standing up for him.

'That shows how much you know,' he remarked. Thoughtfully he tapped his fingernail against his teeth. 'And what about you?' he said suddenly. 'What are you using Alexander for?'

'What do you mean?'

'Why are you marrying him? Is it to buy yourself somewhere safe and secure and far away from Eden, so that you won't ever need to—'

'I didn't come here to fight,' she broke in. 'Just give me the scarf and the brooch and I'll go.'

'Why should I?'

301

'Because you don't need them. You've got what you wanted. You're just keeping them to make a point.'

'Am I? And what point is that?'

'To show us all how powerful you've become.'

He laughed. 'And you think I need a couple of trinkets to do that?'

'Apparently, yes.'

Abruptly his smile vanished. He got to his feet and came round to her side of the desk and leaned against it with his arms crossed on his chest, looking down at her. His eyes were glittering. 'You're so quick to think the worst of me,' he said in a low voice

For a moment longer he looked down into her face. Then he pushed himself off the desk and moved past her to the bookshelf, opened a large cedarwood box and took out a small brown paper parcel. He tossed it onto the desk in front of her. 'There you are,' he said. 'One scarf. One brooch. Both slightly used. Just like their owner.'

She took the parcel and stood up to go. 'Thank you,' she muttered.

He moved back behind the desk, and opened the doors onto the south verandah, and stood with his back to her, looking out. 'If she's angry with me,' he said over his shoulder, 'it's not because I met her at the burying-place. It's because I didn't.'

She stared at the package, then back to him. 'What? You mean—?'

'She waited, but I didn't turn up. There. Now you know.'

She thought of Sibella's outraged face. *I feel so humiliated. I wrote to him. I begged. There was no reply.* You . . . you never intended to meet her there. Did you?'

He laughed. 'Oh, I wouldn't go that far. The truth is, I didn't think too much about it. It was sort of a spur-of-the-moment decision.'

Again she looked down at the parcel in her hands. 'If I hadn't come and asked for this,' she said slowly, 'would you have sent it back anyway?'

'Probably not.'

'But . . . you would have ruined her.'

Again he laughed. 'Isn't that a bit melodramatic?'

She shook her head. 'What's happened to you, Ben?'

He shot her an impatient glance.

'Look at you. You've got everything. An enormous house. Fine clothes. Beautiful horses. But inside, something's gone.' She tapped her breastbone. 'In here. It's gone.'

In the glare from the doorway his face was dark. 'I think you'd better go,' he said quietly.

'What happened to you? Did getting rich burn it all away?'

He turned back to the doorway. 'It wasn't the money that did that.'

Evie had been back only an hour or so, but already she was in her old place on the aqueduct wall, leaning against the trunk of the ackee tree. While she was regaining her strength up in the cave, she had thought a lot about revenge. She'd promised her mother that she would never confront her father, Cornelius Traherne, and she intended to keep that promise. And yet . . . she craved justice from the Trahernes. Justice for herself and for her mother, and for the child she'd sacrificed.

Who was she? That was the question. Until she decided that, she wouldn't know what to do.

She wasn't white. She was mulatto. She was the four-eyed daughter of Grace McFarlane. Wasn't that something to be proud of?

A gust of wind stirred the ackee tree above her head. She looked about her at the creeper-clad ruins of the old slave village—the village that Jocelyn Monroe's grandfather, Alasdair, in his murderous rage, had burnt to the ground after the Rebellion. Then an idea came to her.

Maybe that's it, she thought. Her heart quickened with excitement.

CHAPTER TEN

To reach the burying-place at Fever Hill, one crossed the lawns at the back of the house and took the path over the crown of the hill and halfway down the other side. But if one continued on past the burying-place, the path snaked through a thicket of ironwoods, and finally ended at a creeper-choked ruin in a dark little dell. People shunned this place, for it was the ruin of the old hothouse or slave hospital. A place of duppies and evil memories: some long-ago, some not so long-ago.

Precisely because no one went there, it also possessed a curious kind of peace. At least, it did for Ben. That was why he'd caused the three coffins to be placed here beneath a temporary bamboo shelter, until the mausoleum could be built. It was also why he'd come here to be alone, after fetching Evie. He sat on a block of cut-stone with his elbows on his knees, watching a centipede working its way along the coffin that held his brother's remains. It was peaceful in the clearing, but not at all quiet. The rasp of the crickets rose and fell like the soughing of the sea. A flock of jabbering crows flew raucously overhead.

Life was going on all around him. Busy, indifferent, beautiful. So why couldn't he find peace? After all, he'd achieved what he wanted. He'd found Robbie and Lil and Kate, and brought them out to the warmth and the light. Why wasn't that enough?

'What do you want from me, Kate?' he said aloud. 'I made the wrong choice and you paid for it, I'm sorry. I've tried to make amends. What more do you want?'

Ben sat on in the clearing, while the rasp of the crickets intensified. He was dizzy with fatigue and still half drunk, and still disgusted with himself. That look on Sophie's face. *What happened to you, Ben?*

He'd bought Fever Hill in order to get her back. He saw that now. He'd bought it because she'd lived here once, because she loved it. Perhaps that was why he'd fallen in love with it too. *What happened to you, Ben? Inside, something's gone.*

Was she right? Was that why Isaac had left, and Austen? Ah, but what was the good of wondering? What was the point?

Slowly he got to his feet, and started back up the path.

He'd crested the hill and was wading through the long grass towards the burying-place when a flash of white caught his eye. He stopped. His mouth went dry. Below him, sitting on the bench beneath the poinciana tree, was a ghost.

She was dressed in vaporous white, in the fashion of twenty years before. A high-necked blouse with leg-of-mutton sleeves, a bell-shaped skirt cinched in at the waist, and a beribboned straw bonnet. What little he could see of her face was a waxen yellow.

Then she turned and smiled at him, and he breathed again.

'Hello, dear,' she said calmly. 'I was wondering when we'd bump into each other.'

He took off his hat and went down towards her. 'Hello, Miss Clemmy.'

'I hope you don't mind my coming unannounced. But your letter did say that I might visit at any time.'

'I meant it,' he said. 'I'm glad to see you, Miss Clemmy.' He meant that too. He didn't want to be alone any more.

He'd only met her once before, and that had been years ago when he was a boy, and she'd summoned him to Fever Hill on an errand. At the time he'd thought her mad and slightly pitiful. But she'd treated him with the courtesy with which she treated everyone, and he'd never forgotten.

She patted the bench beside her and asked if he'd care to sit down. She sounded as cheery as if she were at a tea party, not communing with the spirit of her infant son. Ben tossed his hat in the grass and sat down.

Miss Clemmy folded her pale hands in her lap, and watched a yellow butterfly sunning itself on a tomb at the far end of the burying-place.

Ben said, 'You're looking very well, Miss Clemmy.'

'Thank you, dear,' she said, still watching the butterfly. 'I hear that you've brought out your brother and sisters to be with you.'

She made it sound like a jolly sort of picnic, and he had to smile.

'And where shall you put the mausoleum?' she asked.

'To tell the truth, Miss Clemmy, I don't think I'll build it.'

'But why? I'd heard that the plans are all drawn up.'

'They are. And on paper it seemed like a good idea. But it's not for them. It's too grand.' He looked about him at the simple barrel tombs dreaming away the decades in the long grass. 'Maybe the Monroes got it right after all,' he said, indicating the big barrel tomb where the butterfly was still sunning itself. 'Maybe I'll build something like that instead.'

'Oh, don't copy that one,' said Miss Clemmy with startling energy. 'That's old Alasdair's tomb. That wouldn't do at all.'

'Why not?'

'Oh, he was a dreadful old man. Perfectly dreadful. Died of apoplexy just after they freed the slaves. His servants hated him so much that they built that tomb especially for him. Walls two feet thick, and special cement made with ashes from his own great house, and a few other things that it doesn't do to mention.'

He glanced at her in surprise. 'How do you know all this?'

'Why, because it was Grace's mother, old Semanthe, who helped them build it. The aim was to keep him inside, you see. To stop him walking.'

Ben considered that. 'Did it work?'

'Oh, heavens, yes. Jamaicans know a thing or two about ghosts.'

Watching the butterfly lift off from the tomb, Ben thought how odd it was—how odd but how universal—that people attributed such importance to the body of a corpse. Semanthe McFarlane had gone to enormous lengths to keep old Alasdair's corpse from walking. And he, Ben, had gone to endless trouble to find what remained of his brother and sisters and bring them out. For what? To set them free? To have them with him? To atone for the crime of being alive, while they were dead?

He turned to Miss Clemmy, and asked if she believed in ghosts.

'Why, of course, dear. Don't you?'

'I never used to. But then a few years ago Evie saw something. Something I can't explain. Since then, I haven't known what to believe.'

Miss Clemmy was shaking her head. 'That poor child. She was always seeing things. Absolutely hated it. Used to come to me in tears.'

Ben smiled. 'Did you give her ginger bonbons?'

She looked delighted. 'As a matter of fact I did.'

A cling-cling alighted on the tomb of Alasdair Monroe, extended a glossy blue-black wing and began to preen.

Miss Clemmy lightly touched Ben's shoulder. 'Who is Kate?'

Ben opened his mouth to reply, then shut it again. He shook his head.

'It's just that I saw you at the old hothouse,' she said. 'I always come that way and, as I was passing, you were saying sorry to Kate.'

Ben reached for his hat and turned it in his hands. Then he tossed it back into the grass. 'Kate was my older sister,' he said.

'Ah. And why were you saying sorry?'

He had never told anyone about it. Not even Sophie. But there was something about Miss Clemmy's gentle directness that made one feel one could say almost anything. So he told her. About his father, and the day Kate left, and about Pa forcing him to choose between her or Robbie. 'So I told him where she was,' he said simply. 'I thought she'd be able to look after herself better than Robbie.'

'And . . . were you right about that?'

'No. You see, I'd forgotten that she was in the family way. I'd forgotten about the blackstick. That's a kind of lead, Miss Clemmy. The girls buy it and roll it into pills to . . . to get them out of trouble.'

'Oh,' said Miss Clemmy, and folded her hands neatly in her lap.

'It turned out that it had made her sick. Really bad. So when my father caught up with her, she was too weak to protect herself.'

'What happened?'

He shook his head. 'I don't know. She was dead when I got there. Lying in the gutter with one side of her face smashed in.' He cleared his throat. 'She'd gone through the window. I supposed he'd thrown her out. I don't know. When I got there he was holding her in his arms, crying his heart out.' He paused. 'Funny, that. I never remembered it till now.'

Miss Clemmy made a clucking sound that was both wholly inadequate and extremely comforting.

'I made the wrong choice,' he said. 'I should've found a way to save them both. To save Robbie and Kate, both.'

'But how could you have done that? You were only a child.'

'I could've taken him on. Not just told him where she was.'

'But surely . . . surely then your father would have killed you instead.'

He nodded. 'That's what I mean. I made the wrong choice.'

The cling-cling spread its wings, lifted off from the tomb of Alasdair Monroe and headed north.

It flew over Fever Hill great house, and over the cane-pieces of Alice Grove. It crossed the Fever Hill Road and flew west into Parnassus

Estate. But as it was passing over the cane-pieces of Waytes Valley, something glittering caught its eye. It swept down, then abruptly swerved up again. What from the sky had looked like a seductive, glittering thing was in fact a lighted match in human hands. With an indignant squawk the cling-cling headed east, towards the stables at Parnassus.

Back in Waytes Valley, a sea breeze ruffled the uncut cane, and the flame crackled and spat as the hands put it to a cluster of dry leaves.

The breeze fanned the flames higher. A hand fed more dry leaves to the fire. The leaves curled and smoked. Sparks flew upwards.

The wind carried the sparks inland. They flurried south, into the dry, rustling, uncut cane.

CHAPTER ELEVEN

'WHEN THERE'S A DUPPY around,' Quaco had told Belle as he helped her up onto Muffin, 'you get a sudden hot wind in you face, and a sweet-sweet smell. That's when you got to run quick-time and throw lot, lotta salt. But you know all this, Missy Belle. Why you wanting to hear it again?'

'Just to make sure,' she'd told him.

But he was right, she did know it already. She knew that duppies live in ruins and burying-places, but mostly in silk-cotton trees. She knew that on moon-full, all the duppy trees in Trelawny remove from their own place, and go up to the forest to reason with each other. All except the great duppy tree on Overlook Hill. The other trees come to him.

It wasn't going to be moon-full tonight, which was good. Besides, darkness was hours away, for it was still only tea-time. At least, it was tea-time in the outside world. But here in the forest on Overlook Hill, it was half dark. And there was a horrible listening stillness that made her catch her breath. It shouldn't *be* so quiet in a forest. There should be birdsong, and the hum of insects. But the small creatures knew to keep away from the great duppy tree. All Belle could hear was her own breathing.

She raised her head and gazed into the upside-down world of the duppy tree. The great outstretched limbs blotted out the sky: wide enough to accommodate a whole nest of duppies. She swayed. The duppy tree leaned closer. On the enormous buttressed trunk she saw the black, sunken pits where nails had been hammered in. Quaco said that, when somebody got sick bad, it was because the obeah-man had stolen their shadow and nailed it to the tree. She wondered if the shadows were still here, wriggling on the nails.

Her heart began to pound. She wondered if the duppies were here too, watching her. Was Fraser among them? Was he one of the rare good duppies, the kind Quaco called a 'good death'? Would he protect her because she was a relative? Or was he the other kind of duppy, who threw rockstones and put hand on people? She felt in her pocket for the rosemary and the bag of salt. She wished she'd brought Muffin along instead of leaving her tied up at the crossroads so that she wouldn't get scared. She wished she could run away. But she had an offering to make.

She slid the satchel off her shoulder and took out the bottle of proof rum she'd bought from a higgler near Bethlehem. That had been only a couple of hours ago, but it felt like days.

She had slipped away from Quaco just as she'd planned. They'd set off for town after lunch, and stopped halfway at the village of Prospect for a cool drink. It had been easy to persuade Quaco to take a little nap. Then she was off. She'd turned east through Greendale Wood, crossed Greendale Bridge, and then looped southwest through Bethlehem, keeping to the cane-tracks so as to avoid passing too near the Maputah works or home. She'd been proud of herself for finding her way, and when she'd stopped at Tom Gully to give Muffin a drink, it had felt like an adventure. But all that seemed a world away now.

She cast a doubtful glance at the bottle of rum in her hand. What was she doing here? How dare she ask the duppy tree for help? And how did one make an offering, anyway? Should she pour the whole bottle onto the roots? Or just leave it uncorked, so that the duppy tree could have it when it liked? She decided to compromise by pouring half onto the roots, then propping the bottle against the trunk. She did it all with the greatest of care. If you knock against a duppy tree, it might get vexed, and put hand on you. How does a tree 'put hand on you'? She didn't like to think.

When the half-full bottle was resting securely in a fold of the trunk, she took her list of requests from the satchel and unfolded it. Her heart was pounding so hard that she felt sick.

'This is my list,' she said. Her voice sounded horribly loud in the stillness, and she could feel the duppy tree leaning closer to listen. '"Mamma and Papa to be happier and never quarrel again",' she mumbled. '"Sugar prices to go up or treasure to be found, so that Papa will not have to work so hard. Aunt Sophie to come for a visit and make up with Mamma."' She cleared her throat. 'That's the end of my list.'

She wondered if she should say any more. It seemed presumptuous to say 'thank you' when she didn't know if the duppy tree intended to help. But it would be awful to appear ungrateful. 'Thank you, great duppy tree,' she said, and gave a respectful bow. Then she folded the list and tucked it behind the half-full bottle of rum.

The stillness was deeper than ever. All she could hear was her own breathing, and the fall of a leaf in the undergrowth. Then another one brushed her hand. Glancing down, she saw that it wasn't a leaf at all, but a large black flake of ash. Puzzled, she looked up.

The duppy tree was dripping with black ash. Big black flakes, rocking silently down through the canopy, and coming to rest with a soft pattering on the ferns and creepers of the forest floor.

For one terrible moment she thought this must be some kind of sign that the duppy tree was angry with her. Then one of the flakes brushed her face, and she smelt the bitter tang of burnt sugar. Cane-ash, she thought in a rush of relief. It's just someone setting a normal, everyday cane-fire, to burn away the trash and make it easier to take off the crop.

And yet . . . there was still something a little odd about it. For one thing, it was too early in the day for setting a cane-fire. For another, who was doing it, and where? Papa hadn't said anything about setting a fire. And Fever Hill wasn't due to start taking off the crop for another couple of weeks; Papa had mentioned that at breakfast.

She needed to know where the fire was, because it would affect her route back. She decided to make a quick reconnaissance on foot to the western edge of the forest, and get a bird's eye view of which cane-piece Papa was burning, so that she could avoid it.

Down on the Fever Hill Road, a clump of giant bamboo caught fire. Flames scurried up the canes like lizards. The dry leaves crackled and flared. Then the culms exploded in a deafening fusillade of rifle shots. Ben's big bay gelding skittered and squealed.

'Shut up, Partisan,' he said between his teeth, 'it's not here yet.' Ben reined him in and drew out his watch. Half past four. Only half an hour since they'd first got news of the fire, but it felt like hours. A blur of orders and hurried evacuations. Scarcely time to take it in. *Cane-fire*. A vast, hungry animal sweeping towards them from Waytes Valley.

He yanked Partisan's head round and put him into a canter up the track to the works. Already he could smell smoke, and a light scattering of black ash floated down into the red dust like hellish snow.

To his relief, the works were deserted, and so was the settlement behind it. He doubled back to the carriageway, then cantered along the track by the aqueduct to check the old slave village. That too was empty, thank God. Grace and Evie had got out. Once again Ben cantered back to the carriageway, this time putting Partisan up the hill towards the great house. A glance over his shoulder told him that the royal palms down by the gates were already blazing like torches. It didn't seem possible.

The first they'd heard of the fire had been a scent of burnt sugar in the air and a light sprinkling of ash. Minutes later, a panicky field hand had clattered in from Waytes Valley on a mule. The fire was sweeping south towards them at terrifying speed. Months of hot, dry weather had created the perfect conditions, and now a gentle breeze was wafting in from the sea and fanning the flames steadily south and east.

Parnassus had been caught completely unawares, and so was Fever Hill. There was no time to set a controlled fire along the Fever Hill Road, and thereby burn a firebreak to contain the blaze. In the end he'd sent half his men out west to burn an east–west break to protect the cane-pieces of Glen Marnoch, and the other half to start burning a break along the Eden Road, from the edge of Greendale Wood all the way south to Romilly Bridge. He wasn't too hopeful about saving Glen Marnoch, but if the second break held, it would at least save the eastern cane-pieces of Greendale, as well as Cameron Lawe's land at Bullet Tree Walk.

He'd also sent a handful of riders on all available horses to warn Isaac at Arethusa and Cameron Lawe at Eden, and to evacuate the settlements in between. Finally he'd sent a rider to Parnassus—ostensibly for more information on the fire, but really to check that Sophie was safe.

As he'd hoped, he found the great house on Fever Hill deserted. He'd evacuated it immediately, dispatching the men to help with the fire-breaks, and the women in a wagon across country. Now he checked the cookhouse, the laundry-house, the servants' quarters. All deserted.

Back in the carriageway, he reined in for a last look at the house. After the months of renovation it appeared stately and serene, like an elderly lady who'd once been beautiful, and still possessed a faded elegance.

For the first time the enormity of the fire came home to him. This house that he loved was right in its path, and there wasn't a damn thing he could do to save her. This house that, only a few months ago, had welcomed him back with gentle old-fashioned grace, and made him feel at home for the first time in his life. And now he was losing it.

Everything's going up in smoke, thought Ben.

But not quite everything, he reminded himself. At least Kate and Robbie and Lil are still all right. With a last look at the house, he turned and dug in his heels and cantered off towards the stables. Then, having satisfied himself that they too were deserted, he crossed the trickle of the Green River and headed east through the cane-pieces of Bellevue.

He'd gone less than a quarter of a mile before he caught up with the ox wagon bearing the coffins. It was tilting dangerously, with one back wheel stuck in an irrigation ditch. The four field hands who'd been detailed to get it to safety were standing around shaking their heads.

'Hey, Amos!' he shouted as he skittered to a halt. 'What the hell are you doing?'

'Just fixing to pull her out of the hole, Master Ben.'

'So what's stopping you?'

'That fire's running quick as black ant, Master Ben. Why, we just seen Garrick and Caesar come through here, they say that firebreak over at Alice Grove never go hold, they say the whole of Glen Marnoch go burn.'

'Then thank your lucky stars that you're not in Glen Marnoch,' snapped Ben. 'Now get that wheel out of the ditch!'

Gingerly the men moved forwards and put their shoulders to the wagon. With a sinking feeling Ben realised that, if he hadn't happened along, they'd probably have abandoned the wagon and run.

He bit his lip and glanced back over his shoulder. To the north he could see a vast pall of grey smoke at least a mile wide. Amos was right. The fire was scything through Alice Grove towards the house, and after that it would swallow Glen Marnoch to the west, and Bellevue here in the east.

He glanced at the coffins on the wagon. Out here in the open they looked much smaller and more vulnerable. And with only oxen to draw the wagon, progress would be achingly slow, much slower than the fire. If they had horses, they could make it. But all the horses had been needed by the messengers. Where was he going to get any more?

A couple of miles up ahead, he could just make out the guango tree and the giant bamboo that marked the Eden Road. 'Right,' he said to Amos, 'you get the wagon back on the track, no hanging about, and I'll go and see if I can't borrow a couple of horses from someone. Then I'll come back and ride along with you, and we can all get to safety, quick-time.' Without waiting for an answer he dug in his heels and put Partisan into a flat gallop along the cane-track towards the Eden Road.

Oh, thank God. There was a carriage in the distance, coming from town. Whoever it was, they'd lend him the horses without question. An uncontrolled cane-fire threatens everyone, so everyone helps.

But as he drew nearer, he saw to his horror that the 'carriage' was Miss Clemmy in her pony trap, heading straight for the path of the fire. When she recognised Ben she reined in.

'Miss Clemmy,' he panted when he reached her, 'what are you doing?' She blinked. 'Why, dear, I'm going to Eden—'

'There's a *fire*, Miss Clemmy. Can't you see? It'll cut off the Eden Road before you get there.'

'Oh, I know that,' she said, startling him. 'I met a boy on a mule and he told me all about it. He said Cameron and that nice Mr Walker's men from Arethusa are burning a firebreak along the western edge of the road—'

'I know,' he broke in impatiently. 'I've sent men to help. And that's just why you've got to turn round and go back. It'll be chaos up there.'

'I won't be *taking* the Eden Road,' she insisted. 'In about a quarter of a mile I shall turn off and take the track east through Greendale Wood.'

'Miss Clemmy—'

'But I must,' she said with surprising firmness. 'You see, Belle has gone off on Muffin on one of her secret missions into the hills, so I—'

'What? Belle Lawe? Madeleine's little girl?'

'She can be so naughty! She was supposed to join Madeleine for tea at the Mordenners', but Quaco lost sight of her on the way, and then his horse went lame. That's when I bumped into him, on my way to the Mordenners'. Wasn't that lucky? I thought I'd better go after her myself. So here I am.' She looked up at him with a triumphant smile.

Ben kneaded the point between his eyes. 'And you think you do know where to look?'

'Oh, yes. She's either gone to that cave at Turnaround—yes, dear, she did mention it to me—or to Fraser's burying-place on the slope at the back of the house, or to any of half a dozen other places I can think of.' She leaned forward and added in a conspiratorial whisper, 'Madeleine's still with the Mordenners, and doesn't know a thing, thank heavens. But I really do feel that I ought to go and help Sophie look.'

'*Sophie?*' cried Ben.

Miss Clemmy looked worried. 'Didn't I mention that? I met her just after I'd bumped into Quaco. She was going into town, but of course, as soon as I told her, she turned round and headed off to find Belle, so I—'

'Where? Where was she heading?'

'Why, to Eden, of course. On that little grey mare of hers. I think she calls her Frolic.'

Christ, Sophie, what are you thinking? Eden on your own in the middle of a cane-fire? His thoughts raced. He glanced at the brave, silly woman in the pony trap, then back over his shoulder to the cane-pieces.

Sophie was heading into the path of the fire. But surely, as soon as she realised how bad it was, she'd turn round and head back to town to fetch help? Where was the sense in his going to look for her now? He'd never find her in all this chaos. And as for Belle Lawe, he could get a message to her father, and he'd be sure to find her.

He thought of Robbie and Lil and Kate, stuck out in the middle of Bellevue with the fire scything towards them. He couldn't lose them again.

He turned to Miss Clemmy, who was waiting for him to decide. 'Miss Clemmy,' he said, 'you've got to turn round and go back to town.'

'But—'

'No buts. Listen to me. I've just come from Bellevue. I've—'

'I know, the boy on the mule told me. You're getting your brother and sisters to safety.'

He licked his lips. Then something behind her caught his eye. About a quarter of a mile down the road, a cartload of field hands was approaching. He turned back to Miss Clemmy. 'I need you to promise me that you'll turn round and go back to town.'

'But what about Belle?'

'There's a party of field hands coming up behind you, d'you see it? I'll ride over now and get them to unhitch their horse, and send a man to Mr Lawe, quick as he can, to tell him that Belle's gone missing. Now you've got to promise me that you'll turn round. If you don't promise, I can't leave you on your own and go back to the ox wagon.'

She gazed up at him with worried china-blue eyes. 'Of course I promise. But are you sure that you're doing the right thing?'

'What?' he snapped, impatient to be off.

'I mean, I should hate for you to make the wrong choice all over again.'

He reined in and brought Partisan about. 'What d'you mean?'

'Well, you seem to think that Sophie might be in some kind of danger,' she said in her gentle, devastating way. 'So going back to the ox wagon might be the wrong choice. Mightn't it?'

Partisan was angrily tossing his head, and when Ben glanced down he saw that he'd been unconsciously sawing at the reins. It took an effort of will to loosen his grip. 'Sophie will be fine,' he said quietly. 'Now, please, Miss Clemmy. Turn round and go back to town.'

Sophie will be fine, he told himself again, as he dug in his heels and headed up the road towards the field hands. She'll turn back when she sees the fire. She isn't completely mad.

How bizarre, thought Sophie as she cantered through Greendale Wood, that you chose this of all days to go and see Maddy at Falmouth.

It was supposed to have been an opportunity to meet her sister on neutral ground, and re-establish some kind of contact. Instead, here she was, crashing through a wood with a cane-fire somewhere behind her, on her way to Eden. She clattered across Greendale Bridge, then turned Frolic south. The cane-pieces were eerily deserted, the black ash softly falling. Ash this far east? But surely Clemency had said that the fire had started at Waytes Valley? That was miles away.

She didn't want to think about what that meant—or about what might be happening elsewhere. 'Fever Hill all ablaze, Missy Sophie,' the boy on the road had said. *Fever Hill ablaze*. So where was Ben?

And what about Cameron? And *Belle*?

She didn't meet anyone on the road until about a quarter of a mile from Bethlehem, when she came upon a small party of men. They told her they were from Simonstown, on their way south to lend a hand. None of them had seen Belle, or even heard that she was missing. But the eldest man said they'd heard that Master Cameron was burning a firebreak in a great north–south line, to protect the house and the eastern cane-pieces and the Maputah works.

'Where's Master Cameron now?' she asked him. 'D'you know?'

He shook his head. 'Maybe down at Romilly. Maybe further north. But you better turn back now, Miss Sophie. Too much smokes up ahead. And not to frighten about Missy Belle. Master Camron go find her quick-time.'

She bit her lip. In the distance up ahead she could see the roof of Bethlehem chapel pushing above the trees. Three miles beyond that lay Eden great house. The man was probably right: she should turn round now and go back to town. She certainly wanted to. And in all probability, Cameron would find Belle without any help from her. He'd probably found her already, and sent her off in disgrace to her mother.

But what if he hadn't? What if the news that Belle was missing hadn't even got through? There didn't seem to be any way out. If she turned back now and something happened to Belle, she'd never forgive herself.

She wished the men luck, and told them to keep an eye out for Belle. Then she gathered the reins and put Frolic into a canter towards Bethlehem. When she reached the village she found it deserted. She slowed to a trot, and crossed the silent clearing in front of the chapel.

'Belle?' she shouted. Her voice echoed eerily from house to house. She trotted to the edge of the village and reined in at Tom Gully, the shallow stream that marked the boundary between Bethlehem and Eden land. Frolic put down her head to drink. Sophie was thirsty too, but she knew that she couldn't drink. Her throat was too tight to swallow. No more than a yard away, on the other side of this shallow ribbon of rusty brown water, lay Eden.

It's only land, she told herself as her heart began to thud. There's no need to feel like this.

It didn't work.

You're just a miserable coward, Sophie told herself. Belle needs you.

How can you even hesitate? She glanced over her shoulder at the deserted village. Then she looked ahead to the track that led to the works at Maputah, and on to Eden great house. She took a deep breath and put the mare forward across the stream.

Nothing is real any more, she thought as she cantered up to the house. She felt as if she were trapped in a dream, as if she were the only one left alive. From force of habit, she rode round the side of the house and into the garden, where she dismounted and tethered Frolic at the bottom of the steps. It all looked achingly familiar, and eerily untouched by the catastrophe that threatened to sweep it away.

'Belle?' she called.

No answer.

Everything was weirdly peaceful, and alive with birds. She caught the emerald flash of a doctorbird, the smoky blur of a bluequit. At Eden, life was going on in terrifying innocence of the fire about to sweep it away. It was almost as if there was no fire. Except for the black ash, softly falling.

She turned and ran up the steps.

'Belle?' Her voice echoed in the empty house. Quickly she checked the bedrooms. The spare room and the nursery were empty. She ran into Cameron's and Madeleine's room. It too was empty.

She was turning to go when a group of photographs on the bedside table caught her eye. There were three of them, in a little tortoiseshell cluster. The first photograph was of an eight-year-old Belle, scowling into the camera. The second was of Fraser. He wore his sailor suit and he was hatless, his curly hair a pale halo around his eager little face.

She dragged her eyes away from Fraser to the third photograph. With a jolt she recognised herself. She hadn't expected that. Madeleine had taken it seven years ago, on the day of the Historical Society picnic. In the photograph, Sophie stood beneath a tree fern, looking painfully self-conscious in her unflattering pale green dress.

That picnic. She remembered the drive back to Eden with Ben. He hadn't spoken a word all the way to Romilly, and then she'd forced him to talk, and they'd had a row. She pressed her hands to her mouth. First Fraser. Then Ben. Not *now*. There wasn't time.

She ran out onto the steps at the back of the house, and stood irresolute, not knowing which way to turn. Clemency had said that Belle had gone off on a 'secret mission into the hills'. But where? Would she really have gone to the cave at Turnaround, as Clemency believed? That seemed unlikely, given that coming across Evie in the cave had given Belle the fright of her life.

So what about somewhere closer to home? Where would a child with a morbid streak go on a 'secret mission'?

Fraser was buried quite close to the house, only a short way up the slope. Could Belle be up there?

She never seems to play with her dolls, Madeleine had said once. *She just holds funerals for them.*

A cold sweat broke out on Sophie's forehead. She couldn't go up there. No, not to the grave . . . But she drew a deep breath and ran up the well-worn track to the burying-place.

It was beautiful. A small oval clearing enclosed by tree ferns and wild almond and cinnamon trees, and planted with a dazzling profusion of flowers. She saw powder-blue plumbago, the subtle mauves and greenish whites of orchids, and the brilliant cobalt and orange of strelitzia, Fraser's favourite flowers. In the midst of it stood a small white barrel tomb with a stark inscription:

FRASER JOCELYN LAWE
1897–1903

Finally, after all these years, she was standing by his grave.

She watched a flake of black ash float down and settle on the marble. Tentatively, she put out her hand and brushed it off. The stone felt smooth and cool. Not terrifying at all, but strangely comforting.

'I'm so sorry, Fraser,' she whispered. 'I'm so sorry I couldn't save you.'

She looked about her, and stooped and broke off a sprig of orchids, and laid them on the marble. And as she did so, something inside her lifted and broke free.

Now at last she understood what had compelled Ben to bring his dead out to Jamaica. He had decided to stop running from them. He had invited them back.

She squared her shoulders and wiped her eyes with her fingers. Then she began to make a search of the clearing. But she could find no sign that Belle had been here. No ritual herbs. No cut limes or other antiduppy measures such as a child might be able to muster.

And she, Sophie, should know all about that. As a child, she too had had a morbid streak. She'd lived in terror of duppy trees, and had never been without her sprig of rosemary or Madam Fate.

She froze. *Duppy trees.*

A snatch of conversation came back to her. *Did you ask a duppy tree?* Belle had asked at Parnassus, as she gazed intently at Sophie with her big dark eyes. *Did you give it an offering?*

Suddenly, Sophie knew. Belle's 'secret mission' had nothing to do with

Fraser's grave. She'd gone to make an offering to the great duppy tree on Overlook Hill. She was up there right now.

A cold wave of dread washed over her as she realised what that meant. Cameron was somewhere to the north, hard at work with his men to burn a firebreak all the way from Greendale Wood to the cross-roads and beyond. His aim was to block the fire's eastward march, so that it had nowhere to go but south. South to Overlook Hill.

Belle wasn't at the duppy tree. But she'd been there recently. Sophie was sure. There was a half-full bottle of proof rum propped up against the trunk, and round its neck a scarlet hair ribbon tied in a neat, crisp bow.

'Belle?' she shouted. '*Belle!* It's Aunt Sophie! Where *are* you?'

Nothing. Ash pattered down into the undergrowth. To the north she could hear a distant roar. The roar of the fire. Ahead of her the track wound on through the trees towards the western edge of the forest. Sophie put Frolic forwards, heading west.

It was hard going, for the path was overgrown, and she was forced to dismount and lead, stopping often to untangle the stirrups from the undergrowth, and talking to the mare to calm her. But Frolic would not be calmed, for she'd scented smoke. Her ears were flattened against her skull, and she kept tossing her head and tugging the reins. After ten minutes' hard going she caught a glimmer of dirty white sky between the trees. She quickened her pace, dragging the reluctant Frolic after her.

She reached the edge of the forest with startling suddenness, and the stench of burnt sugar hit her like a wall. Frolic squealed and jerked back, nearly pulling Sophie off her feet. The fire was terrifyingly close: a roaring, crackling wall of fierce orange, only half a mile distant. Behind it the cane-pieces of Orange Grove had disappeared in a pall of smoke.

Tugging Frolic after her, she picked her way between the boulders and round the flank of the hill. Somewhere on the southwest slope was a track that wound down to the bridge at Stony Gap.

On this side of the hill, the fire wasn't quite so close. But through the bitter blue haze she could only just make out the giant bamboo that marked the Martha Brae, little more than a mile from where she stood.

'Belle!' she shouted. 'Belle!' Her voice sounded weak and ineffectual.

'*Here!*' yelled a voice, so close that she nearly fell over.

Belle was about twenty feet below her on the track. She was filthy, her face and riding costume covered in dust and soot. 'Aunt Sophie, I'm *really* sorry!' she cried. 'I was trying to get round to see how far it had gone and I slipped and bumped my knee and then I tried to find another way up and sort of got lost.'

She seemed exasperated rather than frightened, and after the first shattering upsurge of relief Sophie was tempted to run down and give her a good shaking.

'It doesn't matter,' she said, raising her voice above the roar of the fire. 'Are you all right?'

Belle gave a tight nod. 'What do we do now?'

Sophie licked her lips. 'Stay where you are. I need to think.'

From where she stood, the track wound steeply down the bare western slope of the hill towards Belle, with a steep drop on the left of about fifty feet into a thorny defile. But if they could make it down to the bottom of the hill, they might reach Stony Gap before the fire closed off their escape, and then cross to the safety of the cattle pastures on the other side of the river.

The alternative was to head back up the track and into the forest again, retracing their steps past the duppy tree, to the crossroads. Every nerve in her body cried out for the primeval shelter of the forest. And yet, she thought, what if we can't make it through in time? What if they found themselves cut off by the very firebreak intended to protect Eden?

'Stay where you are,' she told Belle. 'I'm coming down to you.'

Belle looked horrified. 'But what about Muffin? We can't leave her!'

'What?' shouted Sophie, intent on picking her way down without losing her footing. Behind her a reluctant Frolic tugged on the reins.

'I tied her up!' cried Belle, jumping up and down. 'She won't be able to get away! She'll be burnt!'

'No, she won't,' said Sophie unconvincingly. She slipped on a loose stone and nearly lost her footing. A trickle of pebbles rattled and bounced down the slope and lost themselves among the boulders at the bottom. She licked her lips. The track was steeper than it looked. 'I didn't see Muffin as I was coming up,' she called down to Belle, 'so she must have broken free and run away.'

'Are you sure?' said Belle doubtfully.

'Absolutely.' Frolic tugged on the reins.

'Aunt Sophie—'

'*What?*' she snapped. Yet another tug on the reins. Dust and pebbles rained down on her. 'Frolic, come *on*,' she shouted without turning round.

'Aunt Sophie!' screamed Belle. 'Look out!'

A rock struck her shoulder with bruising force. She glanced over her shoulder just in time to see the mare going slowly down onto her knees—slowly, slowly, as if in a nightmare—then tumbling neck over crop, and sliding down the track towards her.

Ben reached the crossroads before Cameron Lawe's men, but with not much time to spare. He could hear them through the thickening haze of smoke, a few hundred yards to the north. The air was acrid with the stench of burnt sugar. To the west he could hear the crackling roar as the fire engulfed Orange Grove and swept towards them.

The men didn't stop working when he rode up, nor did he expect them to. It wouldn't be much longer before the fire reached them, and if the break didn't hold, the flames would burst through and engulf the great house, the works at Maputah, and the rest of the estate.

To his dismay, none of them had seen either Sophie or Belle. But they told him that Master Cameron was further down towards Romilly, so maybe he should ride over and talk to him in person?

No time, thought Ben as he yanked Partisan's head round and galloped back towards the crossroads. *Don't make the wrong choice again,* Miss Clemmy had told him. Why hadn't he listened to her at once, instead of wasting time riding back to the wagon?

He reached the crossroads and skittered to a halt in a shower of dust and ash. Which way? Which *way*? According to Miss Clemmy, Belle was heading for the cave near Turnaround. But what if Miss Clemmy was wrong? Or what if Belle had gone one way, and Sophie another?

He dismounted and started circling the crossroads, looking for tracks. Partisan threw down his head to cough, then plodded wearily after him. In the dust near the crossroads he spotted a hoofmark: a mare's, by the size of it. A few yards further on he found the small, neat crescent moon of a pony's print. But from the little he found, it was impossible to tell whether Sophie and Belle had been together, or which way they'd gone.

Come on, Ben, which way? Turnaround? It had to be. Where else would Belle have gone? He got back into the saddle and was heading east when a terrified squeal behind him pulled him up short. Partisan pricked his ears and gave an answering whinny.

Belle had hidden her pony with care, tethering her securely to a young guango tree in a clearing just off the track that led up the wooded eastern flank of Overlook Hill. The fat little chestnut had long since smelt smoke, and was white-eyed with terror and tugging frantically at the reins. A bundle of wilted herbs on her browband was tossing wildly.

Ben's heart sank. Wherever she was, Belle must be well out of earshot. She'd never leave her beloved pony squealing in terror.

'You must be Muffin,' he said as he jumped down, tethered Partisan, and advanced slowly towards the pony. 'Where's your mistress gone, eh, Muffin? Where's she gone, then?'

The pony sidestepped and rolled her eyes, but her ears swivelled round to listen to him.

'Rosemary and Madam Fate,' he remarked as he unbuckled the girth and slipped the saddle off the broad, sweaty back. 'What did she want with that lot, eh, Muffin?'

Talking continuously, he unbuckled the cheekband and slipped off the bridle, keeping the reins looped over the pony's neck so that he could still control her. Then he led her—or rather dragged her—back onto the open track. 'Go on, then,' he said, slipping the reins over her head and giving her a slap on the rump. 'And don't hang about!'

Muffin didn't need to be told. She flicked up her tail and clattered off down the road towards the Maputah works.

Rosemary and Madam Fate? thought Ben as he got back into the saddle and started once again for Turnaround. What did Belle want with that? Was she warding off duppies? But what duppies? And where?

Suddenly he remembered Sophie's childhood terror of duppy trees, and the pieces fell into place. *One of her secret missions into the hills.* Duppies. The duppy tree on Overlook Hill.

Oh, Christ. Christ. Straight into the path of the fire.

He turned Partisan round and galloped back to the crossroads, and put the gelding up the track to Overlook Hill.

He crouched low against the hot, sweaty neck as the gelding heaved through the undergrowth. Branches whipped at his face. Memories crowded in. Sophie's expression as she'd stood in the glade of the duppy tree, seven years before.

It's over, Ben, she had said.

No, it bloody well isn't, he told himself grimly. There's still time.

Another parrot flew screeching over the canopy. *Ah-eek! Ah-eek!* Belle and Sophie exchanged taut glances and ran on through the forest.

Surely, thought Sophie, the duppy tree can't be much further ahead? Did you do the right thing, going back into the forest? Or is this the last of your about-turns to go catastrophically wrong?

The breath rasped in her lungs. Her forearm throbbed where she'd fallen and scraped it raw. She was tired. She was beginning to limp.

The roar of the fire was closer now—she could hear branches crackling somewhere to her left—but how close? At the foot of the hill? Halfway up the slope? Fifty feet away?

She pushed aside the tattered leaves of a philodendron, and burst through into the clearing of the duppy tree. 'Thank God,' she panted, stumbling over to the tree and collapsing onto one of the great folded roots. From here it couldn't be more than twenty minutes to the bottom of the hill. Provided, of course, that they still had twenty minutes.

Belle looked frightened. 'You shouldn't sit there,' she said, hardly moving her lips.

'Just for a moment, to catch my breath.'

'You shouldn't sit on its roots. It isn't safe.'

Sophie gave a spurt of laughter. Safe? Nowhere was safe.

Belle tugged at her hand. 'Please can we go now? Please?'

Sophie drew a deep breath. Ash pattered down around her. Up ahead, a horse squealed.

A horse?

Suddenly a big foam-flecked bay gelding crashed through the ferns into the clearing. Sophie leapt to her feet as Ben—*Ben*—jumped down and ran over to her and gripped her shoulder so hard that it hurt. 'Christ, Sophie, Christ. What the hell d'you think you're doing, just sitting there on a tree root?' He was out of breath and covered in soot and sweat, and there was a long bloody slash down his cheek.

'I wasn't . . . I mean . . . I found Belle.' She held up Belle's grimy little fist.

'I'm sorry,' muttered Belle with a sideways glance at the duppy tree.

'Christ,' said Ben to no one in particular. He let go of Sophie and turned away, and put both hands on the bay's sweaty neck, and shook his head. Over his shoulder he said, 'What did you do to your arm?'

'I fell,' said Sophie. 'How did you find us? Did you—?'

'Did you find Muffin?' said Belle. 'I tied her to a tree where nobody would see, and she'll be really sca—'

'I found her,' he said. He turned back to Sophie, and whipped out his handkerchief and wrapped it round her forearm so tightly that it hurt.

She yelped, but he ignored her. He'd already turned back to Belle. 'I untacked her and let her go,' he told her. 'She'll be halfway to Simonstown by now.'

'Oh, *thank* you!' Belle sighed with relief. Clearly she was no longer worried, now that her pony was safe, and she had two adults to look after her.

Sophie struggled to loosen the handkerchief on her forearm. 'Have the men reached the crossroads yet?' she asked Ben.

'Not yet, but soon.' He threw the reins over the bay's head in readiness to mount.

'How soon?' said Sophie.

'Ten minutes? I don't know.'

'We won't make it.'

'Yes we will, if we ride hard.' He turned to her. 'Where's your horse?'

Sophie opened her mouth, then shut it again.

'She fell,' said Belle.

He stared at them blankly. 'What d'you mean?'

'We were trying to get down the western slope,' said Sophie, 'towards Stony Gap. It was too steep and she fell. It was all I could do to get out of the way.'

He looked down at her as if he couldn't understand what he was hearing. For the first time she saw how exhausted he was. His face was drawn, and there were bluish shadows beneath his eyes.

'She twitched when she hit the rocks,' muttered Belle, 'and then she stopped. We think she broke her neck.'

Ben wasn't listening. He was looking from Sophie to Belle, then back to the gelding. Then he rubbed a hand over his face. 'Right,' he said.

He went over to Belle and grabbed her under the arms and swung her up into the saddle. Then he turned to Sophie, and before she knew what he was doing he'd given her a leg-up and propelled her into the saddle behind Belle. 'Keep your head down,' he said as he shortened the stirrups for her, 'and use your heels. His name's Partisan and he's had enough, but he'll get you past the crossroads. But whatever you do, don't stop. Just keep going . . . and yell, both of you, so that the men know you're coming. You'll make it through all right.'

Then it dawned on Sophie that he wasn't coming with them. Until that moment she couldn't have imagined that things could get any worse. She leaned down and grabbed his shoulder. 'What about you?'

'I'll take my chances,' he muttered as he flicked up the saddle flap and started tightening the girth.

'I'm not leaving you here.'

'For Christ's sake, Sophie,' he burst out, 'use your head! One knackered horse isn't going to carry a man, a woman and a child!'

'I'm not leaving you,' she said again.

Tears stung her eyes. In front of her, Belle clutched handfuls of mane and started to shake.

'Look,' said Ben more quietly, 'for once in my life I'm making the right choice. I'm not going to let you spoil it now. All right?'

'Choice? What choice? What are you talking about?'

But he only shook his head, and threw the reins over Partisan's neck, and closed her hands over them with his own.

Another explosion of bamboo. The gelding sidestepped in alarm.

'Go on,' said Ben, grabbing hold of the bridle and turning Partisan round. 'Get out of here.'

But Sophie reined in, and leaned down and grasped his hand. 'There's something you've got to know,' she said fiercely. 'Nothing's changed. I mean, about you and me. What I feel . . . it's just the same as it's always been. Always.'

He looked up at her and his eyes were glittering. 'I know, sweetheart. Same with me.' Then he pulled her down towards him and kissed her hard on the mouth. 'Better late than never, eh?'

'Promise me . . . *promise* you'll be right behind us.'

He didn't reply.

'Ben, I won't go unless—'

'Just keep going and don't look back. Now go on, go!'

'Ben, *please*—'

He slapped Partisan on the rump. 'Go *on!*'

Her last sight of him, through a stinging blur of tears, was as he stooped for the bottle of rum by the duppy tree, and took a long, slow pull. Then the bitter blue smoke closed in around him.

CHAPTER TWELVE

IT WAS STILL RAINING when Sophie and Belle left Eden great house and started slowly along the riverbank towards Romilly. The wind had changed a couple of hours before, bringing in rain from the north. Not a tropical downpour, but a steady, penetrating drizzle.

'Shouldn't we have waited at the house?' said Belle in a small voice. She was huddled in front of Sophie in her mackintosh, and clutching handfuls of mane, for Partisan was stumbling with fatigue.

'Your papa needs to know that you're safe,' muttered Sophie. It was true, but it wasn't the whole truth. The truth was, she couldn't have stood the empty house another moment.

They had reached the crossroads at the same time as Cameron's men, and made it across to the sound of ragged cheers. Cameron himself wasn't to be found, and no one seemed to know where he was. The men had suggested that she go and wait at the house.

She had found the house deserted, and just as she'd left it hours before. After fetching bread and milk for Belle, she had run out onto the verandah to wait for Ben. He didn't come. She had leaned out as far as she could, straining to penetrate the cloud of smoke and steam and drizzle that shrouded Overlook Hill, telling herself that he'd got through.

But nobody came. And she kept remembering the look on his face as he'd told her to go without him. *For once in my life I'm making the right choice.* What did he mean? It sounded horribly like an epitaph.

Now a gust of wind shivered the giant bamboo, showering them with raindrops. Partisan shook his mane and plodded on, and Sophie gritted her teeth. Dimly she perceived that she was wet, cold and exhausted, but she didn't really feel it. She was in a long, dark tunnel with only one way forward: find Cameron, leave Belle with him, then go and look for Ben.

Voices up ahead. They must be nearing Romilly. They reached the creeper-clad enclosure of tumbled cut-stone in which, seven years before, Ben had built himself a fire. She looked for cockleshell orchids, but couldn't see any. It felt like the worst kind of omen. She lacked the strength to convince herself that it didn't mean anything.

Suddenly they were out of the bamboo and into the clearing, and Partisan was picking his way between little groups of astonished field hands resting on the ground.

'Look, there's Papa!' cried Belle.

Cameron was down by the bridge, and hadn't seen them yet. He was hatless and soaked, and had plainly just run down to meet the rider who'd ridden up from town. It took Sophie a moment to recognise her sister. Madeleine too was hatless and soaked, and incongruously dressed in a bronze-coloured afternoon gown, which was smeared with soot and had been hitched up to her knees so that she could ride astride. She must have just dismounted, for she was gripping Cameron's shoulders, and they were staring into one another's faces.

As Sophie rode down towards them, their voices drifted over to her.

'But I thought she was with you,' said Cameron.

'She *was*,' cried Madeleine, 'at least, she was with Quaco till she gave him the slip. God knows where she is by now—' Her voice broke.

At that moment Belle scrambled down into the mud. 'I'm fine! Here I am! I'm saved!'

They turned and saw her at the same time. Madeleine pressed both her hands to her mouth. Cameron went forward and scooped up his daughter and held her up fiercely, high above him, as if he couldn't believe it was really her. Then he set her down with a splash, and Madeleine went down onto her knees in the mud and seized her by the shoulders. 'Where have you *been*?' she cried, shaking her.

Belle was disconcerted. 'The duppy tree,' she mumbled.

'The *duppy* tree?' cried her parents in horror.

'What were you doing up there?' said Cameron.

'I was making an offering,' said Belle, who was beginning to realise the trouble she was in. 'There was nobody at home so we thought we'd better come and tell you.' She glanced at Sophie for corroboration, but neither Madeleine nor Cameron took their eyes from their daughter's face. 'You're all sooty,' Belle said to her mother. 'Did you ride through the fire to save me?'

'Of course not,' snapped Madeleine, who was fast recovering her composure. 'It was over by the time I got there. What sort of offering?'

'I had a list,' said Belle defensively. 'Aunt Sophie was absolutely *brilliant*! She followed me all the way to Eden, and guessed about the duppy tree, and found me in the forest—well, not actually in the forest, because by then I'd . . .' While she went on breathlessly, Madeleine raised her head and spotted Sophie.

Sophie dismounted and handed the reins to Moses, and went over to her. She felt numb and cold and distant, as if she were seeing her sister from a long way away.

Still on her knees in the mud, Madeleine reached up and grasped her hand. 'Thank you,' she whispered.

Sophie shook her head. She tried to pull away, but Madeleine kept hold of her hand. 'Thank you,' she whispered again.

'. . . and Mr Kelly was so brave,' Belle was telling her father. 'He lent us his horse, his name's Partisan, because Aunt Sophie's had fallen down a ravine, *and* he saved Muffin. Have you found her yet?'

Cameron shook his head, clearly struggling to take it all in.

'And he wouldn't come with us because he said a knackered horse can't carry a man, a woman, and a child. So we had to leave him behind.'

Cameron turned to Sophie. 'Is this true?'

She nodded. 'That's his horse,' she said, jerking her head at Partisan. 'He was supposed to follow us on foot,' she went on, her teeth beginning to chatter, 'but I don't think he got through.'

Madeleine came and put her hands on Sophie's shoulders.

'There wouldn't have been time for him to get out, would there?' Sophie said shrilly. 'I mean, we only just made it ourselves, and we were on horseback. Did the fire . . . did it go all the way to the hill?'

Cameron nodded.

'Perhaps he found another way down,' said Madeleine.

Sophie's teeth were chattering so hard she could scarcely speak. 'I'm going to look for him,' she said, turning back to Partisan.

Cameron stepped in front of her. 'No, Sophie,' he said.

'But I've got to. I've got to find him—'

'Sophie,' he said gently, 'in ten minutes it'll be dark. You're exhausted. And this horse isn't going anywhere. I'll send a man out to look for him.'

'Come on, Sophie,' said Madeleine behind her. 'There's nothing more you can do tonight. Come back to the house.'

Sophie looked from Cameron to her sister, then back to Cameron. 'Does he have a chance?'

'I don't know,' he said bluntly. 'We'll know by morning.'

She was in her old room at Eden, trying to sleep. She was also at Romilly, curled up on Ben's blanket, waiting for him to return.

After a while she felt him behind her, settling down against her back. She was so tired that she couldn't move. She wanted to put out her hand and touch him, but her arm was too heavy. She couldn't even summon the energy to open her eyes. 'I'm glad you're back,' she mumbled.

'Sophie,' whispered Madeleine.

She woke up with a start. 'What? What?'

It was dark in the room. By the light of the single candle on the bed-side table Madeleine's nightgown was a pale blur. 'He's all right, Sophie,' she said, sitting down beside her. 'Ben's all right. We've just got word.'

Blearily, Sophie rubbed her face. She felt heavy and sick with fatigue. 'Where? Where is he? Is he hurt?'

Madeleine shook her head. 'I think he's spending the night in the cattle pastures. He sent a boy to check that you and Belle were all right.'

Sophie leaned forward and put her face on her knees.

'After leaving you on the hill, he found his way to Stony Gap,' said Madeleine. 'He got there just before the fire. Apparently he jumped off the bridge into the river. That's what the boy said. Anyway. He sent a note.'

Sophie drew a deep breath. 'What does it say?'

'D'you want me to read it?'

She nodded. She heard the rustle of Madeleine's nightgown as she leaned closer to the candle. '"In the end, the River Mistress saw me through. Ben."' Madeleine paused. 'Does it mean anything to you?'

Sophie nodded. After a while she said, 'What time is it?'

'Three in the morning.' Madeleine folded the note again and handed it to her. 'It'll be light in a few hours. Then you can go and see him.'

Sophie took the note and nodded.

'You'll be all right now,' said Madeleine, stroking her hair. 'Now you can get a proper sleep.' She rose to go, but Sophie grasped her hand.

'What about you? Are you all right? And Cameron? And Belle?'

She saw the gleam of Madeleine's smile. 'We're all fine, thanks to you.'

'No, I didn't mean that—'

'Yes, but I do. I do.'

There was a silence. Then Sophie said, 'What about the estate?'

Madeleine laughed. 'The estate! Oh, don't worry about that. Cameron says if he works round the clock he can get in quite a bit of Orange Grove before it spoils. And we've still got Bullet Tree Piece. So it seems that we're not absolutely ruined just yet.' She paused. 'You know, there's a rumour that it was started deliberately.'

Sophie yawned hugely. 'Really?' Sleep was stealing up on her again. She could hardly keep her eyes open.

Madeleine patted her shoulder. 'You go back to sleep.'

On the morning after the fire, Alexander Traherne awoke from his first decent sleep in weeks, feeling peaceful and relaxed. Still in his nightshirt, and before even tasting his cup of chocolate, he dashed off three short notes. The first was to Sophie, telling her that she was absolutely right, and releasing her from her promise. The second was to his insurers, informing them of the destruction of his house and property at Waytes Valley, and instructing them to pay the compensation monies forthwith to his account. The third was to Guy Fazackerly, announcing that the whole of the debt would be repaid on New Year's Day. Then, business concluded, he went down to breakfast.

To his surprise there was no one about. At length the butler brought a message from his father, to say that he was wanted in the study.

To his relief, the governor hailed him cheerily and seemed in an excellent humour, although Bostock, his man of business, wore the haggard look of a man who'd been up all night. The governor lit a cigar for himself and indicated the humidor to his son, and for a while they smoked in silence. Bostock sat a little apart, staring at the floor.

Alexander felt mildly curious as to what this was about. He and the governor weren't in the habit of sharing companionable silences. When it had gone on long enough, he flicked a speck of lint off his knee and remarked that it was a bad business about that fire.

To his surprise, the governor waved that away. 'These things happen. It simply means that I shall be taking off the crop a little quicker than I'd intended, and spending a lot more on labour to do it.' He leaned back in his chair and chuckled. 'Just as well Waytes Valley ain't yet yours, eh, my boy? Or you'd be getting a snap introduction to the art of taking off the crop at speed!'

Alexander paused with his cigar halfway to his lips. 'I rather thought that it *was* mine,' he said with careful nonchalance.

'Oh, no, old fellow. Not until you're actually married.'

'Ah,' murmured Alexander. A setback. Definitely a setback. Particularly since he'd just sent that note to Sophie.

But still. She could be brought round easily enough. Although it was a confounded shame about the insurance monies. Out loud he said, 'So crop time will cost you a bit, will it? Shall you be put to much expense?'

'Quite considerable, I'm afraid. I shall need to bring in hordes of coolies from St Ann to get it done, and those brutes never come cheap.'

'But won't all that be covered by the insurance?' said Alexander.

'I doubt it,' said the governor, examining his cigar. 'They tend not to pay up when it's a question of arson.'

Alexander nearly choked on his cigar. 'Arson?'

'Odd, isn't it?' said the governor without looking at him. 'Bostock tells me that a man was seen with a box of matches. "Acting suspicious".'

Alexander shot a startled glance at Bostock, but the man of business went on staring at the floor.

'Of course,' said the governor, turning his cigar in his fingers, 'if they find the fellow who did it, he'll hang. And I shall take the greatest pleasure in going along to watch.'

Alexander ran his tongue over his lips and forgot to breathe.

'Still,' said the governor briskly, 'that's not what I wanted to talk to you about.' His small blue eyes were markedly less genial than before. 'I don't suppose you saw Parnell this morning?'

Alexander shook his head. How could he think about Parnell at a time like this? *Hanged?* For a few miserable sticks of cane?

'That's because he left,' said his father. 'Rather early this morning. In an absolute funk.'

Alexander dragged his mind back to the present. 'What?' he murmured. 'Where did he go?'

'Back to England. At least, that's what his note said. Some balderdash about urgent business. Didn't even have the courage to tell me to my face.' He drew on his cigar, narrowing his eyes against the smoke. 'It goes without saying that the match with your sister is off. In fact, everything's off. Including my own spot of business with him. Which, I might add, puts me in a decidedly tricky position just at present.'

'I'm sorry,' said Alexander mechanically.

'So am I. Particularly as it seems that I have you to thank for it all.'

Alexander went cold.

'D'you know what put him in a funk?' said the governor. 'No? Shall I tell you? It seems that he got to hear about you and some mulatto girl.'

Alexander made no reply. He wasn't that stupid.

'So you see, Alexander,' said his father, stubbing out his cigar, 'thanks to you, your sister has just missed out on a most advantageous match, and I shall be compelled to draw in my horns rather considerably. I may even have to sell some of the property.'

Alexander's thoughts darted in panic. In four days the world would know that he'd welshed on a debt of twenty thousand pounds. Added to which was the threat of . . . unpleasantness over that wretched fire. And clearly he could expect no sympathy at home. Despite the governor's false calm, he was incandescent. It was all so horribly unfair.

The governor got to his feet and drew out his watch. 'I'm glad we've had this little chat,' he said, 'but I mustn't keep you any longer. Your boat leaves in just over an hour.'

'My boat?' said Alexander weakly.

'Coastal steamer to Kingston. It should get you there in time to catch the packet to Perth.'

'*Perth?*' cried Alexander. 'But . . . isn't that in Australia?'

'Well *done*, Alexander.' The governor went over to the humidor on the side table and selected another cigar. 'You can check the details with Bostock on your way to town,' he said without turning. 'Oh, and he has some papers for you to sign. Relinquishing your rights. That sort of thing.'

A spark of rebellion kindled in Alexander's breast. 'I shall relinquish nothing, sir,' he said proudly.

His father laughed. 'Oh, I rather think that you will! Insurers can be horribly persistent in investigating a fire.'

Alexander opened his mouth to protest, then shut it again.

'Chin up, old man,' said the governor crisply. 'You'll get an allowance of twenty pounds a month—'

'Twenty pounds a month?' cried Alexander. 'I can't possibly live on that!'

'Twenty pounds a month,' went on the governor imperturbably, 'on condition that we never . . . never . . . see you again. Now off you go.' He turned back to the humidor and shut the lid with a thud. 'And say goodbye to your mother on your way out.'

It's early morning at Salt Wash, and Evie's helping to dole out breakfast for the field hands before they make a start on taking off the crop.

There's sort of a holiday feeling in the village. Everybody's staying with everybody else, and they're all pulling together to help out. Even her mother's not taking the loss of her place so bad as she'd expected. 'I can get new things,' she said with a shrug. 'It's time for a change.'

Yes, thinks Evie as she spoons green banana porridge into each out-stretched bowl. It's time for a change. And she bites back a smile.

Inside, she can't stop smiling. For the first time in months, she's fizzing over with good humour. Revenge tastes *good*. Early that morning she went out for a walk along the Coast Road, and two carriages passed her by, and now the memory of them is like a kernel of heat in her belly.

The first carriage carried Master Alexander on his way to the quay. Lord God, but that man was white! Staring in front of him, like he'd just seen his own self duppy. The carriage had almost passed her by when he glanced down and saw her. And that was best of all: seeing the knowledge in his face that she was the one who'd brought him down.

The second carriage came along a little later, when she'd already turned back for Salt Wash. It was heading in the opposite direction, towards Montego Bay, and in it sat that Mr Austen who used to be secretary to Ben, and his new employer, Mr Augustus Parnell.

Mr Parnell glanced at Evie as he passed, but he didn't really see her. To him she was just some coloured girl on the road. How was he to know that she was the writer of the little note that had finished it all?

Strange how simple it had been, and how effective! All it had taken was the revelation that Cornelius Traherne had a coloured daughter—a darkie half-sister for Miss Sibella—and he had fled. Apparently, the notion of being connected to a mulatto was just too horrible to bear.

Strange, strange. Over the past few days she'd toyed with all kinds of moonshine schemes for revenge on the Trahernes. Poison. Shadow-taking. Each notion crazier than the one before. Then it had come to her in all its simplicity. What her mother had passed on wasn't just about being four-eyed and putting hand on people. It was about being her own self. Evie Quashiba McFarlane. And once she'd got that sorted out, everything else just fell into place. Humming under her breath, she went to the cookhouse and fetched more porridge, then returned to the head of the queue. She was just getting back into the rhythm of doling it out again, when the next man in line snarled things up by not moving along. 'Go on, now,' she said without looking up.

The bowl stayed where it was.

'What's the matter with you?' she said. 'You want breakfast or not?'

'Yes, ma'am,' said Isaac Walker, 'I certainly do.'

She blinked.

He looked tired, and his fancy clothes were crumpled and black with soot. And he was just standing there at the head of the queue, not smiling, but looking as if he was ready to smile.

Evie's good humour evaporated. There was something about this man that made her afraid. Something about the way he looked at her with his small, clever eyes: not as a man usually looks at a pretty woman, but as one human being looks at another when they want to make friends.

But she didn't want to make friends with him. She didn't want to make friends with anyone. 'If you want your breakfast,' she said tartly, 'you'd better go and eat it, Master Walker. Now move along, I've got work to do.'

'I just wanted to make sure,' he said in his quiet, gentle way, 'that you and your mother are all right.'

'We're fine,' she snapped. 'Mother's over at cousin Cecilia's. That's the second house on the right. Why don't you go and look in on her?'

'No, thank you,' he said politely. 'I came to see you.'

Her hackles rose. 'I'm busy,' she snapped.

'I can see that,' he replied.

His expression was hard to read, but he was clearly undeterred. Suddenly she wondered how many people in the past had mistaken his gentleness for weakness. She frowned. 'I'll be a very, very long time,' she said forbiddingly.

'Take as long as you like,' he said. 'I can wait.'

It was an eerie experience to ride north along the Eden Road. On the right lay the rainwashed cane of Bullet Tree Piece—untouched except for a sprinkling of ash—while on the left lay the desolation of Bellevue. Life and death side by side, thought Sophie, with only a strip of road in between.

It was a horrible thought. It kept coming back to her that if things had been just a little different yesterday—if Ben had been slower in deciding what to do or where to go—she wouldn't be heading up the road to see him. She'd be going to his funeral.

She found him a couple of miles in, by the blackened ruins of the wagon that Clemency had told her about. He was hatless, sitting on the ground, contemplating the remains. The heat of the fire must have been intense, for all that was left of the coffins was a pile of smoking cinders.

At her approach he turned and watched her, but to her surprise he didn't get up and come towards her.

Feeling suddenly awkward, she dismounted. 'I got your note,' she said.

He nodded. He wore the same riding clothes as the day before, and his face looked shadowed and drawn.

She stopped a few feet away from him. 'According to Madeleine, you jumped in the river to escape the fire.'

He nodded. 'It seemed the best thing to do.' His voice sounded rough. She wondered if that was from the smoke or from crying. She badly wanted to go down on her knees and put her arms round him, but something told her to keep her distance. He didn't seem to want her here.

As lightly as she could, she said, 'Belle wants to know if you met an alligator.'

He tried to smile, but it wasn't very successful. 'How is she?'

'Contrite. And she keeps telling everyone that Partisan's a hero. This morning she made him and Muffin one of her special hot-molasses mashes, and when I left she was braiding their manes.' She knew she was talking too much, but she couldn't help it.

'So you're back at Eden now,' he said.

'Yes. Well. It's a start.'

He nodded. 'That's good. It's good that you're back.'

'Madeleine wants you to come and stay, until you can rebuild. So does Cameron.'

'Do they?' He shook his head. 'I don't think they do. Not really.'

'You're wrong. And Madeleine knew you wouldn't believe me, so she wrote you a note.' She handed it to him, and watched him get to his feet and walk a few paces away to read it. He stood there reading it for a long time. Then he folded it and put it in his pocket. He cleared his throat. 'Tell her thank you,' he said over his shoulder, 'but it's better that I don't.'

'Ben, what's wrong?'

He flicked her a glance. Then he stooped for a handful of ash, and opened his hand and watched it drift away on the breeze. 'Look around you, Sophie. It's all gone.'

'But . . . surely you can get in at least some of the cane? And—'

'It's not that,' he broke in. 'Of course I can get in at least some of the cane. Of course I've still got money in the bank. It isn't that.' He paused. 'It was the Monroe great house. Your grandfather's house. Then it was mine, and now it's gone.' He glanced at the blackened remains of the coffins. 'It's all gone. I couldn't save any of it.'

'What do you *mean*? You got every single person out alive. You got me and Belle out alive.'

He did not reply. She watched him walk to the other side of the wagon, break off a fragment of charcoal and crumble it in his fingers. And at last she began to understand. This wasn't about the destruction of the house, or even the loss of his brother's and sisters' remains. Or rather, it wasn't *only* about those things. He'd simply reached the end of his resources. She had always thought of him as someone with an unlimited capacity for fighting back. No matter what happened, he would always get up and start again. Now she realised that nobody can do that, not all the time.

She followed him round to his side of the wagon. 'Yesterday on Overlook Hill,' she began, 'you told me that this time you were making the right choice. I didn't know what you meant until this morning.' She paused. 'Clemency came just after breakfast. She told me about Kate. About the choice you had to make when you were a boy.'

Again he forced a smile. 'Everything I do turns to ashes.'

'If you weren't so exhausted, you'd know that's absolutely not true.'

He nodded, but she could see that he didn't believe her.

She tried a different tack. 'You said once that you're like your father. That you destroy the things you love. Do you still think that's true?'

He didn't answer at once. 'Poor bastard,' he said at last. 'You know, when he died, he was only a couple of years older than I am now. He didn't live long after Kate.'

'Does that mean you've forgiven him?'

'I don't know. Maybe.'

'Don't you think it's time you forgave yourself?'

He hesitated. 'Sophie, I brought them out to be with me. I know it sounds odd, but it meant something. Now look at them. Just ashes, blown away.'

'What's so bad about that?' she said with deliberate bluntness. 'They're out here in the sun and the fresh air. It's a good place to be.'

He did not reply.

'Ben . . .' She put her hands on his shoulders and turned him round to face her. 'Look at you. Coming out here all on your own, when you're exhausted. When did you last get any sleep?'

He frowned.

'Added to which, you probably haven't eaten anything since God knows when, and you've just lost your home. Of course you're feeling low.' She put her palm against the roughness of his cheek. Then she stood on tiptoe and kissed his mouth.

He didn't return her kiss.

'Come back to the house,' she said quickly, to cover her confusion. 'I mean, come back to Eden. Have something to eat and a proper sleep, and I promise you'll feel better.'

He was looking down at her, still frowning. Suddenly he took a deep breath and put his arms about her, and pulled her hard against him. He held her so tightly that she could hardly breathe. She could feel his heart racing, and the heat of his breath on her temple. She could smell his clean sharp smell of windblown grass and red dust and Ben. She put her arms round him and buried her face in his neck.

When at last they drew apart, they were both blinking back tears.

'Whatever happens,' he muttered between his teeth, 'you're not going to marry Alexander Traherne.'

It was so unexpected that she laughed. 'What?'

'I mean it, Sophie. He—'

'I know! I broke it off on Boxing Day.'

He looked bemused. 'What?'

'At your Masquerade.'

'But . . . you never told me.'

'You never gave me the chance. You were too busy seducing Sibella.'

'I didn't actually seduce her—'

'I know, I know.' She was starting to feel happy again. Bickering was always a good sign.

'Tell me honestly,' he said, looking into her eyes. 'Do you truly not mind about the house?'

She gave his shoulders another shake. 'No! We'll build another house. And next Christmas we'll give an enormous party, and invite everyone in Trelawny. Including Great-Aunt May.'

He was watching her intently, as if he still wasn't quite ready to believe that she was in earnest.

'And we'll sort the replies into three piles,' she went on. 'One pile for acceptances, and one for regrets, and one for "never in a million years."'

Ben laughed.

MICHELLE PAVER

From the moment she learned to read, Michelle Paver dreamed of becoming a writer—and at the age of five she had produced her first story. 'It was a rip-roaring adventure about an escaped Tyrannosaurus rex and a rabbit called Hamish,' she recalled with a smile when I met her recently near her home in Wimbledon. 'My mother has an old trunk in her loft full of everything I have written since childhood.' Some years later, when Michelle was at Oxford University, she skipped as many of her biochemistry lectures as she could and spent the time writing novels, which, she admits now, 'were never published and with good reason.' After she graduated, with a first-class degree in science, she decided to follow a career in law and joined a City firm. 'It was high pressure, of course—sixteen-hour days, nonexistent weekends, a health-free diet of Chardonnay, Kit-Kats and crisps.' After five years, she was made a partner but, despite earning, as she describes it, 'silly money', she was unhappy. Eventually, she decided to take a year's sabbatical, during which she wrote her first novel, *Without Charity*. When she returned to work she realised that she just did not belong there any more and handed in her notice.

The Law's loss was Publishing's gain, and Michelle Paver has gone on to write a further three novels, *Fever Hill* being the second in her *Eden* trilogy, which began with *The Shadow Catcher*. 'I have so enjoyed writing the trilogy,' she told me. 'I love myth and superstition and found plenty of it in

Jamaica.' Is the author herself superstitious? 'About my writing, very much so. I have a black plastic bat—like a Jamaican ratbat—that my sister gave me about twenty years ago. When I am writing it sits on my computer and it travels with me wherever I go. I don't know what I would do if I lost it.'

Although she gave up the pressurised world of the City, Michelle Paver is not averse to pressure. She has just signed a massive £1.5 million deal to write a six-book saga for children, *Chronicles of Ancient Darkness*. 'It's a different pressure now,' she told me. 'I am in control.' The saga is about a boy and a wolf and their adventures. 'It was an idea that I had at university and that I have now resurrected twenty years later—good job I kept everything in that trunk! I'm writing for myself when I was a ten-year-old, when I desperately wanted to have a wolf as a pet. Since we lived in Wimbledon, my parents, not unnaturally, dissuaded me.'

So does Michelle Paver have any regrets about changing careers? 'I have bad days, when I sit for hours over a blank sheet of paper and novel-writing seems about as enticing as unblocking the sink,' she admits. 'But I can honestly say that I have never, not for one moment, ever missed my old life. I now spend my entire time daydreaming, and getting paid for it. It's no wonder I love it.'

Jane Eastgate

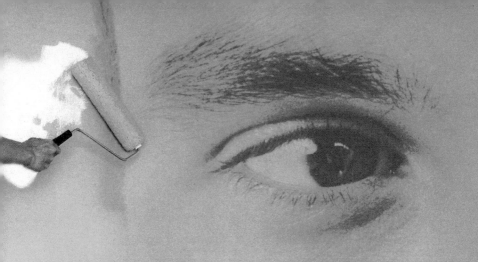

NICCI FRENCH
SECRET SMILE

Splitting up with a boyfriend is
never easy, but when you know
things are not working out it just
has to be done. And Miranda
believes a clean break is best.
Unfortunately, her ex has
other ideas . . .

1

I'VE HAD A DREAM RECENTLY, the same dream, over and over again, and each time I think it's real. I'm back at the ice rink on the afternoon I first met Brendan. The cold stings my face, I can hear the scrape of the blades on the ice and then I see him. He's glancing over me with that funny look of his, as if he's noticed me and he's got something else on his mind. I see all over again that he's good-looking in a way that not everybody would notice. His hair is glossy black like a raven's wing. His face is oval and his cheekbones and chin are prominent. He has an amused expression on his face, as if he has seen the joke before anybody else, and I like that about him. He looks at me and then gives me a second look and he's coming over to say hello. And in my dream I think: *Good. I've been given another chance. It doesn't have to happen. This time I can stop it now, here, before it's even begun.*

But I don't. I smile at what he says to me, and I say things back to him. I can't hear the words and I don't know what they are, but they must be funny because Brendan laughs and says something, and then I laugh. And so it goes, back and forth. We're like actors in a long-running show. We can say our lines without thinking, and I know what's going to happen to this boy and this girl. They have never met before, but he is a friend of a friend of hers and so they are surprised that this is the first time they have come across each other. I'm trying to stop myself, in this dream which I both know and don't know is a dream. An ice rink is a good place for a boy and girl to meet, especially when neither of them can skate. Because they have to lean against each other for support and it's almost compulsory for the boy to put his steadying arm around the girl and they help each other up and laugh at their joint predicament. When the group starts to break up, it's only natural that the boy asks the girl for her phone number.

The girl is surprised by a moment of reluctance. It's been fun, but does she need something like this at the moment? She looks at the boy. He is smiling at her expectantly. It seems easier just to give him the number and so she does, even though I am shouting for her not to. But the shouting is silent and in any case she is me and she doesn't know what is going to happen. But I do.

I'm wondering how it is that I know what is going to happen. I know they are going to meet twice—a drink, a movie—and then, on her sofa, she'll think, well, why not? And so I'm thinking, if I know what's going to happen, it must mean that I can't change it. Not a single detail. I know they'll sleep together twice more, or is it three times? Always in the girl's flat. After the second time she sees a strange toothbrush in the mug next to hers. A moment of confusion. She will have to think about that. She will barely have time. Because the next afternoon, her mind will be made up for her. It's at about that moment—the girl coming home from work, opening the door of her flat—that I wake up.

After weeks of greyness and drizzle, it was a beautiful autumn afternoon. A blue sky just beginning to lose its electric glare, a sharp wind that was shaking bright leaves from the trees. It had been a long day, and I'd spent most of it up a ladder painting a ceiling, so my neck and right arm ached and there were splashes of white emulsion over my knuckles and in my hair. I was thinking about an evening alone: a hot bath, supper in front of the TV in my dressing gown.

So I opened the door to my flat and walked in, letting my bag drop to the floor. And then I saw him. Brendan was sitting on the sofa or, rather, lying back with his feet up. There was a cup of tea on the floor beside him, and he was reading something that he closed as I came in.

'Miranda.' He swung his legs off the cushion and stood up. 'I thought you'd be back later than this.' And he took me by the shoulders and kissed me on the lips. 'Shall I pour you some tea? There's some in the pot. You look all in.'

I could hardly think which question to ask first. He hardly knew what job I did. What was he doing, thinking about when I finished work? But most of all, what was he doing in my flat? He looked as if he had moved in.

'What do you think you're doing?'

'I let myself in,' he said. 'I used the keys under the flowerpot. That's all right, isn't it? You've got paint in your hair, you know.'

I bent down and picked up the book from the sofa. A worn, hard-backed exercise book, faded red, the spine split. I stared at it. It was one of my old diaries.

'That's private,' I said. 'Private!'

'I couldn't resist,' he said with his roguish smile. He saw my expression and held up his hands. 'Point taken, I'm sorry, it was wrong. But I want to know all about you. I just wanted to see what you were like before I met you.'

'You shouldn't have.'

Another smile. 'I won't do it again then,' he said in a playfully apologetic tone. 'All right?'

I took a deep breath. No. I didn't think it was all right.

'It's from when you were seventeen,' he said. 'I like to think of you at seventeen.'

I looked at Brendan and already he seemed to be receding into the distance. He was on the platform and I was on the train which was pulling away and leaving him behind for ever. I was thinking how to say it, as cleanly and finally as possible, when almost before I knew what I was about to do, I said, 'I don't think we should go on with this.'

For a moment, his expression didn't alter. Then he stepped forwards and laid his hand on my shoulder. 'Miranda,' he said.

'I'm sorry, Brendan.' I thought of saying something else, but I stopped myself.

His hand was still on my shoulder.

'You're probably exhausted,' he said. 'Why don't you have a bath and put on some clean clothes.'

I stepped away from his hand. 'I mean it. I'm not playing games.'

'Miranda.' He had a coaxing tone to his voice, as if I were a frightened horse and he was approaching me with sugar on his outstretched palm. 'We've been too happy for you to just end it like this. All those wonderful days and nights.'

'Eight,' I said.

'What?'

'Times we met. Is it even that many?'

'Each time special.'

I didn't say, not for me, although it was the truth. I shrugged. I didn't want to make a point or discuss things. I wanted him to leave.

'I've arranged for us to meet some mates of mine for a drink this evening. I told them you were coming.'

'What?'

'In half an hour. Just for a quick drink.'

'You really want us to go out and pretend we're still together?'

'We need to give this time,' he said.

It sounded so ridiculous, so like a marriage guidance counsellor giving glib advice to a couple who had been together for years and years and had children and a mortgage that I couldn't help myself. I started to laugh, then stopped myself. He managed a smile that wasn't really a smile at all, but rather lips stretched tight over teeth, a grimace or a snarl.

'You can laugh?' he said at last. 'You can do this and still laugh?'

'Sorry,' I said. My voice was shaky. 'It's a nervous kind of laugh.'

'Is that how you behaved with your sister?'

'My sister?' The air seemed to cool around me.

'Yes. Kerry.' He said the name softly, musing over it. 'I read about it in your diary. I know. Mmm?'

I walked over to the door and yanked it open. The sky was still blue and the breeze cooled my burning face.

'Get out,' I said.

'Miranda.'

'Just go.'

So he left. I pushed the door shut gently, so he wouldn't think I was slamming it behind him, and then I suddenly felt nauseous. I didn't have the meal in front of the TV I'd been looking forward to so much. I just had a glass of water and went to bed and didn't sleep.

My relationship with Brendan had been so brief that my closest friend, Laura, had been on holiday while it was going on and missed it completely. And it was so entirely over and in the past that when she got back and rang to tell me about what a great time she and Tony had had—well, I didn't bother to tell her about Brendan. I just listened as she talked about the holiday. Then she asked me if I was seeing someone and I said no. She said that was funny because she'd heard something and I said, well, nothing much and anyway it was over. And she giggled and said she wanted to hear all about it and I said there was nothing to tell. Nothing at all.

It was two weeks after Brendan had walked out of my door. It was half past two in the afternoon, and I was up a ladder and just reaching up with the brush to get into the corner when my mobile went and I realised it was in my jacket pocket and that I didn't have my jacket on. We were working on a newly constructed house in Blackheath, all straight lines and plate glass and pine. I scrambled down and put the brush on the lid of the tin of paint.

'Hello?'

'Miranda, it's Kerry.'

That was unusual enough. We met fairly regularly, every month or so, usually at my parents. I live less than a mile from the house I grew up in and I work for my uncle Bill. Maybe once a week Kerry and I would talk on the phone; I was always the one who rang her. She asked if I was free that evening. I'd half arranged something, but she said it was really important. So of course I had to say yes. I started to discuss where we should meet, but Kerry had it all worked out. A very basic French restaurant had just opened in Camden, fairly near where I lived, and Kerry would book a table for eight o'clock. I was completely baffled. She'd never arranged anything like that before.

I arrived at La Table at about one minute past eight and Kerry was already there. She was sitting at the table with a glass of white wine and the bottle in a bucket by the side, and I knew immediately that this was good news of some kind. She looked illuminated from the inside and it showed through her eyes. She'd changed her appearance since the previous time I'd seen her. I have my hair cut quite short. I liked the look anyway, and it made particular sense when I was working so that my hair wouldn't get dipped into resin or caught round a drill. Now Kerry had had her hair cut short as well and it suited her. Almost everything about her was different. She was wearing more make-up than usual, which emphasised her large eyes. She had new clothes—dark, flared trousers, a white linen shirt and a waistcoat—and an elfin, eager look about her. She waved me over to the table and poured me a glass of wine.

'Cheers,' she said. 'You've got paint in your hair, by the way.'

I wanted to say what I always want to say to this, which is that naturally I have paint in my hair because I spend half my life painting. But I never do and I especially wasn't going to this evening when Kerry looked so happy and expectant. Expectant. It couldn't be, could it?

'Occupational hazard,' I said. I took a sip of wine. 'This place seems nice.'

'I was here last week,' she said. 'It's great.'

'So how's things?'

'You're probably wondering why I called you,' she said.

'There doesn't have to be a special reason,' I said, lying.

'I've got some news for you,' she said. 'Some pretty startling news.'

She *was* pregnant. That was it. I looked at her more closely. A bit surprising to see her drinking, though.

'I've got a new boyfriend,' she said.

'That's wonderful, Kerry. That's great news.'

I felt more puzzled than before. I felt happy for her, because I knew that she hadn't had a boyfriend for some time. It was something that worried her. My parents were always a bit concerned about it, which didn't help. But for her to announce it in this formal way was bizarre.

'It's a bit awkward,' she said. 'That's why I wanted to tell you before anybody else.'

'How could it be awkward?'

'That's right,' she said eagerly. 'That's what I've been saying. It really shouldn't be a problem at all, if we don't let it become one.'

I took another sip of wine and forced myself to be patient.

'What problem?'

'He's someone you know.'

'Really?'

'Actually, it's more than that. It's an ex-boyfriend of yours.'

I didn't respond to this because I started thinking frantically. Who could this be? Lucas and I had had a massive bust-up and he was with Cleo anyway. I'd been with Paul for a year and he'd certainly met Kerry once or twice. But wasn't he still in Edinburgh?

'It's Brendan,' she said. 'Brendan Block.'

'What? What do you mean?'

'Isn't it amazing? He's just about to arrive. He said he thought it would be good if we all got together.'

'That's not possible,' I said. 'Where did you meet?'

'I'll tell you,' she said. 'I'll tell you everything. But I wanted to tell you something quickly before Bren arrives.'

Bren?

'I just wanted to say straight away that Bren has told me all about it, and I want you to know that I hope it won't be embarrassing.'

'What?'

Kerry leaned across the table and put both her hands on mine. She looked at me with big, sympathetic eyes. 'Miranda, I know that Bren broke up with you. He's told me how upset you were, how angry and bitter. But he says he's fine about it.'

'He says he's fine about it?'

And at that moment Brendan Block came into the restaurant.

Kerry met Brendan in the middle of the room, and he bent down to kiss her lingeringly on the lips. She closed her eyes for a moment, looking tiny beside his tall, bulky figure. She stood on tiptoe and whispered something in his ear, and he nodded and looked across at me with his head slightly to one side and a very small smile on his lips. He gave a nod and walked towards me.

'Miranda,' he said. He put his hands on my shoulders and stared me in the eyes. 'Oh, Miranda.'

He bent down to kiss me on the cheek, too near my mouth. By this time Kerry had managed to wrap her arm round Brendan's waist, so she bobbed towards me too, and for one awful second we were all a few inches from each other's faces. So close I could smell his soap and her perfume and something sour in the air between us. I pulled myself free and sank gratefully back in my chair.

'So Kerry's told you?' By now he was sitting too, positioned between me and Kerry so that we were crammed round a small segment of the table, our knees touching. He put a hand over Kerry's as he spoke, and she looked up at him with her shining eyes.

'Yes. But I . . .'

'And it's really all right?'

'Why shouldn't I be?' I said and realised I'd answered a question that hadn't been asked. It made me sound tense, rattled. 'I mean, it's fine.'

'I know this must be hard for you.'

'It's not hard for me at all,' I said.

'That's very generous of you,' he said. 'I told Derek and Marcia you would be like this. I told them not to worry.'

'Mum and Dad?'

'Yes,' said Kerry. 'They met Bren a couple of days ago. They really liked him. Troy did too, and you know how hard he is to please.'

Brendan gave a modest smile. 'Sweet kid,' he said.

'And you told them . . . ?' I didn't know how to finish the sentence. I suddenly remembered a phone call the night before last, when both my parents had talked to me, one after the other, and asked me how I was feeling at the moment. A small tic started up under my left eye.

'That you would understand because you were a big-hearted woman,' said Brendan.

I felt myself getting angry now at the thought of these people talking behind my back about the way they thought I would react.

'The way that I remember it is . . .'

Brendan held up a hand—large and white, with hairy wrists. Hairy wrists, big ear lobes, thick neck. Memories bobbed to the surface and I pushed them down again. 'Let's not go any further right now. Give it time.'

'Miranda,' said Kerry pleadingly. 'Bren just told them what we thought they needed to know.' I looked across at her and saw on her face the luminous happiness that I wasn't used to. I swallowed hard and stared at the menu.

'Shall we order, then?'

'Good idea. I think I'll have the *daurade*,' said Brendan, rolling his 'r's at the back of his throat.

I didn't feel like eating anything.

'I'll just have the steak and chips,' I said. 'Without the chips.'

'Still worried about your weight?'

'What?'

'You don't need to,' Brendan said. 'You look fine. Doesn't she, Kerry?'

'Yes. Miranda always looks lovely.' For a moment she looked sour, as if she'd said 'Miranda always looks lovely' too many times. 'I think I'd like the salmon and a green salad.'

'We'll have a bottle of the Chablis, I think,' said Brendan. 'Do you want a glass of red with your steak, Mirrie?'

That was another thing. I'd always liked the name 'Miranda' because it couldn't be shortened. Until I met Brendan. 'Mirrie'. It sounded like a misprint.

'White's fine,' I said.

'Sure?'

'Yes.' I gripped the table. 'Thanks.'

Kerry got up to go to the ladies, and he watched her weave her way through the tables with that small smile on his face. He ordered our meal before turning back to me.

'Miranda.' He just smiled, then laid a hand over mine. 'You two are very different,' he said.

'I know that.'

'No, I mean, you're different in ways you couldn't possibly know.'

'What?'

'Only I can make comparisons,' he said, still smiling at me fondly.

It took me a few seconds to understand. I pulled my hand away.

'Brendan, listen . . .'

'Hello, honey,' he said over my head, then stood up to pull back Kerry's chair for her. The food arrived. My steak was fat and bloody and slid round the plate when I tried to cut it. Brendan watched me, then lifted a finger to a waitress as she passed. He said something to her in French, which I didn't understand, and she brought me a different sort of knife.

'Brendan spent time in Paris,' said Kerry.

'Oh.'

'But you probably knew that?' She glanced at me then looked away.

'No, I didn't.' I knew very little about Brendan. He'd said he was between jobs. I'd never been to his flat, never met his friends. We had been approaching the stage when you start telling each other about your lives when I'd caught him finding out about my life in his own way.

'So,' I said to Kerry. 'How did you two meet?'

'Oh,' she said, and glanced up at Brendan sideways. 'By accident, really.'

'Don't call it accident. Fate,' said Brendan.

'I was in the park after work one evening and it started to rain and this man—'

'That would be me . . .'

Kerry giggled happily. 'Yes. Bren. He said he knew my face. "Aren't you Kerry Cotton?" he said.'

'I recognised her from your photograph, of course. Then there she was in front of me in the rain.'

'He told me he knew you. Then he offered to share his umbrella—'

'Like the gentleman I am,' said Brendan. 'You know me, Mirrie.'

'We carried on walking together, even though it was belting down with rain and our shoes were squelching with water.'

'But we kept on walking through the rain,' said Brendan, and put his hand on her hair and stroked it. 'Didn't we?'

'We were soaked through, so I invited him to come and get dry at mine . . .'

'I towelled her hair for her,' said Brendan.

'That's enough,' I said, lifting up my hand, pretending to laugh. 'We'll stop with the getting dry, shall we?'

'I can't tell you how relieved I am that you know,' said Kerry. 'When I discovered about you two, well, for a bit I thought it would ruin everything. I would never do anything to hurt you. You know that, don't you?'

There was a small pain in my chest. 'You deserve to be happy,' I said, turning my back on Brendan and speaking only to her.

'I am happy,' she said. 'We've only known each other for a few days, ten to be precise, but I can't remember being so happy.'

'That's good,' I said. Ten days, I thought.

We ate our meal, drank our wine. Glasses clinked. I smiled and nodded, and said yes and no in the right places, and all the time I was trying not to remember the way his tummy bulged slightly over his boxer shorts; the black hair on his shoulders . . .

Finally I looked down at my watch and gave a fake start of surprise at the time it was, though it was only just gone nine thirty, and told them I had to get back—early start tomorrow; long drive, no time for coffee, so sorry . . . We had to go through the whole rigmarole of saying goodbye, with Kerry hugging me hard and Brendan kissing me too close to my mouth and I resisting the urge to wipe the dampness away with the back of my hand, and both of them saying how we must meet again very soon, oh yes, how lovely I'd been, how kind, how *good*.

He walked me to the door of the restaurant.

'It's been raining,' he said.

I ignored him. 'It's an incredible coincidence,' I said. 'I break off with you and a few days later you meet my sister in the park and you start going out. It's hard to believe.'

'There's no such thing as coincidence,' said Brendan. 'Maybe it's not surprising that I'd fall in love with someone who looked like you.'

I looked over Brendan's shoulder at Kerry, still sitting at the table. She caught my eye and gave me a nervous smile. When I spoke to Brendan I smiled too, so that our conversation would look friendly to Kerry.

'Brendan,' I asked, 'is this some kind of weird joke?'

He looked puzzled and a bit hurt. 'Joke?'

'If you're playing with my sister as some way of getting at me.'

'That sounds pretty self-centred,' said Brendan, 'if you don't mind my saying so.'

'Just don't hurt her,' I said. 'She deserves to be happy.'

'Trust me. I know how to make her happy.'

I couldn't bear to be with him another second. I walked home through the damp streets, breathing in deeply, letting the air cool my face.

I often think of positions in families, the difference it makes to you. Would I have been someone else if I'd been the oldest? What about Kerry, if she'd been in the middle, instead of me? Would she have been more confident and extrovert, more like me? Or, at least, more like the me the family assumed I was? And Troy, the baby of the family, who came along nine years after me? If he hadn't been all on his own, the obvious mistake, what would that have meant for him? Or if he'd had brothers who could teach him how to kick a football and play violent computer games, instead of sisters who petted and ignored him?

But we were stuck with what we'd been given. Kerry had come first and had to lead the way, although she hated being a leader. And I was second, impatient to grow up and chafing to be first, always trying to push her out of my way. And Troy was third and the only boy—thin-shouldered, wide-eyed, dreamy, strange.

I let myself into the flat. It was true that I had an early start tomorrow, but for a while I couldn't get to sleep. I lay in bed, shifting to different positions, turning the pillow to find a cooler spot. There was no photograph of Kerry in my flat, of course there wasn't. But then I hadn't believed Brendan's story anyway, so what did it matter? He had tracked down Kerry because she was my sister. Considered from a certain angle, it might seem romantic.

As I drove home from work the following day, the buildings wavered in the drizzle, the skyline was soft and blurred. If it were this time in summer, then it would be light for hours more, but now people were drawing their curtains, turning lights on. In my flat, I pulled off my overalls and stood under a tepid shower for thirty seconds before dressing in a baggy pair of jeans and a long-sleeved T-shirt. I stood in front of the mirror and pulled in my stomach. What had Brendan said about my weight? I turned sideways to the glass and gazed at myself, dissatisfied. Maybe I should start running. Every morning before going out to work, perhaps. What a horrible idea.

The phone rang as I was leaving to meet Laura.

'Miranda?'

'Hi, Mum.'

'I tried calling before, but there was never any reply.'

'My answering machine's packed up.'

'How are you? Are you all right?'

'Fine.'

'Sure?'

I wasn't going to help her.

'I'm fine, Mum. Just a bit tired. I've been busy at work.'

'I spoke to Kerry. She said you'd had a lovely dinner together.'

'It was nice to see her.' I paused and then relented. 'And Brendan.'

'Miranda, you're being very good about this. I just wish you'd told us when it all happened. I hate to think of you being miserable and not telling me.'

'There wasn't anything to tell. Everyone's got the wrong idea.'

'If it's any consolation, Kerry is transformed. You saw what she looked like yourself. She's like a different person.'

'They both seem very happy,' I said.

'So are you really all right?'

'Really. But I'm running a bit late.'

'Yes, but before you dash off, will you come over at the weekend? How about Sunday lunch? Then we can all get together.'

My stomach clenched.

'I'm not sure I'm free then.'

'We could make it Saturday lunch. Or even the evening if that suited you better. Or are you going away for the whole weekend?'

'All right. Sunday,' I said, defeated.

'It'll be very casual. You'll be fine.'

'I know I'll be fine. I'm not anxious. Not in the least.'

'Maybe you can bring someone with you.'

'There isn't anyone at the moment, Mum.'

'I suppose it's still early days.'

'I've got to go now.'

'Miranda?'

'Yes.'

'Oh, I don't know. It's just . . . well, you've always been the lucky one. Let Kerry have her turn. Don't stand in her way.'

'This is stupid.'

'Please.'

I imagined her fist clenched tightly round the receiver, her frowning, intense face.

'It'll all be fine,' I said, just to stop her. 'I promise I won't do anything to stand in Kerry's way. Now, I really do have to go. I'll see you tomorrow when I pick up Troy, though.'

'Thank you, dear Miranda,' she said emotionally. 'Thank you.'

'I never met him, did I?'

We were sitting cross-legged on the floor, backs against the sofa, eating jacket potatoes. Laura had dotted sour cream on hers, but I'd split mine open and mashed several large knobs of butter into it, then sprinkled grated cheese over the top. It was very comforting. Outside it was dark and wet.

'No, it was so brief. When you went to Barcelona it was before the beginning, and when you came back it was after the end.'

'*You* finished it with him?'

'That's right.'

'So why do you mind?'

'Because it's creepy. It feels incestuous. And the way my mum and presumably everybody else thinks I'm heartbroken. It makes me want to smash things.'

'I can see it must be irritating, but it's quite funny too.'

'No,' I said. 'Not in any way at all. She calls him "Bren".'

'Well . . .'

'And he called me "Mirrie".'

'Families,' said Laura vaguely. She wiped her chin.

'Mirrie,' I repeated. Then, 'Am I overreacting?'

'Maybe.'

I'd eaten all the potato and only the crisped skin was left. I took a large swallow of wine. I didn't want to move; it was warm in here and I was full up and pleasantly tired.

'How are things with Tony?' I asked, after a while.

'Oh. All right. I suppose.'

I looked at her. She'd pushed her glossy dark hair behind her ears, and her face looked very young.

'You suppose? What does that mean?'

'They're OK. You know. It's just sometimes I wonder what happens next.' She frowned and poured the last of the wine into our two glasses. 'I mean, we've been together for nearly three years. Do we just continue like this? I think that's what Tony would like, just to go on year after year, being comfortable together, as if we were already married—except with separate houses. Or do we start living together—properly, I mean. You have to keep moving forwards, don't you?'

'I don't know. I've never been in a relationship that long.'

'That's the thing. You have all these dramas and excitements in your life. Things beginning and things ending.'

'And things not happening at all.'

'Yes,' she said doubtfully. 'But I'm only twenty-six. Is that part of my life all over? Is this it?'

'Do you want to move in together?'

'Well, sometimes I think it'd be . . .'

But then there was the sound of a key in the lock and the door swung open.

'Hello,' Tony called cheerfully, dropping his bag on the hall floor with a thump. He came into the room, hair damp on his forehead, cheeks reddened from the air. 'Oh, hi, Miranda. How are you?'

He bent down and kissed Laura, and she put one hand up to his cheek and smiled at him. It looked all right to me.

He was out of the door before I'd even parked the van, and running down the garden path. He couldn't wave because he had a bulging plastic bag in one hand and was holding his backpack by the other, but his pale face was shining, and he was grinning.

'Hi there,' I said as Troy pulled open the door and clambered into the passenger seat, his bag getting tangled up with his angular body in the process. 'How's it going?'

'Fine. Good. Really good.' He wrapped the safety belt round himself and his baggage. 'I've been teaching myself to play the guitar, you know. Do you remember your old guitar? I found it in the junk room. Anyway, I thought I'd cook us supper tonight, all right? I brought the stuff with me. You haven't got any other plans, have you?'

'No,' I said. 'No other plans. What are we having?'

'Savoury profiteroles first of all,' he said. 'I saw them in this recipe book of Mum's and it says they're really simple. I haven't got any filling for them, but you must have something I can put in. Cheese, maybe? Or tuna fish. Even you must have a tin of tuna in a cupboard somewhere. Then kebabs. I have to marinade them first, though. I'll start when we get to your flat. I haven't thought about pudding. Do you actually want pudding?'

'No pudding,' I said. I could already picture the chaos that lay ahead.

Every Thursday I see Troy. It's been a pretty constant arrangement for the past two years, when he was fifteen and in trouble. I collect him from Mum and Dad's after work, and I bring him back later in the evening, or else put him up for the night on my sagging sofa bed. Sometimes we go to the movies or to a concert. Occasionally he meets some of my friends. Last Thursday I took him to the pub with Laura and Tony, and a couple of others. Sometimes he seems paralysingly shy, at other times he just doesn't bother.

Quite often we just go back to my flat and do stuff together. In the past few weeks he's become keen on cooking, with varying results. His enthusiasms flare up and then they die away again. In the summer he was fanatical about jigsaw puzzles then, suddenly, he became bored. 'What actually is the point of doing jigsaw puzzles?' he said to me. 'You work for hours and hours, and then when you complete one you break it up and put it back in the box.'

Where did it go wrong? That's what my mother says sometimes, especially when Troy is silent and withdrawn, skulking in his bedroom, his face a sullen mask. He was always clever, sometimes baffling, dizzyingly clever, talking at one, reading at three, put into classes with children who were one, two years older than him—and two feet taller than him as well because he never seemed to grow. He was tiny, with bony knees and sticking-out ears.

He was bullied. I don't just mean pushed around in the playground or jeered at for being a swot. He was systematically tormented by a group of boys and excluded by everyone else. He never told anyone, and by this time Kerry and I were so much older than Troy that we occupied entirely different worlds. He didn't complain to the teachers or to my parents, who just knew that he was quiet and 'different' to the other boys in his class.

Finally, when he was thirteen, my parents were summoned to the school because he'd been discovered throwing firecrackers at boys in the playground. He was wild with rage, weeping and swearing at anyone who came near him, as if the results of eight years of abuse had surfaced all at once. He was suspended for a week, during which time he broke down and 'confessed' to Mum, who stormed round to the school. Boys were hauled in front of the head, given detentions. But how can you tell children that they have to like someone, particularly when that someone is like my little brother: shy, scared, socially dysfunctional, crippled by his own particular brand of intelligence?

I had left college by this time. I didn't understand how serious it was until Troy did his GCSEs. He was expected to do well. He said the exams had gone fine, but he was vague about them. It turned out he hadn't done a single one. He'd sat in the park near his school, throwing bread to the ducks. The counsellor said it was his cry for help.

He didn't go back to school. He goes three times a week to a woman with letters after her name to talk about his problems.

'How's it all going?' I asked as I made us a pot of tea and he cut red peppers into strips. Already the kitchen was a mess. Rice bubbled ferociously in a pan. Eggshells littered the table. There was flour on the lino.

'Have you noticed,' Troy asked, 'that people always ask me how I am, in that careful, tactful kind of voice?'

'Sorry,' I said.

'I'm bored to death with talking about me. How's it going with you?'

'OK.'

'No, you're supposed to really tell me. That's the deal. I tell you, you tell me.'

'Actually, "OK" is the right word. There's nothing much to report.'

He nodded. 'Brendan's going to teach me to fish,' he said. 'He says one day we can go to the sea, where a friend of his has this boat, and fish for mackerel. He says you just haul them out of the water, one after the other, and then cook them at once over a fire.'

'Sounds good.'

'He says even if it's raining, it's nice to sit in a boat waiting for a tug on the line.'

'Have you seen him much, then?'

'A couple of times.'

'And you like him?'

'Yes. Can't imagine you with him, though.'

'Why not?'

Troy shrugged. 'He's not your style. You're more of a cat person than a dog person.'

'I don't have a clue what you're on about.'

'He's more like a dog than a cat, don't you reckon? Eager, wanting to be noticed. Cats are more independent and aloof.'

'Am I independent and aloof, then?'

'Not with me you're not. But with people who you don't know so well.' He started threading alternating chunks of lamb and pepper on to skewers. 'Brendan once had a kind of breakdown as well.'

'Did he? I didn't know that.'

'He said he never tells anyone. But he told me because he wanted me to know that pain can be like a curse and like a gift, and that it's possible to turn it into a gift.'

'He said that?'

'Yes. He's a bit of a hippy, really.'

'Has Brendan said anything to you about me?' I tried to keep my voice casual.

'He said he hurt you.'

'Ah.'

'Did he?'

'No.'

'And he said you were too proud to admit it.'

'Are you all right?' asked Mum, as she opened the door to me.

I was all right. But the way she kept asking me, that sympathetic tone in her voice, it was like glass sandpaper being rubbed on my skin.

'I'm absolutely fine,' I said. 'There's no problem about any of this.'

'You're looking lovely, Miranda,' she said.

I was looking all right, but it had been a delicate balance. There's the old cliché that when you're dumped—and of course I hadn't actually been dumped, but that was neither here nor there—you should make yourself look dazzling to show the person who has dumped you, or whom people think has dumped you, what they're missing. But because it's an old cliché, which everybody knows, then making a huge effort in those circumstances can end up looking slightly pathetic. It should have been easy, but it wasn't, and the only way I could decide what to wear was to think back to the last time I'd been out to meet someone socially (not counting Kerry and Brendan) and wear what I'd worn then. It had been a casual night out at a bar and I'd worn jeans and a white shirt and my new denim jacket with the suede collar, and that would do fine for a Sunday lunch at my parents.

'Is Troy here?' I asked.

'Yes. He seems quite well. A bit less hyper than on Thursday, but on an even keel.'

The sun was shining, as if in honour of the occasion, and although it was October everybody was out in the long, narrow back garden. Everybody except Troy, who was uncomfortable in groups. Even so, the small garden seemed crowded. Bill and Judy were there as well. My parents hadn't told me they were inviting my boss. So he knew as well.

Know: there should be a different word for knowing something that isn't actually true.

The weather was so good that Dad had lit a barbecue. I could see him at the end of the garden, standing over it, poking at the coals with—yes, there was no doubt about it—with Brendan. The two of them were talking to each other with great animation. Kerry was standing with Judy. She was wearing baggy black trousers and a tight-ribbed pink top, and she looked happy and confident.

I decided to put off any potential awkwardness for as long as possible and walked over to Bill, who seemed like the most neutral person in the garden. He gave me a friendly nod.

'Hi, Miranda,' he said. 'How are you doing?' He handed me a bottle of beer from the table next to him.

'I don't see you here very often,' I said to him.

'Marcia was most insistent.'

Sometimes it's hard to think of Bill as my uncle because he is so unlike my father. He has long hair that he sometimes wears in a ponytail, and he hardly ever shaves. What's more, rich and trendy people queue up to employ him. My father still calls him a painter and decorator, and when I was a child I remember him working with a ragtag collection of no-hopers, usually driving a dodgy van. But nowadays Uncle Bill—which I never call him—has a company, a lucrative agreement with a team of architects and a waiting list that you can hardly even get on to. I took a sip from the beer and looked up at the back of my parents' narrow terraced house, which was covered by scaffolding.

'What do you think?' I said.

'If it wasn't being redone it wouldn't be standing by next year.'

'That bad?'

'Worse. You can almost see that crack growing.'

'Miranda,' said my father, appearing suddenly from the side. 'How are you?'

I ignored the question, especially as Brendan was at his elbow.

'Hi, Dad,' I said. 'Lovely to see you.'

'I've got to admit that Brendan is a master with the barbecue,' he said. He patted me on the back awkwardly.

'It's all about piling up the coal,' Brendan said. 'You make the briquettes into a pyramid and put several fire lighters underneath and then really get it all burning.'

'Bill and I were talking about the house,' I said.

'You should pay attention to Brendan,' Dad said. 'You might learn something.'

'I don't make many barbecues in my flat,' I said.

'You might need to one day,' said Brendan.

'I've always thought it was something men liked doing,' I said.

'We never had a barbecue, did we, Mirrie?'

I was tempted to say: 'No, Brendan. We never had a barbecue because we only went out for about nine days, so we didn't have time for that or indeed almost anything at all.' I didn't. I made myself take a deep breath.

'No, we didn't,' I said.

'I'm afraid that I've been boring Brendan,' said Dad. 'He's been letting me talk shop.'

'Boxes,' said Brendan and rubbed his hands together. 'So simple, and yet imagine life without boxes.'

Bill gaped. Even my father looked startled by such enthusiasm.

'Yes, well,' he said. 'I don't know about that. I'm a practical man. I've always been interested in problem solving. Finding solutions. You can do that with the packaging business.'

'I know exactly what you mean,' said Brendan. 'On the face of it, packaging sounds obvious. But a few years ago, this man called Harry Vermont and I set up this dotcom company.'

'What company?' my father asked.

Brendan laughed ruefully. 'One of those that was going to make us all millionaires,' he said. 'But it's gone now.'

'What did it do?' asked Bill.

'The point of it,' said Brendan, 'was that people could order different sorts of consumer goods from the website and we would deliver them. We would be middlemen. I thought it was all about technology, but once it started I realised it was also about packaging and delivery. You had to get the right packaging at the right place, you had to source it and do the actual packing, and then you had to deliver it on time.'

'Who did you source it from?' asked Dad. 'Packaging in this country is quite a small world. Maybe you were dealing with someone I know.'

'We were only in the planning stage,' said Brendan. 'Then the dotcom collapse happened and we lost our funding.'

'If you're interested, Brendan, I'll show you around some time,' said my father.

'I'd love that,' said Brendan. 'Meanwhile, I reckon it's time to get the food on the barbecue.'

As it turned out, it wasn't time to put the food on the barbecue. While we had been talking, the barbecue had gone out. Brendan said that this sometimes happened when the briquettes had been left in the shed and had become damp. My father looked pleased and said that he wouldn't have been able to bear it if there was somebody in the family better than him at lighting barbecues.

I was disconcerted by that notion of Brendan being 'in the family' and I fell silent. I finished my beer and opened a second one, and then I started to feel more mellow about it all. I stood apart and looked at the family and looked at Brendan bustling around, and suddenly I was touched by the sight of Brendan going to so much effort. He helped my mother with sorting out the marinade for the chicken and salmon pieces. He went into the house and tracked Troy down. Somehow he chivvied him out and persuaded him to carry plates to the table, and the different salads that Troy and my mother had made that morning. It made me think about myself and I felt a little ashamed.

By the time I was on to my third beer, I was feeling thoroughly forgiving of almost everybody in the world, and certainly everybody in this garden, though not necessarily in the most coherent way. Brendan brought me a plate with grilled chicken and salad, and I ate it eagerly. I needed something to soak up the beer. I looked over at Kerry and she sensed my looking at her in that way people do, and she turned to me and smiled. I smiled back. We were being a happy family.

2

I REMEMBER, when I was thirteen or fourteen, going with Bill to a house in Finsbury Park as his unpaid assistant. It was small, with poky rooms and brown furniture. We stood in the living room and he gave me a sledgehammer and told me to smash it through the internal wall, into the kitchen on the other side. He had to tell me twice because it seemed impossible to me that I could do this. The wall looked so solid, the room so unchangeably square and drab, and surely you couldn't just break through structures like that, so casually? But he nodded and stood back, so I heaved the hammer, which was almost too heavy for me to lift, behind my left shoulder and swung it as hard as I could into the centre of the wall, wrenching my arm. Plaster crumbled on to the floor and a crack appeared. I swung again and a hole opened in the surface, jagged and the size of my fist. Again and the hole widened. I could see the centre of the kitchen, and beyond that a fractured piece of the small garden, with the bay tree at the end of it. And I felt all at once tremendously excited—to be opening things up like this, new vistas with each swing of the hammer, light suddenly flooding into the dreary room. I think it was what first made me think that I'd like to do what Bill did, though when years later I tried to say that to him he patted me on the shoulder and said: 'We're just painters and decorators, Miranda.'

Every so often at work I still had that feeling of euphoria—like a bubble of air in my chest, like a wind blowing through me. Knocking walls down always fills me with fresh energy. And every so often I have the same elation in my personal life too. It goes along with transition and change, spring, falling in love, travelling to a new country.

After that lunch, I came home and I made two resolutions: I was going to clean up my flat and I was going to start running. I wrote them both down on the back of an envelope and then I underlined each of them twice. I thought I'd start with the flat.

I changed into some baggy trousers and a T-shirt and put on some music. I rather like tidying my flat, which is on the first floor and very small: just my bedroom, the living room—with a table up against one wall—a galley kitchen with windows overlooking a patchwork of narrow gardens, and the bathroom. Clean surfaces, dishes all put away, a vacuumed carpet, washed floor, neat piles of paper on my desk, laundry in the basket, clothes back in the wardrobe, the gleaming bath, the smell of bleach, polish, lavatory cleaner, soap. My arms and forehead were slick with sweat by the time I'd finished, and it was late. Afternoon had become dark evening and, now that I'd stopped racing around, I could feel the air had the slicing chill of a cloudless October night.

Some of my friends don't like living alone. It's what they're doing until they no longer have to. But I do. I like the feeling I get when I close the door behind me and go upstairs and everything's quiet and waiting. I don't need anybody's permission to lie in a bath for two hours or go to bed at half past eight or listen to music late into the night, or pour myself a glass of wine and watch a trashy quiz show. When friends come round I either cook chicken breasts with garlic, rosemary and olive oil—you just have to put it in the oven and wait for half an hour—or we get a takeaway.

Maybe one of the reasons that Brendan had got on my nerves when we were going out was that he had so quickly made himself at home in my flat. As if it were his home too. But I told myself not to think of Brendan any more. Things were going to be different now.

At a shop called Run Run Run in Camden High Street, I bought a rather lovely silky blue singlet, a pair of white shorts, black suede shoes and a book called *Run for Your Life*, written by a man called Jan. Then I went to the off-licence and bought a bottle of white wine, cold from the fridge, and a packet of expensive crisps fried in an especially healthy kind of sunflower oil. I fastened the chain on the inside of my door and lay in the bath with a bowl of the crisps and a glass of the wine and read my running book. It was very comforting. The first chapter seemed to be aimed at people who were even less fit than I was. It suggested starting your running schedule with a brisk walk for ten minutes and then running very gently for a hundred yards, followed by another ten-minute walk.

I set my alarm clock half an hour earlier than usual, and the following morning I ventured out in my new singlet, shorts and shoes. I walked for five minutes. No problem. I ran hard for about a hundred yards and then the pain began, so I followed Jan's advice and stopped. I walked for a few minutes more and then started to run again. The pain began more quickly this time. My body had started to realise what was being done to it. I slowed down to a walk again and headed for home.

I ran three times that week and I didn't notice any discernible difference. My lungs still hurt as soon as I jogged more than fifty paces; my legs still felt like lead and my heart a stone jolting around inside my ribcage. But at least I persevered, and I felt good about that.

On Friday evening, I went out to a party given by my friends Jay and Pattie, I danced and drank beer and then wine, and then some strange schnapps from Iceland that Pattie found at the back of her cupboard, when most of her guests had left and we were at the lovely stage of the night when you don't need to make an effort any more. A dozen or so of us sat round in their dimly lit living room and sipped cautiously at the schnapps. There was a man I'd met, his name was Nick. He sat cross-legged on the floor in front of me, and after a bit he leaned against my knees, relaxing his weight. I could feel the sweat on his back. I waited a few minutes and then I put my hand on his hair, which was short and soft and brown, like an animal's fur. He gave a little sigh and tipped his head back so I could see his upside-down face. He was smiling faintly. I leaned forwards and kissed him quickly on his smile.

When I left, he asked me if I'd like to see him again.

'Yes,' I replied. 'OK.'

'I'll call you.'

'Do that.'

We looked at each other. Beginnings are so very lovely, like smashing that first small hole in the wall and glimpsing a world on the other side.

Nick did call two days later. We arranged to meet the next evening at a bar in Camden Town. I was five minutes early and he was a few minutes late. He was wearing faded jeans and a checked shirt that hung loosely under his leather jacket. He was unshaven and his eyes were dark brown.

'You're a decorator,' he said. 'Pattie told me. And I can see some paint in your hair.'

I rubbed my hair self-consciously. 'There's nothing I can do about it,' I said. 'However much I check, there's always a spot I've missed.'

When I meet people, they become improbably excited by the fact that I'm a woman doing the work I do. You'd think I was defusing bombs. And it's a bit like being a doctor. I get asked for my advice. People ask me about how they should do up their homes.

Then Nick asked me what I wanted to do after.

'After what?' I said, pretending not to understand.

'Well, I mean—do you want to always be a decorator?'

'Yes,' I said simply. 'This is what I want to do.'

'Sorry. That probably sounded really patronising.'

Yes, it did, so I just asked Nick what he did. He told me that he worked for an advertising company. He said that they were the ones who'd done the commercial with the fluffy talking pig. Unfortunately I hadn't seen it. I asked what he was working on now, and he replied that they'd recently won a huge account with an oil company.

But it didn't matter. What mattered were the things going on underneath the conversation, the things we weren't saying. After what seemed like a short time I looked at my watch and was surprised we'd been talking for over an hour.

'I've got to go,' I said. 'I'm having dinner with this old of friend of mine. Laura,' I added, to make it clear that I wasn't off to meet a man who might be a boyfriend.

'I'm sorry,' he said. 'I hoped that we could have dinner. Or something. What about, I don't know, Thursday?'

I had arranged to see Troy on Wednesday that week, so Thursday sounded fine. I walked out of the bar thinking, yes, I was sure, almost sure at least, that something was going to happen. I had another thought as well, almost a scary one: maybe this was the best bit. Probably for the next few days or weeks we would have the excitement of a new object in our lives, exploring it, finding out about it. And then what? Either it would fade away or just end quickly, or we would become a couple, and even then we would have to subside into some sort of normality in which we got on with our jobs and had anniversaries and had joint opinions about things. It could be good. People say so. But it could never have the sheer possibility of the beginning.

When I saw Laura, she knew straight away that something was up, which it wasn't, not really.

'You don't need to say anything,' she said. 'I can tell just by looking at you.' I tried to tell her not to be ridiculous. I thought he seemed nice, but I couldn't tell yet.

I was more convinced than I let on. Thursday was good as well. We ate at a place just round the corner from my flat and the evening went by almost without my noticing, until we were the only people left in the restaurant and the chef was out from the kitchen with a glass of wine chatting with us. Twenty minutes later we were in the doorway of my flat, kissing each other. I pulled back from him and smiled.

'I'd like to ask to you up,' I said.

'But?'

'Soon,' I said. 'Really soon. It was such a nice evening. I had a great time, I really like you. I'm just not—'

'Sure?'

'Ready . . . I'm sure, Nick.'

'Can I see you tomorrow?'

'Yes, of course . . .' Then I remembered. 'Sorry. I've got to . . . You won't believe it, but I've got to go round to my parents. Things are a bit complicated. I'll tell you about it, but not now.'

'What about the day after tomorrow?'

'That would be so lovely.'

I arrived at my parents' house feeling sulky. My mother had phoned me just before I left, asking if I could dress up. I'd pulled off my trousers and top and put on the blue velvet dress that I'd had so long its hemline had gone wavy.

'You look lovely, dear,' said my mother, as she let me in.

I growled something in response. At least she hadn't asked me how I was. My parents were also decidedly dressed up. Troy was there as well, in corduroy trousers and a faded green sweater.

'It's good to see you, Miranda,' said my father. 'We're seeing a lot of each other, aren't we?'

'So where are the lovebirds?' I asked.

'They should be here any . . .' my mother said, but before she could finish the sentence, the doorbell rang.

'Why don't you go?' she said to me, smiling.

I opened the door and there were Brendan and Kerry on the doorstep, entangled, laughing, in love. They gave me another of their group hugs as they spilled into the house. When I saw them in the light of the living room, they looked startlingly smart. Kerry was wearing a purple satin dress I'd never seen before. It clung to her hips and breasts. When she looked at Brendan, it was with a sort of dazed carnal pleasure. They looked like a couple who had been in bed together about eight seconds earlier. Brendan was wearing an expensive-looking shiny suit and a large colourful tie. He was carrying a shopping bag that clinked. He removed from it two bottles of champagne, glistening with droplets of water. He placed them on the table. There were already six tall glasses there. He picked up one of the glasses and lightly tapped it with his finger so that it rang like a little bell.

'Without further ado,' he said. 'I'm so glad you're all here. Kerry and I wanted you to be the first to know.' I felt a lurch in my stomach. 'Yesterday, I took Kerry out to dinner. And I regret to say that I caused a sensation just before the dessert. I knelt down beside her and asked if she would marry me. And I am very glad to report that she said yes.'

Kerry smiled shyly and held up her hand to reveal a ring. I looked at my mother. Tears were spilling from her eyes. She moved towards them with both arms outstretched and, after they'd hugged, I stepped forwards as well.

'Kerry,' I said, 'I'm so happy for you.'

'Hang on, hang on,' said Brendan. 'That can wait. I just wanted to say one more thing. I spent most of my life moving from foster parent to foster parent. I was a lonely little boy, and I didn't know what it was like to belong to a family, to be loved and welcomed and accepted for what you were.' As he spoke, two huge tears welled up in his eyes and rolled symmetrically down his cheeks. He didn't wipe them away. 'When I first came here,' he continued, 'when I met you, Derek and Marcia, I felt I had come home. What more can I say? Thank you. And now I've brought some champagne so that you can toast our happiness.'

It was all chaos. Brendan opened the champagne in between hugs from my mother and handshakes from my father. Troy gave a shrug and said it was really good and wished them luck. When the champagne was poured and distributed, my father gave a cough. Oh God, I thought. Another speech.

'I'm not going to say too much,' he said. 'It's all been rather quick, I must say.' He smiled at my mother, a shy smile that made him look like a boy. 'But then, if I remember rightly, some other people in this room acted rather impulsively.' My parents met at a wedding of a friend in 1974 and were married two months later. 'Sometimes we should trust our instincts. And one thing I know: I have never seen Kerry look so happy and so beautiful. Brendan, I think you're lucky to have her.'

'I know,' he said, and we all laughed.

'What I really want,' said my father, 'is to drink to the happy couple.'

'The happy couple,' we all said and clinked each other's glasses.

I looked at Kerry. She was almost crying. My mother was definitely crying. Brendan was blowing his nose on a handkerchief. Even my father looked suspiciously near to tears. I made myself a promise. I would let this work. I felt a prod at my elbow.

'A penny for your thoughts,' said Brendan.

'Congratulations,' I said. 'I'm very glad for you.'

'That's important to me.' He looked round. Mum and Dad and Kerry and Troy were in a group at the far end of the room, talking, laughing. Brendan leaned closer to me. 'When I made the announcement, I was looking at you,' he said. 'You looked shocked.'

'Surprised,' I said. 'It's been sudden.'

'I can see it's difficult for you,' he said.

'It's not difficult at all.'

'When I was talking, I was looking at your mouth,' he said.

'What?'

'You've got a beautiful mouth,' Brendan said. He moved closer still. I could smell his breath, sour against my face. 'And I was thinking that I'm marrying your sister but I've come into that mouth.'

'What?' I said, too loudly.

The others stopped talking and looked round. I felt something on my skin, hot, feverish.

'Excuse me,' I said, my mouth feeling clammy. I put my glass down and walked out of the room quickly. I heard Brendan saying something. I went into the lavatory. Just in time I pushed my head towards the bowl and vomited in spasms, again and again, until there was nothing left.

'Are you sure you're all right to do this? Miranda?'

'What? Yes, quite sure. It'll be fun.'

My mind was elsewhere entirely. In bed with Nick the night before, all night. Sleeping at last, then waking in the hours before dawn, dazed with tiredness, and feeling for each other in the darkness. I blinked and smiled at Kerry. My lips were sore, my body tingled.

'There are four of them I've arranged to see,' she was saying, 'and I've worked out how to do it most efficiently. It'll only take an hour or so.'

'I can take you out for lunch after, if you like.'

'That would be lovely. I said I'd meet Brendan. We can just call him and he'll join us wherever we decide to go. He wanted to come this morning, except he'd promised Dad to help him with moving all their furniture before the workmen arrive tomorrow morning and tear the house to bits.'

'Let's see what time we're through with this,' I said, back-pedalling. 'Maybe I'll just have to dash off anyway. I've got a loft extension waiting.'

'It's Sunday,' she protested. 'You work too hard.' Happiness had made her generous. She wanted everyone else to be happy too. 'You look tired.'

'Do I?' I reached up and touched my face gently, the way Nick had done. 'I'm fine, Kerry. Just a bit of a late night, that's all.'

We'd gone to see a film. It wasn't much good, but that didn't matter. We'd leaned into each other, Nick's hand on my thigh, my head pressed against his shoulder. Every so often we'd turned our faces to each other and kissed each other, just lightly: a promise. We'd both known it was tonight, and the film was just about waiting in the dark, emptying our minds of the other things. For me that meant trying to forget what Brendan had said to me the evening before. The way he'd leaned forwards and whispered it to me. Smiling and saying that thing. I mustn't think of it; I had to get it out of my mind, where it was buzzing like a fat, unclean fly. So I gazed at the images flickering across the screen, glanced at Nick. Every so often closed my eyes.

When we wandered into the foyer, it was dark outside. Nick lifted my hand and kissed the back of it. 'Where now?'

'My flat's nearer than yours,' I said.

We got a bus there and sat on the top, right at the front. I pressed my forehead against the window and felt the vibrations and looked at the people on the streets beneath me, walking with their heads bent against the gusts of wind. I felt nervous. Soon, I would be making love with this man who was sitting beside me now, not speaking, who I'd only met twice.

'This is our stop,' I said.

He stood up and then pulled me to my feet. His hand was warm and firm. He smiled down at me. 'All right?'

It was all right. This time it was better than all right. It was lovely. Just thinking about it now, in Kerry's car, made me feel liquid with desire. Then we'd had a bath together, legs tangled up in the small tub, my foot pressed against the inside of his thigh, grinning like idiots at each other.

'What are you grinning at?'

'Mmm? Oh, nothing.'

'Here. This is the first one.' Kerry pulled up and squinted at the sheet of paper dubiously. 'It says it's a two-bedroom maisonette, retaining many period features.'

'Does it say it's next to a pub?'

'No, it doesn't.'

'Let's go and see, anyway.'

It's dangerous buying houses. You know before you set foot inside whether you like them. It's almost like a relationship, when they say it's the first few seconds that count, that instant, pre-rational impression. You have to fall in love with the house you buy. Everything else— whether the roof's sound, the plumbing good, the rooms numerous enough—is almost irrelevant at the start. You can knock down walls and install a damp-proof course, but you can't make yourself fall in love. I was here as the expert, as the voice of caution.

Kerry knocked and the door flew open as if the woman had been standing with her eye pressed to the spy hole, looking for our approach.

'Hello, come in, mind the step, shall I show you round or do you want to do it yourself? Except there are a few details that you might miss, here, come in here first, this is the living room, sorry about the mess . . .' She was large and breathless and spoke in a headlong rush, words spilling over each other. She careered us from room to tidied room, over frantically patterned carpets. She pulled open doors with a flourish, showed us the dimmer switches in the tiny master bedroom, and the spare bedroom that looked more like a broom cupboard and had clearly been built by cowboys. I pushed the wall surreptitiously and saw it shake. Kerry looked around her with bright eyes. She was proba- bly already putting a cot in the spare bedroom.

'Does the pub bother you?' I asked the woman.

'The pub?' She acted surprised, wrinkled her brow. 'Oh, that. No. You hardly hear it. Maybe on a Saturday night . . .'

As if on cue, the first burst of music thumped through the wall, the bass notes shaking in the air. She flushed, but then carried on talking. I glanced at my watch: it was eleven thirty on a Sunday morning.

'What do you think?' asked Kerry as we left. 'If we—'

'Definitely not. Not for half the price.'

'It's falling down,' I said as we left the second house.

'But—'

'That's why it's so cheap. That's why the sale fell through. You might be able to afford to buy it, but you'd have to spend the same again.'

'It's such a nice house.'

'It's a wreck. She's got someone in to plaster and paint over the worst bits in the hall, but there's damp everywhere, probably subsidence. Do you have the capital to do it up?'

'Maybe when Bren, you know, finds a job—'

'In the meantime, he's got nowhere to sell, and it's just what you get from your flat and your income.'

'Mum and Dad have been very generous.'

'Have they?' I tried to suppress the stab of resentment I felt when I heard that. 'No more than you deserve. But don't blow it on that house.'

The third place was filthy and smelt of cigarettes and years of unopened windows. The walls were brown and stained, or had faded flowery wallpaper covering them. The living room needed to be knocked into the kitchen-dining room, to create a huge open space. The plasterboard needed to be ripped away from the fireplace.

'You could have a huge sunroof over the kitchen, and maybe open it out even further into a conservatory. It'd be fantastic.'

'Do you think so?'

'With that garden, definitely. It must be about sixty feet long.'

'It's big for London, isn't it? But it's just nettles.'

'Think what it could be like!'

'It's more spacious than I thought we could afford. And all the cornices and mouldings and proper sash windows—'

'It looks pretty solid to me, as far as I could tell. I'll help you with it.'

'Really? And you think it's the right place for us?'

'It's your choice. You've got to want it and what I think doesn't matter. But you could make it really lovely.'

Kerry squeezed my arm. 'I can't wait to tell Brendan.'

Tony and Laura and Nick and I went to the pub together. That was the stage we'd jumped to, going out as a couple, in a foursome. Everyone was very friendly to each other, wanting to get along, and then, just when things were going so well, I found myself talking about Brendan.

'I should be happy,' I said. 'I mean, Kerry's over the moon.'

'Who are we talking about?' asked Nick amiably, putting a crisp into his mouth and crunching it.

'Brendan. Kerry's boyfriend,' I said. 'Or rather, her fiancé? They've only known each other a couple of weeks and they've got engaged.'

'That's romantic.'

'It makes me and Laura seem a bit staid and dull,' said Tony cheerfully, and Laura shot him an angry look that he blithely did not notice.

'But there's something really really wrong about him,' I said. 'He gives me the creeps.'

'Didn't you go out with him, though?' asked Tony. Laura shot him another look.

'Not for long,' I said. 'It wasn't anything.' Most of me knew that I shouldn't be having this conversation, so I don't know why I then said: 'I finished it with him. It wasn't the other way round whatever he goes around saying.'

Nick looked puzzled and seemed about to speak, but Tony got there first. 'So what's the problem?'

'Well, for an example, he said this thing to me, when they announced they were going to get married.'

'What thing?'

'It was sick. He said—' I stopped dead. I could feel a flush burning its way up my body. 'He said something gross.'

'What? Go on!' Tony didn't seem to be feeling any discomfort. Laura was glaring at me, and Nick was looking down at the table, fiddling with his beer mat.

'It was stupid. I don't know why I mentioned it.'

'Come on, Miranda. Otherwise I'll just have to imagine it!'

'I don't want to say.' How prissy did that sound? 'Let's drop it.'

'Gross, as in sexually suggestive?' Tony persisted.

'He just said I had—' I hesitated, then said, 'He said I had a nice mouth.'

'Oh.' There was a pause. Nick put another crisp into his mouth. Tony stared at me. 'Well, that's not so bad, is it?'

'No,' I said weakly. 'Just leave it now. Forget it.'

A few days later, they arrived unannounced, ringing my doorbell when I'd just sunk into a bath after a sweaty day up a ladder. I cursed, pulled on an old towelling robe and opened the door. Kerry had an eager smile on her face, and Brendan was brandishing a bunch of flowers.

'Is this a bad time?'

'I was just having a bath.' I pulled my robe tighter.

'We can make ourselves at home while you finish,' said Brendan. 'Can't we, Kerry?'

I stepped back reluctantly and they followed me into the living room. Kerry sat on the sofa, but Brendan stood squarely in the middle of the room, gazing around proprietorially.

'You've changed where the furniture is.'

'A bit.'

'I liked it better the way it was before. Don't you want to put the flowers in water?'

'Yes. Thanks.' Actually, I wanted to jam them into the overflowing bin.

'Have you eaten?' he asked, as if I were the one who'd come barging in, not him.

'No. I'm not really hungry. I'll have a snack later.' I took a deep breath, then said, 'Do you want a coffee? Or something alcoholic?'

'Wine would be nice,' he said.

I took a bottle from the fridge that Nick had brought round.

'Shall I open it for you?'

'I can do it fine.' I stabbed the corkscrew into the cork.

'We should have brought a bottle round ourselves,' said Kerry, as I poured three glasses. 'Because, actually, we have a favour to ask.'

'Yes?' I asked warily.

'Well, something amazing's happened. You know that man who was coming round a second time to look at my flat on Sunday?'

'Yes.'

'He's made an offer. Only a bit less than what we were asking.'

'That's brilliant,' I said.

'He seems really keen. And he's a first-time buyer. He's not in a chain.'

'But he is in a hurry,' interjected Brendan.

'Ah,' I said. I had a horrible feeling that I knew where this was going.

'He seems to think,' said Kerry, 'that he can exchange and complete in a matter of a week or two.'

'It has been known,' I said dully.

'But Bren's already given up the place he was renting and we can't move into our new house by then,' said Kerry.

'So,' said Brendan, smiling at me. He took a slurp of his wine.

'So we're in a bit of a fix,' said Kerry. 'And we wondered if we could come and stay at yours. For a week or two at the very most.'

'Of course we'd go to Derek and Marcia's,' said Brendan, 'except their house is going to be a complete bomb site for the next few months.'

'Would it be possible, Miranda?' asked Kerry.

I wondered why Kerry wanted to stay with me in the first place. If it had been the other way round, I would have tried to keep a safe distance between Brendan and his ex-girlfriend.

'My flat's so small,' I said hopelessly. 'I haven't even got a spare bedroom.'

'You've got your sofa bed,' said Brendan.

'Haven't you got friends with a bigger place? Where you'd be more comfortable.'

'Miranda, you're my sister.' Kerry had tears in her eyes.

'Perhaps Mirrie is still finding it painful,' said Brendan softly.

'What?!'

'We shouldn't have asked you,' continued Brendan. 'It wasn't fair. Maybe you're not ready for this.'

I squeezed my wine glass so tightly I thought it would break.

'But you do kind of owe it to Kerry, don't you?' His voice was still soft and insinuating. 'After what happened. Mmm? Mmm?'

'Sorry?' said Kerry.

I stared at Brendan. There was red behind my eyes and I thought of throwing my wine into his face, of smashing my glass against his cheek, of kicking him in the legs, punching him as hard as I could in his belly.

'Miranda?' said Kerry. 'Just a few days?'

I turned to her and tried to focus on her reproachful face. I thought of lying in my bed and knowing Brendan was a few feet away, on the sofa, with my sister. Bumping into him on my way to the bathroom . . . But maybe I could stay with Nick for a night or two, or even with Laura.

'All right,' I said. 'One week.'

Kerry gripped my hand, and Brendan came towards me with outstretched arms. I ducked out of reach.

'I'm going to have that interrupted bath now,' I said. 'Finish your wine.'

The water was tepid, but I closed my eyes and sank beneath the surface, where I waited for my heart to stop battering itself against my chest. A few moments later, I heard the front door shut.

3

I LEANED OVER the dishes of curry and cleared my throat.

'There's something I want to say. It's nothing serious,' I added, seeing his suddenly wary look. 'I just felt that when we were talking with Laura and Tony, things came out wrong. I want to be completely straight with you.'

'Weren't you being straight?'

'I was, but I want to tell you about it in a clear way.'

I took a sip of wine and then gave him a basic digest of what had happened with Brendan and Kerry and my family.

'You see,' I said. 'He was someone I had no strong feelings about, except maybe that by the end I thought he was a bit of a creep. But now he's with my sister and everybody's going on about how she's happier than she's ever been, so . . .'

'So maybe you're starting to wonder if you made a mistake, breaking up with him.'

I pulled a face. 'Oh God, not for a single second. I broke up with him assuming I'd never see him again, and now he's part of the furniture.'

Nick cut a piece of tandoori chicken with his fork and ate it with deliberation. 'So why did you go out with him if he's a creep?'

'We only saw each other a few times. Then I stopped going out with him.'

'It's strange to think of you with someone like that.'

'Have you never started going out with someone and then once you've got over the attraction found that there was nothing left?'

'I'm just wondering what you'll think when you get to know *me*,' said Nick.

'I think I know,' I said. 'That's why I'm going to such trouble to explain it to you.'

'You don't need to explain anything to me. Let's go home.'

Later, we lay side by side, the room dark except for the glow of the streetlights around the curtain edges. I lay with my head on Nick's chest, stroking his stomach softly down to the edge of his soft pubic hair. His breathing was slow and regular, and I thought he might be asleep, but then he spoke.

'What did he say?'

'What?' I said.

'Brendan,' Nick said. 'I mean, what did he *really* say?'

I raised myself on an elbow and looked down at his face. 'Some things aren't good to know. Sometimes you can feel contaminated by knowing something.'

'But it's hard not to think about it. It can't be so bad.'

I felt a chilliness on my skin, like I'd once felt cold while suffering from a fever. 'He said . . .' I drew a deep breath. 'He said he was thinking how he had come in my mouth. I felt—well, I left the room and threw up. So now you know. Now you know the truth.'

'Jesus,' he said. There was a silence, and I waited. 'Did you tell anybody?'

'I'm telling you.'

'I mean, why didn't you tell someone? They'd have thrown him straight out.'

'Would they? I don't know. He might have denied it. He might have said I'd misheard. He'd have thought of something. In any case, I couldn't think clearly. I felt like I'd been punched in the face and the stomach simultaneously. So was that worse than anything you'd imagined?'

'I don't know,' he said, and then we didn't speak. I didn't fall asleep straight away, though, and I'm not sure if he did. I just lay there beside him looking at the car headlights sweeping across the ceiling.

When my mother walked into the bar, I suddenly realised that it wasn't just Kerry who had changed. She looked lovely and somehow younger. Her hair was brushed up onto the top of her head and she was wearing a belted mac that swished as she walked, dangling earrings, dark red lipstick. She smiled, raised a gloved hand as she crossed the room. When she bent to kiss me, I smelt perfume, face powder.

'I've got a bottle of white for us,' I said.

I filled her glass and she clinked it against mine, inevitably toasting Kerry and Brendan. I tried not to mind; tried to banish inside me the five-year-old Miranda who wanted to be toasted and made a fuss of.

'Kerry's told me about your help with the flat-hunting and letting them stay and everything,' she said. 'I know she's not good at expressing her gratitude, but it means so much to her. And to me as well.'

'It was really nothing,' I said.

'I feel so happy about Kerry that I can hardly bear it. I wake at night and just pray and pray that it will be all right.'

'Why shouldn't it?' I asked.

'It seems too good to be true,' my mother said. 'As if someone's waved a wand over her life.'

'It's not a fairy tale. He's not a knight in shining armour,' I said.

'I know, I know. But I have always thought with Kerry that all she needed was self-confidence and then she could do whatever she wanted. That's what Brendan's given her. I never thought that way about you. Whatever the ups and downs, I knew you'd be all right.'

'Oh,' I said dully. Somehow that didn't make me feel cheerful.

'It's just Troy now,' said my mother. 'But I can't help feeling it's going to be OK now. Like we're getting into a virtuous circle.' She tipped the last of her wine down her throat and I poured her another glass. She waited until I was done, then took a breath and said, 'Talking of Kerry and Troy, it seemed like a good moment to talk about things that your father and I have never discussed properly with you.'

'What things?' I asked as I was suddenly filled with an ominous feeling.

'We all know that Troy is always going to need financial help. You know that we have been paying money into a trust fund for him.'

'He may get a job,' I said dubiously.

'I hope so, Miranda, I hope so. But that's not our immediate problem. Now Kerry and Brendan will be getting married in two months' time, and it's going to be a very modest ceremony. But the two of them will be as poor as church mice for a while. Derek has talked with Brendan and he's very impressed with him. He has a large number of plans. But they will need help with buying their flat, so we are going to help them.'

'I'm glad,' I said. 'But why are you telling me?'

'You're doing so well,' said my mother, squeezing my hand. 'I've been talking with Bill. He thinks the sky's the limit for you.'

'So what are you saying?' I knew what she was saying.

'All I'm saying is that we're allocating special resources to Troy and Kerry, and I hope that you agree with us about the need for that.'

What she meant of course was that she was taking money from the slice of the family pie that was allocated to me and giving it to Troy and Kerry. What could I say? No, don't help my brother and sister?

I wanted to cry. It wasn't the money, or I don't think it was. It was the emotions behind the money. We never grow up enough not to need our parents looking after us, taking care of us. I smiled broadly. 'Sure,' I said.

'I knew you would understand,' my mother said fervently.

'I guess I'll need to find a rich husband,' I said, still smiling.

'You'll find whatever you want,' said my mother.

They arrived before I was expecting them, so I was still in my dressing gown, drinking coffee. I'd been running. I'd puffed my way through five miles on the Heath on a glorious late October morning, sharply cold, but bright too, with soggy leaves underfoot. I had planned to paint my toenails and ring up Nick to arrange to meet him for lunch. That way, I could welcome them and then have an excuse to rush off.

But then the bell rang, in three assertive bursts. Before I could answer it, I heard the scrape of a key in the lock. I'd given Kerry a spare key already, but I felt a twinge of resentment. I felt they ought to have let me admit them like guests. I stood up, tightened the belt on my dressing gown and opened the door, pulling Brendan in with it, holding on to the key that was still in the lock. He was wearing a thick coat that belonged to my father, and a long, speckled scarf that looked like one I'd given Troy last Christmas. His eyes were bright, his dark hair glossy. His mouth looked redder than usual.

'Hi,' I said curtly, standing back to let him in, but he simply took a step towards me, as if he were a partner in some dance, and stood looking down at me. I felt his breath on my cheek.

'Hey there, Mirri,' he said. He lifted a thumb and before I could stop him, his red lips were on my cheek. I smelt mint, and underneath it something sour. I turned away and wiped the spot where his lips had been, then retreated further into the hall. Brendan followed. Behind him, stood Kerry, in a bright red duffle coat. Her cheeks were flushed, her fair hair was tied in a little girl's pigtails.

'Don't close the door,' she said. 'We've got loads more to get out of the car. And Mum and Dad and Troy are bringing the rest over.'

'Don't worry,' said Brendan. 'Just essentials.'

'I'll put some clothes on and then I'll help you with them.'

'Why don't you make us some coffee instead?' said Brendan. 'And we haven't had breakfast yet, have we, Kerry? We were in such a rush.'

'*You* were in such a rush. I don't know where you get your energy from.'

He smirked, then said, 'Just some toast and jam would be fine.'

I sat on my bed and breathed deeply. Then I dressed and made my bed. The phone rang, but someone picked it up in the other room.

The front door was still open when I came out of my bedroom, and now my parents and Troy were there as well. There was a small television on one of the chairs. On the kitchen table were a computer with its printer, a portable CD player and a pile of CDs beside it, a bedside lamp with its cord trailing onto the floor. Three large and bulging hold-alls stood by the door. For me, the detail that I found almost horribly intimate was the heap of shoes, his and hers, mixed together. Tennis rackets stood against the wall. An exercise bike blocked the entrance to the bathroom. There was a clutter on the kitchen surfaces: two electric toothbrushes, antidandruff shampoo, a make-up bag, another toaster, an electric iron, a framed photograph of Brendan and Kerry sitting on a wooden bench with their arms round each other, piles of holiday brochures. How had they managed to accumulate so much so quickly?

I stood for a moment on the threshold of the room and looked at them all. Brendan was grinding coffee beans in the kitchen, Kerry was making toast and jam for everyone, and a comforting burnt smell filled the air. Mum was dressed more casually than I was used to, in an old pair of corduroys and a plaid shirt. She was carrying a bright bunch of dahlias. Brendan came up to her and put his arm round her and she laughed and leaned against him and held the flowers under his nose. I looked at my father, but he didn't seem to mind. He was beaming.

Troy was sitting on the floor in the sitting room on a folded-up duvet, with his back against the sofa. He was fiddling with a puzzle I'd given him last Thursday, a set of polystyrene shapes which, so it said on the box, fitted together in a cube. I looked at his face as he concentrated. He looked thin and pale and tired. He slotted in the final shape—yes, it really did make a cube—and gave a smile of satisfaction before taking it apart again. Tenderness rose in my throat and I suddenly wanted to burst into tears.

'Hello, everyone,' I said. I kissed my parents on the cheek and ruffled Troy's hair.

'Coffee's up,' said Brendan cheerily.

'Where do you want to put everything?' I asked Kerry. 'There's nowhere really to hang your clothes.'

'Dad's giving us one of those rails,' she said. 'Just for the smarter stuff and my work clothes. We can stand it behind the sofa. The rest we can just keep in the bags.'

I couldn't manage anything more than a weak, acquiescent shrug. I watched Mum stuffing the dahlias into a tumbler and tried to swallow back a spasm of self-pity. She hadn't given me flowers when she last came round.

'Here we are,' said Brendan. 'Milk, no sugar, right?' He gave a sort of wink, as if he had answered a quiz question correctly.

I sat down next to Troy and watched Kerry put cereal boxes into cupboards. Brendan lifted a heap of books off a wide shelf and inserted the tiny television. 'We can watch it in bed,' he said. 'Is your sofa bed comfy, Mirri? I've never slept in it.'

'How are you?' I asked Troy. I could see how he was: subdued, all the energy gone, so his face looked blanched and his body limp.

A burst of music filled the room.

'Mozart,' said Brendan, stepping back from the CD player. 'We love Mozart, don't we, Kerry?'

'All right,' Troy said. 'Fine.' He picked up the polystyrene pieces again and started fiddling.

'Here we are, mate,' Brendan squatted down beside him. 'You need blood sugar.' He put his hand under Troy's chin and lifted up his face. 'You're tired, aren't you. Couldn't sleep?'

'Not much,' said Troy.

'That's no good. Have some toast and jam. Later we can all go for a brisk walk. That'll help with insomnia. Mmm?'

'I don't know,' said Troy. He looked away from Brendan and bit into the toast. 'I don't know if I feel like a walk.'

'I ought to warn you,' I said. 'I've got to go out quite soon. Sorry. It was an arrangement I made before I knew when you were coming.'

'What a pity,' my mother said. 'You can't cancel?'

'Who are you meeting?' asked Brendan.

'No one you know.'

'Miranda,' said my mother. 'I know you don't mean to, but that sounded a bit rude.'

It took an effort not to say something back to my mother that really was rude.

'He's called Nick,' I said.

'Nick?' Brendan raised his eyebrows.

'Yes.'

'How very strange. I just spoke to him on the phone. When you were getting dressed. Sorry . . . I should have said at once. He rang and I said you'd ring him back—but he didn't seem to know about your prior arrangement. Mmm? On the spur of the moment, I invited him over to supper here. With all of us. I knew you wouldn't mind. We thought we could make a party of it, like a mini house-warming. He said he'd love to come.'

'You seem to have got it all sorted,' I said.

'You don't need to do a thing,' said Brendan. 'We're going to spoil you. Our treat, Mirrie.'

I went out anyway. I couldn't stay in the flat. My flat, though it didn't feel like mine any more, with Brendan's shaving cream in the bathroom, Kerry's television on my bookshelf, their night things slung over the back of the sofa.

I strode over the Heath, feet scuffling up leaves, breath curling in the clear air. A beautiful day and I'd met someone I liked and I should be happy and all I could feel was this sensation eating into my stomach lining like acid. I couldn't stop myself thinking of Brendan sitting on my lavatory, lying in my bath, eating food a few feet away from me, nuzzling up to Kerry, to my mother . . . His hand on my shoulder, his breath on my cheek. I walked even faster, trying to burn off the anger and disgust.

My mobile rang in my pocket.

'Hello.'

'Miranda, it's me.'

'Nick. I was going to call you.'

'I'm looking forward to this evening, though it's a bit daunting meeting your whole family at once. Brendan sounded very friendly.'

'Oh, did he?'

'No, really. I think he was making a big effort with me.'

'It might be better to meet my family another time . . .'

'What are you worried about?'

'Nothing.'

'It's Brendan, isn't it? You don't want me to meet him.'

'I was just thinking about you.'

'I said I'd come and I'm coming.' There was a pause, and he added stiffly. 'If that's all right with you, that is.'

'Why wouldn't it be?'

'Good. Seven o'clock, then?'

'All right.'

Kerry and Brendan had stayed behind to tidy up the flat, while Troy and I were shopping for the supper. But when we returned in the late afternoon, the light fading and the rind of a moon already on the horizon, the mess had hardly been touched. For a blessed moment I thought they'd gone out, but then I heard the rumbling of pipes and voices coming from behind the closed bathroom door. They were having a bath together. A very long bath, which continued as I helped Troy crush the garlic, chop the vegetables. We worked in comfortable silence. Every so often the pipes would rumble again as more water was used, or there would be a squeal of pleasure. I glanced across at Troy. It sounded to me as if sex were going on, sporadically and splashily, in there. I put on some music, quite loud, and returned to the sink. My shoulders ached and I felt sweaty. I wanted to have a bath too before Nick arrived, wash my hair and put on some make-up. I looked at my watch and considered banging on the door, but restrained myself.

When they finally emerged, wrapped in towels, they were pink and damp. Fragrant steam billowed out behind them.

'I'm just going to take a quick bath myself,' I said, laying down the sharp knife.

There was no hot water. I washed my face in the basin and cleaned my teeth, but, just as I was about to go into my bedroom to find something to wear, the doorbell rang. Brendan flung the door open on Nick and my parents, smiling awkwardly at each other on the threshold.

'Nick,' said Brendan holding out his hand. 'Come in.'

'Hi,' I said to him. I thought about going over and giving him a kiss, but instead hovered by the cooker. 'You've probably worked it out already, but the chef here is my brother, Troy.' Troy turned from the hob and lifted a wooden spoon in the air. 'And my parents, Marcia and Derek. My sister, Kerry.' Who, I now saw, was looking gorgeous, in a red velvet dress with a choker that made her neck long and slender. 'And Brendan.'

Everyone said hello and shook hands, I pulled the duvet and the coats off the sofa, but nobody sat down. I cleared my throat.

'Good day?' I said brightly to Nick across the room.

'Fine,' he said.

'It was lovely weather, wasn't it?'

We stared at each other, appalled.

'Drinks,' cried Brendan. He took the two bottles of wine I'd bought out of the fridge and opened them both, with a flourish. 'Get those crisps, Kerry. It's always nerve-racking, meeting the parents, isn't it?' he said. 'When I first met Marcia and Derek I was petrified.' He gave a happy shout of laughter.

'Were you?' asked my father. 'We certainly didn't notice that.' He turned to Nick. 'Miranda tells me you're in advertising.'

'Yes,' said Nick. 'And you're in packaging.'

'Yes.'

'I once thought about advertising as a career,' said Brendan into the pause. 'But then I worried about having to advertise things I didn't agree with. Like one of those multinational petrol companies.' Nick gave me a sharp glance, obviously suspecting I'd told Brendan about his commission.. 'Here's your wine.'

'It's a bit like being a lawyer,' said Nick. 'You can't just pick the things that you agree with.'

'You mean that even bad companies deserve good advertising,' said Brendan, taking a large gulp of wine. 'That's an interesting thought.'

Sitting round the small table, everyone pressed against their neighbour, forks scraping against unmatching plates, the third bottle of wine opened and poured. Nick ate slowly and was quiet, but Brendan wolfed down his helping and asked for more.

'You'll have to teach me how to cook it,' he said to Troy. He turned companionably to Nick, 'Has Mirrie ever cooked for you?'

'Once.'

Brendan grinned. 'Let me guess. Chicken breasts with garlic and olive oil?'

'In fact, I mentioned it to Kerry,' I said.

'Right,' said Nick. He smiled at me affectionately.

'And when she put it down in front of you, she went like this.' Brendan's voice climbed higher. He raised his eyebrows. '*Da-daaa!* Make the most of this, mister.' Even I could hear that it sounded a bit like me.

He laughed. I looked across the table at Nick. He was smiling, a bit. And Kerry. Everybody. I stared down at my plate.

'You OK?' It was Kerry, next to me, laying her cool hand over my sweaty one. Her smell of soap and perfume in my nostrils.

'Fine.' I took my hand away.

'Mirrie?'

Suddenly they were all looking at me.

'I'm fine,' I repeated.

'We're family,' said Brendan gently. 'Family. It's all right.'

I turned on him. '*I finished it with you,*' I heard myself say. '*I was the one who finished it.*'

The room was silent, except for the sound of Nick's fork, scraping on the plate.

'What was that about?'

We were walking along the street towards the underground, having made a hurried exit.

'I don't know. I just felt oh, I don't know. Stifled.'

'Nobody was being nasty to you. You just flared up.'

'You don't understand, Nick. It's all the things that lie between the lines. Things that aren't spoken, but I know are there.'

'That sounds a bit paranoid to me. Brendan was trying to be kind.'

'Right. That's what he wanted you to think. He wants to get you on his side.'

'Christ, Miranda, you should listen to yourself.'

'Oh, forget it,' I rubbed my eyes. 'I made a fool of myself, I know that. I don't want to have a post-mortem over it.'

'Very well.' His voice was cool.

We reached the underground station. A warm and dirty wind blew up from below. I took Nick's hand. 'I'm sorry,' I said. 'Can we let it go now?'

'I can,' he said. 'Can you?'

'Go on, Miranda,' said Kerry. 'It'd be so easy for me to set up; you could be on a plane tomorrow evening! Go on.' She paused, then added almost bossily: 'I think you need a break.'

'I'm fine,' I said snappishly.

'I'm only trying to help you,' she said. 'We're all a bit concerned.' I clenched my fists and told myself to stay calm.

I opened my mouth to say no, but then I thought, why not? Why not escape for a few days? Long nights, deep baths, pavement cafés, room service, new sights, new faces, sun on the nape of my neck, oysters, carafes of wine . . . And when I returned from work, no Brendan. Calling me 'Mirrie'. Whispering things into my ear. It had only been one night and one day and already I felt as if I could barely breathe. Just now I had sent him to the shops to buy some toilet rolls, and for the few minutes he was gone I felt as if a boulder had been lifted off my chest.

'All right,' I said. 'Just two or three days. After all, I might as well make use of having a travel agent for a sister.'

'Good. It's just what you need. Where do you fancy going? It can't be too far if it's only for a short time.' She stood up and collected her briefcase from behind the sofa. 'Look, I brought these back on the off-chance. We do these mini-breaks and there are always spaces at this time of year. I could get you one for a quarter of the price.' She spilt several brochures onto the table. 'What about Prague? Or Madrid?'

'Italy,' I said, picking up a brochure and opening it. I looked at the glossy pictures. Pink and grey churches, canals with gondolas, hotel rooms with large beds.

'Hang on,' I said. I picked up the phone and dialled.

'Nick, it's Miranda . . . yes . . . yes, I feel much better, thanks. I don't know what came over me, tired I guess . . . Listen . . .'

It rained. It was raining when we arrived at the airport and queued for the water bus that would take us to the city. The sky was steel grey. Rain poured down our necks. Nick's hair was plastered to his skull. It rained all the way on the boat, and our first view of the city was a blur . . . a ghost city rising from the water. It was a five-minute walk from our stop to the hotel, and we lugged our bags, full of light clothes and no water-proofs, along a narrow canal where all the boats were tethered to the side, covered in tarpaulins.

It rained every day. We ran to churches and art galleries, and in between we sheltered in little cafés drinking double espressos or hot chocolate. I'd dreamed of long, slow walks through the labyrinth of canals, leaning together on bridges to watch the boats go by, sex under thin sheets with the shutters closed against the sunlight. We spent too much money on lunches, which were meant to have been picnics of bread and cheese, or slices of pizza, because it was better to sit inside for a couple of hours with the tourists' three-course menu and a jug of house wine. Nick bought me a leather wallet and I took photographs of him standing damply on the Rialto Bridge. At night we ate in tiny restaurants and went to bed with the sound of rain clattering against the small windows of our room.

Every so often, the rain momentarily stopped and the sun half appeared through a gauze of clouds. The puddles glistened and the swollen canals rippled in the light. It was the most silent, beautiful city I had ever been in, and I found myself wishing that I was here alone, not having to make an effort. I would have walked and walked along the deserted paths. I wouldn't have minded the rain.

They were still there when I got back on Sunday afternoon. Indeed, they seemed more firmly installed than ever, their belongings spreading along shelves, their laundry in the washing machine, toothbrushes in my London Underground mug. In two thick piles on the table were wedding invitations: Saturday December 13, at 4 p.m. They were making lists of who to invite, of decisions to make, tasks to be done. There was an air of bustle and excitement about them.

I unpacked, made myself scrambled eggs and a cup of tea and took them into my room, shutting the door behind me. I sat in bed, hearing the television next door, the phone ringing and being answered, laughter, the springs on the sofa bed creaking. I poked at my scrambled eggs until they were cold and unappetising, and stared at my bookshelves and the piles of paper on my desk. Was I imagining things, or did it all look a bit different, as if someone had been tampering with things? I turned off my light and lay in the dark. Brendan laughed very loudly, as if he wanted me to hear him.

The next morning they left early to go to the house they were buying. They said they wanted to measure up for curtains and bookshelves, before Kerry went to her office at ten. I decided to arrive at work later than usual, so that I could spend some time alone in my flat.

Later on, I went over and over it in my mind, everything I did in that lovely, quiet, empty hour before leaving. I tidied the kitchen and living room, pushing the duvet and sheets into the tall corner cupboard, folding up the sofa bed, washing plates and glasses. I opened the windows wide to air the room and vacuumed the carpet. Then I had a long bath and washed my hair. I pulled the plug and cleaned the bath out before sitting down to breakfast in my dressing gown. Afterwards, I got dressed, cleaned my teeth, picked up my overalls and left, locking the door behind me. I know I did all of that. I clearly remember.

I was still working on the big house in Blackheath. Bill dropped in at lunchtime and took me out for a salad. I finished at half past five, cleaned my brushes and drove home. I wasn't seeing Nick that evening, and Kerry had said something about going to a movie, so I thought maybe I would be able to spend time on my own, which I was craving. I could get a takeaway and listen to music, perhaps. Read a book. Mooch.

It was nearly six thirty when I pulled up outside my flat. There were no lights on, and the curtains were still open. My heart lifted. I ran up the stairs and even as I pushed the door open I heard it. The sound of dripping, tinkling. A tap running.

There was water everywhere. The kitchen floor was an inch deep in it and the carpet was sodden when I stepped on it. There was water pouring from beneath the bathroom door. I opened the door and stepped into the flood. There was a steady waterfall cascading over the rim of the tub. The hot tap was half-on. I waded across the room and turned off the tap, then plunged my arm, still in its jacket sleeve, into the water to find the plug. I felt ill and sick and consumed with anguish, and then I thought about the flat below and I felt worse. I found a dustpan and started sloshing water off the floor, into the emptying bath.

It took forty-five minutes to get the worst of the water off the bathroom floor. I laid newspapers everywhere to soak up the rest and started on the kitchen. Then the bell rang.

He was yelling before I'd even got the door open. He sploshed across the carpet, still shouting at me. His face was quite purple.

'I'm so sorry,' I kept saying. I couldn't even remember his name. 'So sorry. I don't know how . . .'

'You'll sort this out, do you hear? Every last thing.'

'Of course. If you give me the details of your in—'

At that moment Brendan and Kerry appeared, arms wrapped round each other, faces glowing from the night air.

'What on earth?' began Kerry.

'You may well ask.' I whirled on Brendan, 'Look what you've done. You stay here, you clean out my fridge, you drink my coffee and my wine, you take up every inch of space so I can't move without bumping into you. You have bloody baths in the middle of the day and then . . .' I was spluttering with rage. 'Then you go and leave the plug in and the water running. Look! Look!'

'And that's nothing compared to downstairs,' said my neighbour grimly.

'Miranda,' said Kerry. 'I'm sure . . .'

'Whoa!' said Brendan, holding up his hands. 'Calm down, Mirrie.'

'Miranda,' I said. 'Miranda. There's no such name as "Mirrie".'

'Don't get all hysterical.'

'I'm not hysterical. I'm angry.'

'I haven't been here today.'

'You must have been.'

'No. Now sit down, why don't you, and I'll make us all some tea. Or maybe a drink would be better.' He turned to my neighbour. 'What about you, Mr, er . . . ?'

'Lockley. Ken.'

'Ken. Whisky? I think we've got whisky.'

'All right, then,' he said grudgingly.

Brendan pulled the whisky bottle out of the cupboard.

'You must have been here,' I said to his back. 'You must.'

'I went to look at the house with Kerry, then I went shopping. Then I met Kerry for lunch.' Kerry nodded. She still looked shaken by my outburst. 'Then I went to Derek and Marcia's to see Troy.' He put his hand on my shoulder. 'Did you have a bath before you left, maybe?'

'There's no way I left the plug in and the tap running.'

'It's so easy to do. We've all done something like that at one time or another.' He turned to Ken. 'Haven't we, eh? I'm sure Miranda will make sure everything's dealt with. And she's in the building and decorating trade, so maybe she can help you with the painting and stuff. Mmm?'

'But I . . .' I stopped. A tremendous weariness came over me. 'I remember cleaning out the bath.'

'Don't worry,' he said gently. 'We'll help you sort this mess out.'

'I don't understand.' I felt tears sliding down my cheeks.

'There, there,' Brendan cooed in my ear. 'There, there, Mirrie. I'm here.'

I closed the bedroom door and picked up the phone. 'Laura!' I said. I kept my voice low, so they couldn't hear me. 'Listen, Laura, this thing's happened. I need to speak to someone about it . . .'

'Are you telling me,' said Laura when I'd finished, 'that Brendan crept back into your flat and *on purpose* flooded your flat?'

'Yes.'

'Why on earth?'

'Because he's weird; he's got this thing about me.'

'Oh, come on. I've let the bath run over loads of time,' she said. 'It's really easy to just forget about it.'

'But I don't do things like that.'

'There's a first time for everything. It's a more likely explanation than yours, isn't it?'

'I remember cleaning out the bath. Vividly.'

'There you are, then. You put the plug back in, hosed down the tub, then left the water running a bit.'

I gave up trying to persuade her. It was starting to seem possible even to me, and I'd been there and knew it hadn't happened. And anyway, it was just too tiring.

4

KERRY HAD MADE macaroni cheese with peas and bits of mince added. It was stodgy and too salty. Brendan opened a bottle of red wine with a flourish and poured too much into my glass. He lifted his glass. 'To the cook,' he said.

'To the cook,' I said, and took a very small sip.

'And to you,' said Kerry, looking at me. 'Our host.'

They both smiled at me and clinked their glasses on mine.

'It's a pleasure,' I said because they seemed to expect me to say something.

'That's good, in the circumstances,' said Brendan.

'What do you mean?'

'There's something we've got to ask you,' said Kerry. 'Our house has fallen through.'

Suddenly my face felt like a mask made out of hardened clay. 'What happened? You were about to exchange, for God's sake.'

'They were pissing us around,' said Brendan.

'In what way?'

'You don't want to hear the details,' he said. 'The main point is that we walked away.'

'*You* walked away,' said Kerry with sudden sharpness.

'Whatever.' He waved his hand in the air. 'I'm afraid that we'll have to trespass on your hospitality for a little more.'

'Why did you walk away?' I persisted.

'Lots of things,' said Brendan.

'Miranda? Is that all right?' said Kerry. 'We feel terrible. We're desperately looking for somewhere else to move to.'

'Don't worry about it,' I said drearily.

I didn't say much for the rest of the meal. The food had started to taste like wallpaper paste and it took all my concentration to eat it without vomiting. Kerry had bought a frozen lemon-meringue pie for pudding, and I ate half of a small slice and then said I had a headache and I had to go to bed.

When I got to my room I threw the window open and took several deep breaths as if the air in my room were contaminated. I had the most terrible night. I was awake for what seemed like hours making feverish, deranged plans for the future. At around three in the morning, I seriously considered emigrating and New Zealand seemed especially tempting. This dissolved into a dream in which I had so much to pack that I was never able to escape from my room. Then I was staring into the darkness and wondering if something had woken me up and then I cried out. Befuddled as I was I could make out the shape of Brendan looking down at me. I fumbled for the light and switched it on.

'Ssshh,' he said.

'Don't "sshh" me,' I hissed, shocked and angry. 'What are you doing?'

'I, er . . . I was looking for something to read.'

'Get the hell out—'

He actually put his hand over my mouth. Then he leaned down and spoke to me in a whisper. 'Please don't shout. You might wake Kerry. It might look strange.'

I pushed his hand away. 'That's not my problem.'

He smiled and looked round the room as if it were all a bit of a game.

'I think it is, really,' he said. 'You know, Miranda, I was once looking at you. It was the second time we slept together. I took my clothes off more quickly than you did and got into the bed. *This* bed. I lay where you're lying now and watched you. When you unclipped your bra, you turned away from me, and when you turned round you had a funny little smile on your face. It was beautiful and I wondered if anybody but me had ever noticed it before. You see, I remember things like that.'

If I had been in love with Brendan, this would have been tender and beautiful. But I wasn't in love with him and I felt physically repulsed. I felt as if he were a parasite that had crawled into my flesh and I couldn't rid myself of him.

'This is quite wrong,' I said. 'You've got to leave.'

'None of this matters,' he said. 'Didn't you hear what I said? There's this secret smile you have. I've seen it. I know you in a way that nobody else does. We share that. Good night, Miranda.'

The next morning I woke with a headache and a stabbing sensation behind my eyes. I had a shower, dressed and drank a black coffee. Nobody else was up. Before I left for work, I returned to my bedroom. I looked at the bookshelves, trying to determine by sheer force of concentration whether anything had been moved. I reached for an old novel I had been given as a girl. It's my special emergency hiding place. Tucked inside the book was some money. I counted it out. Seventy-five pounds. I replaced it. I tried to think of something to do. I remembered something I had seen in a film once. I tore a small strip of paper an inch long and maybe a quarter of an inch wide. When I closed the door I wedged the piece of paper in the crack, exactly at the height of the lower hinge.

It kept coming into my mind all day and I tried and failed to push it away. What good would it do me, whatever I found out? If I found the paper still in place, would that reassure me? If I found it lying on the floor, what would that prove?

When I got back to my empty flat and ran to my room, I found something I hadn't even considered. The slip of paper was held fast in the door, but now it was fully a foot higher than where I had left it that morning.

'Nick,' I began.

'Mmm?'

We were walking across the Heath, our feet kicking up crackly amber leaves. The trees were almost bare now, the sun pale and low in the sky. It wasn't yet four o'clock, but the clocks had just been turned back and it was dark early now. My cold hand was in his warm one, my breath steamed in the air. We'd met in a bistro near his flat for lunch—a bowl of pumpkin soup with crusty bread, a glass of wine each and later on that evening we were going to a party thrown by a friend of his. Then I was going to stay the night at his place, though he didn't know it yet. I had my toothbrush and a spare pair of knickers stuffed into my bag.

'I was wondering . . .'

'Yes?'

I slowed down. 'Well. You know Kerry and Brendan need to stay with me a bit longer?'

'You want to come back to my flat rather than the other way round? Is that it?'

'There's that, yes, but . . .'

'I was going to say the very same thing. We need a bit of privacy, don't we?' His hand tightened on mine.

'What if I came and stayed with you? Just until they move out.'

I looked up at him just in time to see the smallest frown, a momentary tightening of his mouth.

'Forget it, it was a bad idea,' I said, at the same time as he said, 'If you're really desperate . . .'

'I shouldn't have asked.'

'Of course you should ask,' he said, too heartily. 'You know how small my flat is, and it's a bit early days, isn't it, but—'

'No. Forget I ever asked.'

He wouldn't forget. And I knew then what I'd known anyway, since Venice at least, that it wasn't going to last. It wasn't going to be a big affair after all, but a nice interim fling. We'd fallen for each other, with that lovely rush of happiness that almost feels like coming down with flu. For a week or so, we'd maybe thought that the other might be the one for us. But no: it would be over. Not today, not this week, but soon enough, because the tide that had rushed in on us was ebbing again.

Tears stung my eyes and I started walking more briskly again, tugging Nick after me. I knew it wasn't really him I was going to miss, so much as being with someone. Rushing home from work, full of anticipation. Planning things together. Being wanted. Being beautiful. Being in love. That's what I didn't want to end. I blinked fiercely.

'Come on,' I said. 'It's getting too cold.'

'Miranda, listen, if you need to stay . . .'

'No.'

'I don't know why you've suddenly got all offended, just because I didn't immediately . . .'

'Oh, don't,' I said. 'Please, don't.'

'What?'

'You know.'

'I don't.' He pursed his lips.

I was filled with a sudden foreboding that if we went on pulling at each other's words like this then everything was going to unravel right now and I'd be alone by nightfall.

'Let's go and have a bath together,' I said. 'All right?'

'Yes.'

'Can I stay the night?'

'Of course. I want you to. And if you need . . .'

I put a hand across his mouth. 'Ssssh.'

'Laura?'

'Miranda? Hi.' There was music in the background and Tony's voice calling something. It made me feel homesick for my flat where Kerry and Brendan were now sitting, eating supper in front of a video. I'd told them I was going out to see friends, but it hadn't been true, and instead I was crouched in a chilly little café down the road, drinking my second bitter cup of coffee, wishing I'd put on warmer clothes.

'Is this a bad time?'

'Not at all. We were about to eat, but that's fine.'

'I've got a big favour to ask. Can I come and stay at yours?'

'Stay?' There was a violent crunching sound, as if she'd stuck a piece of apple in her mouth. 'Sure. Tonight you mean? Is everything all right?'

'Yes. No. I mean, everything's kind of all right. And not necessarily tonight, maybe tomorrow or the next day. Just for a few days.'

'Hang on, you're not making sense, I can hardly hear you anyway, and the pan's boiling over. Wait there.' There was a pause, then the music was turned down. 'Right.'

I took a breath. 'Kerry and Brendan's house has fallen through, as a result of which they can't move out, so I've got to.' I heard my voice rise. 'I've *got* to, Laura, or I'll do something violent.'

'I get the picture,' said Laura. 'How long for?'

'Just a few days, I hope.' I swallowed. 'Will Tony mind?'

'It's got nothing to do with him,' said Laura defiantly. 'But of course you can come. Tomorrow, you say?'

'If it's all right.'

'Really, fine. You'd do the same for me.'

'I would,' I said fervently. 'And I'll keep out of your way. And Tony's.'

'It's all a bit drastic, Miranda.'

'It's like an allergy,' I said. 'I just have to avoid him and then I'll be all right.'

'Hmmm,' said Laura.

I didn't want another cup of coffee and it was too early to go back home. I wandered up the high street until I came to the all-night bagel place. I bought one filled with salmon and creamed cheese, still warm in its paper bag, and ate it on the pavement, while people milled past me. Sunday evening and probably they were on their way home to a hot bath and something cooking in the oven, their own bed waiting.

'I thought it would be better this way,' I said to Brendan and Kerry. 'You need to have time on your own.'

Kerry sat down at the kitchen table and propped her chin in her hands and stared at me. She didn't seem so radiantly happy any more. Her face had a pinched, anxious look to it, the way it used to have in her bad old days, before Brendan came along and made her feel loved.

'We can't let you leave your own home, Miranda,' she said.

'If it's what Miranda wants,' said Brendan softly.

'Is it so terrible for you, having us here then?'

'It's not that. I just thought it was the obvious solution.'

'Have it your own way,' she said. 'You always do anyway.' Then she stood up and left the room, banging the door shut behind her. We heard the front door slam.

'What are you playing at?' said Brendan, in a horribly amiable tone of voice. He came and stood over me.

'What do you mean?'

'You don't get it, do you?' he went on. 'You can't win. Look.' He picked up a tumbler still half full of lime juice and banged it hard on the table so the liquid splattered across the table and shards of glass spun on to the floor.

'Oh shit,' I said. 'What do you think you're doing now?'

'Look,' he repeated and sat down and started squeezing the broken glass in his hand. 'I'll always win. I can stand things you can't.' He smiled at me, though his face had gone rather pale.

'You're mad!' I grabbed hold of his fist and started to pull it loose. Blood seeped out between his fingers and ran down my wrist.

'You have to ask me to stop.'

I looked at the blood gushing from his hand. I heard the front door open again, Kerry's footsteps coming towards us. She started to say she was sorry that she'd stormed out like that and then she stopped and began to scream wildly. Brendan was smiling at me still. Sweat ran down from his forehead.

'Stop,' I said. 'Stop!'

He opened up his hand and shook the glass out onto the table. Blood puddled into his outstretched palm and overflowed onto the table.

'There you are,' he said before he passed out.

At the hospital they gave Brendan twelve stitches and a tetanus jab. They wrapped his hand in a bandage and told him to take paracetamol every four hours.

'What happened?' asked Kerry for about the tenth time.

'An accident,' said Brendan. 'Stupid, eh? It really wasn't Mirrie's fault. If anyone was to blame it was me.'

'It wasn't . . .' I began. 'It didn't . . .' Then I ground to a halt, choked by all the things I couldn't say because no one would believe me.

Brendan was smiling in a drowsy and contented way. His head was on Kerry's shoulder and his bandaged hand lay in her lap. His shirt was covered in splashes of blood.

'You two girls should make up,' he said. 'It's very nice of Mirrie to give us her flat for a while, Kerry.'

Kerry stroked his hair off his forehead. 'I know,' she said softly. She looked up at me. 'OK,' she said. 'Thanks.' Then she looked back at Brendan as if he were a war hero or something.

I left Kerry with him and went home to pack.

Moving out had seemed like an essential response to an emergency, like pulling the communication cord on a train. But like so much in my life, it hadn't been properly thought out. I had exited at high speed without a plan.

On my second evening at Laura's I sat up late with her, drinking a bottle of whisky that I had brought from home with me, along with half a dozen bottles of wine, some fresh ravioli and sauce from the deli near where I was working, and a couple of bags of prepared salad. Tony was spending the evening doing something laddish, so I made a meal for just the two of us. It took me back to when we were at university, staying up all night. But we weren't at university any more and I wondered how long it would take before her patience started to wear thin. I poured some more of the whisky for both of us.

'You know,' I said, 'I associate whisky with moments like this.' I was starting to slur my words a bit, but then so was Laura. 'When I think of whisky and me and you, I think of very late nights and one of us would be crying and then the other one would start crying as well and we'd probably be smoking too. Like that time when I was on my bike and a taxi ran into me, remember?'

'Sure,' said Laura taking a sip, and flinching with the expression of pain that people display when they have taken a bigger gulp of whisky than they meant to. 'Why was it always whisky?'

'Why not?' I said, then added, 'Am I mad?'

'Is this still to do with the whisky?' said Laura.

I took another sip and shook my head.

'Look at the facts,' I said. 'I break up with Brendan. Next thing, he's engaged to my sister. Next thing, he's living in my flat. Them living in my flat is awful. Next thing, I've moved out. So after days of manoeuvring, the result is that a man who makes me want to throw up when I'm around him is living in my flat and I've become a vagrant.'

'You're living here,' said Laura. 'That's not being a vagrant.'

I put my arms round her and hugged her. 'That's so lovely,' I said, overflowing with emotion.

'I must say, I'm curious,' said Laura. 'You make this Brendan sound so appalling that I'd actually quite like to see him. It's like one of those exhibits in an old circus. Do you dare see the bearded lady?'

'You think I'm exaggerating?'

'I want to see him in action,' Laura said with a laugh. 'I want to see what it takes to make you vomit.'

The next day I was at work early, wanting to give Tony and Laura a bit of time together. I went back to the Blackheath house because the owners kept changing their minds about what they wanted. They'd decided that all the lights in the living room were wrong. The Venetian red in the bedroom was too dark. Maybe they should have gone for the pea-green colour after all . . . The man of the household, a Sam Broughton, had arranged to come back to the house at lunch to discuss the fine details, and I spent the morning painting doors and skirting boards.

Sam Broughton had just arrived from the City, insistent that he only had twenty minutes to spare, if that, and we were walking through the house, me with my notepad, when my mobile rang.

'Sorry,' I said to him. 'I'll turn it off after this. Hello?'

'Miranda? Thank God you're there.'

'I'm just in the middle of a meeting, Mum. Could you call back in a—'

'I wouldn't have called except it's an emergency.'

I turned away from Broughton's impatient face and looked out of the window at the branches of a chestnut tree outside. 'Tell me.'

'I've just had a phone call from Troy's tutor and she says that Troy's not come in.'

'That's not really an emergency, Mum.'

'He's not come in for days.' She paused. 'Most of last week.'

'That's not good.'

'It's like before. Pretending he's going there and then not turning up. I thought he was getting better.' I heard her gulp. 'I'm worried, Miranda. I called our house and he's not there, or at least there's no reply, and I don't know where he is or what he's doing and it's cold and raining outside.'

'What do you want me to do?'

'I'm stuck here at the dental surgery. I can't really get away. I tried your flat, but there was just an answering machine. So I thought you could just pop over and see if you could find him.'

'Find him?'

'It's much easier for you to get away and Bill wouldn't mind. And if something's happened . . .'

'I'll see if I can find him,' I said.

'I can't bear all of this any more,' said my mother. 'I thought it was all going to be all right.'

'It will be all right,' I said, too loudly. 'I'll go now.' I ended the call and turned to Broughton. 'I have to leave,' I said.

His glare deepened. 'Do you realise how expensive my time is?' he said.

'I'm very sorry,' I repeated. I wanted to say that my time was valuable as well, to me, at least. But I didn't.

I went to my parents' house first. The workmen weren't there, though the ground floor looked like a building site—well, it *was* a building site. I went from room to room, calling him. In his bedroom I opened the curtains and shook out the crumpled duvet. A book about the migration of birds lay open on the floor. I put it on his pillow.

I didn't really know where to look. Where would I go, if I were him, and hanging around waiting for the end of the day? I walked to the high street and peered into cafés, record shops, the local bookstore. I tried the library, but it was closed. I looked into the mini-arcade, where several boys—other truants, I assumed—were playing the fruit machines in the smoky, bleeping gloom. Troy hated places like that.

I walked to the park and wandered around in the rain. No Troy. I went to the playground in case he was taking shelter there, but it was deserted.

Really, he could be anywhere. I rang Mum at work and she'd heard nothing. I rang Dad, who was in Sheffield on business, but his voice kept breaking up until it eventually crackled into silence.

When you're looking for someone, you see them everywhere. Out of the corner of your eye, and then you turn and it's an old man. In the distance, but as they get closer it's nothing like them after all. In the end, wet and chilly, I went back to collect my van from outside my parents' house and, on the off chance that he'd returned, went in.

The hall doorway was slightly open and through it I could see Troy seated on the old sofa. His hair was plastered to his skull, and he was draped in a thick tartan blanket, under which he was naked. He looked so shrunken and desolate, sitting there, that I could hardly bear to approach him. He lifted his head and looked up and gave a half-smile at someone I couldn't see, and a figure moved across to block him from my view. I pushed the door fully open and stepped into the room.

'Troy,' I said. 'Brendan. What's going on?'

I don't know what I was thinking, but my voice was sharp. I pushed past Brendan and knelt by Troy, clutched him by his narrow shoulders.

'Sweetheart,' I said as if he were a baby still. I wanted to cry. 'What happened?'

He didn't reply, just looked at me, through me.

'I've run your bath,' said Brendan. 'Nice and warm. And I'll bring you hot chocolate while you're in it. OK, mate?'

Troy nodded.

'And I better ring your mum, all right?'

'I'll take you up to your bath,' I said.

I left Troy in his bath and went to the kitchen, where Brendan was standing amid the builder's wreckage microwaving a jug of milk for Troy's chocolate. It was a clumsy process because he could only use his unbandaged hand.

'I got Marcia's message on your answering machine. Clearly she doesn't know you've moved out,' he said. The microwave bleeped and he took the jug out, stirred the cocoa and sugar, and whisked it till it frothed. 'There.' He took a little sip and added more sugar. 'So I thought I should go and look.'

'Where was he?'

'Down by the derelict warehouses. I don't know why I went there—I just had a feeling he was there, like an instinct. I *knew*. I think some people have that gift, don't you?'

I shrugged.

'Who knows what might have happened if I hadn't been there. I think I was meant to save him. It was fate. And so I've made a decision.' He poured the drink into a mug. 'I'm going to put off looking for a job until Troy's all right. Troy will be my job.'

'Oh, no,' I said, 'I don't think that's a very good idea. Troy doesn't need you. The very opposite. What Troy needs, apart from anything else, is you out of his—'

'I'll take him his chocolate,' Brendan cut in. 'You really don't need to stay if you're busy.'

'I'll wait,' I said furiously. 'I'm not leaving him.'

'As you like,' he said.

'I thought you were getting better. I thought things were getting back to normal at last.' My mother was pacing the room in an agitated fashion. Her hair was half unloosed from its bun and hanging down in strands.

'What does "better" mean, exactly?' asked Troy. 'And what's normal? No one's normal.' He was sitting on the same sofa I'd found him on, in the same slumped position.

'Oh, for God's sake,' snapped my mother.

'Calm down, love,' said my father, who was standing with his back to the window. He'd come home early from Sheffield and was still wearing his suit.

'Calm down? Is that all you've got to say? Why don't you say you'll make us all a nice cup of tea?'

'Marcia—'

'I want someone else to take charge here, not always me.'

I glanced across at Troy. He felt my eyes on him and looked up, raised his eyebrows and gave a little smile. 'Tea would be nice, actually,' he said. 'And I'm quite hungry. I haven't had anything to eat all day.'

I stood up. 'I'll get us all something in a minute,' I said. 'Toasted cheese sandwiches?'

'Thank God Brendan was here,' said Mum fervently. I flinched. I'd been there too, hadn't I? 'If he hadn't found him . . .' She sat down on the sofa and took Troy's hand.

'I wasn't going to kill myself or anything,' said Troy.

'So what were you up to?' asked Dad. 'Skipping lessons, wandering around.'

Troy shrugged. 'I wanted to be left alone,' he said. 'I couldn't bear everyone fussing over me all the time.'

'You mean me,' said my mother. 'I'm the one who fusses. I know I fuss. I try to stop myself, but I can't help it.'

'You should trust me.'

'How can we trust you,' asked my father, 'when you skip lessons and lie to us?'

'It's my life,' said Troy mutinously. 'I'm seventeen. If I want to skip lessons, that's my choice. You treat me like a little child.'

'Oh,' said my mother. It sounded like a moan.

'I'll make us those sandwiches,' I said, backing into the windy, half-wrecked kitchen.

When I came back in, carrying a tray loaded with toasted sandwiches oozing melted cheese, and four mugs of tea, my mother had red eyes and had clearly been crying. She said, 'Troy says he'd like to stay with you for a while.'

'Oh,' I said. 'Well, I'd love that, Troy. It'd be great. The snag is, I'm not living there at the moment, Brendan and Kerry are.'

'Not for long, though,' said Troy. 'I can stay there with them for a couple of weeks or so, and then you'll be back. Right?'

'You know how much I want you to stay,' I said, 'but can't you wait just for a week or so?'

'Why?'

I stared at him helplessly. 'Are you sure you'll be all right with Kerry and Brendan?'

He shrugged. 'They'll fuss too much as well. It'll be better with you.'

'So wait.'

'I need to move now.'

'I'll be around,' I said. 'Just call me when you need me, OK?'

'OK.'

The following day I took time off work and went with Troy to the Aquarium. We spent two hours there, noses pressed against the glass. Troy loved the tropical fish, glinting like shards of coloured glass. Afterwards I drove him to my parents' house to pack his stuff. Brendan and Kerry were going to collect him in a few hours' time.

I hugged him hard. 'I'll come and see you there very soon,' I said. 'A day or two.'

In fact, hardly an hour passed without me discovering something that I'd forgotten, so after work the next day I went to my flat. Inside, I found Brendan and Troy playing cards in the main room. They looked over at me in some surprise. Brendan said something, but I couldn't hear him over the music. I marched across the room and turned it down.

'I just popped in to get some stuff.'

'That's fine,' said Brendan. 'Go ahead.'

The very idea of Brendan airily telling me to go ahead in my own flat made me want to boil a kettle of water and pour it over his head.

'How are you doing, Troy?'

'Pretty well, aren't we?' said Brendan. Troy smiled at me.

I went into my bedroom. Unsurprisingly, this was where Troy was sleeping, and in only a day my room had started to look the way that his bedroom always looked. The bed was unmade, there were clothes on the floor, books lying open, a funny sweaty smell. I threw some things into a carrier bag I'd brought with me, then I pushed the door gently to and climbed up and reached for the book where I had hidden the money. I counted it and felt my skin crawl as I did so. Sixty pounds. I counted it again. Sixty. Couldn't he just have taken it all? What was he doing with me? I put the rest of the money in my purse and went back out into the main room.

'I had some money in my bedroom,' I said.

Brendan looked round cheerfully. 'Yes?'

'Some of it's gone. I wondered if anybody had borrowed it.'

Brendan shrugged. 'Not guilty,' he said. 'Where was it?'

'What does that matter?'

'It might have got lost or fallen down the back of something.' He turned to Troy. 'It's your deal.'

I started going over it all in my head, and I tried to explain it to Nick. I told him how I'd put the slip of paper in the door and how it had been in a different place when I checked it. I took a gulp of wine. We were sitting in a wine bar on Tottenham Court Road, just round the corner from his flat. It felt like I was drinking more than Nick was. He was sitting there being all calm and sober, and I was talking and drinking. I took another gulp of wine. 'The difficult thing for me was the slip of paper being back but in an obviously different place. Do you see what I mean?'

'No,' said Nick.

'The thing is,' I said. 'Most people wouldn't notice the piece of paper at all. And maybe, like five per cent of people would spot the paper and they would make a huge effort to put it back exactly where it had been left in order to disguise that they'd opened the door. But Brendan is playing with me. He put that piece of paper there deliberately so that I knew that it had been put back. But also so that I knew that he had put it back so that I would know that he had not tried to conceal that he had been in my room.' I took another gulp of wine. 'He was sending me a message. He was saying: "You were suspecting that I was looking in your room; I want to show you that I know; I also want to show you that I don't care that you know; also, you don't know what I've actually been up to." That's another thing. I left seventy-five pounds hidden in a book. It's my secret stash. Now, any normal thief would just have taken all the money. But Brendan just took fifteen pounds. He was teasing me. He's trying to get into my head.'

'Into you head?'

'And now here I am. He's living in my flat and I'm sitting here pissed.'

There was quite a long silence now. I felt like a comedian who was doing his act and nobody was laughing. There was just silence out there in the audience.

'I can't do this,' Nick said, finally.

'What do you mean?' I said, except I knew.

'Do you know what I think?'

'No, I don't.'

'I don't think,' said Nick. 'I know. You're still in love with Brendan.'

'What?' I said. This I really hadn't expected.

'You're obsessed with him. He's all you talk about.'

'Of course I'm obsessed with him.' I said. 'He's tormenting me.'

'Exactly. It was lovely, Miranda.'

'Was,' I said dully.

Now, finally, he took a sip of wine. 'I'm sorry,' he said.

I wanted to shout at him. I wanted to hit him. And then suddenly I didn't. I fumbled in my purse and found a twenty-pound note and put it by my empty glass. I leaned over, a bit unsteadily, and kissed him.

'Bye-bye, Nick,' I said. 'It was really the wrong time.'

I walked out of the bar. Another of these sudden exits. I had meant to be staying the night with Nick. That was what I had promised Laura.

5

THE NEXT DAY, I lay for a while on Laura's sofa before making myself get up and face the morning. Outside, it was windy and still half-dark. I was cold, I was tired, my tongue felt too thick in my mouth. I hadn't run for days and my limbs felt stiff with disuse. I shut my eyes and listened to the companionable murmurs coming from Laura's bedroom and felt as if I were on a slope, and sliding down it, unable to stop myself.

I thought about the day ahead. I had to go to the bloody house in Blackheath again and paint a red wall green. In my lunch hour I had to collect Kerry from her work and look at an overpriced flat with her. And I'd come back here as late as possible, so Laura and Tony didn't start getting irritated by my presence. I sighed and with an immense effort threw off the duvet.

Later that morning, I got to Journey's End, the travel agent's where Kerry worked, a bit early and shouldered the door open, grateful to be out of the blustery weather. Kerry was at the far end of the room talking to a man in a long overcoat, and although he had his back turned to me I saw it was Brendan and stopped in my tracks, a few feet from them.

'I'm overdrawn already,' Kerry was saying, pleadingly.

'Forty quid should see me through.'

'But . . .'

'Kerry.' His voice was soft and heavy. It made me shudder just to hear it. 'Do you begrudge me? After everything I've done.'

'You know it's not that, Bren.' And she started fishing around in her purse for money. 'Here. This is all I've got. Take it.'

'How can I, now?'

'Please, Bren.' Kerry held out a handful of notes and at the same time looked up and saw I was there. Her cheeks flushed and she looked away, back at Brendan.

'I must say, you look a bit washed out today,' he said as he took the money and stuffed it into his pocket. 'Mmm?'

I saw Kerry flinch as if he'd slapped her.

Forty-five minutes later, after viewing the flat, Kerry and I were drinking coffee in a shabby little café in Finsbury Park.

'You look lovely in that coat,' I said.

'Do I?' She fiddled with the collar self-consciously. 'You don't think it makes me look pasty?'

'It's November. We're all a bit pale. You look great.' I spoke cheerily, as if she were a convalescent in a hospital ward.

'Thanks,' she said with a humility that made me want to shake her.

'Anyway, you'll soon be on your honeymoon, soaking up the sun—where is it—Fiji?'

'Yes.' She made herself smile with an effort.

'Fabulous.'

There was a pause and I picked up my empty coffee cup and pretended to drink the dregs.

'Has Brendan decided what he's going to do?'

'You mean, what kind of job?'

'Yes.'

'He says he's going to put Troy right first.' She sounded listless.

'That sounds like a really, really bad idea to me. Troy wants to be left to himself more,' I said. 'That's why he's moved out.'

'I know.' She bit her lip nervously. 'I told Brendan that.'

'Are you two all right?'

'Of course,' she said curtly. 'Why shouldn't we be?'

'Anyway, he should start thinking of you two; that's where his first priorities lie. What's he done before?'

'Well,' said Kerry. She chewed the corner of a nail. 'He studied psychology for a bit, and then he did some kind of job connected with that dotcom company which didn't work out. And he was involved in various business ventures. He takes risks with things. And he travelled, of course.'

'Of course,' I said. 'I see.'

I tried to remember things he had said. And out of memory's darkness came a name, spoken over a barbecue in my parents' garden. I held on to it: Vermont. That was it. Harry Vermont and the dotcom company. When Kerry had left, I picked up my mobile and dialled Directory Enquiries.

At half past eight the next morning I was sitting in a large, warm office with huge windows that would have overlooked the Thames if they had been on the other side of the building. Instead, the view was of a council estate with doors and windows boarded up. Harry Vermont offered me coffee, but we were both in a hurry—and anyway, when it came down to it, it didn't take very long. I told him that I knew Brendan Block.

'Oh, yeah?'

'You and Brendan set up a dotcom business, didn't you?'

'What?'

'I wanted to find out about the work you did together.'

He took a cigarette from a packet on his desk and lit it. He took a drag from it. 'The work we did together?' he said sarcastically.

'Is there a problem?' I said. 'Can you talk about it?'

'Yeah,' he said. 'I can talk about it.'

'Did you lose much money when your dotcom business collapsed?' I asked brightly, then popped a piece of crumbly Stilton into my mouth. It was Bill's birthday and we were all round at his house for lunch. Outside, it was misty and cold, but inside it was beautifully warm and a large fire burned in the hearth. Judy and Bill had produced a vast game pie, lots of red wine, and now cheese and biscuits.

'Too much,' said Brendan and laughed ruefully, a man of the world.

'What about the others?' I said. I drained my glass and plonked it back on the table. I raised my voice so that Kerry and Judy looked across at us. 'Did everyone lose money? Like that Harry person you told us about once, what was his name?'

Brendan looked momentarily confused.

'Vermont, that was it, wasn't it?' I said.

'How on earth did you remember that?' My mother laughed, pleased with me. I was taking an interest, being polite.

'Because I remember thinking Vermont like New England,' I said.

Bill refilled my glass and I took a large mouthful and swallowed.

'Poor old Harry,' said Brendan. 'He was wiped out.'

'I talked to him,' I said.

'What?'

'He said he met you, briefly, but you never actually worked together.' I took another large gulp of wine.

'You went and talked to Harry Vermont?' Brendan spoke softly. 'Why would you do something like that?' He shook his head from side to side in wonderment, taking in the whole watching room. 'Why?'

'Because you weren't telling the truth,' I said. A sick feeling rose up in me. My forehead felt clammy.

'Harry Vermont let down everyone he worked with,' said Brendan. He sat back a bit, addressing everyone now; his tone was one of sorrowful resignation. 'He wanted the glory but not the responsibility. But I forgave him. He was my friend.'

'He said—'

'Miranda,' hissed my mother, as if everyone couldn't hear every word. 'That's quite enough now.'

'I wanted to find out—'

'Enough, I say.' She slapped her hand on the table's surface so hard that cutlery rattled. 'Stop it. Let's have coffee.'

Judy glared at Bill and nodded at him. They both stood up and went out. In the kitchen, someone dropped a glass.

I thought about making a run for it, but I was wedged between the table and the wall. So instead I said, 'You were deceiving us,' I turned to the table. 'He was deceiving us,' I repeated desperately.

Brendan shook his head. 'Maybe I didn't tell you the whole ugly story because I was protecting him. But I wasn't deceiving you. No, Miranda.' He paused and smiled at me. 'You do that, though, don't you?'

Outside in the hallway, I could hear the grandfather clock ticking.

'Like the way you deceived Kerry.'

'Let's stop this,' said Troy. 'I don't like it. Please stop.'

'What?' Kerry's voice came at the same time, sharp with fear. 'What do you mean?'

'I'm sure Kerry forgave you, though. Because that's what she's like, very forgiving. Mmm?'

'What are you talking about? Tell me.' I saw Kerry's face across from me.

'You know, when Miranda went off with your boyfriend. What was he called? Mike, wasn't it?'

The silence deepened around us.

Brendan put his hand over his mouth. 'You mean you didn't know? Miranda never said? I had no idea. I just thought—if she told me so early on in our relationship, and so casually—I just assumed you all knew too and it was one of those family things . . .' His voice trailed away.

I opened my mouth to say I'd never told him, he'd read it in a diary that was private. But I didn't because who cared how he knew. It was true.

'Kerry,' I said at last. 'Let's not do this here. Can we go somewhere and talk?'

She stared at me. 'I get it,' she said. 'You're trying to do it all over again.'

I left the house, though Judy tried to hold me back at the door, and I got in my van and drove to the bottom of the road where I pulled in at a bus-stop. I felt cold to the bone, but sweaty at the same time, and my hands were trembling so badly that I could barely turn the ignition off. There was a nasty taste coating the inside of my mouth: game pie, blue cheese, red wine, dread. For a moment, I thought I would be sick. I sat for a while, just staring ahead but barely seeing.

A loud horn sounded behind me, and I glanced in the rear-view mirror to see a bus waiting. I started up the van and edged out into the road. I wanted to be alone, desperately. So I just kept on going, not turning left or right, heading east out of London, past shops selling old fridges, mobile phones, catering equipment. After I'd passed a flyover and several arterial crossroads, the surroundings grew more prosperous again. Lights were beginning to go on. Streetlights glowed in the greying dusk. At last there were fields, large trees with scarcely any leaves left on them, a river running by.

I took a random left up a small road, then left again up a smaller lane, and stopped the van in the entrance to a field where cows were standing in the far corner. When I opened the door I could feel the cold biting through my jacket. I wasn't dressed for outside, wasn't wearing the right shoes, but it didn't matter. I started to walk along the lane and welcomed the sting of the wind, the way my hair whipped against my face. I started to think and to let myself remember.

When Kerry was nineteen, she was pretty but she didn't think she was, so of course people rarely noticed her. At least, boys didn't. Michael wasn't her first boyfriend, but he was the first she really let herself fall in love with, and maybe he was the first she had sex with. It was in the summer holidays, just before she went to university, and in the meantime she was working in the local café. He was about three years older than her, studying civil engineering at Hull, but home for the holidays, and he saw her a few times and then one day he leaned over the counter and asked her if she'd like to go out for a drink.

She was very taken up with him. She seemed proud of herself as well because he was older than her, and he made her feel more worldly and glamorous than she'd felt before. She visibly bloomed, in much the same way, I thought, pounding along the lane with the darkness falling, that she had bloomed with Brendan.

And then . . . I had spent too many years trying not to think about this, and I had to wrench my mind round to contemplating the forbidden memory. I don't think I flirted with him exactly, but I remember a look he gave me one day—a suddenly appraising look, right over the head of Kerry. I was five maybe six years his junior, and I was a virgin. I remember even now how I was filled with a rush of triumph and violent self-loathing all at once. But I glowed with secret, guilty pleasure.

We had sex, one afternoon after school, on my bed, while Kerry went round the corner to buy cigarettes for him. It took about two painful, horrible minutes, and even before we'd begun I realised I was making the biggest mistake of my life. I kept out of his way after that. I waited for the flooding shame to subside. A week or so later, when he'd gone back to Hull, Kerry started university and Mike stopped calling her. I tried to find ways of justifying my actions so they weren't so bad, but never succeeded. I'd never told anyone about it. Except for my diary. I had written it down almost as a way of getting it out of my head.

What I wanted to know now was this: had I done it because he was going out with my elder sister? I came to a stile going over a fence and sat down on it, feeling the dampness of wood through my trousers. I closed my eyes and put my thumbs against my ears to seal me into my own interior world. Because if I had done that, what did that make me? And what strange, ugly replica of that event was being played out now?

More to the immediate point, what was I going to do now? I opened my eyes and stood up. I saw it was cloudy dark, with no moon. Here I was, on some remote lane in the middle of fields and woods, and I had no idea of what to do next. A part of me just wanted to run away so I didn't have to deal with any of this. But, in the end, I returned to the van and got in it, then turned on the ignition and drove back the way I'd come.

I bought milk and cocoa powder and digestive biscuits at the corner shop a few minutes from Laura's flat. When I let myself in, I could hear the sound of taps running in her bathroom, so I made myself a mug of hot chocolate, with lots of sugar in it, and sat on the sofa with my legs curled up under me and drank it very slowly, trying to make it last.

I plucked up courage and rang my own flat, and Brendan answered. My heart plummeted, but I said hello.

'Are you all right, Miranda?' he said.

'What do you mean?'

'It must have been painful for you.'

'Whose fault is that?' I said and then cursed myself immediately. I was like a boxer who had deliberately let his guard down. The punch in the face duly arrived.

'Miranda, Miranda, Miranda,' he said in a horrible soothing tone. 'I wasn't the one who betrayed Kerry.'

'You learned that by reading my diary,' I said. 'And then you lied. You said I told you about it.'

'Does it really matter how I learned about it? But maybe it's all for the best, Miranda. Secrets are bad for families. It's cleansing to get them out into the open.'

For a moment I wondered if I was going insane. It wasn't just what Brendan was saying that made me want to gag. I felt as if his voice was physically contaminating me, even over the phone, as if it were something alive and slimy, oozing its way into my ear.

'I was ringing to say I'm coming round tomorrow to pick up some of my stuff.' I paused. 'If that's all right.'

'Do you know what time?'

I was going to ask why it mattered, but I just couldn't be bothered. 'I'll come over on my way back from work.'

'Which will be when?' he said.

'I guess about six thirty,' I said. 'Does it really matter?'

'We always like to have a welcome ready for you, Miranda,' he said.

'Is Kerry there?'

'No.'

'Can you ask her to call me?'

'Of course,' he said affably.

I fastened the laces of my trainers and drank a glass of water before opening the front door. It was half past six in the morning, still dark outside and much colder than the previous day. There was a glint of frost on the pavement, and car windows were iced up. For a brief moment, I allowed myself to think that this was masochistic, but I set aside that thought, pulled the door shut behind me and set out on a run that would take me up the small roads to the park.

It had been a long time. At first I felt chilly and a little stiff, but gradually I settled into a rhythm, and as I jogged—past the newsagent that was just opening up its metal shutters, past the deserted primary school, the recycling centre—I watched the dawn turn to day. Lights came on in houses; streetlights turned off, the sky that had been dark grey became gradually lighter and streaked with pink clouds. All of a sudden I felt a small stab of happiness, to be running along the empty London streets as the sun rose on a glorious late autumn day.

I stopped at the bottom of the road on my way back to pick up a pack of streaky bacon and some white bread. In the flat, no one was stirring yet, so I had a quick shower and pulled on trousers and a jersey that was old and warm and raspberry pink. I put on the kettle for coffee and started to grill the bacon. Laura's door opened and her head poked round. She looked half-asleep still, like a young girl, with mussed hair and rosy cheeks. She sniffed the air.

'Coffee and bacon sandwiches,' I said. 'Do you want it in bed?'

'It's Monday morning!'

'I thought we should start the week well.'

'How long have you been up?'

'An hour or so. I went running.'

'Why are you so cheerful all of a sudden?'

'I'm going to chuck them out,' I said.

Laura looked at me with a puzzled expression. 'What?'

'I've got too caught up in all of this,' I said. 'I haven't been thinking straight. Now I'm going to act like a normal person. I'll find somewhere for Kerry and Brendan to stay, even if I have to put them up in a hotel.'

'You can still stay with us, you know,' said Laura. 'But it's good to hear you talk like that. Why the sudden change?'

I laughed. 'I'm taking my life in hand,' I said. 'This is the new me.'

'Good,' she said, and withdrew her head. A moment later she had joined me in the kitchen, wrapped in a thick dressing gown.

She sat at the kitchen table and watched as I put the rashers between thick slices of bread, and boiled milk for the coffee. She nibbled at her sandwich cautiously. I chomped into mine.

'What are you up to today?' she asked.

I slurped at my coffee. Warmth was spreading through me.

'I'm going to ring round our customers who I know are going to be out of the country for a bit. I'll ask if they want a responsible couple to house-sit for them. There's at least one family with loads of pets that someone would have to feed twice a day anyway. Maybe they'd be glad of Kerry and Brendan staying. So . . .' I poured myself another cup of coffee and topped it up with hot milk, then took another sandwich. 'I'm going to find them somewhere else to live because they're obviously not going to do it themselves, are they? And then Troy can be with me like we'd planned. Then I'm going to my flat to collect a few things and tell them when they've got to be out by. So I'll be out of your hair soon.'

'I like you being here.'

'You've been fabulous, but I feel in the way. I want to leave before you're wishing me gone.'

'Shall I cook us supper?'

'I'll buy a takeaway,' I said. 'Curry and beer.'

Laura left for work and I cleared up breakfast, put a clothes wash on and vacuumed the living room. I promised myself that I'd buy her a big present when I left.

I went to Bill's office and started making phone calls. The family with pets had already arranged for a friend to house-sit. The young woman who lived in Shoreditch didn't really want someone she didn't know living in her flat. But the two men with a small house on London Fields were interested. They'd call me back when they'd talked it through.

It didn't take long before the phone rang. They were going to America in eight days' time for three months, maybe for longer if everything went well. They hadn't thought of getting someone in, but as it came through a personal recommendation, and as long as the new kitchen was still done while they were away, and as long as Kerry and Brendan paid some rent, kept the house clean and watered the date palm in the bathroom, then that would be fine.

'Eight days?' I said.

'Right.'

Their house was far more spacious than my flat, and overlooked a park. It had a circular bath and deep-pile carpets. There could be nothing that Brendan could find to object to, surely. In eight days I could be back in my flat. I'd paint my bedroom wall yellow and change all the furniture round. I'd clean windows and throw things out.

'That's great,' I said. 'Really, really great. You've no idea.'

I called Troy on my mobile and told him. I could hear him smile.

I arrived at my flat a bit early. There was a light on in one of the windows, though I could see no sign of Kerry's car. I inserted the key in the lock and pushed open the door. If they were in, I could tell them about the house in London Fields and try to talk to Kerry. Yesterday I had felt that she would never forgive me, but today it looked different to me. Nothing had happened, except inside me.

I went up the stairs and pushed open the living-room door. It banged against something that clattered out of the way as I pushed harder.

What did I see? What did I feel? I don't know, really. I never will know. It's jumbled up together in a foul twist of memory that I'll never lose.

Scuff-toed boots that I'd seen hundreds of times before, but a foot above the floor, and then his canvas trousers, stained at the knee, and a buckled belt round the waist. A chair on its side. Fear a thick eel in my throat. I couldn't look up. I had to look up. His face above me, tilted to one side, his mouth slightly open. I could see the tip of his tongue. His eyes were open, staring. I saw the rope that he was hanging from.

Maybe he was still alive. Oh God, maybe he was; please, please, please. I righted the chair and clambered onto it, half falling over, and there I was pressed up against his body, trying to hold him up to relieve the pressure of the noose on his neck and trying to undo the knot. Fingers trembling too much. His hair against my cheek. His cold forehead. The slump of his body. But people can be alive when they look dead, you read about it, bringing them back to life when all hope is gone. But I couldn't undo the knot and he was so heavy.

I jumped down from the chair, leaving his body swaying there, and raced to the kitchen. The bread knife was in the sink. I grabbed it and ran back to Troy. Standing on tiptoe on the chair I began sawing at the cord while still trying to hold his body. Suddenly he was free and we fell onto the floor together in a ghastly embrace.

I pushed him off me and hurled myself towards the phone. Jabbed the buttons. 'Help,' I said. 'Help. He's hung himself. Please come and help. Please. What shall I do?'

The voice at the other end of the phone was quite calm. It asked questions and I gabbled answers, and all the time Troy lay an arm's length away and I kept saying. 'But what shall I do, what shall I do?'

'The emergency services will be with you as soon as possible,' said the voice.

'Shall I give him the kiss of life? Shall I pump his chest? Tell me what to do.'

I looked at Troy while I was saying it. His skin was chalky white, except where it was blue round the lips. The noose round his neck was slack now, but there was dark bruising where it had been. My little brother.

'Hurry,' I said in a whisper. 'Hurry.'

I put the phone down and crawled across to where he lay. I put his head in my lap and stroked the hair off his forehead. I leaned down and kissed him. I picked up his hand and cradled it between both my own. In a minute I would pick up the phone and call my parents. How do you say: your son is dead. I shut my eyes for a moment, drenched with the horror of it.

His sweater was draped over the back of the sofa. The clock ticked on the wall. I looked at it: twenty-five past six. If you could turn the clock back through the minutes and the hours until it was before Troy had stood on that chair with the noose round his neck and then kicked off, into death. If I'd arrived before . . . I ran my fingers through his hair. Nothing would ever be all right again.

The doorbell rang and I laid Troy's head gently back on the carpet and went to open the door. While they were clustered round Troy, I picked up the phone.

'Mum,' I said. Then before she could ask me how I was, or tell me any of her news, I said. 'Listen . . .'

Everything was disjointed, skewed, in a strange light, a foreign language. My flat didn't feel like my own flat any more. It was like being out in the street when there has been an accident. People were bustling in and out who had nothing to do with me. There were three people in green overalls, who at first were very urgent and quick and shouting instructions, and then suddenly were slow and quiet because, after all, there was nothing to be urgent about any more because we were all too late. Someone handed me a mug of something hot and I sipped at it and burnt my lips. It felt good. I wanted it to hurt.

There was a hand on my arm, a young female face looking into mine. She was a police officer, pale-faced. Was I all right? I nodded. She wanted details. Troy's name. Age. My name. I started to get angry. How could they ask stupid questions at a time like this? Then I stopped getting angry. I realised that these were questions that needed to be asked.

There would be so much to organise, I thought. Forms to fill out, people to be informed. At that moment it hit me, like a warm, wet wave that ran through every cell. I had to open my mouth wide and gasp, as if the air in my flat was suddenly hard to breathe. My head felt light and I started to sway, and the woman's face appeared in front of me.

'Are you all right, Miranda?' she said. She took the mug out of my hand. Some of it had already splashed onto my trousers. It had stung and felt hot, but now it was cold. 'Are you all right?'

All I said was 'I'm fine' because I couldn't say what I really felt, which was that I had suddenly felt that this was the end of Troy's story. My head was buzzing with thousands of memories of Troy, but now they had all ended in the same way. All the roads from all those memories led to my flat and a rope and a beam and that thing that was Troy and also wasn't Troy any more, lying on my floor, with people he didn't know and who didn't know him clustered round him.

The policewoman appeared once more. She was clutching handfuls of tissues and I realised that I was sobbing and sobbing. I pushed my face into the tissues, wiping the tears away and blowing my nose, but I couldn't stop myself crying. We'd failed, we'd all failed. It was like for the whole of my life we had watched Troy drowning, but in the end he had just slipped below the water and it was all for nothing. Gradually my sobbing gave way to a few snuffles and then I felt squeezed out.

The police officer told me that she was called Vicky Reeder. A man in a suit was standing next to her. He was a detective inspector called Rob Pryor. He asked me some questions about how I had found Troy. Afterwards, he and a man in uniform looked up at the beam. Then the detective came back to me. He talked to me in a low respectful voice, as if he were an undertaker. He told me that they would now be taking Troy's body away. This might be upsetting for me, and he wondered if I might like to step into another room for a few minutes. I shook my head. I wanted to see everything.

One of the green-uniformed men from the ambulance unrolled a bulky plastic bag along the length of Troy's body. It was like a very long pencil case. He looked up at me self-consciously as if he were doing something indecent. It was all very crude. They lifted him, holding him by the feet and the shoulders, and moved him the few inches across to the bag. The bag took some adjusting around him, the end of the cord around his neck had to be tucked inside and then the large zip was pulled shut. Now he could be carried out to the ambulance without members of the public being alarmed.

At that moment I heard voices outside and my parents came through the door. They had walked up without ringing. They looked old. My father was in his suit. He must have driven from work and picked my mother up on the way. My mother looked down at the bag and that was one of the bad moments again. She had an expression of shock and disbelief. The detective introduced himself and then he and my father moved away and spoke in a murmur. I felt a sort of relief at that. I could be a child again. My dad would sort things out. I wouldn't have to make the calls, fill out the forms.

My mother knelt down by the side of the bundle that once had been Troy. She put her hand very gently on the place where his forehead would be, then she stood up and came over to me. She sat beside me, holding my hand but not meeting my eye. When the ambulancemen picked up the bundle, I looked over at my mother. She wasn't crying, but I could see her jaw flexing.

My father said goodbye to Detective Inspector Rob Pryor as if he had helped him change a tyre. I saw Pryor write something on a piece of paper and give it to my father, and they shook hands and then everybody left and we were alone. I still hadn't said anything to my parents.

'Troy,' I said, then stopped. There was nothing to say; everything.

Dad was businesslike, in a mad kind of way. He made tea for us all and then found some paper and a pen. He began to make a list of everything that needed doing and it appeared that there was a lot. There were people to be told, arrangements, decisions to be made. So many. A whole side of paper was covered with his precise, square handwriting.

On top of the horror, it was a strange situation. The three of us were sitting in my flat. My mother hadn't even taken her coat off. My father had made his list. There was so much to do, but there was nothing to do. Nobody wanted to eat. Nobody wanted to go anywhere. It was as if we needed to sit there together and hold the secret to us a while longer before letting it out into the world. We just talked in fragments, but if there was any awkwardness, I wasn't aware of it. I felt as if I'd jabbed my fingers into an electric socket and the current was just pulsing through me over and over again.

It was just before nine when I heard a noise downstairs and voices and laughter on the stairs, and then Brendan and Kerry burst into the room, arm in arm, laughing. They were cheerfully startled to see us.

'What's up?' asked Brendan with a smile.

6

IT WAS DAMP and weirdly warm. In less than four weeks it would be Christmas. Shop windows glittered with tinsel and baubles. There were already Christmas trees outside the greengrocers' shops, leaning against the walls with their wide branches tied up with string. Some doors in the street where I lived had holly wreaths on them. The shelves in the supermarkets were loaded with crackers, mince pies, Advent calendars, boxes of dates. The brass band played 'O, Little Town of Bethlehem' outside Woolworth's. Women in thick coats rattled collection tins in the cold.

What would we do this Christmas? Would we put up a tree in my parents' half-demolished house or in my living room, where nine days ago Troy had killed himself? Would we sit round a table eating turkey with chestnut stuffing and sprouts and roast potatoes and pull crackers? How do you ever return to normal life, when something like this has happened?

Troy's funeral wasn't crowded. He'd been a lonely boy and a solitary young man. There was Bill and Judy, and my mother's sister Kath who'd come down from Sheffield with her family, and then there were the relatives my parents saw once or twice a year. A friend of Kerry's called Carol came; and Tony and Laura.

We were there of course: Mum and Dad, me and Kerry. And Brendan. Brendan looked more stricken than anyone, with his red eyes and a faint bruise on his forehead turning yellow. Even I had to admit that he'd been wonderful over the past week: inexhaustible, indispensable, solid. 'Wonderful' in quotation marks, though. There was more to Brendan than I'd seen before. He had a radar for what everyone around him needed just at that very instant. He'd answered the phone, filled out forms, made pots of tea, gone shopping, shifted his and Kerry's stuff into my parents' house again, so I could move back in to my flat. They were moving to the house I'd found for them in just two days.

A week after the death, we talked about the wedding. Kerry wanted to postpone it, but my parents said that love was the only thing that would get us through. Brendan nodded at that and held Kerry's hand, stroking it and saying in a wise, reflective voice, 'Yes, yes, love will get us through,' his eyes shining. At any other time it would have driven me insane with irritation. I still knew it was irritating, but now there were layers of numbness between the irritation and me.

'Here you are, better than tea.'

Bill pushed a tumbler of whisky into my hand and stood beside me while I took a large, fiery mouthful. We had all come back to my parents' house and were standing in the draughty living room, drinking mugs of tea and not really knowing what to say to each other.

'Thanks.'

'Are you all right?'

'Yeah.'

'Silly question. How could you be?'

'If he'd died in an accident, or of an illness or something, that would have been one thing . . .' I said. 'He shouldn't have killed himself.'

'Well, of course not.'

'I mean, I don't understand it. Mum keeps saying she thought he was getting better. And he was getting better, Bill.' I took another gulp.

'He was a troubled young man.' Bill refilled my glass and took the whisky bottle across to Dad.

I wandered out of the crowded living room, into the building site that used to be the kitchen, then through the hole in the wall where once there was a door and into the soggy garden. It was slightly misty, every outline just a bit blurred, but maybe that was the whisky.

After my conversation with Bill, I was in a state wide open for doubts to crash in. The autopsy had been straightforward. Suicide by hanging. I thought of the last conversation I'd had with Troy on the phone that morning, when he'd sounded tired but quite cheerful. I'd told him about finding the house for Brendan and Kerry, and we'd talked about our plans. My stinging eyes filled with tears again, though I had believed I was all cried out. I heard Brendan asking me, the day before, what time I would be collecting my stuff from the flat, and me replying it would be about half past six. I let myself remember pushing the door open at the appointed time and seeing Troy's body hanging there; his chalky face and sightless, open eyes; the chair upturned by his feet.

I was hysterical, I told myself. Mad. I so badly wanted Troy not to have killed himself, so badly wanted not to have to blame my parents and myself for his death, so wanted not to have to imagine the despair that had led him to that moment, that I was inventing gothic fantasies instead.

A few drops of rain fell on me. I drained my whisky and went back through the kitchen and into the living room. Kerry was standing with her arm through my father's. Her mascara had smudged and there were red blotches on her neck. Across the room, Brendan was on his own. Our eyes met. He looked away and his face crumpled. I suddenly felt that he was staging this just for me, a private drama. Tears coursed down his face; he stuffed a fist into his mouth and doubled up as if he were muffling a great howl.

It was Laura who went up to him and put a hand on his shoulder. She just stood there like that while his bulky body shook. After a while he stood up straighter, and she took away her hand. I saw them talking.

I turned away and went upstairs to find my mother, who had disappeared from the gathering. She was sitting in Troy's old room—Kerry and Brendan's room now, I supposed, for their bags were by the door. She was sitting on his bed and staring ahead into nothing. She looked tired. Her face was full of lines and pouches that I hadn't seen before. I went and crouched beside her and put a hand on her knee.

'I thought I'd leave them to it,' she said. 'Nowhere seems the right place to be.'

'I know what you mean.'

'Miranda?'

'Yes.'

'He was getting better. He was.'

'I know.'

I crouched there for a little longer, then went back to the thinning crowd and to the whisky bottle.

Laura took me home because I'd drunk far too much whisky to drive myself. She steered me upstairs to my flat and took off my coat, then sat me on the sofa and pulled off my shoes.

'There,' she said. 'Now: tea or coffee?'

'Shame to let the drink wear off,' I said. 'Whisky?'

'I'll make coffee,' she said firmly. 'And I'll run you a bath.'

'That's nice of you.'

'It's nothing.' She filled the kettle with water and plugged it in.

'What did Brendan say, then?'

'Say?' She looked confused.

'You were talking to him. After he'd done his great weeping act.'

'That's not fair, Miranda. He's heartbroken but doesn't think he can show it in front of all of you. He has to be strong for the family.'

'That's what he said?'

'Yes.'

'Oh well, who cares?'

'He does,' she said. 'I know what you feel about him, but he cares a lot. After all, you're the only family he's got. He thought of Troy as his little brother.'

'You too,' I said, infinitely tired. 'He's got you on his side too.'

'It's not a question of sides.'

'That's what he says too, but he's lying. He's on one side and I'm on the other. You can't be on both sides at once you know. You have to choose.' There was a pause. 'You've crossed over, haven't you?' My head was aching with the whisky and the wretchedness.

'Miranda, you're my best friend. Don't say things like that.'

'Sorry,' I said. But I couldn't let it go. 'You liked him, didn't you?'

'I felt sorry for him.' She poured boiling water over the coffee grounds and stirred vigorously.

I stood up and fetched the whisky bottle from the shelf. 'Look at that,' I said. 'How've I drunk all of that since the day before yesterday?'

I was almost proud of myself. It was an achievement, of a kind. I sloshed a generous measure into a glass, closed my eyes and drank.

'You'll feel lousy tomorrow,' said Laura.

'One way or another,' I said.

'Do you want me to stay the night?'

'No. You've been lovely.'

'Are you going to work tomorrow?'

'Obviously. It's a working day.'

'I'll ring you in the evening, then.'

'What would I do without you?'

At about half past nine the next morning, I made an attempt to get up and then lay down again. No hangover had ever been quite like this one. I had the usual symptoms, in a more intense form: the parched leathery tongue; the headache which felt as if small rodents were eating my brain from the inside; the general feeling of being poisoned, a shivery creepy-crawly sensation over my skin. People didn't die of hangovers, but they did die of alcoholic poisoning. Could it be that? I remembered that I had a book about medical problems.

I staggered across the flat to get the book and then took it back to bed. There was no entry for alcoholic poisoning, but there was one for hangovers. The book recommended me to drink plenty of water, to go for a brisk run 'even if you do not feel like it'. If nauseous, and I felt very nauseous, I was to take something called magnesium trisilicate. I could barely lift my legs to get my foot into my shorts. I pulled a T-shirt over my head. It hurt my head. It hurt my arms. I tied the laces of my shoes slowly, trying to think how to do it. I clutched a five-pound note in my hand, went downstairs and shuffled out onto the pavement.

The chemist was only a couple of hundred yards away. I asked the pharmacist, a very tall Sikh, for the magnesium trisilicate. It had a sickly minty taste, but I sucked it desperately and headed for home in an approximation of a jog. I had a shower, put some grown-up clothes on and lay on my bed to think.

There was no doubt about it. I was in slightly less of a dreadful state. The day could now begin. What was the time? I reached out to the bedside table for the watch, Troy's watch, which was lying there. Quarter past ten. That was another thing. I knew why the watch was there. Even in his good times he would have big sleeps in the afternoon, like a small child or a cat. He didn't just flop in a soft chair. He pulled the curtains, took his clothes off, got into bed. It was like night-time. When he was medicated he was almost in a coma. He had been sleeping in my bed, and he had taken his clothes off and put his watch on my bedside table. His clothes were on his dead body, but not his watch. He may have forgotten. He was depressed, after all.

There was another thing. I closed my eyes and made myself do it. I pictured my dear, lost Troy hanging from that beam. The rope. It was easy to remember: shiny green, synthetic, rough. I remembered the strands as I'd cut it through with the knife to bring him down. For the first time I thought of suicide as a human activity that needed organising. You need to plan it, you need to obtain materials.

I felt clear-headed now. I got up and felt a wave of nausea and dizziness, but it passed quickly. I didn't have the time to be ill. I had things to do. My flat was so small that there wasn't much to search. I couldn't remember having seen that rope before, but I had to make sure. Under the sink there was a bucket, some washing cloths, various bottles of cleaning fluid. In the cupboard there was the vacuum cleaner, a broom and a mop, a shoebox containing screwdrivers, a hammer, nails, screws and a couple of plugs. I looked on top shelves, behind the sofa, under my bed, everywhere. There was no rope. It could be that he just found a length of rope and used all of it. Or . . .

I phoned my mother and asked if I could come round and she said, yes, that would be good. On the way, I thought of something else. A few months earlier I'd been stuck in a tube train on the Piccadilly Line for more than an hour. An announcement came over the tannoy apologising to all customers and informing us that there was a customer under a train at the next station. Of course, that is a euphemism for throwing yourself in front of the train and lots of unimaginable things happening to the person on their way to being underneath. I had a lot of time to think about it and one of the things I'd thought about was: do you owe anything to anyone when you kill yourself? If you throw yourself under a tube train, the driver is only about three inches in front of you as you go under, with whatever godawful scrapes and bumps and crunches that ensue. The tube driver takes early retirement after a suicide, mostly.

I let a thought come into my mind that I had managed to exclude until that moment. In my flat. Troy had killed himself in my flat. I wondered if even thinking this was an obscenity, but I couldn't stop myself. He had hanged himself in the space where I slept and ate and lived my life. How could he do that? I loved Troy. And, surely, even when his fog of misery was at its thickest, he loved me. Would he have done that to me? Something I could never forget? I made myself consider the possibility that Troy's suicide, and the manner of it, and the place of it, was a statement to me: There, Miranda, there. You thought you understood me. You thought you could help me. Well, here you are. Here is what I've come to. Do something to help me now.

I expected my mother to start crying when she saw me, but her mind seemed somewhere else. 'I'm glad you came, Miranda,' she said, but it sounded as if she were speaking lines someone else had written for her. 'Your father's out.'

'What about Kerry and Brendan?'

'They've gone out. Would you like some tea?'

'Love some. I'll just pop upstairs.'

That's the good thing about your parents' house. It's still sort of your home. You can go anywhere in it, open cupboards. I was going to do something terrible. My mother had gone to the kitchen and I ran up the stairs and into the bedroom where Kerry and Brendan were staying. I felt a tension like electricity in me. My ears were humming with it. I could hear my pulse, hear the blood rushing through my veins.

The arrangement in the bedroom was obviously temporary. They had barely unpacked. Kerry's dressing gown and nightie were tossed over the bed. A suitcase was half open, leaning against the wall, her clothes neatly folded. Next to the bed was a closed suitcase. I laid it flat on the floor, flicked the catches and opened it, revealing Brendan's clothes. It wouldn't take a minute. One by one I lifted shirts, trousers, underpants and turned them over so that I could replace them in the right order. The case was almost empty when I felt as much as heard steps running up the stairs. I didn't even have time to move from my knees when the door opened and Brendan appeared. At first he just looked surprised, and no wonder, with me rooting around in his case, his clothes arranged around me.

'Miranda?' he said. 'What the—?'

I tried to think of something, but my brain had turned to soup. 'I'd forgotten something,' I said randomly. 'I mean I thought you'd taken something by mistake.'

Now his face turned angry. 'What the fuck?'

And then Kerry appeared behind him. 'Brendan?' she said. 'What—?' And then she too caught sight of me.

'The rope,' I said. 'I thought you'd taken my rope by mistake.'

'What?' said Kerry wildly. 'What rope?'

She took a step forwards so that she was glaring down at me. She had her hands on her hips and her face was scarlet. It was as if all her natural reserve and timidity had been burned away by grief and rage. I got up from the floor and stood there, surrounded by Brendan's clothes.

'I don't know,' I said. 'I just thought . . .' I trailed off.

'Let me get this straight,' said Brendan. 'You're going through my things'—here he kicked at his clothes with a foot, so they spread out on the floor—'to find some rope. Yes?'

'I was confused,' I said in a mumble.

'Confused?' said Kerry. 'You come over here, you make a special journey, to poke around in Brendan's case—'

'It'd be better if I went now,' I said.

Brendan took a step forwards so that he was barring my way. 'You're not going anywhere until we've got to the bottom of this.'

'What's going on?'

My father had appeared in the doorway.

'I'll tell you what's going on.' said Kerry. 'She'—she pointed a finger at me—'she was going through Brendan's case.'

'Miranda?' said my father.

'Looking for rope,' added Brendan.

'Rope?'

'That's what she said.' Brendan squatted down and started folding up his scattered clothes and putting them neatly back in the case.

'I think I should go,' I said.

'I think you should explain yourself,' my father said in a voice tinged with disgust. He looked around for somewhere to sit down.

'I was simply trying to get things in order,' I began, then stopped.

'The rope,' prompted Brendan. 'Mmm? Secretly going through my belongings looking for some rope?'

I didn't have anything to say.

'What rope?' asked my mother, entering the room.

I sat down on the unmade bed and put my face in my hands, like a small child trying to keep the world out of my head. Kerry started telling my mother what she'd found me doing, stoking up her outrage all over again, and I stared through the crack in my fingers at a patch of carpet and the legs of the chest of drawers, trying to block out the words.

'I don't know you any more,' my mother said in a flat voice, once Kerry was done.

'Please,' I said. 'I'm upset. We're all upset.'

'What I want to know,' said Brendan, 'is what rope it was. I mean—when you say "rope", well, the word only means one thing to all of us now. Mmm? Only one thing.'

There was a horrible silence in the room, then he went on: 'Is that what you mean by the rope—you mean, the *rest* of the rope? Mmm? Why did you think it would be here? Mmm? Among my things? Is there something you want to tell us?'

'No,' I said in a whisper.

'It's obvious,' said Kerry sharply. 'She's obsessed with Brendan. She's always been obsessed with him. I tried not to see it. I tried telling myself it didn't matter. I thought she'd get over it. Even when she went on and on about their relationship and wouldn't let go of it.'

'Say "you",' I said, hysteria rising up in me. 'Don't say "she" when I'm right in front of you.'

Kerry talked over me. Everything she'd stored up was cascading out now. Her voice was high and hoarse. 'Even when she started going all peculiar and flooding the bathroom and then accusing Brendan of doing it. Or tracking down old friends, like a spy, a bloody spy. I still thought it would be all right. Stupid of me, I see that now. Stupid, stupid, stupid.'

She started sobbing till her thin shoulders shook. Brendan went across to her and wrapped his arm round her waist.

'It's not about you, Kerry,' he said softly. 'Don't you see? When you say she's obsessed, that's probably exactly the right word. I blame myself for not doing anything about it. She's like a stalker. If she weren't family, I'd be calling the police by now, asking for protection. I've read about things like this. She probably can't even help herself.'

'No,' I said. 'Don't say things like that.' I turned to my father. 'You don't think I'm obsessed, do you?'

'I don't know what I think any more,' he said. 'But I know one thing. You'll start off by apologising to Brendan for the way you've behaved. Just because there's been a tragedy in this family doesn't mean that we're going to stop behaving like decent human beings.'

'But I—'

'Whatever it is you're about to say, I don't want to hear,' he said. 'You apologise to Brendan. Do you hear me? That's the least we expect.'

I looked at his caved-in face. I looked at my mother's empty eyes. Then I stood up and faced Brendan. He stared at me, waiting. I clenched my fists and dug my nails into my palms.

'I'm sorry,' I said.

He bowed his head slightly, in recognition. 'Mirrie, I'm sorry too. I'm sorry for you. I pity you.'

I turned away.

'Can I go now?' I asked.

We all trooped downstairs together in silence. Kerry was still sobbing. At the front door, I stopped.

'I left my bag upstairs,' I said. 'I'll get it and then be out of your way.'

I took the stairs two at a time, in spite of the pain banging round inside my skull, and pushed open the door to Brendan and Kerry's room. I knelt down in front of the chest of drawers and pushed my hand under it, into the narrow space I'd been staring at from my position on the bed. And I pulled out the coil of green rope.

Detective Inspector Rob Pryor was nice, like a normal person that you might meet in the real world. He had curly blond hair and a relaxed, almost lazy manner. He brought me coffee from a machine just outside his office. He introduced me to colleagues. Vicky Reeder, the WPC who had looked after me, came over and said hello. Then Rob—he asked me to call him Rob, and I asked him to call me Miranda—took me into his office and shut the door.

I said I was devastated, that we all were, and he nodded and said he understood. 'It's difficult to deal with,' he said.

'It's funny,' I said. 'I thought you'd be puzzled to see me and that you'd just tell me to go away. But you're acting as if you were expecting me.'

He gave a sympathetic smile. 'I wasn't. Not exactly, but it's not a complete surprise. When tragedies like this happen, people go over and over them in their head. They ask themselves if they could have done that or this to stop it. They become obsessed. They need someone to talk about it with. Sometimes they come in here and go over it with us without being exactly sure what they want. It feels so like a crime against them, they can't quite believe it isn't.'

'So you think I'm using you as some kind of therapy?'

He took a sip of coffee. 'You were the one who found your brother. That's a big thing to deal with.'

'That's not it,' I said. 'I've got things to tell you.'

He leaned back in his chair and looked at me warily. 'What things?'

I told him my suspicions. I'd even brought the rope with me. I took it from my bag and placed it on his desk. When I'd finished, he gave a little shrug. 'As I said, these things take time to get over. Troy was suffering from intense depression.'

'He was in a good phase. He wasn't in the mood to kill himself.'

'Depression can be difficult to assess from the outside. Sometimes suicide can be the first visible symptom.'

'This isn't just a feeling. There were all the other details I mentioned to you. There was the watch.'

He looked at me with a questioning expression. 'You're not serious about this, are you? So he forgot to put his watch on after his afternoon sleep. You forget things when you're depressed.'

'There's the rope.'

'What do you mean, the rope?'

'I didn't have any rope. This was bought specially. Brendan said he knew nothing about it and then I found this in his room. As I told you, I was looking for it when I was found by him.'

'I don't understand,' he said. 'What is it you really believe, Miranda?'

I paused. I wanted to express this calmly. 'I think that, at best, Brendan encouraged Troy to kill himself. At worst he, well . . .' I couldn't say the words.

'Killed him? Is that what you're trying to say?' Rob's tone was harsher now, sarcastic. 'And what? Staged it?'

'That's what I've been thinking about. I think it's worth looking into.'

There was a long silence. Rob was gazing out of the window, as if something had caught his interest. When he turned back to me, I sensed a barrier between us.

'Troy took pills,' I said. 'He had terrible trouble sleeping. When he had taken his pills, he was out for the count.'

Rob picked up a file from his desk. 'Your brother had traces of barbiturate in his bloodstream. He was taking medication. There was nothing beyond what you'd expect.' He tossed the file onto his desk again. 'Come on, Miranda. What would *you* do?' he said. 'I mean, if you were me.'

'I'd investigate Brendan,' I said. 'To see what you find.'

Rob looked irritably puzzled. 'What is it with this guy, Brendan? Have you got some problem with him?'

'It's a bit of a long story.'

He was definitely wary now, glancing at his watch. 'Miranda, I'm a bit pressed . . .'

'It won't take a minute,' I said, and I gave him the quick version of the story of Brendan and me as the view from his window darkened behind him. It was one of those dark December days. When I finished, it was harder to make out his expression.

'So?' I said.

'You've had a tough time,' he said. 'One of the things I don't do is get involved in private disputes.'

'Until a crime has been committed.'

'That's right. I'm a policeman.'

'Do you want more evidence? Is that it?'

'No, no,' he said urgently. 'Definitely not.' He stood up, walked round his desk and put his hand on my shoulder. 'Miranda, give it some time. In a few weeks, or months, it will seem different. I promise.'

'And you're not going to do anything at all?'

He patted a large pile of files on his desk. 'I'm going to do a lot,' he said.

Laura looked gorgeous. She'd just had her hair done and, streaked and tousled, it glowed like a beacon on this horrible grey day. It seemed to light up the bar. She looked smart as well. I'd met her straight from work and she was wearing a suit and a white shirt with a ruffle down the front. I had an uneasy feeling that I didn't look particularly presentable. I didn't seem to have had the time for a few days.

I brought the bottle of wine over to the table. Now that was another issue. I was going to start keeping track of my drinking. Not now, though. I had other things to sort out first. As I poured the wine, Laura looked at me and with a flicker of a smile she took a packet of Marlboro Lights and a lighter from her bag.

'You've started again,' I said.

'I used to love smoking so much,' she said, taking a cigarette from the packet and placing it between her glossy red lips. 'And suddenly I thought: Why not? I'll give up again when I'm old . . .' She flicked the lighter and sucked the flame into the end of the cigarette and then ejected a dense cloud of smoke. 'You want one?'

I was very tempted. The smell of it brought back late nights in a fog of drink and talk and laughter and intimacy. But I shook my head and took a gulp of wine to take my mind off it.

'I'd hoped we could go for a walk,' I said.

Laura looked through the window with an expression of distaste. 'In this weather?'

'I wanted to breathe some cold air,' I said. 'Clear my head.'

'You can do that on your own,' Laura said. 'I'm not dressed for that.'

I had planned what I was going to say to Laura, so that it would seem coherent and sane, but it all came out wrong. I talked about Troy and Brendan and going to the police and it turned into a chaotic exercise in free association, hopping from one subject to another as ideas occurred to me. By the time I was finished, Laura was on her third cigarette.

'This isn't like you, Miranda,' she said. 'I'm so sorry about Troy. We all are. But listen to yourself. I know what it's like to be dumped by someone. When Saul broke up with me, you remember what I was like. I couldn't get it out of my head. I even came up with schemes to get him back. Do you remember?'

'Of course I do, but this isn't just a break-up and, as you know, *I* broke up with Brendan, but I don't want to get into that again—'

'For God's sake, Miranda. I've talked to Brendan. He's puzzled by all this, as much as I am.'

'What?' I said. 'Brendan? Have you been discussing *me* with Brendan?'

'Miranda—'

'You've gone over to him. That's it. I can tell. You think he's charming? A nice guy? How dare you? How dare you talk about me to him? What have you told him? Have you given away things I've said to you about him?'

'Miranda, stop this, this is me.'

I stopped and looked at her. She was beautiful and slightly evasive. She took a drag on her cigarette. She was avoiding my eyes.

'You like him, don't you?'

She gave a shrug. 'He's just an ordinary, nice guy. He's concerned about you.'

'That's it,' I said. I rummaged in my purse and, dimly feeling I'd done all this before, in a dream, found a ten-pound note and threw it down on the table. 'There. I'll be in touch. Sorry. I can't say anything more. I've got to go. I can't be doing with this.'

There were sixteen days to go until Christmas and four days until Kerry and Brendan were to be married in the register office half a mile from my parents' house. I woke to darkness outside my windows and the sound of rain, and for several minutes I couldn't make myself get out of my warm bed. I thought of having to scrape the ice from the van's windscreen, of hammering nails into floorboards in an empty and unheated house in Tottenham with bare, numb hands, and squirmed deeper under my duvet.

I heard the sound of mail being pushed through the letterbox and thumping onto the floorboards. In twelve days, it would be the shortest day of the year, and then the days would start getting longer again.

There was grey showing at the edges of the curtains. I forced myself out of bed, sliding my feet into my slippers and putting on my dressing gown, and collected the letters from the floor. I made a large pot of coffee and poured myself a cup. Then I sat down at the table and opened my mail. There were nine Christmas cards, two appeals from charities, a credit card bill, a bank statement and an envelope with Kerry's writing on it. I slid my finger under the gummed flap and lifted out the letter inside. *Dear Miranda,* I read. *Brendan and I thought it might be a good idea if you would be one of our witnesses on Friday. Please let me know as soon as possible if this is all right with you. Kerry.* That was all.

I grimaced and a little corkscrew of pain wound itself round my right eye. That would be Brendan's doing. Getting me to stand beside the happy couple and sign my name by theirs. Pose for the camera. Smile at Brendan, my brother-in-law, part of my family.

Perhaps I should just say no. Perhaps I should simply stay away from the wedding altogether. They'd be better off without me there anyway.

But of course I had to be there because not being there would just be read as yet another hysterical gesture on my part: mad, obsessed, lovesick, hate-filled Miranda; the ghost at the feast.

I sighed and stood up, tightening the belt of my dressing gown, crossed the room to the phone, dialled.

'Hello?'

'Mum. It's me.'

'Miranda.' The flat tone I'd become used to since Troy's death.

'Hi. Sorry to ring so early. I really just wanted to speak to Kerry. About being a witness.'

'She said she was asking you.' There was a pause, then, 'I think it is a very generous gesture on her part.'

'Yes,' I said. 'Can I talk to her?'

'I'll go and call her. Before I do, though . . . We thought, Derek and I, that we should have a small gathering for them before Friday. There'll be no party on the day. This would be just family, really, to wish them well. Are you free tomorrow?'

It wasn't really a question.

'Yes.'

'About seven. I'll get Kerry for you.'

I said to Kerry that I'd be a witness and Kerry said she was glad, in a cool, polite voice. I said I'd see her tomorrow and she said 'good', like a verbal shrug. I had a sudden memory, like a bright shaft of sunlight shining through the dreariness, of Kerry and me swimming in the waves off the Cornish coast, both of us sitting in large rubber rings and letting ourselves be tossed on to the shore. I remembered us laughing together, laughing at each other, squealing with gleeful fear.

'I'm thinking of you,' I said in a rush.

There was a silence.

'Kerry?'

'Thanks,' she replied. Then, 'Miranda?'

'Yes?'

'Oh, nothing. See you tomorrow.'

At exactly seven the next evening I was knocking at the door of my parents' house. Kerry answered. She was wearing a gauzy pink shirt with beads round the neck. I kissed her on her cold cheek and stepped inside.

Work had stopped on the house. The gaping hole in the kitchen wall had been crudely boarded up and there was thick polythene billowing over the side window. Everything had stopped at the moment when Troy had been discovered strung up on my beam.

Bill and Judy were there, sitting in a cluster with my parents round the fire Dad had made. Looking at my depleted family together, I realised they had all become thinner. But not Brendan. When he arrived, a few minutes later, I saw he had put on weight. His cheeks were pudgier, his paunch strained at his lilac-coloured shirt. His hair seemed blacker and his lips redder than ever. He met my eyes and inclined his head, with a half-smile.

He was less ingratiating now. There was the touch of the bully in his tone when he told Kerry he needed a stiff drink. When he mocked my father about the rather feeble fire, there was contempt in his voice.

In other circumstances, we would have been drinking champagne, but Dad brought out red wine instead, and whisky for Brendan.

'What are you going to wear tomorrow, Kerry?' I asked after a moment.

'Oh.' she flushed and looked up at Brendan. 'I'd planned to wear this red dress I bought. I'm not sure it suits me, though. I don't know if I can carry it off.'

'You can carry anything off you want to,' I said. 'It's your wedding day. Show me.'

I put my wineglass down. The two of us filed up the stairs together, into their room. The last time I'd been in here was when I'd found that rope stuffed under the chest. I pushed the thought away and turned to Kerry. She reached into a large shopping bag, unwrapped tissue. My face ached. I wanted to cry. It all felt so wrong.

'It looks gorgeous. Try it on for me,' I said. All my anger at Kerry had gone. I felt only helpless love for her now.

She wriggled out of her trousers, pulled her pink top over her head, unclasped her bra. She was so thin and white.

'Here.' I passed the dress across to her and as she reached out for it we both became aware of Brendan standing in the doorway. No one said anything. Kerry started struggling into the dress, and for a moment her head was obscured by the red folds, only her skinny naked body was visible, shining in its whiteness like a sacrifice. It felt perverse that Brendan and I should be watching her together. I turned sharply away and stared out of the window.

'There,' she said. 'Of course it needs high heels and I'd pin my hair up and put make-up on.'

'You look lovely,' I said, although she didn't; she looked washed-out, obliterated by the bold red colour.

'Hmmm,' said Brendan. He stared at her appraisingly, then a little smile flitted over his face. 'Oh well. They're all waiting to toast us downstairs.'

'I'm coming.'

'Back to being friends, are you?'

It was as if his words had lit a fuse and now anger was burning up towards my centre. I turned to him. 'We're sisters,' I said.

For the few moments that we gazed into each other's unblinking eyes, I felt that there was nothing left inside me except for hatred.

On Friday morning, I got up early, had a bath and washed my hair, then I went into my bedroom and stared at the clothes in my wardrobe. What do you wear to the wedding of your sister to a man you hate that is taking place only days after your brother has died? Eventually I pulled a lavender-coloured dress out of the cupboard. If I put my nice raw silk shirt over the top it would do. I applied make-up, blow-dried my hair and clambered into the dress. I looked at myself in the mirror, grimaced at the whey-faced, hollow-eyed creature I saw there.

We were all going to walk to the register office together from my parents' house, so I drove there through the traffic and parked a few doors down. I half ran through the drizzle, lifting my dress to keep it clear of the puddles. Even as I lifted a fist to hammer at the door, it opened.

'Miranda,' said my father.

I was startled. He was in his tatty tartan dressing gown and unshaven. Had I got the time wrong?

'We've got to leave,' I said.

'No,' he said. 'No. Come in.'

My mother was sitting on the stairs, in a pair of baggy leggings and an old turtleneck jumper. She lifted her head when she saw me. Her face was all folds and creases. 'Have you told her?'

'What?' I said. 'Told me what? What's going on?'

'He's called it off.'

'What do you mean?'

'He wasn't there when Kerry woke and he phoned her at eight o'clock. He said . . .' For a moment the dull monotone of her voice cracked. She shook her head as if to clear it, then continued. 'He said he'd done his best to help us all, but it was no good. He said he was tired of carrying all of us and he could do no more.'

I sank onto the step beneath my mother.

'Oh, poor Kerry.'

'He said,' she went on, 'that he'd found the opportunity of happiness with someone else and he knew we'd understand that he had to take it.'

'Someone else?' I spoke dully.

My mother looked at me suspiciously. 'Didn't you know? She's your friend, after all.'

'No,' I said. 'Oh, no.'

'So,' said my mother. 'There we are.'

'Laura,' I said.

I went up to Kerry's bedroom. The lights were off so that the room was dim. She was sitting on the bed, still in her pyjamas. I sat beside her and stroked her hair and she turned her glassy gaze on me.

'Stupid of me,' she said in a brittle voice. 'I thought he loved me.'

'Kerry, listen—'

'He just loved you.'

'No.'

'And then your friend.'

'Kerry,' I said. 'He's not a good man. He's not. There's something wrong with him. You're better off without him and I know you'll find—'

'Don't you dare say I'll find someone better,' she whispered.

'All right.'

'Everything's ruined,' she said softly. 'It was ruined already, when Troy killed himself. Brendan's just knocked over the last few stones. There's nothing left.'

I thought of Brendan trampling over my family, grinding his boots over all our hopes. I put my arm round my sister, felt her eyelashes prickling against my skin and tears on my cheek. But I couldn't work out if the tears were mine or hers.

Some things, when you look back on them, seem like a dream. But this wasn't a dream, although later I remembered it like a moment snatched out of time and haunting my memory for ever.

I woke and, although it was still dawn, a soft light filled the room. Climbing out of bed, I opened the curtains onto a world of snow. Large flakes were still falling, floating and spinning down on the other side of the glass. I hastily pulled on warm clothes and opened the front door on to the unmarked street. Snow lay thickly on the cars, dustbin lids, low garden walls, its pristine thickness occasionally marked by cats' paw prints, the claw marks of small birds. The world was monochrome, like an old photograph, and foreshortened. There was no horizon, just the steady flicker of falling flakes. As I walked there was no sound, save for the slight creak of my shoes against the snow. Everything was muffled, mysterious, beautiful. I felt entirely alone.

It was still not fully light, and there was nobody on the Heath. I walked up the hill and stood there for a while, watching the snow fall all about me. Soon enough, there would be crowds here, throwing snowballs, building snowmen, tobogganing down the hill. But for now it was just me. I tipped back my head and was blinded by the falling snow.

As I made my way back down the hill, I saw a woman, a figure, walking slowly along the path that crossed mine. She had on a thick coat, a large hat pulled down over her eyes, a scarf wrapped round the lower half of her face. Nevertheless something about her was familiar to me. I stopped where I was, with a tightness about my heart. Perhaps she felt my eyes on her, for she stopped too, and looked up. She turned her head towards me and then she took off her hat and put a hand to her eyes, to see better. Flakes fell onto her dark hair. For a few moments, she didn't move, and neither did I.

I wanted to call out her name: 'Laura! Laura!' I wanted to cover the distance between us so I could see her face properly. And she too seemed to be drawn towards me. She took an uncertain half-step, her hat still dangling from her mittened hand. But still I didn't move.

Then Laura put on her hat and once more started walking along the path, away from me. I watched her as she became a shadowy figure. I watched until, like a lonely ghost, she faded into white.

Somehow, days passed. Months passed. Then something happened.

I was dreaming that I was falling, falling through the air, and then I woke with a start. The phone was ringing. I half noticed, as I fumbled with the receiver, that it was dark outside.

Someone started singing into my ear. 'Happy birthday to you, Happy birthday to you . . .'

I sat up in bed and clutched the phone. Behind the relentlessly cheery tune there was another noise: a rabble of voices; music and loud laughter.

'Happy birthday, dearest Miranda . . .'

'Don't,' I mumbled.

'Happy birthday to you!'

I twisted my head round to see the green glow of the numbers of the clock: 12.01 clicked into 12.02.

'I wanted to be the first to say it. March the 8th. You didn't think I'd forget did you? I could never forget.'

'I'm going to put the phone down now, Brendan.'

'You're always in my thoughts. Not an hour goes by. And I'm always in your thoughts, aren't I?'

'You're drunk.'

'Just merry. And on my own now.'

'But Laura . . . ?'

'On my own and thinking of you. Just thinking of you.'

'Fuck off,' I said and put the phone down.

7

UNBELIEVABLY, UNFORGIVABLY, I arrived late at the church. I had a fistful of excuses. I'd been thinking what on earth I should wear, and whether it mattered, and suddenly I realised I'd been sitting on the edge of my bed staring at the wall for forty-five minutes and I didn't know what I'd been thinking about. The church was down in New Malden, where Laura's parents lived, and it turned out to be much farther than I thought.

There were two different doors to the church, both closed. I could hear people singing a familiar hymn inside. I didn't know which door to take. I took the smaller entrance, down the side. I was worried I'd come out in some prominent place where I'd be stared at. I pushed at the door, but there was some resistance. As it opened, I realised that the small church was full and people were standing in front of the door. A bearded man in a dark trench coat moved along to allow me inside.

The hymn finished and someone I couldn't see started to speak. I looked around for familiar faces. It was a collection of strangers and I wondered for a horrible second if I had blundered into the wrong church, but at the back I saw Tony, gaunt, harrowed, but weirdly embarrassed as well. I hadn't been concentrating on the speech and now I made myself listen. I just picked out phrases: 'happy young woman', 'first flush of youth', 'spring morning'. They seemed nonsensical to me. From the artificial tone. I assumed this must be a vicar who didn't really know Laura, who had only heard about her. 'Sometimes we want to ask God questions,' said the voice. 'We want to ask why bad things happen to good people. Why innocent children suffer. And now, why this beautiful, sunny young woman should die, so cruelly, so unfortunately, so unnecessarily. An accident of this kind would be horrible at any time, but for a woman like Laura, newly married, it is almost too much to bear.'

Through the fog of confusion and misery I felt a steely jab. 'Newly married.' I hadn't known that. So they had got married. Laura had got married.

'And so,' the vicar continued. 'Our thoughts and our prayers must be with, not just Laura's parents, Jim and Betty, but with Brendan, her new husband.'

I could see him now. I leaned across and saw the front row of pews. I

425

could only see them from the back. A grey-haired woman leaning forwards, a grey-haired man with his arm round her, and on her other side, sitting upright, facing forwards, Brendan. I could only see the back of his head, but I could exactly picture his expression. He would be the best mourner in the church. The world champion mourner. I saw him turn slightly to Laura's mother. Exactly. In the midst of his suffering he would be helping others. What a star.

When the coffin was carried past me, I hardly connected it with Laura at all. I just thought about how heavy it must be and wondered how they chose the men to carry it. Laura had been my best friend, but I had never met her parents, so when they followed the coffin out, it was the first time I had ever seen their faces. Laura's mother, round-faced and fleshy, didn't look like her daughter. Laura had been the image of her father. She had been a beautiful woman and he was handsome.

Behind them was Brendan. He almost made me gasp, he looked so handsome. Everything about him was right. He was holding his hands together in front of him, slightly clenched, as if he were in pain but trying not to show it. His black suit was beautifully brushed, without even a hair or a speck of dust on it. He had on a white shirt and a rather gorgeous crimson tie with a large knot. His hair was tousled, which clashed slightly with the care and precision of his dress, but that was appropriate too, as a signal of his grief and his passion, a note of elegant disarray.

The parade passed by and out through the door. There was some awkward shuffling and murmuring while we waited to be sure that the family members were gone and safely away. Last in, I was one of the first out, blinking in the sunshine.

The one person I wanted to see and to hug was Tony, but when I arrived at the house I couldn't see him anywhere. I assumed he must have slipped away after the ceremony. Laura's parents were leading an old woman across the living room into a corner and helping her into an armchair. I thought of offering my condolences and then thought how could I possibly without getting myself lost in horrendous explanations. But then I told myself I ought to talk to them anyway. This argument with myself was still going on when I became aware of someone's presence beside me. I looked round. The face I saw was so unexpected that for a moment I had trouble placing him. It was the detective, Rob Pryor.

'What on earth are you doing here?' I asked.

He didn't answer, just handed me a cup of tea. 'I know what you're going to say,' he said.

I took a gulp of tea. It was scaldingly hot and it burned my mouth and almost everything else as I swallowed it.

'What am I going to say?'

'I thought you'd be here,' he said. 'I thought it was important that I head you off.'

'I don't know what you're talking about.'

'I've looked into this,' Rob said. 'I've talked to the investigation officer. Laura's death is terribly sad. But that's all.'

'Oh, for fuck's sake, Rob,' I said. 'Don't insult my intelligence. I come to you with my suspicions about Troy. You pooh-pooh them. Fine. Then Brendan dumps my sister for my best friend and runs off with her. A few months later she's dead. Do you see a pattern here?'

Rob sighed. 'I'm sorry, I'm not very interested in patterns. Facts are stubborn things. Laura died by accident. She'd been at a party,' he explained. 'She was clearly intoxicated. She had some sort of altercation with Mr Block. She left early. She returned to their flat alone. She ran herself a bath. She slipped and struck her head while the bath was running. She drowned. The bath overflowed and, at just before twenty past midnight, Thomas Croft, who lived in the flat beneath, became aware of water coming through the ceiling, ran up, found the front door of the flat unlocked and discovered Mrs Block dead in the bath.'

I hated to hear him call Laura 'Mrs Block'. It was another way that Brendan had got his clammy hands into somebody's life. I looked round to make sure nobody could overhear us. 'That's exactly what he did when he and Kerry were living in my flat. He deliberately let the bath overflow. It's a message to me.'

Rob Pryor looked at me almost with an expression of pity. 'Mrs Block's death was a message to *you*?' he asked. 'Are you insane?'

'It's easy to bang someone over the head,' I said. 'Hold them under the water. Were people at the party keeping track of Brendan every minute?'

Rob gave an impatient frown. 'It's a twenty-minute walk from the party at Seldon Avenue back to their flat. Maybe twenty-five. Anybody who left the party to kill her would have been away for about an hour.'

'He could have followed Laura back to their flat.'

At that very moment I felt hands on my shoulders. I looked round and a face leaned into mine, kissing me on both cheeks, hugging me too close. It was Brendan.

'Oh, Miranda, Miranda, Miranda,' he murmured in my ear. 'What a terrible thing. It's so good of you to come. It means a lot to me. It would have meant a lot to Laura.' He looked over at Rob Pryor. 'Rob has been a good friend to me, ever since the business with Troy.' He looked back at me. 'I'm sorry, Mirrie. I'm so sorry. I seem to bring bad luck wherever I go.' I didn't reply. I couldn't. 'I needed to talk to you,

Mirrie.' He smiled at me, looking me in the eyes. 'You're the one who understands me. Better than anyone else. There's something strange. Has Rob told you?' He looked over at Rob who shook his head. 'Almost at the moment when it—you know, the thing with Laura, I can't bear to say it—do you know what I was doing?'

'Of course I don't,' I said.

'You do,' he said. 'I was talking to you.'

Dearest Troy,

There's this memory that keeps coming back to me. When you were about nine you insisted on waking me up at four in the morning to listen to the dawn chorus. I staggered blearily out into the garden in my dressing gown even though it was freezing cold and the grass was soaking wet. You were all dressed up in jeans and Wellington boots and a big jacket, and you had Dad's binoculars hanging round your neck. We stood at the end of the garden in the dawn and all of a sudden—as if a switch had been thrown—the birds started to sing. A great wall of sound all round us. I looked at your face and it was so incredibly joyful that I forgot to feel cold. We stayed out there for ages and then we went into the kitchen and I made us hot chocolate and scrambled eggs. You said, with your mouth full: 'I wish it could be like this all the time.'

Of course you can't read this, but I'm writing to you because you're the only person I really want to talk to. I talk to you all the time. I'm terrified that one day I'll find that I've stopped talking to you, because that will mean you're dead.

'I don't really know why I'm here,' I said.

The woman opposite me didn't answer, just looked at me until I looked away, down at my hands screwed together in my lap; at the low table between us where a box of tissues stood ready.

Katherine Dowling must have been in her late forties or early fifties. She had steady brown eyes, strong cheekbones, a firm jaw. She was focused on me, or trying to see into me, and I didn't know if I liked it. 'Tell me what brought you here.'

'I've got no one else to talk to,' I said and noticed the unsteadiness in my voice. 'The people I want to talk to are gone.'

'Gone?'

'Dead.' I felt my throat begin to ache and my sinuses thicken. 'My little brother and my best friend.' I made myself say their names aloud. 'Troy and Laura. He killed himself, or that's what everyone says, though

I think, I think . . . well, never mind that. I found him, in my flat. He hanged himself. Laura died just a few weeks ago. She was only my age. The last time I saw her we didn't speak. I keep thinking if I'd said something to her, if I'd done things differently, this wouldn't have happened. I know that probably sounds stupid to you, but it's what keeps coming back to me.' I was weeping in earnest now and my voice was coming out in hiccups. 'Sorry,' I said. 'Sorry, but it seems so unfair.'

'Unfair on you?'

'No. *No!* I'm not dead, am I? I'm one of the lucky ones. Unfair on them, I mean. I'm the carrier!' I cried out, blotting my face. 'Don't you see? I brought him into my world, and that's my problem and I had to deal with that. But it was their world as well and he's infected them, destroyed them, wrecked their lives. He even made me into his alibi,' I muttered. 'God he must have laughed!'

'Listen!' Katherine Dowling said, and I subsided. 'You are making a pattern that isn't there. You are trying to find a meaning, an explanation, take responsibility, place blame. In the past few months, you have lost two people who you loved a great deal. And you have been through a painful and disturbing episode with a man. This Brendan. Because these things have happened together, you connect them, like cause and effect.'

'I *do* connect them,' I said.

'Now: we can talk about what happened with Brendan; in fact, I think that might be helpful. We can talk about your bereavement, and why you feel such guilt. But we will be looking at *you*—at what is going on inside you after these traumas. We will not be looking at why these two young people had to die one after the other. They died. Now you must mourn.'

I made myself consider what she had said.

'Sometimes I have felt that I was going mad,' I said at last. I felt like a rag doll lolling on the chair. 'Everything seems hostile and out of kilter. It's like a nightmare, but I can't wake up out of it. It just goes on and on.'

'Well, we can talk about that too,' she said. 'We should. Would you like to come again, Miranda?'

I nodded. 'Yes,' I said, 'I think I would. But in a few months.'

The next morning I woke early and knew before I even opened my eyes that it was a warm day outside. The strip of day between the curtains was blue and, for the first time in a long while, I didn't fell clogged with tiredness, but alert, as if there were something that I had to do. Although it was a Saturday and I didn't have to go to work, I got up at once.

I had a quick, hot shower, washed my hair vigorously and pulled on a denim skirt and a shirt. I put on Troy's watch, but for once the sight of it didn't make my eyes well up with tears. I made a cup of peppermint tea and tore a hunk of bread from the loaf, eating it just as it was. I vacuumed the carpets, plumped up the pillows on the sofa and opened the windows to let in the bright day. Before I could change my mind, I pulled on a jacket and walked to the underground.

Kerry was already behind her desk when I walked in. A woman was sitting across from her, leafing through brochures and pointing things out, so she didn't see me immediately, and when she did her face flickered through various emotions: surprise, discomfort, pain, welcome.

I watched her as she leaned across the desk, pointing at pictures with a finger whose nail was a delicate pink. She looked rosy and plumper. Her hair fell in blonde waves round her smooth, pale face.

'Fancy a cup of coffee?' I said, when the woman left, clutching a pile of brochures, and I eased myself into her seat. Kerry's skin was satiny, her lips glossy, and she had tiny gold studs in her ears. Everything about her seemed considered, delicate. I looked down at my hands on the desk, with their dirty, bitten nails, and saw the cuffs of my shirt were frayed.

Kerry hesitated, looked at her watch. 'I don't know if I can.'

'Go on,' called a woman at the next desk. 'We'll be busy soon and then you won't have the time.'

We didn't talk until we got to the café down the road. We took our coffee downstairs, where they had a sofa and armchairs, and looked uncertainly at each other over the rims of our steaming mugs.

'Sorry I haven't been in touch,' I said eventually.

'You've been busy.'

I waved away the polite words. 'That's not the reason.'

'No, I suppose not.'

'I didn't know where to begin.'

'Miranda—'

'You said something to me—just after he, you know—just after Brendan walked out. You said everything was ruined and he'd just kicked over the last few stones. Something like that.'

'I don't remember.' She put her mug down on the table. 'You shouldn't think about him so much, Miranda,' she said. 'You should let him go.'

'What?' I stared at her.

'I have,' she said. 'He's out of my life. I never want to think about him again.'

I was startled by what she had said. 'Don't you want to talk about it at all?' I asked. 'Don't you want to understand what happened?'

'To understand?' She blinked at me. 'Our brother killed himself. My fiancé left me.'

'But—'

'I'm not saying it wasn't terrible. I'm saying that I don't know what there is to talk about.'

I sat for a few moments. All the waves of emotions and hatred and despair that had battered our family, was now a calm, dark pool.

'What about us?' I asked at last.

'Us?'

'Us, you and me, the two sisters. I want to make it all right between us,' I said, then, realising I sounded like a two-year-old asking to be kissed better, I added, 'I just want you to understand that I was never trying to wreck things between you and Brendan, never; he was the one who was . . .' I let my words trail away, realising what I sounded like. 'Like you said, that's all finished with. He's out of both of our lives. I wanted to know if you're all right, that's all. And that we are all right. It would be terrible if we allowed him to alienate us from each other.'

'I know,' she said in a small voice. Then she leaned forwards and for the first time her face lost its smoothness. 'I should tell you something.'

'What?'

'It feels almost wrong. I thought I'd never be happy again. And it's all happened so suddenly.' She blushed. 'I've met someone.'

'You mean—'

'A nice man,' she said. 'He's quite a bit older than I am, and he really seems to care for me.'

I put my hand over hers, 'I'm very, very glad,' I said warmly. Then: 'No one I used to know, I hope?'

The stupid attempt at a joke fell flat. 'No. He's a junior hospital manager. His name's Laurence. You must meet sometime.'

'Great.'

'He knows about everything—'

'Of course.'

'And he's very different, from, you know—'

'Yes. Good. Great.'

'Mum and Dad say they like him.'

'Good,' I said again hopelessly. 'Really good. I'm so happy for you.'

'Thank you.'

I bought a big bunch of tulips and daffodils and irises and hopped on a bus that stopped a few hundred yards from my parents'. The scaffolding had finally gone from the outside of the house, and the front door had been painted a glossy dark blue. I knocked and listened: I knew that they'd be there. When they weren't working my mother sat in the house watching television and my father spent hours in the garden.

There was no reply. I walked round to the back and pressed my nose against the kitchen window. Inside everything gleamed: stainless-steel surfaces, white walls, spotlights on the ceiling. Dad's favourite mug stood on the table, beside it a folded newspaper. Everything the same, and everything changed utterly.

I turned the handle and opened the back door. In the kitchen I found a vase and filled it up with water and crammed the flowers in, gazing out at the garden that just a few months ago had been a mess and now was neatly tended and planted out. Then I heard footsteps on the stairs.

'Hello?' It was my mother's voice. 'Who's there?' she called from the hallway. 'Who is it?'

'Mum? It's me.'

'Miranda?'

My mother was in her dressing gown. Her hair was greasy and her face was puffy with sleep.

'Are you ill?' I asked.

'Ill?' She rubbed at her face. 'No. Just a bit tired. Derek went out to get some garden twine and I thought I'd have a nap before lunch.'

'I didn't mean to wake you.'

'It doesn't matter.'

'I brought you some flowers.'

'Thank you.' She glanced at them without taking proper notice.

'Shall I make us some coffee?'

'That'd be nice.' She sat down on the edge of one of the chairs.

'And then we could go for a walk.'

'I can't, Miranda. I've got, well, things to do.'

'Mum—'

'It hurts,' she said. 'The only time it doesn't hurt is when I'm asleep.'

I picked up one of her hands and held it against my face. 'I'd do anything,' I said, 'anything to make it better.'

She shrugged. The kettle shrieked behind us.

'It's too late for anything,' she said.

'I loved her,' said Tony. He was on his third beer and his words were slurring together. Everything about him seemed to have slipped a bit— his cheeks were slack and stubbly; his hair was slightly greasy and fell over his collar.

'I know.'

'I wasn't good at saying it, but she knew I did.'

'I think—' I began.

'And then,' he lifted up his beer and drained it. 'Then when she ran off like that, just a note on the table, I wanted her dead and she died.'

'That's not connected, except in your mind.'

'Your fucking Brendan. Charming her. Promising her things.'

'Promising her what?'

'You know—whirlwind romance, marriage, babies. All the things we used to argue about in the last few months.'

'Ah,' I said.

'I would have agreed in the end, though. She should have known that.'

I sipped my wine and said nothing. I thought of Laura, laughing, her head tipped back and her mouth open; her white teeth gleaming and her dark eyes shining with life.

'Now she's dead.'

'Yes.'

On Sunday, I ran seven miles through drizzling mist. Then I worked on the company accounts. I was restless and agitated. I didn't know what to do with my spare time. I didn't want to see anyone, but I didn't want to be on my own. I sorted through old correspondence. I threw out clothes that I hadn't worn for over a year.

At last I rang Bill on his mobile and said I'd like to talk to him. He didn't ask me if it could wait till tomorrow, simply said he was in Twickenham but would be back by six. We arranged to meet in a bar near King's Cross. I got there fifteen minutes early. When he arrived, he kissed me on the top of the head and slid into the seat opposite. He ordered a spicy tomato juice and I had a Bloody Mary, to give me courage. I started asking him how his weekend had been.

Bill held up a finger. 'What's this about, Miranda?'

'I want to stop working for you,' I said.

Reflectively, he took a sip of his drink and put it back on the table. 'That sounds like a good idea,' he said.

'What!' He just smiled at me in such a kind and tender way that I had to blink back tears. 'Here I was plucking up the courage to tell you and all you can say is that it sounds like a good idea.'

'It does. You need to start over.'

'That's what I've been thinking.'

'Away from the whole family thing.'

'You're not like family.'

'Thanks.'

'I meant that in a good way.'

'I know.'

'I feel like my life's one great big enormous ghastly mess and I need to scramble free of it.'

'What are you going to do?'

'I guess I'll try to get a job with an interior decorating company, something like that. Shall I give you three months' notice, or what? And will you be my referee?'

'"I've known Miranda Cotton since she was one day old." Stuff like that?'

'Something like.' I swallowed and fiddled with my drink. 'Bill?'

'Yes.'

'I never was in love with Brendan. It wasn't the way people thought.'

Bill gave a shrug. 'I never thought much of him. The way he would always squeeze my arm when he was talking to me and use my name three times in a sentence.'

'Do you believe me, then?'

'On the whole,' he said with a half-smile. 'More or less.'

'Thanks.' My eyes burned with tears again. I felt floppy with gratitude. 'I think I'll have another Bloody Mary.'

'Well, I'm going home. Drink all you like, but we start on the new house in Bloomsbury at eight.'

'I'll be there. Eight sharp.'

He stood up and kissed the top of my head once more. 'Take care.'

I did it. I made myself do it and I did it. I put my flat on the market and it went more smoothly than anything I've ever done in my life. A young man with a clipboard came and looked around and raved about how saleable it was. The very next morning, a woman came to see it. She reminded me of me, except a bit richer, a bit more grown-up. She had a real job. She was a doctor. I saw the flat through her eyes. So much had been moved out that it had a minimalist look to it that made the space seem brightly lit, larger than it really was.

She said that the flat had a good feel to it. I took a deep breath and said yes and thought about Troy hanging from the beam. Half an hour later the estate agent phoned saying that Rebecca Hanes had offered ten thousand less than the asking price. I said no. He rang back ten minutes later and said she had offered the full amount, but she wanted to move in straight away. I said I didn't want to be hurried. I would move in a month. He rang back after a few minutes and said that would be fine. As I put the phone down, I wondered: Is that the secret of doing deals? Is that the secret of life? If you care less than the other person, then you win?

I was pretty far along in the process of jettisoning my old life, but I had done nothing about getting myself a new one. I had no particular family connection with anywhere outside London. I wasn't constrained. Should I draw a line an inch around London? Two inches? Three inches? Would I like to live beside the sea? And, if so, which sea? Village or town? Or open countryside? My freedom was like an abyss in front of my feet. It was almost awesome. It was also the wrong way round. I needed to think about work. What I needed to do was to find a job or jobs. I needed to make some calls.

I made a resolution. I would contact two people every day who might be of some help in finding me work. I sat down with a piece of paper and after five minutes' thought I had a shortlist with one name on it: a guy called Eamonn Olshin, who had just finished training as an architect. So I phoned him up and asked if we could meet up so I could pick his brains about work. Eamonn was surprisingly—almost ridiculously—friendly. I had been seeing the world as a hostile, treacherous place for so long that it was startling when someone just sounded pleased to talk to me. He said he was having people round for supper that very evening and why didn't I come along? My immediate impulse was to say no because I wanted to spend the rest of my life living in a hole in the ground and because it would make me seem pathetically needy. But I was needy. I said yes, all right, trying not to sound too desperate.

Eamonn's flat was down in Brixton. I wanted to arrive fashionably late, and then lost my way so I was ludicrously late. When I finally walked through the door, just before nine o'clock, there were eight people sitting around the table, two or three of whom were vaguely familiar. Eamonn introduced me to them in turn. The first was his girlfriend, Phillippa, which was a relief. He really had invited me because he wanted to see me. After I had regained my concentration, it was too late. I'd missed all the names.

They were halfway through the meal and I said I'd quickly catch up, but I helped myself to just a token portion of lasagne. I sat next to Eamonn and talked briefly about my plans. He was very encouraging, but he had assumed I was looking in London. I told him I was going to move away, probably to the countryside. He looked baffled.

'Where?' he said. 'Why?'

'I need to get away,' I said.

'That's fine,' he said. 'Take a weekend break. There are some great deals. But don't go and live there.'

We chatted for a bit and then the conversation lapsed and I felt a nudge. It was the man sitting on the other side of me. He was one of the ones who had looked familiar. Of course I hadn't caught his name. Unfortunately he remembered mine.

'Miranda,' he said. 'It's great to see you.'

'David! Blimey!' I said. He'd cut his hair short and had a small moustache over his upper lip.

He waggled his finger at me roguishly. 'Do you remember where we last met? I saw you sitting on your arse on the ice at Alexandra Palace.'

A wave of nausea swept through me. Oh, yes. He had been one of the group on the day I met Brendan. What was it? Was God punishing me? Couldn't he have given me a single evening free of this?

'That's right,' I said.

David laughed.

'A good day,' he said. 'It's the sort of thing you ought to do more often and you never really get round to it. Didn't you? . . .someone said that you had a thing with that guy who was there.'

'Yes,' I said. 'Briefly.'

'What was he called?'

Couldn't he shut up?

'Brendan,' I said. 'Brendan Block.'

'That's right. Strange guy. I only met him a few times. He was an old friend of one of the guys, but'—David laughed—'the stories I heard about him. Amazing.'

There was a pause. I knew, I just knew, that I should start talking about anything except what I was going to say.

'Like what?'

'I don't know,' said David. 'Just odd things. He'd do things the rest of us wouldn't do.'

'You mean, *brave* things?'

'I mean things you'd think of as a joke, he'd actually go ahead and do.' David looked uncomfortable. 'You're not still together, are you?'

'As I said, it was just a brief thing.'

'I just heard about this from someone who was at college with him. Somewhere in the Midlands, I think. Apparently Brendan's idea of hard work was to photocopy other people's essays. He was doing one course where the tutor got so pissed off that he failed him altogether. Brendan knew where he lived and he went round there and saw his car parked outside the house. He'd left one of the windows wound down about an inch. What Brendan did was to put some rubber gloves on and spend the entire night going round the area picking up dog shit and pushing it through that crack in the window.'

'That's disgusting,' I said.

'But amazing, don't you think? It's like a stunt in a TV show. Can you imagine coming down in the morning and opening your car door and then trying to clean the car. I mean, try getting *that* smell out of the car.'

'It's not even funny,' I said. 'It's just horrible.'

'Don't blame me,' David said. 'He wasn't *my* friend. And then there was another story about a dog. I'm not exactly sure of the details. I think they were renting a house somewhere and a neighbour was getting on their nerves. He was some old guy with one of those scraggly, mangy dogs. It used to run around the garden barking, driving everyone mad. So Brendan got hold of the dog and he put it in the back of some builder's lorry. Someone came along and got in the lorry and drove off, with this barking coming out of the back. Insane.'

'So this man lost his dog?'

'Brendan said he was testing those stories you hear about in the local papers about dogs finding their way home from miles away. He said he definitely disproved it.'

'How cruel,' said a woman from across the table.

'I must admit,' said David, 'that the story came out sounding less funny than I thought it was going to. This guy was always talked of as a practical joker, but you don't want to be on the receiving end of his humour.' David leaned closer to me and spoke in a murmur. 'Not someone you want to get on the wrong side of. And if you do, roll your windows up, if you get my meaning.'

'That behaviour sounds psychotic. I wish I'd heard these supposedly amusing stories about Brendan before I went out with him.'

'It might have put you off.'

'Of course it would have put me off.'

'Does it really matter? You said you weren't seeing him any more.'

'I think it does matter,' I said. 'You said he was an old friend of one of the guys. Which one?'

David thought for a moment. 'Jeff,' he said. 'Jeff Locke.'

'Do you have his phone number?'

David started to rummage in his pockets.

When I woke, I was drenched in sweat and my heart was thudding. I had been dreaming, but the dream was breaking up and sliding away. I sat up in bed, drawing the duvet round my shoulders. It was just past four, but there was still orange light from the streetlamps and blue light from the moon shining through the half-open curtains into my room. I waited for the panic to subside, then hauled myself out of bed, pulled on my dressing gown and padded into the bathroom. In the mirror, my forehead looked shiny with sweat and my hair was damp, though I was now shivery with clammy cold. I rubbed a towel over my face, then went into the kitchen and made myself a mug of hot chocolate, which I took back to bed with me, along with an *A to Z* of London. I opened it at the right page and squinted down at the tiny letters, the network of roads. When I'd found what I had been half dreading I would see, I put it on my pillow and lay down. I closed my eyes. Soon, it would be light and the birds would be singing and the sounds of the morning would start.

I had to be in Bloomsbury by eight thirty, so I got up at half past six, pulled on my shorts and singlet, and put a sweatshirt over the top. I had two glasses of water and then went out to my van. The traffic wasn't thick yet, so it took me only fifteen minutes to drive to Seldon Avenue in E8. It was a broad road, with apartment blocks and terraced houses on either side. I parked directly opposite number 19. I took off my sweatshirt and got out. It was still quite cool and there was a slight mist softening the horizon. I jogged on the spot for a few minutes to warm up and loosen my limbs, then ran up and down the road twice, getting ready to start properly.

I looked at my watch: 7.04. A deep breath and I set off, quite fast: halfway down the road, right onto a side road, right again and then up through a small alleyway with scrub land on one side and houses on the other. It led to a housing estate, and I dodged round the fire gates, into the parking space and out the other side. Along the small road with lockups and a railway bridge; left through a narrow cutting that led onto a pedestrian bridge over the railway line. I knew exactly where I was now. I'd been here hundreds of times. I sprinted along the street, turned right and stopped, panting for breath. Kirkcaldy Road. Laura's road. Laura's house. I gazed up at her window. The curtains were not drawn, but no lights were on. I looked at my watch: 7.11. Seven minutes.

I waited for a minute or so and then ran back, retracing my footsteps. This time it took just over six minutes. It would take around twenty minutes, maybe, if you followed the streets, which went the long way, along a railway embankment, across a bridge and round a series of builders' yards. But the direct pedestrian route, the alley, cutting through the flats, the one you couldn't see if you were driving around in a squad car, that was a quarter of the distance at the most. Not twenty-five minutes in any way at all.

I arrived at eight in the morning at the flat in Bloomsbury, letting myself in with the key I'd been given. I was going to sand the floorboards. It wasn't my favourite job: it's noisy and stirs up a storm of dust. I covered the shelves with sheets and put on my ear protectors and mask, and for three hours I moved steadily up and down the spacious living room.

At last I was finished. Squatting on the floor, I ran a finger over the wood, which was full of new patterns and knots. Once it was varnished, it would look beautiful. I stood up, pulled off the headphones and mask, and shook myself, like a dog coming out of water. I opened the large windows to let in the spring air and the buzz of traffic. I swept up the sawdust and then vacuumed the floor, making sure the nozzle got into all the corners. I pulled all the sheets off the bookshelves and started to vacuum them too.

The first shelf was full of general things—two thick atlases, several dictionaries and encyclopedias—but as I lifted the nozzle up to the second I saw titles such as *The Addictive Personality, Forensic Perspectives on Erotic Obsession* and a thick green tome called *The Handbook of Clinical Psychopharmacology*. I turned off the vacuum cleaner and pulled down a book with the title *Erotomania and the Sexualisation of Torture* and opened it at random. Karl Marx was being quoted: 'There is only one antidote to mental suffering and that is physical pain.' Was that true?

I heard a movement behind me. I was surprised in different ways at the same time. I had assumed the owner was at work. Not only was he not at work, but also he was wearing striped flannel pyjamas of the sort that I hadn't seen since visiting my grandfather when I was a small child. How could anybody have slept through what I'd been doing in that flat? He looked as if he had just woken up after several months of hibernation. He had long dark curly hair and 'tousled' was an inadequate word to describe its state. He rubbed his hand through it and made it worse.

'I was looking for a cigarette,' he said.

I reached down a packet from a bookshelf.

'And matches.'

I found a box on a loudspeaker. He lit a cigarette, took a couple of deep drags on it and looked around him.

'I hope you're not going to say that I've got the wrong flat,' I said.

'You're not Bill,' he said.

'No,' I said. 'He subcontracted the job.' I looked at my watch. 'Did I wake you? I didn't know you were here.'

He looked puzzled. He didn't seem entirely to know that he was here either. 'I had a late night,' he said. 'I've got to get to work at twelve.'

I looked at my watch again.

'I hope it's nearby,' I said. 'You've got thirty-five minutes.'

'It's very nearby,' he said.

'Still, you'll probably be late.'

'I can't be,' he said. 'There are people waiting for me. I've got to talk to them.'

'You're giving a lecture?'

He nodded his head. 'Interesting book?' he asked.

'I was just . . .' I gazed down at the book in my hand, then pushed it back into its space on the shelves.

'Coffee?' he asked.

'No, thanks.'

'I meant, could you make some for me? While I'm getting dressed?'

I was tempted to say that I wasn't his butler, but this was obviously an emergency.

He flinched as he took his sip of the coffee. 'You've done a good job,' he said, looking at the boards. 'Not that I'd know the difference between a good job and a bad job.'

'It's the machine that does it,' I said. 'I'm sorry I was messing with your books. Are you a doctor?'

'In a way. My name's Don.'

'I'm Miranda.' I sipped at my coffee. It tasted chocolaty. 'Do you deal with mental illnesses?'

'That's right.'

'I know you must get really pissed off with people asking you stupid questions, but can I ask you a stupid question?'

'What?'

'It's about a friend of a friend.' I put a shortbread into my mouth. 'Of a friend,' I added thickly.

'Yeah, right,' he said with a faint smile.

I started to tell Don about Brendan. I began with the dog turds and then I went on, and when I got to the bit about the bath flooding and was saying: 'And then she went back and found that her bath was over-flowing when she *knew* that she hadn't . . .' Don held up a hand.

'Hold on,' he said. He lit a second cigarette. 'This is you, right?' he said. 'The woman?'

'Well, yes, in fact.'

'Go on with the story.'

So I did. Even though time was getting short before his lecture, I told him everything. And then, at the end, I told him about Troy and Laura—but very quickly, so I wouldn't start weeping again. When I finished I picked up my mug and took a last gulp of stone-cold coffee.

'So what do you think?' I asked. My heart was hammering.

'You're well rid of him.'

I gave a snort. 'I could say that. What I want to know is, is he a psychopath? Could he be a murderer—'

He held up his hands in protest. 'I don't want to be pompous and say that I would have to conduct my own investigation before making any comment like that. And I don't want to start throwing technical, clinical terms around. The point is, it doesn't really work that way. I can't say that this pattern of behaviour means that he is a murderer.'

'*Could* be a murderer,' I interrupted.

'The way it would work is if someone were found to have committed certain types of violent acts then I wouldn't be surprised to find the kind of behaviour you've described.'

'So there we are,' I said.

'No, we aren't,' he said. 'The majority of murderers show earlier signs of dysfunctional behaviour. But a very large number of people display dysfunctional behaviour and the vast majority of them don't cross the line.'

'But if he has crossed the line, which is what I think, even if nobody else agrees with me, is that it? Is he finished? Is he still dangerous?'

Don sipped at his coffee. 'You're piling assumptions on assumptions here,' he said. 'I'm sorry. This is all about hindsight. When people have acted, when they have committed a crime and been caught and imprisoned, then the psychologists and the psychiatrists come out of the woodwork and do their tests and pronounce their verdicts with great authority. And you'll be able to find experts to argue for or against any issue you want.'

'Thank you,' I said dully. I noticed that he was looking at me kindly.

'Keep away from him,' he said.

'Yes.'

'Are you all right?'

'I don't know.' I looked at my watch. 'You've got four minutes.'

'I'd better go,' he said. 'You don't look happy.'

'It doesn't make it all right that it might be just a stranger, does it?' I started to gather up the sheets. 'You can't just sit on the bank and let people drown.'

Don looked as if he were going to say something, but had changed his mind.

'What are you going to talk about?'

He frowned for a moment. 'A very rare psychological syndrome. Very, very rare. Only about four people have ever had it.'

'So what's the point of lecturing about it?'

'If I started asking myself questions like that,' he said, 'then where would I be?'

You didn't kill yourself, did you? Of course you didn't. I should never have let myself doubt that, not even for a second. You didn't kill yourself and Laura didn't bump her head and drown. I always knew it. The question is, what should I do now, Troy? I can't just not do anything, can I?

The weird thing is, I should be scared myself, but I'm not. The truth is, I don't care any more. Not about my safety. I feel like I'm standing on the edge of a cliff in a howling wind and I don't mind if I fall off or not. Sometimes I think I almost want to.

I hope it didn't take too long. I hope you never knew.

8

I COULDN'T LET GO. God knows I had plenty to do with work and looking round at estate agents and making huge decisions about my life. Even so, I rummaged in the pockets of jackets hanging in my cupboard and found the number that David had scrawled on a ripped-off corner of a newspaper, the number of the person at the skating rink who had known Brendan. Jeff Locke.

'Brendan Block? The guy who used to order weirdly flavoured pizzas?'

'Did you think there was something odd about him?'

'Sure.'

'You should have warned me about him.'

'You can't go about like a policeman. Anyway, didn't he get married?'

'She died.'

'What? You mean his wife?'

'She was a friend of mine,' I said.

'I'm sorry.'

'That's all right.' Then I asked him, 'How did you meet him?'

He had to think for a moment. 'I think a guy called Craig McGreevy was an old friend of Brendan's. He works for the Idiosyncratic Film Distribution Company in Islington.'

'Hi, sorry to trouble you. My name's Miranda Cotton and I'm a friend of Brendan Block. I need to reach him urgently. Can you help me?'

'I'm not sure,' McGreevy said. 'I haven't seen him for ages. I've got a number.'

I couldn't resist a smile when he read out my phone number to me.

'I've tried that one,' I said. 'He's not there any more. Maybe someone else could help me? How did you get to know Brendan?'

There was a pause that I had become used to. Is it like that with all friends or was there something particular about Brendan? When I thought of my friends, I just knew where I had met them. Craig McGreevy gave me a couple of names and numbers. One of them didn't answer, but the other did and put me onto someone else who put me onto a man called Tom Lanham who, as soon as I mentioned Brendan, said: 'Are you ringing about his stuff?'

'His stuff?'

'When he moved out, he left some boxes. He said he was going to collect them, but that was about a year ago.'

'You shared a flat with him?'

'He stayed here for a bit, then took off. Are you a friend?'

'That's right. I might be able to help you with his stuff. I could take it to him.'

'Are you sure?' Tom said. 'That would be great.'

'Could I come round and talk to you?'

'Can you come round tonight?'

I was disconcerted by his eagerness. How much stuff was there?

'Where do you live?'

'Islington. Just off Essex Road. I'll give you directions.'

I took down the details and three hours later I was knocking on his door. Tom had obviously just returned from work. He escorted me in and offered me a drink. I asked for coffee. It was very good, very strong, so that it made me wince as I sipped at it. He poured himself a glass of wine in a large glass.

'Why do you want to find Brendan?'

'I'm worried about him,' I said.

Tom smiled. 'I thought he might owe you money.'

'Why?'

'Because he owes *me* money. He was meant to be contributing towards the mortgage, the heating, the phone, but he never quite got round to it. He went off to work on a film somewhere. He said he was helping with some location scouting.'

'When was that?'

Tom sipped at his wine. 'About a year ago. Someone came to stay in the room he'd been using, so I put his things in a couple of empty wine boxes.'

'I'll take it off your hands.'

'Why are you doing this?' he asked.

'It's a bit like you and the money he owes you,' I said. 'Except it's not money.'

Tom looked at me with a puzzled expression. 'I suppose what it *is* is none of my business?'

I tried to make myself smile as if none of this was very important. 'It's like with you,' I said. 'Not a big deal.'

As soon as I got home I tipped the boxes onto the floor of my living room and sifted through the pile. At first it looked enticing but, as I sorted through each item, it quickly began to seem disappointing. It was just a collection of objects. There didn't seem to be anything that connected, no touch of anything personal.

Except, right at the end, there was a handwritten note on lined paper that looked as if it had been torn from a notebook. The writing was a childish scrawl. It said: *Nan's in St Cecilia's*. This was followed by an address in Chelmsford and a room number.

I looked at the piece of paper and I wished I'd never seen it. If I'd had a friend—a friend like Laura—sitting with me now she would have asked me what I was doing, and I would have said to her: 'I don't know.' She would have said: 'He's gone. Let him go. What's it to do with you?' I might have said: 'I'm in a zoo and by mistake I open a cage and let a dangerous animal escape. He scratches and bites me and then he is gone. Should I just be glad and get on with my life or is it still my responsibility?' My friend would say to me: 'You're worrying about people you don't know, people you'll never see.'

And I would say: 'Yes. Stupid, isn't it?'

St Cecilia's was a residential home. As soon as I opened the swing door I was hit by a smell of cleaning fluid and all the smells that the cleaning fluid was trying and failing to cover up. Nobody was at the front desk. I looked around. There was another door which led to a corridor. An obese woman in a light blue nylon housecoat was mopping something up. I cleared my throat and she looked round at me.

'Hello,' I said. 'Have you got a Mrs Block here?'

That was a guess. I wondered if Nan was a relation.

'No,' said the woman.

'Her first name's Nan,' I said.

'There's no Nan here,' she said and returned to her mopping.

I took the letter from my pocket.

'She's in room three, Leppard Wing.'

The woman gave a shrug.

'That's Mrs Rees. Along the corridor, up the stairs, first floor, along the corridor past the TV room. She might be watching TV.'

I went upstairs. In room three there was a bed and a chair and a table in the corner. There was a basin, a wastepaper basket, a window with a crack in the top corner and a nice view over a playing field. Mrs Rees was sitting in the chair with her back to the door. She was in her dressing gown. Her face was directed towards the grey light outside.

'Mrs Rees?'

I moved into her line of sight, but she didn't respond. I knelt by her chair and put my hand on her arm. She looked at the hand, but not at me.

'I'm here about Brendan,' I said. 'Brendan Block. Do you know him?'

'Tea,' she said. 'It's tea.'

'No,' I said, more loudly. 'Brendan. You know, Brendan.'

'It's tea,' she said.

'Your nightie?' I said.

She just gave a whimper. This was a disaster. I didn't even know if this was Mrs Rees. I didn't know if Mrs Rees was the woman referred to in the note. But if this was the right woman, it was immediately obvious that she wouldn't be able to tell me anything about anything. In desperation I stood up and walked round the room. Above the table, stuck on the wall with tape, were two photographs. The first was an old picture of a man in uniform. He wore his cap at a jaunty angle. Husband probably. In the other a woman stood holding the hands of two children. I looked closely. It was the woman in the chair, years ago. The boy, about ten years old, smart in his school blazer, grinning at the camera, was unmistakably Brendan. I took the picture from the wall and showed it to the woman.

'Mrs Rees,' I said, pointing at the photograph. 'That's Brendan.'

She frowned and stared. 'That's Simon.'

'Simon?'

'Simon and Susan.'

I tried to ask more questions, but she started talking about tea again. I tried to stick the picture back on the wall, but the tape was too old and dry. I just leaned it against the wall. I tiptoed out of the room and then ran down the stairs. The woman was gone from the corridor. I found her in a room behind the front desk. She was pouring water from a kettle into a mug.

'I talked to Mrs Rees,' I said.

'Yeah?'

445

'I need to talk to her daughter, Susan.'

'Granddaughter.'

'Yes, of course. I've got something important for her. Could you give me her address?'

The woman started to rummage through a box of filing cards.

Susan Lyle lived at 33 Primrose Crescent, which was on the eastern outskirts of the town, near a cemetery. It was a row of beige and grey houses. Number 33 had closed curtains, a peeling red door and its bell, when I pressed it, rang out a tune: a few notes from 'How Much is that Doggie in the Window?'

I was taken aback when the door opened almost immediately and a woman stood in front of me, filling the entrance. For a moment, all I could think of was her size. She had a vast stomach that looked misshapen in blue leggings; her white T-shirt, on which was written in bold pink DO NOT TOUCH!, was stretched across her bulky chest; her neck was thick; her chin fell in folds; her hands were dimpled. I felt myself blushing with a kind of shame as I tried not to look anywhere but into her eyes, small in her wide, white face. In her grandmother's photograph she had been skinny and knock-kneed; what had happened in life to make her like this?

'Yes?'

'Susan Lyle?'

'That's right.'

I heard a child's wailing come from behind her.

'I'm sorry to disturb you like this. I was wondering if I could have a quick word with you?'

'What's this about? Are you from the council? They already checked the premises, you know.'

'No, not at all. Not the council, nothing like that. You don't know me. I'm . . . my name's Miranda and I know your brother.'

'Simon?' She frowned. 'You know Simon?'

'Yes. If I could just . . .'

I took a small step forwards, but she didn't budge from the entrance. The wailing inside grew louder, joined by a high-pitched shrieking.

'You'd better come in before they kill each other,' she said at last and I followed her into the hall.

It was dim in the living room because the curtain was drawn, so it took me a few minutes to make out exactly how many children there were in the stuffy, cluttered room. There was a baby sitting placidly in the playpen among a giant heap of soft toys, dummy in its mouth. There was a wailing toddler with a damson streak down its bib strapped into a high chair, and an upturned bowl on the floor. There was another toddler on the sofa, staring at the television screen where there was some kind of game show going on, though the sound was turned down. She was gripping a lollipop in her fist. I peered into the carrycot on the floor and there was a baby in there, fast asleep in spite of the noise.

'What a lot of children,' I said brightly. The smell of nappies and air freshener clogged my nostrils. I felt a sense of acute oppression, a thickness in my chest. 'Are they all yours?' As soon as I asked this, I realised it was a stupid question, mathematically impossible.

'No,' she said, staring at me with mild contempt. 'Just the one.' Then she added with pride: 'I have three more who come after school three days a week too. I make a good living. I'm registered.'

Tenderly, she lifted the screaming boy out of the high chair and wiped his mouth with a corner of the bib. 'Quiet now,' she said. 'Shush!' And he immediately quietened, his smeared mouth breaking out into a grin.

Perching the child on the great swell of her hip where he clung like a tiny koala, she said: 'So—Simon?'

I hadn't rehearsed an opening, so it came out abruptly. 'When did you last see him?'

'Are you police?'

'No.'

'Social?'

'No, I just—'

'So what gives you the right to barge into my house and stand there looking as if there's a bad smell under your nose and ask me questions?'

'Sorry. I didn't mean to . . . I'm just worried and I'd be really grateful if you could help me.'

'Has he dumped you or something?'

'What?' For a ghastly moment I thought that perhaps Brendan had even got to his sister before me and told her his version of our relationship.

'Why else would you come running to me for help?' She lowered herself onto the sofa with the boy, picked up the remote control and flicked through channels randomly before saying, 'Not for ages. We've gone our separate ways. He's got his life and I've got mine. Why? What's it to you?'

'Like I said, I know Simon. I've known him for nearly a year now. And I'm a bit worried about him.' I sat down on the edge of the sofa. 'I think he might not be very well.'

'He should go to a doctor. What am I supposed to do about it?'

'I don't mean ill like that . . . I mean . . . well, his behaviour has been rather disturbing and—'

'Oh, I *see*. You mean ill in the head, do you? Mmm?' She suddenly sounded like Brendan. 'Who do you think you are?'

'I didn't—'

'Get out!'

'I just want to help,' I lied.

The anger suddenly went out of her. 'I could do with a fag,' she said. She stood up with surprising agility and the children fell back into the depths of the sofa, letting out yelps of surprise. I followed her into the kitchen, where she sat down heavily on a chair. She poured herself a large glass of fizzy lemonade and lit a cigarette. 'Is he in trouble?'

'I don't know,' I said cautiously, aiming for a vague and misleading truthfulness. 'It's more that I want to prevent trouble, if you see what I mean. So I thought I'd come here and just talk to someone who knew him before he got taken into care.'

'What? Care?' Her laugh was a high, thick wheeze. 'Where did you get that idea from?'

'You mean, he didn't get sent away?'

'Why would he, with our mum and then our nan there to look after us? We were never in care.' She pulled on her cigarette and then released a trail of blue smoke. 'Si wasn't a bad boy.'

'What about school?'

'Overton. What about it? He was good at lessons, but he hated people telling him what to do or criticising him. He could have done all right if they hadn't . . .' She stopped.

'If what?'

'Never mind.'

'Did they punish him.'

'They don't like boys like him being clever.'

'He was expelled?'

She ground out her cigarette, swilled back the remains of her lemonade and stood up. 'I'd better see what they're up to in there,' she said.

I stared at her. 'What happened then, Susan?'

'You can see yourself out.'

'Susan, please. What did he do after he was expelled?'

'Who are you, anyway?'

'I told you, I know Brendan.'

'Brendan? *Brendan*? What is all this?'

'Simon, I meant.'

'I've had enough of people poking their noses into our business. I don't believe you want to help Si. You're just *snooping*. Get out of my house before I call the police.'

Children were coming out of Overton High School, weighed down by backpacks, carrying musical instruments and PE bags. I sat and watched them for a few minutes. Then I got out of the van and wandered over to a couple of women standing by their cars chatting.

'Sorry to bother you,' I said.

They looked at me expectantly.

'I'm moving to the area,' I said. 'And my children . . . well, I was wondering whether you'd recommend this school?'

One of them shrugged. 'It's all right,' she said.

'Is there much bullying?'

'There's bullying in every school.'

'Oh,' I said, stumped. Then: 'I had a friend who came here about, let's see, twelve or thirteen years ago. He mentioned something about an episode.'

'What d'you mean?'

'I can't remember now what it was, exactly. Just, he said something . . .' I allowed my words to trail away.

'That'd be the fire,' said the other woman. 'It was before our time of course, but people still talk about it.'

I turned to her, my skin prickling. 'Fire?'

'There was a fire here,' she said. 'You can see. A whole Year Eleven classroom was burnt to the ground, and half the IT area.' She pointed across the yard to a low red-brick building that was newer than the rest of the school. 'Never caught no one. Probably kids fooling around. Awful what they get up to nowadays, isn't it? There's my Ellie now.' She raised an arm to a lanky girl in plaits walking our way. 'Good luck with the move. Maybe see you again, if you decide to come here.'

I got back into the van and put a Polo into my mouth. I sucked on it, feeling its circle become thinner and thinner until it broke and dissolved. I turned on the ignition, but still sat with the engine idling, staring at the new classroom, imagining a blaze of leaping orange flames. Simon Rees's revenge. Like a sign I knew how to read, like graffiti scrawled on the wall: *Brendan woz 'ere.*

Don was his own worst enemy, in all sorts of ways. He smoked too much. He kept irregular hours. He existed in a general state of vagueness which I began to think was largely deceptive, but not entirely. When I was sealing the floor, he wandered in with two mugs and I had to wave him back before he caused disaster. I joined him out in the corridor and he handed me a coffee and started thinking aloud about other things that needed doing in his flat. Did I think the window frames looked a bit worn? (Yes, I did.) Could anything be done about the cracks in the living room door? (Yes, if money weren't an object.)

'It's dangerous to think of things as you go along,' I said. 'That's how costs spiral out of control.'

'I've heard that,' Don said, sipping his coffee. 'The problem is that it's easier to think up ideas once the work has started. Don't you find that?'

I shook my head. 'There's always more you can do,' I said. 'Always something else that can be fixed. What I like is getting a job finished.'

'You don't want more work?'

'That's a funny thing,' I said. 'I have this feeling that not only *I* should be working at the moment. Shouldn't you be as well?'

Don looked a bit shifty.

'I have this problem,' he said. 'I suffer from attention deficit disorder.'

'Is that a real illness?'

'It's more like an excuse with a long name. This is my day when I work from home. I think and write and make plans.'

'What do you do the rest of the time?'

'Bits of teaching. I see some patients, other stuff.'

'You look too young for that,' I said.

'You mean "immature"?'

'You should learn to take a compliment,' I said. 'I was saying I was impressed.'

'I think it's cleverer to be able to do what you do,' he said.

'You don't know the half of it. Remember Brendan, that man I told you about?'

'Yes.'

'I found his sister. She lives in a council house in Chelmsford.'

'You went to see her?'

'Yes.'

'Why?'

I couldn't think of a short answer, so I told him what I'd done. I told him how Brendan wasn't his real name, about what he did to his school. 'Isn't that scary?'

'Are you scared yourself?'

'Me?' I shook my head. 'This isn't about me. This is about other people, don't you see?'

'It's hard to tell.'

'You said yourself he sounded dangerous. He set fire to his school. Would you admit that that's a symptom of mental disturbance?'

'You didn't say what happened. Was he charged with arson? Did he receive any kind of treatment?'

I took a deep breath. 'He was never caught.'

'Did the sister tell you he did it?'

'Reading between the lines, it's obvious. Can't you see the pattern? Everything fits. Is it true or is it not true that setting fires as a child is one of the earlier signs of being a psychopath?'

I'd finished my coffee and Don gently took the mug from my hand. 'This conversation isn't going the way I planned,' he said.

'What do you mean?'

'I was going to work my way around to saying that it's fun having you working here and how I wondered if we could have a drink some time. I was also going to apologise as well because it's probably difficult for a woman like you because you can't do your job without being harassed by people like me.'

I couldn't help smiling at this. 'Instead I started going on about this psychopath I used to know.'

'That's the thing,' said Don. 'I don't want to offend you.'

'I'm not easily offended.'

Don paused and looked at me as if he were trying to decide if I were telling the truth. 'I worry that you misunderstood what I told you before. I don't think you should have gone to see those women. You should be careful about interfering in other people's lives.'

'I've told you,' I said, with a harder tone in my voice. 'Brendan is dangerous. Do you disagree?'

'There's no magic checklist, Miranda. You wouldn't believe how many people I see who are on the edge. You can tick all the boxes. They have been bullied and beaten and sexually abused. Yes, they may have set fires. Whatever the profilers say, that doesn't make you Jack the Ripper. Above all, he's out of your life and it's not your business any more.'

'Don, if you had sold a car and then you got a report that there was something dangerous about it, would it not be your business?'

Don looked genuinely troubled by this, 'I don't know, Miranda. I just want to say two things. The first is that people aren't like cars. And the second is, what are you actually going to do?'

'It's very simple,' I said. 'I want to find out if he's going out with anybody else. If he is, then she will be at risk and I'll warn her.'

'She may not be grateful,' said Don. 'I have to say I admire you for doing this. You're being a good Samaritan for someone you don't know. But a gesture like that could be misconstrued. And you may be putting yourself in danger.'

When he said this, I felt a shiver go through me. It wasn't apprehension, though, more like a surge of exhilaration. I had a strange sense of stepping out of my life and all the things that trapped me.

'That's not important,' I said to Don.

'Will you be careful?'

'Yes,' I said, meaning no. I wouldn't be careful; I would be unstoppable.

I wanted to find Brendan without his knowing I'd found him. It was more difficult than I expected. I phoned Laura's parents. I talked to Laura's mother. I told her my name and that I was an old friend of Laura's.

'Yes,' she said. 'I think Laura mentioned your name.'

'I was at the funeral,' I said. 'I'm so sorry. It's a terrible thing.'

'Thank you,' she said.

'I wanted to get in touch with Brendan,' I said. 'Is he staying in Laura's flat?'

'No,' she said. 'It's being sold. We haven't seen him. He said he needed to go away.'

I couldn't believe that Brendan had left his parents-in-law without even a forwarding address. I could think of only one thing to do, but I felt a lurch of apprehension as I did it. I phoned Detective Inspector Rob Pryor and indeed he sounded a long way from pleased to hear from me.

'Don't worry,' I said. 'I've just got a simple question. I know you've become friendly with Brendan. I need to get in touch with him and I wondered if you could tell me where he is?'

'Why?'

'I've got some stuff he left behind in a flat he lived in.'

'*Your* flat?'

'*A* flat.'

'How did you get it?'

'What is all this?' I said. 'What business is this of yours?'

'I don't know what's going on with you, Miranda, but I think you should give it up and move on.'

'I just want his address.'

'Well, I'm not going to give it to you.' Another pause. 'I'll tell him to call you. If I speak to him.'

'Thank you.'

'And don't call me again.'

I put the phone down. That hadn't gone very well.

Why do phones always ring when you're in the bath? I left it for ages, but it went on, insistent, until at last I wrapped myself in an unsatisfactorily skimpy towel and headed for the living room.

'Hello?'

There was a short pause, during which I knew for a certainty who was on the other end. I pulled my damp towel more tightly around me.

'Mirrie?'

At his voice, just the utterance of that single word, I felt the familiar, choking disgust. It was as if the air were suddenly thick and dirty, and I could barely breathe. Sweat prickled on my forehead, and I wiped it away with a corner of my towel. 'Yes.'

'It's me.'

'What do you want?'

'What do I want? It's what you want, I think.'

'I don't . . .'

'Or what you have for me.'

I clutched the receiver and didn't reply.

'Rob just called me,' he went on. 'I hear that you're looking for me.'

A kind of groan escaped me.

'You want to give me something. Something I left behind. I wonder what that can be.'

'It's nothing.'

'It must be important, if you're going to all this bother. Mmm, Mirrie?' He waited and when I didn't answer said: 'You just can't let go, can you?'

For a moment, everything went misty.

'Cut the crap,' I said. 'This is me. Nobody else is around. You know what I know about you. You know and I know you know and every hour of every day I think about what you did to Troy and Laura and Kerry, and if you think . . .'

'Hush,' he said in a soothing voice. 'You need help. Rob thinks so too. He's very concerned about you. He says that in his opinion there's a word for what you've got. For your syndrome.'

'Syndrome? Syndrome? Give me your address and then piss off.'

'I don't think so.' I could hear him smile.

'Jesus,' I said, with a sob of rage. 'Listen . . .'

But I was talking on a dead line. Brendan had put the phone down. I gazed at the receiver in my hand, then rammed it down on its holder.

I climbed back into the tepid bath. I ran hot water and then, holding my nose, slid underneath it. I listened to the booming of the pipes and the beating of my heart. I was so angry that I felt I would fly apart.

I came up for air with a thought that made me leap from the bath and run naked and slippery back to the phone, crouching low as I passed the window so no one would see me. I dialled 1471 and waited until the automated voice told me the caller's number. It was a 7852 number. Where was that? Somewhere in south London, maybe.

I shuffled on all fours under the window, then went to my bedroom, yanking out the bath plug on my way. I dressed in baggy cotton trousers and a loose top and then started flicking through my address book, looking for those four digits, trying to find out which bit of London Brendan was in now. There had to be a better way of doing this. I found a telephone directory and ran my finger down the lines and lines of names, looking for the area code. My eyes were starting to swim with the effort until I found the area: Brackley.

What now? I couldn't wander around Brackley looking for him. Maybe I should call the number and—well, and what? Talk to Brendan again? Just the thought of it made me tremble. I turned on my laptop computer. Two minutes, a couple of search engines and I was looking at the name Crabtrees, a café in Brackley. I looked at my watch: 7.35.

Now that I knew it was a café, I did risk calling the number. It rang and rang and just when I was about to put the phone down, someone answered. 'Yes?'

'Is this Crabtrees?'

'Yes. It's the payphone. You want someone?'

'Oh, well, can you tell me the opening hours?'

'I dunno exactly. Eight till late, that's what it says on the board outside.'

'OK, thanks.'

'It's not a pub, though.'

'No.'

'You can't get drinks—it's all cappuccino and latte and those herbal teas that taste like straw.'

'Thanks. You've been very helpful.'

I didn't stop to think. I picked up my denim jacket and left. No underground goes to Brackley, so I drove there, through the balmy evening.

Crabtrees was in the upmarket bit, between a shop that sold candles and a shop that sold bread. I drove past it and then found a place to park a few minutes' walk away.

I walked slowly past the café, with the collar of my jacket turned up, feeling excruciatingly visible. I cast a few rapid glances through the glass, but didn't see him. Then I turned round and walked past once more. The café was practically empty and he didn't seem to be in there.

I went inside. It was brightly lit and smelt of coffee, vanilla, pastry, herbs. I ordered a pear juice and a flapjack and took it into a corner. What would I do if he walked in now? I should have brought a large newspaper to hide behind.

After half an hour of nibbling at the flapjack and sipping at the juice,

I paid up and asked the young woman behind the counter what time they closed.

'Nine,' she said. She had silky blonde hair twisted on to the top of her head, a scattering of clear freckles over the bridge of her nose and a lovely candid smile. She glanced at the watch on her delicate wrist: 'Just seven more minutes, I'm glad to say.'

'And what time do you open in the morning?'

'Eight o'clock.'

'Thanks.'

I knew it was ridiculous, but I was back at eight, with a newspaper. I ordered a milky coffee and a brioche and took up my seat again, wedged behind the coat stand so that if Brendan did come in he wouldn't see me. There were two middle-aged women behind the counter this time, and a man in the kitchen, behind the swing doors.

I stayed an hour and a half, and had two more coffees, and then, shaky with caffeine and fatigue, went outside and sat in my van for a bit. I called Bill and said I wouldn't be at work for a couple of days, and then I left a message on Don's machine apologising for not turning up to finish the job, but promising I'd be back soon. I didn't say when, because I didn't know when and I didn't want to think about the hopelessness of my task. Brendan may have been passing by and would never return to the café again, and I was hiding in a corner, camped out behind a newspaper, waiting with a dry mouth and a pounding heart for something that wouldn't happen. Or he could be just across the road, at an upstairs window, looking down. Maybe he was coming along the street now and if I didn't hurry I'd miss him. Maybe this was what going mad was like, crouching in a café, hiding in my van, pacing the streets in an area of London miles from home.

I went to the candle shop and took my time choosing and buying a glass bowl and some floating candles in the shape of water lilies, all the time peering out at the street. I went to the baker's and bought a wheel of brown sourdough bread. I walked very slowly up the street and down again. I went into a bookshop and bought a book of walks in and around London. I poked around in a hardware shop until the glares of the man behind the counter drove me out. I bought a pad of ruled notepaper and a pen at a stationer's, and some toffees to suck during my vigil. I returned to Crabtrees once more, which was filling up now.

As well as a couple of waiters, who looked like students, the young woman from last night was back. She nodded at me in recognition when I ordered white bean soup and a glass of sparkling water. I sat in my

455

obscure corner and leafed through the book of walks. I ate very slowly, and when I'd finished got myself a cup of tea. When the door opened I would bend down, as if tying my shoelace, then peer round the bottom of the table to see who was coming in. At just after two, I started trudging up and down the streets again, wretched with the impossibility of my task. I told myself I'd give it until closing time and then call it a day.

At half past four, the young woman looked mildly surprised to see me again. I had a pot of tea and a slice of lemon drizzle cake.

At seven, I came back for vegetable lasagne and a green salad, but I just pushed it round my plate and left. I got the van and parked it near the café and huddled in the dying light, waiting for it to be closing time. On the spur of the moment, I rang Don again and when he answered, before I could change my mind, said: 'That drink you mentioned, did you mean it?'

'Yes,' he said without hesitation. 'When? Now?'

'Not now. Tomorrow?'

'Great.'

He sounded genuinely pleased and the glow of that stayed with me after I'd said goodbye.

I must have dozed off because I woke with a start and found the light had faded and the crowds on the street had thinned, although there was still a pool of people outside the pub up the road. It was just before nine, and I turned the key in the ignition, switched on the headlights, put the gear into reverse, released the handbrake, glanced in the rear mirror . . . and froze.

If I could see him in the mirror, could he see me? No, surely not. I turned off the ignition and the headlights and slid down low in the seat. I held my breath in the dark. He stopped at the door of Crabtrees, where the young woman was turning the 'Open' sign to 'Closed'. When she saw Brendan, her face lit up and she lifted a hand in greeting before opening the door to him. I sat up a bit straighter in the seat and watched as he took her in his arms and she leaned into him and he kissed her.

She was very beautiful, Brendan's new girlfriend. And very young— not more than twenty-one or -two. I watched her as she pushed her hands into his thick hair and pulled his face towards her again. I closed my eyes and groaned out loud. Whatever Don had said, whatever my common sense told me, I couldn't leave it—not now I'd seen the freckles on her nose and her shining eyes.

The woman collected her coat and shut the door. She waved goodbye at someone still inside and then she and Brendan walked arm in arm down the road, back the way he'd come. I waited until they were nearly out of sight, then got out of the van and followed them, praying he wouldn't turn round and see me. They stopped outside a door between a bicycle shop and an all-night grocery and broke apart while the girl fumbled in her pocket for the key. Her flat, then, I thought. That made sense. Brendan was the cuckoo in other people's nests. She pushed the door open and they disappeared inside.

The door swung shut and a few moments later a light in an upstairs window came on. For a second, I saw Brendan standing, illuminated. He closed the curtains.

9

IT WASN'T EXACTLY an orthodox first date: poking around in an abandoned church in Hackney that a few years ago had been turned into a reclamation centre. Don was at one end of the church, where the altar used to be, bending over an iron bath with sturdy legs, and I was down the aisle looking at stone gargoyles.

'Why have I never been in this place before?' he called out to me, gesturing around him at the stone slabs, the vast wooden cabinets, the boxes full of brass handles and brass padlocks.

'Because you're not a builder.'

'I want everything here. Look at these garden benches, this bird bath.'

I grinned across at him, feeling suddenly dizzy with unfamiliar happiness. 'You don't have a garden.'

'True. Do you have a garden?'

'No.'

'Oh well. Tell me what I should get, then.'

'What about a pew.'

'A pew?'

'It would go perfectly in your room. Look here.'

He walked down the aisle and stood beside me. But he didn't look at the old wooden pew with carved arms. He looked at me. I felt myself blushing. He put his hands on my shoulders. 'Has anyone ever told you you're gorgeous?'

'Never in a church,' I said. My voice caught in my throat.

And then he kissed me. We leaned against a wood-burning stove and I put my hands under his shirt and felt his warm skin beneath my palms. Then we sat down on the pew, and when I looked at him he was smiling at me.

I was at Crabtrees at eight the next morning, but she wasn't there. Instead, one of the men I'd seen two days previously was behind the counter, serving up double espressos, hot chocolates, camomile teas. I perched on a tall stool, ordered a coffee and a cinnamon bun, and then asked if the young woman who'd served me before was coming in soon because I might have left a scarf behind, and maybe she'd picked it up.

'Naomi? No.'

'When will she be in next?'

'I dunno. She only comes in a couple of days a week. She's a medical student. She didn't say anything about a scarf, though.'

'Don't worry. I'll come back later,' I said.

I joined the rush-hour queue at the bus-stop a few yards down the road from the door I'd seen Naomi and Brendan enter. The curtains in the upstairs room were still drawn. I stood there for fifteen minutes, shifting from foot to foot and watching the buses arrive and go. Eventually the curtains in the flat were opened. If I waited long enough, one of them had to come out. If it was Brendan, I'd knock at the door and hope she was there. If it was Naomi, I'd catch up with her and talk. If it was both of them together . . . well, I'd think about that when it happened.

In the event, it was Brendan who emerged. He was wearing baggy black trousers and a grey woollen jacket and carried a silver rucksack over one shoulder. I pressed myself against the bus-stop, among the crowd, worried that he might be coming my way. He passed by on the other side of the road, walking with a jaunty step and whistling to himself.

I waited until he was out of sight, then crossed the road and went up to the door and rang the bell. When she opened the door, she was wearing a white towelling robe and her hair was bundled up in a towel.

'Hello?' she said, peering through the gap. 'Can I . . . ?' Then recognition and puzzlement came into her face. 'Aren't you the woman in Crabtrees?' she asked. 'What are you doing here? How did you know where I lived?'

'Can I come in? Then I could explain. Just a few minutes.'

'Who are you?'

'If I could just—'

'Tell me your name.'

'Miranda,' I said. I saw her eyes widen and inwardly cursed. 'You may have heard of me.'

'Oh, yes, I've heard of you all right,' she said in a hostile tone. 'Now I think you'd better go.'

She started to push the door shut, but I put my hand against it. 'Please,' I said. 'I wouldn't be here if it weren't important.'

She hesitated, biting her top lip as she stared at me.

'There's something I have to tell you,' I said. 'Please.'

At last she shrugged and stood back to let me pass. I followed her up the stairs and into the tiny living room. There was a bunch of bluebells in a jam jar on the table, and medical textbooks. A man's leather jacket was slung over the chair. She turned to face me, hands on her hips, and didn't ask me to sit down. 'I know that you used to go out with Ben,' she said, and I blinked at her. He was 'Ben' now, was he? 'And I know you couldn't let go when he ended it; that you made his life a misery.'

'What about Laura?' I demanded. 'Did he tell you about her?'

'Of course. Laura was his wife and she died and his heart was broken.' I saw tears start up in her candid grey eyes.

'And Troy? He's told you about Troy, has he?' I asked harshly.

'He still has nightmares about it.'

'Naomi, listen. You don't know what you're getting into here. Brendan . . . Ben . . . there's something wrong with him. Really wrong.'

'How dare you say that. He's suffered more in his life than anyone has a right to suffer, but it hasn't made him bitter or closed-off. He's even nice about *you*; he understands why you've behaved like you do.'

'He makes things up,' I said. 'He lies, Naomi. But there's more to it than that.' I felt quite sick with frustration and wretchedness.

'I don't want to hear any more.'

She actually put her hands to her ears as she said this. I raised my voice. 'I think you're in danger.'

'You're talking about the man I love.'

'Listen. Just hear me out. Please. Then I'll go. But please listen, Naomi, *Please*.' I put my hand on her arm and when she tried to pull away, gripped her harder.

'I don't think she wants to listen. No one wants to listen to you any more, do they? Mmm? Now take your hands off her.'

I turned.

'Ben,' said Naomi. 'Oh, Ben!' She crossed the room and put her arms round him.

'I wonder how you found me? You must have gone to a lot of effort.'

I glanced quickly at Naomi. All I could think of was that, in trying to save her, I might have put her in greater danger.

'I'm very sorry that you've been dragged into this,' Brendan said to Naomi. 'I wanted to protect you. Are you all right?'

'Oh, you don't need to protect me!' she said. She gazed at him tenderly and put a hand up to touch his cheek. 'Anyway, it was my fault. I let her in.'

'I'll go,' I said.

'Do that,' said Brendan. He took a few steps towards me, until he was gazing down at me. He had a very faint smile on his lips. 'My poor Mirrie.'

Three days later I got a call from Rob Pryor.

'I thought we weren't meant to talk any more,' I said brightly.

'We need to talk now,' he said.

I felt a ripple of alarm. 'Has something happened with Naomi?'

'No,' he said. 'Nothing has happened with Naomi. I couldn't believe that you'd been to see her. That you were watching her.'

'I had to,' I said. 'It felt like a moral duty.'

'I want you to come and see me. This whole business with you and Brendan. It can't go on like this.'

'I know what you mean,' I said. 'I feel like someone with a disease.'

'We're going to sort it out,' he said.

'When do you want me to come?'

'One other thing first, Miranda. Do you have a solicitor?'

'What do you mean?'

'I think it would be useful if you had some sort of legal representation.'

'The only time I've had a solicitor is when I bought my flat.'

The whole idea seemed laughable, but Pryor didn't give up. He asked me if I knew anybody at all who was a lawyer. I thought for a moment and then remembered an old college friend, Polly Benson. Pryor said it would be a good idea if I brought her along.

I began to get suspicious. 'Is there some problem?'

Pryor's tone was soothing. 'We're going to sort this out,' he said, 'but you may benefit from some advice. Talk to your friend, then phone me. We'll make a date.'

I phoned Polly and she gave a cheerful scream when I identified myself. She was so excited. We hadn't been in touch for ages. We must get together. We must have a drink. I said that would be great, but first I had something I needed to talk to her about. I asked her if she could come with me to see someone. In fact, a detective. She said sure, no problem, straight away. I said I would pay her, just like a normal client, and she laughed and said to forget it and, anyway, I wouldn't be able to afford it. She asked me what was up, so I gave her the two-minute version of the Brendan story while she murmured sympathetically.

'What a creep,' she said, when I'd finished. 'But you don't know what's up?'

'Brendan's become friendly with this detective. He may have made some complaint.' I laughed. 'Or maybe he's going to confess to murder.'

'Maybe Brendan objects to what you've been saying about him,' said Polly. 'You have to be careful about things like that.'

'I'm a bit worried about needing a solicitor,' I said.

'Then it'll be good that I'm there,' she said.

I wasn't sure if that really answered my question, but I found a time she was free the next day and also a time we could meet for a drink later in the week. I phoned Rob Pryor and that was fine and so, weirdly, the next afternoon found me standing outside the police station talking with Polly. She was wearing a grey pinstriped suit and with her jet-black, very straight hair and brown skin she looked stunning.

A uniformed officer showed us through to Pryor's office. Brendan was there and a middle-aged woman, also formally dressed, who Pryor introduced as Deirdre Walsh, Brendan's solicitor. She looked at me with a puzzled expression, as if I weren't the person she was expecting. I introduced Polly to them and tried hard not to look in Brendan's direction. Pryor asked if Polly knew about the situation.

'I filled her in,' I said. 'But I'm not quite sure what this is all about.'

Pryor was fidgeting with a file on his desk. He flipped it open.

'At Mr Block's request,' he said. 'This is an informal meeting.'

'What does that mean?' I said.

'You'll see,' said Pryor, picking up a sheet of paper from the file. 'We all know what's been going on, more or less. But it might be worth going through some of the salient episodes.' He pursed his lips and hesitated for a moment before continuing. 'Last year the two of you had a brief, intimate relationship, which Mr Block ended.'

'That's not true,' I said.

'Please, Miss Cotton, let me just—'

'No. I'm not going to sit here and nod to a lie like that. It was simple. I caught Brendan reading my diary.'

'Please, Miss Cotton, Miranda, let me go on and then you may have your say.'

I clenched my teeth hard and said nothing.

'According to Mr Block, he ended the relationship. Maybe unfortunately he then began a relationship with your sister and then with a mutual friend . . .'

'She was *my* friend,' I said.

'. . . a relationship'—said Pryor, as though I hadn't spoken—'that ended tragically.'

'For *Laura*,' I said. 'Not for Brendan.'

There was a sort of angry sigh from Deirdre Walsh and I saw that she was actually glaring at me.

'Please, Miranda,' said Pryor.

Polly leaned over and put a hand on my arm. I nodded at her.

Pryor continued. 'I won't go through all the episodes of tension during the time when Brendan was engaged to your sister. I'll only mention the occasion when you were caught searching through Brendan's possessions in his bedroom.'

I looked round at Polly. I hadn't mentioned that to her. She was looking entirely impassive.

'Mr Block admits that his severing of ties with your sister was a painful process, but he was, at least, no longer connected with your family. However, your erratic behaviour only intensified. There were, for example, the wild accusations you made against him to people—well, to people such as myself. Even when I went to the trouble of showing that the accusations—for example, concerning the death of Laura— were demonstrably false.'

'That's just not true,' I said. 'It all depended on time, and you got the route wrong. I checked it, and, if you took the direct route through the council estate, Brendan could easily have got there in ten minutes.'

There was a silence. Deirdre Walsh leaned forwards and spoke for the first time. 'I'm sorry, Miss Cotton. I'm not sure I've got this right. Do I take it that you have walked the route yourself and timed it?'

'Someone had to,' I said.

'Excuse me,' said Polly to the others, and leaned close to my ear and whispered to me. 'I think it would be better if you didn't respond to these claims point by point until the detective has finished.'

'Why?' I said.

'Please,' said Polly.

'All right,' I said. 'Go on, then.'

Pryor took another piece of paper from his file. 'Do you know the name, Geoffrey Locke?'

I thought for a moment. It sounded familiar. 'Oh, you mean Jeff? I've met him.'

'You phoned him about Mr Block.'

'I wanted to reach him.'

'Craig McGreevy?'

'I don't see the point in just reading these names out.'

'You actually visited Tom Lanham.'

'I'm sorry, I don't see the problem.'

I looked over at Brendan. He had the very, very faintest of smiles on his face. It reminded me of the way he looked at me when we first met, when I first suspected that he really liked me. I looked at Pryor. He had no kind of smile on his face.

'You didn't just talk to Lanham. You took property of Mr Block's away with you.'

I looked at Polly again. She didn't catch my eye.

'If I saw him,' I said. 'I could give it to him. That was the idea. Tom just wanted to get it out of his flat. And if you talked to him, you'll also know that Brendan skipped without paying rent.'

Pryor looked at his file again. 'Mr Block's grandmother, Victoria Rees, is severely demented. You visited her at her nursing home.'

'Yes.'

'Did you think she would be able to give you Mr Block's address?'

'I wanted to find out about his childhood. For various reasons.'

'And you called on his sister,' said Pryor. 'And you asked offensive and invasive questions.'

'I wouldn't say that.'

'After all the tragedies he has suffered, Mr Block is trying to put his life back together. He has a new relationship. You approached his new partner. You had been spying on her and you threatened her.'

'I did not threaten her.'

'It was agreed with Mr Block and his legal representative that I would coordinate this meeting and speak on his behalf. But I just want to call on Mr Block to say what this has meant to him.'

Brendan gave a cough. 'I'm sorry, Mirrie,' he said. 'I feel sorry for you, I really do. But I've felt'—there was a pause as if this were all too painful to talk about—'violated, threatened, invaded, unsettled.'

'Ha! My heart bleeds for you,' I said angrily.

'Miranda,' said Polly sharply.

'I have one more thing to say,' said Pryor. 'Ms Walsh and Mr Block came to see me with this information. Much of it I knew already. I have to say that, in my professional opinion, there is no doubt whatsoever that harassment has occurred. Your solicitor will be able to tell you that harassment is a summary offence with a penalty of up to six months' imprisonment or a fine of up to five thousand pounds, or both. I would be quite within my powers to arrest you here and now.'

I was so dismayed and angry and shocked that I could barely speak.

'That is just such a travesty,' I said. 'I just—well, for a start, in no way have I harassed Brendan. I talked to friends of his.'

'The harassment isn't defined in the Protection from Harassment Act of 1997,' said Deirdre Walsh in a chilly tone. 'If you believe you are being harassed and a reasonable person, such as a magistrate, agrees, then harassment is proved. I must say that I have never seen a clearer case.'

'Ms Walsh is right,' said Pryor. 'It was my view that the case should proceed. I consider you a possible threat to Mr Block. But he was eager to settle the case informally. If this case reached a criminal court, you would be subject to a restraining order. If it was a civil court it would be a restraining injunction. It doesn't matter. They amount to the same thing. Mr Block is willing to accept a personal commitment from you. If you won't make such a commitment, we'll think again.'

'You mean, you'll arrest me?'

'That's right,' said Pryor.

'This is completely insane,' I said. 'If anything, Brendan is the one who has been stalking me. I was the one who broke off with him and then he insinuated himself into my family, into my life. I should take an injunction out against him.'

There was quite a long, awkward silence.

'You're going about it in an unconventional way,' said Pryor. 'And now I think you might like a few moments with your legal adviser. We'll leave you alone together.'

The three of them stood up and walked past me. I had to stand up to leave space for them.

'That isn't exactly what I was expecting,' I said.

Polly was staring down at the carpet. She turned to me. Her face was drained of colour. 'I'm not sure if I'm right for this,' she said. 'You may need someone more senior.'

'I just want your advice, Polly.'

She bit her lip. 'Is this true?' she said. 'Did these things happen?'

'They're not exactly false,' I said. 'In themselves. But the idea that I was stalking Brendan is grotesque.'

Polly stood up. She seemed reluctant to meet my gaze. 'I shouldn't have agreed to this,' she said. 'We know each other. It's not professional. I didn't realise . . . But look, Miranda, I think—apart from everything else—you should see someone.'

'If you mean a therapist, I have been talking to someone. I was talking to her about my feelings after losing my brother and my closest friend.'

'You didn't tell me that,' said Polly. 'Among other things. You should have told me.'

'So you could have discounted what I said as some psychological symptom?' Polly didn't reply, but she didn't deny it either. 'I'm not going to accept this.'

Polly shook her head urgently. 'No, Miranda, stop that. They are being generous with you.'

'Let them prove it in court.'

'Miranda!' Polly grabbed my arm with a grip that almost made me cry out. 'If you go to court you will lose. Let me tell you, you do not want to be cross-examined on what that detective read out from his file. You will be convicted, I promise.' Polly was looking at me with a pity that revolted me. 'I don't know what's happened, but I'm so so sorry. Miranda, let me be your lawyer for five minutes and we'll just accept whatever they're offering. Whatever it is, they're letting you off easy. Will you let me ask them back in?'

I could hardly speak. My skin felt hot and clammy, while my mouth was dry. 'All right,' I said.

On the way out I caught sight of Brendan in the corridor. He was in conversation with Rob Pryor. He caught my eye and then he smiled. He raised his right index finger and wagged it slightly at me, like a teacher reproving a pupil. Then he passed the finger across his neck. Around the neck. What did that mean? Was it like a knife across a throat? Was it Troy's noose around the neck? Was this a warning? *Don't mess with me.*

'Did you see that?' I said to Polly.

'What?' she said.

Nobody but me ever seemed to see.

Afterwards, back on the steps outside, Polly said I should be very relieved. I had signed an undertaking drafted by Deirdre Walsh according to which I promised not to approach or contact Brendan or his friends or members of his family. Polly also said on my behalf that I was sorry and that I'd been under a lot of pressure and that I was already receiving psychiatric help. Before we parted, Polly held out her hand.

'I don't mind any of this,' I said. Polly looked puzzled. 'It's all crap. Brendan was always going to outwit me at something like this. I think you gave me good advice. I had to sign that document. So I should thank you for saving me from going down in flames. But I need to ask one thing: do you believe me?'

Polly seemed unwilling to speak.

'Well, do you?'

She made an unhappy gesture. 'I'm sorry, Miranda,' she said.

That evening Polly rang me, cancelling our drink.

I went to a newsagent along the road and bought a pad of notepaper. The only shade they had was some awful sort of violet. But, after all, what did the colour matter? I sat at the table in my flat. Soon everything would be packed away, and I already felt like an emigrant leaving my old life behind. But there was something important I needed to do. I began to write:

Dear Naomi,

If you're reading these words, that means at least that you didn't throw the envelope in the bin, so that's something.

As you probably know, if you give this to Brendan/Ben or to the police—it amounts to the same thing—then I'll be arrested and charged with harassment. That's what they told me. I hope you don't. I don't want to go to prison. But if you do hand the letter over, could you read it first? And I want you to read this promise as well: this is my last message to you. I'll never contact you again. It's up to you now.

I'm not going to attempt some defence of my behaviour to you. It would all be too complicated and this letter would have to be as long as a book and I probably wouldn't have the words to explain it, anyway. All I can do now is to be as clear as possible. I've been accused of being a threat to Brendan. I happen to believe that it's the other way round. I wake in the night and every creak I hear, I think he may have come to finish me off. I'm frightened for myself but I'm even more certain that you are in danger. Maybe not today, maybe not tomorrow, but if things go wrong, the way things go wrong in relationships. I don't think Brendan can take it when things don't go the way he has planned it.

What am I saying to you? I was going to send you a sort of checklist. Do you think he is telling the truth? Is he caring for you or controlling you? Is he being secretive? Are there hints of anger? Violence? Do you know what he's doing when he's not with you? How much do you really know about him? Do you believe what he tells you?

But this is all rubbish. Forget all I've said. You'll know.

You'll never hear from me again and I wish you happiness and that you'll never want to contact me. I'm about to leave my flat. I don't know where I'm going, yet. But if you ever want to contact me, I'll put some numbers of various people at the bottom of this letter. One of them should be able to put you in touch with me.

I'm afraid that I think you've had bad luck. But I wish you good luck.
Miranda

Before I could change my mind I put the letter in an envelope, addressed it to her care of Crabtrees and walked out and posted it in the box on the corner.

10

'HELLO! MIRANDA?'

His voice boomed up the stairwell, and then I heard his footsteps, taking the steps two at a time. I applied one last precise lick of gloss paint along the skirting board then laid my brush down on the lid of the paint pot.

'The paint's still wet,' I said as he came through the door, loosening his tie as he did so. 'Don't touch anything.' I stood up and crossed the beautiful bare room.

'Except you,' he said. He put his hands on my aching shoulders and kissed me and bit by bit all my stiffness eased away. I thought: How is it possible to feel excited and safe all at the same time; to know someone so well and yet feel there's so much more to know?

'Good day?' I asked.

'This is the best bit. I've got exactly fifty minutes before I have to get back to work. I've bought us some sandwiches from the deli.'

'Shall we have those in a bit?' I said and took him by the hand. I led him up the next narrow flight of stairs, along bare boards and fresh-painted walls, into the small attic room I was using as a bedroom, where a mattress lay under the window and my clothes were stacked in wooden boxes. I took off his jacket and tie and he unbuttoned my over-alls and we grinned at each other like idiots because here we were on an ordinary Wednesday lunchtime, about to make love in an empty, echoey house. Light fell through the blinds in bars across the room. I hung his suit on a hanger for him. He tossed my paint-stained gear into a corner.

'I'd like to stay here the rest of the day,' I said a bit later, stretched out on the mattress while he lay propped up beside me and stroked my hair.

'Roasted vegetables with mozzarella or farmhouse Cheddar and pickle?'

'Half of each?'

'OK.'

'We can have them in the kitchen, then I can show you what I've done since you were last here.'

I had tried to move out of London, to the country. I really had. I'd burnt my bridges, leaving Bill, selling my flat in record time, putting my stuff into storage. I'd thought about relocating to Wales and Lincolnshire and even, for a few days, Brittany, where apparently lots of English people were desperate for a builder-cum-interior designer to revamp their picturesque farmhouses. But I was now living in a tall, narrow house just south of King's Cross, renovating it while the owner was in America for nine months. When he'd offered me the job—an extravagant modernist conversion of the kind I'd dreamed of, with free accommodation thrown in—it had seemed like too good an opportunity to pass up. I'd started at the bottom and moved upwards, and eight of the nine months had now elapsed. Only the attic room where I slept was still to be plastered and decorated and opened to the skies.

'You've done a great job,' he said, posting the last of his sandwich into his mouth and pulling on his jacket.

'It's all right, isn't it?'

'And now you're nearly finished.'

'Yes.'

'Miranda?'

'Yes.'

'After that—'

But then my mobile phone started bleeping from the bedroom, so we said goodbye hastily, and I pounded up the stairs to get it, while downstairs I heard the door slam shut. I caught up the vibrating phone. If I stood on tiptoes and craned my neck, I could just see him from the dormer window, walking briskly along the street. He'd forgotten his tie.

We went for a bike ride in the early evening and had coffee, sitting on the pavement outside even though it was getting chilly. We'd been together nearly one year now, all the seasons. He'd seen me through the anniversaries . . . Troy's death, Christmas, Laura's death. He'd met my beaten-down, bewildered parents; met Kerry and her fiancé. He'd let me wake him up at three in the morning to talk about the things I tried not to talk about in the day. I looked at him as he biked beside me, and he felt my gaze, glanced up, swerved. My heart contracted like a fist.

At his flat, he made supper for us—smoked mackerel and salad with a bottle of white wine—while I sat on the church pew he'd bought at the reclamation centre and watched him. When he sat down he took a small bite, but then pushed his plate away. 'Um . . . what I was saying this afternoon . . . about your plans, you know. Well, I was thinking . . . you could move in with me.'

I started to speak, but he held up a hand. 'Hang on. I'm saying this all wrong. I don't mean, you could move in with me. Well, I do of course, but that's not what I'm really saying.'

'You're confusing me.'

'I'm nervous, that's why.' He took a breath and then said, 'I very much want you to come and live with me.'

He twisted the wineglass round by its stem. 'I want you to marry me, Miranda.'

Happiness bubbled up in me like an underground stream finding the surface. Unlooked for, undeserved happiness that had come into my parched life when I met him.

'I want to have children with you,' he continued.

'Don,' I said.

'I want to grow old with you. Only you. Nobody but you. There.'

'Oh,' I said.

'I've never said anything like this before.' He gave a grimace and rubbed his eyes. 'Now you're supposed to reply, I think.'

'Listen, Don,' I said.

'Just tell me.'

I leaned towards him and put my hands on either side of his lovely, clear, kind face; kissed him on the eyelids and then on the lips. 'I love you too,' I said. 'I love you very, very, very much. Only you.'

'That's good,' he said. 'Isn't it?'

'Can you wait a bit?' I held his gaze.

'Well, of course I can wait . . . but does that mean you're not sure?'

'No. It doesn't mean that at all. I used to wonder how you knew when it was the real thing. Not any more.'

'So why?'

'It's complicated,' I said evasively.

'Are you scared?'

'Do you mean of commitment or something?'

'Not exactly. But after everything you have been through, maybe you feel it's wrong to be happy. Or maybe you feel you're not safe, and therefore anyone who's with you isn't safe either. We've talked about how you felt you were the carrier. Is that it? Everyone you love dies.'

'You're the psychologist,' I said.

'Because I don't mind,' he said. 'Everything's a risk. You just have to choose the risk you want to take. I chose a long time ago. Now you have to as well.'

I put my hands over his, turned his palms upwards, kissed them both. 'I have chosen,' I said.

'You're crying,' he said. 'Into your food.'

'Sorry.'

'Of course I'll bloody wait.'

I've met a man. Don. I wish you could meet him as well. I think you'd like him. I know he'd like you. It feels odd, unsettling, not right, to be in love with someone again. I never thought it would happen, not after everything. I thought all of that was over. And sometimes . . . well, a lot, really . . . I get this sudden rush of panic that it's wrong. Wrong to be happy, I mean, when you're not here and Laura's gone and Mum and Dad are wrecked. It was me who spread the terrible contagion. I can see that sardonic expression on your face when I say that, but nevertheless it's true. I'll always miss you, Troy. Every minute of every day of every week of every year that's left. So how is it possible that I can allow myself to be happy? Maybe it isn't. We'll see.

My eyes were closed, hard, my breath coming in gasps. My heart was beating so fast that my body seemed to hum with it. I was sweating. I could hardly feel the pain. I knew it was there. On my face, around my jaw. I could taste blood, warm, metallic. Around my neck, the scraping. My ribs, sore, bruised. My eyes still closed, afraid of what was in store. I felt the sounds of someone approaching, the vibration of footsteps on the stairs. The touch, when it came, was gentle on my face and cheeks, but it still made me flinch. I didn't open my eyes. I murmured something.

'Jesus, Miranda!' said the voice. 'I heard glass breaking . . . What the fuck? Miranda?'

I opened my eyes. The light hurt them. Don. Don's lovely face looking down at me, close, distressed. He ran over to the window. I spoke in a murmur, but Don couldn't make it out. He leaned closer to my face.

'Said he was going to kill me,' I said in little more than a whisper.

His expression darkened. 'Was it him? Brendan?'

'Said he'd come for me.'

I felt him gently touching my face, stroking my hair, unfastening my shirt, assessing the damage.

'You're bleeding.'

I just groaned. He was looking around.

'There's blood on the . . . What did that bastard do to you? I'm calling the police. And an ambulance.'

'No.' I said, half raising myself and flinching at the pain it caused me. 'Don't . . . It's not . . .'

'What are you talking about?' Don said, almost angrily. 'I'm sorry, Miranda. I'm not listening to you.' I heard three little bleeps as he punched the numbers in his mobile phone. I sank back almost sobbing, partly with the pain, partly at the thought of what was to come.

I wasn't there when the police examined the room, when they dabbed at the blood on the wall and picked hairs off the carpet and put the knife in a plastic bag. I was grateful for that. It would be like the death of Troy all over again. Don told me about all that later. He had wanted to come with me in the ambulance, but a policeman told me he ought to stay and help to identify objects at the scene.

Meanwhile I had been taken away in an ambulance with a female police officer for company. She was like a free pass that took me to the front of the outpatients' queue. Within two minutes a consultant in a white coat and a spotted tie arrived.

He examined my face and the inside of my mouth. 'What were you struck with?' he said.

'A wall,' I said.

'Do you know who did this?' he asked.

I nodded.

He turned to the police officer. 'You'll need to photograph this. The neck as well.'

'He's on his way,' said the WPC.

'We'll be taking an X-ray, but the cheekbone is probably fractured.'

I gave a cry because as he said it he had given a dab on my cheek with his finger, as if to test his theory. He shone a light into my eyes and into my ears.

I was X-rayed and I was photographed and then I was taken to a private room with a vase without flowers and a window without a view. The doctor said they wanted to keep me under observation for a night. The WPC said that they would like to take a statement. She said they could wait if I didn't feel well enough, but the sooner I could manage it the better. I said I could do it immediately. Within the hour a detective knocked on my door, took his jacket off and removed a sheaf of paper from his bag. He was called Seb Brett and he looked pale. He pulled a small table alongside my bed and started to take dictation.

I gave him the story in every detail: Brendan ringing at the door, forcing his way inside, grabbing the back of my head and slamming my face into the wall, pulling the knife from somewhere and pushing it against my throat, my pleading, his smile and telling me that this was the end, then the sound of the door, Brendan jumping up in alarm, running, I couldn't see where. The incident had only taken a few minutes, but it took a couple of hours and fourteen pages to make the statement. At the end I was exhausted, but Detective Brett asked me to read through it and sign at the end of each page. My words seemed different in Seb Brett's rounded, precise handwriting. They were all mine, but he had selected particular phrases and made alterations. I found it difficult to concentrate, so this was a slow process as well. Halfway through there was a knock at the door. It was Rob Pryor.

'Miranda,' he said. 'I just heard. I came straight over. How are you?'

'Shaken,' I said.

'I'm not surprised.' He walked over to the bed and picked up the pages I'd finished with. 'Do you mind?'

I looked across at Brett, who just gave a shrug. So I said I didn't mind. Each time I signed a page, he would take it from me and read it with a tut-tutting sound that I found infuriating. I signed the last page and passed it over to Pryor, but he gave it straight back.

'You need to sign it immediately where the text ends,' he said. 'Just here.'

'Why?'

'So some wicked policeman can't add a bit at the end saying "I woke up and it was all a dream", and you would have signed it off.'

I signed my name hard against the last word, which was 'police'.

'How did you get here so quickly?' I asked.

'Mr Block is being questioned. He rang me.'

I turned to Brett. 'Is this legal?' I said. 'Pryor is a friend of Brendan's.'

Brett looked quizzical. Pryor walked across and they had a whispered conversation that I couldn't quite hear. It went on for several minutes with puzzled looks from Brett. At the end of it he nodded and looked at me. 'DI Pryor has asked if he can have a quick word with you. Is that all right?'

'What about?'

'It'll only take a minute,' Pryor said.

'I don't believe this,' I said, looking at Brett. 'Do you realise who this man is? This is like letting Brendan's lawyer come in and nobble me when everything has just happened.'

'I was telling Seb about your previous connection with Mr Block.'

'So?'

Pryor walked across and sat by my bed. It was like having Brendan himself there. His proximity made me want to gag.

'What time did the attack happen?' he said.

'You've read the statement.'

'Your boyfriend made the call at—what was it—five past seven this evening.'

I didn't speak. I wasn't going to be drawn into a conversation.

'Your boyfriend,' said Pryor. 'Some sort of doctor, isn't he?' I only shrugged. He leaned in closer, his eyes narrow. 'You know what? I don't believe you.'

'What?'

'Did he help you? Your boyfriend? He could do it, couldn't he? A few bruises, things that would show, but not too much damage.'

'What the . . . ?' I stuttered. 'What are you saying?'

'There was a knife,' Brett said. 'He dropped it. We're checking the prints.'

'They lived together,' said Pryor. 'She could have saved it.'

'We never lived together,' I said. 'What the hell are you doing?'

He was so close to me now that I could almost smell him.

'He's got an alibi,' he said.

I took a deep breath. I had to control myself.

'His girlfriend, Naomi Stone.' He looked at me with an expression of mild triumph. I'd seen it before. 'You don't seem very concerned.'

'Maybe I'm used to being disbelieved,' I said. 'As I said, I was the one who was there. He had his knife against my throat. Look.' I lifted my chin.

He clapped his hands gently.

'Oh, very good,' he said. 'It's a brilliant performance. Dignified. Not overdone. Pretty convincing. But then you've had a bit of practice.'

I tried to concentrate. Don't let him rile you. 'Have you ever thought that it's just possible that you could be wrong and that Brendan could be dangerous?'

'None of this matters,' said Pryor. 'He couldn't have attacked you. He was at home. He was at home when the police called and Ms Stone places him there for the entire evening.' He picked up the statement and glanced at it once more. 'You mention a dark blue shirt. When I saw him a few minutes ago, his shirt looked brown to me.'

'He might have changed it,' I said. 'Did that occur to you?'

He shook his head and smiled. 'Mr Block is making a statement. If you really want to know—' And now Pryor was interrupted by the ringing of his mobile phone. With a sigh of exasperation he took it from his pocket. 'Yes?' Suddenly his expression changed. 'What the hell are you talking about?' He looked at me with glassy eyes as he listened to the phone. 'I'll be right there.'

He mumbled something to Brett and then walked out of the room, banging the door behind him, Brett pulled a face at me. I think he was on my side, mostly. He ran out after Pryor. I was alone for several minutes and I lay back and stared at the ceiling, trying to empty my mind. When the door opened I barely looked round. It was another female police officer. She sat in the corner, but made no attempt to start a conversation. I closed my eyes so I wouldn't be bothered.

Much later, it must have been after an hour, the door opened and I was aware of someone by the bed. 'Are you awake?'

I opened my eyes. Brett.

'Sort of,' I said. 'You look cheerful.' There was a pause. 'So what's happened? What happened with Pryor?'

The smile spread across Brett's face. 'He's not a happy man,' he said. 'My colleague was talking to Naomi Stone. She told her about some of the hairs recovered at the scene. And the knife.'

'So?'

'She's withdrawn her alibi. And, better still, we've found the dark blue shirt. It was in the bottom of a rubbish bag outside his house. It has some stains on it. They are as yet unidentified, but we already know they are drops of blood. Human blood.'

'Mine?'

'We'll see. I told Rob Pryor that he should come and apologise to you.'

'What did he say?'

'He had a previous engagement. Off the record, I think I can tell you that we shall be filing charges against Brendan Block in the morning.' He took my hand. 'We'll leave you now.'

11

ON A BRIGHT AND FREEZING New Year's Day I got up early, kissed Don's cheek very softly so he didn't wake. Before I left, I looked down at him. Yes. He'd do. I took the van and drove out of London. The roads were almost empty. I went over Blackfriars Bridge from where I could see the dome of St Paul's shining in the icy light, through New Cross, Blackheath, and on to the A2. I felt calm and, in the brightness of that winter's day, things took on a clarity and precision.

I joined the M2 and a few miles later exited towards Sheerness. I could see the Medway estuary now, the mud flats and shabby clusters of houses with a few bare trees bending in the wind and the sky vast and empty of clouds. Soon I was crossing onto the Isle of Sheppey. I pulled over and consulted my map, then drove a couple of miles farther, onto a bumpy minor road, left towards the church, which was the one vertical marker rising out of the marshy land. At the church, I parked and looked at my watch. It was ten o'clock; I had about two miles to walk and just less than an hour to do it in.

It was bitterly cold when I opened the door, and I could hear the desolate call of sea birds on the wind. I pulled on my thick jacket, my scarf, woollen hat and thick biking gloves. I started to walk. There was nobody around; just a few sheep grazing at the tufts of grass, birds picking their way delicately over the mud with long, hinged legs. I turned my back on the sea and walked towards the inland marshes.

After about forty minutes, I saw a dot on the level horizon. The dot became a woman in a heavy coat with blonde hair escaping her hat and whipping round her pale cheeks. Neither of us made a signal or lessened our pace. We just continued walking towards each other across the marshes until we were a few feet away from each other.

'Naomi,' I said.

'Hello.'

'Everything go all right?'

'I was careful, like you said.'

I had not seen her since those days in court, when I'd tried so hard not to look at her. Once, our glances had touched for a second, less, and then we had both looked hastily away as if we had been scorched. She had lost weight and her pallor was striking.

'Shall we walk, just for a bit?' I said and she nodded and turned back on her path. We went single file for a bit, until the wide estuary lay before us. There were pebbles and broken shells at the water's edge, and also old cans, broken bottles, shredded plastic bags.

'Was it easy to get away unnoticed?'

'There's no one really to notice any more.' Her voice was quiet and flat; I had to strain to hear it. 'What about you?'

'I told Don I was inspecting an empty property.'

'Oh.'

For a few minutes there was just the crunch of our feet over frosted grass. I was sure we were remembering the same thing . . . that strange hour when we'd met and like the two witches muttered plans and exchanged tokens. From her bag, she'd produced a little sandwich bag with some coarse dark hair inside that she'd pulled from Brendan's brush, and the jagged-edged carving knife wrapped in soft paper towels that she'd handed over by the bottom of its blade, careful not to touch its handle. And then she'd unfolded a dark blue shirt and laid it out before us. I'd held out the index finger of my left hand for her, and she'd taken a safety pin, opened it, and, biting her lower lip, jabbed the point into my finger. A dark ball of blood had welled up and after a few seconds I'd shaken it over the shirt and its collar and then wiped it there as well.

'Can I ask something?' Naomi said at last.

'Sure.'

'How did you do that to your cheek? You looked awful in court, even all those weeks after.'

It all seemed a long, long time ago.

'When I saw Don pulling up outside, I smashed my face against the kitchen door as hard as I could, as if someone were holding me by my hair and doing it to me. I did it over and over until I couldn't see for the blood.'

'How could you do that?' she said in a whisper.

'I thought of Troy . . . Laura as well, but mostly Troy. Then it was easy; welcome, even. It was nothing.'

Naomi nodded as if she understood.

'Now tell me something,' I said. 'Something I never had time to ask before.'

'Yes?'

'How were you so certain about Brendan?'

She hesitated. 'Are you sure you want to know?'

'Tell me.'

'He told me what he'd done to Troy. He said he'd do it to me too, if I left him.'

There was a pain in my stomach and a burning sensation behind my eyes when she said this. I squinted into the wind and kept on walking. 'He actually told you about Troy?'

'Yes.'

'Why didn't you go to the police?'

'I thought of what had happened to you. I couldn't be sure.'

'What did he say?'

'He said he'd filled him up with pills and strung him up on the beam and left him to die there. He said . . . he said he'd tried to call out.'

'What?' My voice was a whisper.

'He'd tried to say your name.'

I went on walking. One foot in front of the other. It's hard to understand how it's possible to keep on walking when you hurt so much and you just want to bend over with your arms around your stomach, curl up into a tight ball and wail like a baby. He called out for me because he thought I was coming home soon. I'd promised him I'd be there and he must have thought I could rescue him. But I was late.

'Are you all right?'

I managed a noise of assent.

'I think this might have been his.' Naomi pulled one hand out of her pocket; she was holding a bracelet made of leather, with three dull wooden beads on it. 'Was it?'

I took the bracelet in my gloved hand. 'Yes. Since he was small.' I held it against my cheek for a moment, then slipped it over my wrist.

Naomi said, 'My car's not so far from here.'

We stopped and looked at each other.

'What are you going to do?' I asked.

'I caught his eye in court,' she said. 'When I gave evidence. He smiled at me. One of his nicest smiles. That's when I was certain about what to do. I'm leaving everything. Starting over from fresh.'

'Can you do that?'

'Why not? I've got no family. Maybe that's why I fell in love with Brendan . . . I thought we were these two orphans who'd come together to protect each other in the wicked world.' She gave a harsh laugh, more like a bark, and then shook her head as if to clear it. 'One day he'll be free again and then he'll try to find me.'

'Where will you go?' I asked.

There was a pause and she looked at me as if she were committing my face to memory. 'Abroad. But it's probably better if I don't tell you.'

'Good luck,' I said.

'What will you do?'

'Nothing. I've got six years. I'll take that, a day at a time, and I'm going to try to love as well as I have hated. After that? Well, I'll see. Pryor said they're going to reinvestigate Laura and Troy's deaths, so . . . well, who knows?'

'Oh,' she said faintly. 'So you're still waiting?'

I winced. But in a way of course she was right. I was still waiting for Brendan and when he came I would be ready for him, like a soldier who can feel his enemy approaching even in his sleep.

'We'll never meet again, will we?' I asked her.

'I guess not.'

'This is goodbye,' I said and smiled at her for the first time.

We both reached out at the same time; our hands met in a fierce grip. We stared into each other's eyes and didn't look away. It was like looking into the abyss.

'It was probably wrong, wasn't it?' she said. 'I try to imagine myself justifying it to people and I'm not sure I could, except—'

'To save your life,' I said.

'I hope so,' she said. 'So what about you? Are you telling your . . . your boyfriend?'

'Don?' I said. 'I think I should. But I won't. I'd better keep it to myself.'

There was nothing really left to say. We let our hands drop back to our sides.

'Goodbye,' she said.

'Goodbye.'

She turned and walked back the way she had come and I watched her figure getting smaller. Then I turned, too, and went back over the bleak marshland under the circling birds, back to the old grey church and my van. Back along the small road to the larger one, to the motorway; back to the teeming city where my life was. Back up the stairs to Don.

'I'm home,' I said listening to the word as I spoke it. I repeated it, to make sure. 'Home.'

'I missed you.'

'Well,' I said, kissing him. 'I'm here now.'

Dearest Troy,

I think I need to let you go now. I don't know how I'll manage without you, but I'm going to try.

I'm sorry.

NICCI FRENCH

Nicci French is the pseudonym of the unique husband-and-wife writing team, Sean French and Nicci Gerrard. The couple met in 1989, when they were both journalists at the *New Statemen*. Nicci was the literary editor and Sean a weekly columnist and leader writer. At the time, Nicci was recently separated and coping with a baby and a toddler. She admits to being 'scrawny, raw, angry . . . quite unready for love', but well remembers a day when she'd had to bring her children into work, and Sean, who often dropped into her office for a chat, 'bent down to them and talked to them shyly and sweetly'. It was the start of a deeply involving and passionate love affair, and they were married within a year.

It was then that the couple decided to start writing fiction together. 'We talked about whether two people could write a novel that had one voice,' says Sean. 'Then we both had an idea at the same time and we just thought we had to do it together.'

'We really wanted to create a third writer, with her own unique style,' adds Nicci. 'It's not just a bit of Sean French and a bit of Nicci Gerrard pushed together. When we get letters addressed to Nicci French, this non-existent woman, saying they really enjoyed a book, it's the best reward we can get.'

What was it that made them choose to write psychological thrillers like *Secret Smile,* their seventh novel? 'There's something about the narrative

shape of a thriller,' Nicci reflects. 'It's a very satisfying structure into which you can put lots of ideas. I'm interested in the effects of crime and what lies beneath the surface. The thrillers that we write are about ordinary people who have extraordinary things happening in the middle of their lives, and the way that they have to change to resolve things.' It's intriguing to note that each of their novels features a female, rather than a male hero. 'Yes, we decided right from the beginning that a woman was a more interesting person to have at the centre of a psychological novel,' Sean explains. 'I don't know whether perhaps it's the feeling that women are more vulnerable than men in modern society . . .'

Sean French and Nicci Gerrard now live in Suffolk with their two children and Nicci's son and daughter from her first marriage. They find it works best if they settle down to write as far away from each other as possible—Nicci works at the top of the house, Sean at the bottom. 'We agree the structure of a book, then one of us writes a chapter and hands it to the other, giving them the total right to change anything.' Their main objective is that the story should be read as if it had been written by one person.

'People ask us if we argue, and of course we do. But it's rarely about handing over our beloved words,' Nicci says.

Anne Jenkins

Printed and bound by Maury Imprimeur SA, Malesherbes, France

601-025-1